1944
2ND PRINTING

W9-DAA-805

PRESIDENTIAL AGENT

PRESIDENTIAL AGENT

Upton Sinclair

The Viking Press · New York
1944

THIS EDITION IS PRODUCED IN FULL COMPLIANCE WITH
ALL WAR PRODUCTION BOARD CONSERVATION ORDERS

COPYRIGHT 1944 BY UPTON SINCLAIR

FIRST PUBLISHED BY THE VIKING PRESS IN JUNE 1944

SECOND PRINTING JUNE 1944

PUBLISHED ON THE SAME DAY IN THE DOMINION OF CANADA
BY THE MACMILLAN COMPANY OF CANADA LIMITED

PRINTED IN U.S.A. BY THE AMERICAN BOOK—STRATFORD PRESS

TO

MARY CRAIG SINCLAIR
MY BELOVED WIFE

Into your hands I place the five Lanny Budd
books with whatever honors they may have
won. Without your wisdom and knowledge
of the world they could not have been
what they are. Without your cherishing love
through times of stress and suffering their
author could hardly have been alive.

Author's Note

IN THE course of this work of fiction there occur several scenes with Franklin D. Roosevelt. When the author was a candidate for the governorship of California, he had the pleasure of a two-hour conference with President Roosevelt, but since that time he has had no personal contact with the President, and has no first-hand knowledge as to his reasons for this or that action or attitude. The scenes in this book are fictional, and neither the President nor his wife has been consulted concerning them. The description of the President's appearance, mannerisms, and surroundings the author can certify to be accurate, but the speeches attributed to the President represent merely the author's guesses as to his mind. The author hopes they are good guesses, but does not wish anyone to assume that he speaks for the President or is in a position to reveal his secret thoughts.

Some of the local color and atmosphere toward the end of the story have been derived from a gay and informative record of the time, *Munich Playground* by Ernest R. Pope, a correspondent who covered that field. Thanks are due to the author and to the publishers, G. P. Putnam's Sons. Many other records have, of course, been consulted, and thanks are due to several refugees from Germany and Austria who have contributed their experiences. For the story of Zaharoff's treasure hunt the author is indebted to the autobiography of Charles Courtney, *Unlocking Adventure*, published by Whittlesey House.

Contents

Book Five:
Extravagant and Erring Spirit

Book Six: A Full Hot Horse

Book Seven:
The Things That Are Caesar's

BOOK ONE

Seats of the Mighty

1

Sweet Aspect of Princes

I

LIKE two ships that rest for a while in some port and then sail away to distant seas; years pass, decades, perhaps, and then by chance they meet in some other port; the two captains look each other over, wondering what time has done to an old-time comrade, what places he has visited, what adventures have befallen him, what losses, what gains he has made. So it was when Lanny Budd caught sight of Professor Alston in the lobby of one of New York's luxury hotels. "Long time no see," he said—for it was the fashion of the hour to be Chinese; you greeted your friends with the words: "Confucius say," followed by the most cynical or most absurd thing you could think of.

"Really, Professor," Lanny continued, seriously, "I'm ashamed of having lost contact with you. You can hardly guess how important a part you played in my life."

"Eighteen years almost to a day since we parted in Paris," calculated the other.

"And almost half my life up to now," added Lanny.

Alston still thought of him as a youth, and saw now that the ensuing years had dealt kindly with him. There were no lines of care on the regular and agreeable features, no hint of gray in the wavy brown hair and neatly trimmed little mustache. Lanny was dressed as if he had just come out of a bandbox, and he had that ease of conversation which comes from having known since earliest childhood that everything about you is exactly as it ought to be. When you are so right, you can even be wrong if you want to, and people will take it as an amiable eccentricity.

What Lanny saw was a rather frail little gentleman with hair entirely gray, wearing horn-rimmed spectacles and a linen suit with some of the wrinkles which these suits acquire so quickly. "Charlie" Alston would never be exactly right; he had been a "barb" at college, so Lanny's father had told him, and he would never be free from the consciousness that the people who had always been right were watching him. He was a kind and also a wise old gentleman, and that helps somewhat but not entirely, as all the smart world knows. Lanny recollected that he had come upon the mention of Charles T. Alston as one of the active New Dealers; so perhaps he was no longer teaching classes in college.

"I have heard from you indirectly," said Alston; but he didn't elaborate the remark. It might have been from the newspapers, for the ex-geographer added: "I hope your divorce didn't hurt you too much."

"My ex-wife has moved up the social ladder, and I was one of the rungs." Lanny said it with a smile; he didn't really mean it, for he was satisfied with the position on the social ladder assigned to a grandson of Budd Gunmakers and son of Budd-Erling Aircraft.

II

"What has life been doing to you?" the older man wanted to know.

This was an overture and called for a cordial response. "Have you anything to do for the next hour or two?" Lanny inquired, and went on to say that he had an appointment to view a collection of modern paintings which might soon come on the market. "That's how I have been earning my living. There are people who are naïve enough to trust my judgment as to what paintings are worth, and that enables me to spend the rest of my time as an idler and parasite." Again he said it smiling.

The ex-geographer replied that he would be happy to inspect works of art under the guidance of such an authority, and they left the hotel and took a taxi. A short drive and they stepped out in front of one of those establishments on Park Avenue where you either own your apartment or pay several thousand dollars a month rent. A personage who might have been one of Frederick the Great's grenadiers opened the taxi door for them; a clerk wearing a boutonnière took Lanny's name; a young woman with shiny red lips spoke it over the telephone; an elevator boy with several rows of buttons shot them toward the skies; and an elderly caretaker admitted them to a tier of rooms which apparently went most of the way around the building, and gave a hawk's-eye view of Manhattan Island and its environs.

The family was away in midsummer; the furniture was shrouded in tan-colored robes and the shades were drawn, but the caretaker raised one, and the visitors stopped to admire a penthouse rose garden. Then they strolled from room to room, examining paintings, each with its separate "reflector" which the caretaker turned on. They would stand for a while in silence, after which Lanny Budd would begin one of those well-modulated discourses with which he had learned to impress the most exclusive sort of people, those doubly élite who possess both wealth and culture.

"You observe the aristocratic aura with which Sargent could surround his model. You note that the head is somewhat small in proportion to the rest of the lady. Mrs. Winstead wasn't really that way, I can assure you, for I knew her; nor was it any blunder of the painter's, for I knew him even better. I watched him work in the hills and valleys around my mother's Riviera home, and can testify that he was able to get his proportions exact when he thought it desirable. It was his aim to select the salient characteristics of his subject and bring them to your attention. If you wanted literal exactness, he would say, a photographer could get it for you in the fraction of a second. It was the business of a painter to portray the soul of his subject."

"Not entirely overlooking what the subject might choose to believe about his soul," remarked Alston, with the trace of a smile.

"Surely not," agreed the other. "As far back as the days of ancient Egypt painters learned to make the masters taller and more impressive than the slaves. It is only in recent times, beginning perhaps with Goya, that painters have ventured to mingle a trace of humor with their subservience."

"Would you say that was the case here?"

"This was a sad lady, as you can perceive. They were enormously wealthy and correspondingly proud. They lived on an immense estate, and their two lovely daughters were brought up with great strictness and chaperoned in all their comings and goings. The result was that one of them eloped with a handsome young groom and the other made a marriage hardly more satisfactory. The haughty old father never consented to see either of them again. He has been one of my clients and I have had chances to observe his sorrow, in spite of his efforts to conceal it. I have no doubt that John Sargent, a kindly man in spite of all his brusqueness, thought that if there was any way of bringing a moment's happiness to Mrs. Winstead, there would be no great harm done to art. In his later years he wearied of such charity and refused to paint the rich at all."

III

"Charlie" Alston realized that this was the same informed and precocious Lanny Budd who had accompanied him to the Paris Peace Conference and shared a six months' ordeal. A youth who had lived most of his life in Europe; who not merely could chatter in French, but knew the subtle nuances, the argots, even the bad words; who knew customs and etiquette, personalities, diplomatic subterfuges; who could stand behind the chair of an "expert" during a formal session and whisper things into his ear, point to a paragraph in a document or write the correct word on a slip of paper—thus equipping a one-time farmboy from the State of Indiana to be something less than helpless in the presence of the age-old and super-elegant treacheries of Europe.

Now Lanny Budd was the same, only more of it. He had lived nearly two more decades between Europe and America, meeting the prominent ones of all lands and learning to take care of himself in all situations. Art to him was not just art; it was history and social science, psychology and human nature, even gossip, if you chose to take it that way. You had to get used to the fact that he really knew the "headliners," and that when he mentioned them he was not indulging in vainglory but just trying to make himself agreeable.

"Here you have an interesting contrast, Professor: a John and a Brockhurst side by side, and both dealing with the same subject. It is as if our host had wished to decide the question who is the better painter—or perhaps to provoke a perpetual debate. This is one of Augustus John's earlier works, and in my opinion they put him in a contemporary class by himself. Poor fellow, he is not taking good care of himself nowadays, and his work is not improving. Gerald Brockhurst is technically a sound painter, but I imagine that he himself would admit the supremacy of John at his best. Brockhurst's success can be attributed to his firm line and to his color. Both these characteristics have increased with the years, and that, I am sure, is why he has just been chosen to paint a portrait of my former wife. She has become Lady Wickthorpe, as you perhaps know, and is engaged in renovating a castle whose former châtelaines were painted by Gainsborough. Irma will be delighted with a portrait which will make her appear like a cinema star."

So once more an ex-geographer perceived that art was also psychology and even gossip!

"You have children?" he felt privileged to inquire.

"One daughter," was the reply. "She is seven, which is old enough to make the discovery that to live in an ancient castle is exciting, and that titles of nobility are impressive. It will be her mother's duty to see that she marries one of the highest."

"And you, Lanny?"

"I am the father, and, for having achieved that great honor, I am allowed to visit the child when I wish, and am shown every courtesy. It is taken for granted that I will not do or say anything to break the fairy-story spell under which the little one is being brought up."

IV

With the hot copper sun sinking low behind the long stone canyons of Manhattan Island, the two friends strolled back to the hotel where they had met. Lanny had a room there and invited the other up; he ordered a meal, and when it was served and the waiter withdrew, they lingered long over iced coffee and conversation. So many memories they had to revive and so many questions to ask! A score of men whom they had worked with at the Peace Conference: where were they now and what had happened to them? Many had died, and others had dropped out of sight. Alston spoke of those he knew. What did they think now about their work? He had been one of the dissidents, and Lanny had gone so far as to resign his humble job in protest against the misbegotten settlement. A melancholy satisfaction to know that you had been right, and that the worst calamities you had predicted now hung over the world in which you had to live!

Better to talk about the clear-sighted ones, those who had been courageous enough to speak out against blind follies and unchecked greeds. Lanny's Red uncle, who still lived in Paris—he was now a *député de la république française*, and once or twice his tirades had been quoted in the news dispatches to America. Lanny recalled how he had taken Alston and Colonel House to call on this uncle in his Paris tenement, this being part of President Wilson's feeble effort to bring the British and the French to some sort of compromise with the Soviets. "How my father hated to have me go near that dangerous Red sheep of my mother's family!" remarked Lanny. "My father still feels the same way."

They talked for a while about Robbie Budd. Alston told with humor of the years in college, when he had looked with awe upon the magnificent plutocratic son of Budd Gunmakers, who wore heavy white turtleneck sweaters, each with a blue Y upon it, and was cheered thunderously on the football field. Alston, on the other hand, had had to earn his living waiting on table in a students' dining room, and so was never "tapped" for a fashionable fraternity. Lanny said: "Robbie isn't quite so crude now; he has learned to respect learning and is even reconciled to having one of his sons play the piano and look at paintings instead of helping in the fabrication of military airplanes."

"And your mother?" inquired the elder man. When informed that she was still blooming, he said: "I really thought she was the most beautiful woman I had ever seen."

"She was certainly in the running," replied the son. "Now she contemplates with grief the fact that she is in her late fifties, and with a seven-year-old grandchild she cannot fib about it."

V

The ex-geographer was persuaded to talk about himself. He had made an impression upon his colleagues in Paris and had been offered a post in Washington. Among the acquaintances he had made there was the then Assistant Secretary of the Navy, a tall, robust young man of ability and ambition who appeared to have a weakness for college professors. "Likes to have them around," said Alston; "has an idea they know a lot, and that their knowledge ought to be used. A novel idea in American public life, as you know."

"It is one that annoys Robbie beyond endurance," replied Robbie's son.

"When F.D.R. became governor of New York State, he invited me to come to Albany and take a minor post—not to have much to do, but so that I could have a salary and be at hand to consult with him about the problems of his office, more complicated than any one man could deal with. A strange destiny for a geographer, but you know how it was in Paris; we all had to be politicians and diplomats, linguists, ethnographers, jurists—or anyhow we had to pretend to be. It is the same in government; you have to study human nature and the social forces that surround you, and apply your common sense to whatever problems arise. F.D. seemed to think that I was reasonably successful at it, so he brought me to Washington, and now I'm one of those 'bureaucrats' whom your father no doubt dislikes."

"Don't get within earshot of him!" exclaimed Lanny, with a grin.

"What I really am is a fixer. I have a subordinate who runs my office reasonably well, and I keep myself at the President's disposal, to find out what he needs to know, if I can, and to straighten out tangles if anybody can. When two self-important personalities fall to quarreling I go quietly to see them and persuade them that the Republicans are the only people who will profit by their ill behavior. All kinds of disagreeable and disillusioning jobs like that—and every now and then I get sick of it and decide that this shall be the last; but more troubles arise, and I am sorry for an overburdened executive who is trying to keep a blind world from plunging over a precipice."

"You think it's as bad as that, Professor Alston?"

"I think it's as bad as possible. What do you think, Lanny?"

"You mean about this country, or about Europe?"

"It's all one world—that is one of the things I learned as a geographer, and that the American people have to learn with blood and tears, I very much fear." It was the summer of 1937.

VI

Lanny, as he listened, had been thinking hard. His thought was: "How much ought I to tell?" He was always restraining the impulse to be frank with somebody; always having to put a checkrein on himself. Now, cautiously, he began:

"You remember, Professor Alston, that I was an ardent young reformer in your service. I didn't give up even after Versailles. I used to travel to one after another of the international conferences—I believe I went to a dozen, and met the statesmen and the newspaper fellows, and served as a go-between; I used to smuggle news—whatever I thought needed to be made known. I really believed it would be possible to instruct the public, and bring some peace and good fellowship to the unhappy old continent where I was born. But of late years I have been forced to give up; I was antagonizing everyone I knew, breaking up my home—it was like spitting against a hurricane. You must understand, I have built up something of a reputation as an art expert; I have played a part in making great collections which I have reason to hope will be bequeathed to public institutions, and thus will help in spreading culture. I persuade myself that this is a real service, and that taste in the arts is not just a fantasy, but an important social influence."

"Yes, Lanny, of course. But can you not also have political opinions and exercise some influence on the side of humanity?"

"It would be difficult, almost impossible. Most of the persons for whom I buy pictures are conservative, not to say reactionary, in their opinions. I have met them because I move in my father's world and my mother's, and in neither of these would I be received unless I kept a discreet attitude on the questions which now inflame everyone's mind. I don't doubt that you know how the people of money and fashion abuse and defame Roosevelt."

"He is trying to save them, and they will not have it."

"Not under any circumstances. Every man of them is a Louis Seize and every woman a Marie Antoinette, hellbent for the chopping block. I made enemies by pointing this out to them, and now I have learned to let them do the talking and reply that I am a nonpolitical person, living in the world of art. They take that as my professional pose, and assume that I am after the money, like everybody else. You see I lead a sort of double life; I talk frankly only to half a dozen trusted friends. I'd like to have you as one of them, if you consent; but you must promise not to talk about me to anyone else."

"I use many devices to keep my own name out of the papers, Lanny —so I can understand your attitude."

"You surely will when I tell you that one of my best-paying clients is Hermann Wilhelm Göring."

"Good grief, Lanny!"

"You may recall hearing me speak of my boyhood chum, Kurt Meissner, who became an artillery officer in the German Army. Now I am free to tell you something I was not free to mention at the time—that while I was serving as your secretary I ran into Kurt on the street in Paris; he was there as a secret agent of the German General Staff, and my mother and I sheltered him and saved him from the French police. Afterwards he lived in our home on the Riviera for a matter of eight years, and became a well-known pianist and composer. Then he went back to Germany and became a Nazi; through him I met many of those high in the Party, including the Führer, whose favorite Kurt still is. You see my position: I could tell my boyhood friend what I really think of his party and his cause, and thus break with him; or I could take the color of the Braune Haus and listen to what they told me, on the chance that what I learned might some day be of use outside. So I have played Beethoven for 'Adi,' as Hitler's intimates call him, and General Göring finds me a gay companion, invites me to his hunting lodge, and pumps me for information about the outside world. I tell him what I am sure he already knows, and I market for him the pictures which he has stolen from the wealthy Jews of his Third Reich. My father goes in and leases his airplane patents to the fat Exzellenz, and they try their best to outwit each other, and laugh amiably when they fail. *Geschäft ist Geschäft.*"

"It is a terrible thing to be giving the Nazis the mastery of the air over Europe, Lanny."

"Don't think that I haven't warned my father, and pleaded with him to change his business policy. But he answers that he went first to the British and the French, and they wouldn't pay him enough to keep his plant running. 'Am I to blame because it is the Nazis who have the brains and the foresight?' he asks, and is too polite to add: 'What business has an art expert trying to determine the destiny of nations?' Rob-

bie insists that he believes in freedom of trade, and quotes Andrew
Undershaft on 'The True Faith of an Armorer.' But, alas, when I put
this creed to the test, it didn't stand up. My father would not, either
directly or indirectly, permit the democratically elected people's government of Spain to purchase a Budd-Erling P9—not for cash on the
barrelhead."

"You know Spain, Lanny?"

"Not so well as I know France and Germany and England, but I
have visited it three times in the past year. Each time I brought out
paintings, but also I met and talked with all sorts of people, and kept
my eyes open. I saw the putting down of the Franco uprising in Barcelona and the arrival of the International Brigade for the defense of
Madrid."

"What do you think will be the outcome of that fight?"

"The people will certainly be crushed if we continue our refusal to
let them buy arms, while at the same time we permit the Italians and
the Germans to send Franco everything he asks for. I cannot understand our country's diplomacy, and I wish that you would tell me:
Why is it, and what does it mean?"

"The answer is not simple. There are so many forces, some pulling
one way and some another."

"But the President himself, Professor Alston! He is the head of the
government and is responsible for its policies. Can he not see what he is
doing to Europe when he permits the Nazis and the Fascists to combine
and murder a democratically chosen people's government?"

"The President is not the ruler of Europe, Lanny."

"No, but he is the head of our State Department, or ought to be, and
has the say about our foreign policy. Why has he reversed what has
been international law since the beginning; that any legitimate government has the right to purchase arms for its own defense? Why did he
go to Congress and demand that the arms embargo be extended to apply to the Spanish Civil War? Why does he go on supporting the
farce of Non-Intervention after he has had a whole year to see what it
means—that we keep faith with Hitler and Mussolini while they keep
faith with nobody in the world?"

VII

The ex-geographer was gazing into a pair of earnest brown eyes and
listening to a voice that was always well modulated, even when it was
full of concern. They seemed to him young eyes and a young voice;

the same as he had observed them in the conference rooms of the Hotel Crillon, where the grandson of Budd Gunmakers had labored so hard to save the district of Stubendorf, the home of his friend Kurt Meissner, from being turned over to the Poles. Now here was this Lanny in the summer of 1937, nearly twice as old, but still stating a complex problem in simple terms. Or, at least, so it seemed to a "fixer" of high state affairs. Why doesn't President Roosevelt see this? Why doesn't he do that? A fixer hears such questions all day and most of the night; and perhaps he doesn't know the answer, or perhaps he's not free to tell it.

Alston listened until this friend had finished pouring out his demands; then, after a moment's pause, and with a trace of a smile, he said: "Why don't you ask him yourself, Lanny?"

"I have never had that opportunity, Professor."

"You could have it quite easily, if you wished."

The younger man was startled. "You think he'd have time to talk to me?"

"He is a great talker; he loves it. Also, he likes to meet people, all sorts—even those who disagree with him."

"I hadn't thought of the idea," said Lanny; but he was thinking now while he spoke. "It would be a great honor, I know; but I might get into the newspapers—and then what would Robbie say?"

He stopped, and the other laughed. "You might go to sell him a picture. He might really buy one, to make it all right!" Then, more seriously, he explained that the President was at Krum Elbow, his mother's Hyde Park home, which was not so closely watched by the newshounds. "They make their headquarters in Poughkeepsie, some distance from the estate, and they don't haunt the grounds as they do the White House. The President could easily instruct his secretary that your name was not to be included among the daily list of visitors. That might be of advantage to him, also—for it's possible that he might have something confidential to say to a friend of Hitler and Göring."

VIII

It doesn't take long to arrange an appointment when the telephone service is working—and when you are the right person. Early next afternoon Lanny left his hotel, driving a sport car which was at his disposal whenever he visited his father's home in Connecticut. His route took him through Central Park and up Riverside Drive; across a great tall bridge from which he had a breathtaking view; then up the valley of the Hudson River, known to history and legend. Here Major André had been hanged and General Arnold had fled to avoid hanging; here mysterious Dutch figures had played at bowls in the night, thus causing the thunder, and Rip van Winkle had anticipated Freud with his "flight from reality."

The Dutch settlers had moved up this broad valley and with bright cloth and glass beads and other treasures had purchased large tracts from the Indians. Wars and revolutions had left them undisturbed, and now their tenth generation descendants were gentlemen farmers, living in dignified leisure and voting the Republican ticket. Once in a while comes a black sheep to every fold, and so in this staid Dutchess County was a family of Democratic Roosevelts whom their relatives and neighbors looked upon with horror, referring to the head of it as "That Man." The Nazis had changed his name to Rosenfeld and said he was a Jew; millions of worthy Germans believed it, and Herr Doktor Josef Goebbels, who had started the story, had chuckled over it to Lanny Budd.

A well-paved boulevard winds along the edge of the hills, now losing sight of the river and then coming again upon a sweeping view. Every few miles is a village, with houses surrounded by lawns and shaded by ancient trees. Cars are parked in front of general stores, and loungers sit in front of them, chewing cigar stubs, whittling sticks, discussing their neighbors and the doings of their politicians. In the heat of a midsummer afternoon everything is still that can be; only the bees hum, and the motor of a car speeding along the highway at the customary rate of ten miles faster than the law allows.

When Lanny neared the little village called Hyde Park, he found that he was ahead of time, and stopped for a while in a shady spot and waited, going over in his mind for the tenth time what he was going to say to the man who held the destiny of the Spanish democracy in his hands. Would this busy man give him time to say it all? On chance that he wouldn't, what was the first thing to make sure of? Ever since the spring of 1919 Lanny Budd had been trying to change the history of the world—off and on, of course, and in between playing the piano, looking at paintings, and making himself agreeable to the smart friends of his mother and father.

IX

The old Dutch farms run from the highway to the bluffs which confine the river, a distance which may be half a mile or more. Each has its own gates and perhaps a porter's lodge. Lanny drove slowly until he came to gates having a sentry-box with two State troopers on guard. He stopped and gave his name to one who came forward; the man nodded, and Lanny drove on, up a long treeshaded avenue, like a thousand other approaches to mansions that he had visited in the course of his playboy life. This mansion was modest, according to playboy standards: a two-story structure which had been lived in and added to; part frame and part stucco, with towers; the sort of house which really rich people discard as no longer big or elegant enough.

Lanny parked his car in a shady spot on the circular drive. A colored butler opened the door before he rang, and a woman secretary came to meet him in the entrance hall. When he gave his name she led him without delay along the hall and down half a dozen stairs having a ramp alongside. These gave into the library, a spacious room which appeared comfortable and much used. The books were mostly legislative reports; there was a Winged Victory in marble against one of the walls, a model of a ship under glass, and a lady's sewing-bag hanging over the back of one of the overstuffed chairs. These details Lanny Budd took in with swift and practiced eyes. Then he saw a large flat-topped desk near the fireplace, and seated at it, facing him—That Man!

A large man with a large head, powerful shoulders and arms, wearing a white pongee shirt open at the throat. In his middle years he had been stricken with the dread disease called poliomyelitis, and as a result his legs were shrunken; he had to wear braces, and in public you observed him leaning upon the arm of a strong companion. In his home he used a wheelchair, which was the meaning of the ramp leading into the library. Such a stroke would have crushed most men; but one who had the courage to defy his fate, the power of will to persist and train his shrunken muscles all over again—such a man might come out of the ordeal stronger and more self-possessed. Many persons had doubted whether it could be possible for a man so handicapped to stand the strain which the office of President inflicts upon its victims, but F.D.R. had managed to enjoy the job. He was blessed with a buoyant disposition and could make jokes, look at movies or postage stamps, and not lie awake at night trying to solve problems of state.

He was seated in a large leather chair, and offered a cordial hand and welcoming smile. Lanny was to be exposed to the famous "Roosevelt charm," and had wondered: "What will it do to me?" He had encountered various kinds of charm on the old continent where he had been raised; many kinds false, some dangerous, and he had learned to distinguish among them. He saw at once that here was a man genuinely interested in human beings and in what they had to bring him. On his

desk within close reach was a stack of reports and documents a foot
high. These would be hard going; but when somebody like the grandson of Budd's came along, having traveled all over the cultured world
and met its élite—someone who shared F.D.'s own joy of living and his
prejudice in favor of the "forgotten man"—then his face lighted up and
his eyes sparkled and it was as if he had had a glass or two of champagne. "You two are made for each other"—so Alston had said to each.

X

They talked about the ex-geographer; the President said that he had
found him a highly useful man, and Lanny replied: "I made that discovery when I was still in my teens." He described himself, a youngster
who hadn't even finished prep school, plunged suddenly into the cal-
dron of old Europe's hottest hatreds. Everybody connected with the
American peace delegation, even a secretary-translator, had been pulled
and hauled this way and that by national interests, racial interests, business interests. With his father's help Lanny had come to recognize the
real forces behind that conference: the great cartels which controlled
steel and coal and shipping and banking and above all munitions
throughout Europe; which owned newspapers in the various capitals,
subsidized political agents, and moved governments about as their
pawns. Stinnes and Thyssen in Germany, Schneider and the de Wendels in France, Deterding in Holland, Zaharoff in all countries from
Greece to Britain—these were the men who had had their way, and had
broken the heart of Woodrow Wilson.

Zaharoff, munitions king and "mystery man of Europe," had been
no mystery to Lanny. He told how this Knight Commander of the
Bath and Grand Officer of the Legion of Honor had tried to buy a
young American secretary, offering him the most tempting of bribes to
betray his trust and reveal the secrets of the peacemakers. Later, not
being entirely pleased with the treaties, Zaharoff had subsidized a private war of the Greek nation against the Turks. Lanny told how, with
the help of Robbie Budd, he had tried to buy the Bolsheviks at the
Genoa Conference; and how, in Lanny's presence, he had burned his
diaries and private papers and thus set fire to the chimney of his Paris
mansion. When his beloved wife had died, this munitions king of Europe had taken to hiring spiritualist mediums. Lanny had brought him
one, but the seance had produced, instead of the hoped-for wife, a
horde of soldiers shouting vilifications. Among them had been one who
proclaimed himself the Unknown Soldier, buried under the Arc de

Triomphe. He had declared himself a Jew—something which would surely have distressed the anti-Semitic military cliques of France.

A President who had distressed the numerous anti-Semitic cliques of his own country listened with manifest pleasure and remarked: "These are tales out of the Arabian Nights. I command you to come and tell me a thousand and one of them."

"Under penalty of having my head chopped off?" asked the visitor, and they chuckled together.

XI

One who had studied the social arts in France would not make the mistake of doing all the talking. Franklin D. Roosevelt had had his own Arabian Nights' adventures, and Lanny let him tell them. "We have our masters of money on this side of the water, too," he said. "They know just what they want, and are greatly shocked because they cannot get it from me. They were not entirely without influence in the previous administration, as you no doubt know."

"Indeed yes, Mr. President."

"You would be amused to hear of the efforts they made to trap me, after I was elected and before I was inaugurated. The country was in the midst of a panic, and if only I would consent to meet with Mr. Hoover and give him some idea of what I wanted done! The scheme was, of course, that I should be assuming responsibility, taking the panic over as my panic instead of my predecessor's. I let him have it all, up to the very last moment."

"It took nerve, and I admired yours."

"You can't imagine the pressure; it never let up, and hasn't let up yet. They persuaded me into a World Economic Conference in London right after the inauguration, if you remember, the idea being to preserve the gold standard and fix all currencies at the then-existing levels. France and Britain had devalued their currencies and wanted to keep the dollar at the old level, so they could take over the trade of the world. When I realized what it was all about I dumped the chess-board, and I don't expect ever to be forgiven for it. You doubtless know the sort of stories they tell about me."

"I have had them straight from the horse's mouth."

"I am supposed to be drunk all the time, and in spite of my physical deficiencies I maintain a large harem."

"Have you heard the one about the psychiatrist who died and went to heaven and was invited to psychoanalyze God?"

"No. Has that something to do with me?"

"St. Peter explained that God was suffering from delusions of grandeur—He thought He was Franklin D. Roosevelt."

The President threw back his head and laughed heartily; he put his soul into his enjoyment of a joke, and it was a good thing to hear. Lanny remembered that Abraham Lincoln had sought the same kind of relief from too many burdens.

"Just now," said the Chief Executive, "I am in the midst of the hottest fight yet, brought on by my efforts to reform the Supreme Court. Those nine old gentlemen in their solemn black robes have blocked one after another of our New Deal measures, and the whole future of our program depends upon my efforts to break that stranglehold. I have called for an increase in the number of the justices, and this is called 'packing the court,' and is considered the opening wedge for Bolshevism. There is nothing the enemies of this plan will not do or say." The President told some things they had done, and after one tale of senatorial skullduggery he asked: "What do you think of that?"

Lanny said: "I think it shows you are almost as indiscreet as the previous Roosevelt." This brought another burst of laughter, and after it they were friends.

XII

The son of Budd-Erling judged that it was time to bring up the subject which lay nearest to his heart: the peril to the democratic nations involved in the Nazi-Fascist preparations for war, and the demonstration of their program they were now giving on the Iberian peninsula. Lanny told about the trips he had made into Spain, and what he had learned there.

"It is called a 'Civil War,' Mr. President, but it is nothing of the sort; it is an invasion of a free people by the Italian and German dictators. Its purpose is to give them practice in the use of their new tanks and airplanes, and to establish landing-fields and submarine bases to attack the shipping of the free nations when the real war begins."

Lanny described the Spanish ruling classes. "I have played tennis with King Alfonso; I know his set on the Riviera and I have met many of the same sort in Paris and London and in Spain itself. I believe they are the most ignorant, vain, and arrogant aristocracy in Europe. The younger set have learned to drive motorcars, and a few of them to fly, but that is as far as they have got with anything modern; I would have difficulty in naming half a dozen among them who have read a book.

Their interest is in playing polo, shooting tame pigeons, gambling, and chasing women. They are superstitious, and at the same time utterly cynical; about government they know nothing, and if their man Franco wins this war they will turn the country into a paradise for Juan March and speculators like him, and a dungeon for every enlightened man and woman."

"I have no reason for doubting your opinion, Mr. Budd. If I could have my way, governments in many parts of the world would be changed. But I am not the ruler of any part of Europe."

"I believe, sir, that you have the say about the matter which is of greatest importance to the Spanish people's government. I am told that up to this year it has been the invariable rule in international affairs that any established government has the right to buy whatever arms it needs for its own defense. That rule was rescinded last January, and it was you who urged Congress to do it. I couldn't understand it then, and I understand it even less now, when you see that it means the death of one of the most enlightened and progressive of governments."

It was a challenge, deliberately made bold; Lanny all but held his breath while he waited for the reaction of the great man in front of him.

The great man paused to think, and to light a cigarette in a long thin holder. The smile had gone out of the blue eyes, and a grave look had come upon the genial features. "Mr. Budd, you ask me about what has been and still is one of the most painful decisions of my life. I am called a dictator, but you know that such a role is farthest from my wishes or my thoughts. I am the duly elected executive officer of a great democratic people; I am pledged to uphold government by public opinion, and I can do only what the people will let me."

"Of course, Mr. President; but you can sometimes lead the people."

"Up to a certain point, but never beyond it. I can present them with one or two new ideas at a time. If I go too fast or too far, and lose contact with them, then I am powerless to accomplish any of the things I wish. The constant study of my life has to be: 'How fast can I move? How far will the public follow me? Dare I do this? Dare I do that?' Such is the art of government in a democracy, Mr. Budd; often it does not seem heroic, but it is the best way that I know of. It is slow, but also it is sure."

XIII

The President took a couple of pulls at the long thin cigarette holder; at the same time watching his hearer, seeking to read the effect of his words. He resumed: "Call me statesman or politician, the fact remains that I must keep in power or I accomplish nothing. And I am not operating in a vacuum, but in a set of circumstances which I am unable to alter. I am the head of the Democratic Party in the summer of 1937. Have you made any study of this party?"

"I am afraid I don't know my own country as well as I ought to," replied this foreign-born and foreign-raised American.

"In my thoughts I compare myself to a man driving three horses; they had such a hitch-up in old-time Russia—a *troika*. I cannot go anywhere unless I can persuade the three horses to take me; if any one of them balks, the *troika* comes to a halt. One of these horses is young and wild; that is my New Deal group, backed by organized labor and its sympathizers, the intellectuals; they want to gallop all the time, and I have to put a curb-bit in that horse's mouth. The second is much older, and inclined to be mulish; that is my block of Southern states. Those states are run by a land-owning aristocracy, and by new industrialists who are still in the pre-labor-union stage of political thinking. The poor, whether white or black, are largely disfranchised by the poll tax; therefore, the majority of congressmen and senators from the South are always looking for a reason to desert the New Deal. Right now they are finding one in the 'court-packing' program. You have read some of their utterances, I suppose."

"I have."

"And then my third horse, a nervous and skittish steed which I seldom dare to mention by name. You will consider my naming it confidential, please?"

"Of course, Mr. President."

"My Roman Catholic charger. There are twenty million Catholics in this country, and the great bulk of them think and vote as their Church advises. That is especially true of those of foreign descent—Irish, Italians, Germans, Poles. They are strong in our great cities, New York and Boston, Chicago and St. Louis and San Francisco, and their vote determines any close election. They have been told that General Franco is defending their faith against atheistic Reds."

"What they have been told is Franco propaganda, and mostly false."

"That may be so—but will they believe it from a Protestant? I must have their support for my domestic program; so there I am."

That was all the President said; but later on Lanny learned from Professor Alston that the heads of the hierarchy had come to Washington and "talked cold turkey"; in other words, votes. They had said: "Either you keep arms from the Spanish Reds or else we defeat your party."

They could elect Republicans to Congress next year and bring to nought F.D.'s Supreme Court reform plan. They had threatened in so many words to do it.

"Mr. Roosevelt," remarked the visitor, "what you say is almost identical with what Léon Blum has told me. He carried an election on a program of domestic reforms, and is very proud of having pushed them all through. But he had to pay the price which the reactionaries exacted—no aid for Spain. I have warned him in vain—what good will it do him to nationalize the armament industry of France while Hitler is permitted to arm and prepare to overwhelm him? What will be the position of France with a Fascist Spain at her back door and German submarines using harbors on the Atlantic and the Mediterranean?"

"The danger to France is plain enough, because Hitler is just across the border; but you can't use that argument with Americans, three thousand miles away from trouble. Believe me, Mr. Budd, the great mass of our people have just one thought with regard to the European mess: they want to keep out of it. They have no ifs, ans, or buts on the subject; they just say: 'Let Europe go to hell in its own way, but keep us out.' They fly into a fit at the thought of anything that might get us in—such as, for example, the sinking of an American ship carrying munitions to either side in the Spanish war."

"Will they feel that way, Mr. President, when they see the Reichswehr rolling into Paris, and General Göring's bombing planes destroying London?"

"The American people will believe that when they see it; and meantime there's no use in you or me trying to tell it to them. I can say to Congress: 'These are dangerous times, and we must have ships and planes to defend ourselves,' and I can get away with that; but if I should say one word about defending the interests of any other nation or group, I would raise up a storm that would bowl me over. Believe me, I know my master's voice, and when I hear it, I have no choice but to obey. If you want to save Spain, persuade your French friends to stick out their necks; or better yet, persuade Mr. Chamberlain and his Cabinet, the real authors and sustainers of the Non-Intervention policy. If the British cannot see that it is their fight, surely nobody can ask *me* to take it on *my* shoulders."

XIV

So that was that. Lanny was just about to get up and offer to take his leave, but his host had something on his mind and said, abruptly: "Charlie Alston has told me a lot about you, Mr. Budd, all of it good. He thinks I ought to make some use of your abilities."

Lanny wasn't entirely surprised; he had guessed what was in his one-time employer's mind. He said: "I am afraid, sir, I haven't enough training to be of any real use to anybody."

"Very few of us have had training for the work we are doing, Mr. Budd; it is all too new. We have to learn as we go along; we try things and see what happens."

"Mr. Roosevelt," said the grown-up playboy, earnestly, "you are paying me a compliment, and I would hate to seem not to appreciate it. I believe with all my heart in what you are doing, and I would love to be of use to you. But I have ties which compel me to return to Europe and make it impossible for me to settle down to a regular life."

"There might be things you could do for me in Europe, and they wouldn't have to be 'regular.'"

There was a silence, with Lanny thinking hard. He glanced about him to make sure they were alone in the room; then, lowering his voice, he began: "There is something I should have to tell you about my own life, before I could be of any service to you. It is so much of a secret that I didn't mention it to Professor Alston; I haven't told even my father and mother, whom I love. Not merely my own life but many others might depend upon it."

"I am used to receiving confidences, Mr. Budd; and you may be sure that I keep them."

"This must never under any circumstances be told or even hinted to any other person."

"I promise—unless, of course, it is something contrary to the interests of the United States."

"It is nothing of that nature. Many years ago I met in Berlin a young couple, artists, also ardent Social-Democrats, working for freedom and enlightenment in their country. When the Nazis came in, this couple took up what is called underground work; the man was caught, and no doubt has been dead for years. The woman went on with her dangerous tasks in Berlin, and I used to give her money which I earned as commissions on picture deals. When the Gestapo had got all her associates and were hot on her trail, I managed to smuggle her across the border. A year or more later we were secretly married in England. You can see how that dominates my life, and makes it impossible for me to be 'regular.'"

"You mean that she is still going on with her activities?"

"Nothing could induce her to stop. I ramble over Europe, buying pictures for American clients and earning sums of money which I turn over to her. I needn't go into details about what she does; it is a question of getting the truth into a country which has fallen into the hands of the Prince of Lies."

"I quite understand, Mr. Budd; and naturally I sympathize with such efforts."

"I make use of the social position of my mother and father, and of their friends; also, of course, the reputation I have been able to build up as an art expert. That gives me a legitimate reason for going into any country, meeting prominent persons, and hearing what the insiders are saying. I have visited Hitler at the Braune Haus in Munich, and at his Berchtesgaden retreat. I have been on hunting trips with General Göring, and had him try to hire me as his secret agent. As I told Professor Alston, I refuse his money, but promise to tell him things in friendship; what I tell him is news I am sure he already knows, or that won't do any particular harm."

"Fabulous, Mr. Budd! Might it not be worth while for you to visit *me* now and then, and tell me what you learn from General Göring?"

"I have thought of it, sir. What I am afraid of is, it might kill my opportunities in Germany, and put the Gestapo on my trail. You live of necessity in a glare of publicity; and because I was until recently married to a very rich woman, I too have had more than my share of attention. Many reporters know me, and how could I come to the White House without its arousing curiosity? I don't need to tell you that the German embassy has its swarm of spies, and that everything of interest is cabled in code to Berlin."

"All that is true; but it happens that I often have to act secretly, and I have ways of arranging it. There is a so-called 'social door' to the White House, and my friends often slip in unobserved. Also, I have among my personal bodyguards a man whom I have known from his boyhood, and whom I trust. He wouldn't have to know your name; we would agree upon a code word, and any time you got in touch with him and gave that word, he would report it to me and I would set a time for him to bring you. You would be known as a 'P.A.,' that is, 'Presidential Agent,' and would have a number. I believe the next number is 103."

"Very well, Mr. President. If you feel that I can be of use to you in that way, I will do my best."

"Keep an expense account; it will come out of my secret fund."

"No, that is not necessary. I am able to earn plenty of money; I have to, because that is my camouflage."

"But you like to use the money for your cause, do you not?"

"I sometimes earn more than can be safely spent by my wife and her associates; and what I do for you would add nothing to my expenses. Let me be one of your dollar-a-year men."

XV

F.D.R. pressed a button on his desk and the woman secretary appeared. "Missy," he said, "I want to speak to Gus at once." When the woman had gone he said to Lanny: "Choose a code name. Something unusual and easy to remember."

The visitor thought. "How about Zaharoff?"

"Fine!" said the other, with a chuckle. "How long do you plan to be in this country?"

"A couple of weeks. I am here to report to some of my clients."

"Will you be able to see me again before you leave?"

"Certainly, if you wish."

"I may be able to think up a list of questions to ask you, and matters about which you might try to get information for me."

"You will hear from me without fail."

A youngish man built like a college fullback entered the room. "Gus," said the President, "this gentleman is a very special friend whom I shall be seeing now and then. Look him over carefully so that you will know him whenever you meet him. You are not to know his name; we have chosen a code name which he will make use of over the phone, or by mail or wire. The name is Zaharoff. Fix that in your memory."

"Zaharoff. O.K., Chief."

"Whenever he calls or wires you, you will name a time and place where he can get you again in a few hours, and then you will come to me, and I will make an appointment so that you can bring him to me. Nobody else is to know anything about him, and you are not to mention him under any circumstances. Is that clear?"

"O.K., Chief."

"You will give him the phone numbers of your hotels in Washington and in Poughkeepsie, and any other place where he is likely to find you." Then, turning to his visitor: "Could you make it convenient to call in a week or two?"

"You bet," replied Lanny, doing his best to make himself at home in the land of his fathers.

"His name is Gus Gennerich, and he used to be a New York cop.

Talk to him a little, so that he will know your voice over the phone."

Lanny turned to the ex-policeman, who had never taken his eyes off him for a moment. "Mr. Gennerich, I have just been spending a couple of the most interesting hours of my life. I have been meeting a great man and a wise man whom we can trust. He is doing a job for all of us, and we have to be ready to protect him with our lives. You agree with that, I am sure."

"I do, sir."

"The name we have agreed upon is that of a Greek peasant boy who was born in a Turkish village and who came to be at one time the richest man in the world. He was called the munitions king of Europe, and he was the embodiment of everything that we in America dislike and distrust. Z-A-H-A-R-O-F-F, with the accent on the first syllable. You think now you will know me and my voice?"

"I think so."

Lanny took out his notebook and jotted down the phone numbers which the man gave him. The President said: "That is all, Gus," and the man went out.

"Mr. President," declared Lanny, "you have done me a great honor, and I appreciate it."

"A lot of my friends call me 'Governor,'" replied the other. "It is easier to say, and reminds me of the days when I had only one forty-eighth of the burdens I have now. May I follow Charlie Alston's example and call you Lanny?"

"Indeed you may; and be sure that if you give me a commission, I will do my very best to carry it out. Unless I am mistaken we have hard and dangerous times ahead of us, and you will need men whom you can trust."

"I need more of them right now, Lanny, and if you know any, tell me about them. I meant to invite you to stay and have afternoon coffee with us; that is a sort of institution in our family, and you would meet my mother and a couple of my secretaries. But in view of the plans we have in mind, I think you had better just walk out quietly."

"I understand, Governor."

"Don't fail to call Gus a week or two from now, for I shall do a lot of thinking in the meantime. Good-by and good luck to you."

Lanny went out and got into his car and drove away, saying to himself: "By heck! I have fallen for the Roosevelt charm!"

2

Wise as Serpents

I

NORTHWARD up the valley of the Hudson and into that of the Mohawk, Lanny began one of those motor trips in which he combined business with pleasure. He had learned to drive as a boy, and loved the gentle purring of a well-cared-for motor. He enjoyed the variety of landscapes slipping by; his subconscious mind was pervaded by the presence of nature, even while his thoughts were occupied with his personal problems or the destiny of the world. If the mood took him he might turn on the little radio in the car, a combination of inventions by which music could be brought to millions of homes and to travelers on all the world's highways.

Lanny Budd had learned to enjoy those pleasures of the mind and imagination which cost very little and do no harm to any other person. He had learned to take care of himself in a world that was often dangerous. He had learned what he could do, and tried not to grieve because it wasn't everything. The world was tough and stubborn and changed very slowly; just now it evidently meant to grow worse before it grew better. Jesus, who had lived in a time not so different, had said to his disciples: "Behold, I send you forth as sheep in the midst of wolves: be ye therefore wise as serpents, and harmless as doves."

In the trunk of Lanny's car was a cardfile listing hundreds of paintings with their prices, also a couple of bags containing photographs. He was what the English call a "bagman" and the Americans a "drummer," but never in either land had there been one so exclusive. He would travel a couple of thousand miles and call upon only half a dozen clients, all of whom had invited him to visit them whenever he could. In each case he had telephoned to make sure the visit would be convenient. He would arrive at a country estate and the servants would carry in his bags; he would spend the night or a week-end, making himself the most acceptable of guests. He would tell about the great ones overseas and what they were doing and saying. He would inspect his host's

24

art treasures, and would say what he thought with judicious and precise discrimination. He would linger over the last treasure he had purchased for this client, asking how it was "wearing"—meaning whether the client still found pleasure in looking at it. If there was any uncertainty in the tone of the reply, Lanny would say: "You know I could probably get you an offer for it."

When the time came to settle down to business and tell this client what the bagman or drummer had in mind for him, it would be one special item which Lanny had come upon in some old castle of the Rhineland or château of the Loire country; something that had caused him to exclaim: "This belongs in the Taft collection"—or whatever it might be. Sometimes he would come in his father's station-wagon, bringing the painting with him; if he came early, ahead of his host, he would make bold to have the butler take down a painting from the head of the staircase and hang the new treasure, so when the host came in there would be a vision of glory hitting him between the eyes.

It was Lanny's practice to let the work speak for itself; never, never could anyone say that he tried to force a sale or revealed anything but critical impersonality. "Be sure, this work will find a home before I get back to Connecticut." And the host would know this was true, for money was free in America again; the fortunate few had floods of dividends rolling in, and it was a problem to know what to do with them. If you were collecting old masters and wanted an expert to bring you choice items, you behaved in such a way as to earn his respect: that is, you sat down promptly and wrote a check for twenty or forty or possibly a hundred thousand dollars.

All his life Lanny Budd had been learning how to handle the rich and powerful. In earliest childhood he had watched his father and mother doing it. In those days Robbie had been selling the instruments of killing. Generals and cabinet ministers had been the customers, and duchesses and countesses had been flattering and cajoling and "pulling them in," all for a fee, of course. Early in his twenties, Lanny had discovered his own line; the sums were smaller but the techniques the same, and the psychology of the victims. The excessively rich were as shy as wild birds; everybody was hunting them and they took wing at the least hint of danger. They were abnormally sensitive and had to be handled as if they were made of wet tissue paper. They would absorb flattery like sponges—but only that subtle kind which assured them that they were above flattery. Each client was a separate problem, and love of beautiful art and love of wonderful self were tied up together in a knot of many complications.

II

The last stage of this tour was Pittsburgh, where Lanny's friend Harry Murchison made and sold immense quantities of plate glass, and was always interested in the latest news about glass-shattering in Europe. Harry had gained about two pounds avoirdupois every year since the outbreak of the World War, when he had come so near to becoming Lanny Budd's stepfather. Now he was married to his former secretary, and Lanny never tired of observing the speed and certainty with which American women acquire the social arts. Adella Murchison was now a stately matron, perfectly sure of herself and her leadership in the cultural life of her grimy home city. Lanny had provided her with the lingo of the arts, and every time he came visiting she acquired a fresh supply with which to impress her friends. She was willing to pay generously, and when Harry objected: "Where on earth will you put another painting?" she replied: "I have heard you say that no excursion steamer is ever so crowded that there isn't room for one more passenger."

Adella was at their place in the Adirondacks, and Harry said: "I have got me the wings of a dove and I fly to my beloved every weekend." He invited Lanny to come along, and when Lanny explained that he had an urgent engagement in Washington, his friend countered: "I'll deliver you in Washington on Monday morning before I come back here." When Lanny asked about his car, Harry offered to have a man drive it to Washington. When the rich want something, they get it.

Harry's dove proved to be a comfortably equipped private plane with seats for a pilot and three passengers. It rose from the Pittsburgh airfield just after business hours and settled gently down on the Lake Placid airfield before sundown. Harry's secretary had phoned to announce their coming, and Adella was waiting, driving the car herself; they wound through pine forests laden with pungent odors and came to what was called a "camp," a quite sumptuous slab-sided mansion on a remote little lake. They supped on a platter of fried black bass which had been swimming in those blue waters a couple of hours previously. The couple plied their visitor with questions—Harry about the prospects for more glass-shattering in Europe, and Adella about the friends he had met and the paintings he had discovered on that unhappy but interesting old continent.

Presently it came out that the Murchisons had seen a play about Queen Elizabeth and the Earl of Leicester, and Lanny perceived that

Adella's imagination had been captured by the brilliant and willful figure of the queen's lover. "I can tell you where you can get a portrait of his wife," remarked Lanny, "the unfortunate Amy Robsart. She was married when they were both mere children, and she was killed by falling down a flight of stairs. There were whispers that somebody had thrown her down, as a means of freeing her husband to marry the queen."

"Is it a good painting?" asked the plate-glass lady.

"The painters of that time were none of them of the best. This is supposed to be the work of Marc Gheeraerts, whom the English call 'Garrard.' I am not sure if the attribution is justified, but it's an interesting work. The painter was apparently more concerned with the subject's elaborately jeweled clothes than with her character. All those Tudor ladies were so stiff in their corsets that it is hard for us to imagine them as having any life."

"Where is the painting?"

"It is at Sandhaven Castle. The owner's wife is Rosemary, my old flame; they neither of them care much about paintings, and every time Bertie gets into debt she invites me to tea and brings the conversation around to the price of old masters."

So it was that Lanny carried on his business, having a cardfile of paintings and another of customers, and matching a card from one with a card from another. Adella lit up right away; she had met Rosemary Codwilliger, pronounced Culliver, and had driven by the castle, and now she asked questions about both, and then about the unfortunate Amy Robsart. Lanny said: "You can read all about her in Sir Walter Scott's *Kenilworth*." He knew that this would make a hit, because Adella liked to have stories about her pictures, things that she could use to interest and impress people.

"What do you think it could be bought for?" she wanted to know, and he told her he hadn't asked for a price, but his guess would be something less than a thousand pounds.

"I'd better not cable, because that might sound as if you were anxious. I am sailing for England at the end of the week and I'll pay a call on Rosemary and take a stroll along the gallery and lead up to the subject tactfully. The Robsart family was connected with Bertie's—I don't remember just how and he probably doesn't either."

"You have sold us so many men," remarked Adella, referring to her two Goyas and her double Velásquez suspected of being a del Mazo. "It's time you got me a woman. Is she really pretty?"

"Sweet and rather pathetic," replied the subtle expert. "I'll send you a photograph, and you can decide whether you'd like to have the lady in your home."

So it was that Lanny made money for the underground movement against the Nazis in Germany. So also it was that Adella made sure of receiving visits from a charming man who lightened the smoke-laden atmosphere of that city where she had been born and had raised herself from far down in the social heap to the very top.

III

Set down at the Washington airport on Monday morning, Lanny got busy on the telephone and gave the password. "Gus" told him to call again at noon, and when he did so the order was to be at a certain street corner at a quarter to ten that evening. It happened to be raining, and Lanny with overshoes and umbrella stood watching the speeding traffic, standing back far enough from the curb so as not to be too badly spattered. A car drew up, and the President's bodyguard looked out and nodded.

"Not a very good night," Lanny remarked, as he stepped in. The other replied: "I'll say!"—and that was all the conversation. They rolled up Pennsylvania Avenue, and into the "social door" of the hundred-and-forty-year-old building which had housed all the Presidents of the United States but the first. At the gate there was apparently no guard; at the door, which is the main front door under the white pillars, the guard looked at Gus and said: "Hello." Avoiding the elevator, they went up a flight and a half by a rather narrow, red-carpeted staircase. An aged Negro servitor passed them, saying: "Evenin', Mista Gus." They stopped at one of the doors which was ajar; Gus tapped gently, and that warm voice which all the world had learned to know over the radio called: "Come in."

The President was lying in bed, wearing pajamas of blue pongee, covered by a knitted blue sweater, crew-neck style. His head was propped up, with a reading lamp at his left shoulder and a "whodunit" lying on the sheet which covered him. "Good evening," he said to his visitor, not naming him; then, to the other man: "Thank you, Gus." As the man started to retire, the President added: "Close the door, please."

So the two conspirators were alone. Lanny took the chair by the bedside, and the other coughed slightly and reached for his handkerchief. "I am supposed to have a cold," he said. "I am growing suspicious of my subconscious mechanism, for I notice that I develop the sniffles whenever I have a tiresome schedule like today."

"I hope I am no part of the cause," replied Lanny, grinning.

"You are what I wanted to be free for. Have you had time to think about the subject of our talks?"

"I have been motoring most of the time, and I've thought about it constantly."

"Needless to say, Lanny, I haven't had that much time: but I have made notes of several things I want to ask about."

"Shoot!" replied the other; and without further preliminaries they got down to business.

Said F.D.R.: "There has grown up a practice on the part of our leading American industrialists to make secret deals with the big European cartels, whereby they share one another's processes and inventions upon a strict monopoly basis. It appears from the social point of view a highly undesirable practice. I am not sure what I can or should do, but it seems clear that with wars threatening as they are, the government ought to get all possible information on the subject. Do you happen to know about it?"

"I have heard my father discussing it with his friends and associates. I know that such deals have been made with I. G. Farben Industrie and with A.E.G., the great electrical trust of Germany. I have been told that the du Ponts have such arrangements, also a prominent lead company and Standard Oil of New Jersey, I believe having to do with artificial rubber."

"I am not proposing that you should do detective work," explained the President. "That is the business of our Intelligence, and usually they get what they go after. But often we can save a lot of time and wasted effort if we know where the big booty is hidden and where to start digging. A casual remark dropped by one of the insiders may be worth more than tons of documents."

"Quite so," replied the other. "I have heard such remarks, and could easily make note of them. My father talks to me freely and tells me what this or that one has told him. I could be present on such occasions; the only reason I haven't is that I am bored by talks about making money, even in the biggest amounts."

"Do you intend to tell your father about these meetings with me?"

"I plan not to tell anyone, even my wife. It wouldn't do any good, and the wisest and most loyal person might drop some hint by accident. In the case of my father, he is very bitter against your policies: income taxes in the higher brackets, and what he called 'doles,' and your 'court-packing'—a long list. Just now the C.I.O. has got into his plant and is threatening a sit-down strike, and that makes him sore as the devil. If I told him I had met you, it would be the occasion of a long discourse, every word of which I already know by heart. My father is a kind and generous man, and has a sense of humor; you, Governor, would find him very good company, if only it weren't for politics and your threatening his control over what he considers his private affairs."

"It is something I have often observed," remarked the "Governor," with a sad smile; "the conservatives have the best manners and are the easiest to get along with."

"I have speculated about it. They have everything they want, whereas the advocates of social change are apt to be fanatical and narrow, and sometimes motivated by jealousy, one of the meanest of qualities. The conservative has a whole community behind him and he obeys its rules; that makes for serenity and pleasant feelings. The radical, on the other hand, has to make his own rules; he makes many mistakes, and tries his own temper as well as other people's."

IV

It was as Alston had said; these two were "made for each other." Both had grown up in comfort and near-luxury, never knowing deprivation; both were generous by nature and dreamed of a kindlier world; both had met with disappointments and disillusionments, but were stubborn and did not easily give up their dreams; now both were fighting-mad in their hearts, but kept a smile on their lips because that was good form, that was "sporting." Also, they both liked to talk, and were tempted to ramble into the fields of philosophy and literature and what not. But the time was short, and they would jack themselves up and come back to business.

Lanny told about his Paris friends, the de Bruynes, to whom he was related in a peculiar French way. Denis was a leading financier, growing always richer; his cousin had been chosen one of the governing board of the almighty Banque de France—and then Léon Blum had broken the private control of that institution. Lanny could hear all the secrets of France talked in Denis's drawing-room; he could meet Laval, Bonnet, Tardieu—any of the other scamps.

He told about his friend Kurt Meissner, who had become one of the top Nazi agents in Paris. A distinguished German musician and composer, Kurt had access to the highest circles, and everywhere he went he talked persuasively about the problems of the two countries. Why should Frenchmen let themselves be used as pawns by the English in their policy of keeping the Continent divided? Was it not easier to shake hands across the Rhine than across the Channel? France and Germany represented the two highest cultures in the world, and why should they not unite? And why should Frenchmen of breeding and social position permit themselves to be ruled by demagogues and Jews, the dregs heaved up from the bubbling kettle of social hates? Hitler was the man who had solved the problem of labor unionism, and his solution was good for all countries. Hitler was the one enemy of Bolshevism who really meant business; what greater crime against the true interests of French culture than to let the Jew demagogues draw them into alliance with Russia, the arch-enemy of all culture and indeed of all civilization?

So thought Frenchmen, especially rich young Frenchmen, the *jeunesse dorée*, after they had talked with Kurt Meissner in drawing-rooms. Lanny said: "I can never be sure how much Kurt trusts me now. He is secretive, but I watch him through the minds of his victims, and I know that he will be worth an army corps to the Nazis when their invasion starts."

"When will it start, Lanny?"

"The day they are ready. Powder deteriorates, planes get out of date, so why wait an hour after your machinery is set to go?"

"You are certain that Hitler means war?"

"Many of my friends cannot believe it, and I put it to them this way: A man who is poor starves himself and spends all his time and labor to build a bicycle. What are you to assume about his purposes? Do you assume that he is intending to sail on the sea? Or to play music? Or to give his friends a banquet? No, because you cannot sail on a bicycle, nor play tunes on it, nor eat it. A bicycle is good for only one thing, to ride a bicycle; every part of it is made for that, and no part of it is good for anything else whatever."

Lanny told of conversations with his client and host, the head of the Luftwaffe. Hermann Göring was a man of many pleasures but of only one business, which was preparing to make war from the air. Lanny described the huge new office building of the Air Force in Berlin, with three thousand rooms; he told about the airports with hangars hidden underground—Robbie Budd had visited one at Kladow, and had been staggered by the completeness of it. Said the son: "Robbie thinks the fat general is making a grave mistake by building short-range fighter planes when he should have bombers to bring England to her knees. But Hermann only laughs and winks. What he means, of course, is to put troops ashore in England and fly those planes from English fields."

"How can he do it while the English control the seas?"

"He expects to do it by parachutes, and by submarines and dive-bombers sinking the British fleet. He figures that it won't take long to ferry troops across twenty miles of water, and they will be specialists, with weapons the like of which has never been seen in the world before."

"The reports I get differ widely, Lanny. I'd like very much to know the real numbers of the German Air Force; I mean actual first-line planes of the different types."

"I think my father comes pretty near to knowing those figures. But you must bear this in mind, Governor—what counts at this stage is not so much the number of planes as the machine tools, the jigs and dies, the stocks of aluminum and rubber and so on. Hitler isn't ready for war yet, and won't be for two or three years. Meantime he tries one bluff after another, but is ready to back down before any strong move of Britain or France."

"The British tell me they daren't move, because they're not prepared."

"That is the statement of public men who have lost the habit of action. Military expenditure in Germany now is two and a half times that of Britain. What good does it do to delay when you're falling behind at that rate?"

V

Twice Lanny offered to leave, but the President wouldn't let him. "I'll sleep late," he said; then, grinning like a schoolboy playing hooky: "I have a cold and won't be able to keep appointments." He lighted one cigarette after another in the long thin holder—certainly not a therapeutic procedure—and went on asking questions about the old continent which was managing its affairs so badly and might again be calling upon America for help. F.D. had discovered here another self, a self that had lived abroad and knew all the people who were in the headlines there. It was as if the morning newspaper had come suddenly to life, and the persons in it stepped out and started talking.

"Tell me about Hitler," said the President; so Lanny described that strange portent, half-genius, half-madman, who had managed to infect with his mental sickness a whole generation of German youth.

"Years ago I made a remark in a woman friend's hearing: 'There will be nothing to do but kill them.' The remark horrified her so that I promised never to make it again. But it is literally true; they are a set of blind fanatics, marching, singing, screaming about their desire to conquer other peoples; it is their God-given destiny, and they have no room for any other idea in their heads. They have a song: 'Today Germany belongs to us, tomorrow the whole world.' The German word for belongs is *gehört*, while the word *hört* means hears; so in Germany they sing 'belongs to us' and abroad they sing 'hears us,' which sounds less alarming. That is typical of the Nazi technique. Hitler has written in his book that you can get any lie believed if you repeat it often enough; and especially if it's a big lie—because people will say that nobody would dare to tell one as big as that. It is no exaggeration to say that he has made Germany into a headquarters of the Lie; he has told so many and so often that nobody in his country has any means of distinguishing truth from falsehood."

Lanny described the Führer in the early days of his movement, coming onto the platform of a crowded beer cellar in Munich, the living image of Charlie Chaplin with his tiny dark mustache and ill-fitting pants. In those days he always wore a rusty brown raincoat; he was the proletarian leader, the rabble-rouser, the friend of the common man. "People here make a grave mistake," Lanny said. "They think of Nazism as a reactionary movement, an effort of the capitalist class to put down labor and the Communists; but Nazism was a revolutionary movement—that is the only way any movement can get power nowadays. Hitler promised the redistribution of landed estates without compensation, the abolition of what he called 'interest slavery,' the whole program of populist revolt."

"We had such a man in this country—Huey Long."

"I'm sorry I didn't meet him."

"Believe me, I did! He was all set to be my successor. He once had me waked up at one in the morning to give me hell over the telephone from Baton Rouge for some appointment he didn't like. I refused to cancel it and he was my mortal enemy forever after."

"There will be others like him," replied Lanny, "unless we solve the problem of poverty in the midst of plenty. The German middle classes, the little men like Hitler, were being wiped out, and he offered a millennium, also a scapegoat, the Jews. When he got the votes, he took them to the big industrialists and sold them for more campaign funds."

That aspect of the movement had few secrets for Lanny, because his father, a steel man himself in those days, had heard the German steel men talking about the sums they were turning over to their new political boss. "Thyssen alone put up five million marks."

"And now he's very unhappy, I am told," remarked the President.

"Don't let that fool you. Hitler is a wild horse and has taken the bit in his teeth—but he's galloping in the direction the big industrialists

want him to go. They are finding it a wild ride, but they expect to arrive at their destination, which is the integration of the industry of the
Continent and its control from Berlin."

"Control by the Hitler gang?"

"But under the rules of the big business game. A big industrialist
wants to turn out unlimited quantities of goods, and have an unlimited
market for them at what he calls 'fair' prices, that is, prices which allow
him a profit. He wants to take these profits and reinvest them in his
plants and turn out more goods, and so on, over and over—he calls it
the 'turnover,' and as long as he can make it he's happy. That is the situation in Germany for every man who can produce war goods; also for
every worker who has any sort of skill. Naturally, they all think it is
herrlich, and that the Führer who has brought this about is some sort
of magician, or an emissary from on high."

"It is really Hitler who is directing it?"

"It is the technical men of German industry, and the officers of the
general staff of the Wehrmacht. They are probably the most highly
trained military men in the world, and of course it is *herrlich* for them,
because for the first time all German industry, both capital and labor,
does exactly what they, the members of the Herrenklub, direct. Emil
Meissner, Kurt's brother, is a member of that club. He was doubtful of
Schicklgruber, the demagogue, but now he worships Hitler, the inspired master of the German destiny. I have seen Emil rise from lieutenant to general in less than twenty-five years, and today he is probably
the happiest man I know; he has everything exactly the way he wants
it. The Communists, the Socialists, the democrats and pacifists are all
dead or in concentration camps; every good German is hard at work,
living frugally and investing his savings in government bonds; and all
the money the wizard Schacht can create is going into the building of
that bicycle I was telling you about a while ago, the machine on which
the German Army is going to ride to world mastery."

"It is a terrible picture you paint, Lanny."

"I assure you, Governor, I am no painter. I am only a transporter of
paintings. When I come on one that seems to me worth while, I bring it
to this country and show it to my friends. The most important one for
you to look at is the picture of this German war machine being tried
out in Spain. Hitler is sending his tankmen, his artillerymen, and above
all his airmen there in relays; nobody stays more than three or four
months, just long enough to learn the new techniques of swift and
deadly mechanized war; then he goes back to Germany, and tells it to
his superior officers, and on the training fields in the Fatherland he

teaches it to hundreds of others. The Italians are doing the same, but they're not so good; they don't really like war and nobody can make them. But the Nazis like nothing else, and the result is going to be that they will have a large army of trained and eager professionals, while all the other peoples, except perhaps the Japanese, will be bungling amateurs. The Nazis are training some of their stormtroopers right here in America; I have seen them in New York, and they may be doing it even in Washington. You tell me you can't prevent what is happening in Spain, Governor, but surely you ought to be able to do something in America."

Said the President: "I think I can assure you we're not entirely over-looking that part of our duty."

VI

It was after two in the morning when the great man released his visitor. The last thing he said was: "Make your reports as short as you can. One man sent me a long one, and when he asked if I had read it, I told him I hadn't been able to lift it!"

He pressed a button, and told his colored valet to summon Gus Gennerich. The man came promptly, and escorted Lanny out of the building by the same door they had entered. The rain had stopped, the moon had come out, and Lanny said: "It will be a pleasant day." The reply was: "Looks like it." Evidently this ex-policeman didn't consider it his duty to make conversation with "P.A.'s." He drove Lanny to his hotel.

Much later that same morning the art expert turned secret agent set out on the crowded highway to Baltimore. He reached New York before sundown, having approached the city by the Pulaski Skyway, and crossed the George Washington Bridge. He was heading for Newcastle, Connecticut, for he had already engaged steamer passage and desired as much time as possible with his father.

He had phoned that he was coming, and there was always a warm welcome for him. He had allowed his "Pink" ideas to sink into the background and be forgotten; he had kept his second marriage secret, and to his stepmother and half-brothers and their families he was the art expert and man of the world, lover of music and friend of famous and important people. He didn't mention that Franklin D. Roosevelt had been added to the list. He talked, instead, about his art adventures, and especially about the Murchisons, whom Robbie knew. To fly to the Adirondacks for a week-end was a decidedly swanky thing, and

Lanny's half-nephew, Robert Budd III, piped up: "Why don't you build us some passenger planes, Grandfather?"

Grandfather was sixty-three, an age at which most men think of retiring; but Robbie Budd was just getting ready to conquer the world, by way of the air above it. As a preliminary, he had more than once conquered himself. In his youth he had been "wild," or so his stern Puritan father had judged him. Lanny was the product of that wildness, and as a result was still looked upon askance by the older generation of Budds; they were a long-lived and long-memoried tribe. Again, a decade or so ago, Robbie had been "playing the market" heavily, and drinking much more than was good for him as a result of the strain, also of the bitterness in his heart against his father and his oldest brother.

But now all that was over; Robbie's father was no more, and Robbie was on his own, nourishing colossal hopes. He had broken with Budd Gunmakers, which had been taken over by a Wall Street crowd and was making mostly hardware and "specialties." Robbie's heart was set on the dream that some day the new firm, his creation, would have a bigger turnover and pay higher dividends than the family firm which had been wrested from them.

Robbie Budd lived and breathed and ate and talked airplanes: catwalks and bulkhead segments, stabilizers and de-icers, sub-assemblies and spot-checking—a whole new vocabulary which the members of his household had to learn. Robbie's conscientious wife, who had suffered at the spectacle of his weaknesses and had even had to take Lanny into her confidence, now shared his high ambitions, and did everything to encourage and help him: inviting the plant engineers to dinner, and even studying the highly technical reports which determined the obsoleteness of the B-EP10 and the expected supremacy of the B-EP11.

Robbie Budd was a football and polo player who had taken to golf, and had added fifty pounds and a load of dignity. His gray hair became his florid complexion; his manner was hearty, and he enjoyed talking, provided it was with some person who liked to listen to what Robbie liked to talk about. If left to himself, he might have grown slouchy, but his wife kept him in order by the simple device of causing his used garments to disappear and new and spotless ones to be in their place. She kept his home the same way, causing cigar stubs and ashes and used whisky glasses to disappear. The house was large and elegant, but slightly suggestive of a Puritan meeting-house, with plain papered walls and furniture of the sort which Esther's forefathers had made. On the walls of the drawing-room hung several paintings by Arnold Böcklin which Lanny had found in Germany, knowing that they would please his stepmother because they embodied or were supposed to embody philosophical ideas.

VII

Into this household came Lanny on his secret errand. He must get his father to talking, and carefully guide the conversation to the subjects which had been listed for him by That Man in the White House —who was Robbie's pet peeve and the embodiment of all evil and destructive tendencies of the time. Lanny mustn't make the mistake of showing too much interest in any one subject; he must let his father ramble along. No notes could be made, but Lanny would fix names and figures in his memory, go to his room and jot them down, and then come back for another load.

It seemed a mean sort of job, spying on one's father. But Lanny wasn't going to report anything which could do Robbie any harm; he was only going to harm the cause which Robbie had taken for his own, the cause of bigger profits for businessmen all over the land; also the maintenance of that autocratic control of industry which Robbie considered essential to its progress, and which Lanny considered a menace to the higher sorts of progress, political, social, intellectual. There was no use arguing the point, no use trying to reconcile or explain two opposite points of view. Nobody could tell Robbie Budd that the workers had any capacity or any right to meddle with the control of industry; Robbie considered that the workers belonged exactly where they were and were getting exactly as much pay as they were worth. Robbie didn't really consider them competent to have anything to say about politics either, but he was reconciled to that system, having found that he could make deals with the political bosses in his town and county and state. He hadn't been able to control the Presidency or the Congress, in spite of expensive efforts in combination with other Republican big businessmen; they had tried their best and a few months ago had got a sound licking. Now every time Robbie thought about it he got so hopping-mad that it made his veins swell out dangerously.

Lanny had to say to himself: "I am a traitor to my family's ideas; I am a snake in the grass." He had to say the same thing in the home of his ex-wife and her friends in England, and with most of the fashionable ladies and gentlemen who came to his mother's home on the French Riviera. He had to take with them the pose of art lover and ivory-tower dweller to whom politics was a base trade, far beneath a gentleman's notice. He had to listen to the expression of the most reactionary opinions, and if someone asked him a direct question: "What do you think about it, Mr. Budd?"—or Herr Budd, or Monsieur Budd as the case might be—he had to be ready with some playful answer, something that would pass for a *mot* in the smart world: "Well, all sorts of people manage to make politics pay, and I suppose we shouldn't be too much surprised if labor tries the same thing."

VIII

What Lanny did with his father was to ask how things were going in the plant; his father told him they had just installed the "mating jigs" for the new model. Lanny expressed interest in this odd form of the reproductive process, with the result that Robbie offered to take him and show him the latest devices. Next morning he was escorted through that quite extensive plant which had sprung up in a few months on what had until recently been a mosquito-breeding marsh. He gazed down from a balcony into a great room which appeared to be a jungle of complex machines, each one beating and pounding out its own individual tune. Lanny knew, of course, that every machine had been placed exactly on a spot which engineers had measured to the hundredth part of an inch; he knew that the motions of those machines were determined in some cases to the hundred-thousandth part of an inch, and that the finest watch had never been built with such care as the pieces of steel and aluminum and magnesium and what not which were here being stamped or ground or polished amid such a variety of sounds that it all became one, an infinitude of racket which, so Lanny was assured, the ears of the workers soon ceased to record at all.

Down a long line appeared, in process of growth, a row of swift and deadly fighter planes which would be able to hurl themselves through the air at the rate of a mile every fifteen seconds or less. There weren't nearly as many on that assembly-line as Robbie had hoped to see, and the line wasn't moving fast enough to please him; but he stubbornly clung to the belief that old Europe was soon going to war, and then everybody would be calling for Budd-Erling pursuits. Robbie had seen it magically happen in Paris at the end of July 1914, and Lanny had been there, helping as well as a precocious lad could do. Neither had forgotten any detail of it, and so now they could talk to each other in shorthand. Robbie said: "God knows I'm not asking for it, but it's coming." Lanny wondered: Was it humanly possible to stake one's whole fortune on a gamble, and in one's secret heart not be hoping to win?

Inside that fabricating plant was order, but outside was chaos. Going and coming, Lanny passed through a string of real-estate subdivisions full of jerrybuilt cottages and shacks of varied ugliness, with gas stations and sodapop stands and "eateries" scattered along the main road. It had grown that way, because that was the way Robbie Budd had willed it; Robbie was not afraid of chaos, but saw danger in any sort of order except his own. Lanny's heart ached, because in England he had seen garden cities, and in Vienna beautiful blocks of workers' apartment houses built by the Socialist municipality. Why couldn't something of that sort have been done in Connecticut?

But Robbie Budd had his God called Individualism, and this ugly nightmare was His temple. Robbie wanted no government and no workers' movement of any sort in or near his place; if he could have had his way he would have forbidden all meetings and organizations of any sort whatever. But now the C.I.O., most radical of mass movements, was spreading in his plant, and Robbie was fuming and raging, considering it treason and conspiracy. None the less so because it was backed by the power of the United States government—or as Robbie preferred to put it, by a gang of political shysters who had got hold of the government and were using it to wage a war of vengeance against those who owned property and carried the responsibilities of industry. No doubt whatever of the perfect sincerity of Robbie Budd's opinion of the "New Deal"!

IX

In between tirades Lanny gathered details about the arrangements existing between I. G. Farben, the great German chemical trust, and the Standard Oil Company of New Jersey for the sharing and exchange of patents and technical secrets in the production of artificial rubber from petroleum. He learned about similar deals in other industries, and got the names of various persons who had such secrets locked in their bosoms or their safe-deposit vaults. Lanny would say: "Do you really know that, Robbie?" and his father would reply: "Thyssen told me himself"—or perhaps it would be Krupp von Bohlen, or one of the de Wendels or the du Ponts. Oddly enough Robbie Budd himself had somewhat the same arrangement with Göring; Robbie had his men in Göring's plants and the fat Exzellenz had his in Newcastle—Lanny could be sure of it, for he met them. But he didn't intend to mention that in his reports to F.D.R. The President had agreed with his new secret agent that it was all to the good to have an aircraft fabricating plant hidden up one of the navigable rivers of Connecticut, and a force of American technicians and workers acquiring the "know-how" in that vitally important industry.

Also Lanny collected information as to the present status of the Luftwaffe. Some of it came from Robbie, and some from those Nazi technicians, who knew about the younger Budd's connections in Hitlerland, and thought of him as a friend of their cause. He spoke a fluent German and could tell them about visits to Karinhall and Berchtesgaden. They were bursting with pride over the achievements of their Third Reich, and what more natural than that some of their bursts should be aimed in Lanny's direction?

After listening, the investigator would retire to the room which had been his since his first visit twenty years ago; he would set up his little portable machine and type out the report, not forgetting to make it short. He would seal it in an envelope marked "No. 103," and put this into another envelope addressed to Gus Gennerich at the ex-policeman's Washington hotel.

X

Duty done, Lanny was free to enjoy himself. Early next morning he bade good-by to his father's family and drove half-way to New York, stopping at the home of the Hansibesses, as he called his half-sister and her violinist husband. Hansi Robin was giving a concert for a workers' group in New York that evening, and Lanny's steamer was sailing at midnight. So everything fitted nicely; Lanny would drive the musicians in, after the concert they would see him off, and Bess would drive the car back to her father's next morning.

The Hansibesses had a baby boy, now a year old; they had called him Freddi, in memory of his uncle whom the Nazis had murdered. He was Lanny's half-Jewish half-nephew, with the lovely dark eyes and hair of his father, whom Lanny had called a shepherd boy out of ancient Judea. He was learning to toddle about and to say new words every day, and kept his parents in a state of constant admiration. His grandmother came over from her home to have lunch and meet her adored Lanny, and point out qualities in the treasure-child which might otherwise not be noticed. Hansi was composing a sonata, and he and Bess played the first movement for their visitor, and Bess indicated features in it which her husband was too diffident to mention.

In the afternoon the grandfather came out from the city. Johannes Robin, formerly Rabinowich, was making money again, though on a far more modest scale than that which he had known in Germany. Upon him rested some of the responsibility for keeping that great

Budd-Erling plant going. He had charge of the sales office in New York, and took flying trips to France or Holland or Turkey, to South or Central America, or Canada—for Budd-Erling was making not merely fighter planes, but also an "all-purpose job" which was carrying supplies to mines in the high Andes and to prospectors in the far northern wilderness. Johannes didn't sell anything to Nazis or Fascists —he left that to his long-time partner, Robbie, who had a stronger stomach. Johannes was tireless in reading newspapers and technical journals, watching out for large-scale business enterprises which perhaps had never realized how they might speed up their work by the use of airplanes.

A greatly changed Johannes Robin from the eager and rather egotistical person whom Lanny Budd had happened to meet on a railroad train in Europe nearly a quarter of a century ago. Now he was subdued and humbled, content to be alive and to have got his loved ones away to this safe corner of a deadly dangerous world. It no longer worried him that his surviving son and the son's wife called themselves out-and-out Reds. Johannes would have turned anarchist if he had thought that was a way to bring justice upon the heads of those Nazi barbarians who had murdered his son and come so near to murdering himself. Lanny didn't have to use any subterfuges in asking a one-time *Schieber* for information as to the secrets of European *haute finance* and its deal with the new masters of Germany. Johannes would pour it out in floods, and would have been greatly pleased if he had known what use was going to be made of it.

XI

Lanny drove them all in to the concert, which was held in a hall on the East side, its purpose being to collect funds for the aiding of Jews who had escaped into the countries bordering on Hitlerland. The place was packed to the doors with Jewish men and women, some of them old but most of them young, a few bearded but most smooth-shaven, a few well-to-do, but most poor. Jews of all sorts and sizes, but mostly undersized; Jews with dark curly hair and some with red; Jews with Jewish noses, but many who might have been taken for Russians or Poles or Hungarians or Italians or Spaniards. They had been mixed up with all the European tribes for a thousand years, but alas, it hadn't done them any good. Once upon a time, long ago, a group of Jewish holy men in a fanatical mood had called for the killing of another Jewish holy man, and by an odd quirk of fate posterity had remembered the executed one, but had forgotten that he was Jewish. He was God, and only those who had called for his death had been Jews; so now in the slums of this crowded Manhattan Island tough little Irish boys and tough little Italian boys would frighten little Jewish boys by yelling: "Christ-killer!"

In Germany this hatred had become a mental disease, and Jew-baiting a substitute for social progress. So there was grief in the faces of this crowd and they had come as to a synagogue. It was a labor crowd, and most of them had broken with their ancient faith, but the spectacle of wholesale torture and humiliation had brought them back to the Ark of their Covenant. Hansi Robin, tall and dark-haired, might have stepped out of any of the books of the Old Testament; he stood before them, grave and priestlike, playing the Jewish music that he loved: *Kol Nidre* and Achron's *Hebrew Prayer*, and Ernest Bloch's *Nigun*, from the *Baal Shem* suite. The audience listened spellbound, and many sobbed, and the tears ran down their cheeks. This was a people who made no secret of their woes; who in the old days had rent their garments and wailed, put on sackcloth and sat in their backyards sprinkling their ashpiles over their heads. "My confusion is continually before me, and the shame of my face hath covered me, . . . Behold, I was shapen in iniquity; and in sin did my mother conceive me. . . . Deliver me from bloodguiltiness, O God, thou God of my salvation: and my tongue shall sing aloud of thy righteousness."

Hansi's accompaniments were played by his wife, who was a grand-daughter of the Puritans, and thus had derived a great part of her moral being from those ancient Jewish scriptures. As for Lanny, he had lived most of his life in the Midi; he loved to laugh and sing and dance, and it came hard to him to lament and torture his soul. But he had committed himself to the Jews by sanctioning his half-sister's marriage, thus helping to bring a half-Jewish baby into the world; he had taken Hansi's brother Freddi Robin as his comrade, and in his efforts to save Freddi had got himself into a Nazi dungeon and seen an elderly Jew beaten close to death. So Lanny was bound in soul to that unhappy race; he had to listen to their music and share their torments, to stand by their Wailing Wall and climb to the summit of their Calvary.

XII

There were still parts of the world where the Jews were not tortured and degraded; where they were citizens and free men and women. One of them was America, and another was the Soviet Union, where Hansi and Bess had visited several times. Whenever they played for the workers, which they did frequently, the couple always closed by playing the *Internationale*. Always the audience would rise and cheer, even those who were not Communists; for, whatever their creed might be, they knew that this hymn meant battle against the oppressors. These New York Jews wanted to fight Hitlerism with any and every weapon they could lay hands upon.

After Hansi had exchanged greetings with one or two hundred workers, the three went out to their car, and Lanny drove them west to the pier where a great steamer lay waiting for its passengers. They had an hour or so for a final chat; then the deep whistle sounded, and the two musicians went out to the pier and watched the steamer towed out into the river. A great harbor, and, half-way out of it, the Statue of Liberty with her blazing torch. Lanny had first seen her in the midst of World War, and she had been welcoming him to the land of his fathers. Later, departing from New York during the Wall Street panic, he had thought that she was drunk. Now she had reformed, but was sad, because so few looked at her or thought about her any more. She might have liked to send back a message to her native land of France, which was facing such a dark and uncertain future. Her torch was wavering in shreds of fog, and it might have been a signal.

But Lanny Budd wasn't on deck to see it. He was down in his cabin, hammering away on his little portable, making notes of statements which Johannes Robin had made and which were to be sealed up and marked "No. 103," and sent by the little boat which took the pilot back to land.

3

Trust in Princes

I

IRMA BARNES, once Mrs. Lanny Budd and now the Countess of Wickthorpe, had at last found a way to spend some real money. She had been handicapped for years because Lanny hadn't cared about spending it, but preferred to live in a little old villa on the shore of the Mediterranean. Now Irma was engaged in modernizing one of the most famous of English castles, part of it dating back to Tudor days. She was taking out pretty nearly everything but the walls and floors, and putting in every gadget she could think of, or that was suggested by a lively young architect whom she had met in a New York night club. Wickthorpe Castle was going to show the English upper classes what they had been missing all these years. She went every day to watch the work, and to imagine the sumptuous entertainments she was going to give when it was completed. Meantime the family was living in Wickthorpe Lodge, adjoining the estate. She had rented it years ago and lived there with Lanny; a convenient arrangement, because it had enabled her to get acquainted with her second husband before breaking with her first.

Irma had crowned her career by being taken into the English nobility; everybody showed her deference, the servants addressed her as "my lady," and it was all delightful. She was going to bear an heir to an earldom; at least, she had a fifty-fifty chance of doing so, and was praying for luck. At the same time she was having her portrait painted by Gerald Brockhurst, a painter who was well recommended and who charged accordingly. One hour every morning she sat for him; not being a chatty person, she sat for the most part in silence, considering whether the armor room of the castle should be left in its present gloomy condition, or should be done over in batik or something else cheerful.

The daughter of J. Paramount Barnes was happy. She had had the responsibility of a great fortune placed upon her shoulders in childhood, and now at last she felt that she was making proper use of it. Her husband had an important post in the Foreign Office—he was a careerman in spite of being an earl, something out of the ordinary. He worked hard and took seriously his duty to protect the future of the British Empire in unusually trying times. His wife would help him by entertaining splendidly but at the same time with dignity; she would spread his influence, and get him promoted. Ceddy couldn't become Prime Minister, but he might become Viceroy of India. Mary Leiter had made it —why not Irma Barnes? In any case she would help to preserve an ancient and honorable tradition, and hold in check the forces of discontent which were undermining property and religion in England as everywhere else. Irma was only twenty-seven, but had lived a great deal, so she considered; she had come close to those satanic forces, and been shocked to the depths of her otherwise placid being; she hated them, and knew that she was going to devote her influence, social and political as well as financial, to combat them.

II

In the midst of these labors and planning came a wireless message from her former husband, on board a ship. "Arriving day after tomorrow will it be convenient for me to see Frances reply Dorchester Hotel regards Lanny." Brief and to the point; polite beyond criticism, but Irma knew that inside the velvet glove was the mailed fist. Lanny had a fifty per cent interest in Irma's child; he could claim fifty per cent of the little one's time, and of the control of her rearing. He could come to see her when he pleased, and everything must be made pleasant for him. If there was any hint of disharmony, he might suggest taking the child away with him, and that filled both Irma and her mother with distress. To be sure, the "twenty-three-million-dollar baby," as the newspapers called her, was no longer anywhere near that rich, for Irma's fortune had been reduced by the depression, and she had settled a chunk of the remainder on her new husband and their future offspring. But kidnapers mightn't know that; and while there was said to be none in England, what was to prevent the child's father from taking her to France, where she had been born, or to New York, where Irma herself had been born? No law that Irma's solicitors could find for her!

Irma really knew her former husband. She knew that he called himself a "Pink," using the word jestingly. Irma herself declined to recognize shadings; she called him in her heart a "Red," and generally with the double adjective "out-and-out." No amount of play-acting on his part, no talk about art for art's sake or ivory-tower residences, could fool Lanny's ex-wife. She could be sure that whatever political facts Lanny might pick up from the lips of her highly placed guests he would carry off and repeat to his friend Rick, the bitter and aggressive left-wing playwright and journalist.

But what could Irma do about it? She had agreed with Lanny in their parting that she would not mention his political opinions as the cause of their break. She had granted this in return for Lanny's promise not to propagandize the child with his ideas. Irma had taken her mother into her confidence—and Fanny Barnes cared very little about the safety of the British Empire but very much about her prerogatives as grandmother. Fanny was urgent on the subject—her daughter must not do the slightest thing to irritate Lanny and cause him to assert the prerogatives of the other grandmother. Lanny was socially acceptable, wasn't he? He knew how to make people like him, and most of Irma's friends did like him. All right then, let him come as a guest and treat him like any other guest.

In America it was supposed to be "sporting" to take divorce lightly and remain friends; and Irma, as an American, would take that right. Nobody, save perhaps the rector of Wickthorpe parish, would be shocked to meet her ladyship's first husband at dinner in her home; and Fanny Barnes would take the rector off, explain matters to him, and require him to show a true Christian spirit. If Lanny pretended to be in sympathy with the ideas of the other guests, that was his concession to harmony, his effort to avoid causing embarrassment. For heaven's sake, let him get away with it, and don't say a word, don't even frown, but make him feel that he is the most appreciated of personalities!

So Lanny would have a cottage on the estate; he would have servants to wait on him and prepare his meals; and if an innocent child wanted him to come to lunch with her and her mother and grandmother, she would have her way. Lanny would entertain them with news about the Budd family, whom Irma knew well, and the Budd-Erling plant, in which Irma owned a million-dollar block of stock. Lanny would play the piano for his daughter, dance with her the farandole which he had taught her in Provence, and take her horseback riding on the estate, of course with a groom to follow them.

Seven-year-old Frances Barnes Budd was a happy child, and healthy like her two parents. She had dark brown eyes and a wealth of dark brown hair like her mother; a vigorous and active body, eager for every sort of play, but not much impulse toward the life of the mind—again like her mother. She adored her father, who came to her like a prince out of a fairy story, always with adventures to tell, and music and dancing and games. She had been guarded from every evil thought, including that of trouble between her parents, or that there was anything unusual about having two fathers.

She was the incarnation of six years of marriage, with their joys and sorrows. Lanny could put all these out of his thoughts when he was out in the busy world, but when he came here he saw them before his eyes. Being of an imaginative temperament, he would fall to thinking: "Could I have saved that marriage? And should I?" Six years of shared experience are not to be wiped out of the soul, which has depths beyond the reach of any eraser. He would wonder: "Could I have been a little more patient, more tolerant? Could I have made more allowances for her youth, and for the environment which made her different from me?" He would wonder: "Is she thinking such thoughts now? Is she remembering our old happiness?" He would never ask such questions, of course, for that would be a breach of good form, a trespassing upon her new life.

He had not come to visit Irma, but Frances. He would play with the child, devote himself to her—but how could he help seeing the mother in the child? He would start thinking his "Pink" thoughts about their offspring. Poor little rich girl! Some day she would awaken to the fact that she was set apart from other children, and that what was supposed to be a great good fortune was in fact an abnormality and a burden. She would discover that friends could be mercenary and designing, and that love was not always what it pretended to be. She would discover the secret war in the hearts of her mother and father, and that this war extended over the whole earth and divided all human society, a chasm deeper than the Grand Canyon of the Colorado, or those which lie at the bottom of the ocean floor. Frances' mother was content to live on her own side of that social chasm, while Frances' father insisted upon crossing from one side to the other and back again—a most unstable and nerve-trying sort of life. But he must never let the child know about it—for that would be unsettling her mind, that would be propagandizing!

III

In the evening Lanny would be invited over to the house which for a year or two had been his home and Irma's. Perhaps it would have been tactful for him not to come, but he had his secret purposes in coming. He had known Ceddy since boyhood, and Ceddy's friend and colleague in the Foreign Office, Gerald Albany, who lived near by. They knew that Lanny had been tinged with Pinkness, and they were used to that in their own ranks; they took it for granted that as men acquire experience, they learn how hard it is to change the nature of men and nations. When Lanny said that he had decided to leave politics to the experts, they took that to mean themselves, and the arrangement was satisfactory.

So they talked freely about the problems facing the British Empire. They had a "line," which Lanny understood perfectly: British governments change, but foreign policy never, and that was why Britannia had ruled the waves over a period of four centuries. If in the course of the conversation the American guest put in the suggestion that it might now be necessary for the old lady to give some thought to the air above the waves, that was taken good-naturedly; it was well known that

Lanny's father had airplanes to sell, and one might reasonably assume that the son had an interest in the business. Commercial men weren't looked down upon as they had been in old England; for, after all, this was an industrial age, and business and politics were pretty thoroughly mixed. The recent Prime Minister, Mr. Stanley Baldwin, had been an ironmaster, and the present Prime Minister, Mr. Neville Chamberlain, was an arms manufacturer from Birmingham.

There existed at this time a peculiar situation in the inner shrine of the British government. Intelligence Service, most secret of all organizations, was turning in one report after another showing that the German Air Force had outstripped the British; also, that the German Navy was disregarding its pledged word to limit construction to one-third of the British. Prime Minister Chamberlain, who believed in business and called it peace, was solving the problem by sticking the reports away and forgetting them. But Anthony Eden, Foreign Minister, was on the warpath against this course, and Sir Robert Vansittart, the highest permanent official of the Foreign Office, was backing him up.

Gerald Albany, the embodiment of propriety, would probably not have mentioned this delicate subject in the presence of an American; but Lanny let it be known that he had heard about it. So then they talked. Ceddy declared that the trouble was due to the inability of some statesmen to face frankly the fact that Hitler had made Germany into a great power, and that she was again entitled to cast her full vote in the councils of Europe. Irma supported him, speaking with that new assurance which had come with her title. It was her idea that her new country should make a gentleman's agreement with Hitler covering all the problems of Europe, and should use this as a lever to force France into breaking off the Russian alliance. Thus, and only thus, could there again be security for property and religion. Lanny, listening to her emphatic phrases, thought: "She is still quarreling with me in her heart!"

IV

The basic principle of British policy for a couple of centuries had been to maintain a balance of power on the Continent, and to fight whatever nation attempted to gain dominance there. Before the World War that power had been Germany. After that war, it had been France, which had accumulated a huge gold reserve and used it to build up a "Little Entente" in Central Europe and to demand a share of the oil of the Near East. Thus it had become necessary for the British to lend money to Germany and build it up as a counterweight. Now there were many in Britain who thought the counterweight was growing dangerously heavy, and that France should again receive the support for which she was clamoring, and for which Léon Blum had come a year ago to beg in vain.

The problem was complicated by the upsurgence of Russia, which most British statesmen had written off as a derelict after 1917. Russia now had an alliance with France, but didn't know whether to trust it or not, and the British didn't know whether the French meant it, and whether they should be encouraged to mean it or to sabotage it. French policy, unlike the British, did change with the government, and that was a bad thing for the French, and for their friends and backers. Many persons in Britain took the position that the question of Russia was not merely a political issue, but a moral one; they refused to "shake hands with murder." Gerald Albany, a clergyman's son, was among these; but Ceddy spoke cautiously, saying that in statecraft it was not always possible to be guided by one's moral and religious ideas. "We should have had a bad time at the outbreak of the last war if we hadn't had the aid of Russia; and surely the hands of the Tsar had bloodstains enough."

The fourteenth Earl of Wickthorpe was about Lanny's age, and everyone agreed that he had a brilliant career before him. He was tall and fair, with delightful pink cheeks and a little blond mustache of which he took care. He was quiet and serious, a good listener and slow speaker. He considered himself modern and democratic, meaning that in his own set he did not exact any tribute to his rank. In his dealings with those below him it had never occurred to him to do anything but to say what he wanted in the fewest words and to be at once obeyed.

He had known Lanny well, and had excused Lanny's free and easy ways on the ground that Americans were like that. When he had met Lanny's wife, at one of the international congresses, he had the thought that she had made a poor match, and it was a pity. He wondered if she had realized it, and before long he decided that she had. He had known about the American practice of easy divorce, but the idea had been repugnant to him, and he had been rigidly correct in his attitude to his friend's wife all through the period when they had rented the Lodge and had the run of the castle.

Only when he heard the news that Irma was in Reno getting a divorce had he allowed himself to think about her seriously. Evidently she liked him, and evidently liked the thought of being a countess. He wasn't pleased by the idea of having a second-hand wife or of being a stepfather; but, on the other hand, he was pleased by the idea of getting out of debt and being able to preserve his great estate in spite of outrageously high taxes. He had contrived to be sent to "the States" on a diplomatic errand, and had invited the blooming grass widow to become his bride with the same grave courtesy as if it had been a proposal to lead the grand march in a ballroom. She had been very generous; the trustees of her estate had sat down with his lordship's solicitor and inquired what settlement was desired, and had agreed to everything with no more than a casual reading of the somewhat elaborate document.

V

There were not many guests at week-ends, because of the lack of room in the Lodge; but friends dropped in in the evening and there was talk about the problems of the world. Just now it was Spain, which resembled a bunch of firecrackers going off in the vicinity of a powder-keg; no one could tell which way the sparks were going to fly and when all Europe might blow up. A publisher of newspapers, a little man who himself resembled a bunch of firecrackers going off, urged Wickthorpe to talk to friends in the Cabinet and bring about the recognition of General Franco as a belligerent without further delay. Lanny, who had been informing President Roosevelt that the British and French governments were conniving at the destruction of the Spanish people's government, now heard this powerful British publisher maintain that the British and French governments were favoring the Spanish Red government so outrageously that it amounted to driving Italy and Germany to war against them. "It will come, and we shall be to blame for it," declared Lord Beaverbrook, who had once been plain Max Aitken, company promoter of Canada. He had made a million pounds there, and now he owned *The Daily Express* and the *Evening Standard*, and from his state of mind you would have thought that the Bolsheviks were in the act of laying siege to these valuable properties.

Nearly a year ago the various governments had formed what was called a "Non-Intervention Committee"; it was meeting in London and had held something like seventy sessions, every one of them an acrimonious wrangle. The Italians and the Germans, who had intervened in Spain from the first hour, meant to go on intervening, while steadily denying that they had ever thought of such a nefarious action. Lanny had heard a story of a Kentucky Colonel who knocked a man down, and when asked: "Did he call you a liar?" replied: "Worse than that; he proved it." That was the situation before this Committee, which refused to receive complaints from individuals, but couldn't prevent representatives of the Soviet government from proving that the Italians and the Germans were systematically sending in troops and matériel to General Franco. Then the Italian and German delegates would fly into a fury and fight their share of the war in London.

A German cruiser off the coast of North Africa had been attacked by what Berlin called "Spanish-Bolshevist submarines." Berlin now demanded that Britain and France take part in a naval demonstration off Valencia. France, patrolling the French frontier with Spain, demanded that Portugal should patrol its frontiers, through which Italy and Germany were pouring in supplies; when Portugal refused, France withdrew her patrol officers and left her highways open into Spain. That was the way it went; one crisis after another, and no way to stop them. It was obvious to insiders of every nation that Franco alone could not conquer his people; if "Non-Intervention" were actually enforced, the Fascists would be licked. Italy and Germany were determined that this should not happen. At any and all costs, their man was going to win.

What did the British want? They had great difficulty in making up their minds; all choices were painful. Obviously they couldn't permit the Reds to build themselves a fortress on the Atlantic seaboard, enclosing all Europe in two prongs of a pincers. The British owned immensely valuable properties in Spain—Rio Tinto copper, for example, indispensable in making munitions—and certainly they didn't want strikes and Red commissars in those mines. On the other hand it might be fatal in wartime to have German submarines based on the Atlantic, and France enclosed in a pair of Nazi pincers. On the whole it seemed best to let the two sides fight it out and exhaust each other, and then a compromise government could be set up, the sort the British could lend money to. The only trouble was, neither side was willing to admit that it was exhausted; this was a war to the death, a kind which is bad for trade and every sort of vested interest.

In Downing Street there had been one crisis after another, and people's tempers were beginning to be frayed. Even in the most exclusive drawing-rooms, among English ladies and gentlemen, there were exhibitions of bad manners. Among the guests at Wickthorpe Lodge was an author of novels very popular in smart London circles; he had airy manners and was a great ladies' man, in spite of the fact that he was growing bald. In his thinking he was for practical purposes a Fascist, and did not resent the label. Lanny had met him here and there at parties, and knew that he was a confidant of Lanny's Fascist brother-in-law, Vittorio di San Girolamo. When Gerald Albany remarked that the trouble was that nobody could depend upon the word of Mussolini, he was "such a gutter-rat," this novelist blew up. "My God, man, what sort of world do you think you're living in? Do you imagine you can handle those Italian Reds like members of your Sunday-school class? They are bomb-throwing, knife-sticking anarchists, and before Mussolini put them down they had seized half the factories in Italy. Do you imagine you know how to deal with people of that kidney? And when you have to find men to do the same job in England, do you imagine they'll be polite church members like yourself?"

"I'm not telling Mussolini how to govern Italy," replied the Foreign Office man mildly. "But when he asks for the right to blockade Spanish ports and keep British ships out of them, I naturally have to consider what he offers in return, and whether I can believe what he tells me."

"All I can say is," retorted the novelist, "when there's a killer in your house and you call for the police, you expect them to shoot first and present their character certificates afterward."

VI

Lanny Budd would listen and say little; only now and then a well-chosen question, to steer the conversation if it could be done. He fixed in his memory details which might be of importance; the character of statesmen and their secret purposes, the attitude of great industrialists, the state of popular movements, the military preparations of this country and that. Alone in his room, he would type out the data and address them to Gus Gennerich, not putting the letter in with other mail that went out from the castle, but saving it to be posted in a public box.

Having done this, he would have moods of satisfaction, followed by others of depression. He had fallen for the Roosevelt charm, but the spell did not last all the time. Professor Alston had warned him that F.D.R. was of an "impressionable" temperament. He had been full of sympathy for Spain while listening to Lanny's story, but could it be that next day he had received a visit from someone high up in the hierarchy of the Holy Church and had heard stories about nuns being sprinkled with oil and burned by Spanish Reds? And would he believe these stories—or at any rate let the prelate depart in the belief that he believed them?

Anyhow, even with the best of intentions, could he absorb all the facts which came to him? What a brain would have to be in that large head to classify and retain them all! The President of the United States must have hundreds of people working for him and bringing him information; thousands must be sending it on their own impulse. Where did it all go? Who read it and heeded it? Lanny saw a vision of his reports being handed in by Gus and added to the pile on the desk. Something else would cover them up in a few minutes, and would they ever be uncovered again? Lanny would have to go back and find out if F.D.R. had ever heard of them, or if they had been lost in the files! And suppose the great man happened to be too busy to see him—what then would become of an art expert's bright dream of changing world history?

"Put not your trust in princes," the psalmist had advised, and Lanny was not heeding the warning. In those old days princes had had to take measures to keep other princes from poisoning them; the surest way was to poison the other princes first. Nowadays princes had to think about raising campaign funds and getting re-elected, keeping control over Congress in the off years, and matters such as that. They wanted to make the world safe for democracy, and at the same time to keep the country out of war. When they discovered that these aims were incompatible, they were in a predicament, and what wonder if their words one day contradicted the words of the previous day, and if their actions were not always in accordance with the campaign platforms of their party?

This much Lanny had already learned: that the favor of princes is a very tempting thing. For princes can act, whereas art experts can do nothing except talk in drawing-rooms. One gets so tired of futility, and of seeing things going the wrong way. If only somebody who *could* do something *would* do it! That had been Lanny's thought for more than half his life, ever since he had seen a world war burst upon a horrified humanity. Now he saw another getting ready to burst; black thunderclouds on the horizon, rolling rapidly upward, shutting out the sunlight; and people going about, heedless, as if in a dream; as if they were blind and couldn't see the darkness, deaf and couldn't hear the rumble of the thunder—those guns and bombs in Spain, to abandon the simile and deal with plain facts. The grandson of Budd's had been close enough to the first World War to have shell splinters fall near, and the son of Budd-Erling had already been close enough to the second to see houses destroyed by shellfire and hear bullets whining past his ears. How could he help being nervous about the prospects?

VII

Lanny couldn't visit England without paying a call at The Reaches, one of his half-dozen homes. A lovely thing to have friends, and to know that you have chosen well and aren't going to have to sever precious ties and mutilate your own life; to know that marriage isn't going to change your friend, nor political disagreements, nor weaknesses of character. To see a family grow, and yet always be the same; to see a tradition surviving and being passed on to new generations; to see knowledge increasing and loyalty never failing—yes, if you have a friend like that, and his adoption tried, you grapple him to your heart with hooks of steel.

Sir Alfred Pomeroy-Nielson, Bart., was in his seventies, but as lively as ever and as interested in what was going wrong in the world about him. He had filled two rooms of his rambling old red-brick house with original documents on the contemporary English drama, and was still dreaming that he might find somebody to help him pay the expenses of this unusual sort of collection. His wife had died not long ago, but he had three children and twice as many grandchildren, all living in England and dutifully visiting him now and then. His oldest, Rick, lived with his family at The Reaches; Nina kept the house, a task not too difficult, since servants were plentiful. In 1937, as in 1914, there were young people dancing and singing all over the place, playing tennis, punting on the Thames, and in the evening sitting out in the moonlight, listening to distant music and experiencing thrills the like of which they were sure had never before been heard of in the world. As always, they considered themselves a unique and original and vitally significant generation; they were respectful to their elders, who held the pursestrings, but slightly sorry for them, as being so backward and out of date, preferring Beethoven to hot jazz, and Tennyson and Browning to Auden and Spender.

Rick was no good for punting, on account of his knee which had got smashed while helping to save England; but his oldest son was at home, vacationing from Oxford, and Alfy's long legs and digestion were sound, in spite of his months in a Franco dungeon. It was the first time Lanny had seen him since their parting on the right bank of the Tagus River several months ago; Lanny hadn't really seen him then, just a dark form stepping out of a boat and scrambling up the bank, dislodging the stones of Portugal. Of course Alfy had written, pouring out his thanks, more ardently than he could do now that he was face to face with his rescuer. But he managed to get out: "I'll never forget it, Lanny; and be sure that if I ever have a chance to return it in kind, I'll be there."

"I hope I'll never be in a fix as bad," replied the family friend. "But if I do, I'll holler."

"And be sure I'm going to earn that money and pay it back," added the youth.

"That was a contribution to the cause, Alfy; and both you and I will make more of them, I don't doubt."

"You will make them all until I have paid you back," declared the baronet's grandson. He said no more, for the subject of money wasn't dwelt upon in his world. Rick had already sent an installment of what it had cost to buy the lad out of a Fascist dungeon, but Lanny had returned it, knowing that the large family was in debt and not likely to get out of it, with Rick deliberately refusing to write "potboilers," as he called the sort of plays his rich friends enjoyed seeing.

Lanny said: "I've come on something interesting in the States; a way to put some of our ideas across. But I'm pledged not to talk about it."

"That's all right," replied Rick; "if it's a secret, the fewer who know it the better."

"There's nothing to prevent my passing information on to you as always," added the visitor. He told some of the news from his Connecticut home, and bits of what he had heard at Wickthorpe Lodge.

"The Beaver is on the warpath, privately as well as publicly," commented the playwright. "They call him flighty, but you notice that he never wavers from loyalty to his fortune."

"And to Empire Free Trade," added Alfy. It was the scheme of having parts of the British Empire trade with one another, to the exclusion of the rest of the world; "the Beaver" had been tireless in its advocacy ever since his Canadian days.

"It's all the same," replied the father. "It means that greed and jealousy continue to rule the world, and people spend their substance building fences to keep the rest of the world out."

Eric Vivian Pomeroy-Nielson was a saddened man. He was only a couple of years older than Lanny, but already there were touches of gray in his wavy dark hair and lines of care in his forehead. He had had his success as a playwright, but that had been a fluke, so he declared, and wasn't likely to happen again. He had his ideas of what was decent, and he followed them, even though he saw the rest of the world traveling another road. He slaved to collect material and organize it into a thoughtful article, and then he sold it to one of the weeklies for five or six pounds. He might have got ten times as much from one of their press lordships, Beaverbrook or Rothermere or Astor, on the single condition that he would write what they told him instead of what he believed.

Alfy was tall like his father, more slender, and had dark wavy hair;

his features were thin and sensitive and his spirit high. He had absorbed his father's ideas, and took them with desperate intensity; he had proved it by going off to Spain to fight in the air for the people's cause. Now he was under a sort of parole and couldn't go to Spain again; he had taken up the idea of the law as a career, and Lanny knew that it was as a means of repaying his debt. Lanny didn't think that this idealistic lad would ever be a moneymaker in any field, but he let the matter rest until Alfy should have finished at Magdalen College, pronounced Maudlin.

VIII

The grandson of Budd's was accustomed to refer to himself playfully as an amphibious animal; one of those prehistoric lizards whose ancestors had always lived in the water, but which was now climbing out onto the rocks and painfully learning to breathe air in its pure state instead of air that was hidden in the interstices of drops of water. The Lanny lizard could manage it for a while, he said, but every now and then the effort would become too great and he would have to slip back into the element which was his natural home.

By that element he meant the world of fashion and pleasure. It was a world where everybody had, or at any rate was assumed to have, all the money he could possibly want. It was the "leisure-class" world, and the people in it were proud of the fact that they had never done and didn't know how to do anything useful. The farther back they could trace an ancestry which had never done it, the more distinguished they were. To them the world provided every luxury the ingenuity of men had been able to devise: delicious foods and rare wines, with skilled cooks to prepare and trained servants to serve them; soft and delicate fabrics, cut always in a manner having esoteric significance; fast motorcars, swiftly gliding yachts—and not merely physical satisfactions, but intellectual and moral and aesthetic; great music and literature and art —in short, all the delicate and gracious things that life had to offer. The best examplars of that leisure-class life were truly delightful companions.

The Lanny lizard would crawl out of this agreeably warm ocean onto the hard rocks which were called "reality," into the rare and cold atmosphere known as "social reform." Here people slept in uncomfortable beds, ate poor food badly served, and wore clothing entirely without distinction. They were frequently worried about money and forced to borrow it from someone who had it—which usually meant the Lanny lizard. They worked hard and had few pleasures; they were frequently embittered and hard to please; they were jealous, not merely of the idle rich, but sometimes, alas, of their own comrades whose labors had won too great appreciation. They played little and studied and read a great deal; they were apt to be proud of their knowledge, and had invented a jargon of their own, more adapted to repel than to enlighten.

In short, it was a difficult atmosphere to breathe, and the lizard would find himself getting dizzy and yearning for his old-time home. It was fatally easy to slide back into that pleasure ocean; and moreover, it was from there that he got his food; he had to go back for what were called "business reasons," and his friends the reformers were glad to have what he brought out of it. The result was, Lanny was one of those creatures which have both gills and lungs, and spend their time splashing in the tide-waters, being caught by the waves and bumped against the rocks, and never sure what they are or where they belong.

IX

In this world of fashion and pleasure one of the conspicuous activities was the making of love. To these elegant ladies and gentlemen love had become a game; something to cultivate and experiment with, always in refined and elegant ways, of course. It was something which pervaded their beings, like a perfume always in the air, like soft music heard from far off, while eating, sleeping, or conversing. The ladies of fashionable society prepared themselves elaborately for the practice of this gracious art. Their costumes were carefully devised to stimulate and suggest it, by revealing exactly the proper portion of their "charms." Ideas of what was permissible differed widely in different lands, but in those of the West it had been the custom to reveal the face, the arms and shoulders, and the upper part of the bosom; of late years the entire back down to the waist had been added to this list. When stimulation began to fail, exposure must be increased.

The same sort of changes had been observable in the dance. A little more than a hundred years ago Englishmen had considered it grossly indecent to stand face to face with a lady and put one arm around her and hold her ever so lightly while going through the movements of a dance; Lord Byron, usually no prude, had written a vehement protest against a vile new procedure known as "waltzing." Now this practice had had its day and lost its charms; it wasn't tantalizing enough or mimetic enough to interest anybody. Dancing had become still more obviously a form of love play, a way of titillating the most basic of all instincts, of suggesting the most universal of pleasures.

Reflections upon this subject of love and love-making were passing through the mind of Lanny Budd for the reason that he had promised his friend Adella to get a price on a painting in the fine Georgian home of his old sweetheart, Rosemary. She was a year older than Lanny, which meant that she was at the age called "dangerous" for women, and therefore not entirely safe for men. Lanny had been keeping away from her on purpose, but now business drew him to her. He could come near to guessing her thoughts, for he knew her as well as he ever could know any woman. She had been his first love, and memories of her perfumed nearly all his haunts. She had sat with him by the river-bank at The Reaches, and on the shore at Bienvenu, his mother's estate. She had motored with him through France and Germany, and sailed on the yacht *Bessie Budd* all the way to the Lofoden islands.

She was gentle and kind, and had accommodated herself to his eccentricities. When the time had come for her to marry, she had considered that she owed it to her family to choose a member of her own class; at least, that is what she told Lanny, though he suspected that she had wanted to become a countess, and had enjoyed that eminence. Anyhow, she hadn't wanted to hurt him, and didn't see why he should be hurt. The ladies of her class made such state marriages—*mariage de convenance* was the French phrase; they bore their children and then considered their duty done; after that they could be free if they wished, and as a rule they did. Bertie, the earl, had had his affairs, when and as he pleased; in the course of the years Rosemary had become certain that he would play fair and not object to what she did, provided she observed reasonable discretion. Such was the fashion in the smart world, and if you didn't like it you could stay out of it—which you probably had to do, anyway.

Rosemary and Lanny had been happy for a couple of years, and then, after a ten years' interval, for another year or two; why not for a third period? She knew that he was divorced, and she would be frank and straightforward in "propositioning" him. And what was he going to answer? He couldn't say: "I am married again," for that was a secret which he shared with only three persons, Rick and Nina and F.D.R. He couldn't be mysterious and say: "Sorry, old dear," for Rosemary would ask straightway: "Is there another woman?" and if he was the least bit vague about it she would draw her own conclusion. She knew many of his friends, and it was a part of their modernism to talk with frankness about their own and others' sex lives. The story would go out: "Lanny Budd has another woman, and who is she?" Everybody would be watching him, and the longer he kept the secret the hotter would become their curiosity. Reserve was one thing your smart friends wouldn't forgive; it was a mark of distrust and opened you to the suspicion that you were involved in something disgraceful.

On the other hand if he said: "I am no longer interested in you, Rosemary," that would be wounding her intolerably. He couldn't say: "I have adopted a different moral code," for either she would know it was an evasion, or else her curiosity would be aroused; that was one of her characteristics, and she would want to know all about these new ideas and where had he picked them up. He thought of telling her that he wasn't well, but he knew that his looks belied it. In short, he couldn't make up his mind what to say, and had to leave it to the inspiration of the moment, a dangerous thing for a person of sympathetic nature.

X

Rosemary had taken care of herself, as ladies of her world know so well how to do. She did not look her age; a bit "matronly," but nowhere near to "plump"; Lanny knew that it meant heroic dieting, the foregoing of a lesser pleasure for the sake of a greater. She had always had a wealth of straight flaxen hair; she had scorned to bob it in the bobbing season and now she scorned to wave it in the "permanent" season. She was as Nature made her, trusting that great mother and with good reason. She permitted few cares to disturb her, for she had "inherited that good part."

She received him in her sitting-room, newly done in pale blue silk. Windows were open and a gentle breeze stirred the curtains; a bird sang on a branch almost inside. "He gets paid with breadcrumbs," said Rosemary. "Oh, Lanny," she added, "it's so good to see you! Why don't you come often?"

It was a bid at the very outset, and he chose to evade. "This bird has to travel long distances for his breadcrumbs. I have just come from America." He talked about Robbie Budd, who had always been her friend, and who sent his warm regards. He told news about the Robin family, and his mother, and other mutual friends; that was the sort of conversation she liked; she could take an interest in general ideas if she had to, but she found it rather exhausting and rarely did it if the other person would let them alone. She told him about Bertie, who was fishing in Scotland, and about her children, who were nearly grown, depriving their mother of the last hope of concealing her age.

Presently he asked: "Have you any more paintings you would like to get rid of?"

"Oh, Lanny, you are going to make me talk about horrid business things!" But she resigned herself without difficulty, and they strolled through the gallery. She remarked that Bertie was always spending more than he made; women were always "working him" for presents. When Lanny came to the unhappy Amy Robsart he looked at her for a while and then said: "I know a woman in the States who might be interested in that, if you would put a reasonable price on it. The woman has been reading *Kenilworth*."

Possibly Rosemary had never heard of that novel, but she wouldn't be *gauche* enough to reveal the fact. "What is it worth, Lanny?"

"I'm not the one to tell you, because I'd be getting my commission from the purchaser and I'd have to represent her."

"I know, Lanny, but you're my friend, and I have to ask someone I can trust. Tell me what you'd be willing to pay if you were buying it from a dealer."

"Bless your heart, darling, I'd pay the least I thought the dealer would take, and the dealer would ask the most he thought I'd pay. There really is no fixed value for a painting."

"Tell me the highest price you would recommend as fair to your client."

"Well, if you would quote me eight hundred pounds, I'd feel justified in advising anyone to take it—that is, assuming that the person wanted such a painting."

"It's a very old thing, Lanny."

"I know; but the old houses of England are full of old paintings, and unless they have a well-known name they're just curiosities. I have grave doubts whether this is a Garrard, as it is supposed to be, and I wouldn't offer it as such."

"I'll have to telegraph Bertie; you know it's his property."

"Of course." Lanny knew Rosemary made her husband allow her ten per cent commission for her cleverness in making these deals. That didn't hurt Lanny.

They went back to the sitting-room, and after tea was brought, they were again alone. She looked lovely in a Japanese silk teagown which matched the pale blue of her room, and had golden herons and clumps of bamboo on it; he wasn't sure if he ought to look at her, but of course that was what she was made for. Suddenly she exclaimed: "Lanny, we used to be so happy! Don't you suppose we might be again?"

There it was, "plain and flat," as he had expected and feared. "Darling," he replied, "I'm in the same fix as you were when you were young; I have to think about my parents. My mother is so anxious **for** me to settle down, and I've made her so unhappy with my entanglements; my break with Irma was a blow."

It was a "red herring," cleverly dragged out for the emergency. Rosemary asked: "What was the matter between you and Irma, Lanny?"

"Well, you know how it is: Irma wants one kind of life and I want another. I think you had something to do with it. She saw how high you had flown, and she wanted to sit on the same perch. Now she's got there, and I hope she has the fun she expects."

"She'll probably find it isn't so romantic as she imagined. Do you think you'll ever go back to her, Lanny?"

"I'm quite sure that is finished. My mother is begging me to find the right sort of wife and stick by her. You know my habits; I've never stayed very long in one place in my life, and I'm afraid it would be hard to find a wife who could stand me."

A second red herring, brought into being by inspiration! It worked even better than the first. "Why don't you let me try to find you a wife?" inquired his old sweetheart.

"Bless your heart, dear, how could I stay here long enough? I have some picture business in Paris now, and after that I have to go to Germany."

It amused her very personal nature to talk about him, and the sort of woman who could make him happy. So long as it wasn't a married woman, this was a safe topic while he was drinking his tea. When he was leaving she said: "I'll let you know about the painting—and also about the wife!" Then she added: "You'd be conceited if you knew how much I think about you, Lanny. Come again soon!" It was always hard for her to face the idea of not getting what she wanted.

XI

Once every week while Lanny was on his travels he wrote a letter to his wife in Paris. She had had a number of names; just how she was Jeanne Weill, pronounced as the French pronounce it, Vay. She was supposed to be from Geneva, and Lanny had got her a book so that she could read up on that old city of watchmakers and moneychangers, not to mention the League of Nations, which was clinging feebly to life in a magnificent palace recently completed for it, which Rick in an article had called its mausoleum. Trudi occupied a small studio on Montmartre, and did sketches which were sold on commission by the proprietor of a tobacco shop near by; she lived on the proceeds, and talked about her work to the concierge and the tradespeople, thus maintaining an adequate camouflage.

Lanny's letters to her were always on cheap stationery, always addressed by hand, and with nothing distinctive about them; the contents were designed so that any agent of the Nazis in Paris might read them and learn nothing, save that a person named Paul was well, and that he had made so-and-so-many francs, and expected to be in Istanbul on such-and-such a date. The city on the Bosporus was code for Paris, and the francs were supposed to be multiplied by thirty; that is, they meant dollars, and Trudi would know from this what plans her underground friends were to make for the future. Lanny had never sent her a cablegram or even a telegram; he had never stopped his car near her place and never entered the building except after elaborate precautions. Nazi agents had found her once in Paris, and they weren't going to find her again if he could help it. She no longer had any contacts with other refugees, except for the one man whom she met at night and to whom she turned over the money and her occasional writings.

Trudi Schultz was one of those persons who, in the words of a German poem which Lanny had quoted, "belong to death." When he left her, he could never know if he would see her again; when he received a note from her saying she was well, it couldn't satisfy him completely for the reason that it was several days or weeks late, and he could never know what might have happened in the interim.

How does a man love such a woman? The first thing to be said is that, unless he is extremely neglectful of his own interests and peace of mind, he doesn't. Lanny had got into this position because of that weakness which his mother and father and all their friends so greatly deplored: a sentimental streak which made him oversorry for the underdog and overanxious concerning evils which have been in the world a long time and are beyond the power of any man to change. Hitler had seized Germany, and his nasty Nazis were beating and torturing poor Jews and others who opposed them. When you met some victim of that terror you were sorry for the poor devil and helped him to get on his feet again; but when it came to declaring a private war on the Hitlerites and setting out to overthrow them—well, Don Quixote tilting at the windmills was a sensible citizen in comparison with such a person.

But this art expert had got himself in for it; he had gone and got married to an "underground" worker so that he could take her away to America—if only he could persuade her to come, which so far he hadn't had the nerve to try! Did he really love her? Could any man really love a woman who led him such a life; who gave him only little snatches of joy, and no comfort or peace of mind whatever? Lanny hadn't told a single one of his smart friends about it, but he could hear their comments just as well in his mind. "Good God, a man might as well fall in love with a buzzsaw!" A woman whom he couldn't hold in his arms without the thought that a gang of bullies might break in the door and murder them both! Whom he couldn't think of when he was away from her without seeing images of her stretched out naked on a table, being beaten with thin steel rods! It was indecent even to know about such things!

Trudi had foreseen all this; she had warned him about it, over and over, in the plainest words. She hadn't wanted to marry him, she hadn't wanted even to live with him. She had insisted that the things she had seen and experienced made it impossible for her ever again to be a normal woman, ever to give happiness to a man. But he had thought that he could give happiness to her; he had argued that men going off to war clutch eagerly at the joys of love before they depart, and why could it not be the same with a woman soldier? Was it because men are naturally more selfish? Or was it because women are not meant to be soldiers, and are less able to bear the strain of belonging to death? *Wir sind all' des Todes Eigen!*

He had given her a lot of happiness, of that he could be sure. He had picked her up on obscure street corners by appointment and driven her out into the safe countryside; they had stayed in little inns and he had seen that she got substantial food. He had given her love, of mind and soul as well as body; he had kept the faith with her and helped to renew her courage. Yes, she had said sometimes that she couldn't have gone on without him. But even while she said it, a cloud would darken her features and she would fall silent; he would know that she was thinking about her comrades who had fallen into the clutches of the German secret police, and about the horrors which even at this moment were being perpetrated upon them.

XII

Did Lanny Budd really love Trudi Schultz, alias Mueller, alias Kornmahler, alias Corning, alias Weill, *et aliae,* or was he just sorry for her and full of respect for her intelligence and integrity of character? It was a question he asked himself, a problem he wrestled with in his own soul. He could never love her completely, for she was a creature of the hard rocks and the rare cold atmosphere, while he had been playing in the warm soft ocean of pleasure. Trudi could never give him what Rosemary had given, or Marie de Bruyne, or Irma Barnes. All these had been "ladies"; they had known how to dress and how to dance, how to talk and how to behave in the fashionable world; they had known how to "charm" their man. Trudi, while she had come out of the German middle class, had voluntarily joined the workers in order to help them; her very names were commonplace—Schultz, while it meant a village magistrate, had become the name for a butcher or a grocer, while Trudi was a name for a serving maid.

Lanny's Trudi had been an art student of great talent, and had worked hard to develop it; all Germans worked hard, whether it was in the cause of God or the devil, and Trudi had lived a Spartan life from the time that Lanny had first met her in Berlin. She had been severe in her moral judgments, even of the Social-Democratic movement to which she belonged. She had not glorified self-sacrifice as an ideal, but had accepted it as a necessity of her time and circumstances. The workers were not going to get freedom and justice without heavy sacrifices, and those who aspired to guide them must be prepared to think wholly about their cause and not at all about their pleasures.

Somewhere inside Lanny Budd a bell rang whenever he thought these thoughts; a great gong with quivering tones which sent shivers all over him. Yes, that was the way to speak, that was the way to live; that was honest and decent, fair to one's fellow humans; that was the way to pay the debt you owed for being a civilized man, an heir to culture, instead of a savage, dirty and diseased, living in a hut with pigs and chickens. Lanny had felt that high regard for Trudi from the very first hour; she had renewed his distrust of the fashionable world and all its beliefs and practices. Lanny had said: "Yes, I know; I am a parasite; we are all parasites. I ought to get out of it and get something useful to do."

But the trouble was, circumstances wouldn't let Lanny get out. Time after time, something had turned up that he could do for the cause, but only by staying on in the leisure-class world, keeping the role of playboy, art expert, moneymaker. It had taken both money and social intrigue to get Freddi Robin out of a Nazi dungeon, and again to get Alfy out of a Franco dungeon. Even Trudi hadn't wanted Lanny to break with his family and his wealthy friends; no, for the underground had to have money for paper and printing and radio tubes and what not, and had even been willing for Lanny to sell General Göring's paintings in order to keep them in funds.

So while other people were tortured in prisons or starved in concentration camps, it was Lanny Budd's agreeable duty to travel first-class on steamships or airplanes, to stop at de luxe hotels, to put his feet under the dinner tables of the richest and most exalted persons. Boredom was the worst of hardships he had to endure—unless you counted that of having to make the greater part of his life into an elaborate lie, to watch every word and every facial expression for fear of revealing his real sentiments. Whatever you did in that *haut monde* you must always be smiling and *insouciant*, and you must always agree that disturbers of so perfect a social order had to be put down with a firm hand.

XIII

Lanny put all doubts and disharmonies away in a cupboard of his mind and locked them with a secret key. He was on the way to his beloved; he ached for her presence and his thoughts were of the interesting things he would have to tell her. She rarely had much news for him, but he was a messenger of the gods, who came from Mount Olympus and their other haunts, laden with the latest installments of international mythology.

He took a taxi to his customary hotel and deposited his belongings. He got his car out of the garage where it was stored, and drove to a spot three or four blocks from his wife's humble lodgings. The concierge who opened the door for him knew him, and had received her proper tip now and then. "Mr. Harris" was the name he had given, so he was "Monsieur Arreece." Now the woman looked at him with concern and shook her head. "*Hélas, monsieur, mademoiselle est partie.*"

"*Partie!*" exclaimed Lanny. "When?"

"I do not know, monsieur. She must have gone out, and she has not returned. It has been nearly a week now."

"Her door is locked?"

"It was locked, monsieur; but yesterday I became alarmed and notified the police. They brought a locksmith and opened the door, but there is no sign of her. Apparently nothing has been disturbed."

"They have no trace of her?"

"No, monsieur; they nor anyone."

Lanny couldn't say that he was surprised, for he had talked about this contingency many times with Trudi. She had said: "Go away. Do not involve yourself. If I am alive I will get word to you." She had his mother's address at Juan-les-Pins, his father's address in Connecticut, his best friend's address in England. He had no way to find her, but she could always find him.

"What did the police say?" he inquired.

"They asked many questions, monsieur. I told them there was an American gentleman who sometimes came to visit mademoiselle. They told me if you came again, I was to notify them."

"It would do no good to do that. I have not heard from mademoiselle and there is nothing I could tell them."

"*Mais, Monsieur Arreece!* It would be a serious matter for me not to obey the police."

"No one will know that I have been here," replied the visitor. He took out a hundred-franc note, which he judged the right size for the cure of such anxiety. "You say nothing and I'll say nothing and it will be O.K."—the French all knew those two letters.

"*Mais sa propriété, monsieur; ses articles!*"

Lanny knew that Trudi didn't have many *articles;* a few sticks of furniture, a few pieces of clothing suitable to the poorest. She never kept a letter or any scrap of paper; when she wrote something for the underground, she took it away or mailed it at once. The only things she might have were a few sketches, and Lanny would have liked to have these, but he dared not take the risk. He would not trust the French police in any matter having to do with leftwing refugees; also, they had records of his own distant past which he wouldn't care to have dug up.

He took out another note and handed it to the concierge. "Keep her property for a while," he said. "If she comes back she will pay you. *Merci et bonjour.*" He turned away and got out of that neighborhood, never to return.

4

Plus Triste Que les Nuits

I

LANNY'S first step was to get his mother on the telephone. Had there come any letter from his friend? The word in English carries no connotation of sex, but Beauty knew whom he meant; her sharp eyes had not failed to observe the weekly letters, which she dutifully forwarded as directed. She had questioned Lanny and succeeded in getting a few details, but not all that she wanted. Now she told him there was no letter. He tried to keep anxiety out of his voice; no use worrying her. "If a letter comes, please phone me to the hotel at once."

He called Rick, with the same results; nothing there. He hadn't expected it, for he had told Trudi that he was on his way to "Istanbul." To Rick he could say: "She has disappeared. I fear the worst." Nothing more over the phone.

Rick was full of concern; he knew what anguish of mind this meant to his friend. "If there's anything we can do, let us know and we'll come at once." But of course there wasn't. "God bless you, old fellow!" the Englishman exclaimed. He didn't really believe in God, at least not that he knew of; but he had to say something different from the ordinary.

Lanny and Trudi had talked this problem over in advance. She had asked, and he had promised, that in the event of her disappearance he would stay quiet for a while, to give her a chance to communicate with him if she could; also, that he would never do anything that might reveal his connection with her, and thus imperil his ability to serve the cause. He had assented to her stern formula that this was a war in which the cause was everything and the individual nothing. That was the Nazis' own law, and the anti-Nazis would have to match them in firmness of purpose.

The husband went over again and again in his mind the circumstances which governed this case. The Nazis were on the aggressive, all over Europe; they were intriguing and deceiving, seducing and corrupting; undermining the power of their opponents and building up that of their supporters, and no law of God or man meant anything to them, only the question of results. When they approached persons of social standing, they sent a fine musician like Kurt Meissner, able to play Beethoven and even to compose Beethoven, and to speak the exalted language of international cultural solidarity. When it was a question of leading bankers and industrialists, they sent a financial wizard like Hjalmar Schacht to show how Germany had solved the problem of unemployment and crisis; how German big business was thriving as none other had ever thriven, even in America in its boom days; how there were no more unions and no more strikes, no more class war, no more political demagogues levying blackmail. When it was a question of the newspapers of France, always for sale to the highest bidder, they sent Otto Abetz with an unlimited expense account and a briefcase full of plausible editorials in the most highly polished Parisian, setting forth the advantages of permanent friendship between France and Germany, and the treason to European culture involved in the alliance with Bolshevism.

Paris was full of refugees from both Germany and Italy; Jews especially, but also Socialists, Communists, democrats, liberals, pacifists, every sort of idealist; all quarreling among themselves as they had done at home; all insisting that their way was the only way to fight Fascism-Nazism. These refugees smuggled news out of Germany and Italy and smuggled in what they called their "literature": newspapers, pamphlets, leaflets. And of course their enemies were fighting back with fury; the Hitlerites had their little Gestapo in Paris, and Mussolini his little OVRA; Dr. Goebbels had his Personal Department B, and the SS had their Braune Haus. German agents came under every sort of disguise: scientists and journalists, teachers of music and languages, students, traveling salesmen, importers, laborers, even refugees. Agents would be trained to pose as leftists; they would be sent to concentration camps in Germany and beaten there, so that the other prisoners would see them and word would go out to the underground that they were all right; then they could "escape" to Paris, and be welcomed by the anti-Nazi groups, and be in position to collect names and addresses of the "comrades" both at home and abroad. The former would be shot, and the latter would be intimidated and silenced by whatever measures it took.

II

What would be the attitude of the French police toward this foreign civil war going on under their noses? The French police represented property, as police are apt to do all over the world. There were Frenchmen who held the same ideas and behaved in the same manner as the refugees, and the police regarded them as public nuisances and potential criminals; if they got any protection, it was because they had strong influence with labor and commanded numbers of votes. The head of the Paris police, the notorious Chiappe, was to all intents a Fascist, in open sympathy with the Croix de Feu and other native organizations, and perhaps with the Cagoulards, the "Hooded Men," whose murder gangs were patterned on the Blackshirts and the Schutzstaffel. The Nazis were helping to subsidize these groups in France and would not fail to have their friends and secret representatives in the Sûreté Générale and the Deuxième Bureau.

Of course there were limits to what could be done in a supposedly free republic. If refugees of prominence were molested, it made a scandal; the Reds and the Pinks had their newspapers with large circulations and they loved nothing so much as having martyrs. Just a month or two ago Mussolini had arranged the murder of his two leading opponents among the refugees, Carlo and Nello Rosselli, editors of the Italian-language anti-Fascist newspaper in Paris; they had been kidnaped and beaten to death in the woods—the same method which had been used in Rome to get rid of the Socialist editor Matteotti, soon after Il Duce had seized power. Lanny had been there at the time, and his efforts to tell the outside world about it had caused his expulsion from the new Roman Empire. Now the newspapers of Paris had been full of the Rosselli story and it had even reached Connecticut. It was bad publicity for both Fascism and France; it served to alarm the outside world, and the police certainly wouldn't want any more of it.

Lanny was in a position to make another Rosselli case by the simple operation of telephoning any one of the American newspapermen whom he knew in Paris. The story would be flashed to the ends of the earth and would make the front page wherever there was a *grand monde* and a proletariat which loved to read about it. AMERICAN SOCIALITE IN PARIS REVEALS SECRET WIFE DISAPPEARANCE, CHARGES NAZI KIDNAPING. Nothing less than a local murder or the outbreak of a world war would take precedence of that. They would bring in Budd Gunmakers and Budd-Erling, J. Paramount Barnes and Irma and Frances and the fourteenth Earl of Wickthorpe. Under the glare of such a searchlight, the French police might conceivably get busy and find what was left of Trudi Schultz, alias Mueller, alias Kornmahler, alias Corning, alias Weill, pronounced Vay. But what would it do to the picture business, and to Lanny's access to the top-flight personalities of two continents? What would it do to his new job as Presidential Agent 103? Obviously, all that would be *fini, kaput,* knocked into a cocked hat. For the Nazis it would be a major victory— for of course what they really wanted was not to get Trudi, but to find out where she was getting the money.

If they had her, that was why they had her, and they would be working right now to draw the secret from her. She had said many times that she would die with it in her heart; that was the first duty of every conspirator, the first pledge they all made. But who could tell what any person would do under the most cruel tortures that modern science could contrive? Who could say that in some delirium she might not cry out the name of Lanny? Who could be sure that she might not be hypnotized and told that she was speaking to her lover? Many things might happen, and Lanny Budd had plenty of time to imagine them. If the torturers managed to break the secret, they wouldn't be apt to kidnap the son of Budd-Erling, but they might slug him on some dark night and it would be an ordinary case of robbery; they might force his speeding car off the road and it would be a lesson to other reckless drivers.

III

The unhappy husband went to his hotel and inquired if there had been any call for him. Then he went to his room and sat there; when he got tired of sitting, he got up and paced the floor for a while. He didn't want to go out, because there was the possibility that Trudi might call on the telephone. She had done that once, to this very hotel; the time when strange men had been following her on the street, and Lanny had had to think quickly and tell her how to evade them.

Waiting; just waiting. Like a man deprived of all his senses, and of all powers, but who still retains his consciousness; who knows that something terrible is happening, but cannot find out what it is and cannot do anything about it. He didn't want to eat, he didn't want to read, he didn't want to see anybody; his thoughts were altogether occupied with Trudi. Her image floated before him; those fine, exquisitely chiseled features, expressive of intelligence, of sensitiveness, of moral fervor. She was a saint; he had often told her that, half teasingly, for she didn't like the word with its ecclesiastical connotations. But religion takes different forms; new faiths are born, spurning the outworn faiths of the past. Trudi was a saint of the new religion of humanity, of solidarity, co-operation, and justice. Her image was that of an early Christian martyr, with trembling eyelids and the sweat of anguish upon the forehead; a Nordic blond martyr with fair hair and blue eyes. He had no photograph of her; the only one she had let him have made had been put in a sealed envelope along with their wedding certificate and sent to Robbie Budd, to be put in his safe and opened only in the event of Lanny's death.

But Lanny didn't need any picture; he had an art critic's trained eye and memory. He knew every detail of her features and her form; he knew them as line and color, he knew them as living things, expressions of a mind and character. He had come to Paris with his senses warmed by the thought of her embraces; now he paced the floor of a hotel room like a wild creature caged, tormented by the thought of her torments. He had a vivid imagination, but needed none on this subject. He was back in that dungeon in the basement of the Columbus Haus in

Berlin, its floor slimy and stinking with stale blood; he saw the heavy wooden bench with the elderly Jewish banker—"Jewish-Bolshevik plutocrat" was the Nazi phrase—stretched out naked on his fat stomach and being whipped on his flabby white buttocks with thin steel rods. Lanny heard the rods whistling, four of them, like the wind in a chimney on a stormy night; heard the shrieks, the moans, the gabble of the tortured old man.

Quietly, methodically, mechanically the Nazis did that to people; they did it to long strings of men and women, one after another, until the whippers were dripping with sweat, until they became exhausted and had to be replaced. The victims would fall unconscious and be dragged away and dumped into another room, piled sometimes on top of one another. A wholesale procedure, the mass production of suffering, intended to terrorize all Germany, and then the whole continent of Europe. *Heute gehört uns Deutschland, morgen die ganze Welt!*

They had called in their eminent physiologists and psychologists to tell them how to humiliate and degrade human beings, to break their wills and subject them to the National-Socialist will. They built chambers of concrete of a carefully devised crookedness, so that a human being could not stand up or sit down or lie without having sharp corners sticking into various parts of him; they would throw him in there and leave him for days, for weeks. They would bring him to an inquisition chamber and strap him in a chair with a bright light glaring into his eyes, and there they would question him, with relays of inquisitors, giving him not a moment's rest for days and nights. At intervals they would burn his flesh with cigarettes or stick slivers of wood under his fingernails to liven him up and make him more attentive. They had ascertained scientifically the exact amount of heat and humidity which would reduce the human will to impotence and turn the mind to putty.

Now they had Trudi Schultz somewhere, and were putting her through that sort of ordeal. Doubtless they would rape her—why not? It was one more way to horrify and shock a woman, one more way to subjugate her, one more way to impress her with the might and majesty of the *Neue Ordnung.* They made a sort of ceremony out of it; both Freddi and Trudi had described such scenes: the Stormtroopers in their shiny black boots and shiny leather belts lined up awaiting their turn, dancing with amusement, cracking their jokes and roaring with laughter; the women victims, also awaiting their turn, compelled to witness unspeakable obscenities, sometimes fainting with horror and having buckets of water dumped over them so that they might miss nothing. If all that didn't cause them to talk, their loved ones would be brought in and tortured before their eyes; a child one day, an old mother or father the next. *"Nun, sag'! Wer ist's, was ist's?"*—whatever the inquisitor wanted to know. With Trudi it would be just two things: "Who gave you the money?" and "Who got it from you?" Perhaps they already knew the latter; perhaps that was how they had got Trudi. Or perhaps they would pretend to know; they would tell her that her comrades had betrayed her, and why should she continue to spare them? They would have an endless string of devices, psychological as well as physical; they would never give up until they found out who had been putting up the money for the hundreds of thousands of anti-Nazi leaflets and pamphlets that had been smuggled into Naziland.

IV

Such was the technique in Nazi Germany. Could it be that the same things were being done to German refugees in Paris? Trudi's comrades had informed her that there was a Prussian nobleman connected with the Embassy, a man of wealth who in the normal course of his life was entitled to reside in a fine château. He had rented in the environs of Paris an historic place with splendid grounds and a high spiked fence around them. No residence of such pretentiousness would be without its wine cellars, and in these places the Nazi agents could carry on their operations under the shelter of diplomatic immunity. Of course they couldn't do it wholesale, but they could handle a special case—and one was enough for Lanny's imagination.

He told himself that he couldn't stand it. But he had to stand it; what else could he do? He would resume the nerve-racking experience of waiting for something to happen. He had begun it when the Nazis had seized the Robin family in Berlin and Lanny and his friends were in Calais, expecting the yacht *Bessie Budd* to arrive. Then again in Berlin, with endless waiting for Freddie Robin to telephone—and he didn't. The same with Trudi, in Berlin several times; and now again. He mustn't see any of his friends, because he couldn't trust them with his secret and he couldn't hide his agitation. He wouldn't attend to business, for what was the sense of making more money if Trudi wasn't there to put it to use?

Remorse seized him, because he had let this woman go to her terrible fate. He ought to have stopped her at all hazards. But what could he have done, except to wreck her peace of mind and her health? He had known what she was doing before he had tied his life to hers. And what could he have said to her, except arguments of selfishness which would have shamed them both? Loyal comrades were in the clutches of the enemy; many of them murdered, others suffering the whole gamut of abuse. Freddi Robin and Lanny had helped to maintain a Socialist school in Berlin; in the carefree old days they had pledged their faith to a cause and its supporters. Trudi and her former husband had been among these, and Lanny's memory was full of names, faces, personalities of scores whom he had met there—students, teachers, guests. Most of them were now paying the price, and Lanny and Trudi owed them what support and assistance it was possible to bring. How could the Nazi monster ever be overthrown, if those who had the weapons were to turn tail and run away from the battlefield?

The very idea of doing so was a humiliation; it was a bourgeois idea, born of primitive selfishness and nurtured in the system of competitive greed. Dog eat dog! Look out for number one! Each for himself and the devil take the hindmost! Such were the maxims of the business world; a shame to humanity, a denial of the fatherhood of God and the brotherhood of man. On what basis could Lanny have said to his wife: "Come off with me and forget our comrades and their needs. I have money, and we can spend it on ourselves and be happy together."

Such ideas belonged in that world which called itself the "great world," the "high world," the "select world,"—all in French, the language of elegance and corruption. Lanny had come to hate that world, and now he hated himself because he had been born in it and was flesh of its flesh. His conscience tormented him because he hadn't been good enough for Trudi; because sometimes—frequently, in fact—he had wondered if he hadn't made an unfortunate marriage; if he wouldn't have preferred having a wife who knew how to dress and could go to dinner parties in the fashionable world and exchange polite conversation with his elegant friends. Yes, sometimes he had actually been bored with the life of heroism and self-sacrifice! Sometimes he had wanted to make love to his wife, while she had wanted to talk about the comrades and their sufferings and needs! Many times he had been all too human and had had to lie persistently in order to keep his superhuman wife from finding it out.

Well, now he had no wife; now he was free to slide back into the warm ocean of pleasure. He could forget Trudi Schultz and let Rosemary and his mother find him the right sort of darling, perfectly "finished" in a high-priced school and equipped for the offices of leisure-class wifehood. He sat with his hands clenched and tears running down his cheeks, vowing that he would never commit that act of treason to his ideals. No, he would stick by Trudi, or at any rate the memory of

Trudi, and by her cause. He would move heaven and earth to help her. But then, as soon as this grandiloquent phrase came to him, he realized that he had no lever and no fulcrum to move even a small portion of the earth. He sat in a hotel room waiting for a telephone call which was never coming, and he tried in vain to think of a person who could give him real help. Those who were willing wouldn't be able, and those who might be able couldn't even be trusted with his secret.

V

Trudi had forced her husband to anticipate this situation, and to agree upon his course of action. "Some day they will get me," she had said. "They get all of us in the end." She had given him the name and address of the middle-aged German teacher of the clarinet who was the medium whereby commissions on picture sales were converted into anti-Nazi literature. Professor Adler was not his real name, but that under which he lived and worked in Paris. He earned meager sums by his teaching, and he lived on those so as to awaken no suspicions. If at any time Trudi were to be missing, Lanny must never go near the garret where this musician lived, but mail him a note enclosing one of Trudi's sketches by way of password, and appointing a place on the street for a meeting at night. This professor had never been told where or how Trudi got her large sums of money, but he had been told that in the event of anything happening to her, he would receive a letter which would enable him to get into contact with the source of the funds. That was the way the underground was built, in separate units, each having contact with no more than one or two others.

Lanny had asked: "What if they should get the professor?" and Trudi's reply had been: "I know another name, but I am not permitted to reveal it. If both Adler and I should be caught at once, it will be up to you to try to make contact through some one of the French comrades whom you can trust; or give your money to them, to be used for the propaganda here." She added: "God knows they need it! They are at the same stage as we Germans were a year or two before Hitler struck."

Lanny spent most of his time in the hotel room, and whenever the phone rang, his heart hit him a blow underneath his throat. Several friends called up, inviting him out, and he made the excuse that business tied him down; when people called on business, he made the excuse of social engagements. Never did he hear the one voice that he wanted; his grief told him that he never would hear it again. For why should she fail to telephone, unless she was in the hands of the enemy? And if she was in their hands, what chance was there of her escaping? He would go out and walk for a while, turning unexpected corners and stopping to look in a shop window to see if anybody was trailing him. But the only persons who paid attention to a well-dressed and young-looking American were the ladies of the *trottoir*.

After four days he could wait no longer, and wrote on his typewriter the fateful note which he and Trudi had agreed upon. He asked Professor Adler to be on a certain obscure street corner in Montmartre at ten o'clock on the following evening and to wear a blue flower in his buttonhole. The letter was signed "Toinette," in the hope that if it fell into the hands of the enemy it might be taken for an assignation. At the hour appointed Lanny walked to the place, taking every precaution to make sure that he was not being followed. He strolled past the spot, looking for a smallish German with prematurely gray hair and a blue flower. There would be, of course, the chance that it might be a Nazi agent taking the musician's place; but this chance had to be taken.

However, there was nobody resembling a professor of clarinet playing. Lanny passed the corner several times, and then, thinking that the musician's knowledge of geography might be defective, he crossed to the other corners—but in vain. He went back to his hotel and wrote another note, making another appointment for the evening after next; he went again, and walked as before, seeing no blue flowers and no one who looked like either a musician or a Gestapo agent—Lanny had met a number of both. His notes doubtless went to the dead-letter office and were burned, along with thousands of other attempts at assignations.

VI

Lanny might have told himself now that he had done all he could; he might have written finis to that chapter of his life and closed the book. But the very fact that he hadn't loved Trudi as wholeheartedly as he ought to have loved her bound him to her memory. Now that it was too late, he really yearned to live the heroic, the saintly life! The fact that he had held a martyr in his arms poisoned his thoughts of the fashionable world which beckoned him from the Riviera, from Biarritz and Salzburg and Davos, and the other places where his mother's friends were to be found in late summer.

Day and night his mind was obsessed by one thought: "How can I save her?" His reason told him that the chance must be slim, and growing more so. What would they do with such a prisoner? Chloroform her and drop her body into the Seine, so that she would pass for one of those unfortunates who every night put an end to themselves in all the great capitals of an unhappy world. Or put her in a closed car and drive her by night to the border—say at Strasbourg, where there was a bridge which Lanny knew well—one half of it France and the other half Germany, the only thing owned in common being a barrier painted with black and white stripes. With the diplomatic immunity which Nazis enjoyed and shamelessly abused, there would be no chance of search; a prisoner well gagged, perhaps unconscious and hidden under a robe, would be safely restored to the land of her origin.

Who would help Lanny Budd? He thought first of his powerful father. Robbie had said that he would be coming to Germany before long. If Lanny had cabled: "I am in serious trouble please come immediately," Robbie would have taken the first steamer. If Lanny had added: "Bring Bub Smith," Robbie would have understood that the trouble was serious indeed, and would have put someone else in charge of his company police force at the Budd-Erling plant and brought with him an ex-cowboy from Texas who was a straightshooter in both the literal and figurative senses of the word. Bub was getting on in years, but he could still toss a silver dollar into the air and hit it with a pistol shot. He had done many kinds of confidential work for Robbie in France, including the bodyguarding of Baby Frances. He had learned to talk the lingo, also to know many kinds of people, including the *flics* both in Paris and on the Riviera.

If Robbie had said: "Bub, I want to know all about the Château de Belcour, which the German Graf Herzenberg maintains in Seine-et-Oise, and where I understand they have a woman prisoner,"—Bub would have said: "O.K., Boss, I'll see what can be done." Robbie would put some new one-thousand-franc notes into Bub's hands, and add: "There's more where these came from, but don't spend them without changing them, for they can be traced." Bub would grin and say: "I'm no sucker, Boss," and that would be enough. Lanny would have been willing to wager that before the week was over Bub Smith would have one of the Graf's servants drunk, and it might be right in the servants' quarters of the château.

Lanny, being of an imaginative temperament, lived through this whole episode. Having included in his cable a request to his father to bring the sealed letter from the safe, Lanny opened the letter and showed the marriage certificate and the photograph of Trudi. Robbie, who had been raised in New England where they grow saints and ascetics wholesale, looked at the portrait—all this in Lanny's imagination, of course—and recognized the sort of woman his susceptible son had "fallen for." He understood without argument the peril in which the wife now stood, for he had been in Germany and knew the Nazis, and had heard the story of Johannes Robin from Johannes himself, and the story of Freddi from Lanny. He was ready with his answer even before his son had finished outlining the situation. "Yes, Son. It looks pretty black but I'll do what I can for you. But you'll have to understand that this is the last straw, and I won't move a finger unless you give me your word that both you and your wife will settle down and drop all sorts of radical activities from now on."

And of course Lanny couldn't say that. Trudi would never make such a promise, and wouldn't admit Lanny's right to make it for her. As for Lanny himself, he had given up one wife because of his unwillingness to make that same promise, and now, apparently, he would have to give up another. He said: "I'm sorry, Robbie; it's no go." The father demanded: "Then what on earth did you bring me across the ocean for?" Lanny replied: "I didn't"—and so ended that abortive piece of imagination!

VII

The bewildered husband's thoughts turned to Léon Blum, who had ceased to be Premier of France a couple of months ago but had become Vice-Premier, and therefore was still chained to the whims of a Cabinet. Lanny had had with Blum much the same sort of session as recently with Roosevelt: that is, he had challenged Blum on the issue of the Spanish war, and heard the defense of a Socialist who held power only on the sufferance of capitalist politicians; of a pacifist and humanitarian who found himself confronted by a many-headed hydra of war; of a Jew who saw anti-Semitism being spread like an artificial plague all around him, and who questioned his right to put that added burden upon his overburdened party.

But Blum was still the leader of that party, and still dreaming of justice in a world of maniacal greeds; still pleading for peace with two psychopathic dictators bent upon war. Privately he could be a friend and wise adviser; if Lanny should go to his apartment and tell him the painful story, Blum would respect his confidence and might be able to give helpful advice. He might name some trustworthy police agent who knew the ropes in Paris and could go to work among the Nazis. It would cost money, of course, but Lanny wouldn't mind that—the money he had brought with him was burning a hole in his pocket, and it seemed to him he would never again have use for it if he couldn't save Trudi. But the more he thought over the plan, the more unlikely it seemed that any police official could permanently keep such a secret as Lanny had to impart. Sooner or later there would be a leak; and anyhow, Lanny would be always in dread of it, and would no longer dare go into Naziland and do his work. He had pledged Trudi that never under any circumstances would he imperil this privilege he enjoyed; and now, since he had become a "presidential agent," he was more than ever committed to preserving it.

So it would have to be some comrade, and preferably someone of the underground. An image arose in Lanny's mind, and he relived a scene of three years ago when he had sat in a tiny second-story bedroom of a workingman's home in the Limehouse district of London, talking in whispers to a German sailor with a round shaven head and a typical Prussian neck that came up in a straight line in back. A tough, hardfisted fellow, this Bernhardt Monck, and Lanny had been suspicious of him; but Trudi had sent him from Berlin, and Lanny had given him money for Trudi's work, and since then nothing had happened to Lanny—which would hardly have been the case if Monck had been a spy of the Nazis. Less than a year ago Lanny had seen him marching at the head of a company of the International Brigade on that forever glorious day when it entered Madrid and stopped the Moors of Franco at the little Manzanares River. Certainly no man was going to walk into any such deadly scrimmage unless he believed in the cause for which it was fought!

There had been many scrimmages since then; and was Monck still alive? If so, perhaps he had earned a furlough, and Lanny could bring him to Paris and put him to work, meeting him secretly and guiding his efforts. Lanny could find out about him through Raoul Palma, his Spanish comrade who for many years had run the workers' school in Cannes, and who was now in Valencia with the Loyalist government. One of the letters which Lanny had found awaiting him in Paris had been from Raoul, telling him the news and pleading with him to move the British government so that the embargo might be lifted and the besieged people of Spain might purchase arms. Just a little thing like that was all a retired school director wanted from his one friend among the ruling classes of the world!

If it hadn't been for war and censorship, Lanny would have got Raoul on the telephone and asked him the whereabouts of Capitán Herzog, the name under which Monck was going in Spain. But with conditions as they were, mail, telegraph and telephone were "out" so far as this matter was concerned. Lanny would have to go to Spain;

and the question which troubled him was, suppose he went, and in the meantime Trudi were to smuggle a letter to him, or try to get him on the phone at this hotel!

VIII

Lanny couldn't sleep. He paced the floor of his room, tormenting himself with thoughts about his wife in the Château de Belcour. He had forgotten to eat; then he decided that he ought to eat, and ordered some food, but found that it had lost its savor. He went out and walked the pavements of Paris in the small hours of the morning; then he came back, and lay down on the bed without undressing; he had managed to exhaust his body but not his mind, and he lay with his eyes closed, thinking every terrible thought possible about Trudi.

Did he doze, and then awaken? He would never be sure. People would tell him in after years that perhaps he had been asleep all the time; but he knew that he was awake and in full possession of his faculties. A strange feeling began to creep over him and he opened his eyes slowly, and there at the foot of his bed was what appeared to be a trace of light, a sort of pillar of cloud, so faint that he couldn't be sure whether it was the first glimmer of dawn coming in at the window. But dawn doesn't come and gather itself into one spot, nor does it make one begin to shiver. The thought flashed over Lanny: "It's happening again!"

It had waited twenty years to happen again. Twenty years ago to this very month Lanny had lain in bed in his father's home and had had this same feeling, and seen a pillar of light turn into the form of Rick, who had been flying in battle over France. One of the most vivid memories of Lanny's whole life, something he could never forget if he lived to be as old as Methuselah. Hundreds of times he had wondered if it would happen again, but it had never happened.

This time it was Trudi; standing there, full size, dim, but otherwise real as life; wearing a plain blue gingham dress with which Lanny was familiar, a dress for which she had paid perhaps twenty-five francs, less than a dollar; with her blond hair drawn back tightly from her forehead and doubtless hanging in two braids—though Lanny couldn't see these, because she was facing him and never moved. She was two or three feet from the foot of the bed, looking at him, slightly downwards; her face pale, her expression gentle, sad, not to say grief-stricken.

When this had happened to Lanny the first time, he had been a youth, entirely uninformed in the strange field of psychic phenomena.

The feeling of grief had overwhelmed him and he had thought: "Rick is dead!" But in the course of twenty years he had read many books on the subject and had tried series of experiments with various mediums, weighing evidence and trying one hypothesis against another. He knew that "apparitions" or "phantasms" have been appearing to men since the beginning of recorded history. What do they mean and how do they arise? From the mind of the beholder or of the person beheld? Are they hallucinations? If so, why do they so often correspond to facts which the beholder cannot normally know? If you say they are "hallucinations telepathically induced," you have to decide what you mean by telepathy and how it works; otherwise you are just fooling yourself with a long word.

Twenty years ago Lanny had said: "Rick is dead!" But Rick hadn't been dead; Rick had been lying on the field of battle, badly hurt and near to death. The apparition had borne a bleeding wound across the forehead—and Rick carried the scar of that wound to this day. Rick had been in France and Lanny in Connecticut; a circumstance which took more explaining than either of them had ever been able to find in any book. Now Lanny looked at this vision of his wife and saw that she had no wound of any sort; just an expression of infinite sorrow. She would have felt that, of course, because she was separated from him, and knew that he would be suffering because of her; that he would forget to eat and wouldn't be able to sleep.

The vision of Rick had filled the youthful Lanny Budd with awe. For twenty years since then he had been thinking: "If I ever see another, how shall I behave?" He had decided that he would not have the least fear or excitement, only scientific curiosity; he would make the most of every instant, like an astronomer during an eclipse of the sun. The astronomer prepares for years and travels half-way around the earth—all for a few seconds. Now Lanny had the seconds and he found that he was awed, even frightened, in spite of himself. Trudi of course would never hurt him; but Trudi came from another world, Trudi represented a break in those veils which hide mankind from its destiny and conceal secrets which may well be unbearable. Lanny felt that his skin was creeping and crawling; he couldn't know that his hair was rising, but it felt like that, a sort of tickling. He was staring hard, and at the same time thinking—the thoughts of twenty years in a few seconds.

He had called out to Rick, and the apparition had faded. So he had decided that he wouldn't speak the next time. But he found that the impulse to speak was hard to resist. To lie there staring at his wife and see her gazing at him—that wasn't normal, it wasn't the part of love. He had become familiar with the idea of thoughts being communicated without words, so he decided to try that. He said: "Trudi!"—moving his lips, perhaps, but not making any sound that he could hear. It seemed to him that the apparition leaned forward slightly and turned its head, as if trying to hear. He said again, soundlessly: "Trudi!"—and could it be that her lips were moving, that she was speaking to him without sound? He had no knowledge of lip-reading, but he imagined that she was saying his name. Afterwards, when he tried the experiment, he discovered that you do not move your lips in saying "Lanny" —you say it with the tongue.

"What shall I do, Trudi?" he thought—and that takes a lot of moving. Did he deceive himself when he imagined that she answered: "Do what I have told you." An obvious enough thing for her to say; any wife, alive or dead, would say it to her husband if she thought that by any chance he would heed. Did he imagine that he heard: "Talk to me in your mind"? That, too, was obvious enough—with a husband who for twenty years had been speculating about psychic phenomena, visiting mediums, persuading his friends to do the same, and making elaborate records of significant communications.

Anyhow, there it was in Lanny's mind, and it stayed while the apparition slowly faded into the light of dawning day. Lanny found himself with a dew of perspiration on his forehead and a chill which was in no way normal in Paris at the end of summer. He found himself with an almost irresistible conviction that Trudi had been there; at least something of Trudi, or from her, and that she had put something into his mind. Nothing that he had read or thought had inclined him toward "spiritualism," but now he was thinking: "Suppose it could be!" And again: "Suppose the Nazis couldn't kill her!" Lanny recalled the *Visit of Emmaus*, so vividly painted by Rembrandt. "And he said unto them, Why are ye troubled? . . . These are the words which I spake unto you, while I was yet with you, that all things must be fulfilled."

IX

Intellectually Lanny didn't know any more about apparitions after this experience than he had known before it. Had this been Trudi—the body, the mind, or the soul of Trudi—or had it been his own subconscious mind, building up a synthesis of ten thousand memories of Trudi? He would never be able to say. But emotionally, Trudi had been there. She had made herself real to him; she had brought his ten thousand memories into active life; and moreover, she had given him a directive.

Lanny had always been, from earliest childhood, a ladies' man. His father he had seen but rarely; it had been his beautiful and warmhearted mother who had shaped his personality, and when she had gone off to take her part in the social whirl, she had left the child with women servants. She had come back trailing clouds of glory—she and her lady friends, dazzling and fascinating creatures, birds of paradise, whose conversation resembled a gramophone wound up and set to run at its highest speed. They had made a pet out of one bright little boy, the only one in a household, and he had watched them primping and powdering, getting armed for their forays into the masculine world—Lanny drinking in words which would never have been spoken if the gay ladies had dreamed that a child could understand them.

Then Rosemary had come into his life; a second mother, but more than a mother, initiating him into the mysteries of love. She had been gentle and kind—they were always that way with Lanny, because he was that way with them. She might have stayed with him for life, only the world wouldn't let her. The world was far more powerful than any individual; it was stern and harsh and made demands upon you which you disobeyed at your peril. *Le grand monde, le haut monde, le monde d'élite*—Lanny had heard these phrases from childhood, and it had taken him many years to understand this *monde*, how it had come to be, and from what its overwhelming authority was derived.

Then had come Marie de Bruyne, one of the creatures and agents of that authority. A lady of high position in Paris, she had been his *amie* in the French fashion, and had handled him with the tact of the woman who accepts intellectually the supremacy of the male creature and does not admit even to herself that she is managing the life of the man she loves. Whenever Lanny did or said anything that was not in accord with the conventions of Marie's class, she had not scolded, she had not even mentioned it; she had just become unhappy, and when Lanny observed it, he decided that it was hardly worth while to do or say or even believe too strenuously that forbidden thing.

And then Irma Barnes, who had come out of the so-called "New" world, and gave no heed to the conventions which bound the women of aristocratic France. Irma had never hesitated to say what she thought; and far from considering herself subject to the male creature, she took it for granted that this creature existed to dance attendance upon her and keep her from being bored. But she had been placid and easygoing; out of her superabundance she had been willing to give Lanny anything he might want, and her only complaint was that he wouldn't make adequate use of his opportunities. What had broken up their marriage was the black crisis which was now gathering over their world. No longer could one just live from day to day and ask no questions; one had to take sides—and Lanny had taken the side opposite to his wife's.

That was how Trudi had come into his life. She represented that other side of his nature, the side which Irma couldn't and wouldn't tolerate; the gullible and softhearted side which made excuses for what called itself "social justice," but which Irma called class jealousy and plain organized robbery. Trudi was—or had been—like Marie de Bruyne in that she had her creed, her set of beliefs and code of conduct from which it was unthinkable to depart. In Trudi's view the workers of the world were struggling to release themselves from age-old servitude and to build a co-operative society, free from exploitation and war. That effort called for the utmost loyalty and consecration, and any weakening in one's efforts was a form of moral decay. Trudi had managed her newly acquired man in much the same way as Marie; she never scolded or found fault, but Lanny would see the distress in her features and would hasten to withdraw the evil words and to suppress the evil tendencies which derived from his leisure-class upbringing and made it so difficult for him to become a singlehearted champion of the oppressed.

X

And now, from the spirit world—if that was it—Trudi was renewing her control of the susceptible Lanny Budd. A new religion had been born and a new martyr was saying: "I am with you alway, even unto the end of the world." A new evangelist was preaching: "Be sober, be vigilant; because your adversary the devil, as a roaring lion, walketh about, seeking whom he may devour: Whom resist stedfast in the faith, knowing that the same afflictions are accomplished in your brethren that are in the world." This world, it appeared, had changed very little in nineteen hundred years; the same human weakness confronted terrifying tasks, and the same moral efforts had to be made, the same injunctions to be laid down, over and over, world without end, Amen.

Without speaking a word, Trudi had said everything she had wanted to say to Lanny—or would have wanted to say if it had really been Trudi instead of Lanny's subconscious mind! Lanny's subconscious mind knew Trudi extremely well and would have no difficulty in making up words for her. So now, for the rest of Lanny's life, Trudi was going to be standing at the foot of his bed, asking: "What have you done for the cause today? Are the workers any nearer to freedom from exploitation and war because of your efforts? Have you really had your mind upon it or have you just been having a good time as in the past?"

Unconsciously, automatically, in Lanny's mind these exhortations would shade into those of the old-time religion which he had read in his boyhood and which his Puritan grandfather in Connecticut had hammered home in a Sunday-morning Bible class. "I beseech you therefore, brethren, by the mercies of God, that ye present your bodies a living sacrifice, holy, acceptable unto God, which is your reasonable service. And be not conformed to this world: but be ye transformed by the renewing of your mind," and so on. "Not slothful in business; fervent in spirit, serving the Lord; Rejoicing in hope; patient in tribulation; continuing instant in prayer; Distributing to the necessity of saints"—this last word would have to be altered, of course, for they were no longer called saints, but comrades and fellowworkers. Their necessity was exactly the same, however, and Lanny had been one of the "distributors," to the endless exasperation of his mother and her friends, of Rosemary and Marie and Irma, each in her turn resenting the coming of ragtag and bobtail to their homes, the flood of begging letters and of leftwing publications with flaring incitements and indecently bitter cartoons.

These begging visitors and letters came no more of late years, for Lanny was pretending to have lost interest in the "cause," and only half a dozen friends shared his real thoughts. What Trudi now exhorted him was: "Get in touch with the underground again, and give them money so that the work may go on. Do not try to save me, because I am beyond help. Do not waste your time in grief or regrets, because what has happened cannot be changed, and your duty is to the future."

Yes, he heard it all and knew it by heart. Trudi had said it, and he had assented, and must now obey her stern directive. He hadn't intended to tell her about President Roosevelt, but in that ghostly meeting he had known that it was all right to tell her, and she had replied: "That is a truly important thing for you to do. If you can persuade That Man and bring him along with us, it will be the greatest service to the cause."

"But can we trust him? Will he really do anything to help us?"—so he had asked, wavering in his soul.

"Nobody can be sure; perhaps he doesn't know himself. But do what you can to open his eyes, and watch him and see what use he makes of your efforts."

This from the Trudi-ghost bore a striking resemblance to what Lanny himself had been thinking. But that wasn't evidential, for Lanny's own thoughts had borne a close resemblance to Trudi's. She had been occupied during a year of marriage and several years preceding marriage to make certain that this should be the case. She would hardly give up the effort now that she was in the spirit world—or was she in that world? Where was she, and what was she? Find out if you can!

BOOK TWO

Wrong Forever on the Throne

5

Forward into Battle

I

LANNY took up his life where he had left off. Zoltan Kertezsi, Hungarian art expert who had taught him his trade, had been to Salzburg for the festival and now arrived in Paris. Lanny dined with him in his apartment, and they talked shop through the meal; what paintings they had bought, or sold, or had orders to buy or sell, and the prices paid or offered. It might happen that Zoltan knew of something that met Lanny's requirements, or vice versa; they helped each other, and would argue over a share in the profits, but reversing the usual procedure, the receiver insisting that he hadn't really earned that much. Lanny had never told his friend what he was doing with his money, but the other must have guessed that he was giving it away for some purpose.

They talked about politics. Zoltan despised that vile world, but just now there was so much murder in the air of Europe that the smell of it reached even to the highest ivory-tower dweller. The urbane and gentle art expert described the plight of Salzburg, famous for its baroque architecture and its music festivals, conducted, as it were, just below the entrance to an ogre's den. Hitler's retreat at Berchtesgaden was a couple of miles up in the mountains, barely across the Austrian border, and now the Führer was summoning the statesmen of various small nations and setting forth his demands—which meant in every case that they should cease their resistance to Nazi agents who came in as tourists and occupied themselves with throwing the affairs of the country into turmoil. Every day Hitler felt himself stronger, and with each concession he wrung from others he was stronger yet.

When the two art lovers could no longer bear these painful thoughts, they played music. Zoltan was a violinist; no great artist like Hansi, but with a fine style of bowing and a lovely tone. He played the sort of music which corresponded to his gentle nature and delicate tastes. Lanny accompanied him, and it was just what he needed to soothe his

88

hidden grief. They played early Italian arias by Tenaglia and Pergolesi, and the haunting cry, *Have Pity, O Lord* (*Pietà, Signor*'), which is said to have been written by the tenor Stradella. After that they played the slow movement from the Mendelssohn concerto, and when the tears ran down Lanny's cheeks, he could exclaim: "Oh, how lovely!" without seeming affected or sentimental to his friend.

Before they parted, the American remarked: "By the way, Zoltan, do you happen to know anything about the Château de Belcour? I met someone who told me about interesting old French paintings there."

"I have never heard them mentioned," replied the other.

"The party I was talking to is no judge of art, but the descriptions sounded interesting, and I thought we might go some time and have a look."

"Do you know the owners?"

"I think I have met the Duc de Belcour; but I understand the place has been rented to Graf Herzenberg, who is connected with the German embassy."

"Not so good," said the Hungarian. "But if you like I'll make inquiry among some people who might know, and see what I can find out."

"Good, and I'll do the same. Be as quick as you can, because I have a deal that may take me to Valencia, and I'd better go before Franco gets any nearer."

"That's a pretty dangerous trip just now, Lanny."

"I suppose so, but people get afraid that their art treasures are going to be destroyed by bombs and they offer them at bargain prices. One of my American clients has been tempted by some of the things I described to him, and he's anxious for me to have a try at getting them out."

II

From there the investigator went to call on his Red uncle, tough old warrior of the class struggle, who had been the means of seducing the youthful Lanny away from the faith of his fathers, suggesting to him that *la belle France* was not the altogether admirable lady she had seemed. Jesse Blackless still lived in the tenement on Montmartre, among the humble people whose cause he had espoused; he had moved to an apartment on a lower floor, because the climbing of stairs was too hard on his heart. His faithful wife had given up her work in the Party offices and was helping him as secretary; with the class struggle intensifying, there were more speeches to be made, more documents to be filed, more funds to be raised.

Jesse hadn't seen his sister Beauty Budd in a long while, and Lanny told the news from his home on the Riviera and the one in Connecticut. Jesse, for his part, rarely had any news, except on that filthy subject of politics. He was even more contemptuous of it than Zoltan, for he knew its real insides; but somebody had to clean the Augean stables, and a third-rate portrait painter had made himself into a first-rate muck-rake man. He had lost nearly all his hair, and his scalp, which had once been browned in Riviera sunshine, had been bleached in the close atmosphere of the Palais Bourbon, which housed the deputies of the French parliament. Député Zhess Block-léss, as the French called him, was wrinkled and lean, but his tongue was as sharp and active as a whiplash.

He had always talked freely to his nephew, who was not to be converted to the uncle's Communist Party line, but was a good listener and also a mine of information about the class which Jesse desired to "liquidate." Just now the deputy was especially stirred up, for the civil war in Paris appeared to be near the boiling point. The French Fascists were split among themselves by the ambitions of their rival leaders; and, said Uncle Jesse: "When thieves fall out, the Reds come into their own!" A story had come to the deputy's ears, and he was collecting evidence with the intention of blowing it wide in the Chambre. The Cagoulards, the "Hooded Men," who had been beating and murdering their opponents, were preparing their final coup to overthrow the French republic and set up a dictatorship of the Right. They had got arms from both Germany and Italy, and had them hidden in hundreds of places all over the land.

It was the Franco procedure all over again, and among the conspirators were Marshal Pétain, the hero of Verdun, and General Weygand, who had been Foch's chief of staff; also Chiappe, the Corsican head of the Paris police, and Doriot, former Communist leader said to have sold out his party and bought himself an estate in Belgium with money got from the Nazis. CSAR was the name of this group—*Comité pour Secret Action Révolutionnaire*—and their funds were coming not merely from abroad but from anti-labor forces in France, including the tire manufacturer Michelin, and Baron Schneider, the armaments king. Again the parallel with Spain; Franco having got his funds from Juan March, ex-smuggler who had become tobacco king of that country, and his guns and tanks and planes from Hitler and Mussolini.

Uncle Jesse said: "The de Bruynes ought to know a lot about all that. Can't you get them to talk and bring me their story?"

"Sure," said Lanny. "But for heaven's sake, don't mention my having been here. And by the way, Uncle Jesse, here's a story that may be of use to you. I have heard a report that the Nazis have a château not far from Paris, where they take people from the underground and hold them. Do you know anything about it?"

"I have heard such stories more than once, and I don't doubt them. Manifestly, the Nazis aren't going to let the underground operate without hindrance."

"The story I was told is quite specific. It has to do with the Château de Belcour, which has been leased by someone in the German embassy. The person who told me doesn't want it talked about at present, because he believes they have an important prisoner there, and if they are alarmed, they'll take the prisoner into Germany."

"I'll see what I can find out," replied the Red deputy.

"And one thing more," added his nephew; "I want to go to Valencia on a picture deal. Can you get the visa for me?"

"Any time you say," replied the uncle, who had close connections with the Spanish embassy in Paris because his party in Spain was collaborating in the national defense.

"Make it as soon as you can," said the nephew. "Things look bad there and later might be too late."

III

Next on Lanny's list was one of his oldest friends, Emily Chattersworth, châtelaine of the very grand estate known as Les Forêts. A childless woman, Emily had tried to find happiness in a career as *salon-nière;* now her health was failing and she was sad, because in the rage of these times she saw the death of urbanity, dignity, even common honesty in that France which was her adopted home. She loved Lanny as a son, and he could never pass through Paris without driving out to see her. Old friends are a part of life's treasure—also old places, such as this château with an artificial lake behind it, and a lawn shaded by plane trees, where Anatole France had sat and discoursed upon the scandals of the long-dead sovereigns of his country. Inside was a drawing-room where Isadora Duncan had danced to Lanny's piano playing; also where Bessie Budd had fallen in love with the violin playing of Hansi Robin.

Emily now had snow-white hair and a slowing step; a stroll in her rose garden was all that she was equal to. She had invited two nieces from the Middle West to live with her, and both of them were fine young women whom Lanny might have invited to go for a drive with him; he was in the embarrassing position of being supposed to be "eligible" when he wasn't. What he did was to tell the three ladies the news he had collected in America and England and Paris, omitting for the most part the distressful subject of politics. He talked for a while about paintings and finally said: "By the way, Emily, do you know the Duc de Belcour?"

"He used to come to my salons, but I haven't seen him for years."

"I understand he has some paintings that he might like to get rid of. He has rented his estate, you know."

"I heard so—to some German."

"No doubt I can get Kurt to introduce me to the German; but first I'd like to make sure the comte approves my inspection."

"I don't know where he is now," said Emily; "but I'll give you a letter to him with pleasure."

"Thanks, darling," replied the art expert. It is convenient to know people who can introduce you to anybody in the great world. It is like having a large library at your disposal; you don't know everything that is in every book, but you know what book to go to.

As a matter of precaution he asked: "Can you tell me anything about his politics?"

"I haven't heard of late. He's *le vrai gratin*, so doubtless he's a Royalist."

"A Royalist these days can be anything from an intellectual bandit like Maurras to a devotee of the Church."

"Belcour was a reserved and proper little man. I cannot imagine him joining the *enragés*."

"Thanks again," said Lanny.

IV

His next duty was to call up Denis de Bruyne. He had promised Marie on her deathbed that he would help to guard and guide her boys —and little could that dear soul have dreamed the use he would make of the intimacy! Denis always invited him out to the château; he would call at Lanny's hotel on Friday afternoon and return him on Monday morning. On the way out they talked about the two families; Denis, a business associate of Robbie Budd and a heavy stockholder in the airplane enterprise, was interested to hear all news about the plant. The head of the family was nearing seventy; his spare frame erect and active, his white hair and little mustache always neatly trimmed, his manner that of a grave *père de famille*. The château was no more than a fair-sized villa, with lovely but unpretentious grounds. A long wall facing the south was covered by carefully trained grapevines and peach and apricot trees. The house was of red stone, and its furnishings had been handed down through half a dozen generations. The place had been one of Lanny's homes, and whenever he came here he lived over his happy years with Marie de Bruyne.

On the drive out, Denis imparted a strange item of news to his guest. He lowered his voice, even though there was a glass shield between him and the chauffeur, and though this chauffeur, the son of an old family servant, had been jokingly described as "the most conservative man in France." "You will find changes on the place," said the master. "I hope you won't be too greatly distressed."

"What are they?" asked the guest, who understood that all changes are distressing to a conservative Frenchman.

"We have felt it necessary to protect ourselves, and have erected a small fortification in the garden."

"Good God!" Lanny wanted to say; but he had learned to guard his tongue, and remarked: "Not for the *boches*, I suppose—but for the *canaille?*"

"Precisely," replied his host. "I have reason to feel sure that the present tension cannot continue much longer."

"But why should you think that troublemakers would pay any special attention to your home?"

"We have something in storage that they will surely be interested in."

"I see," said Lanny. There was nothing in this idea to startle him unduly, for there was a partly underground storage room at Bienvenu, once used as an ice-house, and ever since Lanny could remember Robbie had kept it full of machine guns, rifles, carbines, automatic pistols, and ammunition for all of them. Robbie had never had any idea of using these weapons, except for demonstrations; they were samples of what he had to sell, and he meant for people to use them a long way off, in China, South America, or the Balkans.

When they reached the château, Denis took his guest and showed him a perfect little "pillbox" of reinforced concrete with firing-slits on all sides. It stood on a knoll which commanded the rest of the estate and a valley slightly below it. Only the wall with the vines and fruit trees stood in the way, and Denis remarked, casually: "We shall have to blow that up, of course."

V

Lanny learned what this was all about when he met the sons at the family dinner table. Denis *fils*, now over thirty, had a gentle and well-bred wife who ran the household; they had three children, who had been taught to give Lanny the honorary title of "uncle." Charlot, two years younger, was an engineer, and had been put in charge of the technical side of a plant which his father had recently taken over; his wife and two little ones were also part of the household. Charlot was especially fond of his mother's former *ami*, considering him as his teacher in political and economic affairs. In fulfillment of his duties as a sort of foster father, Lanny had tried to awaken a social conscience in these two boys. As time passed, he had come to realize that he couldn't make them think as he thought, and that if he did so, he would be only breaking up their home life; so he had given up and let them travel their own way. But they had not forgotten his early attempts, and had the idea that they were applying the lessons in their own fashion. Of late years, since Lanny had decided to crawl "underground" and hide, he had assented to everything the de Bruynes had told him; so now he was, in their estimation, one of themselves.

The children had their supper earlier and apart, and the young wives listened while the men of the household discussed the state of public affairs. The franc was declining again, labor was seething with revolt, and *la patrie* was in dire straits. For all of it they held the "Reds" responsible; and by this term they meant anybody who expressed dissatisfaction with the existing economic system or proposed any change which would weaken the control of the country by the present owning class. More than any other person they blamed Léon Blum, the Jew, whose utopian dreams were a subtle camouflage for the scheme of that oriental race to seize the mastery of the world. "Better Hitler than Blum!" was the cry of the conservatives. They didn't really mean that, of course; they were just trying to say the worst possible about a Socialist vice-premier.

Frenchmen were going to keep their country French; they were going to preserve the Catholic religion, the institution of the family, and the private property system; they were going to teach the young to be loyal to *la patrie* and the ideals which made her great and kept her so. Because the democratic system put the ignorant mob in control and put the country at the mercy of venal unprincipled politicians, that system was accursed and must be abolished. The de Bruynes had put their faith in Colonel de la Roque, who had promised action. Because of Charlot's efforts at action as a member of the Croix de Feu, he bore an honorable scar across his face. But now, Lanny learned, they had lost faith in their former leader; he had yielded to the blandishments of the politicians and had pledged his organization to a fraudulent device known as *légalité*.

The de Bruynes were at the point of espousing the program of the Cagoulards, a sort of Ku Klux Klan of France. The noblest, the best names in the land had been enlisted in that cause; arms were being smuggled in from abroad—for since Blum had been able to put through his cunning scheme to nationalize the munitions industry, it was no longer so easy to get them from French factories. Depots were being established at strategic points all over the country; officers of the Army and especially of the Air Force were being won over, and *le jour* was being prepared. The Third Republic would be dumped into the dust-bin of history, the rascal politicians would be jailed, and a committee of responsible persons would restore order, stabilize the franc, and bring back prosperity to *la patrie*. Denis named the persons: Pétain, Weygand, Darlan, Chiappe, Doriot—the very same men whom Jesse Blackless had listed.

A few years ago Lanny would have said that his old friends had gone mad; but he had seen Hitler come, and after Hitler anything was pos-sible, even probable. What he said now was: "What will Hitler be do-ing while you are carrying out this program?"

"It will take only a few days," replied the eager Charlot, who talked more than he should, seeing that he was the youngest of the men. "No longer than it took Hitler to move back into the Rhineland."

The *père de famille* added: "We have very positive assurances that Hitler will find nothing to object to in our program. Why should he? He has said many times that he has no quarrel with France, except for the Russian alliance, which commits us to the anti-Nazi side, as well as to every evil that plagues our domestic life. It is either we or the Com-munists, and the decision cannot be delayed much longer. One more series of strikes, and the situation may get entirely out of hand; the Reds may have our factories and repeat everything they did in Russia."

"How soon will the concrete in your pillbox be set?" inquired Lanny of the young engineer. He meant it playfully, but the answer was given without a smile: "It was poured three weeks ago. That is enough time for safety."

VI

"Baron Schneider dines with us tomorrow," said Denis. "Do you know him?"

"He was in my home when I was a boy," replied Lanny, "but I don't suppose he would remember me. He knows my father, of course."

That was Schneider of Schneider-Creusot, famous throughout the world. Since Zaharoff had retired, he had taken over the title of munitions king of France. But not content with that high rank, he had aspired to be emperor. That was always the way, apparently; when you owned so much, why shouldn't you have the rest? The advantages of large-scale management were so obvious, and likewise the painfulness of letting somebody else get profits which might be yours. Baron Schneider of Schneider-Creusot was getting close to his end, but his hands itched as Zaharoff's had done and he could not keep them from reaching out and clutching at power.

"I think he expects to persuade me to join actively in his CSAR," remarked Denis.

"Doubtless he needs your moral support," responded Lanny, tactfully, and added: "He probably won't want me present."

"I'll tell him you're to be trusted. You of course understand the highly confidential nature of what we are discussing."

"*Cela va sans dire*," replied the American. He had a distaste for lying, and never told a whopper unless it was absolutely unavoidable. By way of a diversion he added, quickly: "I suppose it's all right if I tell Robbie."

"Of course," assented Denis. "Robbie is going to have to do something of the sort himself before long."

It was natural for Lanny to wish to know all about the great man he was to meet, so he asked questions about the Baron Charles Prosper Eugène Schneider, who had a German name but belonged to a family which had been in the business of manufacturing munitions in France for just about a hundred years. "As long as Budd Gunmakers," remarked the American. "Our family has lost its heritage, and I suppose the Baron feels that he has lost his." This was a reference to the recent nationalization procedure.

"He owns more plants outside of France than in, so he's in no danger of starvation."

"How many, do you suppose?"

"It must be over three hundred. He has formed a colossal holding company, the Union Européenne Industrielle et Financière." Denis himself had formed such a company, though on a far smaller scale; he went on to sing the praises of the cartel, as it was called—the "vertical trust," the greatest of all social inventions, according to the Frenchman. It was an institution which would continue from generation to generation, and give society the benefits of mass production without any of the risks incidental to the system of inheritance. "The managers will always be competent technical men, so it doesn't matter whether the owners know anything about the business or not. The owners can go off and get drunk if they want to."

"That seems helpful to everybody but the owners,"—so Lanny would have liked to say, but it was the sort of remark which he had learned to choke back into his throat. "Is Le Creusot the biggest of his plants?"

"I think Skoda, in Czechoslovakia, is bigger. It has been French policy to build up the defenses of the *cordon sanitaire*, to protect not merely France but all Western Europe against Bolshevism. Schneider has built great plants also in Poland."

"I always understood that Skoda belonged to Zaharoff," remarked Lanny.

"Zaharoff wanted to sell, and Schneider was ready to buy. You know how these great enterprises are built; it's purely a matter of having credit."

"Oh, don't I know it!" replied the son of Budd-Erling. "I went around with my father while he was raising the money for his start."

"Your father didn't keep enough for himself," commented one of the father's investors. "He should have started by getting control of some bank. That way, you get thousands of investors without the bother of going to call on them; they don't even know what they're investing in. That is what Schneider did, and you can be sure he kept a sufficient share for himself. He built up this huge cartel in the last thirty or forty years; the family business was comparatively small before that."

"Naturally he wants to hold on to it," remarked Lanny; to which his host replied: "*Vraiment.*"

VII

Baron Schneider of Schneider-Creusot proved to be a dapper and most elegant aristocrat in his late sixties. He wore a neat little white mustache, and had that feature which had struck Lanny about Zaharoff —a prominent nose, like an eagle's. Robbie had said: "It is used for smelling money." Like Zaharoff, the Baron was soft-spoken and mild of manner; no doubt, when he smelled money and was demanding it, he would scream, as the eagle does, and as Robbie had said Zaharoff would do. But Lanny had never heard Zaharoff scream, nor did he ever hear Schneider.

A munitions king was by virtue of his job the man of intrigue, the man who pulled wires behind the scenes of history, putting up the money to protect his properties both at home and abroad. Since this protection had to be intellectual and political as well as financial, Schneider had purchased *Le Temps* and *Le Journal des Débats*, the two newspapers of Paris most influential with those who governed Europe, and whom the Baron must persuade if he was to have his way. Since his business was on an international scale, his intrigues had to be the same. It was not enough for him to control the government of France; he had to make sure of those countries with which France was allied and for which he was providing magnificent new machinery for the manufacture of the machinery of killing. Having bought so many politicians in his day, the Baron could hardly be blamed for taking a cynical attitude to the breed; now, since they were refusing to stay bought, he could hardly be blamed if he had decided to get rid of them.

That was why he had come to have dinner at the Château de Bruyne on a Sunday evening; not because he was interested in the dinner, or impressed by a modest estate, but because Denis, who had begun by owning the taxicabs of Paris, had come into control of other enterprises, including a couple of banks. His sons were active rightists, and the Baron, being old, needed some who were young. He addressed Denis by that name and Denis called him Eugène. He was embarrassed to find a stranger present, and directed his conversation to this stranger, giving him an opportunity to reveal his point of view. Lanny, knowing the ways of the world, took occasion to say: "I believe you know Emily Chattersworth, who has been a sort of godmother to me."

Yes, indeed, the Baron knew this leader of the Franco-American colony, and how during the World War she had taken leadership in aiding the French *blessés*. Denis, who also knew the ways of the world, mentioned that Lanny had had unusual opportunities to know both Adolf Hitler and General Göring personally. The Baron was quick to reveal his interest, so Lanny explained how in boyhood he had been a guest at Schloss Stubendorf, and had come to know a young German who had been one of "Adi's" earliest converts and had visited him in prison after the *Bierkeller Putsch* in Munich. Thus Lanny had been taken several times to meet the Führer of National Socialism; the last time he had seen him was at Berchtesgaden two years ago.

The Baron warmed up quickly. He had sent emissaries to both Hitler and Göring, it turned out, but what they had brought was of necessity formal stuff; they had met the Führer and the Chief of the Luftwaffe on dress parade, as it were. Schneider wanted to know what sort of men they really were, their private lives, their weaknesses, and possible ways to reach and influence them. Evidently the new munitions king of Europe looked upon the son of Budd-Erling as something of a "find"; he occupied most of the time at dinner in drawing him out on the subject of the National Socialist German Workingmen's Party and what it meant to France.

What was Lanny to say? He might have stated flatly: "In my opinion the Führer is definitely psychopathic. His whole being is dominated by irrational phobias. First of all he hates the Jews, and after that come the Russians, then the Poles, then, I think, the French. It may be the Czechs come ahead of you, I'm not sure. He has said in his book that the annihilation of France is essential to the safety of Germany, and there can be no doubt he means it; he didn't mind saying it, because he has a sort of double cynicism: he tells the truth in the certainty that that is the last thing anybody will expect or believe. He is infinitely cunning, and will make you any promise, for the reason that no promise means anything to him. He has only one faith and one idea in the world, and that is the Germans as the master race, destined to conquer the world under himself as the inspired Führer. That is the magnetic pole to which his being turns, and the one thing you can count upon in dealing with him."

That was the truth, but it was surely not what the munitions king wanted to hear. Was Lanny there to convert him? *Could* Lanny have converted him? It seemed most unlikely. If Lanny had said it, the Baron would have made up his mind that the American guest was some kind of Red or near it. He would have dropped the conversation, and after dinner would have requested the opportunity to talk privately with Denis; Lanny wouldn't have heard a word of the things he wanted to hear, and as a presidential agent he would have been the world's worst flop.

So, following his usual practice of telling no falsehood where it could be avoided, he explained that "Adi" was a complex personality, highly emotional, and that his actions were difficult to predict. He had written bitterly about France, but had shown in other cases that he could change his policy when his interests required it. In Berchtesgaden he had assured Lanny that he desired friendship with France, and that the only thing which stood in the way was the treasonable alliance with Russia.

"*Précisément!*" exclaimed the Baron. "We may find Hitler hard to trust—but surely not so hard as Stalin!"

"*Malheureusement*, I have not had opportunity to know Stalin," replied Lanny. He said this with his best smile, and the young de Bruynes helped him out by laughing as if it were an excellent *mot*.

VIII

So now the son of Budd-Erling was not merely a left-handed member of the de Bruyne family, but also of the Cagoulards, the "Hooded Men." When the meal was over they adjourned to the library, where the ladies tactfully refrained from coming, and for two or three hours the five gentlemen discussed the state of Europe and the part which France was playing and about to play therein. First in their thoughts was Spain, which the Reds were trying to get into their clutches.

"I had occasion to be in Seville last spring," remarked Lanny, "and to visit General Aguilar, just returned from the Jarama front. He was quite sure the Reds would not be able to hold out beyond the end of this year."

"They have all been free with their promises," responded the Baron. "The Reds can hold out so long as they are allowed to get arms from Russia; and it is going to bankrupt us all if it is allowed to continue. Ten billion francs is my guess at the amount of the bill."

Lanny wanted to be sympathetic with the so-nearly impoverished armaments maker, but he was afraid of sounding sarcastic. He managed to think of something apposite: "It is too bad that Zaharoff had to die before he saw this victory. He told me he was contributing his quota."

"Basil was inclined to be optimistic when telling about himself," remarked Eugène, dryly. "I can assure you from personal knowledge that he set his own quota, and the rest of us thought it was far from adequate."

Lanny smiled again. "The old gentleman always pleaded poverty; you would have thought he was on the verge of actual hunger. He became one of my father's heaviest investors, but I personally never had any sort of business dealings with him, so we were able to remain friends. He even came to see me after he was dead."

Naturally, the Baron looked startled and Lanny felt it was permissible to laugh. "You may have heard that Sir Basil used to visit spirit mediums, in the hope of receiving communications from his deceased wife. I happened to know one such medium, and in a séance she reported that the spirit of Sir Basil was present, and was crying for his duquesa, but couldn't find her because she was 'twice dead,' whatever that could mean. It was the first news I had had of the old gentleman's passing, which had taken place a few hours previously; so naturally I was startled."

"It is strange how those things happen," commented the old gentleman's successor.

IX

However, Baron Schneider hadn't come there to learn about spiritualism. He had come to plan for a repetition of the Spanish coup, but with more finesse and better management, so that civil war could be avoided, and *la patrie* might become an equal partner of the German Führer, instead of a vassal, as Spain was bound to be. The Baron was emphatic about that; he had received assurances on it and talked freely about the program. It was a most respectable conspiracy; the names involved were literally holy, since they included high dignitaries of the Catholic Church, whose publications, all the way between Warsaw and Brooklyn, were repeating stories about Spanish nuns having been soaked in oil and burned by the Spanish Reds. The name of Marshal Pétain was the most honored in the French army, and that of Admiral Darlan in the navy. There were a score of other high generals and naval officers involved, to say nothing of politicians, including ex-Premier Laval. Schneider called the roll, because he had come to enlist the de Bruynes and to have the *père de famille* promise an adequate "quota" without having to be asked for it.

There was one question which Lanny wanted to have answered; the most delicate of questions, to be approached with infinite tact. "Permit me to venture a suggestion, Baron Schneider. It happens that the piano virtuoso and composer Kurt Meissner is one of my oldest friends; in fact, he lived in my home on the Riviera for many years after the war, and is accustomed to say that he owes his career to the support which my family gave him. He has been in Paris for some time, and I have reason to feel sure that he would be interested in what you are now planning."

Lanny was aware that this statement would appear naïve to the great man, and he wanted it to be just that. Said the Baron: "I thank you, M. Budd; it so happens that I enjoy the honor of Herr Meissner's acquaintance. He has given me valuable help in the organizing of our Comité France-Allemagne."

"What I have in mind," continued the double-dyed intriguer, "is that

Kurt is one of the Führer's intimate friends, plays music for him frequently and enjoys his confidence. He would be the best of persons to put your proposals before Hitler and to explain your point of view."

"Your suggestion is excellent, M. Budd, and I am indebted to you for it."

The other continued: "I hope I am not intruding, Baron,"—knowing, of course, that the Baron would be forced to say that he wasn't. "The subject is delicate, and I am merely making suggestions, to which you need not feel compelled to reply. I realize that Hitler has even more reason to desire a change of government in France than in Spain, for France is his neighbor, and is extending credits to Russia, his one permanent enemy. If Hitler is finding it worth while to put up billions of francs to support General Franco, it seems to me he would be financially interested, as a cold business proposition, in securing a government in France which would promise to seal the Spanish border and stop the present flow of supplies to the Reds. Wouldn't it seem so to you, monsieur le Baron?"

Eugène Schneider's keen dark eyes were fixed intently upon this presumptuous American's, as if he were reading every one of the thoughts written upon the mental scroll behind them. Lanny knew that trick well, and knew that a skillful rascal must meet the gaze with one equally firm. At last the munitions king replied: "M. Budd, the subject is, as you say, one of great delicacy. I can only tell you that that aspect of the matter has received our careful consideration."

"I respect your reticence, Baron. I am told that the decline of Doriot's influence is due to the fact that he has been accused of receiving German funds, and has apparently not felt in position to deny it. All I wish to say is that I have known Kurt Meissner since boyhood, and there is a certain warmth of intimacy one attains then that can never be entirely reproduced in later life. Let me tell you, in the strictest confidence, that Kurt was a secret agent of the *Generalstab*, operating in Paris at the time of the Peace Conference. Prior to that he had been an artillery officer, and was wounded, and lost his wife and baby because of war privations; so you can understand that it is difficult for him to love the French. He came into Paris in civilian clothes on a false passport, and as it was still wartime, he would surely have been shot by your police, who were on his trail. My mother helped me to smuggle him into Spain and thus saved his life, something which Kurt has acknowledged many times. I tell you all this so that you may understand why he would trust me more than he could ever bring himself to trust any Frenchman."

"Your story is most interesting, M. Budd."

"What I have in mind to say is that if the suggestion meets with your approval, I should be happy to talk over with Kurt the plans we have been discussing tonight and to bring you his reactions and advice."

The cautious magnate turned to his host. Having been a member of the *haut monde* of Paris all his life, the Baron was no stranger to the practice of *la vie à trois*, and must have heard rumors as to the situation in the de Bruyne household years ago. "*Eh bien, Denis?*"

Said the *père de famille*: "I could not think of a better method of procedure."

"You understand, M. Budd," said the other, "you are dealing with the most inviolable secret of our movement. The political life of all of us depends upon its being preserved religiously."

"You do not have to tell me anything about that, Baron," replied Lanny—again avoiding an outright lie. "I have lived the greater part of my life in France, and I understand your political relationships fairly well. Also I have enjoyed the confidence of a number of your statesmen, and have never betrayed it."

X

Lanny's first action on returning to his hotel was to call Kurt Meissner's apartment. He hadn't seen Kurt for more than a year, and the composer's pleasure when he heard his friend's voice seemed unfeigned. "Come to lunch," he said, and Lanny replied: "Sure thing."

The presidential agent sat at his little portable and typed out a detailed account of the Cagoulard conspiracy to overthrow the French republic. He didn't say how he had got this information, but he wrote: "This is first-hand and positive." He gave the names of the persons involved and the program, signed it "103," addressed it to Gus Gennerich, and put it into the mail.

To himself he said: "F.D. won't believe it." But of course Lanny couldn't help that; it was his fate to be living in a time when so many things were unbelievable, even after they had happened.

Kurt lived in a fashionable apartment, suitable to his station in the musical world. He had a man-servant to wait on him, a shaven-headed Silesian who had fought under him all through the war and still kept military discipline; the man probably added spying to his other duties, and Lanny got the impression that he disapproved of having foreigners around. Even when Lanny talked about his visit to the Führer, Willi Habicht refused to relent; perhaps he thought the Führer oughtn't to keep such company. Or perhaps it was just that the servant was naturally glum, the result of having fought victoriously for four long years, and then discovering at the very last moment that he was unaccountably licked.

Also there was a secretary in the apartment, a Nordic blond young lady, a devoted Nazi, brisk and efficient. Lanny was left with little doubt concerning her double role in the household. Kurt had a wife and several children at home, and now and then went back and begot another. In the old days he would have considered it his duty to be true to that wife, but now there was a new *Weltanschauung*. The Nazi world was a man's world, and the first duty of woman was to submit. Kurt's superiors would undoubtedly see to it that he had a trustworthy German companion, so that he might be proof against the wiles of seductive enemy ladies. No Mata Haris this time; at least, not working on the Germans! Perhaps also—who could say?—it might be one of the duties of Ilse Vetter to check on Kurt's activities and report now and then.

If so, she could have nothing but good to say; for Kurt was competent, he had the best connections, and he was laboring with single-minded devotion to break down the intellectual and moral defenses of Marianne and bring her into the orbit of the New Order. So true was this that Lanny had come to find his boyhood chum quite intolerable; that long lean face which he had once found grave and even priestlike now seemed to him fanatical, touched with madness. The phrases of abstract philosophy and ethics with which Kurt had so impressed Lanny in his boyhood now sounded hollow to his ears; for of course there could be no general or universal truth in the mind of any devotee of National Socialism. For him the good, the true, and the beautiful were limited to Germany and Germans, and for other peoples and individuals the words were a fraud and a snare. Perhaps in the deeps of his heart Kurt might still have affectionate memories of the little American boy whom he had undertaken to inspire and guide; but if so, he would regard those feelings as a form of weakness to be repressed. Lanny, like everybody else both inside and outside Germany, would be used for the furtherance of Adolf Hitler's dream of glory, and every word that Kurt spoke and every attitude he assumed to the son of Budd-Erling would be for some carefully studied purpose.

All right, since that was the game, Lanny would learn to play it. He would keep his friendship with a respected German musician, and speak no word to him that did not have some carefully studied purpose. For many years Lanny had never voiced his real ideas on political and economic subjects in Kurt's presence. He had made a cautious withdrawal from the field, saying that he realized he was out of place there; he had become an art expert, in Kurt's eyes a money-making art dealer; he had become a dilettante in all the arts, and if Kurt chose to assume that he was playing around with ladies such as the Countess of Sandhaven, that was Kurt's privilege and did Lanny no harm.

In recent years the playboy had been dropping hints that he was following along the path of least resistance, and being impressed by the phenomenal success of Adi Schicklgruber—but of course never calling him by that humiliating name. Adi, the former army *Gefreite* and dere-lict painter of picture postcards, had become not merely the master of Germany but the master politician of Europe. He had compelled all the world to talk about him, to heed his words, and to tremble at his frequent rages; he had sent his armies into the Rhineland and now had it securely fortified; he had restored conscription in Germany and was now militarizing the entire Fatherland. He had got away with both these dangerous moves, in spite of all the threats of his enemies and the fears of his own General Staff. Wonderful man! A twentieth-century Napoleon! If Lanny was impressed, that was a part of his role as a weakling, and if Kurt looked down upon him for it, that was what all Nazis did to all the rest of the world.

XI

During the luncheon with Kurt and Fräulein Vetter, Lanny told the news of his mother and father, and of Rosemary and her paintings. He told about his last trip into Spain, saying nothing about Alfy, but mak-ing it a picture-buying expedition, in course of which he had met many of Franco's officers and witnessed the triumphs of Franco's arms. That he should have been thrilled by them was a proper role for an American playboy. General Franco's class was Lanny's class, and Lanny had slipped back into his proper place in society.

Afterwards, alone with Kurt in the study, and with the secretary's typewriter clicking busily in the next room, Lanny opened his mind completely and revealed the changes which had been taking place in it. Kurt had been right all along, and Lanny had been blundering for the greater part of his life. Kurt had been right about the Versailles Treaty, he had been right about reparations and the cruel inflation which had been forced upon Germany; about the *Schieber* and the Jews, and above all about Adolf Hitler, from the first time they had heard him speak in Munich. Lanny had trusted the Reds, and had found that they were unworthy of his trust; he had hoped for some sort of humane social order in France, but had come to realize that the French democracy was hopelessly corrupt, that the Russian alliance was a device of political rascality, and that the only hope for the French people lay in co-operating with the New Order which Adolf Hitler was successfully constructing.

Of course Kurt was pleased. He said that he had been deeply wounded by the separation from Lanny, who had been like a brother to him in past times. He clasped Lanny's hand, and said that this news had restored his youth to him; he said: "My family will be happy; Heinrich Jung will be happy; the Führer will be happiest of all!"

Did Kurt mean all that? And would he continue to feel that way after he had had time to think matters over? Lanny could never be sure on this point. It was obvious that Kurt would have acted this way, whether or not he believed in his old friend's sincerity. He had probably long ago passed the stage where he gave full faith to anybody, or to anything that anybody said. He would watch his old friend and weigh the chances for and against; Lanny would do the same, and they would continue their intimacy so long as it served the purposes of both.

XII

The time had come for Lanny to reveal the business which had brought him here. He had, he said, news which he thought would be of special interest to Kurt. Last evening he had been in conference with Baron Schneider at the home of the de Bruynes. Kurt knew all four of these persons, but now he pretended to have had no idea that they were engaged in a conspiracy to overthrow the government of their country. A most extraordinary thing! A proof of the decadence which prevailed in France! "I always told you that, Lanny. It was the reason I couldn't bear to live any longer on the Riviera, in spite of all your dear mother's kindness."

"Again you were right, Kurt! That world was falling to pieces."

"Do you mind if I make notes?" Kurt asked; and when Lanny consented, he jotted down the names of all the army and navy officers who were in command of the "Hooded Men," and the great manufacturers and landowners and bankers who were putting up the money to pay for the hidden stores of arms. Lanny wasn't naïve enough to believe that all this was really news to the German; Lanny's guess was that Kurt was riding in the very center of this whirlwind, perhaps even directing it. But Kurt would be glad to check his information by so high-up an authority as the munitions king of France, Czechoslovakia, Poland, Belgium, and other countries. Every detail was important; and of course it was good to know that poor blundering Lanny Budd had at last seen a glimmer of the light. No doubt that he could be made use of, though of course not in the ways he naïvely supposed.

Lanny went on to explain his bright idea. "If it has been worth while for the Führer to put up so much money for Spain, he might wish to do the same for France, and make sure of success at the outset. Of course I understand that you may not feel free to discuss such matters with me, and I'm not suggesting that you should. I told the Baron I would take the matter up with you, and report what you said if you wanted me to—though of course there's no reason why you shouldn't get in touch with him direct. If you send anybody else, you'll have to vouch for him, because a man like Schneider doesn't talk unless he's perfectly sure about the person's credentials. I doubt if he'd have talked before me if he hadn't known my father and if the de Bruynes hadn't vouched for me."

Very tactful of the American, but at the same time a trifle self-important; telling Kurt how to handle his most secret negotiations; taking it for granted that Kurt was engaged in such affairs, something which Kurt had never admitted to Lanny, or to anybody but fellow-members of the service. In short, something of what the Americans call "a buttinski," and the Germans *ein zudringlicher Geselle*.

But of course Kurt would take pains not to let Lanny see any trace of such feelings. He would be deeply grateful and assure an American playboy that his revelations were of the utmost importance; however, Kurt could do nothing but pass them on to the authorities in Berlin who handled such matters. He would promise not to mention Lanny in the report, and if Lanny got any further information he could be sure that Kurt would be grateful and would deal with it in the same ultra-confidential way.

From all this Lanny learned that Kurt wasn't going to trust him, but just use him. Kurt wasn't even going to admit in plain words that he was a Nazi agent! All right; Lanny was keeping his secrets also. It would be a duel of wits, and let the best set win.

"By the way, Kurt," said the art expert, "there is a favor you can do me. Do you know Graf Herzenberg?"

"I know him fairly well."

"I'm told he's connected with the embassy. He has leased the Château de Belcour, and I'm told there are some interesting old French paintings in it. Have you been in it?"

"Many times. I noticed some paintings but didn't pay any special attention to them."

"Emily has given me a letter to the Duc de Belcour, and I've no doubt he'll be willing for me to view them; but of course it will have to be subject to the Graf's approval."

"I'll speak to him about it, if you like."

"As soon as possible, please. I have to go into Spain again, to see some paintings there."

Said Kurt, as if the idea had occurred to him for the first time: "You do really know quite a lot about painting, don't you, Lanny?"

"Some people gamble their money upon it," replied his friend. "And that includes the commander of your Air Force!"

6

Blondel Song

I

WHY was Lanny Budd taking so much trouble to get inside the Château de Belcour? He asked himself the question many times without finding an entirely satisfactory answer. His head told him that Trudi probably wasn't there; but on the other hand, his heart told him that she must have been there; they surely wouldn't have two prisons near Paris. Said head: "If she is still alive, she is in Germany by now." Said heart: "I want to see the place where she was." Said head, with a trace of mockery: "Do you want to sing a song outside her dungeon, like Blondel, the minstrel of King Richard the Lionhearted?" Heart replied: "I went and looked at the old palace where they had Alfy, and I found a way to get him out. Perhaps I might do it again." In the most vital of men's concerns, heart usually wins over head, and this is reprobated by a school of philosophers who call themselves realists, materialists, monists; on the other hand it is sanctioned by another school who call themselves idealists, Platonists, mystics.

The mail brought Lanny a note from the secretary of the Duc de Belcour, saying that so far as Monsieur le Duc was concerned it would be entirely agreeable for M. Budd to inspect the paintings, but that the decision necessarily rested with the occupant. A few hours later Kurt called up, to report that he had made an appointment for Lanny to visit the château at three o'clock the following afternoon. Lanny thanked him cordially, and called Zoltan, who with his customary efficiency had got a lot of information about the art contents of the building. He retailed this to his : iend, but said that unfortunately he had an appointment for the hour Kurt had set. This suited Lanny, who couldn't foresee what situations might arise and might have a hard time explaining them to Zoltan.

Five minutes before the appointed hour, Lanny's automobile halted before the entrance to these very splendid grounds. He gave his name to the porter who, he observed, was a German. The gates swung back, and he drove between two rows of ancient beech trees. In the back seat of his car lay Trudi Schultz, bound and gagged; at least, so Lanny visioned her. His head said: "Perhaps!" and his heart said: "Oh, God!"

The building was of gray granite, four stories in height and quite extensive; it had been built by a cousin of Louis Seize for his favorite mistress, and had to be big enough so that royal personages could be entertained there. It had towers and crenelations suitable to a castle, but its windows were wide for comfort; at that time artillery had made stone walls hopelessly vulnerable, and noble gentlemen and ladies had learned to rely for their security upon the majesty of the kings of France. Now the driveway was paved with asphalt, and motorcars instead of gilded coaches waited in the wide curving spaces.

II

Promptly on the hour Lanny ascended the steps, and the door was opened before he knocked. A German in livery took his name and led him to a high-ceilinged French drawing-room with elaborate frescos and gilding. In front of Lanny's eyes was a Largillière, and he didn't wait for any invitation to begin his art-experting. One eye surveyed a lady of two hundred years ago, having a tower of hair on her head like a Chinese pagoda, her bosom and arms smooth-shining and white, while voluminous folds of cerise silk encased the rest of her. Lanny's other eye was on the door, through which he expected a more modern costume to appear.

It came; a young Schutzstaffel officer, all in shiny black boots and belt, and with the death's head insignia on his sleeve. The instant he appeared Lanny swung about, clicked his heels, threw up his arm with fingers of the hand extended, and snapped out: *"Heil Hitler!"* The young officer could hardly have expected this, but his response was obligatory and automatic: he halted and returned the salute. Then he said: "Herr Budd?"

Lanny replied: *"Lanning Prescott Budd, Kunstsachverständiger seiner Exzellenz des Herrn Minister-Präsident General Hermann Göring."*

The Germans love to string titles like beads on a necklace, and they like to put long words together to make what small boys in frivolous America call "jawbreakers." The title which Lanny had conferred upon himself was no more than "art expert"—but how much more honorific and impressive it sounded! It took all the starch out of the young Nazi's collar, and he said, lamely: *"Leutnant Rörich gestattet sich vorzustellen."*

"Sehr erfreut, Herr Leutnant," replied Lanny. The man appeared to be in his early twenties, and had a round, rather naïve face and closely clipped yellow hair. Lanny's heart cried: "You have been beating Trudi!" His head advised: "No, he wouldn't do menial work; he would direct the rank and file and make sure they did a thorough job."

Employing his very best Berlinese, Lanny explained that he was an old friend of the second-in-command of Germany, and for years had been aiding in the disposition of certain of the General's paintings and the acquisition of others more suited to a great man's increasing honors. At present Lanny had in mind a project to be put before the General for the setting up of a museum of art works illustrating the development of the various European cultures; he was preparing a list of examples suitable for such a grandiose undertaking. Had the Herr Leutnant himself made any study of the subject of historical painting? The Herr Leutnant modestly confessed that he knew very little about it, and Lanny set out to remedy his deficiencies. Each time they stopped before a new work the expert would give his appropriate *Spruch*. Zoltan had given him the names of the painters, and he had refreshed his memory by the reference works in his suite; the same for the château, which was in the guidebooks, with all the dates and information about the Belcour family.

Lanny really looked at the paintings, and formed opinions about them, and expressed competent judgments; but every now and then a part of his brain would be swept by a storm. He would be thinking: "You had her in a dungeon, perhaps under this very spot; and did you violate her yourself. or is that also something you delegate to your *Gemeinen?*" Heart said: *"Nazi Schweinehund!"* Head said: "Perhaps he has taken a fancy to her and is keeping her here indefinitely."

Now and then the lecturer would find some modern simile or allusion and thus lead his discourse away from historic times. Was it a battle scene, with artillery thundering? He would remark: "How startlingly fashions in war have changed! Nowadays you wouldn't stand much chance with a cannon like that." The young officer assented, and Lanny began foretelling that the fighting would be forced into the air; this gave him a chance to mention that his father was Budd-Erling Aircraft, and had leased many of his patents to General Göring, being favored in return with the secrets of the newest Messerschmitts and Focke-Wulfs. Lanny himself had shot stags with the General, and had visited Karinhall, and met the Frau Minister-Präsident General, who was Emmy Sonnemann, the stage star, whom no doubt the Herr Leutnant had seen many times.

"*Ja, gewiss,*" said the Herr Leutnant, and found this conversation most exhilarating.

Or was it a painting by a Spaniard? Lanny had just come from Franco Spain; he had traveled with his brother-in-law, Il Capitano Vittorio di San Girolamo, an officer in the Italian Air Force who had lost an arm in the fighting in Abyssinia. The Italians hadn't shown up so well in Spain, alas; they were having to call on General Göring for more and more help. In the judgment of Lanny's father there was no organization in all the world so efficient as the German Air Force. The founder of Budd-Erling had been taken by Seine Exzellenz to visit Kladow, the new secret air-training base, and had raved about the sights he had seen there. The humble Schutzstaffel officer, who had been prepared to be bored by a culture-seeking American tourist, found himself being lifted up from one Nazi heaven to the next. *Kolossal!*

III

Presently they came to a painting of a wounded soldier with his head in a woman's lap. Said the *Kunstsachverständiger:* "That reminds me of a work by my former stepfather, who was the famous French painter Marcel Detaze. Do you know his work, by any chance?" When the officer had to confess that he didn't, Lanny rattled on: "The Führer is a great admirer of his, and asked me to send him an example. I was giving an exhibition of my stepfather's work in Munich three years ago, and Kurt Meissner, the *Komponist*—you know Kurt, perhaps?"

Ja, the Herr Leutnant was glad to be able to say at last that he had met one of the many distinguished Germans whom this extraordinary American knew intimately.

"Kurt is one of my oldest friends. I visited Schloss Stubendorf the Christmas before the war broke out and ruined Europe. Kurt is the cause of my having met the Führer so early—we went to hear him speak soon after he came out of prison, back in the old days. I didn't become converted at the outset—I used to think I was something of a Socialist at that time."

"We are all Socialists now, Herr Budd," reminded the other; "National Socialists."

"Of course," assented Lanny; "but I had got hold of the wrong kind. Then I visited the Führer in Berlin and he explained matters to me in that marvelous way he has.—But I was telling you about the painting. It is called *Sister of Mercy*, and Kurt and I and Heinrich Jung took it to the Führer at the Braune Haus in Munich. You have been in the Braune Haus?"

"*Nein, Herr Budd, ich bin ein Rheinländer.*"

"*Ach, so?*"—and Lanny talked about that most beautiful country of grapes and old castles, and about Herr Reichsminster Doktor Josef Goebbels, who was from that region, and about the Frau Reichsminster Magda Goebbels and their home and their brilliant conversation. Then he laughed, and reminded himself that he was supposed to be telling about the Braune Haus in Munich; he described the elegant building, which was the Führer's own design; also the Führer's study and its decorations, and how the Führer had admired the *Sister of Mercy*—he had extremely fine taste in art, had been a painter himself and would have liked to be nothing else, so he had assured Lanny; but, alas, the German people had demanded his services and he had been unable to think about his own pleasure.

The Führer had talked with amazing knowledge about French painting techniques—this wasn't true, but Lanny was sure it could do no harm to pile it on extra thick. The Führer had spoken feelingly of his respect for French culture, and his desire that this great people should be reconciled to Germany. All that was needed was the reorienting of French policy, the breaking off of the atrocious alliance with Jewish-Bolshevism.

"That was three years ago," said the art expert, "and you can see the marvelous prescience of the man. Right now the French are beginning to realize the monstrous nature of their blunder. There is a movement under way to change the government of this country suddenly and completely. You can take it from me that it won't be many months before you see the Russian alliance repudiated and a German alliance formed, one that will last for a thousand years—just as the Führer said to me in Berchtesgaden."

For an hour or two the young Schutzstaffel officer had listened to a foreigner ask him if he knew this and that, and most of the time he had had to answer a humiliating No. But here was something about which he was informed, and he said: "I think I know what you mean, Herr Budd. I suppose that you are actively interested in that movement."

"Indeed, yes," replied Lanny; "with everything I have, heart and mind and purse." Then, as if he had committed an indiscretion, he came back to a painting on the wall. "Here we have a David, a later and quite different style from Boucher and Fragonard. He painted charming ladies, as you see; but he became a revolutionist, and did revolutionary scenes, terrible pictures—but no doubt General Göring would wish to have samples, if only as a warning to your German people. All the miseries and corruptions from which France suffers now date from that blind upsurgence of the rabble, which was able to overthrow its rulers by means of pikes and pitchforks, but was not able to keep the control from passing into the hands of Jewish moneylenders and speculators. You agree with that interpretation of French history, Herr Leutnant?"

"*Absolut, Herr Budd.*"

"I am talking too much, I fear——"

"Oh, not at all, I assure you; I have never listened to more instructive conversation."

"I always find myself moved when I come into one of these old buildings. This château, you know, fell into the hands of the revolutionists. Very often they burned the buildings; but somebody had the more sensible idea of turning this one into a revolutionary headquarters. You can imagine the scenes which went on here; the mob of peasants and village people marching in, singing their furious songs, with the bloody heads of their victims on pikes. Probably they broke into the winecellars and got royally drunk—you have winecellars in this château, Herr Leutnant?"

"Yes, of course."

"I suppose you have dungeons, also?"

"There are small rooms in the cellar which may have been used for that purpose."

"With rings set in the masonry, to which prisoners could be chained?"

"I have never looked for them, Herr Budd."

"One sometimes makes gruesome discoveries in these old places. Perhaps it might interest you to go down there with me some day, and see what we could find." The lecturer dropped a hint like that, and then skipped quickly away from what might have been a dangerous subject. He would come back to it later.

IV

They came to the music room, and in one corner was a tiny instrument of French walnut, elaborately carved and inlaid. "Ah, look—*une épinette!*" exclaimed Lanny. "We wouldn't get much music out of it, but doubtless it is priceless as an antique. We have seen in music the same evolution as in war, Herr Leutnant." There was a stool before the instrument, and Lanny said: "Shall I try it?"

He seated himself, raised the cover, and lightly touched the keys. Little tinny tinkling sounds came forth, and Lanny said: "That is what our great-grandfathers' grandfathers considered music. Yet a good many of Mozart's finest works were composed for such—I have seen the little clavichord on which he learned to play, in the humble apartment in Salzburg where he was born."

Lanny played a snatch from a Mozart piano sonata; then he rose and walked across the room to a fine modern French instrument, a grand piano, and seated himself there. He put on the loud pedal and struck the chords, and thunder rolled forth. He played the *Horst Wessel Lied*, the marching song of the Nazis, written by a Berlin Stormtrooper, said to have been a pimp. It has a fine stirring rhythm, and Lanny could be sure that Herr Leutnant Rörich had been brought up on it. Judging by his looks, he had been a youth when his party took power, and his present confidential position indicated that he must have come into the Hitlerjugend as a boy. *Die Strasse frei den braunen Bataillonen*—it was a prophecy which had come true, for when the song was written it was the Reds who had possession of the German streets, and now the last one of them was dead or in a concentration camp. It was a marching tune that would stir anybody's blood, regardless of what he might think of the words.

Lanny stopped and turned to his escort. "*Das klingt besser, nicht wahr, Herr Leutnant?*"—and the other replied: "*Viel besser, gewiss.*"

"Am I taking too much of your time?" inquired the visitor, graciously. "Oh, by no means."

Lanny turned again to the piano, saying: "Let me play you one of the tunes which once rang out in these elegant rooms." Again he pressed the loud pedal and played with vigor another marching tune that would stir anybody's blood, regardless of what he thought of the words. "*Ah, ça ira, ça ira, ça ira!*"—meaning three times over that it is going to go, or to be gone through with, the job is going to be done. In this case the job was to cart the aristocrats "to the lanterns" and hang them from the chains stretched across the streets of French towns. The accent falls on the "a" of *ira,* and when a French revolutionist sang it he hissed and spit it out with hatred to be matched only by the Nazis proclaiming that Jewish blood would spurt from the knife. Alas for the many times the threats of both songs had been made good!

"I don't suppose you ever heard that tune," remarked Lanny, as he rose from the piano. "That is what the mob was singing when it took this château. Have you examined the walls and floors to see if there are traces of aristocratic blood?"

Unspoken in the visitor's mind were far different thoughts. "What are the floors of this château made of? Surely those loud sounds would go through them. Certainly, if Trudi is there, and heard the *Ça ira,* she will know I am here, for she will be sure it would never be played by Nazis. She remembers how I sang it, with comical fierceness. She knows the story of Blondel, too, and will understand that I am sending her a message."

But strange to say, the Trudi-ghost was failing to appreciate this effort on her behalf. What she was saying now was: "Go to Spain and find Monck, and get in touch with the underground again."

V

To his escort Lanny remarked: "It might be the part of wisdom, Herr Leutnant, not to talk too freely about the possible interest of General Göring in these paintings. You know how the French are, a mercenary people, and whenever I ask for a price on any painting, I always have to keep the name of my client a secret."

"I understand, Herr Budd."

"Some day, I doubt not, the commander of the German Air Force may be in a position to compel a reduction in the price of French paintings; but that may be several years yet, I imagine." Glancing at the young officer, Lanny did not do anything so vulgar as to wink; he gave a sly smile, and the other said: "*Jawohl, mein Herr!*"

They had completed the round of the *rez-de-chaussée,* and the escort remarked: "There are paintings in some of the upstairs rooms also, but they are small and I doubt if they are important."

"Probably not," assented the expert. "I am acquainted with an American department-store proprietor in London who has Rembrandts in his bedrooms, but the French are more frugal. However, there is still a favor you may do me, if your patience is not exhausted."

"Surely not, Herr Budd."

"I am interested in this building, as an example of the development in French architecture. We observe in all architecture a gradual process of departure from reality, very interesting to the student of social customs. Some feature originates in a mechanical or historical necessity, and then it becomes accepted and conventionalized, and is continued for centuries after its original purpose has been forgotten. Once upon a time, you know, a château was a fortress, built for defense and compelled to be on the alert day and night. Then, in course of time that strain was relaxed, but a château still had to be a château, because it was the dignified, the aristocratic thing. However, defense features are both expensive and uncomfortable and gradually they came to be replaced by imitations, until now a château is like those Hollywood façades they erect with nothing behind them. If you don't mind strolling with me around the outside of this building, I will show you some of the tricks which the architects of the *ancien régime* in its decadence used to play upon their clients; or perhaps it was the clients playing tricks upon their friends and guests, including members of the royal family who now and then came to visit them."

"Most interesting, Herr Budd. Let us go, by all means."

They strolled to the door while Lanny continued his discourse. "You are perhaps living in a château for the first time, Herr Leutnant, and discovering that it is far from commodious. I venture the guess that the staff of Graf Herzenberg is compelled to send its laundry to be done outside, because the facilities of this magnificent building have been found inadequate."

"You have guessed correctly," laughed the Schutzstaffel officer.

"I recall reading somewhere an old document having to do with the coming of some young princess to marry one of the kings of France. It may have been Marie Antoinette, or possibly Anne of Austria, at an earlier period. Anyhow, the chronicler described the immensity of the princess's escort, a veritable army, with so many hundreds of coaches and so many four-horse wagons, so many servants of this sort and that, forty cooks, perhaps—and the list ended with one laundress. You could see the reason when you came to the items comprising the young person's trousseau: hundreds of elaborate costumes, cloth of gold and of silver, velvet brocade, pure silk from China, and so on—and trailing off at the end to an unimportant item of three chemises."

VI

Discoursing thus entertainingly, Lanny roamed about the grounds of the structure with its many outbuildings, servants' quarters, stables now turned into garages, kennels, aviaries, and what not. Lanny had learned the art of conversation in childhood, and could carry it on while the greater part of his mind was busy elsewhere. How wide were the openings into the basement? Too narrow for a human head to pass through, as in the old castles, or trusting to iron bars, as in later and more orderly days? "Just as I thought, an acetylene torch would cut one of those very quickly! And where does the telephone line run? And the electric light wires? And the servants and workers—all Germans, certainly. No chance of any leak to the outside! And the dogs? Yes, a number of them, and doubtless all turned loose at night!"

Aloud Lanny said: "Beautiful dogs, Herr Leutnant! Are you a lover of these friends of our race? I find it is better to know only one dog at a time—it is just as with a woman, they are jealous, even though they do not show it, even though they perhaps do not know what is the matter with them. Especially these German shepherds. In England they call them Alsatians, and in my homeland police dogs; I do not know why; perhaps people are unwilling to credit the Germans with having created anything so surpassing. May I have the pleasure of being introduced to them? I bought one of these dogs once, from a man who bred and raised him. The man led me to the dog and pointed me to him and said: 'This is your new master; from now on you will have nothing to do with any other man.' And I swear that creature understood the words and took them as his bible. Years later, when I was compelled to be away from my Riviera home for a long period, the dog would not eat and actually perished of starvation. You should have yourself formally introduced to these dogs, Herr Leutnant, so that you can walk out in the grounds at night with safety."

"These are German dogs," replied the Schutzstaffel officer, smiling. "I think they know the German smell."

"Or absence of smell," countered Lanny. "Since you have your laundry done regularly!"

So when they parted they felt themselves to be old friends. Lanny said: "I have no words to tell you how grateful I am for your courtesy. Perhaps you would let me return the hospitality some time. Are you stationed here permanently?"

"So far as I know, Herr Budd."

"*Menschenkind!*—then you might like to join me in Paris some evening and let me show you some of the curious aspects of that city to which the ordinary tourist does not have access."

"*Ich bitte darum.*"

"Just now I have to be away; but a little later, on my return—may I phone you?"

"*Bitte sehr, mein Freund.*" It was a case of *Wahlverwandtschaften*—translated as "elective affinities."

VII

Lanny drove until he was a safe distance from the château, and then drew up in a shady spot by the highway, got out his notebook and pencil, and made maps and elaborate notes of every detail he had observed of the building and grounds, both inside and out. Then he drove on; and the Trudi-ghost said: "You are wasting your time. You cannot help me, and you will risk getting caught. Go to Spain."

Lanny, mannish and stubborn, replied: "I am going to help you. Even if I go and get Monck, it will be to help you."

The Trudi-ghost countered: "Monck will put you in touch with the underground, and you can give them the money."

Lanny, who liked to have his own way but usually gave in when some loved person kept insisting, replied: "Oh, all right, all right; I'll go." It was like still being married.

He telephoned for an appointment and drove to his Uncle Jesse's; parking as always some distance away so as not to attract attention in the neighborhood. All neighborhoods in France are full of curiosity.

The Communist deputy had had his nephew's passport stamped with a visa for Valencia. At the time it wasn't necessary to get an exit permit from the French government, for in one of the shifts incidental to the maneuvers of the Non-Intervention Commission, the border was open into Spain, and the French officials contented themselves with saying: "*C'est très, très dangereux, monsieur, et vous y allez à votre risque.*" The papers of the previous afternoon told of airplane bombs being dropped on the temporary capital of "Red" Spain, and the morning papers told of a cruiser bombardment and the sinking of a merchant vessel in sight of the city. Lanny said: "I won't stay long, Uncle Jesse."

In return for the favor he told his relative a lot about the Cagoulard conspiracy. He didn't mention having met Schneider, and he warned his uncle, as many times before, that he must never let himself be tempted to mention any member of the de Bruyne family, no matter what offenses they might commit. There had been on this point a mutual understanding, never infringed over a period of some fifteen years. The de Bruynes of course knew about the Red sheep in Lanny's family, something he couldn't help and wasn't to be blamed for. Sometimes Lanny would tell them news about the Reds and their doings, treating it playfully for the most part, and confining it to such items as anyone could easily have found out.

There was a curious aspect of this class struggle, even at its fiercest; each side looked upon the other with horror, but this feeling was mixed with a complex of other emotions: fear, awe, curiosity, even amusement. There was something romantic about the idea of actually knowing a real Red; of being able to go to his home and sit down and eat bread and cheese and drink wine with him. What was he really like? What did he talk about when he wasn't making speeches? What did he do? Lanny would answer: "He paints portraits of little street gamins, whom he loves. They are only fairly good as paintings, but people buy them for the benefit of the cause."

Jesse Blackless wasn't doing much painting now; his hands were growing unsteady, he said—he couldn't help thinking about Spain, and that made them tremble. There was a fresh crisis. The Franco invaders who absurdly called themselves "Nationalists" had been trying to get belligerent rights from Britain and France, and failing in this, they had sought to establish a blockade by means of submarines; they were sinking British and French and other neutral vessels seeking to enter Loyalist ports. That of course was "piracy" in the eyes of all neutrals, and it had provoked the first signs of real determination on the part of Britain and France. They had jointly announced that they would sink all submarines in those waters, and they had meant it—with the result that the mysterious pirates suddenly ceased operations about the coasts of Spain.

That was always the way, Jesse said; the moment you took a firm stand with the dictators, they backed down. It was well known that when Hitler had given orders to the Wehrmacht to march into the Rhineland, the General Staff had been afraid of the move, and Hitler had conceded the point that if the French offered resistance, the Germans would at once retire. It would have been the same with Italy in Abyssinia, and it would be the same in Spain, if only England and France would decide to grant real neutrality and let the Loyalist government buy arms like any other.

VIII

Only when Lanny was about to leave, he remarked quite casually: "By the way, Uncle Jesse, did you make any inquiries about the Château de Belcour?"

"I did, and there's no doubt you have a straight tip. The place has been leased by a Nazi named Herzenberg, and they discharged every French employee, even to the laborers, men who had worked there all their lives, and their fathers before them."

"Well," said the nephew, "it strikes me that ought to be a story. I keep hearing reports that this and that member of the underground has disappeared without a trace. Suppose some of them were in the *oubliettes* of that château, surely your Party press would like to know about it! Why don't you find some intelligent and dependable comrade to go to work quietly on this lead? The neighborhood must have reports of what's happening in the place, and there must be ways of finding out more. The Nazis must have gardeners and chauffeurs and what not, and they must come out now and then; they might talk to a woman, or someone might get them drunk."

"You're outlining quite a program," commented the uncle. "It would cost money."

"I know; but I smell what I believe is a sensation, and I'd be willing to put up a good sum."

"How much, for example?"

"First, two conditions: you're never to mention me to anybody concerned; and second you'll keep the story to yourself until I say it can be released. The point is, the tip came to me in confidence, and I haven't the right to jeopardize the life of a person who may be a prisoner in that place right now. It depends on what we find and what chance there might be to do something for the person."

"That seems fair enough."

"All right then. I'll put ten thousand francs into your hands now, and you may draw on me for actual expenditures up to two or three times as much."

"*Sapristi!*" exclaimed the Red painter. "That is a deal!"

"Here's a tip for you," said the nephew. "Make note that the château has its laundry done outside. It might be that some worker in that laundry is a Party comrade."

IX

Lanny was through in Paris for the time being. Early next morning he had his belongings put into the car and took the *route nationale* to the south. He had driven over it perhaps a hundred times, so he knew every landmark. With him rode Rosemary, and Irma, and the Marie-ghost—but not the Trudi-ghost, for she had never seen his Riviera home. Most of the time she had stayed in a small studio; now she stayed in a dungeon beneath the Château de Belcour, where Leutnant Rörich came and tortured her; she clenched her hands and set her teeth and endured it, and now and then heard the singing of the *Ça ira*, and whispered to herself that Lanny was coming—but he shouldn't, for he would surely be caught.

Half-way to his destination, Lanny took the road which parallels the Central Canal, connecting the river Loire with the river Saône; the former flowing to the Bay of Biscay and the latter to the Mediterranean. This is the historic land of Burgundy, rich in coal and iron, as well as in wines and olive oil. The district of the canals is one of Pluto's realms, dingy and smoke-stained; in its valleys grew tall black chimneys instead of trees, and all nature was polluted and defiled. One of its towns is Le Creusot, which means The Hollow or The Crucible—and either might apply. Hither, a century ago, had come two brothers from Alsace and purchased a bankrupt foundry. They had built it up and learned to make arms, and the Crimean War had come at a fortunate time to make them millionaires. The son of one of them had multiplied his riches out of the Franco-Prussian War, and the grandson had done the same out of the World War. Charles Prosper Eugène Schneider had known the right statesmen and the right bankers, also the right words to whisper into their ears; it was rumored that his vast chain of enterprises had drawn sixteen milliards—or what the Americans call billions—of gold francs from the earnings of the French people.

The Schneiders had built themselves a palace called the Château la Verrerie, which means the Glasshouse; the reason not being apparent, since it was made of the most solid stone obtainable. It stood on a hilltop with the village huddled around it for protection, exactly as in medieval days. The hovels in which the workers lived were of materials and style of architecture different from those which surrounded the Budd-Erling plant, but the principles on which they had been erected and the methods by which the community had grown were much the same. The workers of this Hollow or Crucible hated the master of the

Glasshouse, and voted Red on every occasion; so the master feared them, and was financing political conspirators as the only means he could think of to protect himself. The tire manufacturer Michelin and the industrialist Deloncle and the landowner Comte Pastre whom Lanny had on his list were all in the same state of mind and taking the same course.

Lanny had telephoned for an appointment, and the Baron was expecting him for lunch. Afterwards, over the coffee and brandy, he reported on his interview with Kurt Meissner, making it more intimate than it had really been. The *Komponist* had been impressed by the news Lanny had brought him, and had promised to take the matter up with the Nazi authorities. Lanny was on his way south to visit his mother, and on his return in a few days he would see Kurt again and report developments.

After this, Lanny talked about the delicate situation in the British Cabinet with regard to the question of German supremacy in the manufacture of airplanes; he referred to the status of affairs in France at the moment—he had been told that the Deuxième Bureau was getting the same reports on German aerial activities, and that Premier Chautemps was treating the reports in the same way as Chamberlain. Lanny didn't really know this latter fact, but he judged that it was quite certain to be the case, and that Schneider would know it. He took a shot in the dark and it landed in the bull's-eye.

Charles Prosper Eugène, Baron Schneider, confessed that he was greatly worried because modern war appeared to be developing new techniques; leaping into the air and flying over that Maginot Line upon which the French people had based their hopes of security. There came something wistful into the voice of an elderly *entrepreneur* who had invested so many milliards of francs in weapons which might suddenly turn out to be worth so little that it wouldn't pay to move them to the scrap pile. Lanny told how his father had foreseen this development several years ago, and had decided to stake everything he owned on the future of the fighter plane. He told of Robbie's efforts to interest French and British army men—he could give convincing details on this subject, for the dumbness of the "brass hats" had been the theme of his father's lamentations ever since Lanny could remember hearing his voice. French, British, Americans, it was the same with them all; only Germans were on the alert and ready to welcome new ideas.

The Baron sighed and said: "We are compelled to make friends with the Germans, greatly as we fear and dislike them." Then he added: "I think, M. Budd, that it might be well worth your father's while to pay a call upon me the next time he visits Europe."

"I am sure he will be delighted to do so, Monsieur le Baron." Lanny knew that he had achieved a coup for his father, one which might be worth another block of stock for himself if the frightened supermagnate should take up the notion to have a branch of Budd-Erling set up in France. In any case, the son of Budd-Erling had made himself solid with one of the most powerful men in the world. Schneider of Schneider-Creusot would take it as a matter of course that Lanny was trying to promote his father's business, and would respect him for having made an approach in exactly the right manner. That is how the biggest business is carried on, with tact and dignity, and without hurry or worry. Whatever came of Lanny's effort, he would be counted among those who had a right to get the Baron on the telephone, and the Baron would know that Lanny's interest in the Hooded Men was the legitimate and proper interest of one who had property at stake.

"Stop by and see me whenever you are passing this way," said the master of the Crucible and the Glasshouse.

X

Bienvenu was always the same. First came the dogs, clamoring loudly; Lanny had been romancing when he talked about only one, for they kept reproducing themselves and it was hard to find people to adopt them. His mother heard the racket and knew what it meant, for he had telephoned before leaving Paris. But she wouldn't come out into the bright light of late afternoon—she had begun to note the crow's feet in the corners of her eyes, and couldn't endure for even her son to see them. Beauty Budd had never been much of an outdoors person, and now, without making any fuss, she stayed at home in the daytime, and made her social appearances under the protection of the kindly shadows of evening. Everybody said how marvelously she was managing to keep her charms; at any rate that is what they said in her hearing.

Beauty's one serious trouble was, as ever, that known as *embonpoint*. The happier, the hungrier, seemed to be the rule with this one-time "professional beauty." She weighed herself on the scales in her bathroom every morning, and what she saw destroyed her appetite for breakfast; feeling faint in the middle of the morning, she would nibble several chocolates, and at lunch she would gaze longingly at the cream pitcher, which someone always left provokingly within her reach.

She was an intensely personal being; she was curious about every human she had ever known, and always Lanny had to answer a score of questions about how Robbie was, and Robbie's wife, and all their family. Beauty might have had that family herself, but fate in the form of a cruel old Puritan plutocrat had intervened; so Beauty had only her one Budd, whom she adored and watched over and spied upon lovingly. What was the state of his heart now, and was there still no chance of his settling down? He would soon be thirty-eight and it was surely time.

His adoring mother wanted to know, had he seen Rosemary on this trip? He knew what that question meant: "Oh, Lanny, are you going to get tied up with that woman again?" The alternative was even worse, the *affaire* which she knew he was having in Paris, but she wasn't allowed to know even the woman's name; obviously, she was some variety of social outlaw, and a fond mother imagined the worst. She simply couldn't be kept from scheming to get some suitable wealthy debutante to be brought to the house, or to meet Lanny by accident at the home of the former Baroness de la Tourette on the Cap d'Antibes near by.

XI

Throughout most of Lanny's life Cannes had been a winter resort, and Juan-les-Pins, on the edge of which the Budd estate was situated, had been a tiny fishing village. But advertising and real estate promotion, plus the cult of sun-bathing, had turned the whole Côte d'Azur into a summer resort as well. New casinos had been built, for gambling and dancing and dining; colored bands had been imported from America, and all night long the thumping of drums and the moaning of saxophones resounded over the Golfe Juan. People did their sleeping in the morning on the sands of the beach or on apricot-colored mattresses laid upon the rocks of the Cap; the men wearing little more than a G-string and a pair of horn-rimmed dark glasses; the women adding a light brassière. Nature hadn't always constructed them with a view to such exposure, and when you saw them you desired to avert your eyes, but there was no vacant place. Especially was this so when one of the new German excursion steamers arrived and discharged a cargo of a thousand stout Nordic male and female blonds, and they all made a rush for the beaches to eat sausages and drink beer. Lanny fled before such invaders and shut himself up behind the gates of Bienvenu, where he had a little studio with a piano on which he could pound out his discontents.

The older residents of the Riviera, at least those whom the Budds knew, had their estates with private swimming pools, and so did not have to come into contact with what they politely referred to as "the public." Here you saw more tasteful costumes, on bodies which had been bred for good looks and carefully tended since infancy; you listened to polite conversation about other people and what they were doing, and about dancing and dining and travel; you played a lot of bridge and gin-rummy, and ate modest but excellent meals served with decorum. It was all extremely proper, but dull after you had come to know it. Now and then you heard talk about a new book or a forthcoming election, and if you were in your secret heart a Pink like Lanny, you observed that the point of view was always that of the protection of this decorous mode of life and the property ownership upon which it was based. Nothing was to be changed, and the idea had better not even be mentioned; for times had become serious, and with Spain only a couple of hundred miles away, it was a case of "Under which king, Bezonian? speak, or die."

Now Lanny was going into Spain for the fourth time, and it was undeniably dangerous, and gave great distress to his mother. Paintings, yes—but weren't there plenty of paintings in France and other parts of Europe? Couldn't he busy himself with selling Detazes? Beauty could always use her share of the money, and Marceline, his half-sister, was begging for more all the time. By the way, how was Marceline? Beauty reported that the child's husband was still with the Italian troops in Seville, and the child herself was unhappy in that wretched hot climate, with mosquitoes biting her ankles, and fleas, too; everything topsy-turvy in wartime, the price of everything prohibitive, and Marceline cursing the day she had let her one-armed hero come to this place. Couldn't Beauty force Lanny to send at least some pocket money?

Beauty knew that she mustn't scold her wayward son, or try to force him; otherwise his visits to her home might become even fewer. He was obstinate; he had his duties, as he conceived them, and Beauty had to keep his dark secrets locked in her heart. When he came, she was proud of him; all his old friends wanted to see him, he was invited everywhere, and could have been "in the swim" and towed his mother along in his wake; but he had something serious on his mind, she could see at once, and she didn't believe for a moment that it was picture business taking him into Spain. No, he was going on another of his mad errands, and his mother had to hide her anxiety and let him go.

XII

Beauty Budd was married to what she called the kindest man in the world, and one who was firmly convinced that he was married to the most wonderful of women. Parsifal Dingle showed fewer signs of age than anyone of his generation whom Lanny knew; he permitted nothing to trouble him, he loved everybody, no matter how hateful they might be, and when they got into trouble he talked to them about Divine Love, never referring to their past actions, but assuring them that they could have happiness and healing whenever they were willing to open their hearts to receive it. He said his prayers and read his books and papers dealing with the subject of New Thought; also, as part of each day's routine, he carried on psychic experiments with the Polish medium who had made her home with the Budd family ever since Parsifal had discovered her in New York, eight years ago.

Madame Zyszynski, elderly, rather dumpy ex-servant, was slow-minded and left it for others to be interested in her rare gift; she would sink back into a chair and go into a trance, and straightway would begin to speak with strange voices and tell things about which Madame herself knew nothing, either waking or asleep. Parsifal was still accumulating notes concerning a Buddhist monastery called Dodanduwa, on an island off the coast of Ceylon, and the monks who had lived there a long time ago; he had written and learned that there actually was such a place, and now he was sending copies of his records to be checked.

For most of the time, Madame's "control" had been the spirit of an Indian chieftain named Tecumseh. But recently he had got "tired of talking so much," he declared, and his place had been taken by a voice named "Claribel," who said that she had been a lady-in-waiting to the queen of Henry the Sixth of England. She was a poetical lady, and if you gave her any subject, no matter how remote or esoteric, she would burst into a sort of sleepy rhapsody in poetical prose. It might be a vision called up by the words; as a rule it was indefinite, but always it was extraordinary as coming from the mind of this dull Polish woman, whose reading was confined mostly to the pictures in the cheapest sort of papers. Parsifal would go to the encyclopedia and look up the most unlikely subjects, such as "the choragic monument of Lysicrates," or "the Old Slavic Josephus," or a fossil called "glyptocrinus decadactylus." Said Claribel of this last: "With my ten fingers I did shake the world,"—and that was true, since it is true of everything that moves on the earth; but the question was: How did any voice coming out of Madame know the meaning of a long Greek word?

Trudi Schultz had had sittings with Madame, and in the last of them Zaharoff had appeared, announcing his own death, just after it had occurred and before the papers carrying the news had appeared on the streets of Paris. So naturally Lanny had the thought: "Trudi might come to me!" One of his first procedures upon reaching home was to take Madame into his studio and get her comfortably seated in an arm-chair, and then wait with pencil poised over a notebook.

But alas, it wasn't Trudi, only Zaharoff, an unwelcome intruder at this moment. But Lanny mustn't show it; no indeed, for it was Tecumseh speaking, and the two-hundred-year-old Iroquois was extremely touchy in his dealing with the grandson of Budd's; taking exception to his supposed-to-be-scientific attitude, ridiculing him, often teasing him by refusing to tell him the things he most wanted to know. Lanny had learned to be scrupulously polite, talk like a devotee of spiritualism, and omit none of the ceremonies due to a person of royal rank.

"It is that old man who has guns going off all the time around him," declared the chieftain. "Such a racket, it makes my head ache! And people shouting that they hate him. Poor tormented old man, he's always talking about money. What is the matter with him—didn't he have a chance to fix up his business affairs before he left?"

"He left rather suddenly," replied Lanny; "but I know that he made a will. Perhaps he is not satisfied with it."

"He keeps crying: 'Gold! Gold!' Did he have anything to do with gold? He says 'gold at the bottom of the sea.' What is that?"

"I am sure I have no idea, Tecumseh."

"He says it is being covered with sand and mud. It will be lost forever. This old man—Basil, he cries—is that his name?"

"That is his first name."

"He says a human arm floated out in the water and it was from the kitchen—no, he says the Kitchener."

"Was that Lord Kitchener? He was lost at sea."

"He says yes; the ship was full of treasure; he, Basil, tried to bring it up. Was he ever a diver?"

"I doubt it very much."

"He says they got some gold, but most of it is still there. He says it is very important; there were war records."

"Doesn't he know the war is over?"

"It is another war coming. The gold was in the treasure room. It is a fortune for you. The man who can unlock it—his name—I forget the name."

This last was supposed to be Zaharoff speaking to Lanny. The voice was still that of Tecumseh, but the words were supposed to come from the "spirit," and you were supposed to play that game. Lanny said: "You never told me that you had done any treasure-hunting, Sir Basil."

"Many things I never told you. I kept my affairs to myself. The name of the man—he is the key-master."

"Key-master?" repeated the inquirer. "Do you mean the master-key?"—for Lanny had read a few crime and mystery stories.

"Key-master," insisted the one-time Knight Commander and Grand Officer. "He opens all locks. The American. You can find him."

"I ought to have some clue to his name, Sir Basil."

"Huff—is it Huffy—or Huffner? Tell him there is gold—the greatest treasure—it was for Russia—to stop the revolution——"

The voice trailed away, and there was silence. Lanny was afraid the old man would fade out, and he asked quickly: "Sir Basil, have you been meeting any friends of mine?"

"Some of yours, but none of mine," quavered the spirit.

"See if you can find one of my friends named Trudi. Remember the name for me, please." Lanny took that as a tactful way of giving the request to Tecumseh, who might otherwise spurn it.

"Trudi—Trudi—Trudi—!" It died out in a sort of sigh, and quiet followed. The medium began to stir, then moaned and opened her eyes, and the séance was over.

"Did you get good results?" she asked, and Lanny told her: "Very good." That pleased her; she rarely asked more, and he never told her, for that might invalidate later communications. He went away thinking: "A damned strange thing! Kitchener's arm floating in water, and gold at the bottom of the sea." He recalled the name of the cruiser, H. M. S. Hampshire, which was reported to have struck a mine in the North Sea during the World War. That was all he had ever heard, so far as he could now recall. He thought: "I wonder if Zaharoff ever did engage in a treasure hunt."

He tried several times more with Madame Zyszynski, but all he got was Claribel and her prose poems. When he said "Trudi," the lady of old England knew that the name was German, but apparently thought it was a milkmaid, and went into a rhapsody about cows, country lanes, and kisses. To be sure, Lanny had walked in country lanes with Trudi, having motored her out into the remote parts of la douce France, and having assuredly not failed to kiss her. Some people might have called that "evidential," but it wasn't what the researcher wanted now.

XIII

Lanny phoned and made an appointment with the wife of Raoul Palma, who had been running the workers' school while her husband was in Spain. Lanny gave her some money for the school and learned that Raoul was still in Valencia, in a state of terrible tension over the developments in the war. Lanny said: "I am going in there on picture business." Julie Palma answered: "Take him a lot of chocolate. They are living on horse and burro meat in Valencia now."

He had a couple of Detazes to get out of the storeroom and pack and ship to Zoltan. Then, his last errand, he went to call on the Señora Villareal, one of his clients, who lived near Nice. He had tea with this Spanish lady of the old school, who was in his debt because he had brought some of her paintings out from Seville and she couldn't imagine how she could have got along without the money. He told her now that he had an opportunity to go into Red Spain. "With money one can do almost anything with that crowd," he said. "You know how the unfortunate city is being bombed, and it is a ghastly thing that its art treasures should be exposed to destruction. I feel that I should be doing a public service in rescuing some of them."

"Surely, Señor Budd; but is it not frightfully risky?"

"I don't intend to stay long. What occurred to me is that you might know someone in Valencia who has some especially valuable work he might like to have brought out. It couldn't be a large one, for I plan to travel by train. I learned the lesson that a car is too dangerous a luxury in a war-torn land."

"Oh, Señor Budd, it is such a horrible thing! How much longer can it go on?"

"I wish I could make a guess," he replied. "If anybody had asked me at the beginning, I would never have said it could last fourteen months."

"There will be nothing left of my poor country!" sighed the lady. "My estates bring me almost nothing, because the army has to have the produce, and they pay in paper money which is without value in the outside world."

"Keep it carefully; it will surely be redeemed." Thus soothingly Lanny addressed a mother who still had one daughter at the age for marriage but who lacked the necessary *dot*. He led the talk to the subject of refugees from Valencia, and the Señora listed several who owned paintings; they all surely needed money, and presently she telephoned to one and made an appointment for the American expert to call. She spoke of Lanny in the highest terms, explaining that he was no speculator but a gentleman with the best connections; his father was the great manufacturer of airplanes, he was an intimate friend of Mrs. Chattersworth, and so on. That is the way the world is run, and the way Lanny Budd was able to travel to any part of Europe and to earn not merely his expenses but the means of indulging his whims.

XIV

He called upon a Spanish grandee—they don't use the term any more but they have the manners and the ideas. This one was living in obviously straitened circumstances in an unfashionable part of Nice. Señor Jimenes owned lands in the suburbs of Valencia on which oranges were grown, and buildings in the slums for which thousands of laborers had been accustomed to pay high rents. But now everything was in the hands of the Reds, and how could an unhappy grandee hope to maintain his grandeur? He spent an hour or more probing Lanny's mind and soul, and when finally he had satisfied himself that this was a man of good will, he confessed that he owned a Murillo, representing some ragged little boys playing outdoors; a superlatively lovely and absolutely priceless work. Before his mansion had been seized, he had had a trusted servant carry this treasure away and hide it in a hut near the city. If Lanny could get it and bring it out, the señor would agree to let him sell it and pay him a commission.

On account of Trudi, Lanny was in a greedy mood. He said: "Señor Jimenes, those are the terms on which I normally work; but now it is a question of risking my life on an extremely dangerous enterprise. If I, a foreigner, go to visit a former servant of a landlord, I am certain to be observed and very likely to be reported; if they caught me, they would quite possibly find out my record and shoot me as a spy. In any case I might have to pay large sums to officials to get the painting out; I might have to take it directly on a steamer to London or even to New York. The only terms on which I could undertake such risks would be that I had an option to buy the painting outright."

"And what would you be willing to offer, Señor Budd?"

"First, I should have to view the work and satisfy myself as to its authenticity. I do not doubt that you, Señor, believe your little boys to be Murillo's; but that popular painter had many imitators, and I have many times seen owners of art works deceived as to what they had acquired. My proposal would be that you trust me with an order for the delivery of the painting; if I am satisfied that it is genuine, I will assume all the risks from the moment it is in my hands. I will put the sum of one hundred thousand francs into escrow here, and as soon as the painting is delivered to me I will order the bank to release the money to you."

"Oh, but, Señor Budd, the painting is worth many times that much money! Perhaps a million francs!"

"Quite possibly, and I am making no attempt to deceive you. What you have to figure on is what the painting is worth in Valencia today; for that is where I would get it, with all the risks of bombs and Reds and crooked officials and firing squads and ship torpedoings—a whole gantlet to be run, and if you expect the full price for the painting, it is surely up to you to do the running."

Lanny was used to the spectacle of persons of wealth and rank arguing, pleading, haggling, fighting for their money; the sums were larger than if it was the purchase of suspenders or cabbages, but the technique was the same. Courtesy required that you should listen patiently and never cut any statement short; never take offense, and when everything had been said several times to no purpose, you must rise to leave with great reluctance. It was expected that you would make some small concession, in order that the other party might feel that he had gained something by his labors. In this case, the seller was badly off, perhaps not able to pay his rent; Señor Jimenes actually wept when he contemplated parting with his sole transportable treasure—so he described it— and in the end Lanny weakened and raised his offer to a hundred and ten thousand francs. This was, he opined, a real fortune in France; a man might live on it in modest comfort the rest of his days.

It was only when Lanny had given up hope, left the house, and was getting into his car that the Spanish grandee called: "Come back, Señor; it is a deal."

There was nothing new about that, and nothing humiliating. Lanny came, and with entire amiability prepared the necessary papers. He went away knowing that he had a satisfactory story to tell to Kurt or the de Bruynes or Baron Schneider or General Göring, in case any of them should chance to hear about his going into Red Spain. He would get the money needed for his effort to help Trudi, without having to sell any of the securities which he had stored in his father's keeping, and which he couldn't order sold without causing worry to both his parents, and causing them to ask inconvenient questions. His main pur-

pose was, of course. to see Monc'- but to make a profit incidentally could
do no harm.

7

Spain's Chivalry Away

I

LANNY BUDD was traveling on a train, something which he did
rarely. It was the express which ran along the Mediterranean; a rocky
and irregular coast, with now a beach, now a wooded stretch, now
bare red sandstone cliffs, and now a spur of mountain with a black tunnel through which the train darted with a loud racket. There were fishing villages, and pink and white villas built into the rocks, and vistas
of bright blue sea with many small boats, some with white sails and
some with red. When it grew dark there were lighthouses flashing
white and red signals.

They came to the southernmost point of France, and the few passengers who were going on had to get out and walk through a tunnel;
there it was Spain, and they had to stand in line while officials inspected
their papers and luggage. Lanny was traveling light, with only one
suitcase, his portable typewriter, and a large package of *chocolat Me-
nier*, one piece of which would suffice to win the favor of most any
official. Presently he was in an extremely dingy train, having scars to
prove that it had been through battles. Except for the early fighting,
Red Catalonia hadn't seen much of the war, and in the judgment of the
rest of the country wasn't carrying its share of the burden. Catalonia
was anarchist and individualist, and didn't take kindly to the stern discipline which war imposes. The peasants of Catalonia were glad to be
free of their landlords, but didn't want to part with their products
except at war prices, which was why the people of the towns were
having a hard time keeping nourished.

All this was explained to an American traveler by a young workingman who had been into France on some purchasing errand for his col-
lective. He was ardent, full of determination and hope; a new life had

begun for him and his kind, and they had no thought of giving it up. It was the final conflict and each stood in his place; the international party would be the human race. What had been done in Catalonia was going to be done throughout the Iberian peninsula, and when the workers of France saw its success, they too would throw the parasites off their backs. In the next stage, the people of the Fascist lands would discover how they had been misled; they would revolt, and Europe would become one commonwealth of workers and peasants, free, fraternal, and dedicated to the life of reason.

Poor old Europe! Lanny in childhood had thought it was a beautiful and wonderful continent; only little by little he had come to realize that it was a land of hereditary evils too numerous to be counted. Then he had become possessed by the same bright dream of social change as this young workingman; he still cherished the dream, because there was nothing else to live for, but he clung to it now with a sort of desperation, like one who knows that a dream is over and that he has come wide awake. Just recently he had been reading a statement by some historian, that during the past few centuries Spain had spent an average of seventy years of each hundred at war, and France an average of fifty. Idealists preached and promised freedom, but what they got was "man arrayed for mutual slaughter."

Of course Lanny mustn't say anything like that to a workingman of Red Catalonia. He had to explain, as well as he could in his imperfect Spanish, the strange indifference to freedom now being displayed by the great American republic, which all Europe thought of as the land of freedom. Dropping that embarrassing subject as soon as possible, he asked questions about the workers' co-operatives. To what extent were they solving the problems of production? Were they actually getting it, in spite of all the controversy, the politics, the sabotage? That was the test, and the only test, in war as it would be in peace. More production than capitalism could give; more than that thing which Robbie Budd glorified under the name of "individual initiative," and which was really the true anarchy. As Lanny had said to his father: perfect order inside the plant and perfect chaos outside!

Yes, said this workingman, the wheels of the factories were turning and the goods were coming forth. The workers had had more than a year in which to organize and solve their problems; in spite of war and blockade and internal conflicts, they were getting materials and turning out goods. "How do you solve this?" and "How do you manage that?" Lanny would ask; and all the time he was thinking: "I must explain this to F.D.R." The smiling and genial President of the United

States had become little by little the center of Lanny's thinking, his refuge from despair. A man who really had power and who really understood! If Lanny should tell him how the Catalan workers were running their own plants, F.D.'s face would light up, and he would chuckle and remark: "How the National Association of Manufacturers and the United States Chamber of Commerce would like that!" But would he really do anything about it? Would he even say anything about it publicly? And if he did, wouldn't the Associated Robbie Budds of America be able to throw him out on his ear at the next election?

II

From Barcelona on, the young workingman's place was taken by a grim-faced elderly peasant woman who had been to town to nurse a son wounded in the fighting on the Aragon front. She had brought in a load of produce to pay her expenses, and now was carrying home such necessities as salt and kerosene. Lanny had picked up many words of the Catalan language, which is allied to the Provençal of the fisherboys with whom he had played in childhood; and anyhow, he had no shyness about trying to jabber in all the tongues of polyglot Europe. He made out that the peasant woman was dissatisfied because the high prices for farm products were more than balanced by high prices for store products. Lanny knew that this complaint was universal in wartime. He found that this woman didn't like war, and couldn't see that the coming of Franco would make any difference to her—provided only that they wouldn't fight over her hereditary acres! Lanny was interested to understand the peasant mind, which is strictly "isolationist," and as firmly fixed as the boundary-stones of its small plots of land.

The farther south the train went the hotter it was, and the nearer to war. Trains were sometimes bombed; ships and small craft had been torpedoed and beached where you could see the wrecks from the train. Few people went to Valencia who didn't have to, for it was bombed frequently and its defenses were inadequate. It had been the seat of the government ever since the siege of Madrid had begun, ten months previously; now the government was planning to move to Barcelona, so people on the train reported; some departments had already moved. The Italians were pressing in the south, while Franco, with his Moors and Requetes and another large Italian army, was fighting a great battle up on that River Ebro where Lanny had once hidden his car while the Fascists were searching for him. Franco was getting a thumping defeat, so reports indicated, and everybody was exulting in this success.

Raoul's wife had written him that "a friend" was coming with news from home. Raoul had no trouble in guessing who it was, and he was waiting at the badly bombed station. He was several years younger than Lanny, but already his dark hair was streaked with gray and his face deeply lined; he looked years older than when Lanny had last seen him, during the first attack upon Madrid. He had a high forehead and delicate features; a thin nose, with nostrils which seemed to quiver when he was deeply moved, which was often, for he was high-strung and impressionable. People call it the "spiritual" type of face, but to Lanny it meant undernourishment; he was sure his Spanish friend hadn't had a square meal in many a month, and as he handed over a heavy package he said: "This contains chocolate."

"Oh, good!" exclaimed Raoul. "How the staff will welcome that!" Lanny thought, how characteristic! He was going to share it with the whole Foreign Press Bureau! Having foreseen this, Lanny had purchased a goodly stock.

III

The new arrival explained, quickly: "I don't want any publicity about my coming. I have a couple of important errands and then I have to skip out. I don't want to go to a hotel. Can you take me somewhere we can talk quietly?"

"I'll put you up in my room, if you don't mind discomfort."

"Not in the least. Let us go."

The people of Valencia had no *gasolina*, and were eating their horses and burros; but there were a few antiquated cabs at the station, and the two friends and their luggage were driven to one of the smaller hotels set apart for government employees. Raoul had a small room with a single cot, and it was his idea that Lanny was to occupy this while his host slept on the floor. Lanny said: "I won't stay on those terms," and they started an argument, which might have lasted quite a while.

Lanny changed the subject abruptly, saying: "I want to see you eat at least one piece of chocolate." He opened the package, and on account of the heat the contents were soft. It was necessary to unwrap a piece and lick it off the paper. Not a dignified procedure, but a semi-starved man does not stand upon ceremony, and all the time that Lanny talked Raoul licked, and it wasn't long before his mouth and everything around it were smeared a rich shiny brown.

Lanny began: "Do you happen to remember that Capitán Herzog whom we saw marching with the International Brigade in Madrid?"

"Indeed, yes. He has made a good record in the Thaelmann *columna.*"

"He is still alive, then?"

"Well, you know how it is in war. I wouldn't necessarily have heard if anything had happened to him."

"Can you find out?"

"I can find out where he was stationed and if there's any recent news about him. His company is fighting on the Belchite front, I'm fairly sure."

"What I have to do is to have a talk with him. I have a message from the underground in Germany; I'm pledged not to talk about it, but you will understand, it's a party matter, and important."

"Of course, Lanny. It wouldn't be easy to get to the front without publicity. We are taking foreign journalists continually; but if you went along, they would know you, and they wouldn't see any reason for not mentioning you." Raoul called the roll—it was a roll of honor —of American writers who had made the cause of the Spanish people their own, and who were now or had recently been in Valencia: Ernest Hemingway, Vincent Sheean, Dorothy Parker, Eliot Paul, Louis Fischer, Anna Louise Strong, Albert Rhys Williams. They had taken a long and perilous journey in the cause of conscience. They turned their hearts' blood into burning words in the effort to overcome the dull inertia of the masses, to awaken the people of America to the meaning of this rape of democracy.

Lanny said: "I have met many of them, and they would know me. That wouldn't do."

"You must understand," explained his friend, "I'm not the boss. I have to take the matter to my chief. and I have to be able to say something that will convince him."

"Couldn't you say it is somebody with a message for Herzog; say, a family matter."

"The answer would be: 'Let the man write to Herzog, and if Herzog wants to see him, it's up to him to make the application.' All that might take some time."

"Couldn't you get somebody to smuggle me up there?"

"But that's not done in wartime, Lanny. You'd be a spy, and might get into serious trouble. It would certainly mean publicity."

"To be suspected as a Fascist spy wouldn't be so bad from the point of view of what I'm doing. Much better than being a friend of the Reds."

"Yes, but you might have to clear yourself before you could get out.

And it would get me into a mess—it might make it impossible for me to be of any use here. You must understand, I am half a foreigner, because I have lived so long in France. We are bedeviled by spies and saboteurs, and by suspicion and fears of them. Once you are suspected, you are guilty."

"Then perhaps it isn't wise for you to be hiding a stranger in your room here."

"It won't be good if it lasts very long, and unless I can introduce you as a comrade."

They talked the problem over from every angle. Whatever story Raoul told he had to stick by; he couldn't try a second. Also, he was bound by the name Lanny Budd, which was in the passport and could not be changed. He asked: "Will Herzog know your name?" and Lanny answered that there could be no doubt of that.

Finally Raoul said: "The best thing is to be open about it. I will go to my chief and ask permission to get El Capitán Herzog on the telephone. Unless he is at the fighting front, that should be possible. I will say to him: 'Lanny Budd is in Valencia and wishes to see you.' If he will say to my chief: 'Please send this man to me,' it can be done, I am sure. Perhaps I can get permission to go as your escort."

"*Bueno!*" said Lanny Budd.

IV

While Raoul went to carry out this commission, the visitor went for a stroll about the city of the Cid. It is more than a thousand years old, and many of its buildings have been made out of the stones of a previous city a thousand years older; ancient Roman ruins, such as Lanny had been used to seeing in the neighborhood of his childhood home. The less ancient Valencia was built in part by the Moors, and has blue and white and golden domes like Istanbul and other places of the Levant. Like all Spanish cities it had dreadfully crowded slums, and its modern industries were carried on in buildings ill-suited to the purpose. Now these industries were in the hands of the workers, who were learning to run them under penalty of being conquered by Franco's Moors, which meant death for the men and worse than death for their wives and daughters.

Italian and German bombers came over at frequent intervals. The interference was pitifully inadequate, and they could come down and pick their targets. They chose places where there might be crowds, for their purpose was to terrify and break the spirit of the population.

What they achieved was to fix in the minds of all a black and bitter hatred of their class enemies, whether native or foreign. The outside world called this the "Spanish civil war," but no worker in Spain ever thought of it as anything but an invasion by foreign Fascists who were pledged to put down and enslave the workers of all Europe and keep them as slaves for the rest of time. Spanish landlords and great capitalists and high prelates of a degenerate Church had hired this crime and paid for it by pledging the national wealth of Spain, the iron ore and copper and all the products of the soil. Foreign troops were doing the fighting, and the weapons were without exception of foreign manufacture—including all the planes which swarmed in Spanish skies and blasted Spanish homes and tore the bodies of Spanish women and children. Some day there would be justice! Some day there would be vengeance!

Lanny didn't see any of the torn bodies, for they had been carted away and put underground; but he saw the blasted homes by hundreds. The bombs were not big enough to destroy whole blocks, but enough to send one five-story tenement sliding down into the street, or perhaps to blow out the front walls and leave it like a set in a modernistic play, with several rooms exposed: a dining room with a table for the family to sit at, a bedroom with a bed for lovers to lie in, a crib for the resulting baby to sleep in. Sometimes the damage was recent, and gangs of men were clearing away the rubbish, taking down loose cornices and tottering walls; sometimes the ruins were still smoking—for the bombers dropped incendiaries, and many stone buildings had been gutted and left mere shells.

Amid all this ruin the people went grimly about their daily tasks. They were drably clad, the men mostly in well-worn black *blusas*. Lanny never saw anybody smile, even the children, unless he caused them to do so by being a wonderful *señor Americano*, asking questions and distributing centavos. He looked like a "class enemy," but did not behave so, and everybody on the Loyalist side knew that there were a few *simpáticos*, especially from that wonderful land across the sea where every worker owned a motorcar and sent back money to his impoverished relatives. "*La tierra de tíos ricos*," a peasant had once said to Lanny; the land of rich uncles!

V

Back at Raoul's room, Lanny read about the battle of Belchite in a crudely printed newspaper. At last his friend came in, greatly excited.

"I talked with El Capitán," he announced. "We are to start tonight, and I am to take you. *Congratulaciónes!*" But really it seemed that Raoul was the one to receive these; it was a holiday he had earned by fourteen months of incessant labor with few thoughts of himself. Now he gave no heed to possible dangers at the front; when you have been under siege for so many months, first in Barcelona, then in Madrid, then in Valencia, you learn to forget about danger; it is like a thunder-storm—maybe you will be hit and maybe not, but there's nothing you can do about it and no use crawling under the bed.

What Raoul thought of was the chance to be with the wonderful Lanny Budd, who had picked him out of a starvation job in a shoestore in Cannes and given him a chance, first to study, and then to teach others. During fifteen years Lanny Budd had come and gone, and every time he had come it had been with a pocketful of money for the workers' school, and a story of adventures in that *grand monde* which Raoul's Marxist convictions obligated him to despise, but which his human weakness led him to hear about with curiosity.

First they went to a café to get some dinner. Lanny was worried, because he hadn't ever tried the meat of either *burros* or *caballos;* but he learned that, for a much higher price, some fisherman had been willing to risk being machine-gunned. Also there was rice fried with olive oil, and there was the juice of the well-known Valencia orange, and dates which grew in groves of tall palms in the suburbs. Few are the times when one cannot get food in a city if one has a purse full of its currency.

A much-battered Ford runabout had been provided for the trip. The chauffeur, who ordinarily was inseparable from his vehicle (for fear of being drafted into the army), was providentially sick, and so Lanny would be permitted to do his own driving, at his own risk. Raoul had the necessary passes, including a government order for the proper amount of *gasolina*. If you bought it on the black market, you would pay pretty nearly its weight in silver.

Belchite lies in Southern Aragon, something over a hundred miles north from Valencia. It is rather barren hill country, and the front there represented a noose drawn by the invading armies from the west of Madrid to the north and around to the east and southeast. If they had been able to come southwest from Belchite, they would have cut off Madrid from connection with the outside world; if they could have come southeast to the coast, they would have cut both Madrid and Valencia from Catalonia, dividing the Loyalist territory in half. They had marched boldly in full sweep, with one or the other of these plans in mind; but the free men of the Spanish democracy had stopped them cold, and now Raoul brought the latest news from headquarters and was all but dancing with delight. The battle of Belchite, the greatest victory of the war!

VI

Lanny didn't want to sleep; he didn't mind driving on Spanish roads at night, even with a strange car whose motor sputtered ominously now and then. They sped rapidly northward over a wide plain, green with well-tended orchards, the setting sun casting long shadows of tall date-palms across the road. Their destination was Lérida, and Lanny said: "Do you remember—we spent a night there, trying to make up our minds whether to strike north through the Pyrenees, or east to Barcelona. What a difference it made in your life!"

"I'll tell the world!" exclaimed Raoul, who had been perfecting his American in the company of visiting journalists. He talked about the cataclysm of humanity which had turned upside-down the life of an amiable idealistic school director, and made him into a sort of publicity agent in the service of Mars. Incidentally he had met so many famous correspondents and writers that he fancied himself as military expert and authority upon international diplomacy. He was quite sure that Franco had shot his bolt up here in this hard and harsh land; also that Britain and France were at last awakening to the perils of Fascism, and that their stand against submarine piracy would soon be broadened into a policy of true neutrality. Lanny had grave doubts on both points, but refrained from voicing them, for the poor Spaniard had to live and do his work. Let him have hope as long as he could.

Raoul described the manifold duties of a publicity agent of Mars. The head of the Foreign Press Bureau, to whom Raoul tried to be loyal in spite of many obstacles, was a gnomelike little man, pallid-skinned and nearly bald. He was embarrassed because he was assumed to understand the American language but really didn't; therefore he shut himself up in a small room with carefully drawn curtains, wore dark glasses even in that gloom, and left the meeting of foreign journalists entirely to his subordinates. One of these was a charming lady whom Lanny had met in Madrid on his first visit. "Constancia de la Mora. You remember, you bought some art goods in her little shop." Raoul was loud in his praises of this aristocratic Spanish woman, granddaughter of a former premier, who had broken with her old associations and cast in her lot with the people. Her husband had done the same, and was now commander of the Loyalist Air Force.

VII

They climbed into the hills, from which most of the forests had been stripped many centuries ago, leaving the land barren and the population sparse. Darkness stole upon them, except for the feeble rays from their little car, turning this way and that on the winding road and lighting hillsides of red clay and now and then a peasant hut. They reached Lérida soon after midnight, and arousing a sleepy clerk of the Palace Hotel, found that they could have only one room and one bed. In the morning they had orange juice and coffee and *huevos revueltos con tomates*. They bought bread and fruit—for the nearer they got to the front the scarcer food would be.

On the familiar road toward Saragossa they passed those sights of war which Lanny had learned to know so well. The road was worn and rutted, and the dust of vehicles made a reddish-gray fog around them and ahead. Out of this fog emerged trucks carrying wounded men back to the bases, and slow-plodding peasant carts taking families and their belongings away from destruction. Very young children and old people rode, while the rest walked alongside; the men wearing short black trousers and hempen sandals, the women much-worn dresses, invariably black. Sorrow enveloped them, old and young, but they had that patient dignity which characterizes the Spanish people, inured through centuries to every known kind of suffering.

Raoul's papers were in order, and an American visitor was welcomed with old-fashioned courtesy by guard-posts on the way. Always the travelers asked how the fortnight-old battle was going, and made the discovery that the closer you get to war, the less you know about what is happening. Better to stay at home, sitting by a radio! The rumble of the guns grew louder, but there was no way to tell enemy shots from friendly, or which were finding their targets.

La gasolina, otherwise unobtainable, was purchased from government stores, and before noon they were coming down into the valley of the Ebro. The bridge across the river had been blown up, and they went along the bank by a road which had been torn to pieces by shell-fire. There were burned-out wrecks of cars and trucks scattered here and there, and a sickening sweet-rich smell that made one reluctant to breathe. The publicity agent of Mars was put on the defensive, and explained: "They can bury all the human bodies, but not the horses and mules."

As they neared their destination, Lanny apologized: "I have a message for the Capitán which I am pledged not to reveal to anyone else." His friend replied promptly: "I much prefer not to know anything that doesn't concern me. If ever there is a leak, the fewer persons one has to suspect, the better." He went on to state that he would find some of the soldiers to talk to; they would tell him not merely about the fighting, but about the progress of adult education in the trenches. That was Raoul's hobby, about which he was willing to ask questions without end. The government program called for teaching every soldier to read and write, and nothing else could have reconciled a pacifist and idealist to the manifold horrors of civil war. "Even if the Fascists should win," he said, "that is one thing they will never be able to undo."

VIII

The appointment with Capitán Herzog was at an inn called *El Toro Rojo*. Raoul didn't know just where it was, and they stopped to get directions; apparently these were not correct, for they got lost, and finally approached the place by a sandy path in which the car would have stuck if the Spanish official had not leaped out and pushed from the rear. A swinging sign with a fierce red bull told them, as it had told thousands through the centuries, that they had found the right place. It was a building so old that it was sagging in the middle, but it had an inside court with a second-story gallery all around, and carvings which Lanny would have been glad to study if there hadn't been a battle so near.

El Capitán was waiting for them: a solidly built, shaven-headed Prussian, the sort whom Lanny was used to seeing in a brown shirt with shiny black belt and a swastika on the sleeves; but this one was a rebel, a laborer and sailor who had educated himself and become an active Social-Democratic Party worker. He had learned war the hard way, in action, and because of his force of personality had been chosen as leader by the Germans of all creeds and parties who made up the Thaelmann *columna*. The Capitán was clad in a much-worn khaki shirt and trousers tucked into boots, with insignia of his rank sewn onto the sleeves. His face was drawn, and Lanny guessed that he hadn't been back from the front more than a few hours.

Raoul stayed by the car, so there were no introductions. Comrade Monck, as Lanny had learned to call the German, was a man of direct approach. His first words were the same that he had spoken at their first meeting: "*Wir sprechen besser Deutsch.*" When Lanny assented, he said: "*Bitte, kommen Sie mit,*" and led him out of the courtyard and up a hillside path. Under a cork-oak tree, clear of underbrush and giving a view in all directions, they seated themselves. "Bushes may have ears," declared Monck.

Lanny was in the same businesslike mood. He didn't comment on the crash and rattle of gunfire. He didn't even ask: "How is the battle going?" It was enough that the enemy had retired from this field, if not from the atmosphere. "Trudi has disappeared in Paris," he announced.

"*Ach Gott, die Arme!* How long ago?"

"About three weeks. She had made me promise that if ever she disappeared, I would wait a while before I took any action. Then I tried to get in touch with the man whose name she had given me, a clarinetist, Professor Adler."

"I know him; a true comrade."

"I wrote twice, making an appointment, but he failed to show up."

"It must be that the Nazi devils have got him also."

"That is what I feared. Trudi has given me no other name, and you are the only person I could think of who might put me in touch with the underground."

"I guessed as much as soon as I heard you had come," replied the German.

"There is something I must explain at once," continued Lanny; "something rather embarrassing to me. Trudi has always insisted that I have a special value to the movement, in that I am able to get large sums of money. There are others who can write, print leaflets, and distribute them; so she said, again and again."

"The world being what it is, Herr Budd, she is right beyond question."

"She made me promise that never under any circumstances would I take any step that might reveal my connection with the underground, and make it impossible for me to go on with what I have been doing for her and a couple of other trusted friends. It puts a man in an awkward position, to have to see other people risking their lives while he lives in comfort and safety."

"You can put your conscience at rest," declared the Capitán. "From what Trudi told me I would name you as one of the persons indispensable to our movement. You should under no circumstances let yourself be tempted to break your promise."

Said Lanny: "You will understand better how difficult the decision has been when I tell you that for nearly a year Trudi has been my wife."

"Oh, wie schrecklich!" exclaimed the Capitán. Then, gazing into the visitor's face: "Herr Budd, you have my deep sympathy. This is a terrible thing in any case, and beyond words when it is someone we love. It is the time we live in that permits assured happiness to none of us."

"I have known what must be her fate, Comrade Monck; but somehow, it was impossible to be prepared."

"She was a magnificent girl; one of those who should be at the head of the German government, instead of the monsters and madmen who have seized the power."

"You think there is no chance that she may be alive?"

"Alive? Yes, quite possibly; but better dead."

"I wrestle with myself day and night. I ought to be doing something to save her. But what can I do?"

"What can anybody do, except to make war on the Nazis? Here, right now, we are having the satisfaction of putting a number of them where they can do no further harm. We are fighting what is called a holding action; the longer we can keep them busy in Spain, the more time we give the rest of Europe to awaken to its peril. The Nazi-Fascists did not expect this, I assure you, and it has deranged their plans not a little. It may be they will learn what is in the souls of free men and women, and be more hesitant in attacking the next democratic government. At least, that must be our hope."

IX

Lanny realized that he had come to the place of consolation, if any such there was in the world. The noise which filled this air was of a giant sausage machine, grinding up Nazis; here the self-called master-race were being met by the only measures that counted with them, the only argument they understood. If you really wanted to get rid of Hitlerism, these were the weapons and the techniques. The thing to do was concentrate your attention upon them, forgetting everything else.

"You must understand, Herr Budd," went on the Capitán, "I have been seeing men die in Spain for more than a year; men of conscience, of fine minds, many who were or might have become artists, writers, scientists, teachers—intellectuals of all sorts. They didn't have to come here and die; they might have lived quite safely elsewhere. I get to know them, I share their lives—and then in a fraction of a second I see their faces shot off, their guts blown out by a shell burst. I have to go on and leave them; the enemy is out there, and my business is with him. So you must understand, I have got used to death, and I spare my own feelings. There is a limit to the attention I can give to any one person, no matter how worthy."

"I understand perfectly," answered Lanny. "It was exactly the way Trudi felt, and tried to make me feel. It is I who am the weakling."

"That is not the way to put it. Trudi told me a good deal about you, Genosse Budd—may I call you that?"

"Assuredly."

"I have had a rough life, but I managed to hear a little music and read enough poetry to know that there are finer things in this world, and to appreciate people who have been able to live in them and for them. I know the torment you must be enduring, and I sympathize with all my heart. All I can tell you is that the fate of the world—not merely of Spain, but of all the future—is being decided up here in these hot and dusty hills, and we need the sort of help that you can give, we need it worse than any other kind. We cannot fight unless we have the weapons and we cannot get the weapons unless we can get world opinion behind us, unless we can somehow manage to explain why we are fighting—not for ourselves, but for those who are so blind and indifferent to their own danger."

"There is almost nothing I can do, Genosse Monck; I am filled with despair because of my impotence."

"Don't be too hard on yourself. I know about the documents you smuggled out of Germany for Trudi, and I know that they somehow got published and produced their effect. Also, the money you gave us was turned into hundreds of thousands of pieces of paper, and, as a result, millions of Germans know things of which they would otherwise be ignorant. All that will count some day—I don't know when or how, exactly, but we have to keep our faith in the human spirit, in the social mind. I beg you not to let this tragic sorrow weaken your determination and dry up the source of funds for our underground work."

"What it makes me want to do is to stay here and learn to fight like you. It makes me feel myself a coward——"

"To be a coward of that sort takes courage, Genosse Budd, and I beg you to have that special kind. You are one in a million, and you must keep the promise you made to your clearsighted wife."

"I am going to do my best," said the unhappy man. "I have to have your help in getting new contacts with the movement."

"You will certainly have that help. It may take a little time, because I have my duties here, and one cannot write about such matters from a war zone. I do not know how much longer this battle will last, but when it is over, I will apply for a furlough; I have earned it, because

I have been on duty constantly for more than a year. I will come to Paris and meet you and make the necessary contacts."

"That is all right, so far as it goes; but you are taking the chance that you may be killed in the meantime, and I would be left with a pocket full of money and no place to spend it. I do not know anyone else whom I could approach without risk of uncovering my secret."

"Let me think." There was a pause while Lanny listened to the sounds of the guns and endeavored with professional ears to sort one kind from another. Finally the Capitán inquired: "You remember how I identified myself to you, with a little sketch drawn by Trudi?"

"Be sure I shall never forget it."

"You have other such sketches in your possession?"

"Quite a collection."

"Are they signed, by any chance?"

"No; Trudi never put her name on anything."

"Very good; they will serve. I will write a letter to a man I know in Paris; let us call him 'X' for the present. I will say that I have a friend who is an artist; I want X to see his work, which I am sure X will appreciate. That is an innocent-appearing note which should not trouble any censor. I will say that the American art expert, Mr. Lanny Budd, has a collection of these drawings and will be glad to send him samples on request by mail. I will give your address, which Trudi taught me and which I have graven in my memory: Juan-les-Pins, Alpes Maritimes, France. X will guess that this is a party matter, and will write to you and ask to see the drawings you have for him. He knew Trudi in the old days and will recognize her work. In the event that I fail to show up in Paris, you can propose a meeting, and tell him everything and follow his guidance."

"That sounds all right," said Lanny. "But suppose the Gestapo has got this man also? They would undoubtedly make a response to me, and I would hate to be earning money for them to spend."

"The man I am sending you to is a German, about my age, which is thirty-five. He was in the Oranienburg concentration camp for two years. As a result he has a sort of nervous spasm, a tic I believe it is called; his left eyelid cannot be still. The Nazis in their efforts to make him talk used to tie his hands behind his back and then hang him up by the thumbs; that mangled his thumbs and pulled them out of joint; also it broke his shoulders and they healed improperly. You have a right to ask him to show you these various scars."

"I will do so," replied the other. "The Nazis might have difficulty in reproducing such marks at short notice!"

X

They discussed the methods by which they might communicate with each other, without Lanny's having to visit battlefronts. The Capitán said: "You understand that in a war like this, everybody watches everybody else, and often has reason for doing so. Letters may be stolen, or they may be secretly opened and read by others than the censors. We have traitors in our army—and you may be sure that Franco has some in his."

"By all means, Genosse Monck. Let me point out to you how my profession of art expert serves me in this situation. Would it be possible that you have some family heirlooms, old paintings which I might be trying to sell for you?"

"That would not sound likely with a man of workingclass origin."

"You might have a rich aunt—that can happen to the poorest. Let us say that you have a Tante Lize, and I have been to inspect her paintings, and I tell you that I am definitely certain I can sell the one showing the French prisoner of war. You would understand that I have got results from some investigations I am having made as to Trudi's whereabouts."

"Very good, Genosse Budd. I wish I might have a letter from you saying that you have got a good price for the painting showing the prisoner coming out from a dungeon."

"There is no limit to the price I would be able to get for such a painting," declared Lanny, earnestly. "You may assure your friends of the underground that that is the case."

"*Leider, Genosse*, such a work of art is beyond our skill to produce."

"This is one of the subjects I came to consult you about," continued the visitor. "Can you spare me a few minutes longer?"

"Our regiment has been brought back to rest and recuperate; therefore I am entitled to spend a couple of hours sitting under a shady tree talking with a friend from America."

"Even though it is a bourgeois person, and mysterious?"

The Capitán smiled. "This war has received a great deal of publicity, and you would be surprised how many tourists have thought of it as a spectacle for a summer's holiday. By one or another ingenious scheme they wangle a permit to come; they are writers, lecturers, painters, motion-picture directors or actors; sometimes they are businessmen who have goods to sell which we urgently need. Their wives wish to be able to go back to—what are the names of those strange towns in America?"

"Podunk, for example?"

"To Podunk, and say that they have heard the rumble of the cannon and smelled the smoke of powder. They show up here, and have to be fed even though the troops go hungry. They find it highly educational —until they get too close, and the wind brings the stench of human bodies rotting in this blazing Spanish sun. Then they have an attack of nausea and decide that battlefields and picnic grounds are not the same."

XI

Lanny got down to business. "Genosse Monck, there is a member of the German embassy in Paris, Graf Herzenberg, who has rented the Château de Belcour near Paris. Trudi was quite sure that members of the German underground who have disappeared have been hidden there. Have you heard anything about it?"

"No, but I would expect something of the sort to be done."

"It may be an obsession, but I am haunted by the idea that Trudi is in that place. It seems likely they wouldn't kill her so long as there was the slightest chance of getting out of her the information they so badly want."

"That is reasonable, I agree."

"Of course they might take her to Germany; but it might be more convenient to have her in Paris where her statements might be checked against those of others. They wouldn't have much reason to feel worried, for so long as Chautemps is premier of France, the government will be busy with political intrigues, and no one will take any sort of action displeasing to the German ambassador."

"That sounds convincing, also."

"I won't go into details—suffice it that I have social connections whereby I was enabled to make a thorough inspection of the ground floor of the château and of the grounds outside. I have drawn a reasonably accurate plan of the building and its environs. I am now having investigations made to see if I can find out about prisoners inside the place. If I get anything definite, I shall want a dependable man to undertake the job of rescuing Trudi. You understand how I am bound by my promise; I cannot do the job myself, and can only serve as secret paymaster."

"You will have difficulty in finding a man equal to that job, I fear."

"One of the reasons I came up here was the hope of persuading you to get a long enough furlough and make a try at it."

"*Aber!*" exclaimed the Capitán. "How could I work in France when

I do not know the language? I have only my German, and a few words of bad English, and enough Spanish to understand my orders, and to bargain with the peasants for food."

"You are a man of action and judgment. I have contacts with both the Socialists and the Communists in Paris, and could put you in the way to find dependable French assistance. Also, your contacts with the underground might help. Tell me, have you a family?"

"I have a wife and two children in Germany. The wife is working to support the little ones, against the time when I shall have saved up enough to bring them out."

"*Also!* If you will do your best for me, I will, regardless of success or failure, make it possible to bring your family out and to make them secure, at least until you are through with this war."

The Capitán sat in silence for quite a while. "What you are proposing is, in brief, that we shall burglarize a French château?"

"Possibly that, and possibly more, depending upon circumstances. First, we shall find out if Trudi is there, and second, if she is there, we shall get her out by whatever means it takes."

"Have you thought of any plans?"

"I have thought of many, some of them rather wild, I must admit. I succeeded in making friends with a member of the embassy staff, and I have thought that we might kidnap him and exchange him for their prisoner."

"*Aber nein, Genosse Budd!* The Nazis care nothing for individuals, and would sacrifice many lives to find where our underground has been getting its funds. Cross that one off."

"I have thought we might force the embassy man to talk, and perhaps to help us."

"The Nazis have you hopelessly licked at that game, for the reason that they have no scruples, while you have. Do you think you could torture a man?"

"Well, I have the feeling that if I was quite sure the man had Trudi, I would be willing to tear him to shreds to make him talk."

"You think you would, but you would probably find that the effort would wreck your nervous system. Also, you overlook the fact that the embassy would notify the French police as soon as their man was missing; and you do not enjoy diplomatic immunity."

"I have thought that we might have a small vessel and take the fellow out to sea."

"In that case, you would be a pirate, and any nation that caught you might hang you."

"Theoretically, yes; but practically, if you have money, you are sent to prison for a few weeks or months, until the scandal has blown over."

"You are speaking as a member of the leisure classes, Genosse Budd. You are accustomed to having your own way, and are annoyed by the idea of having to submit to law. But you must remember that I am a Socialist and a so-called Red fighter, and we are not privileged to break the laws of France or any other country; if we do, the police are prompt to proceed against us, and what is still more important, the capitalist press leaps to put all the details on the front page. You must bear in mind that our comrades of the underground in France are in that country as guests, and have to proceed with the utmost circumspection. The reactionaries are ceaseless in their watch to get something on us, to support the demand that we be expelled from the country. We face the fact that if crimes are committed against us, the police manifest very little interest, but if we dare to reply with a countercrime, every form of power in the land rises up in wrath against us."

Said Lanny: "All that you tell me is right, and it means just one thing —that in whatever we plan to do, we must not fail."

"In other words, the perfect crime!" replied the officer, smiling for the first time in this colloquy.

XII

They discussed back and forth for quite a while, and at the end Monck said: "I cannot tell how long this battle will last. We have forced the enemy to retire all along the line, but we have not been able to rout him or surround him, and I doubt very much if we have the resources to do either. What happens in such clashes is that we extend our communications as far as we dare, and use up our supplies, both food and ammunition; then we have to halt, and there follows a long wait, perhaps a couple of months, while both sides bring up fresh troops and supplies. During that interval I can with honor apply for leave for a month, and I will meet you in Paris and see what you have been able to discover and what plans you have been able to work out. If you could present me with a really perfect crime, I might be willing to commit it; but I warn you in advance that I will take no chance of compromising our movement, and would strongly urge you not to do it either. That is what the Nazis would most desire, and what Trudi would forbid, if she had a say in the matter."

Sorrowfully Lanny had to admit that this was correct. He asked: "At your best guess, when should I expect you in Paris?"

"I would say three weeks, possibly four."

"That is a long wait for a woman under torture, Genosse Monck."

"You must not put that sort of pressure on me. There will be a long wait for men who are dying up in these hills while we talk, and for the hundreds of thousands of our comrades in all the concentration camps and prisons of the dictators—Spanish, German, and Italian."

"I say no more," replied Lanny. "I will go back to Paris, see what has been learned, and perhaps start further investigations. It may be then that I will take a fast steamer to New York, where I have a chance to get a large sum of money, and also to speak some important words to an influential person. One never knows, in dealing with our governing classes, when one is having any effect. It is like shooting arrows into the dark."

"We in this place do a lot of shooting into the dark. We prefer to use bullets and shells, when we can get them. Do what you can to move the hard hearts of the profit seekers and their politicians, and get us whatever help you can—that is, of course, without endangering your social position."

Again there was a smile upon the face of the speaker; but it faded quickly as there came a burst of machine-gun fire that sounded nearer, up in the hills to the left. "That may be a flanking attack," he said. "I am afraid I cannot talk any longer. *Adios, Compañero!*"

8

This Yellow Slave

I

THE return to Valencia was uneventful. Raoul talked about adult education in the army, and also about the great victory in the making. He was sure the Fascists were finally on the run—all the fighting men agreed on it. Lanny didn't tell him what the Capitán had said; in fact he didn't mention the officer, saying merely that his own purpose had been accomplished and that he was deeply grateful. Raoul said: "Come as often as you can."

They discussed the problem of getting a painting out of Spain. It was against the law, but laws were not being strictly enforced amid the confusions of war, and Raoul knew that the money was meant for the cause. "Our art treasures won't be of any use to us if Franco gets here," he conceded, and went on to say that Lanny might have trouble getting by the border carrying a rolled-up old master under his arm; some official might insist on adhering to the regulations and referring the matter back to Valencia, with endless red tape and delay. "Also it might cause publicity," Raoul opined.

Obviously, the thing to do would be to walk on board a foreign steamer, preferably one leaving for Marseille. No one would pay any attention to the baggage which a passenger took on board; the submarine pirates had been driven away, and the trip would be quick. Raoul undertook to visit steamship offices and make arrangement for the passage; Lanny would drive in the car to get the painting, and then proceed to Raoul's lodgings, pick him up and drive to the harbor of Gráo, where the steamers docked.

The address which Señor Jimenes had given was to the south of the city, beyond the cemetery. *La gasolina* was just about equal to the trip, and Lanny found the peasant home without too great difficulty. The gray-haired old servant was working in a vegetable patch, wearing a black sleeveless waistcoat attached to his cotton trousers with a broad *faja* of dark red. His eyes lighted up with delight when this foreign gentleman offered him a cigarette, something he had not seen for a long time. Lanny said: "I have a letter from the Señor, and he told me to show it only to you."

They found a seat under a heavily laden grape arbor, and the *huertano*, whose name was Tomás, took the letter in his hands and looked at it solemnly; he didn't know how to read handwriting, but was ashamed to confess it. His former master, having foreseen this, had told Lanny how to proceed; he was not to allow the man to take the letter to the village official who served as scribe, but talk to him patiently and convince him that the visitor was a friend of the family. To that end the master had provided various details, and Lanny now told the news about how they were living, the children in school, and so on. Lanny explained that he had agreed to buy the painting if he decided that it was genuine, and described the work as the Señor had described it, including the fact that one of the six little ragamuffins was eating a bunch of grapes. "That will convince Tomás," the owner had said. "He has seen it hanging on the wall most of his life, and his idea of art is the perfect texture of the grape skins."

"*Bueno, Señor,*" said the man at last. Putting the letter into his pocket, together with the carefully extinguished cigarette butt, he led the way into the *barraca*, a cabin with a thatched roof, blue-washed sides, and a cross on top. The three women and as many children were not introduced, but Lanny greeted them kindly; the women bowed politely, while the little ones stared with open mouths. Tomás fetched a stool, and from up among the rafters, carefully concealed by old boards and rags, chains of garlic, of onions, and of dried figs, he drew forth a canvas cylinder about four feet long and perhaps a foot in diameter. The dust of a year was wiped from it and it was spread out and held open before the visitor's eyes.

Ars longa! Nearly three hundred years had passed since oils and pigments had been mixed and spread upon this well-woven cloth; kings and queens had reigned and perished, conquering heroes had been acclaimed and turned to dust—but here were half a dozen street urchins who had survived the ravages of time and were still laughing and full of energy. Their costumes were not so different from those of the little ones in this cabin, but their faces had that softness, that angelic quality of love, which must have been the basic ingredient of the soul of Bartolomé Esteban Murillo, for it manifested itself in everything he painted, whether it was cherubs out of heaven or disorderly little urchins on the narrow and crooked streets of old Seville.

If Lanny carried this painting out of the peasant's cabin he was obligated to release to Señor Jimenes the sum of a hundred and ten thousand French francs, which was something over four thousand dollars. If the painting proved not to be genuine, it might possibly be sold for as much as four hundred dollars. So Lanny was not satisfied with the thrill of beauty; he spread the canvas on the heavy wooden table which stood in the center of the all-purpose room and studied the signature and brushwork under his glass. When he was satisfied that it was an early Murillo, he said: "*Està bien, Tomás,*" rolled up the treasure, and tied it with the ragged hempen cord. He said his "*Buenas dias*" to the women, and saw the man carry the roll out and stow it in the car. He knew that Tomás was in a state of suppressed anguish at the idea of parting with this precious object on the basis of no more than some marks on a scrap of paper; he wasn't used to living by paper, like the *gente de la capital*. Having known the peasants of Mediterranean lands since childhood, Lanny spoke reassuring words, patted the old man on the back, and made him feel better with a whole packet of cigarettes and a ten-peseta note.

II

Raoul was waiting in front of his lodgings. He ran upstairs and got the typewriter and the suitcase, and while Lanny drove he explained that he had found a French freighter due to sail for Marseille that evening. He had engaged passage for the American traveler for the sum of four hundred and fifty francs. "Not very elegant," he apologized; but Lanny said: "It's all right if you got a guarantee against torpedoes." Raoul, having learned the American habit of "kidding" about the most serious subjects, replied: "A life-preserver goes with every ticket."

As a matter of fact, it was perfectly safe, for there was a gray-clad French destroyer patrolling off the port and a British light cruiser visible to the north. Chanticleer had crowed and the lion had roared; the Spaniards might kill one another and sink one another's ships all they pleased, but right at the moment nobody was going to sink French or British ships. Lanny walked on board with his precious roll under his arm and his Spanish friend carrying the rest of his luggage. Nobody asked any questions, and before long the engines of the rusty old tramp began to rumble and pound and she stole out past the long môle with her French flag proudly floating over a load of cork, hides, and other raw materials for the factories of Marseille or Lyons.

Lanny, who liked all sorts of people, made the acquaintance of two officers of the French merchant marine, and of sailors from two or three thousand miles of Mediterranean shore. He told the officers that he had a painting in his cabin, but didn't offer to exhibit it, and no one manifested curiosity. In his tiny cabin, reasonably clean, he wrote some notes for his Big Boss, telling what an officer of Loyalist forces on the Belchite front thought of the prospects of that battle and of the supplies which the opposing forces were getting from Germany and Italy.

The trip took two nights and a day. On his arrival, Lanny's first act was to phone to his mother, to ask if by any chance there had come a letter from his *amie* in Paris. No such luck; so he told her that he was alive and on his way to her. He had to come because his car was there, but of course he wouldn't say anything so tactless to an adoring mother. He asked her to phone to Señor Jimenes and tell him that the painting was safe, and that the money would be released as soon as Lanny could get to the bank. He sent a cablegram to a dear old lady in Chicago who purchased babies in paint, telling her that he was making a special trip to her home in order to show her the half dozen most charming urchins who had ever romped on the streets of old Seville. After which he engaged a taxi as the quickest way of getting himself and the aforesaid urchins to Juan-les-Pins.

III

At Bienvenu there was a letter from Rick in Geneva, where he had been sent by the editor of a leading weekly to report the opening ceremonies of the League of Nations Assembly. Rick enclosed a carbon copy of his first article, in which with quiet irony he contrasted the external splendors of the proceedings with their intellectual and moral bankruptcy. The British Indian ruler, Aga Khan, reputed to be the richest man in the world, was to be chosen President of this Eighteenth Assembly. He was a Moslem god, but the most modern of divinities, owning a famous racing stable and contributing twenty-five hundred quarts of champagne for the Geneva festivities. He spent most of his time on the Riviera, where Lanny had met him many times; he had admirable manners, and gave priceless jewels to the ladies who won his favor.

The new Palace of the League of Nations had been ten years a-building and had cost fifteen millions of dollars. It was magnificent beyond telling, and its murals, paid for by the Spanish republic, had as their subject the freeing of mankind from intolerance and tyranny; alas, the painter had gone over to the Franco side, and the Spanish republic was not sending delegates to the Assembly, on account of the failure of the League to act against Franco's intolerance and tyranny. Rick predicted that this Assembly would demand the withdrawal of foreign troops from Spain, and also the ending of Japanese attacks upon China, but that it would be powerless to enforce its decrees and not one of its members would move to make them good. All this took a couple of months to happen, and meantime the delegates from China went home, and Rick went home also, telling his readers that it was no longer worth his while to write, or theirs to read, about the doings of the League of Nations.

Lanny stayed at his mother's home long enough to have another session with Madame. Alas, he got nothing but the wearisome Claribel, and fragments of he knew not what; confused voices, names which he had never heard, references to happenings of no consequence; the contents of a mental junkshop, with goods molded and cracked and covered with dust. Lanny jotted it down in his notebook, and after a month or two would read it over to see if there were evidences of precognition, such as he had read about in the books of J. W. Dunne. But he didn't stay for more of it now, and wondered if Madame's gift was petering out. Poor soul, she was always afraid that would happen, and Lanny would console her, saying: "You have given us our money's worth already."

IV

Early in the morning Lanny stepped into his self-moving magic chariot, and this time he didn't stop at Le Creusot, but went straight through, reaching Paris in the late afternoon. His hands trembled as he glanced through his mail at his hotel. Nothing from Trudi; nothing from Professor Adler; only the silence of the tomb. So he phoned to his uncle. Having decided that it was no longer wise to visit that center of sedition, he had appointed a certain street corner as a rendezvous. Now he drove to the spot and took the elderly painter into his car.

They rolled peacefully about the drives of the Bois while Jesse made his report. He had an investigator—"Let's call him Jean," he said—"a dependable fellow who is a good mixer and knows how to get acquainted with all sorts of people. I didn't tell him what I expected to find; I just said I wanted to know what those Nazis are doing in that château and why there have to be so many of them. Jean found an old unused water-mill near the village, and he read up on the subject and took up the project of leasing it and putting it back into service. So he has an excuse to visit the peasants and ask if they would bring their grain to him; he sits in the *bistro* in the evening and chats with everybody, and the first crack out of the box they were telling him that it was no use expecting the patronage of the château, because those Germans have nothing to do with anybody. The village is bitter against them because men and women who had been employed there, and their fathers and grandfathers before them, were turned off without ceremony. That is an advantage to us, as you can see."

"Possibly a disadvantage," remarked Lanny. "They will be predisposed to believe whatever they hear, provided it is bad."

"Yes; but with hundreds of pairs of eyes watching, they can't fail to pick up some valid details. The Germans don't trade in the neighborhood, but bring all their supplies from Paris. One of their *camions* had a breakdown and halted by the roadside at night, and a peasant driving his cart stopped to see if he could help. Of course he was full of curiosity—and you know how sly they can be. The Germans said they didn't want any help, but he stood there offering comments, discussing the prospects of a storm, and so on; obsequious, but stubborn, and of course they couldn't order him off a highway in France. Tell me, is the party you are interested in a woman?"

"Why?"

"The peasant declares he heard a groan from inside the *camion*, and it seemed a high-pitched voice. It was a covered vehicle, and he couldn't see anything but what the Nazis illuminated with their flashlights."

"Do the people of the neighborhood believe there are prisoners in the château?"

"They are quite convinced of it. But of course it's a natural assumption; it's what the Nazis do wherever they go. A district like this, close to Paris, is tinged with Red, and naturally the Reds believe the worst."

"Has Jean met any party comrades?"

"Several, he tells me. He has let them have the idea that his sympathies lie their way."

"Did he follow up my tip about the laundry?"

"He has made contacts there. The Nazis bring the laundry and call for it, so there's no chance of getting inside by that method."

"Is he being careful not to excite suspicions by too many questions?"

"He's a clever chap, and used to the role of idle gossiper. Once you have established yourself as a Frenchman of the left, able to remember the last war and what *les sales boches* did, you are permitted to hate them. *Que le diable font-ils dans la patrie?* You can be sure it's nothing good, and that they are paying the pigs of politicians a lot of money to let them stay. That is the way Frenchmen talk in the *bistros* nowadays; they don't trust any of their *cochons*, and all they value politically is the privilege of calling them names."

V

Lanny said: "What you tell me fits in with the story I have heard, so let us get more. I have to run over to Chicago to sell a picture. I expect to be back in a couple of weeks and perhaps one or two days over. Meantime, have your man keep on working. We should have detail maps of the district, and a plan of the château. What could that mill be rented for?"

"I don't know, but it shouldn't be much. It is so run down as to be almost useless."

"We can lease it with an option to buy, and we can take our time and do a lot of discussing about fixing it up. Meantime, we have a rendezvous—and the Nazis would find it as hard to get into our place as we into theirs."

Lanny went to the bank next morning and drew out thirty thousand francs in the form of thirty crisp new notes. They looked immensely impressive, and even Americans had a tendency to be fooled and to forget that a franc was only three or four cents. (It had been doing a lot of fluctuating.) Lanny preferred to handle the sum in cash, because he was sure the banks were co-operating with the police authorities, and the last thing he wanted was to have anyone get the idea that he was putting up money for the Red cause. His uncle promised to stick the money away in an empty ginger-jar, and to change every single one of the notes before he paid them in any sort of transaction.

Lanny called Kurt on the telephone. Speaking English, he said: "On my way to Bienvenu I had lunch with Baron Tailor." Kurt knew both the English language and French geography, and would understand the reason for not saying Schneider. "I told him of my talk with you and he was interested and wants to hear more on the subject. You can follow that up if you wish." Lanny was sure that Kurt was never going to admit to him, directly or indirectly, that the Nazis were paying money to the Hooded Men; the proper role for Lanny was to be free from curiosity on all delicate subjects.

He went on to say that he had visited the château near Paris and had found some paintings of great interest. Also he had met a delightful young German, Leutnant Rörich. "What wonderful young men you have managed to train, Kurt! A quite new sort of men. *Unglaublich!*" He knew how Kurt would beam at that. "He reminded me all the time of Heinrich Jung. You remember when Heinrich was at that age, so full of his early enthusiasm for the Führer?"

They talked about old times for a bit, and at last Lanny informed his friend: "I am running over to Chicago to dispose of a painting. I am taking the *Bremen*, because it will be like a visit to Germany. I have been missing it." He inquired if there was anything he could do for his friend in either New York or Chicago, but Kurt said there wasn't. *Glückliche Überfahrt!*

VI

Lanny took a boat-train for Cherbourg. The great German liner was stopping there that night; she was as fast as any, and Lanny wanted to get the smell of Naziland after two years. Also he might pick up some items of information. He had three purposes in the trip: to sell his precious old master, which he now had carefully wrapped in oilcloth; to tell his father about the interview with Schneider and get due credit for this coup; and finally to visit Washington and make sure that his secret communications were being received and read. He hadn't dared make carbon copies of any of them, but he had them all in his head.

The steamer was magnificent and shiny, like everything the Nazis were displaying, and every German on board was as proud of it as of all the other triumphs of the *Neue Ordnung*. The vessel was crowded, for the most part with Americans on their way home from a summer of culture seeking and finding; they were loaded with it and couldn't resist unloading upon Lanny, even when they learned that he had lived in Europe most of his life. He had been able to get on board at the last moment by sharing the bridal suite, the most expensive apartment, with a manufacturer of machine tools from a city of Indiana. He chanced to meet this large expansive gentleman in the steamship office; they both had money, but shrank from paying twenty-one hundred dollars for a five-day journey, and decided to stand each other's company. The gentleman was a devout Catholic and hung a crucifix over his bedpost as soon as he opened his bags; it had been blessed by a bishop, and would keep him from being seasick in spite of equinoctial storms. He had recently kissed the Pope's toe, and received a rather gaudy medal for his contributions to the building of a cathedral.

Opposite to Lanny at the table sat a plump widow who owned most of the stock of a manufacturing plant in Camden, New Jersey. She had with her a lovely daughter, a bold striking brunette just out of Vassar. How Beauty Budd's heart would have thumped if she had been there, and how quickly she would have convinced the mother of the supereligibility of her brilliant son. Mother and daughter had been doing the grand tour, and it had included at the end a ten-day excursion into Russia, entering by way of Leningrad and coming out by Moscow. The only things they had enjoyed had been the paintings, and the palace of the Tsar and Tsarina with the bedrooms and all the knickknacks and bric-a-brac untouched. All the rest of Russia was dirt and bad smells, dingy clothing and water-spigots out of order. Women actually working on the railroads, shoveling dirt! Women paddling along barefooted in the dusty roads, following their men! Most horrible!

A relief to come out into Poland, and find the stations with counters loaded with every sort of delicious foods. And the army officers, with such gorgeous sky-blue uniforms! The ladies had spent a whole day in Warsaw and hadn't seen a sign of any slums; they hadn't heard there was a ghetto, and were quite sure that stories of pogroms were just made up by the hateful Bolsheviks. Lanny had learned to listen to such opinions and smile amiably. In his mind was the thought: "You should

have stayed a while longer, Miss Gwendolyn, and married one of those
uniforms!"

VII

Studying the passenger list of the steamer, Lanny noted the name of
Forrest Quadratt, the poet whom he had met at Irma's Long Island
home; American-born of German descent, and said to be a left-handed
relative of the Kaiser. He had been a lifelong devotee of *Machtpolitik*
and Lanny was sure that he was now a well-paid agent of the Nazis.
Their last meeting had been in the days of Lanny's suppressed quarrel
with Irma, and he couldn't be sure that she hadn't given the man some
hint of her husband's distressing political attitude. Whenever Lanny
suspected anything like that, he had a deft way of covering it up; he
would say: "I used to have a Pinkish tinge to my thinking, but what I
have learned about the wholesale purges in Russia has cured me. I realize now that Europe has to be protected from the Asiatic hordes, and
nobody but the Germans can do it."

The one-time decadent poet—he said that he had "given up the
genius business"—was in his fifties; rather small and stoop-shouldered,
nearsighted and wearing thick glasses through which he peered out at
you; leaning forward and speaking with rapidity—English, French, or
German, *wie Sie wollen, comme vous voulez*, as you like it. His hand
was soft, warm, and moist, and so was his voice. He had sinned heavily
and written about it boldly; also he had read the literature of sin, and
was cynical about what was in the hearts of men, and what women
were doing when they shut and locked the doors of steamship cabins.

Like all the Nazis, Quadratt was convinced that the mass of mankind was made up of dolts and imbeciles who had to be given orders
and made to obey. He considered that the Germans were the proper
people to take charge of Europe and bring it out of the Middle Ages.
The British had their huge empire, and should be content with that and
not make Germany the victim of their jealousy and greed. As for the
United States, they were the people who most resembled Germans, and
should be their spiritual brothers, as they already were their blood
brothers—owing to the vast immigration of Germans, who had brought
most of the new country's culture. Let America be content with the
Western Hemisphere, upon which the Germans had no designs whatever. If you asked Quadratt why the German propagandists were so
active in all South American countries, he would answer that their attitude was purely defensive, a result of America's having deprived Germany of her hard-won victory in the last war.

But Lanny Budd asked no questions of that sort. Lanny Budd was the spiritual brother of the Nazis, an art expert who had sold pictures for General Göring and shot stags with him; an amateur pianist who had played the *Moonlight Sonata* for the Führer; a gentleman of leisure and fashion who had been the friend and patron of Germany's greatest living *Komponist*. In Lanny's pocketbook was a clipping from the *Münchner Neueste Nachrichten*, telling how the American *Kunstsachverständiger* was directing a one-man show of his former stepfather's paintings in Munich, and how he had taken the *chef-d'œuvre* to the Führer at the Braune Haus and the Führer had certified to the validity of the art work. This clipping included a photograph of the distinguished American, and thus served as a *Legitimationspapier* to any Nazi anywhere.

Lanny wished to make himself rock-solid with this *Nummer-Eins* propagandist in the land of Lanny's fathers; he swore him to secrecy as to the source of his information and then revealed the new revolutionary movement to abolish the Third Republic of France and put an end to the alliance with Russia. Quadratt pretended to know all about it, but obviously he knew very little, and Lanny let himself be deftly led to make revelations; the Nazi agent enjoyed getting the better of anyone, and the presidential agent enjoyed watching a smooth psychological trickster doing his stuff. Lanny was sure it couldn't do any harm for Quadratt to possess this information, and it was a way of getting a Nazi to unveil his innermost soul.

The talk took place in the ex-poet's stateroom, where they could be sure of privacy—at least the ex-poet could be sure. Lanny wondered if there might be a dictaphone, but decided that it wouldn't matter, for he wasn't naming the de Bruynes or Schneider; only those French politicians whom the Nazis had on their payroll. After this steamship intimacy had progressed to the proper point, Lanny ventured: "We're going to have to do something of the same sort in America, I very much fear."

The Kaiser's left-handed relative didn't consider it necessary to play shy like Kurt Meissner; what he played was sad, for he was a tenderhearted man, a lover of culture and peace, and he hated to see violence and cruelty anywhere. Said he: "I am afraid that you are right, Mr. Budd. There are elements in every country today which are deliberately or otherwise playing the Moscow game, and they have no intention of letting themselves be put down without a struggle."

Lanny knew that Quadratt had sounded out Robbie Budd on the question of the Hooded Men of America and the possibility of their being used to overthrow the New Deal. Now Robbie's son threw out a piece of bait, and was amused to see the speed with which the peace-loving Nazi grabbed it. Lanny said he had heard the subject discussed in American drawing-rooms and that some of the most prominent victims of the New Deal were now in a mood to put up money and save themselves from further victimization. Quadratt made plain that he wanted nothing in the world so much as to know the location of those drawing-rooms; and Lanny promised to invite these wealthy friends to meet Quadratt and hear what he had to suggest.

The son of Budd-Erling went on to discuss some of the more prominent public enemies of the New Deal: Mr. Henry Ford, who had spent a fortune to awaken Americans to the menace of Jewish Imperialism; Colonel McCormick of Chicago, lavish in subsidizing those groups which were struggling to keep America out of European affairs; Mr. Hearst, who had interviewed the Führer just recently, and whose newspapers were the Rock of Ages for all friends and sympathizers of National Socialism; Mrs. Elizabeth Dilling, who ran a sort of volunteer intelligence service and had a dossier on every man or woman who had ever given aid or comfort to Moscow. Lanny said he hadn't met any of these persons, but would like very much to meet Hearst and the wife of Ford for business reasons, since both were noted for their interest in painting. Did Quadratt know of any way to bring him together with either of these highly inaccessible persons?

The reason for this proposal was that Lanny knew the world in which he lived, and was sure that Forrest Quadratt would have more respect for him if he believed him to be engaged in making plenty of money like Quadratt himself, and not just traveling about the world indulging a yen to meet celebrities and put his feet under the dinner tables of the rich. When they parted on board that steamer, they were friends who understood each other thoroughly and were prepared to exchange favors. You scratch my back and I'll scratch yours!

VIII

Arriving in New York, Lanny signed an affidavit to the effect that his painting dated from approximately 1645, which meant that he did not have to pay any duty upon it. Then he stepped into a taxicab and was driven to the airport from which a plane left for Chicago almost every hour. He sent a telegram to Mrs. Sophronia Fotheringay, saying that he was coming. Instead of going directly to her home, he went to a picture dealer and had the painting put into an elaborately hand-carved old Spanish frame. When he reached the mansion on Lake Shore Drive he dined with the hostess, and told her the story of his trip into the land of the Reds—the deepest-dyed and bloodiest of all Reds now operating. Manifestly, a painting must be extremely valuable to justify the taking of so many risks as the expert described.

The old master was hung in the drawing-room, with a proper reflector above it. Before they went in to see it Lanny delivered his spiel about a painter who had been the favorite of Spain all his lifetime, and after three centuries was the favorite of all persons everywhere who loved sweetness and light. They entered the room, and the elderly widow was seated in a padded armchair, after which Lanny ceremoniously unveiled the treasure. Of course she was enraptured; she saw in one of those dark-eyed urchins the perfect image of her only son, who had been killed in the Meuse-Argonne and was now waiting for her in heaven. His photograph stood on the piano, and Lanny had to get it and compare them, and admit that the likeness was extraordinary. The coincidence cost the old lady an extra five thousand dollars.

When the visitor mentioned that he was asking thirty thousand for the painting, old Mrs. Fotheringay never turned a hair. When he told her that he would prefer to have her call in some other expert, say from the Art Institute, to pass judgment on the work's authenticity and the fairness of the price, she waved the idea aside, saying that he had risked his life to get it, and she liked it. She didn't mention, but Lanny knew, that she had so much money she literally didn't know what to do with it. Her husband had left her the royalties upon certain basic patents having to do with machine-tools of which she did not even know the names; all she knew was that several million dollars was paid every year into her bank account, and she wrote checks for any amount that came into her head, often without taking the trouble to enter the item in the stub—which made it rather hard for her business manager. Now she wrote a check payable to Lanning Prescott Budd, and he wrote her a bill of sale.

Afterwards he strolled with her about the many rooms of this old-style overdecorated home, and looked at all the painted babies and children, many of which he had bought for her. She told him that she loved them all, and would not part with a single one at any price. She invited him to spend the night, but he said that he was taking a plane back to New York at midnight, so she told her butler to have a car ready for him at the proper hour. He devoted the rest of the evening to telling her about art in Europe and preparing her mind for the next picture he might bring. He had never been mercenary in the past, but now he had become so, on account of Trudi. Gold, "this yellow slave," was going to perform for him the magic service of getting his wife out of a dungeon cell.

So Lanny told himself. It is an ancient doctrine, and highly dangerous—that the end justifies the means. Looking upon the matter through Marxist eyes, he could see it as the automatic operation of economic force. How could any man on earth see that amiable stout old lady with her pen poised to write checks, and not say: "I might as well have it as the next fellow"? If you had any sort of "cause," including a Marxist one, you naturally believed it the best of causes—otherwise you would have had some other!

IX

Back in New York, Lanny called Gus Gennerich at his hotel in Washington, and was told to call back in four hours. He telephoned Hansi and Bess to say "Hello," and then Johannes to invite him to have lunch and a gossip. He called Robbie, and said that he was going to Washington on picture business, and would come to Newcastle on his return. He added that he had "big news," but didn't say what, for when he told about Schneider's "bid," he wanted to see the expression on Robbie's face, and if possible lead the conversation into channels of interest to Robbie's son.

When he called Gus the second time, the man asked if he could take a plane to Washington at once. Lanny said: "You bet!" and Gus replied: "Call me at nine-thirty tonight."

This so wonderfully comfortable modern world was getting smaller and smaller, and those who had the price of its services were getting them more and more prompt and efficient. The porter in Lanny's hotel would phone to the airport for his reservation, and meantime a taxi would be speeding the passenger to a newly opened field which was a marvel of administration. Safe traveling "on the beam" would deliver him in his country's capital in an hour, a journey which had taken the founder of the country at least two weeks.

So it came about that Lanny Budd was again picked up on a street corner and delivered through the "social door" of the White House. The "Governor" was in bed, as before, but this time he had no sniffles; his family and guests were looking at a movie upstairs, while he had begged off on the plea of pressing work. "Hello, Marco Polo!" he exclaimed, when his visitor entered the room; he always had comical names for his intimates, and had been struck by the fact that no two of Lanny's communications bore the same dateline.

They had been numbered serially, and he had read every word, so he declared. "It is better than a Cook's tour; you should have them made into a movie some day." Then, his expression and tone changing as suddenly as any movie actor's, he demanded: "What is going to be the outcome in Spain?"

"The Belchite drive has come to an end," replied the visitor; "just as I wrote you it would. Franco has taken most of the north, with its iron ore that Hitler wants so badly. The rest depends upon the British and French Cabinets. If they continue the farce of 'Non-Intervention' while Hitler and Mussolini send in all the supplies needed, the end is certain. It may take another year, but no people, no matter how brave and determined, can fight airplanes and artillery with sticks and stones. Neither side has the manufacturing resources to fight a modern war, and it's purely a question of how much each can get from outside."

Lanny had been told, definitely and flatly, that the "Governor" wouldn't do anything about that. But he couldn't give up; nobody could give up who had been to the battlefront and seen the bloodshed and agony. He was too tactful to say "Please," or "You must," or anything of that sort; he just told what he had seen with his eyes and heard with his ears, and it was better than any movie which F.D. could have enjoyed upstairs. First Trudi and the visit to the Château de Belcour; then the trip to Spain, and what El Capitán had reported under the sound of the guns. Said Lanny: "This raid is the beginning of a war on civilization, and it won't stop until the last bastion has been knocked out. The best military brains in Europe are planning it and this time they aren't overlooking anything."

This Cassandra in trousers was in a strong position, because only a few weeks previously he had warned his hearer that France was to be the next victim, and now he was able to bring the blueprints of this future operation. He told what he had heard from the lips of the de Bruynes and Baron Schneider in two long talks. When Lanny was speaking to the Nazis he lied carefully, but to the President of his country he would bring the precise truth, and wouldn't hide any name, unless perhaps that of his own father. F.D. was the one who had the right to know, and Lanny must count everything else as second to that service. There were things he couldn't put on paper, but in the privacy of this bedroom he got them on the record.

"There are reasons, Governor, why you should understand my relationship to the de Bruyne family; no Frenchman would need an explanation, but an American does. Marie de Bruyne made me a sort of godfather to those two boys, and they still think of me in that relationship; they keep no political secrets from either my father or myself, and so it has come about that I am in the center of the coming storm in France. I mention this so that when I tell you I know something, you will be sure that I really do know it. In future, when I write, let the de Bruynes be St. Denis, and Baron Schneider be Mr. Tailor."

"Have you made a note of these?"

"I have prepared a list of such names. Kurt Meissner is Kaiser; that is where his loyalties began, and may end again. You understand that Kurt was an officer of the old army; it was that army which sent him to Paris at the time of the Peace Conference. His brother Emil is a general, and Kurt is an agent of that same army today. You must know that the Germans have half a dozen organizations doing their secret work in the Ausland; Goebbels has one, and I'm pretty sure that Göring has his own; Rosenberg, the supplier of the official Nazi religion, has his, and so have the SS, and the Gestapo, or Secret State Police. The old army, the Reichswehr, has perhaps the biggest of all. Those officers are exclusive, and they look upon the Nazis as upstarts and intruders; it's all for the Fatherland, of course, but the old army has its own way of doing things, and keeps its own secrets. I am not sure, but I got hints that Kurt and the Graf Herzenberg are not on the most cordial terms. The fact that it was an SS officer who showed me about the grounds of the Château de Belcour indicates that the Nazis are running the Embassy, while Kurt's organization is serving the army."

"Did Kurt admit to you that the Cagoulards are taking his money?"

"No, and I'm sure he never will. Even if friendship prompted him to, he is under a solemn oath. But you know how it is; you can smell things in the atmosphere. Both Schneider and the de Bruynes made it plain that they want all the money they can get and they don't care who puts it up; also, it goes without saying that Hitler would rather take France by a revolution than by a costly war. You have only to ask yourself—what else would Kurt be doing in Paris? When he left my home on the Riviera and went back to Germany to live, he was a musician devoted to his art and living a most austere life; I doubt if he had five hundred dollars a year to keep himself and his family. But now he lives in a fashionable apartment with a blond secretary and an ex-soldier to wait on him and drive him in a limousine. What is all that for? Manifestly, to find out what high-placed Frenchmen are for sale, and to buy them."

"The Frenchmen know what they are selling?"

"Some do and some don't; Hitler is as cunning as the devil when he wants to be. He is holding out an olive branch with one hand, and keeping his dagger behind his back in the other. Perhaps—who knows?—if the Frenchmen take the olive branch he will not use the dagger. Many of them choose to believe so, and not all have been bought for cash; they want to break the alliance with the Reds, and put down the labor unions and the sit-downs, and Hitler is the one who knows how. It is one ideology and one technique all over the world, and it is spreading fast. The dictators are all blood brothers under their skins."

"Under their shirts," put in F.D., with a smile.

"It makes the Communists wild for anyone to say so, but the fact is that Mussolini took over his technique from the Bolsheviks; the Agitprop, the Gaypayoo, the youth movement, the whole show. When I first met Mussolini he told me: 'Fascismo is not for export'—but that was only until he had got firmly set in the saddle. Then he passed on his bag of tricks to Hitler, and now the two of them have loaned it to Franco, and to the little Balkan dictators. I have been watching the Croix de Feu, the Jeunesse Patriote and all the others in France, and it is a standardized product—if you follow the formula you can produce it in any part of the world where you can raise money for shirts and armbands and banners and drums and the salaries of rabble-rousers. In this country, I am told, the shirts are silver, or gold, or white—more appropriate to a country which can afford laundry bills."

X

That led to Forrest Quadratt and Lanny's negotiations on board the *Bremen*. Like Kurt, the ex-poet had never admitted that he was a Nazi agent, but he had shown wide acquaintance with the art of getting the money of the rich, and also with the names and addresses of persons who might like to see a coup d'état against the New Deal. Lanny said: "He knows exactly what he wants, and again it is the standard product. Quadratt talks to Americans and Kurt talks to Frenchmen, so they have different sets of phrases, but the thing they talk about is identical."

"They really imagine they can make headway in a free country like America?"

"I assure you they are making headway very fast, and are full of confidence. They figure that the New Deal cannot go on piling up public debt indefinitely; and when you have to stop, there will be a smash-up, and that will be their chance. The very freedom we are so proud of is their assurance of success; we are made impotent by it, and cannot imagine taking action against those who use their freedom to destroy ours."

"It is hard to see just what I can do, until they take some overt action." F.D. seemed to be thinking out loud, and Lanny put in quickly: "Are you open to a suggestion, Governor?"

"Always, of course."

"We grant that American citizens who have millions of dollars have a right to use them to poison the public mind; but surely we don't have to grant the right of foreigners to come in and intrigue against us. Why doesn't some congressman propose a law requiring all agents of foreign governments to register, say with the State Department, declaring what government they represent, what payment they receive, and the nature of their duties? If American citizens serve on the payroll of foreign governments, why not make them do the same? That would turn the spotlight of publicity upon them; it would frighten some, and might be the means of jailing a few who would try to keep their doings secret."

"By Jove, Lanny, that's an idea! I'll give some thought to it."

The younger man flushed with pleasure. "You know my position. I can't make any suggestions to congressmen; but you, no doubt, make them now and then."

"Indeed, rather often!" replied the President, with one of his broad grins. "They aren't always accepted, but I keep on trying."

XI

They came back to the subject of Quadratt, and Lanny said: "I believe I have him on the hook, and could get a lot of information about his doings." But the President replied that he had abundant sources of information as to the United States. He wanted the son of Budd-Erling to return to Europe where he had so many carefully cultivated entrées. Roosevelt was really frightened by the prospect of waking up some morning and reading that France was in the hands of the Fascists. He complained that the State Department could hardly be ignorant of these intrigues, and wondered what those well-bred young gentlemen did with such information when they got it.

F.D.R. was a free and easy talker, which was one reason he had so many enemies. He described to his visitor that venerable and somewhat musty building, whose inmates had a tendency to take on the color of their environment. Secretary Hull was the most honorable and high-minded lawyer who had ever come out of the mountains of Tennessee, but he was somewhat old-fashioned in his thinking, and devoted to his idea that freedom of trade would solve all the problems of the nations. He was a former senator, and possessed the confidence of those elder statesmen to a greater degree than F.D. himself; so F.D. had been forced to adopt the method of putting in younger men upon one pretext or another. "But the trouble is, they all take to wearing top-hats and spats, and presently I discover that the new state of the State Department is more stately than the old."

Lanny chuckled. "Perhaps you might like me to investigate them for you."

"No," was the reply; "I know them too well already." Then the laughter went out of the great man's voice and he continued: "I really deplore the spread of these reactionary doctrines all over Europe. I want to know what I can do about it, and when, and how."

This was the opening for which Lanny had been praying, and he stepped into it without hesitation. "May I make another suggestion, Governor?"

"Always, Lanny. Believe me, I am glad to make use of other men's minds. You have lived among these new movements and seen them grow, while to me they are almost incomprehensible; I hear the stories of what the Nazis are doing, and it seems like somebody's nightmare."

"It is primitive barbarism employing all the techniques of modern science. That makes it the most dangerous movement in human history; the last upsurgence of the beast in man against the restraints of civilization. The first step in fighting it is to understand it, and that is where you can help more than any other man. For in addition to being the most powerful executive in the world, you are the greatest educator in the world. And don't think that is just taffy—you can talk to twenty or thirty million Americans any time you wish, and sooner or later what you say reaches every literate person in the world."

"You want me to warn them about the Cagoulard conspiracy?"

"No. The French people would resent your claim to know more about their affairs than they do. I don't mean even that you should name the Nazis, or the Fascists, or the Falangistas, or any other group. But surely, as the spokesman of the world's leading democracy, you can warn our people that the dictatorships which are spreading over the world are an evil force, the enemy of every freedom-loving man and woman. Surely it is your duty, as the leader of the free world, to speak out against aggression, and say that some way must be found to quarantine the aggressors and make it impossible for them to disturb the peace and order of the world."

Lanny had had his say, and he knew when to stop. The President sat staring before him with a frown on his face, and Lanny watched him. A large and decidedly noble head—or so it seemed to an admirer; graying hair, beginning to thin at the front and on top; broad heavy shoulders and vigorous arms lying relaxed on the bedsheet; blue and white-striped pajama coat open over a powerful chest. In that large head was a brain, and inside it, by some process beyond the comprehension of all the scientists on earth, a chain of thoughts was being generated which might change the destiny of the world. Lanny was afraid to breathe or to blink an eyelid for fear of interrupting those thoughts.

At last the President spoke, his voice low and grave. "You are right, Lanny. I believe I will do it. It will raise merry hell, but the time has come for speaking out. I am scheduled to leave for a trip to the west and I shall be making several speeches. Would you like to write one of them?"

All the *savoir faire* that Lanny Budd had acquired in a leisure-class lifetime failed him at that juncture, and he blurted out: "*Me*, Governor?"

"I have a lot to do, and the mark of a good executive is never to do anything that he can get done. You have your mind full of this subject, and why not get it off? I don't say that I won't change it a lot; but you make the first draft."

"O.K., if you say so."

"Let us get the key phrases on paper without delay. Do you use a typewriter?"

"Yes."

"All right, there's one over in the corner. Turn on the light and imagine yourself the greatest educator in the world. You are going to write a few sentences which all literate people on earth will read and give thought to."

"My God!" exclaimed the son of Budd-Erling. "If I am able to hit the keys straight!"

This amiable great man was not above being pleased by his visitor's naïveté, and he had learned to take his multiple duties with a flavoring of gaiety. "Don't use too violent language," he cautioned. "Remember your responsibilities!"

XII

Lanny went to the typewriter and seated himself, took off the cover, turned on the light, and put in a sheet of paper. His head was in a whirl, but the whirl was full of words and phrases, because he had been a talker all his life, and now for many years his talk had been of the perils of Nazi-Fascist dictatorship. Sentences took form, and he found that his fingers were equal to the task of hammering them out. When he had finished, he read: "The present reign of international lawlessness began a few years ago. It began through unjustified interference in the internal affairs of other nations or the invasion of alien territory in violation of treaties; and has reached a stage where the very foundations of civilization are seriously threatened."

"O.K.," said the President, and Lanny's head was more in a whirl than ever. But still, it didn't keep another sentence from coming. He typed it and then read: "Innocent peoples, innocent nations, are being cruelly sacrificed to a greed for power and supremacy which is devoid of all sense of justice and humane considerations."

Again the listener said: "O.K."

Then a third sentence, one which seemed crucial to its author: "When an epidemic of physical disease starts to spread, the community approves and joins in a quarantine of the patients in order to protect the health of the community against the spread of the disease."

"Excellent!" exclaimed the President. "Take that for your keynote. Everybody in the world understands the nature of a quarantine." Then he ordered: "Read it all over to me." After listening he asked: "If I say something like that, will you be satisfied?"

"Oh, Governor! It will make me as proud as a dog with two tails."

F.D. chuckled. "Where did you get that phrase?"

"Somewhere in England they have such dogs." Lanny liked his fun, too.

The President sat in thought, and it was not about dogs' tails. "Consider this for a moment," he said. "The German people have had some real grievances, have they not? There were clauses in the Versailles treaty which couldn't be enforced and shouldn't have been there."

"Indeed yes, Governor. I got myself into hot water by speaking out against them."

"Then suppose we make it harder for the Nazis by admitting that fact. Let us put in a paragraph that will cut the ground from under them. Take this—" and he dictated, phrase by phrase, while Lanny typed: "It is true that the moral consciousness of the world must recognize the importance of removing injustices and well-founded grievances; but at the same time it must be aroused to the cardinal necessity of honoring the sanctity of treaties, of respecting the rights and liberties of others, and of putting an end to acts of international aggression."

Lanny typed those words, and read them back. "Will that do any harm?" the other asked.

"It shows me what it means to be a statesman."

So both were pleased, with themselves and with each other. "I want a speech of say twenty minutes," explained the President, "about ten typewritten pages. How soon could you have that ready?"

"I'll do it tonight. Believe me, I won't do any sleeping till it's finished."

"Get it to Gus's hotel as soon as it's ready. I'll tell him to expect it. I think I'll use it in Chicago, where I'm scheduled to speak at the opening of the Outer Drive Bridge. How Bertie McCormick will foam at the mouth!"

"Don't lose your nerve and back out on me, Governor."

"I'll probably change your text so that you won't know it, but the substance will be there. I've had something of the sort in my noodle for a long time. I tell you in advance, nothing I have said in my entire career has aroused such a fury of opposition as those half-dozen sentences will—and it won't be only among the Republicans!"

XIII

Lanny went to his hotel room, set up his own typewriter, and went to work. He didn't need to order any coffee, for he was in a state of exaltation. Now, at last, he was going to change the world! Everything he had ever done in his life was preparation for this job. His head was so full of ideas that it was hard to sort them out. An exposé of all Fascist aggression, a call to solidarity of all democratic forces—and all in three thousand words!

He paced the floor and ordered his thoughts. The Nazi-Fascist piling up of armaments; the efforts of the peace-loving nations for an understanding; the Covenant of the League, the Briand-Kellogg Pact, the Nine Power Treaty. When he had got it clear in his head he sat and typed—all through the small hours of the morning. He revised and marked out and tore up and retyped, and worked in a fever, until the sunlight was streaming into the room. The final task—the making of a clean copy—he might have entrusted to the hotel stenographer; but he thought: "Suppose F.D. delivers it as I wrote it, and then she remembers it!" No, he had to do it all.

He allowed himself the luxury of one carbon copy, which he would seal up and put away in his safe-deposit box in the First National Bank of Newcastle, of which Esther Budd's father was president. All the earlier drafts were torn into small pieces and sent down into the capacious sewers of the city of Washington. The first copy was sealed in an envelope and addressed to Gus Gennerich's suite in the Hotel Mayflower. Lanny called a messenger and entrusted him with the precious missive, cautioning him that it was important and giving him a half-dollar to stimulate his sense of duty. Lanny waited until Gus had telephoned: "O.K., Zaharoff." Then he pulled down the shades, shut off his phone, hung out his Do Not Disturb sign, and slept the sleep of one who has succeeded in reversing the foreign policy of his country.

BOOK THREE

Most Disastrous Chances

9

His Honor Rooted in Dishonor

I

IN NEWCASTLE, Lanny found his father in a high state of discontent. Budd-Erling Common had lost seven points on the market in the past week. Other stocks had done even worse; business was receding, and another panic was in the air. After all that New Deal spending, nobody had money enough to buy anything, and goods were piling up in the warehouses. Of course Robbie blamed That Man; Lanny, hiding his guilty secret, felt himself more than ever the snake in the grass. He listened politely and didn't say a word while Robbie denounced the madness of trying to bring back prosperity by spending; here we had piled up a huge public debt—and where were we? No place that Robbie Budd wanted to be!

Troubles never came singly. Those C.I.O. organizers who had slipped into the Budd-Erling plant and poisoned the minds of the workers had now got to the stage where they were presuming to demand a conference with Robbie's executives. There was supposed to be something called a Wagner act which compelled Robbie to negotiate with them, but he had set his jaw; he wasn't going to recognize the act, he would close up his business before he would let any gang-leaders come in and tell him how to run it. Lanny wanted to say: "You are the original anarchist, Robbie," but instead he told how he had just sold for thirty thousand dollars a painting which he had bought for a little more than four thousand.

Robbie couldn't but be tickled by news such as that. Better than he had ever managed to do in all his business career! There must be a catch in it somewhere, and he asked: "Won't that old woman find out that you've overcharged her?"

Lanny replied: "Mrs. Fotheringay is a perfect lady, and never mentions what she has paid for her art treasures. I doubt if she remembers for more than a few days. She got something that will bring her happiness every time she looks at it; and nobody found it but me."

The cautious father wanted to know what his son was going to do with all that money. He would have been pleased if the son had answered: "Put it into Budd-Erling." But Lanny was noncommittal; he had something in mind that he would tell about later. The father said: "I hope to God you're not giving it away to those radicals of yours." Robbie cherished the notion that the "radical movement" was in great part the creation of his son's perverted generosity.

Lanny had thought it over and decided to feed his father some of that soothing syrup which he was administering to the rest of the fashionable world. "No," he replied, gravely. "I've about made up my mind that the world isn't going to change as fast as I hoped. I'm definitely done with politics. I'm going to retire and cultivate my own garden." It was pathetic to see how eagerly the father gulped this down. It made him so happy that he forgot the stock market and the C.I.O. for the rest of the evening.

They were settled in his den, and while he smoked a long dark cigar that came out of a gold-foil wrapper, Lanny told about his visit to the de Bruynes and the later one to Le Creusot. He didn't say that he had undertaken to act as go-between for the Hooded Men and the Nazis; he said that he had talked airplanes—which was true—and that the Baron had admitted being uneasy because the Germans were forging so far ahead of his country. Lanny had told him what the new Budd-Erling pursuits were able to do, and now the Baron wanted to have Robbie Budd call upon him. Robbie didn't need to have it pointed out to him that that might mean something really big. "I've been planning to see Göring," he said. "I'll see the Baron first, and that will help me with the General." It is the essence of the munitions man's technique to play two rival countries each against the other.

Lanny told about the Cagoulard conspiracy and the fortification in the de Bruyne garden; also the talk with Quadratt, and the Nazi effort to unite all the different sorts of "shirts" in America. It was Lanny's hope that his father might "open up" on this subject, but all Robbie said was: "The New Deal is doing its best to force something like that on us, and if they keep asking for it, they may get it." Lanny was pretty sure his father had information along this line, but the only way Lanny could have got it was by doing with Robbie what he had already done with Kurt: pretending to change his viewpoint and approve the conspiracy. But Lanny couldn't bring himself to take that step. Robbie would go far enough without any encouragement. With it, he might get himself seriously involved, and Lanny wouldn't take that upon his conscience. Back to the ivory tower!

II

There was another bee buzzing under a psychical researcher's hat. This bee made the noise: "Huff"—and then "Huffy"—and then "Huffner." This bee said: "Key-master," and then "American." Upon Lanny's arrival in New York, it occurred to him to consult the classified part of the telephone book under "Locksmith." He didn't find a Huff, or Huffy, or Huffner; so he looked for a locksmith not too far from his hotel, and strolled there and said to the man: "I have a safe in my home in Connecticut and have lost the combination. What do I have to do?"

"You have to go to a man who knows how to open safes," was the not very illuminating reply.

"Do you know how?"

"No, sorry; I'm just an ordinary locksmith."

"Can you recommend somebody to do it?"

"The best man in New York is Horace Hofman."

Lanny repressed a start. Huff—Huffy—Huffner—Hofman! "Is he an ethical person?"

"He was one of the founders of our American Association of Master Locksmiths. You won't find any better man in the business."

"Where can I find him?"

"He has a place up in Harlem, with more keys in it than any other place in the world, so he claims." The man produced his telephone book and gave Lanny the address. "Hofman with one 'f'" he said, and Lanny thanked him and went to a near-by telephone booth and called the number.

"May I speak to Mr. Hofman?" The voice answered: "Speaking," and Lanny explained: "I am looking for a locksmith who used to know a party named Zaharoff."

The reply set a whole swarm of bees to buzzing in or around Lanny's head. "I used to know a Mr. Zaharoff. I did a good deal of work for him."

"May I ask, did you ever do any deep-sea diving?"

"I did that for Mr. Zaharoff, and very nearly lost my life at it."

Lanny wanted to say: "My God!" But his training in the social arts protected him. "Mr. Hofman, my name is Budd. I used to be a friend of Sir Basil Zaharoff, the armaments manufacturer. Is that the man you mean?"

"That is the one."

"May I come and have a talk with you?"

"Certainly. I am at the shop, unless I am called out on some job." It was a friendly voice, and apparently that of an educated man. Lanny said he would be there in half an hour.

It was a small but well-appointed shop, with large rooms in back. The proprietor was a man with rugged and much-lined features; his hair was white, though he appeared to be under fifty. Lanny introduced himself and was invited into a back room, furnished as a combination of den and museum; its walls were hung with more kinds of keys than Lanny had ever imagined to have existed in the world. "This has been my lifelong hobby," explained the host. "Some of these are the newest and some the oldest keys ever made."

"You are no ordinary locksmith, I take it," replied the visitor. "You might be described as a key-master."

"Now I know that you were really a friend of Mr. Zaharoff's, for that is what he used to call me: *der Meister-Schlosser*."

"I have a strange story to tell you, Mr. Hofman; but first let me ask one or two questions. Did you ever hear of the cruiser *Hampshire?*"

"Indeed yes. That was where I came near to losing my life."

"You were diving for the gold on board?"

"Exactly."

"Was there anything in your experience to correspond to this: Kitchener's arm came floating out?"

"I couldn't know that it was Kitchener's; but a human hand came floating out of a room we opened, and then two corpses. They nearly drove us divers mad, because we thought they were chasing us. The heavy door was swung by the current and we were trapped. One man was killed, another had his back broken. I thought my end had come, and when I came to in a hospital I found my hair had turned white. Did Mr. Zaharoff tell you that story?"

"He never mentioned it during his lifetime; he told me after he was dead."

That statement never failed to make people listen. Lanny narrated how his father had been the European representative of Budd Gunmakers, and how he had met the munitions king at the age of thirteen and become one of his friends. When Zaharoff's duquesa had died, Zaharoff had taken to visiting spiritualist mediums, and Lanny had brought one to him, and many strange and unexplainable incidents had occurred. In one of the latest Zaharoff had revealed his own death, a few hours after it had occurred and before Lanny had read about it in the papers. Recently, at another séance, a voice claiming to be Sir Basil's had told Lanny about the *Hampshire* on which Lord Kitchener had died, and about the gold at the bottom of the sea, being covered with sand, and about a human arm floating out. Lanny had his notebook with him, and read the phrases he had jotted down.

III

The "key-master" told his story in return. He had become known in the capitals of Europe for his skill in opening safes and locks which no one else could master, and some five years ago his exploits had attracted the attention of "Mr. Zaharoff." (Lanny had never heard Sir Basil referred to in that way, but he recognized it as an Americanism, and adopted it politely.) Mr. Zaharoff had invited the key-master to a remodeled old château at Biarritz, and provided for him a very elaborate dinner-party, at which paunchy and gray-bearded financiers from all over Europe drank champagne and danced with young girls until they could no longer stand up but fell asleep piled on top of one another. Mr. Zaharoff himself didn't dance, and very soon realized that he had got up the wrong sort of party for the American; so the two of them sat at the abandoned dinner-table chatting, with a blond beauty wearing a diamond butterfly in her hair sound asleep across the munitions king's knees. "When you invite such young ladies to parties and then don't pay any attention to them, you are considered discourteous," the locksmith explained; and Lanny answered: "I have been there."

What Mr. Zaharoff wanted was for Hofman to take part in an expedition to bring up the ten million dollars' worth of gold which was known to have been in the *Hampshire* strong room. Hofman had sworn off from diving long ago, but now he let himself be tempted by a "fabulous reward." The sunken cruiser had been located and marked by a buoy, and a German salvage ship was fitted out with every sort of modern appliance. The *Hampshire* lay in some four hundred feet of water, and was found to be covered with deep sand; but this was dredged away and entrance was obtained with electric torches. No explosives could be used, because of the huge quantity of munitions inside the cruiser. The strong room was found to be full of great chests containing gold coins, but they were too heavy to be carried by divers and it was necessary to tear them open and scoop the coins into canvas bags, a tedious process. Storms are frequent in the North Sea, and the salvage ship would have to seek port; when it returned, the wreck would be found buried under sand again. It was heart-breaking labor and there were many mishaps, culminating in the steel door of the strong room slamming to on half a dozen divers and bringing them near to death. In all they had got about half a million dollars' worth of the gold. There could be no doubt that the rest was there, just as Lanny had been told in the séance. "But somebody else will have to go for it," remarked the key-master. "My fingers are insured for a hundred thousand dollars—but even so, I don't want to lose them."

"I have no interest in treasure-hunting," replied the son of Budd-Erling, "except to hear about it. The reason I sought you out is not that I wanted to know where the *Hampshire's* gold is lying, but how it came about that an old woman, a Polish ex-servant who lives in my mother's home, came to know that there was gold in the cruiser, and that Sir Basil Zaharoff had sent a diver named Huff, or Huffy, or Huffner, to bring it up."

"You can search me, Mr. Budd," said the Meister-Schlosser.

IV

Lanny found himself attracted to this unusual personality, a man of French parentage who had made his way in the world by the American method of mechanical ingenuity. From childhood he had been fascinated by every sort of lock and had been tempted to take them apart and put them together again. He had made the subject his life study, and now it was his claim that he could open any safe that men could build. This ability had brought him many adventures, taking him to strange parts of the world and bringing him into touch with princes and millionaires. He had not been awed by any of these, but had told them in American fashion that he was pleased to meet them; he had done his job quietly, and at the same time had studied the personalities of his employers and formed shrewd judgments of them.

Lanny invited him to lunch, and listened to stories, some of them humorous, many terrible: children who had locked themselves in chests and were suffocating, butchers and furriers who had got themselves locked in refrigerators and were freezing; bankers who had lost the combinations to their own vaults; misers who had died leaving their fortunes locked up, and heirs who fell to fighting when greenbacks or gold were brought to view. Of course there were unethical opportunities, and it took a strong character and sound judgment to make use of such a talent as Horace Hofman had acquired. He had been called to Moscow to open safes which contained some of the crown jewels, and there had met Stalin, and been allowed to purchase for a nominal sum a wonderful collection of Indian, Chinese, and Russian "animal locks." Taking the gold of the *Hampshire* to Berlin, he had met Hjalmar Schacht, who had invited him to the May Day celebration at which Hitler spoke, soon after his becoming Chancellor. "I was close enough so that I could have stuck a knife into him," said the Meister-Schlosser.

"What did you think of him?" inquired Lanny.

"I wasn't impressed. He was bareheaded, and wore a shabby brown raincoat; he shouted in a high rasping voice—very bad German, I imagine."

"He comes from Austria, the Inn Valley, country of the Steerwashers." Lanny told the story of the peasants who had wished to compete for a prize offered for the best white steer; they had only a black steer, but every day they washed it, and at the competition they had insisted so loudly that it was white that they had carried off the prize.

Lanny himself expressed no opinions about Hitler, but kept the conversation on Germany for a while, so as to discover his guest's point of view. He found that Hofman's mind was not burdened with social theories, but he had the instinctive reaction of a man who has lived in a free country and resents militarism and its trappings. That was enough for Lanny's purposes, and after they had spent part of the afternoon chatting he remarked: "Mr. Hofman, I don't know whether you are able to accept my statement that Zaharoff never mentioned the cruiser *Hampshire* to me during his life. I wouldn't blame you in the least if you couldn't."

"No, I am quite willing to accept it, Mr. Budd. I have heard stories of psychic experiences—though never anything quite so startling, I must admit."

"I have been forced to give thought to the subject, because such things have happened to me many times. It seems to me this case ought to be followed up, and I am wondering if you would be interested to try."

"What do you have in mind?"

"I would like you to try a series of sessions with this Polish medium, and see if you would get any sort of communication from Zaharoff or anybody connected with the treasure hunt."

"Where is the medium?"

"At my mother's home on the Cap d'Antibes. She is getting on in years and I couldn't undertake to bring her to New York, but I would have my mother bring her to Paris, and I am wondering if you, who have done so much traveling, would care to come there as my guest. I would be happy to pay your expenses both ways in return for the satisfaction of my curiosity. Also, you might do a little locksmith work for me; at my mother's estate we have a storeroom in which we keep the paintings of my former stepfather, Marcel Detaze, whose work seems to be acquiring value as the years pass. The keys have been lost, and you may help us to get in. Bring all your tools along, for there might be more work to do on that old place and others."

"That is certainly a generous offer, Mr. Budd. When would you propose for me to come?"

"I am sailing for Southampton at midnight. That is rather short notice, I know, but you tell me you are used to being called at all hours to save people's lives. Is your business in such shape that you could leave it, say for a month?"

"I have a wife and daughter who attend to my affairs when I am away, and we have a competent assistant. It is indeed sudden, as you say——"

"I will be pleased to put a check into your hands, and I will give you bank references."

"That part of it is all right, Mr. Budd; I know your family and also its products. From the point of view of mechanics, there is a certain kinship between a lock and a machine gun. If you are quite certain that you want me to come, and wouldn't be bored before you got through with the experiment——"

"Let me assure you, Mr. Hofman, I have been pursuing this subject patiently since I first got acquainted with this medium, eight years ago. I must have had several hundred sittings with her, and my present stepfather has had one nearly every day. I will show you many notebooks that I have filled, and some of the stories are as strange as any of the real ones you have to tell."

"All right," said the Meister-Schlosser. "You tell me yours and I'll tell you mine!"

V

They traveled on a comfortable English steamer, and all the way Lanny laid himself out to win the confidence of this new friend. He talked psychic research and sometimes art, and in turn listened to locks and keys. He carefully avoided politics, but took the precaution to prepare Hofman's mind for what might be coming, mentioning among

Madame Zyszynski's revelations a young artist couple whom Lanny had met in Berlin many years ago in the course of his business. Ludi and Trudi Schultz were their names, and it must be that they had been opposing the Nazis, for Ludi in a séance had declared that he had been killed by them. Lanny didn't know what had become of the wife, but she had been mentioned and apparently was trying to find her husband, or he to find her. Hofman remarked that the Nazis had evidently found ways to solve the problem of unemployment, but it was hard to excuse their cruelty to their opponents. Lanny answered with words he had heard his father use many times: "The Europeans have not yet learned to change their governments without violence."

They went up to London for a couple of days, because Lanny wanted to see Rick. Nina drove her husband to town, and Lanny told them his story, and a dozen or more of the wild schemes which sprang up overnight like mushrooms in his head. He didn't really know what he was going to do; it depended upon whether the Capitán came, and what that ally would approve. "But I'm never going to rest till somebody gets into the cellars of that château," he vowed.

Rick said: "If there's any way Alfy can help, he will drop his college work and come."

"Alfy is a marked man," was Lanny's answer. "This is no job for him."

He didn't introduce his new friend to the old ones, because Rick, too, was a marked man, and Lanny wished to be rigidly nonpolitical. "Of course I may have to take Hofman into my confidence," he said; "but first I'm going to try to get him to do the work as part of an experiment in psychic research."

"When you get through, give me the story for an anti-Nazi play," said the Englishman.

"You're forgetting the Lord Chamberlain," put in his wife. Nina was a quiet little woman, but now and then she made a remark that showed how well she understood the world she lived in. "Poor Rick! He's always dreaming that if he can get a brilliant enough plot, he can persuade the propertied classes to pay him for threatening their property."

"Beaumarchais did it before the French Revolution," insisted the playwright.

"And then got into trouble, didn't he?"

"He was in jail for a few days, I believe, but he lived to a ripe old age. I hope to do the same, so as to attend the funerals of Mussolini and Hitler!"

VI

Lanny had cabled his mother telling her to bring Madame to Paris for two or three weeks. There was nothing Beauty Budd loved so much in all the world as a trip; she made herself agreeable to her many rich friends so that they would invite her to come along, and one reason she had been heartbroken over Lanny's divorce was that Irma also was a tireless tripper and did it *à la princesse*. This time Beauty was invited to bring her husband, and of course she never traveled without her maid. She guessed that Lanny had had some kind of successful business stroke, and it was like old times to have him spend the money on his mother instead of on some other man's wife or widow.

Arriving at his Paris hotel, Lanny's first thought was of the mail. Nothing from Trudi or Adler, but a note from Monck; he had got a month's furlough, and would be in Paris in a few days. Then Lanny phoned Uncle Jesse and made an appointment to pick him up on the street. Lanny's car had been stored in Paris and now he drove his uncle and listened to the news. Jean had rented the old mill for five hundred francs a month. Also he had found an architectural volume giving the ground plans of famous châteaux, and one of them was Belcour. The Michelin touring maps gave all details about the roads. Jean had become well acquainted with men who had worked in the place all their lives, and he knew several who could be trusted to take bribes.

Another item of information which Lanny had asked for: the Germans who were employed in the château never spent their time off in the neighborhood, but always in Paris, and Jean had found the café which they frequented—a German place, of course. There were several islands of Germans in this great metropolis; Red and Pink and Brown Germans, as Red and Pink and White Russians, and Red and Pink and Black Italians—and so on for most of the nations on the globe. Each of them spoke their home language, ate their home food, read their home newspapers, and argued and fought their home battles; each was a small village, full of intrigue and spying, jealousies and thwarted hopes; each had its heroes and saints, its traitors and informers, and those who lived by pretending to be whatever paid best at the moment.

Uncle Jesse asked no questions; but he was nobody's fool and had his own thoughts. He had known for a score of years that his nephew trailed with the Pinks, at present denounced by the Reds as "Social-Fascists." Jesse knew there was a Socialist underground, just as there was a Communist, and he had no difficulty in surmising that it was some worker of this movement whom the Nazis had seized. Jesse had no idea that his nephew was living a celibate life in Paris, and when the nephew suddenly took to spending a fortune to get somebody out of a dungeon, it was a natural assumption that it was some *Freundin* he was helping.

The deputy knew also that his nephew kept up his old intimacy with Kurt Meissner and the de Bruynes. Manifestly, he couldn't do that without pretending to change his political color, and that was why he had to keep himself in the background. Jesse was willing to play this game for a proper price. He looked upon Lanny in much the same light that Lanny looked upon old Mrs. Fotheringay: a softshell crab that every creature in the sea would take a bite of—and why shouldn't the biggest bite stay in the family? Lanny would bring his uncle large bundles of francs and never ask for an accounting; Jesse would spend part of the money to get Lanny what he wanted, and put the rest away against the time of another election, when a *député de la république française* would have to meet opponents well fortified by capitalist backers. Lanny wouldn't wish to make contributions to Red campaign funds, but he was glad to pay anybody, of whatever political hue, to help him get his Socialist *amie* out of a Nazi dungeon.

VII

In the interest of psychic research, Lanny had agreed not to tell the members of his family anything about Hofman, but merely that he was obliging enough to come all the way from New York to make experiments. Nor would Lanny tell his mother that he was paying the visitor's expenses, because that would excite her curiosity and possibly her discontent. Lanny gave his new friend a check and left it for him to pay his own bills. To Madame he was merely Monsieur Offmah, with a French nasal sound at the end; whenever he requested, she would come to his apartment and take a seat in an overstuffed chair, lean back her head, shut her eyes, sigh and groan a few times, and be in her trance. Lanny said: "I'd better stay out, at least the first few times. It will be interesting to see if Tecumseh connects you with me."

They tried their first séance that evening, and the key-master came out of it quite staggered. The Indian chieftain hadn't appeared, but from the first moment had come a voice which purported to be that of Hofman's mother, who had died when he was a child. She had talked about the farm in the Blue Ridge mountains of Virginia, the house with a red clay floor, the half dozen brothers and sisters, and her own blond hair which had hung in two braids to her knees. She had mentioned various family details, some of which little Horace remembered only dimly. "Really, Mr. Budd, it is most astonishing!" The locksmith had purposely avoided revealing anything about his own origins, and had waited in the full expectation that "Madame" would produce only those episodes of his career about which he had given hints.

"I am glad," Lanny said. "So often the results are disappointing, and I'd hate to have you come all this way for nothing."

Here was a lock that would take the Meister-Schlosser quite a while to open. Was it his mother, or was it only the childhood memories buried in his subconscious mind? The old question of spiritualism versus telepathy; and what was telepathy and how did it work?

Hofman wanted to go right after this problem. He would have liked to have several séances every day, and being a systematic man, he started keeping notebooks like Lanny. He struck up a quick friendship with Parsifal Dingle, who never tired of talking about psychic matters, and had notebooks which would take anyone a long time to study. Parsifal took to attending Hofman's séances, and that brought in the Bhikkhu Sinanayeke, a hundred years dead in a monastery of Ceylon. "Claribel," most fortunately, did not put in her appearance; Parsifal, who had dabbled in hypnotism in earlier years, had tried the experiment of hypnotizing Madame and seeing what he could do with her in that way; all that he got had been Madame's own childhood life, something which had never before come into her séances. He had had the bright idea of giving Madame the hypnotic suggestion that Claribel wouldn't appear any more, and that apparently had ended her.

Lanny in turn had an idea that Madame should be hypnotized and told that Zaharoff would appear. This was done, and the results were startling. "That old man with people shouting at him"—such was Tecumseh's phrase—began speaking with direct voice, and was much pleased to hear the voice of his old friend of the cruiser *Hampshire*. Apparently he had only pleasant memories of this friend, and for the first time since he entered the "spirit world" he manifested that quiet irony which the Knight Commander and Grand Officer had possessed in his life on earth. He mentioned the list of sunken treasure ships which he had shown to Hofman, inviting him to choose the one he would go after; also, he told of the anxiety he had suffered when the salvage-ship came in with one dead and several injured divers, and the time he had had collecting insurance policies and otherwise carrying out his financial obligations to these men. Apparently he was now beyond reach of creditors, and no longer under the necessity of being the "mystery man of Europe."

Horace Hofman got along fine with the "spirits," or whatever they were. He handled them with the same delicate touch he would give to a complicated lock; he spoke in a soft persuasive voice and they responded as if it were magic. He found this fascinating as any game, and remarked to Lanny: "It appears there are stranger things in the deeps of the mind than in the sea."

VIII

Lanny phoned to his friend Leutnant Rörich at the Château de Belcour. "You promised to spend an evening with me"; and the other replied: "You promised to invite me." Lanny explained that he had been to Chicago since their meeting. They made a date for the next evening, and Lanny said: "Bring a friend with you, and we'll make his eyes pop open."

So here came two junior SS officers, prepared to make a night of it. Bruno Fiedler was the name of the other, and he had a tendency to put on fat; his face was round and red, with yellowish bristles which he should have shaved twice a day, but evidently didn't. His eyes were narrow and sly, and Lanny thought at the first glance: "I won't fool you so easily as Rörich."

They were as excited as two schoolboys. They were going to see the real wickedness of Paris, famed throughout the world. Members of the master-race were taught to despise French decadence, but of course they could despise it better if they knew what it was, and they were full of curiosity to find out. Lanny had never gone in for that sort of thing, but he had listened to the conversation of his playboy friends both native and foreign, of artists, journalists, diplomats, munitions buyers, tourists, and the riffraff that came to what they called "gay Paree" in search of thrills which they missed at home.

Lanny took his Nazis to one of the de luxe places of pleasure, where you could have anything for a price. He had ordered a *cabinet particulier* with dinner for six. They noted the extra places and asked who was coming. Lanny replied: "What sort of ladies do you prefer? German?" They said No, they had plenty of German ladies at home. He went on: "Algerian? Senegalese? Or perhaps from Dahomey?" He was being funny; they were starting off on a note of hilarity. They said they wanted French ladies; they had heard reports that French ladies were extraordinarily passionate, but so far they had been disappointed.

Lanny called the waiter and ordered three canapés, three quarts of champagne, and three passionate French ladies. The waiter bowed three times and said "Oui" three times and everybody was merry. Presently there came prancing into the room three ladies, undoubtedly French and reasonably young, all painted and powdered, with bosoms just a trifle more bare than one would find in good society; skirts above the knees, showing embroidered garters slightly soiled, openwork stockings and slippers with abnormally high heels. They came all smiles and dimples, and with practiced eyes each chose her man and made a rush for the seat at his right hand. They gave their first names, and the gentlemen did the same; champagne corks popped and bright conversation in French began quickly. Lanny saw that he had got the youngest and prettiest of the trio, and Leutnant Fiedler didn't like that; in his role of perfect host Lanny said to his lady: "Devote yourself to the other gentleman, Fifi; he is new in Paris and wants more than his share." This was considered delightfully clever, and the fun grew faster.

Lanny left his wine glass almost untouched, and concentrated upon thinking up bright remarks and making his friends have a good time. Presently Hans Rörich noticed that their host was getting less than his share of the delightful sparkling drink, and he said: "You are reneging on us, Herr Budd. Empty your glass!"

"I have to make an embarrassing confession," replied the American. "I cannot drink champagne."

"Why not?"

"It goes straight to my head."

The young Nazis thought that was delightful. An American millionaire, such a man of the world and so self-assured, having to admit that he couldn't carry his liquor! "For shame on you!" cried Fiedler. "Drink it down!" .

"You bring us out for an evening and then spoil all the fun!" put in the other Nazi. Of course that was part of the fun.

"I go clean off my head," Lanny pleaded. "I behave like a fool."

"*Kolossal!*" exclaimed Fiedler; and Fifi clapped her hands: "*Ça sera fameuse!*"

The host flushed with embarrassment. "Really," he said, "you won't like it. I say things that are shocking."

"*Merveilleuse!*" exclaimed Toinette, and Belle and Fifi pounded on the table with their knives and forks: "*Buvez! Dites les choses horribles!*"

In short, they were absolutely determined to see Lanny drunk, and he would have been the poorest of sports if he had refused to oblige them. "All right," he said. "It's your funeral," and quaffed his glass of "fizz-water." The waiter, sharing the fun, filled it up promptly, and they wanted their host to drink that, but he said: "No, no, please. Wait a while." So they waited, watching him covertly while pretending to talk about other things.

IX

In the course of two decades of fashionable life, Lanny Budd had had opportunity to observe the effects of liquor upon a number of fortune's darlings; one of them Dick Oxnard, painter of genius and favorite of New York society, who had drunk himself into an early grave. Lanny knew every symptom; so, in a minute or two, he put a silly grin on his face and then tried hard to get it off but couldn't. The Nazi offi- cers looked at one another and winked; Rörich looked at his one lady and Fiedler at his two, and all were delighted. Lanny would blink and roll his eyes, and then all five would giggle and hardly be able to stop.

"Drink some more!" exclaimed Rörich, and Fifi offered Lanny's glass to him. He took it and held it unsteadily, spilling some. He rose, lifted it high, waved it unsteadily in the air, and proclaimed: *"Heil Hitler!"* Of course the two Nazis rose, and held up their glasses; the French ladies, having been hired to do what they were told, followed suit. They drank the toast and resumed their seats. Lanny blinked, gulped two or three times, and rose again, exclaiming: *"Der grösste Mann der Welt!"* All rose and drank again, and he said: *"Mein Freund Adi! Prosit, Adi!"* and drank a bit more. He took it in small sips, talking wildly in between, which enabled him to seem to be taking a great deal.

Drunkenness affects different men in different ways, and now with Lanny Budd it took the form of singing the praises of *lieb' Vaterland* and all its achievements. Hiccuping now and then, and stumbling over his own tongue, he said that German was the language he liked to speak and Germans were the people he liked to be with; he was one of them in soul, and begged them to let him see them often. He hoped they would excuse him for weeping with happiness when he spoke of his visits to Schloss Stubendorf as a boy, and of Kurt Meissner, who had been getting ready to become the greatest musician in the world; of Heinrich Jung, son of the *Oberförster*, who, without knowing it, had been getting ready to become one of the leaders of the Hitlerjugend. He told how, after the war, Heinrich had visited the great Adi in prison, and had told Lanny about this new Führer, destined to redeem first Germany and then the world.

"The world is rotten," declared the playboy. "France is rotten—look at this and you can see how rotten it is." He waved his hand, indicating the room, the table, the food, the *Damen*. He was speaking German, so the *Damen* didn't know they were *Damen* and wouldn't hear that they were *verfault*. Lanny hiccuped and said *Verzeihung*, and explained that it did him grief when he thought about the corruption of *Frankreich*, and he became *absolut schwärmerisch* when he thought about the virtues of *Deutschland*. He didn't mind piling it on, because he was supposed to be drunk, and by that time his friends were somewhat drunk also.

It was a moving speech, received with many a *Hurra* and a *Heil*. It culminated in the announcement that rotten *Frankreich* was going to be cleaned up and so was rotten *Europa*. Lanny knew all about it, and guessed that his National-Socialist friends knew also; but perhaps they didn't realize how near *Der Tag* had come. "We are ready to act, we Hooded Men,"—and Lanny proceeded to take off his hood and reveal himself as a leader of the coming leisure-class coup d'état, one of its paymasters, and an intimate of the men of action who were going to carry it through. Lanny took another sip of champagne and named these leaders and their important social positions; he told where the arms were stored and named the key places which were to be seized— he didn't have to worry about accuracy, because the young Nazis were in a state of exaltation, seeing their Fifth Column taking possession of France without having to fire a shot, and they weren't in any condition to make notes or remember details. Lanny watched the women, to make sure they gave no signs of understanding German, but were proceeding in the normal way to get as much champagne into them as an American millionaire was willing to pay for.

X

This wasn't the sort of conversation the two Schutzstaffel officers had come prepared for; and presently the befuddled host realized it, and hiccuped: "I'm doing all the talking. I am drunk, by God—just as I told you!" He started to grow unhappy because of his bad manners; but his friends consoled him—it was most intellectual conversation. They wished to prove that they too could take part in such conversation, and assured him that Americans were great people and worthy of sharing Germany's high destiny. Lanny Budd and his guests would be friends for life. Yes, they knew what the Hooded Men were doing, and were ready to help whenever called upon.

"*Nein, nein, wartet nur*—you wait—let the French do it—hic!" Lanny had a different role for his Nazi comrades. "What you do is take care of the Germans—German traitors. You know you got German traitors in Paris?"

The host was started on another confused discourse. There were Reds and all sorts of betrayers of the Fatherland in Paris, slandering the great Führer and noble Nazis, and sending their lies back into Germany. "We Cagoulards have spies among them and we know who they are; maybe you—hic—like me to tell you?"

The Schutzstaffel officers said they didn't need any Auslanders telling them about German traitors; they had their own means of watching the vermin—but all the same they were grateful to their American friend for this warning. The three had another explosion of *Schwärmerei;* they clasped hands across the table—this was easy because the corrupted French ladies were by now sunk back in their chairs, about ready to fall asleep. The three uncorrupted gentlemen sang a song telling the dear Fatherland that it could sleep in peace because its herosons were keeping watch. They sang about the streets being free to the brown battalions, and then about Germany belonging to us today and tomorrow the rest of the world. In between songs the nazified American would sip a few more drops of champagne and renew his offer to find out for his German friends what the traitors and snakes and vermin were doing here in Paris.

"*Nein, nein,*" Rörich insisted. "We have our ways to take care of them—*nicht wahr, Bruno?*" And Bruno, whose face was now the shape and color of a harvest moon rising over dusty fields, replied: "*Du musst es ja wissen!*"

"What do you do with them?" demanded the American. "Take them back to Germany?"

"We take care of them! They don't spill any more poison in the Ausland."

Lanny became excited. "*Pass auf, Menschenkind!* They are fooling you. They are sending stuff into Germany all the time. I have seen it with my own eyes. Heinrich Jung showed me some of it in his office in Berlin."

Maybe that wasn't exactly drunken conversation; but the young Nazis were drunk enough by now so that they couldn't tell the difference. They were being challenged, and had their honor to defend. Rörich mumbled: "Maybe a few"; and Fiedler proclaimed angrily: "Nobody pays any attention to such *Pöbel.*"

"You are mistaken," insisted Lanny. "The Führer told me himself it is a great menace. Do you mean to oppose the Führer's word?"

No, of course; neither of them dreamed of opposing the Führer's word. Neither of them could say that they had ever been spoken to by the Führer; but here this American made the claim, and proceeded to prove it before their eyes. He pulled out the clipping from the Munich newspaper. "Here is an article telling of my visit to the Führer at the Braune Haus, and here is my picture to prove that it was nobody else. I had called on him once before in his apartment in Berlin, and afterwards I visited him for an evening in Haus Wachenfels, at Berchtesgaden. I played Beethoven for him and he had Kannenberg sing songs for me. Do you know Kannenberg?"

They were staring at him, awestricken. They had heard of the fat and jolly *Bierkellner* who was the Führer's steward, but had never laid eyes upon him. How could they stand up before such authority?

"The Führer said to me: 'It is a grave peril to my *Regierung*, the activity of these *Schweinehunde* in the Ausland. They must be rooted out. They lie about us; they poison the outside world against us. *Sie müssen ausgerottet werden'*—hic! That is what the Führer said; and what are you in Paris doing about it?"

XI

This was, for all practical purposes, as if the Führer himself were here, demanding an accounting. The two underlings were greatly distressed. "We are doing our best," pleaded Rörich. "We know these people and we watch them."

"Watching is not enough. They have to be put out of business. They have to be liquidated—purged!"

"There is a limit to what we can do in France, *mein Lieber*."

"There should be no limit. If I, an American, am willing to overthrow the government of France for you—hic—why should you be afraid of a few sneaking traitors hiding in the slums of this city? You should seize them and break them to pieces."

"We have done it a few times, Herr Budd." It was still Rörich speaking. "That is Bruno's job."

"What do you do, Bruno?"

"I give them something they don't forget in a hurry."

Lanny was working himself into a really fierce mood. He stuck out one forefinger and swung it down toward the table. "Woosh! Woosh!" —the whistling of the whip. "You give them *die Peitsche*?"

"*Ja, gewiss.*"

"*Also!* You may believe me, I know about it! Reichminister General Göring sent his staff officer, Hauptmann Furtwaengler, and took me down into the Columbus Haus, and I watched what they did to a fat Jewish *Schweinehund*. Solomon Hellstein was his name, the banker— you know the Hellstein Bank in Berlin?"

"*Natürlich, Herr Budd.*"

"They stretched him out on a bench with his fat fanny bare and they laid it on good and plenty. How that old Jew did yell! You should have a place like that here in Paris."

"*Zerbrechen wir uns nicht den Kopf, Herr Budd. Wir haben so etwas.*"

We have it! Those were the words Lanny wanted to hear, and there was exultation in his voice. "Give it to them good and plenty!" he cried. "Make them talk!"

"Bruno makes them. It is his job."

"You do it yourself, Bruno?"

"I flay them alive."

"You have good muscles?" The son of Budd-Erling got up, stagger- ing slightly, and felt his Nazi friend's arm. "*Ja*, those are tough! Let's try them!" Laughing wildly, he picked up Fifi, who had fallen asleep in her chair, bored by a long conversation which had nothing to do with ladies. She woke suddenly when Lanny turned her upside down over the chair and pulled up her very scanty skirt. "Show me what you do!"

The woman started struggling and kicking and the two Germans started roaring with laughter. It was truly a hilarious scene. Fifi squealed, but Lanny held her down, and kept calling to Bruno: "Go on! Show me!"

"I have no whip," protested the SS man.

"Take a napkin and tie some knots in it." Then to Fifi: "Shut up! He only wants to whip you."

"But I don't want to be whipped!" wailed the girl. She was starting to fight, and seemed capable; but Lanny said: "Keep still. I'll pay you a thousand francs." A girl in her business learns about the whims of rich gentlemen. She became suddenly still, and Lanny turned to Bruno with mounting excitement. "Now! Go to it!"

"*Aber, Herr Budd!*" protested the Nazi.

"What is the matter? Are you afraid?"

"*Nein, Herr Budd——*"

"Don't you know there are women among those Red vermin? Don't you ever have women prisoners to whip?"

"*Ja, natürlich—aber——*"

"And you spare them? You don't break them down—hic—make them tell what they are up to?"

"*Nein, nein*——"

"Have you got softhearted? Afraid to defend your National Socialism?"

"*Natürlich nicht—nimmer, Herr Budd*——"

"*Also, was ist los?* Don't you know that your Führer whips his women? Have you never heard that?"

"*Ja, ja—aber, hier ist nicht Berlin, Herr Budd; hier ist Paris.*"

XII

Lanny, working himself into a passion, was threatening to become ugly, as many drunks do. Hans Rörich, who had known him longer, felt it necessary to intervene. He laid his hands on his host's shoulders pleadingly. "*Bitte, bitte, Herr Budd*—you must make allowances. We are connected with the Embassy, and we cannot have any sort of disturbance in a foreign country. It is not gentlemanly of you—*nicht korrekt!*"

Lanny's mood changed suddenly—this also being a characteristic of drunks. He had been rebuked, and his feelings were wounded. A look of despair came upon his face, and he turned away and hid it in his hands. "*Ach!* I have offended you! You will never respect me again!"

The two Nazis doubtless had handled drunks before, and understood all this. They grinned to each other as they replied: "*Nein, nein, Herr Budd,* don't take it so seriously."

"You made me get drunk! I told you—hic—I would play the fool." Lanny shook with sobs.

"It is nothing, Herr Budd, *wirklich*—it is all good fun. Bruno will forgive you—won't you, Bruno?"

"Of course, I forgive you, Herr Budd—*macht gar nichts.*"

Lanny was hard to console. He sank into a chair and would not show his face, in spite of the efforts of his friends. They would never love him, they would never respect him again. He kept up this little comedy because he wanted them to have something else to occupy their minds; something to laugh over, and thus forget the grave admissions they had made. A crazy American millionaire who wanted to see a woman whipped and who then wept like a spoiled kid because nobody loved him! Were they all as *verrückt* as that? *Ein verrücktes Land*, full of gangsters and bootleggers and cowboys and wild Indians—you could see it in the cinema, and be sure that such a land would be ripe for taking over when the time came.

At last the wild man let himself be comforted. Then he wanted to drink another toast. "*Der Tag in Frankreich!*" he announced, and of course they drank it; the women, too, neither knowing nor caring what the words meant, so long as it was champagne in the glasses. Poor Fifi, who saw her thousand francs vanish like so many champagne bubbles! The host observed her state of melancholy and gave her a hundred-franc note, which she quickly folded up and stuck into her stocking.

To his friends the son of Budd-Erling pleaded: "*Bitte, nicht mehr trinken*—hic—don't let me have any more." They laughed heartily and said they had learned their lesson—they were scared to death of him. To take his mind off the bottles they started petting the girls, who had been so cruelly neglected. Lanny remarked: "There are rooms upstairs. What do you say?"

They said "Yes," with evident satisfaction. As they started to leave the room, Fifi attached herself to the wild American; but he said: "*Non, non—ce monsieur,*" pointing to Bruno, "he wants two." He put her on Bruno's vacant arm, saying to the partly befuddled Nazi: "It's all right; I'll get another." He escorted the five of them to the elevator and saw them inside. Then he stepped back, and the door was closed.

He returned to the *cabinet*. The waiter was there, and Lanny said: "*Addition, s'il vous plaît,*"—and not a single "hic." He examined the account, making sure that it included the rooms and everything. He paid it, together with a generous tip. "*Ces boches sont gentils, n'est-ce pas?*" he remarked. "Those Germans are nice, aren't they!" He took his hat and walked out—strangely enough, perfectly straight, and when an attendant brought his car and started, he didn't weave in the traffic or bump into anything, in spite of the fact that the greater part of his mind was in the cellars of the Château de Belcour. He had got what he had come for—the admission that the Nazis had prisoners there, that they tortured them, and that a woman was among them.

10

Falsely True

I

WAITING for Monck to arrive, Lanny sat in at séances with Hofman and Madame. He sat as still as a mouse, hoping that Tecumseh would ignore him, and for a while this succeeded. Lanny concentrated his mind upon the image of Trudi; he "rooted" as hard as he could for Trudi to come, and this was a worthwhile experiment, whether one chose to believe that there were spirits in the neighborhood or that the subconscious mind of Madame was weaving fantasies. If telepathy was a reality, a medium's mind might receive suggestions just as if it were under hypnosis.

No Trudi; but after Lanny's strenuous mental labor had gone on intermittently for a couple of days, the Indian chieftain said: "There is a man here named Loodveek. That is a German name, is it not? He is young and has blond hair. He has been here before."

Hofman had been posted as to what he should do if such a personality appeared; so now he said: "We are trying to get in touch with Trudi."

"He says that Trudi is not here. He is worried about her."

"Does he know where she is?"

"He says she is in trouble; he feels that, but does not know where. There is an old man trying to help her, and the old man is suffering, too. The old man is stout and kind; he is some sort of servant who does not like what he has to do; he is in a dangerous position. Loodveek tries to give me his name, but he doesn't know it very well himself. It is something like Powell."

"The German name Paul is pronounced Powl. Could it be that?" It was still Hofman asking questions, and Lanny sat there, ready to burst with a dozen others he wanted asked.

"It might be," said the control. "I don't understand these foreign ways of saying things and I don't see any sense in them."

"Can you find out if Trudi is in the spirit world?"

"This man doesn't say. He says Trudi was his wife; I ask him why he says 'was,' and he doesn't answer. He looks like an educated man but very unhappy. Maybe he can't speak but a few words, I don't know why. He says the old man groans all the time."

There was a silence. When that happened, Tecumseh was apt to fade away; it was necessary to keep talking to him. But Hofman had asked everything that Lanny had told him to. So now Lanny ventured a timid question: "Pardon me, Tecumseh, could one of the old man's names be Adler?"

"Oh, so it's you!" exclaimed the Amerindian, dead a couple of hundred years. "I haven't been having the pleasure of hearing from you. Have you been biting holes in your tongue?"

"I have been trying to oblige you, Tecumseh."

"You are trying to fool me. You sit there thinking that telepathy stuff at me all the time."

"Does that bother you?"

"Of course it does; it is the wrong suggestion; it works backwards. You are one of these smart intellectuals and think you have to understand everything with your mind; but there are things older than the mind, millions of years older. When a bee builds a hexagonal cell, does it have to go to an engineer to find out how?"

"How does the bee find out, Tecumseh?"

"He has it already inside him; his intuition. You have it, too, if you would let it work."

"How can I learn to do that?"

"Have you ever heard the saying: 'Except ye become as little children, ye shall not enter into the kingdom of heaven'? What does that mean to you? Put yourself in an attitude of faith and you experience the reality of faith; put yourself in the attitude of skepticism and you become as a hollow nut, all shell and no meat inside. Take that off and pray over it, Mister Worldly Wiseman."

"Really and truly, I am trying to do that very thing, Tecumseh. I am in trouble and I need help. Can't you give me another chance?"

"Just what do you want?"

"I want that man Ludi to talk to me directly. Can't you persuade him?"

"The man is gone. There is something the matter with him that I don't understand. I think he is the same kind of smart-aleck that you are—he cannot believe that he is a spirit, or that he is still alive and can talk if he believes that he can talk."

"Do a man's doubts follow him into the spirit world?"

"The sin of intellectual pride is self-punishing; God doesn't have to do anything to you—you do it to yourself, and this German fellow is doing it, and maybe also that Trudi who was his wife."

Lanny said: "You seem to know the Bible, Tecumseh. Do you remember the story of the man who said: 'Lord, I believe; help thou mine unbelief'? I say that prayer to you. We have known each other a long time, and you must know there is some reason why I come back again and again, in spite of the bad times you give me."

"Well, if you want to get results, stop shooting that telepathy business at me."

"Just what shall I shoot?"

"Tell yourself: 'There are spirits and I know there are spirits, just as live and real as I am, and I want such and such a spirit to come and talk to me.' Ask, and it shall be given you; seek, and ye shall find; knock, and it shall be opened unto you."

"Thanks, Tecumseh. I'll do my honest best."

"That's enough now. You tire me out with all these arguments. Remember, I was nothing but a stone-age man born too late, and I never heard any of these long words that you highbrows have made up. Where do you suppose I got them from?"

"God knows, old friend."

"God knows—but He won't tell!" With that, Madame gave a violent start, and when she came out of her trance, she said: "Did somebody have a quarrel?"

When the two men had left the séance room, the incorrigible intellectual remarked to his locksmith friend: "It seems to me the stone-age man is taking over the whole mental apparatus of my stepfather."

II

The President of the United States kept his promise and delivered that "quarantine" speech in Chicago. The American *Herald Tribune* in Paris reported the event and gave several paragraphs, some of which Lanny recognized. The rest was of the same tenor, and the effect of the speech was what F.D. had foretold. In fashionable society everybody argued pro or con, and a week later came the New York papers, full of the same debate. The policy of the State Department, carefully built up for the past decade and a half, had been dumped overboard in half an hour. "Stop Foreign Meddling!" clamored the *Wall Street Journal*.

Robbie Budd made it a rule to write his son every month, but this was a special occasion, and the fabricator of airplanes poured out his displeasure in a long screed. Here was definite proof that our national and international affairs were in the hands of a madman. We were going to take all the troubles of the world on our shoulders, and be played for a sucker by every tricky diplomat and his mistress. It was Woodrow Wilson all over again, only worse, because we told the world that we could learn nothing from experience. We would carry this burden all alone; for where in the world was any other nation looking out for any interest but its own? Where was there a foreign statesman who would even pretend to be thinking about any other nation? Even the English, the world's masters of hypocrisy, had given that up as *vieux jeu*.

To Lanny this was playing over an old phonograph record; Robbie had been dinning it into his ears all through the Peace Conference of Paris. Robbie wanted his country to be the best-armed in the world, as its wealth and resources entitled it to be, and then to attend strictly to the affairs of the Western Hemisphere. Let Europe stew in its own juice; let Britain and Germany fight it out—from Robbie's point of view it mattered little which of them came out on top. Just make it plain to them that they had to keep out of South and Central America! In the days when Lanny had felt like teasing his father he had asked: "Suppose that some day there should come a nice, carefully contrived revolution in Brazil—not a Nazi revolution, but one of pure native Brazilian Fascism—what would you do about it? And suppose the thing spread all over South America, and you woke up some morning and discovered that the Germans had the continent in the bag?"

But just now Lanny wasn't teasing anybody. Instead, he wrote: "I had lunch with Baron Tailor again and he asked about you. When do you plan to come?"

III

Bernhardt Monck arrived in Paris. He called Lanny's hotel and spoke one word: "Belchite." Lanny said: "Where are you?" The answer was: "I'll be walking on the Rue du Rivoli, where the jewelry shops are."

Lanny hardly knew the Capitán at first glance. He had got himself a suit of old clothes and had gone back to his role of sailor enjoying shore leave. Lanny drove him out into the country, so that no one might see the grandson of Budd's in unfashionable company. They spent the day, having plenty to talk about. This was the man to whom Lanny meant to tell everything, and he found the telling a great relief.

He set forth the different items of evidence he had collected, tending to show that Trudi was in the château. He told about his Red uncle, and about Jean, and the mill; about the drunken party, and the admissions his Nazi friends had made; about Kurt, and the use Lanny hoped to make of this friendship; about the Führer, and the clipping from the Munich newspaper; about the fat General and his paintings—Monck must have all the details in his mind, for there might come some crisis when there would be no time for explanations.

Lanny saved Madame and Tecumseh and the spirits until the last, they being a hard pill for a Marxist to swallow. The founder of this Social-Democratic religion had lived at a time when mechanistic theories of the universe had prevailed in Germany, and he had included them among his ten commandments; therefore "dialectical materialism" and "scientific Socialism" were supposed to be inextricably bound together —whereas, so far as Lanny could see, they had no connection whatever. He knew the materialist mind, as dogmatic as any Pope's, and he became apologetic when he brought up this subject. "You may think it's all superstition and fraud, but it's a part of the story, and before I get through you will see how it may help us in our job. So I beg you to listen patiently."

"O.K.," said the sailor. " '*Raus damit!*"

Lanny went back to the beginning and told how his stepfather had picked up this old Polish woman in the cheapest sort of medium parlor in a cheap neighborhood in New York, and of the things she had told them which she had no normal way of knowing; how Lanny had brought Zaharoff to her without saying one word about him, and she had revealed among other things the fact that this Greek agent had once pleaded guilty in the Bow Street police court in London to having borrowed money on four hundred and sixty-nine sacks of gall belonging to another man. "As God is my witness," said Lanny, "I didn't even know what gall was; but my friend Rick found the record in the *Times*, of a date more than sixty years ago."

He told about Zaharoff's reporting his own death, and then of his revelation concerning the *Hampshire*, and the "key-master" whose name was Huff or Huffy or Huffner, and who could tell Lanny about the gold. Lanny said: "I had never had anything to do with locksmiths, and I supposed the only men who knew how to open safes were burglars. But I found this man Hofman, and here he is in Paris, absorbed in trying experiments with Madame. He has already heard communications about Trudi—and of course you can see how useful he could be to us in the château, if we could persuade him to take the risk."

"Do you think he would be willing?"

"I don't know; I have waited to get your advice before broaching the subject."

"Tell me just what you have in mind."

"Roughly, this. I shall be a guest at the château. Sooner or later those Nazis will have to invite me, and I'll find a pretext to stay overnight. Also, I'll have some way of getting word to you. I will make friends with the dogs—I've already begun at that, and I'll keep them out of the way while you and Hofman either climb the wall, or he picks the lock of one of the gates. I will leave one of the ground-floor windows open, and you and Hofman will go down into the cellars and open the doors of whatever dungeons you find."

"Do they have a nightwatchman?"

"That's one of the things I have to find out. I may have to stay more than one night."

"And suppose we get caught—what happens to us?"

"There mustn't be any fighting; if you can't get away you must give up. My father employs one of the best *avocats* in Paris, and I will go to him as my father's son and put the case in his hands; he will of course keep me out of it—my function will be to guarantee him a thumping fee. He will go to the French police, and so you will quickly be turned over to them. The *avocat* will take up the matter with the German embassy, and I haven't a doubt that he can bluff them into backing down. You see the situation; you are not burglars but political crusaders, trying to save a refugee who is held in durance in defiance of French law. If you are prosecuted, members of the Embassy staff must appear in open court and face cross-examination as to what was going on in the château. The scandal would be terrific, and I feel certain they would never face it. They would just tell the police that it was all a mistake, and request them kindly to drop the matter."

IV

Such was the program; crazy enough, but not so crazy as the ideas Lanny had suggested in Spain. Monck admitted that if Lanny could really manage to spend a night in the château, and if Hofman could be persuaded to do his fancy work, there might be a chance to get Trudi out. The most serious flaw he could find in the plan was that it involved Lanny's taking the locksmith, a comparative stranger, into the most precious secret of his life. "You will be breaking your promise to Trudi."

Lanny said: "I have been worrying over that. It may be that I can get by without telling Hofman anything of the sort. He is not interested in politics, and I don't have to be either. Suppose you come to me, as a former friend of Trudi's, and tell me the horrible story of her being tortured by the Nazis, and I introduce you to Hofman and let you tell it to him. My heart is touched and I offer to put up the money to save her, but I can't be known in connection with the matter, because of my father's business relations with General Göring, to say nothing of my own. That won't make me seem very heroic, but there's no reason why I should, and I surely don't seem it to myself, with all this lying that I hate so utterly. But it seems to be what the situation calls for; Trudi wanted it, and you want it, and—" Lanny stopped himself; he nearly said: "and the President."

"That part of it's all right," said Monck. "When you set out to kill people, as I'm doing, you surely don't mind lying to them, or about them."

"I'm talking about lying to Hofman, who is a fine fellow, I am certain."

"My guess is, he'd prefer not to know that you're a Socialist or have any political connections. If he doesn't know it, then what he does is a purely humanitarian thing. Those Nazis, holding a woman in prison, are criminals, and nobody has to be squeamish in trying to get the better of them."

"All right," Lanny said. "Then let us say, you learned about Trudi's plight, and came to me because you knew that I had been helping to promote her art work. I'll show her sketches to Hofman and convince him that she is a real personality. I think you had better be something a bit higher in the social scale than a sailor. What else have you been?"

"I was secretary of a labor union for a while—a Socialist union, to be sure."

"We can leave off the Pink label. You were the secretary of a union, and you employed Ludi Schultz as a commercial artist, and in his studio you met his wife. Now you've learned from refugees in Paris where she is and came to me to ask financial support. I explained to you my father's position and my own; I will put up the money, but only on condition that my name is never to be mentioned by anyone. I introduce you to Hofman and you persuade him to help you. You don't tell him that I am going to be in the château. You are a German, and you have a confederate who has a job there. All that I'm doing is putting up a bunch of money. You can tell Hofman I'll pay him anything within reason for the job."

"You will confirm that?"

"Of course. But I think the proposal ought to come from you, because you are the one who has dug up the case and has got all steamed up about it. You present it emotionally, as a friend of Trudi's, while I'm interested only because I consider her a great artist. You know how it is with us rich people—we let others do the dirty work."

The ex-sailor and soldier didn't smile often, but this humor was in accord with Marxist ideology, and he answered, in American: "You said it!"

V

The Capitán went over the story a second time, looking for flaws, and finally he said that he was willing to work over it and see how it developed—even to the extent of attending a spiritualist séance for Trudi's sake! Lanny gave him a sum of money and said: "Get yourself a better suit and a room in a hotel. I'll let Hofman bring Madame to you, because he has learned how to conduct these affairs, and Tecumseh is inclined to waste time in discussions with me." Lanny could read the mind of a hard-boiled "monist," hearing a phrase like that; he added: "Take it as a game, and play it according to the rules."

"All right," said the other. "Tell them."

Lanny set forth the proper way to treat Madame and her "control." Nothing of any importance might happen, and in that case it would be tedious, and seem very silly. "Whatever happens, do me the honor to believe that I haven't said one word to the old woman about you, and I shall not. What name will you take?"

"Any you say."

"All right, you are Monsieur Branting. I'll tell Hofman you are a man I met in Berlin many years ago; you want to make a test, and for that reason I am telling him no more about you. You will take my word for that?"

"Yes, surely, Genosse Budd."

"Don't let that slip past your tongue again. Better call me Lanny. When the séance is over, call a taxi and send Madame to a picture show —that is her greatest joy in life—and you get acquainted with Hofman and tell him whatever you feel the circumstances warrant. Take him out to dinner and get him feeling good. From now on you are the boss!"

So they had a séance, and Tecumseh said there was that old man with the guns going off all around him. The old man said he was lonely and still couldn't find his wife. He said he was trying not to worry about all that gold being lost, for after all, when had gold ever made anybody happy? That didn't sound like Zaharoff, but maybe he was becoming spiritualized. Tecumseh remarked: "His gold is sour grapes"—which gave the impression that the stone-age man was becoming sophisticated. Tecumseh had never liked Sir Basil, and when he took his departure the chieftain said: "Boom, boom, boom—twenty-one guns!"

Next there was reported a little girl with blond hair in pigtails, speaking to someone she called "Pay-tah." That gave Monck a jolt, for it had been his childhood nickname; he had been christened Peter. He had had a little sister who had died young and whom he barely remembered. Now she said that she was happy in the spirit world, and kept her love for him. This wasn't exactly evidential, but the name was unusual, and Monck couldn't figure out how anybody in this company could have heard it.

He was hoping for more news from home; but, alas, here came the insufferable Claribel, bouncing and eager to display her poetical talents. She asked for a name, and Monck took a chance and said "Ludi." Evidently she thought he was speaking Latin, for she started on one of her visions, having to do with gladiators marching into an arena and ending with the lament that "Men can still find no pleasure so great as killing their fellowmen." She asked for more, and Monck tried her first with a German word and then a Spanish. She was equal to both, and perhaps would have understood Tagalog or Marathi if his travels had taken him that far. When the tiresome séance was over, Hofman remarked: "Madame will have to be hypnotized again."

VI

Having the locksmith alone in his hotel room, Monck poured out the sad story of a young woman artist of talent which had attracted the attention of experts even in France, and whose only offense had been refusing to accept the dictates of the Nazi tyrants and continuing to circulate exposures of their cruelty. The Nazis had caught her husband, and for four or five years nothing had been heard of him; no doubt he had been murdered and buried in quicklime. The widow had gone on with her activities, first in Berlin and then in Paris. Monck had got some of her literature from friends of the underground, and he gave it to Hofman to read; the highest and purest idealism, he said; a defense of the basic rights of freedom of speech and of religion which everyone in America took for granted.

The Nazi gangsters had kidnaped this woman, and were holding her somewhere under the Château de Belcour. They would torture her to make her reveal the names of her associates, and if she refused, they would never let up till they had killed her. Several refugees in Paris had disappeared, and everyone was satisfied that this was what had become of them; one of the Nazi spies among the refugees had confessed it.

Horace Hofman simply couldn't believe such a tale. He thought he was living in a civilized world, and such things happened only in movies. Why didn't the refugees appeal to the Paris police? Monck proceeded to set forth a still more melodramatic situation: the chief of the Paris police was a Fascist, at present engaged in a conspiracy to overthrow his own government, and permitting the enemies of his country to accumulate stores of arms for that purpose. The government, the army and navy and air force of France were riddled with such disloyalty, and anyone who went to the police on such an errand as Hofman suggested ran a risk of being himself locked up. Certainly someone in authority would give the Nazis a tip, and their victim would be whisked into Germany overnight.

Persuading an ordinary American to believe things like that was a long job of education. Monck had to tell how Göring and his followers had set fire to the Reichstag building in order to blame it on the Communists and justify their campaign of terrorism. He had to tell about the "Blood Purge" and what that meant—that Hitler, who had got power as a radical agitator and then had sold out to the big steel and munitions interests of his country, had murdered in cold blood some twelve hundred of his own followers who had tried to stick to their old program. He had to tell how the Nazis had killed the premiers of Austria and Rumania who had opposed them; likewise the king of Yugoslavia and the foreign minister of France. Hofman had read about these events, but had hardly realized their significance and had already forgotten them. America was such a well-behaved land, and so far off!

When the locksmith asked what they wanted of him, Monck pledged him to secrecy, and told him that he and other members of the underground were attempting to get Trudi out of the château. They had got an agent inside the place who would keep the dogs out of the way and leave one of the windows unfastened. What they wanted of Hofman was to come along and open the doors of whatever dungeons or lockups might be found in the cellars of the building.

"Just as simple as that!" said the Meister-Schlosser, with a smile. "It sometimes takes a lot of time to open a lock that one is not familiar with; it takes tools, some of which it is a near-crime to possess."

"You have them," replied Monck, "and we will carry them in for you and carry them out again."

"And suppose we are caught and these amiable Nazis give us a dose of their torture?"

"Me, yes—but you, no. You are an American, and the last thing they want at this stage is any unfavorable publicity in your country. Our friends will be on watch outside, and if we fail to come out by a certain hour they will go to the American embassy, and more important yet, to the American newspapermen. We have the money to pay a first-class French *avocat*, and of course to pay you."

"I would never think of taking money for anything of this sort. If I did it, it would be because I believe in fair play and decency. I have been asked to commit crimes more than once in my life, and if I did this it would be the first."

"Strictly speaking, it is burglary; but we will go unarmed, and will be acting against kidnapers, who can hardly come into court with clean hands."

"Suppose we opened the doors and found nobody inside, and then we were caught—what then?"

"We would have to produce the evidence we have of various persons who have disappeared in Paris, and what the Nazis have been doing at the château. They would find out what we had on them, and would have to back down; they aren't ready for war, and they don't want to be exposed until that time. I point out that you would be with us in those cellars and could make quite sure that we didn't take anything but Trudi, or some other person we might find being held by force."

VII

The locksmith said he'd have to have time to think this over; and what he did was to come straight to Lanny. "Mr. Budd, I have never in my life let myself be played for a sucker, and if you wish me to have anything to do with this enterprise you will have to deal with me openly. It is one thing if it is supported by a man of property and standing like yourself, and quite another if it is the proposal of a mysterious German who calls himself a 'labor union secretary' and who I suspect is going under a false name. Just what do you know about him?"

"I know him to be a man of good faith, whom I have tested and trust to the limit."

"You believe this Trudi story?"

"I used to know Trudi well, and I did what I could to make her known as an artist of rare talent. You may recall that I mentioned her to you on the steamer. I haven't the slightest doubt that Branting's statements are true."

"This is a serious matter for a man of my calling, Mr. Budd. Such a blunder could ruin me forever. You will have to trust me as I trust you. Are you backing this enterprise?"

"I am backing it to the limit. I cannot come forward myself, because of my father's position and my own business in Germany; but I feel it my duty to help a woman of noble character, of sensitiveness and refinement, who has been made the victim of an outrage. Let me show you her work, which speaks for itself and for her."

Lanny brought out a portfolio of photographs. "I have the originals of these in my storeroom at Juan. Most of them are sketches which Trudi would throw off in a few minutes. She loved to draw children and poor old men and women she saw in the street; she would watch them and then draw them from memory. She has extraordinary fineness and clarity of line, and you see that whether it is pencil or crayon, every stroke counts."

Lanny was launched upon one of his persuasive discourses on art. He dealt with technical matters, but in simple language which an uninstructed hearer could follow. "There is a soul in these drawings," he said. "Hardly one of them is commonplace; each gives you a feeling—weariness or gaiety, sorrow, hunger, despair. When you have looked at them for a while, you begin to know the person who has created or interpreted them; for no artist can make you feel such things unless he himself has felt them. These minute variations of a line do not happen by accident, but because someone has learned exactly what are the indications of a certain emotional state, and how to reproduce them on a small flat surface."

Horace Hofman's life had been lived in other fields than those of art; but he had had to do with fine distinctions and possessed a pair of keen eyes. After he had spent an hour studying these drawings, Trudi Schultz had become a real person, a living presence in the room. He said: "Mr. Budd, this is a dangerous undertaking, and I may be acting foolishly, but I am willing to help you if you can show me any chance of success. Of course I count upon you, in case we should get into trouble, to pay whatever it might cost to defend us."

Said Lanny: "Every dollar I have in the world would be committed to your defense, and if necessary I would borrow from my father. You say that you will not let me pay you, but I assure you that if you do us this service, I will find some way to reward you, and on a liberal scale."

VIII

While these things were going on, Beauty Budd was living at the hotel, having the time of her life, as she always did. She had spent some forty years making friends in Paris, and now they invited her, and she went tirelessly day and night. She had married a "spiritual" man and was quite sure that he had ennobled and reformed her, but somehow that didn't keep her from believing that the *grand monde* was just as great and the *haut monde* just as high as it considered itself. She wanted Lanny to take her about, for he was a charming escort, and when she saw his success with important people she was ready to burst with pride—her corsage being already dangerously tight. Lanny went with her now and then, for that was the way to pick up information as to what was going on; you met the right people, said the right things to them, and guided the conversation into the channels you desired.

At an extremely classy *soirée* he ran into the American ambassador, that same "Bill" Bullitt who had been on the American staff at the Peace Conference, and whom Lanny had joined in protest against what they considered unsatisfactory provisions of the settlement. What a lot of water had flowed under the bridge in eighteen years! "Bill" had been ambassador to Russia, where he had acquired an intense dislike for the regime. Now he had got himself transferred to Paris, where he spoke boldly in opposition to the alliance of France with Russia, at the same time being troubled to discover in what company this brought him. William Christian Bullitt, amiable rich playboy like Lanny himself, had written in his youth a novel poking fun at the solemn snobbery of his native city of Philadelphia. Now he was round-faced and tending to baldness, serious and exactly proper in his evening clothes. He had been one of the original New Dealers, and rumor had it that he sometimes wrote speeches for the President. Lanny might have caused a sensation if he had said: "I wrote the Chicago quarantine speech"; but of course he wouldn't.

He thought quickly, and remarked: "You know, Bill, you are likely to have a new French government to deal with before long."

"You mean Blum again?" inquired the ambassador, ready to talk politics, and thinking that Lanny might have inside information.

"Nothing like that," replied the art expert. "I mean the Cagoulards."

"Oh, my God! You don't mean you take those people seriously!"

"I wish I were at liberty to tell you what I know about their military preparations."

The rest of the fashionable company was forgotten, and Bullitt drew the younger man out onto the terrace. It happened to be a warm evening, though late in the autumn, and they found two chairs. "Listen, old man," said the ambassador. "I am the one person who has a right to know about such matters."

"You must have heard about the plot already."

"People talk to you much more freely than they do to one in my position. Tell me what you have heard."

"It happens that my sources are confidential. You know my father's position, and perhaps you know who my friends are."

"You may count absolutely upon my discretion. I won't breathe your name to a living soul."

"Not even in your dispatches?"

"Of course not. Washington doesn't ask how I know. They are satisfied if I tell them that I do."

Lanny explained: "I can't afford to take sides in these civil wars, because I have business connections in the different countries, and so has my father. But we are Americans, and you really ought to know what is in the wind right now."

So the son of Budd-Erling whispered the news about the arms caches, and the financiers who were backing the enterprise, and the Nazi agents who were pouring in funds. It wouldn't be more than a month before the coup would come off and, in the Hitler phrase, "heads would begin to roll." Bullitt asked many questions, and Lanny chuckled within himself, feeling certain that before the ambassador went to bed that night he would get off a coded dispatch to the State Department, or perhaps to the President direct. F.D. would read it, and know that Lanny Budd had got there first, and so Lanny would be the fair-haired boy!

He had more serious purposes in this bit of play. One good turn deserves another, and in the event that Horace Hofman got into trouble Lanny would be in position to ask favors; also, he wanted to find out what Bullitt knew concerning the Château de Belcour. He said: "I don't know whether it's Kurt Meissner or Graf Herzenberg who is distributing most of the money. I understand one is working for the Wehrmacht and the other for the Schutzstaffel."

"All their agents are stuffed with funds," declared the ambassador. "I wish we had one-tenth the amount for our work."

Lanny asked what he knew about Herzenberg, and the other talked freely. The Graf was one of the early Nazis, and had a strong position in the party, since not many of the aristocracy had come into the movement in those days. Their fellow-aristocrats had rather looked down upon them, considering that there must be something cracked or crooked about persons who really took the Hitler ideas seriously. Now the Junkers had made terms with the Nazis, and were using them, or trying to, but they still looked down their long noses at them and counted the days before they could get rid of this bunch of upstarts and interlopers. Lanny knew all that, but didn't say so; he listened and learned that Herzenberg was a sort of overseer of the German ambassador, like the commissars whom the Russians set to watch their army officers. At the same time he could do the dirty work that it was too dangerous for Embassy officials to do. He had as his mistress a redheaded Austrian actress who was reputed to have some Jewish blood and who very certainly was a spy working in French government circles for Nazi pay.

IX

All that was directly to the point; and driving his mother back to the hotel, Lanny inquired: "Have you ever met Lili Moldau?"

"I met her casually in Berlin, and I believe in Vienna some years ago."

"She is in Paris now, I'm told, as the *amie* of Graf Herzenberg. Would you like to do a little job for me?"

"What is it?"

"You know Herzenberg has leased the château of the Duc de Belcour, who is an old friend of Emily's. I went there and looked at some paintings, and I believe I could find a market for several of them, if Herzenberg were willing to release them. Naturally, nothing of the furnishings could be taken out during the period of his lease without his consent. It happens they are historical paintings and I don't think he can especially enjoy looking at representations of French troops winning victories over Germans. What I thought was that if I met him socially, I might lead him to talk about them, and offer tactfully to get them out of his way. All you'd have to do is to get Lili Moldau to invite you to tea, and I'd bring you. I think I could do the rest."

Beauty Budd had lived a long time in the world—longer than she could be persuaded to admit—and for almost thirty-eight years of that time she had been watching her one precious son. "What is this, Lanny? Are you up to some of your radical tricks again?"

"Bless your heart, old dear! This is a deal on which I would stand to make a few thousand dollars, and I could pay you one of them—or keep you a while longer in this center of the world's elegance."

"Is that the reason you invited me?" she asked, ready to have her feelings hurt.

"Goose!" he said. "You know I have to earn my living." He didn't mind hurting her feelings if he could divert her mind from his "radical tricks."

But he saw that he hadn't succeeded. "When are you going to introduce me to that new *amie* of yours?" she demanded.

"She isn't in Paris now, or I would, honestly."

What was that strange intuition which made Beauty almost impossible to fool? "You don't take your mother into your confidence any more," she lamented. "When did I ever fail to help you when you asked me? I know perfectly well that you're absorbed in something more important than selling pictures. I know you didn't bring Hofman to Paris just to try experiments with Madame."

"I'm busy with a dozen things, dear. Robbie asked me to get some information from Baron Schneider for him, and Rick wants to know whether the French government is going to stand by the Nyon agreement. Hofman wanted to come, and I thought he'd be good company for Parsifal while I took you to parties. Haven't I been behaving?"

Why didn't he take her into his confidence? She would have gone to bat for him, and would have kept his dreadful secret; but she would have worried herself full of wrinkles, and she would have tried to exact from him the same payment as Robbie—a pledge that never, never, never again so long as he lived would he engage in the madness of making war on constituted authority or established property rights. Beauty hadn't much more social conscience than a tigress; only a tigress's love of her own progeny. Moreover, she had what no tigress has, the ability to shed tears and to be unhappy for an indefinitely extended period. Every man knows that is hard on the man's nerves as well as the woman's—so what was the use?

X

Jesse Blackless had taken a sheet of note paper and torn it in halves irregularly, giving one piece to Jean and the other to Lanny. The latter had passed it on to Monck, alias Branting, together with Jean's address. The French investigator had been told that some day a man would come to him with the other half of the paper, and by that token he would know the man he was to trust and obey.

Following Lanny's instructions, Monck rented a small and inconspicuous French car, and drove out to the mill where Jean had installed

himself. Ever since the German had taken on this job he had been dili-
gently making use of a pocket dictionary of the French language and
by now was able to make himself understood. He knocked on the door
of a moss-covered old building which stood perhaps thirty feet from
the road, with an open space and a platform against which carts or
small trucks could be backed up. The creaky door was opened by a
smallish, narrow-chested fellow with a straggly brown mustache and
a cigarette dangling perilously under it. That was Jean as he had been
described; and Monck, having rehearsed the sentence, said: *"J'ai un
papier pour vous."*

He handed out the half sheet, and the other man looked him over,
then took out the paper from his pocket and carefully matched them
against the frame of the door. When he was satisfied, he said: *"Entrez,"*
and Monck stepped into the main room of the mill. It hadn't been used
for a long time, and the white dust had turned gray and moldy. The
water passing over the dam sounded as if it were right in the room;
everything was deadly damp and chilly, but there was a round-bellied
iron stove with a long pipe hung from the ceiling, so presumably the
place could be kept habitable. There was a lean-to at one side which
had been used as bedroom and kitchen, but the roof leaked, and Jean
had fixed himself a pallet on the floor in a dry corner. He had a table
with a little oil stove and some food, and was having a good time camping out, he declared.

He had been told that the purpose of this campaign was to pry into
the secrets of the château, so as to provide the party press with a red-
hot exposé and the député Zhess Block-léss with material for speeches
in the Chambre. Jean was to be allowed to go on thinking this until
the raid was over, and indeed for the rest of his life. The only persons
who were to know the real truth were Lanny, Hofman, and Monck,
alias Branting. At any rate, such was the hope; of course if Lanny
couldn't carry out his wonderful idea of becoming an overnight guest
of Graf Herzenberg, then it might be necessary to bribe one or more
of the former workers of the estate, or possibly even one of the Germans now employed there.

Patiently, and with much consulting of the dictionary, Monck gathered the facts which Jean had accumulated. The Frenchman was a
Communist and the German a Social-Democrat, which normally would
have led to arguments; but Monck, forewarned, had nothing to say
about politics and parties, or where he had come from or what he was.
His only difficulty was to keep Jean from talking fast. *"Lentement,
plus lentement, beaucoup plus,"* the visitor would say, out of his dic-

tionary. French is hard to learn from print, because the look of the words is so different from the sounds; now and then Jean would have to find the word himself and point to it. Monck would say: "*Ah, oui!*" and repeat the word, learning language along with architecture, landscape, geography, milling, and what not.

He took the man in his car and made a circle of the estate, and then through the near-by village and around it. They did this several times, observing the landmarks, and being careful not to make themselves conspicuous. Monck had already familiarized himself with the ground plans of the château and Lanny's crude map of the grounds. Jean had got one of the former workers in the place to draw him a more detailed map by the device of claiming to have been inside and making assertions as to the position of things which irritated the other by their inaccuracy. When Monck cautioned: "You are sure you haven't asked too many questions?" Jean replied, with pride: "I set up the drinks and get them to arguing. They are stupid, or why would they stay in a place like this?"

XI

Meantime, Lanny was working at the difficult assignment of getting himself into the Château de Belcour. He had called Rörich on the telephone the day after the party and said he was afraid he hadn't behaved very well. The SS lieutenant answered that they had had a grand time and were everlastingly grateful. Lanny exclaimed: "I am immensely relieved. I don't remember what I did or said, but it must have been terrible."

He suggested that they must get together again soon, and the other replied: "The sooner the better." So now Lanny phoned to his friends the de Bruynes. The head of the family was away on one of those mysterious affairs about which no one asked questions. To Denis *fils* Lanny explained that he had met two officers of the staff of Graf Herzenberg, and found them well informed as to National-Socialist techniques both political and educational. He thought the family might like to make their acquaintance. He didn't have to say: "In view of the fact that you are seeking reconcilement with Germany."

An engagement was made for the following afternoon, which happened to be Sunday. Lanny called at Belcour for his two friends, which meant that he had another chance to give his name at the gatekeeper's lodge and then to drive through the double line of beeches to the front entrance of the château. He drove slowly, observing everything he could, for every little might help. He didn't get a chance to enter the front door, for his friends came tripping down the steps, dressed in their elegant uniforms, with tall boots and belts newly shined; all, as the Germans say, poured out of the egg. They were young and full of excitement; they were winning a war—by the most agreeable method ever devised. Who could fail in loyalty and gratitude to Führer Hitler and Foreign Minister von Ribbentrop and the other great minds who had discovered how to conquer a nation by drinking tea with ladies and gentlemen of the highest social position?

Lanny had the pair crowded into the front seat beside him, and while he drove he explained that from the French point of view a great honor was being done them, since Frenchmen of this class rarely opened their homes to foreigners. He explained the basis on which he himself stood with this family; the mother had been his *amie* for many years—which, of course, established Lanny as the very devil of a fellow. He said they would have to be on their best behavior. "I don't think they'll serve champagne, but if they do, please don't ask me to drink any." The amused passengers promised that they wouldn't. Lanny added: "I don't know if you know the reputation of the de Bruynes; they are very old, *le vrai St. Germain*, and the father has become a considerable financial power. All three of them are active politically, and have important plans in hand. I am not free to give you any hint of these, but it is possible they may do so themselves if you win their confidence."

The two officers stole a swift glance at each other. *Herrgott!* The man actually didn't remember anything of what he had blurted out the other night! *Jawohl, um so besser!*

XII

Both châteaux being in Seine-et-Oise, the drive was short. The Nazis met two Frenchmen just in their thirties; cultivated, with gracious manners, high technical education, and military training as well. Some day it might be the fate of one pair to meet the other pair on the battlefield—but why should they? Both pairs found it pleasanter to sit on the terrace of this old red-stone building and sip coffee out of delicate porcelain cups and converse about their countries' ideas and aims. Western Europe had a common philosophic and scientific heritage, a common literary and artistic heritage—and it had enemies still close to a state of barbarism, rapidly preparing for one of those raids which had come every century or so throughout recorded history. So, at any rate, these four believed and said.

They talked about the new kind of training which the Nazis were giving to their youth. Lanny knew about it, for Heinrich Jung was one of those in charge, and had raved about it to Lanny for hours on end. Here were two products of that training and they spoke for themselves. Lanny mentioned the "Party day," a celebration held in Nuremberg the first week in September. Fiedler had obtained a furlough to attend these ceremonies, and described them as the most beautiful and moving in the world. A million German youths assembled in one giant airfield; and such decorations, whole forests of banners and standards; such music and singing, such marching, such eloquence of orators and fervor of consecration on the part of auditors—no one who attended could doubt that a nation had had its soul restored.

The French brothers had been through all that themselves. They too were products of a "youth movement," and had marched and sung, worn insignia and sworn oaths under the banners of the Croix de Feu. But on a scale so pitifully small in comparison! They did not conceal their envy of the Führer and his magnificent triumph; they looked upon themselves as a vanguard of such developments at home, dreaming of some magic whereby they might overcome the cruel skepticism and wicked cynicism of the French masses. Denis *fils* and Charlot had no ambitions for themselves, but were ready to be followers of some Jeanne d'Arc who would lead *la patrie* on a new crusade, a Catholic and conservative revolution against the materialistic and individualistic forces of the modern world. Lanny would have liked to tell them that the National Socialist German Workingmen's Party had succeeded because of the second and fourth words in its title, and that the masters of French industry and finance would have to find themselves a rabble-rouser before ever they would see a million youths assembled to swear allegiance to their cause.

The conservative French revolution was to have reconciliation with Germany as one of its goals, and therefore the two Nazis were cordial to it, and glad to reveal the secrets of their colossal success. Privately, they didn't share the hopes of the de Bruynes, because the French were not Germans, and were incapable of such discipline, or of producing a Führer of such genius. But they explained their methods of organization and training—no secrets, since they were available in books, and both Frenchmen read and spoke German. More important, the Nazis told how it felt to be the objects of such efforts, the material of this discipline; how their doubts and uncertainties had been overcome, what had moved them and ultimately persuaded them, and what now, as finished products, they thought and felt and intended to do. All that was deeply interesting from the psychological as well as the political point of view.

XIII

Driving his SS friends home, Lanny found that they had been impressed by the sincerity and intelligence of the two brothers. Rörich said: "It is something that must not be allowed to happen, that Germany and France go to war again. Why should we destroy each other for the benefit of others?"

"It would not be the same next time," said the more practical-minded Fiedler. "The French army will not be such an obstacle."

"It is supposed to be a pretty good army," ventured Lanny, mildly.

"*Lächerlich*," said the Nazi. "We would blow it to pieces in a few weeks."

"It must not be allowed to happen," put in Rörich, quickly. "If we could bring it about that France was governed by such men as the de Bruynes, there would be no excuse for it."

They expressed their gratitude to Lanny for having brought about this meeting. They would be glad to know more such Frenchmen. It was an overture, and he responded at once: "Let us see more of one another."

"By all means," said Rörich, the more genial of the two. Lanny waited to see if he would add: "Will you come to see us at the château?"

But alas, no such luck! The SS lieutenant asked: "Will you be our guest some evening in Paris?" Lanny could only answer that it would give him pleasure.

When they came to Belcour and he stopped in front of the steps, they didn't say: "Won't you come in for a while?" Nothing of the sort; just "*Danke schön*" and "*Auf wiedersehen*." Lanny drove away, completely balked, and reflecting: "That place is a concentration camp, and I might as well expect them to invite me for a social call at Dachau or Oranienburg!"

11

Time by the Forelock

I

IT IS in the nature of social affairs that they cannot be hurried, and so Lanny Budd had to spend a lot of time waiting. He couldn't use it all in living through imaginary scenes in the Château de Belcour, nor yet in listening to Hofman's speculations as to what kind of locks he was likely to find on the doors of that place. There was Madame, always in the hotel, and Lanny kept thinking up schemes to get information by way of the psychic underground.

There were some of his acquaintances who looked upon him patronizingly because he had let himself be drawn into this sort of activity. An aroma of fraud hung about it, and only a weakminded person would waste time on it. Lanny had heard this said by gentlemen who played the stock market and wore out their nerves trying to win great sums of money for which they had no need; by others who got drunk at night, or amused themselves seducing other men's wives. He had heard it also from ladies whose occupation in life was decorating their persons with expensive clothing and jewels, and from others who found diversion in staking their fortunes upon the turn of a card or a roulette wheel. Such occupations were fashionable; but to try to find out something about the mysterious universe you lived in was a waste of your own time and a deprivation to your friends.

Lanny had read enough to know that it was truly a mysterious universe, and the clues to its secrets had been found in odd and unexpected places. An old-time Italian had occupied himself with touching a copper wire to frog's legs and watching them jump; a retired merchant of Philadelphia had taken to flying a kite in thunderstorms—which must surely have seemed eccentric to the neighbors. So it must have been with the grinding of curved glass, which had opened up a universe of the infinitely large and another of the infinitely small. One could list hundreds of men who had watched some puzzling phenomenon—the falling of an apple, the bubbling of a tea kettle, the fer-

218

menting of liquids—and had persisted in asking why and how it happened, and so had expanded man's powers over nature.

And what about the mind, most familiar of our possessions, yet the least investigated? Lanny was coming to the conclusion that his mind was one with all the other minds existing—and this, not because his mystical stepfather had dreamed it, but because of facts which he was observing and for which he could find no other explanation. He saw himself as a bright and lovely bubble, floating on the surface of a vast dark ocean; he was keenly aware of his own existence, and somewhat less keenly aware of other bubbles, dancing in the sunshine all around him; but of the infinite ocean from which he had come and to which he was destined to return, he knew next to nothing, and was considered an oddity because he kept trying to find out.

An ocean of mind-stuff, a cosmic consciousness, or unconsciousness —whatever that could be and however it could function. Some called it evolution and others called it God. Whatever its name, it brought you into existence and kept you going. Very certainly you hadn't made yourself, either body or mind; very certainly you didn't know how to make your own blood or to repair your tissues; your thoughts came, but you didn't know how, and the wisest scientist had no explanation of the process whereby a thought, desire, or act of will could cause your muscles to flex and your hand to move. You had some control over both mind and body; you lived your life, as you said, and did what you pleased; but why you pleased this and not something else was a question you left to the learned psychologists—very few in number, and mostly not agreeing with one another.

Dipping into the subconscious mind of a dull old Polish woman, Lanny had discovered fragments of the minds of other people, mostly dead, but now and then a living one. Were these disembodied minds, spirits, or ghosts, or did they exist as fragments of mind-stuff—just as long-buried fragments of bones exist in the grave? No scientist had to apologize for studying a piece of the skull of a Piltdown man and learning what he could about that ancestral being. Why shouldn't some of them get busy to study the mental fragments of a long-dead Amerindian chieftain, or a Greek munitions king, or a victim of the Nazis murdered in a concentration camp? Nobody could give any reason that satisfied the son of Budd-Erling, so he went ahead holding séances and jotting down notes.

II

He had watched his stepfather hypnotize Madame; he had read books on this subject, and now he wanted to try it once. He asked her permission, and she said Yes without hesitation. She would do anything for this family who had been so kind, solving all her problems for her and granting her every request. In her secret heart she held Lanny as a son, and at the same time as a lover; when she went to the cinema, he was the hero upon the screen, and a lonely old woman dreamed dreams which she would not put into words or perhaps even admit to herself.

With Horace Hofman watching, Lanny seated himself in front of her and fixed his eyes upon hers; he made the gentle passes he had seen Parsifal make before her face, and murmured slow words of command. He was himself surprised by the quickness with which she passed into a trance; quite evidently a different kind from those which she herself induced, tapping a different level of consciousness, or at any rate bringing a different set of phenomena. No "control" and no "spirits"; only passivity and silence. If he had told her that she was a bird flying, she would have got up and waved her arms; but he wasn't interested in parlor tricks. He wanted to find out what sort of mind he now had to deal with. He asked questions, and she answered; she was satisfied and would do what he told her. Yes, she knew about Tecumseh, but he wasn't there now; there were no "spirits" anywhere about, and she didn't know how to get any.

Lanny said, in a quiet, firm voice: "Listen carefully, Madame, and remember what I say. You will have nothing more to do with Claribel. You will take control of Tecumseh"—how Lanny would have liked to find a way to get Tecumseh under hypnosis!—"and ask him to bring me a man named Ludi Schultz whom I very much want to talk to. You will remember the name?"

"I will remember."

"Also his wife, Trudi, if you can find her. They are good people who will do you no harm, but will tell you about themselves if you can find them. You will remember all that?"

"I will."

"And above all no more Claribel. No more Claribel. You will wake up now." Lanny snapped his fingers, and the old woman came to herself. "You feel all right?" he asked—having been worried by the thought that he might put her into a trance and then not be able to get her out. She said she was all right, and he asked her to go into her own kind of trance. She sank back in her chair and closed her eyes, and it worked like magic—there was no Claribel and no Tecumseh, but a voice, speaking German, and saying that he was Ludi, and that he was well and happy in the spirit world.

A most unsatisfactory Ludi, far different from the aggressive Social-Democratic Party worker whom Lanny had known in Berlin. He didn't have very much to tell that he hadn't told in previous séances; he took some time to speak, and his answers were vague and sometimes faint. He said Yes, he knew Lanny Budd, and remembered having met him in Berlin. He, Ludi, had been a prisoner of the Nazis, and had "passed over" a long time ago. The spirits apparently didn't like the word death, and in general were as mealy-mouthed as if they were in church. Ludi said he had had different ideas when he was on earth, but now he had changed. He said Yes, he knew what was happening to his friends on earth—sometimes, at any rate; but he didn't prove it by giving details. He said that he knew some of those he had known on earth, and what had happened to them since they had passed over. Lanny named several persons whom Trudi had mentioned as having fallen into the hands of the Nazis, and Ludi said they were here and they were well and happy. It was a formula.

III

Lanny had found that these fleeting and unsatisfactory beings didn't like to be pinned down and forced to answer questions, and he was taking no chances of having the voice of Tecumseh suddenly break in and scold him. However, there was one subject nearest to his heart and he came to it quickly: "You remember Trudi, and your life with her?"

"I remember her, of course."

"Have you seen her lately?"

"I thought I saw her, but I wasn't sure. I think it must have been her ghost."

"How interesting! Do you mean they have ghosts in the spirit world?"

"Sometimes; at least, some believe in them, but I never did."

"But you saw something that you thought was Trudi?"

"Yes."

"And did she speak to you?"

"A few words. She called my name, and said she was coming."

"Did you answer her?"

"I tried to, but I am not sure if I could."

This cross-questioning went on for quite a while. Lanny was interested to know if Trudi had been near to death and had appeared to her former husband in the "spirit" world in the same way that she had appeared to her second husband in the world which called itself "real." He wanted to know if people appeared on the threshold of the spirit world and then receded into the real world again. He wanted to know how Trudi had looked, and what Ludi had thought about her near-appearance, and why he was so vague in telling about it. "Is it because when you were on earth you were so much opposed to the idea of spirits? Maybe in your heart you are still opposed, and that is why you don't see Trudi and others of your old friends. Could that be possible?"

The voice admitted that it might be, and Lanny proceeded to give him the same advice which Tecumseh had given to Lanny. "Try to change your attitude, and be more receptive to the fact that you yourself are a spirit, and that there are other spirits you might learn to know and love." A strange kind of auto-suggestion, given to beings who perhaps weren't beings at all, but merely imaginings taking form in some mind-stuff, fragments out of the minds of Madame and Lanny or perhaps the former minds of Ludi and Trudi.

Lanny asked about that old man who was said to be helping Trudi; and again it was all vague and unsatisfactory. Ludi said the old man might have been a ghost, too; he had spoken Trudi's name. He was rather stout and had a kind face. Yes, he was called Paul, pronounced German fashion, and Teich, or something like that—it was the German word for "pond." Perhaps it was Teicher. No, Ludi had never met him before, and didn't know where to find him. He would try to find out more about Trudi, and would come to another séance. Lanny, trying to give suggestions, pleaded in the name of friendship, and said he would be glad to have Ludi's company at any time; but Ludi said it wasn't easy to arrange. The man in the real world explained that he was trying to help Trudi without being sure what world she was in. Ludi ought to help them both; but instead of reacting to this with ardor, as Ludi on earth would have done, the spirit voice said that he was *müde*, *erschöpft*—very tired, and his voice trailed away, and it turned into the moanings of Madame, coming out of her trance, something which Lanny had learned to recognize and never to oppose.

So there was one more not very successful experiment. Lanny said to Hofman: "Do you suppose we are shaping all this ourselves? Imagining the way things ought to be, and so getting them that way?"

The locksmith answered: "I admit that Ludi's bewilderment is about what is in my own mind when I try to imagine the spirit world!"

IV

It didn't take Beauty Budd very long to think of somebody who would know Lili Moldau, and she called up this friend and invited her to tea, along with a couple of other ladies so that they could play bridge. Lanny had been to a newspaper office and inspected what they had in their files concerning the actress. Thus it was brought to his mind that he had once seen her in a play in Vienna; he had forgotten the event, but didn't have to tell her that. Posted on the details, Beauty had no trouble in leading the conversation, first to the stage and then to her favorite performer. "She is living in Paris at present," remarked the friend. "Oh, do you know her?" exclaimed Beauty. "I would love to meet her, and Lanny would enjoy it, too."

The friend promised to invite Beauty and her son to tea. That is the way things go in smart society; people are always being "used" for some purpose or another, and they try not to know it, because they have a natural human desire to believe that they are loved for themselves alone. They don't like to become suspicious and distrust other people's motives; but they learn by sad experience, and the older they grow, the less faith in human nature they retain.

A date was made, and Lanny and his mother dressed themselves in their glad rags and he drove her to a mansion on the Boulevard des Malsherbes, and there was the lovely Lili in all her Titian-haired splendor, clad in a sheath dress of green silk with a sort of patina of gold, tight-fitting as if to say: "See how I have kept my figure!" She had been in her time the most charming of ingénues, and now, at an age where that was no longer plausible, she was too proud to take older roles, and preferred to serve as a sort of scout for her lover and patron, exploring the wilds of French public life to find out who was in the market and at what price.

Mother and son laid themselves out to be charming, and they knew all about it. An actress could not but be touched by this off-stage applause heaped upon her; apparently the pair had followed her about from city to city in Austria and Germany; they knew all her roles, and the fine points of her technique. Really, it was extraordinary! "Why have we never met before?" she asked, and it did seem surprising, for they had so many friends in common. Kurt Meissner for example; Lili knew him well, and after they had exchanged reminiscences, Beauty let it be delicately understood that she had played in Kurt's life the same intimate role which Lili played in Graf Herzenberg's. And then the Fürstin Bismarck, and the Fürstin Donnerstein, and Emily Sonnemann —why, they lived practically in the same world! Certainly they must be friends, they must see more of each other.

Lanny didn't take anything for granted. He let the stage star know that they were the Budds of Budd Gunmakers and Budd-Erling Air-craft, and that his mother was the widow of Marcel Detaze. On chance that Lili hadn't heard of him, Lanny told about the Munich exhibition, and the painting of his mother, *Sister of Mercy*, which he had taken to the Führer at the Braune Haus. It would have been cheap to pull out the clipping and display it here; more *comme il faut* to prove it by the intimacy of his revelations concerning the great master of German destiny.

An American art expert made it plain that he had followed the career of Adi with the same fidelity he had given to Lili Moldau. He had been to Berchtesgaden, an honor which had never been vouchsafed to an actress maliciously reputed to have Jewish blood. He had been a guest at Karinhall, and at Göring's palace in Berlin, doors which Lili's shadow had never darkened. He had visited the Goebbels family. "Poor Magda!" he remarked. "The last time I saw her, at The Berghof, she looked very sad."

Lili replied: "You men know what you are!" Tactful, and as far as one should go in referring to the scandals of the *Regierung*.

Also, the Budds had connections in Paris; they were intimate friends of Mrs. Chattersworth, and of the de Bruynes, and the former Baroness de la Tourette; they had once leased the palace of the Duc de Belleau-mont—in short, they represented for the *amie* of Graf Herzenberg a "find" of the highest value. "I would like you to meet *Seine Hochge-boren*," she remarked; "you will find him charming." Beauty replied, with exactly the right degree of *empressement*: "I know I should be proud to meet any friend of Lili Moldau's."

V

So mother and son came home well pleased with themselves. The promised invitation came by telephone next day; to meet Herzenberg at Lili's town apartment, and not at the château. That was no less satis-factory to Beauty, and Lanny had to pretend that it was the same to him. One step at a time—and such long delays in between! Lanny reported progress to Hofman and Monck, and they spent hours figuring over what they would do in the event that Lanny's social ambitions failed. Monck's time was running out, and he insisted that he could not ask for an extension. But how could they venture into the grounds of the château at night unless something could be done to those dogs—to say nothing of the nightwatchman who was almost certain to be on duty? Wait a day or two longer, and we'll see what Herzenberg is like, and whether or not he ever serves tea or gives dinner-parties at his concentration camp! Meantime, let's have another séance with Madame, and see if we can get Ludi to tell us any more news!

Beauty Budd and her preoccupied son dressed themselves again and drove to a fashionable apartment house near the Parc Monceau. There was *die schöne Lili*, playing the ingénue as she had done for twenty years or more, but now ad-libbing, as the American stage folk call it. She, too, must have consulted some "index," for she had learned about Lanny Budd's infatuation with the spirits and was primed for conversation on the subject. Did he know that the Führer and a group of his friends were deeply interested in all such mystical subjects? Lanny said he had heard it. Did he know that in the early days the Führer had always consulted an astrologer named Hanussen before he took any decisive political step? Lanny had been informed of that also. Then the actress inquired, did he believe in astrology? He said he had not had opportunity to investigate this abstruse subject.

Lili had recently consulted a fortune-teller in Paris who charged five hundred francs a sitting, which certainly indicated that she must have something. She had told the actress of incidents in her past too painful to talk about, and then had told her that she was going back to the stage and make a greater success than ever. "Of course every person who has ever had a stage career cherishes that dream, and I am wondering if I should try to make it come true. Would that count a proof of foreknowledge?" Lanny replied that it would be a proof of psychology, at any rate.

Seine Hochgeboren arrived: a shaven-headed Prussian with a dueling scar on his cheek and a monocle through which he surveyed you with what appeared to be a condescending air, though he may not have meant it that way. Certainly he had every reason to be cordial to a mother and son who possessed a knowledge of France and of the French fashionable world which might make them of the greatest use to him. His manners were suave, and your feelings were smoothed, your self-esteem flattered; the conversation was guided so that you were asked few direct questions but were led to reveal your habits and desires. It was as if a master of many servants was investigating a candidate for some especially important and confidential position.

This might be the case, of course, for Herzenberg had dealt with servants from childhood, and now had a large payroll at his disposal. Just what were these Budds and why had they sought an acquaintance with his *amie?* Were they as rich as they appeared? A great many smart people are like movie sets—all façade and nothing behind them. These Americans had a family fortune in the background, but did they command it, or might they be black sheep of some sort, devotees of the gambling tables, for example? If so, what were they prepared to offer, and what pay did they expect?

A Nazi overseer could count upon the certainty that such wordlings knew who he was and what he was doing in France; also, that they were not motivated by pure love of Germany, or of National-Socialist ideals. Lanny, in his turn, could assume that Lili had told her lord and master all that she had been able to learn about the pair. Also, one could be reasonably sure that two young officers of the Death's Head brigade had reported to their superior their clever feat in getting an American playboy drunk and hearing him blurt out the story of the Hooded Men and their plot. Even though Seine Hochgeboren might have known this already, it was confirmation, and held out the hope of future leakages.

So Lanny didn't have to recite that "spiel" with which he was accustomed to hypnotize Nazis, about how many times he had visited the Führer, and being an intimate of the Görings and the Goebbelses and the rest. He could be dignified and aloof, mentioning such mutual friends as Graf Stubendorf, at whose Schloss he had spent half a dozen Christmases since boyhood, and Emil Meissner, Kurt's oldest brother, now a General in the Reichswehr and a Junker of the inner circle. It was as if Lanny had been saying: "These are my credentials; and my way of presenting them lets you know that they are genuine."

VI

This was a busy, hard-driving man, and Lanny wouldn't make the mistake of assuming that he was interested in a tea-party chat. Said the visitor: "I have something on my mind that might be of use to you. My business does not permit me to take an active part in politics, but sometimes I come upon an item of information which seems important, and then it is a pleasure to pass it on. This may be something you know about, and if so, don't feel it necessary to comment. I am not fishing for information, but offering some."

"I appreciate your kindness, Herr Budd."

"I assume that you know Baron Schneider; but it may be that you haven't had contact with him lately. It happens that he is in a frame of mind to be of use to you and your cause. I won't need to say more, for you know what influence he has. Remember, he is not merely Schneider-Creusot, but also Skoda."

"Quite so, Herr Budd."

"I took a message from him to Kurt Meissner several weeks ago, and it may be that Kurt has acted upon it—he hasn't told me. Kurt is one of my dearest friends, my boyhood hero and exemplar; but I have an idea that his unhappy experiences have disturbed his judgment, so that he finds it hard to trust any person of the French race. You doubtless know that he was a confidential agent of the Reichswehr here during the Peace Conference."

"I have heard something about it, Herr Budd, and we Germans are in your debt."

"Forgive me if I explain myself, for I want you really to understand me. I am a man of peace, both by profession and practice. My parents are American, I was born in Switzerland, lived most of my life in France, and had my holidays in England and Germany. In the last war my stepfather was killed fighting for the French and my best friend was nearly killed fighting for the Germans. I don't want to live through such sorrows again, and I believe there can and should be a genuine reconciliation between France and Germany. Kurt taught me that ideal as a boy, and he still accepts it in theory—but when it comes to a concrete case, I have the idea that his reason does not dominate his attitude; instinctively, he simply cannot help disliking Frenchmen. I am mentioning the matter to you with the thought that this may be less true of you."

"It isn't true of me at all, Herr Budd. I respect the French as a great people with a great tradition, and I am deeply obliged for your confidence. I would be glad indeed if I might have a chat with you about these and other matters."

"Certainly," replied the art expert; "whenever you desire."

"I have an apartment in town where my friends come occasionally. I will give you my telephone number, if you like."

"With pleasure," said Lanny—and inside himself he was saying: "*Damn!*" He got out his notebook and put down the number, according to Seine Hochgeboren's request that he consider it confidential.

Then he remarked: "I had the pleasure of visiting your château not long ago and looking at the paintings."

"I heard about it. I hope you found them worth while."

"I had the thought that you could hardly enjoy the daily confrontation with French military glory."

"Oh, well, one can't afford to forget history entirely, even while dreaming of a happier future."

So they played with each other, as two urbane men of the world; and on the drive home Beauty said to her son: "Did you really mean what you told him about your attitude to Germany?"

"Sometimes I think I do," replied the son. "I would almost be willing to turn into a Nazi if it would prevent another war between France and Germany."

"You are a strange fellow," said the fellow's mother. She was not very clear on the subject of the new ideologies, but had read somewhere that the Red dictatorship and the Brown were not far apart in theory and practice. All she could say now was: "If you were going to change your mind, why on earth didn't you do it before you broke up with Irma?"

VII

Lanny was one step nearer to his goal; but the steps were so many, and the time between them irksome! He could call up his new Nazi friend and ask for another view of those paintings, and by imparting information about French affairs and promising to get more, he could gain a position of intimacy with the whole Embassy staff. But would he ever get invited to spend a night at the château? Must he not rather assume that this was something out of the question; against policy, possibly even against orders?

He talked it over with his fellow conspirators. Should he drive to Belcour and there put his car out of commission and claim that it wouldn't run? But they undoubtedly had a well-equipped garage, with a mechanic who would quickly find the trouble—and possibly be suspicious as to its origin. Could he go as a visitor and fall seriously ill? Well, they would call a good German physician, and have a nurse to attend him, or perhaps an ambulance to rush him to Paris. Hardly would they leave him free to be sick by himself, and to wander about the grounds at night as a measure of convalescence!

Monck, alias Branting, had got himself an SS uniform. He was a Hauptmann, the rank he was used to in Spain, and the one befitting his age and solidity of frame. He had got the outfit from a tailor in one of the faubourgs, near to a motion-picture studio; he had said he was aspiring to a role, and the tailor, generously rewarded, had entered into the spirit of the undertaking and turned him out complete with all accouterments, according to a magazine illustration which Lanny had obtained. Now he strutted up and down his hotel room, halted, clicked his heels, threw up his right arm and heiled Hitler. Both his two associates had had opportunities to watch the Nazis in action, and they criticized his behavior, and finally pronounced him able to paralyze the will of any German nightwatchman. But what about the dogs? Rörich had told Lanny that they knew the German smell; but could Monck count upon that? Perhaps he had lost his in exile—and even acquired a Spanish smell!

They had their rendezvous, their car, their maps and blueprints, everything ready; they had figured out the last details of time and place. Their plans were at the stage of an army general staff which receives the order to invade a certain country and has only to reach into a pigeonhole and take out Plan 147B. But alas, all their plans, of whatever number, were timed for 0130, the military way of saying one-thirty in the morning. All depended upon Lanny's being inside the château at that hour, and being there as a guest, not as a burglar. Night after night passed, and he still spent them all in Paris.

VIII

The solution of their problem, when it came, was arranged by a kindly fate without any prodding; it was due to a development in French politics which none of them could have foreseen. A Corsican of Fascist sympathies, Duc Pozzo di Borgo, had fallen out with Colonel de la Rocque, tough leader of the Croix de Feu, and was waging ideological war upon him because of his "legalistic" tendencies, so offensive to the Cagoulards. The once-fiery Colonel had got nine million francs from Pierre Laval and had purchased *Le Petit Journal*, a newspaper of Paris with several hundred thousand readers; this had caused him to make peace with the government and promise to obey the laws. In short, he had become just another politician. The Duc had published the charge that the Colonel had received money from the French Foreign Office to build up his organization; the Colonel had replied with a suit for libel, and now the issue was being fought out in the courts—to the profit of the French public, which read newspapers of all political hues and agreed on only one thing—a delight in scandalous revelations concerning its statesmen, whom it called *cochons*, in English the short and ugly word "pigs."

And now to the witness stand came André Tardieu, recently Foreign Minister of the French republic, and testified that he had indeed paid public funds to Colonel de la Rocque for the upbuilding of the Croix de Feu, and that Pierre Laval, recently Foreign Minister and then Premier, had done the same. An immense sensation and, of course, fury among the "legalistic" sons of the Cross of Fire. Shortly thereafter the French Socialist Marx Dormoy received a visit from a mysterious black-clad gentleman who placed in his hands a heavy portfolio and departed without explanation. Dormoy, Minister of the Interior, was charged with the duty of protecting the republic from its enemies at home; and upon opening the portfolio he found that it contained full details of the doings of the Hooded Men and their plot to overthrow the government; the sources of their funds, and what amounts they had spent for guns in Germany and explosives in Italy; where these supplies were stored in several hundred secret places throughout France, and exactly when and how they were to be used.

Dormoy put all this before the Cabinet, and there resulted one of those seismic disturbances which go on day after day, shock after shock, until people in the neighborhood begin to wonder whether it may not be the end of the world, so often predicted by the prophets of the Christian religion. The Socialists, of course, clamored for exposure of the conspiracy and arrest of all the conspirators; but the conservatives pointed out that the plot involved some five hundred officers of the French army, many of them among the highest—and after such a housecleaning, how much army would France have left?

The Socialists, who had been on the point of overthrowing the Chautemps government, decided to stay on and fight within the Cabinet. Dormoy, blackbearded friend of the people, destined to be murdered by the Nazis in a few years, may have foreseen his fate and resolved to make the most of his time, warning the workers and peasants of the peril in which their Third Republic stood. Rumors began to appear in the papers, and little groups of men to meet and argue on street corners and in wineshops, as they do in democratic countries, to the distress of those who desire the world to stay as it is, and believe that the less the excitable masses know about public affairs, the fewer chances there are of tumults and increases in the income tax.

IX

It was Lanny's birthday, which came in the middle of November. He wasn't having any celebration, or even mentioning the event, out of consideration for his mother who couldn't bear the sight or sound or even the thought of the figure 38. Lanny got up as usual, ordered his orange juice and toast, and looked over his mail and his half-dozen Paris newspapers. Those of the left were full of dark hints of treason and sedition; knowing what it was all about, Lanny thought: "It may break at any moment; and what will it do to my plans?" He knew that Jesse Blackless had his ammunition ready and his guns primed; his speech would attribute the conspiracy to the Nazis, and would frighten those master-intriguers and make them cautious. The nephew had said: "Give me two or three days more."

He was going to send Monck out to the mill that morning. Jean had been told to find out where the Germans got the meat that was fed to their dogs. It would be necessary to poison them; an unpleasant thing to think of, but a human life was at stake. This happening would alarm the Nazis even more, and probably cause them to double their guard; therefore the burglary would have to be committed before the poisoning was discovered, and that meant a difficult job of timing.

A knock upon Lanny's door: a cablegram, which proved to be from Robbie. "Sailing Normandie tomorrow arrive Paris proceeding Berlin hope for your company." There had been a time, long ago, when such a message would have been the happiest event in Lanny's life. Now it was a nuisance, and one reason more for rushing things.

He shaved and dressed, and was about to leave for Monck's hotel, when the telephone rang. A woman's voice, which at first he failed to recognize; a woman in great agitation, breathless, as if she had been running and was barely able to gasp out a word or two; a woman speaking English with a French accent: "No names—terrible—police arresting—friend—best friend—mustn't say names—place in country—pillbox—you understand?"

The word "pillbox" told him; he knew of only one such. The speaker was Annette, wife of the younger Denis de Bruyne. "I ran to neighbors—for God's sake—help us!" She began whispering—as if that would protect the dread secret over the telephone.

"What do you want me to do?"

"Find the others! Warn them—keep out of way. You also! They are taking private papers—reading everything."

"I understand. Is that all?"

"Be quick! Others must not come home—you understand?"

"Perfectly. I will do what I can."

"Good-by."

So, the government had made up its mind to strike! They must indeed mean business, when they were raiding a home of such prominence as the Château de Bruyne. They would see the pillbox in the garden, and would soon find the cache of munitions; they would read whatever papers they could find in the home. They had caught Denis *fils*, but the father and younger son must be elsewhere, and it was up to Lanny to warn them. He called the elder Denis's office; the secretary had just come in, the employer had not. Lanny guessed that when a man is doing such work as overthrowing a government, his private secretary must have some idea of it. He said: "Ask no questions. M. de Bruyne is in very grave danger. It is necessary that you find him at once and warn him to disappear." The secretary replied promptly that he understood and would do his best.

Lanny repeated the procedure for Charlot. He too had not arrived, but the secretary, a woman, promised to find him. There was a club where the young man sometimes kept appointments, and Lanny called there, but without success. There was nothing more he could do; he couldn't be expected to go out and search the streets of Paris for those two. Knowing French politics as he did, he didn't think they were in serious danger, except of publicity and inconvenience—and possibly of blackmail.

Was Lanny himself taking any risks? When he gave his name over the telephone and helped seditious conspirators to escape arrest, he was making himself an accessory after the fact, and making it appear probable that he was an accessory before it. When the police went through those papers at the château, would they find the name of Lanny Budd as one who was carrying messages for the Cagoulards? If they searched the papers of Baron Schneider, they would be very apt to find memoranda concerning a message carried to an agent of the Reichswehr. Annette had said: "You also!"—and no doubt she had something like this in her mind. Lanny had caused her to believe that he was one of the Hooded Men at least in spirit, and the servants must have got the same impression. One of the first acts of the police would be to get the names of visitors from the servants. "M. Budd comes often, and he had dinner here with Baron Schneider!"

A blaze of lightning flashed in Lanny's mind. "By heck, I've got it! I'm a fugitive from justice!" He delayed just long enough to step into the adjoining suite and tell Hofman to get ready, they were going at once to see Branting, the problem had solved itself. He darted back to his own suite and threw a few articles of necessity into a small bag, including a book which he might try to read during a time of great stress. He wrote a note for his mother: "Gone a couple of days. Picture business." Then he and the locksmith bolted to the car.

X

Monck was awaiting them, and the son of Budd-Erling announced: "God has tempered the wind to the shorn Lanny!" He was in a lively mood, tempted to slap the two men on the back and invite them to dance the farandole. "No poison, no trouble at all! I walk right in and stay as long as I please! I have the right of asylum!"

He told them of the telephone warning, which had made him into a fugitive from justice. He had been working in the Nazi cause, and the Nazis knew it, and now, when he was in peril of his life, could they refuse him shelter? "Let them try it! I'll telephone the Führer, if necessary!"

The other two agreed that this did the trick, and they opened the cabinet of the general staff and took out Plan 147B. They had been over every detail a number of times, and now all Lanny had to say was: "Tomorrow morning, if you see the signal, and if not, then the next morning. Good luck, and thank you both with all my heart." They shook hands, making it a rather solemn moment, and Lanny took his departure. Monck was to drive out to the mill and see if Jean had picked up any additional information. Hofman had nothing to do all day, except perhaps to have another séance and see if Ludi or Tecumseh or Claribel had any suggestions to offer.

On the way Lanny stopped to purchase a couple of small bottles of cognac, which he put away in his bag. Then he drove to the Château de Belcour. To the gatekeeper, who knew him by now, he said: "Tell Leutnant Rörich I must see him at once. It is very urgent. *Ohne Aufschub!*" There was a telephone in the lodge, of course, and in a minute or so the gates swung open. Leaving his keys in the car but carrying his bag, Lanny went up the steps of the building two at a time, holding out his arm and saying his "Heil Hitler!" Then he grasped the hand of his Nazi friend. "Come inside," he said. "Something terrible has happened. Take me where we can talk privately."

"Everything is private here, Herr Budd," replied the other.

"I know; but this may be a matter of life and death."

He was escorted into what had once been the steward's office and the door was closed. In low tones the secret agent of the Hooded Men broke the news that his conspiracy had been discovered by the French police and that he and all the other conspirators were on the run. Lanny didn't have to depart from the truth very much. The charming Annette de Bruyne, whose hospitality Rörich had accepted, had telephoned the news that their home was in process of being raided and their papers searched and read. Lanny, at gravest risk, had got word to the other members of the family, and likewise to those persons who constituted his immediate contacts with the organization. It appeared that the whole conspiracy was being blown open; if the government had learned what was going on at the de Bruynes', it was to be assumed that they would know about hundreds of other places where arms were concealed, and would be making such raids all over France. "Being a foreigner," Lanny said, "I am in an especially dangerous position, and I could think of no place to seek shelter but here."

"*Aber!*" exclaimed the SS man, greatly embarrassed. "This is really most unfortunate, Herr Budd. We are in no position to offer shelter to anyone, because Seine Hochgeboren is an official of the Embassy, and his home is under diplomatic status."

"So much the better, *lieber Freund;* I assure you, the French police have no possible way of guessing that I am here. I haven't told a soul— not even my mother."

"*Leider, leider, Herr Budd*—how can I make it plain to you? We simply do not do such things. It is a question of the diplomatic proprieties."

"*Na, na, Rörich,* I am speaking as one *Weltmann* to another. This is for the cause, and we do not stand so strictly upon proprieties when Nazism is at stake. You know only a small part of what I have been doing; and I assure you that I value my life and my ability to work for the Führer more than I do the feelings of any Jewish-Bolshevik democratic republic." Those were the strings you pulled when you wanted to ring the bell in a National-Socialist soul.

"Believe me, *lieber Herr Budd,* I sympathize deeply. But you know I do not have the say in such a matter. I am only a junior officer."

"That I can understand. *Ist Seine Hochgeboren zu Hause?*"

"I believe so. I will put it up to him if you wish."

Lanny wished it; and while the Leutnant was gone, he strolled into the library adjoining the smaller room, and took a good look at the catches which held the French windows. When the head of the establishment appeared, the visitor was examining rows of French classics bound in very fine leather stamped with the crest of the Duc de Belcour. They went back into the smaller room and closed the door—just the Graf and his "refugee." Rörich had doubtless been told to keep out, and wasn't sorry.

XI

It was a funny scene; at least it would seem so in after years when Lanny could look back upon it: an exemplification of the classic formula, an irresistible force meeting an immovable body, and what happens? Underneath the velvet glove of the trained diplomat was the iron hand of the master of men, one of the *Herrenvolk* destined to rule the world. Seine Hochgeboren was absolutely determined that this American stranger or near-stranger should not find refuge in his home, which had been in the past and might be now a small-scale Oranienburg or Dachau. Lanny, for his part, had adopted the ancient French motto: "*J'y suis, j'y reste.*" He was here, and he was going to settle right down and make himself at home, and nothing less than physical force would get him past the door—or one of those French windows of the library, the one Lanny had agreed to leave open that night; the third from the northwest corner of the building, with two catches at the top, two at the bottom, and an extra solid one in the center, holding the two sections together.

All with the most elegant manner—*suaviter in modo, fortiter in re!*—Lanny explained what work he had been doing for the cause of the Hooded Men, identical with that of the National Socialist German Workingmen's Party. He knew all the secrets and named the key names. Quite recently he had had lunch with Baron Schneider at his home, La Verrerie, in Le Creusot, and had been commissioned to offer financial aid to the Nazis through Kurt Meissner. He had been told how the arms were coming from Skoda, not Le Creusot, for better purposes of concealment. (He hadn't been told any such thing, but he knew it was sure to be so.) He had dealt with the key men, and for that reason the French authorities would be seeking him more than any other person.

Patiently Graf Herzenberg replied. The services of Herr Budd were appreciated to the full, and of course he could count upon all sympathy and assistance from the Nazi organization. But it would have to be at some other place than the home of an Embassy official. "We simply dare not offer such provocation to the French government. We do not permit any of our own secret agents to set foot upon these premises."

No less patiently, Lanny made his counter-reply. "I appreciate your position, Graf. I have never before forced myself upon any person, and it pains me deeply to do it now. But this is not a private matter and neither of us is a private person. I came to your estate because I thought of it, not as a home, but as part of the German Reich. I could not go to Kurt's, because it is an apartment house, and I am well known there. If I made a mistake, I am sorry; but I came in good faith, and surely it is your duty to protect me from our enemies."

"I grant all your points, Herr Budd, and, as I have told you, I will see that you are taken to a place of security."

"When you propose that, you are subjecting me to a risk which I feel is entirely impermissible. I do not think I am a coward——"

"I have never intimated such a thing, *mein Freund*——"

"My life has value to your cause, far more than I am at liberty to tell you. It is my duty to protect it, and yours to help me."

"I will see that you are taken in a closed car, and since it is an Embassy car, it will be covered by diplomatic immunity."

"If I am discovered in such a car, it will be exactly as awkward for the Embassy as if I were discovered here. Behind your high fence and inside these spacious grounds I am safe from all observers, and I protest most earnestly against the idea of taking me out upon a public highway during this crisis."

"After dark, Herr Budd?"

"Darkness makes no difference to the French police, for they have fast cars and flashlights. They will consider it far more likely that fugitives will attempt to travel at night, and they are accustomed to block the highways and stop and search all cars. Nor is there any safety in distance from Paris, for we have hidden our arms in all parts of France, and the search for our friends will be nationwide."

XII

So they argued back and forth; and when they had said everything there was, they went back and said it over again. Neither would give an inch; finally Seine Hochgeboren declared, firmly: "I deplore this misunderstanding, Herr Budd; but this is my home and I am charged with the responsibility for the care of it. The decision must be mine, and I can only repeat what I have said before: I cannot permit you to stay."

Said the son of Budd-Erling, with exactly the same amount of firmness: "I appreciate your position, Graf Herzenberg, and it puts me in a most excruciating dilemma. If you knew the facts concerning my duties and responsibilities, you would not dream of turning me from your door. But I am under oath not to reveal these; so what am I to do?"

"I can only act upon the knowledge which I possess, Herr Budd. If you have valid credentials, you must permit me to see them."

"Surely you know, my friend, that the last thing in the world a confidential agent would do is to carry credentials in a foreign country."

"No agent of Germany is working in this country without having some superior who knows him and will vouch for him. Tell me who that person is."

"What I tell you, Graf, is that you are mistaken. I have no superior in this country, I report to no one here and am known to no one here —at least not in my full capacity."

"Surely, Herr Budd, you know enough about our affairs to realize that I cannot accept such a statement without any sort of confirmation."

"All I can tell you is that if you force me to go farther, you will be making a mistake which you will greatly regret. I am a personally appointed and confidential agent of a person whose authority you will recognize."

"You will have to name that person to me."

"Despite the fact that I am under pledge upon my honor as a gentleman to do it under no circumstances?"

"I am fully capable of keeping a secret, Herr Budd; and anyone in Germany who knows me will trust me for that."

"I am sorry, I have to keep my promise. What I ask is that you permit me to telephone to Reichsminister General Göring."

"You mean to telephone from this place?"

"You make it necessary."

"You will give him your name?"

"By no means. I can speak a few words which will identify me to him; and I presume that you will recognize his authority."

"As it happens, Herr Budd, General Göring has no authority over me. I am an official of the Embassy, and my superior is Foreign Minister von Ribbentrop."

"I am sorry that my acquaintance with Herr von Ribbentrop is slight. Therefore, since you make it necessary, I have to ask to telephone to the Führer."

"*Wirklich, Herr Budd?* You enjoy a telephone intimacy with the Führer?" This was really too much!

"I am sorry that you put me into the position of seeming a braggart, Graf. The last time I visited the Führer at Berchtesgaden he was kind enough to give me the telephone number of Haus Wachenfels—pardon me if I am accustomed to speak of it by its old name, whereas you may know it as Der Berghof. Some time ago the Führer asked me to bring him a painting by my stepfather and I have neglected to do him that courtesy. If you will call him wherever he happens to be and say that the stepson of Marcel Detaze wishes to speak with him, he will understand it as code, and I am sure he will tell you that I am a person socially and politically acceptable."

For the first time the immovable body showed signs of being shaken. Said the Graf: "Even granting the truth of your claims, Herr Budd, it seems to me it would be most injudicious to attempt to call the Führer from a foreign country about a matter of so delicate a nature."

"Let me suggest an alternative. Would it be within reason for you to call Kurt Meissner and ask him to come out here at once on a matter of extreme importance?"

"That I could do, but it would be quite futile. Kurt has already assured me of his warm friendship for you, and nothing that he could add would modify the decision I announced."

"Kurt has told you of our friendship, Graf, but has he told you what he knows about the Führer's attitude to me? Unfortunately, Kurt was not present at my last visit to Berchtesgaden, when Herr Hitler was gracious enough to unbosom his soul and tell me of his true feelings concerning the French people. On that occasion he urged me to do everything in my power to avert misunderstanding between France and Germany, and I took that as a commission to do what I have been doing for the past year."

"Is that the confidential mission of which you spoke previously?"

"By no means. That was a public mission. I was charged to tell everyone that I had it directly from the Führer's own lips, and I have told it to hundreds of persons in the highest social and political and financial positions in France. Kurt has heard me say it more than once."

"Is that what you wish Kurt to assure me?"

"What I would like more than anything else, Graf, is to have Kurt tell you what I did for him under circumstances almost identical with those which have driven me to your home. I do not know how much you know about his work for the Reichswehr after the war; I have never asked him about it, and am not hinting for you to tell me. Suffice it to say that he was in Paris in civilian clothes and under a false passport at the time of the Peace Conference of 1919; he was a spy, liable to a military trial and to be shot at sunrise. He asked me for help and I gave it to him, instantly and without question. At that time I was secretary-translator to a member of the American staff at the conference; I was only nineteen, but I had proved my ability, and earned a career if I chose to follow it. I, too, enjoyed diplomatic status, and might easily have pleaded to Kurt the risk I would be running and the higher duties I owed to my country. But I raised no such objections. I took him to my mother, who hid him in her apartment for a week, and then I bought a car and she took him into Spain as her chauffeur. Kurt knows that we saved his life, and has many times said so."

"I do not doubt it, Herr Budd, and all this puts me in an extremely painful position. As it happens, Kurt knows nothing about the special circumstances which determine my position, and nothing that he could say would possibly affect my decision."

XIII

There followed a long and stubborn pause. Lanny was here, and didn't need to talk; he waited to hear what else his host had to say. At last came a new proposal: "Would it come nearer to meeting your wishes, Herr Budd, if I offered to send you into Germany?"

Lanny laughed. "Let me show you something." He took from his pocket the cablegram he had received that morning and handed it over. "You see, I should be very well taken care of in Germany. My father has important business relations with General Göring; he shares in the use of all the new devices and processes which the German Air Force possesses, and you can believe that there are not many persons who enjoy that privilege. The General personally escorted him to Kladow and showed him that wonderful military base. He not only invited me to Karinhall and introduced me to his wife, but he offered to present me with a hunting estate near by. I have never accepted any favor from him, but I have done him many, and when I travel to Germany with my father we shall have the pleasure of enjoying a great man's famous hospitality, and I shall tell him of intimate conversations about political affairs in Washington and New York as well as in Paris and London. Among other things I am sure *der dicke Hermann* will roar with laughter over the story of how I fled for shelter to Graf Herzenberg and what a devil of a time I had persuading him not to kick me out."

"I don't want to kick you out, Herr Budd," interposed the diplomatic official, obviously disturbed. "I, too, have orders which I am not at liberty to disobey, and which General Göring, as a military man, would be the first to understand."

"*Es kommt darauf an,*" said Lanny; the German way of saying that circumstances alter cases. "Now and then emergencies arise, and subordinates have to exercise discretion. I assure you that I don't expect to impose upon you very long—for France, which I know well, is a mercurial country; not for nothing is it called Marianne, a woman's name. Her tempests arise quickly and blow over even faster. I am not in danger of a French firing-squad as Kurt was, or even of a French jail; I am only afraid of their newspapers, which would break that shield with which I have protected myself—my profession of art connoisseur. If you knew what I have been able to do with it during the past few years you would understand that it must be protected against all mischances. That is why I thought I was safe in appealing to a man of culture and taste like yourself."

Lanny by now perceived the signs of weakening of his opponent in this long duel. He chose his most persuasive, *vox humana* tone, and pleaded: "I beg you to be reasonable, *lieber Freund*. I am here, I am safe, and it would be most distressing to have to depart. I assure you, I am a gentleman, and know how to behave myself. I will not meddle in your affairs, nor bore you with my company. I will, if you prefer, stay quietly in a room and read a book which I have brought. You may send me a little food, whatever is convenient, and I will keep your servants content with the proper *Trinkgeld*. When I feel the need of fresh air and exercise I will walk to the rear, completely out of sight of the road. If I may see the newspapers, I will be able to judge concerning this political thunderstorm, and when I perceive that it has blown over, I will take myself out of your way, skirting the dangerous city of Paris and heading for the fine old bridge which crosses the Rhine at Strasbourg. If on the other hand the danger seems likely to last, I will accept your kind suggestion and let you send me into Germany by whatever route you are accustomed to use."

The immovable body was moving—a bad prognosis for the future of the Third Reich! "I am forced to accept that compromise, Herr Budd, and to hope that your assurance of safety within these grounds will be justified by the event."

"*Meinen aufrichtigsten Dank, Graf.* You may be sure I will do everything in my power to repay your kindness." He held out his hand, and they exchanged a clasp. Then, smiling his best, the American added: "Let me assure you that my title of *Kunstsachverständiger* is not just camouflage; I really do know about art, and sometime during the day, if you find that you have leisure, I should be happy to take you about these fine rooms and tell you what I know about the painters represented here, and the historical significance of these different works. Since you have to live with them, it might amuse you to know about them."

"Thank you, Herr Budd. It happens to be a busy day for me, for somewhat the same reasons as for you. I am obliged to go into Paris, but if I am able to return before you leave, I will avail myself of your offer. Now if you like, I will have you shown to a guest room."

12

Observe the Opportunity

I

VICTORY in one battle meant the beginning of another. Lanny lay upon the bed in the pleasant second-story room assigned to him, and talked to himself without words. "Don't take it too hard. You have a lot of time to pass and you don't want your hair turning gray." He had brought with him Hans Driesch's book on psychic phenomena, and now set himself resolutely to reading. It was a subject in which the Führer was interested and that made it respectable; it was in the German language, and Lanny was going to speak, think, and be exclusively German until this battle was won.

There came a tap on the door. It was Rörich, friendly and smiling; might they have the pleasure of his company at lunch? Lanny assented; if they were going to treat him as a guest, that was to the good. As they went downstairs, the lieutenant grinned and whispered: *"Sie sind klug!"* Lanny had performed a feat in getting his own way, and Rörich was amused by it. He was glad to have company. Perhaps it becomes monotonous, running a concentration camp.

The meal was served *en famille*, as it were, in a small room which apparently had been intended for the upper servants. Present were the Third Secretary of the Embassy, the very haughty Herr vom Rath; Rörich and Fiedler, a stoutish Hauptmann Bohlen, a young Doktor Flügelmann with pince-nez and little black mustache; also a humble and quiet male secretary. They had a very unpretentious luncheon, consisting of *Wienerschnitzel* and a salad with a reasonably good *vin ordinaire*, followed by a *compote*. A man-servant waited upon them; Lanny had never seen a woman on the place, and didn't expect to— unless it was Trudi.

The thought of Trudi would come unexpectedly like that, and each time his heart jumped up and hit him under the throat. This was Trudi's place of captivity, and these were her captors, her torturers. Was the sharp-eyed Herr Doktor there to say when she had been whipped enough, and to make sure that she was kept alive? Was the round and rosy Hauptmann there to see that the two lieutenants didn't yield to feelings of a sentimental nature? Did the cold and reserved Rath prepare the reports to Berlin? Thinking such thoughts. Lanny had to smile and smile and let others be the villains. A strange thing, to be sitting in a chair putting stewed fruit into his mouth, and thinking that Trudi might be right under his feet at the moment. One floor down, or possibly two? And what would she be doing and thinking? Should he wangle his way to the piano again, and play the *Ça ira*, to tell her he was here? He must do nothing unusual, nothing to attract attention to himself. Be polite and completely non-invasive, and give no excuse for anybody to wish him elsewhere!

The Hauptmann had telephoned to Paris and learned what the afternoon papers had in their early editions. Tremendous excitement, with headlines several centimeters high. The police had discovered a nationwide conspiracy and were seizing great stores of arms: machine guns and mortars, bombs and grenades, hundreds of thousands of rounds of ammunition. Since it was in the papers, the company felt free to question Lanny, and he told what he knew and more that he had guessed. He wasn't sure if he was a hero in their eyes or a coward; anyhow, he was a personality, and surely nobody would find him a bore.

II

Apparently Rörich had been put in charge of the guest. That suited Lanny perfectly, and after the coffee he said: "Shall we have a stroll?" They went out to the terrace, and he added: "We must go toward the back. I must not be seen from the road." They walked in a grove of plane-trees, which in America are called sycamores; the guest re-marked: "You must be happy, living in such a grand place. I don't suppose you have had it that way always."

"No, indeed," replied the young officer, and revealed that his father had been a shopkeeper, ruined by the postwar inflation; they had

had it very hard indeed. Lanny replied that things were far easier in Germany now, and there was reason to hope they would get better still. He didn't say how, for just then a dog barked, and he remarked: "Those friends of mine! Let us pay them a visit."

Their stroll turned toward the kennels. There were two shepherds and two dobermans, each pair in a separate pen of heavy wire mesh. They were glad to see visitors, and stood with their paws on the wire and their tails wagging briskly. "Oh, the lovely creatures!" exclaimed the American, and talked the language of those who have property to guard and the leisure to play with life. "You know, Rörich, you cannot really understand men until you have had an opportunity to study dogs. I am not joking; it is an amazing thing, how you see all human qualities, both weaknesses and virtues, in these mirrors of our personality. I suppose it is because they have lived by serving man for thousands of years, and have had to accommodate themselves to our dispositions. Whatever the reason, it is the fact that you will rarely in this life find a man who will be as utterly devoted to you and as single-minded in loyalty as a dog. You will find no child more eager for attention, or more ready for a romp, or more quickly aware of any trace of displeasure. As for jealousy, that is really comical. Have you made a special friend of any of these dogs?"

"*Leider*, I haven't had the time."

"Then they will not object to your manifesting interest in me. But I have one of these shepherds at my mother's home who can hardly bear to see my mother kiss me; and as for allowing me to pet another dog, that is out of the question—Pluto simply shoves his nose in and takes the other dog's place. If I order otherwise, he becomes so miserable that I cannot bear the spectacle."

The keeper came, an elderly man whose business it was to know dogs, and what the *Herrschaft* said about them. He and Lanny talked technicalities; Lanny said: "What are they fed?" and "What exercise do they get?" The man replied that they were turned loose at night and ran all over the place. The visitor made a move to open one of the doors, and he warned: "*Achtung, mein Herr.*" Lanny said: "We are old friends by now!" They discussed the instincts of watchdogs and what they could be taught. Lanny declared: "They know exactly what is in your mind. If you are afraid of them, they will give you cause for fear, but if you trust them they will deserve it."

He walked into the pen with the two shepherds; the man went with him, speaking words of command. It was a formal introduction, and the dogs came humbly. Lanny said: "*Schön Prinz!*" and "*Brave Lizzi!*"

He let them smell him to their noses' content; he patted them on the heads, and said: "I shall never have any trouble with anything so beautiful." The bitch was expecting pups, and he asked: "What do you do with them?" The man said: "We shall have to give some of them away," and Rörich added: "Would you like one?" Lanny replied that he would like nothing more, and would take it in his car the next time he went to the Riviera.

There were the dobermans, the old-style German police dogs, smooth-coated, black and tan, lithe and eager. The visitor said he didn't know them so well, and asked about their qualities. They were less excitable than the shepherds; more stolid, but hard fighters. He wished to make their acquaintance, and the keeper asked to go in first. The same introduction was made, and this pair also had full opportunity to learn Lanny's smell, his hands, and his English tweed suit and his shoes from New York. "My dogs remember my friends after years of absence," he said. He would have liked to add: "I suppose you don't need any nightwatchman"—but he was afraid this remark might be remembered if anything went wrong.

III

"Don't let me keep you from your work," he said to his friend. "I have a book, and am used to entertaining myself." He took a seat in one of the great leather armchairs of the library, and started the reading of a learned work by a professor of philosophy at the University of Leipzig. It had been comforting to Lanny that a scholar of this standing had taken the trouble to examine a layman's notes of experiences, and certify to their value as a contribution to knowledge.

In his book Professor Driesch began, as all Germans do, at the beginning of the beginning; he discussed the problem: "How is *knowing* possible," and he pointed out the importance of remembering that the knower is a part of Reality, as well as the known. We are forced to assume that there exists between the knower and the thing known "a primordial relation, which we shall call *knowing potentia*." Somehow the thing known affects the mind, and this affection takes the form of matter, and some matter which comprises what we call a flower affects some other matter which we call our body and our sense organs and our brain. Said the learned Professor Hans Driesch:

"This is a great miracle, and is by no means understood. Think of this: The ultimate result of the affection is a certain rearrangement of the electrons and protons in my brain—and then I 'see' the flower 'outside in space.' This in fact is a real enigma and will be an enigma forever. Things would be much easier for us to understand if the electrons and protons of the brain would 'see' *themselves*, but this, as you know, is not the case."

When Lanny read words such as these he knew that a man who had thought deeply was trying to explain to him in the simplest possible words ideas which were extremely complex. He did not read such words quickly, but stopped and pondered each sentence to make sure he understood its full meaning. He looked up from the page of the book at the very stately library which the Duc de Belcour had inherited from his forefathers, and found it strange to reflect that it was all "an arrangement of electrons and protons."

Lanny's eyes ran quickly over the outsides of hundreds of books, and these outsides affected the electrons and protons which composed his brain in a certain special way, for the reason that in the course of his life he had opened a great many volumes of the French classics, and so had acquired a special kind of "knowing potentia" for the language and history and philosophy and drama and fiction of the French. When he saw the name Racine on the leather binding of a volume, the electrons and protons of his brain began to dance in a certain special way, and when he saw the name Rochefoucauld, they danced in a way entirely different; it might be said with probability that there existed in the whole universe no other assemblage of electrons and protons which would have danced in exactly the same way as those of Lanny Budd. All this, surely, was to be recognized as "a great miracle!"

Some force which was "a real enigma" drew the objects which Lanny Budd called his "eyes" away from the leather-bound and gold-stamped volumes to the floor of the room, and along the floor to the third pair of French windows from the northwest corner. In front of those windows, on the soft carpet of dark green velvet, he saw a small coin lying, a franc, which had formerly been made of silver but was now made of base metal, and has on one side a figure of Marianne, or liberty, or the republic, whatever you choose to call her, sowing seed. Lanny couldn't see this with his physical eye, but he knew that this figure on the coin was turned up. He knew it because there wasn't really any coin there; he was seeing with what Hamlet called his "mind's eye" a coin which was going to be there sometime after one-thirty next morning, as a signal from Monck and Hofman that they were in the château. Ever since this signal had been agreed upon, Lanny had been seeing imaginary coins on carpets in front of windows, and each time the electrons and protons of his brain had been set to cavorting with a special and peculiar sort of violence.

Here was a problem which might have been found worthy of investigation by a professor of philosophy at Leipzig University. If the manner of the vibrations had been exactly the same as if the coins were "really" there, we should have said that Lanny Budd was suffering an hallucination. If such vibrations had continued in the same way for an indefinite period, we should have had to say that Lanny was mildly insane. But because the vibrations were such that Lanny knew they were different, we said merely that he was "imagining" the coin; he knew it wasn't "really" there, but expected it to be there soon, and felt now the things he was going to feel when he saw it "really" there. Yet the emotions he was going to feel were so violent that he couldn't bear them even in imagination, and took his eyes off the carpet and his mind off the coin that wasn't there, and forced himself to go back and read some more sentences from the learned professor's book.

IV

What did this authority have to say about the special kind of problem which had been puzzling Lanny's mind for so many years? Under the heading "Telepathy," he read:

"All our normal knowledge about another mind's contents is reached in an indirect way; we see and hear that the other being moves and speaks, and then infer that his mind is in a certain state. In the realm of psychic phenomena the indirect way is turned into a direct one. Sense organs and brain are excluded. The knowing goes from subject to subject immediately; the relation *knowing potentia*, therefore, must have existed also between them."

A strange thing, whatever way you looked at it. Lanny wondered which would seem the stranger—that we possessors of minds should be compelled to know other minds by the roundabout and complicated method of "inferring," or that we should now be coming to a stage of evolution where we were discovering another, a "direct" method. For hundreds of thousands, perhaps millions of years, men had been using the indirect method, and their minds were so set in it that they were unwilling, perhaps unable, to contemplate the possibility of the direct method. Yet, what a saving of time it would be! What a convenience—or possibly a nuisance! Like any power whatever, it would depend upon who was using it, we or the other person. What a different world it would make if ever it came into general use! A world so different that we couldn't imagine it, and wouldn't know how to live in it; some might prefer to commit suicide and take themselves out of it!

Here was Lanny Budd, for example; seated in a soft leather armchair, comfortably reading a book, or trying to. His wife whom he loved, the dearest being in the world to him, might be only ten or twenty feet away from him, lying on a bench in a stone cell in torment. He had been imagining her, or trying to avoid imagining her, for a couple of months; and here he was, this close, yet powerless to find out a single thing about her. Heavy stone walls lay between them, and the poet had been lying when he said that stone walls did not a prison make nor iron bars a cage. They made a prison for Trudi Schultz, and had obligated Lanny to carry on an elaborate set of investigations and intrigues in order to get this near; it would require a man in a Schutzstaffel Hauptmann's uniform and another with an elaborate set of steel tools to find out if she was there, and what was going on in her mind.

But here came this strange and mysterious possibility of mind reading, or telepathy. If it was a reality, the mind of Trudi would be able to flash a message into Lanny's mind, instantly and directly. Had she done something of the sort, that time when she appeared at the foot of his bed? He himself had tried it many, many times, in all ways and under all conditions: in the stillness of the night, when she might be asleep; when he himself was falling asleep, or just awakening; whenever his thoughts of her became vivid, and she might be thinking of him. Nothing had ever come in reply, but he kept on hoping.

He had read about the experiments of Coué, who claimed that it is not will but imagination which affects the subconsciousness. Since it was easier to imagine Trudi when he had reason to believe that she was so near to him, he sat now deliberately holding her in his mind, employing his art-lover's memory to visualize her. He saw her perfectly chiseled features, expressive of intelligence and of moral conscientiousness, of concern about truth telling and justice doing. He recalled her as he had known her ten years ago, young, eager, full of hope for her cause and for personal achievement in the work she loved; he recalled her as he had known her of late, when hope had been replaced by grim determination, when love of truth and justice had become stern anger against wholesale liars and killers. Fanatical, if you chose to use an unkind word, and by no means easy to live with, but commanding a husband's admiration and immovable loyalty.

He put his arms about her in love; he did not command her to come to him, but told himself happily that she was coming, that she was welcoming him and responding to his embraces. He permitted his senses to be warmed and his thoughts to be dissolved in memories of the oneness they had enjoyed for a couple of years. *Belle nuit, O nuit d'amour, souris à nos ivresses!* And in that sort of semi-trance his conscious mind waited, hiding in a corner as it were, trying to fool itself and pretend that it wasn't there, keeping watch for something that might possibly be a communication, a message from a beloved one who might be buried just beneath him in a dungeon of heavy masonry.

The trouble with all such experiments was, how were you going to know a message if you got it? How were you to distinguish between a thing from outside and the swarm of things you already had inside? Lanny had had a thousand imaginings concerning Trudi in that dungeon; he had had many others of her being elsewhere, including under the sod of France or Germany. How would he know which was the real "hunch" and which was self-deception. Even if he saw her, or heard her voice—how would he know that wasn't an hallucination, the product of his overstrained fancy? Tecumseh had called him a "highbrow," and had bade him become as a little child; but how did one perform that feat? Backward, turn backward, O time, in thy flight!

V

Dinner was a more formal meal, served in the great paneled dining room. The same men attended, but they now had two servants to wait upon them and there were several courses. The Nazis were no ascetics; they did themselves well, as you could see by looking at them. The afternoon papers had been brought out from the village, and everybody had had a glance at them; they all knew French, otherwise they wouldn't have had this assignment. Lanny learned that his efforts in Paris had been unsuccessful; all three of the de Bruynes were in prison, and likewise several of the other leaders whose names he had been hearing and using. All the papers were violent, raging in favor of their special point of view.

So the diners had plenty to talk about, and all expressed their opinions, mainly to the effect that the French were poor organizers and worse keepers of secrets. "It can't be done in a democracy," declared Fiedler; the well-informed Secretary vom Rath supported him: "That is why they are doomed." The consensus was that the chances of reconciliation between Germany and France were greatly reduced.

They wouldn't say in the presence of an American that this meant war, but such were the implications of their talk.

After the meal they repaired to the music room. Rörich had told them that Lanny was a musician, and of course his talents were at their service. "What shall I play?" he asked, and the Leutnant, who had known him first and had taken him up as a protégé, remarked: "Didn't you say you had played for the Führer?" It was up to Eduard vom Rath, the ranking officer, to suggest: "You might play for us what you played for him."

Lanny seated himself at the fine rosewood piano, and began the first movement of the *Moonlight Sonata*. It is a composition laden with grief; and here were five German males, full of good food and wine and ready to sink into a mood of exquisite melancholy. They were separated from the homeland, and from the women they loved; they didn't know when they would go back, and they turned all slow music into a *Liebestraum*. Beethoven had been born in Germany, and the fact that he had chosen to spend most of his life in Vienna was overlooked; that he had been a democrat and in rebellion against authority was quite unknown to these Nazis. They had been taught that he was one of the glories of the *Herrenvolk* and a proof of their superiority over all others. To enjoy him was honorable, and for a foreigner to play him was an act of homage.

When that movement came to an end, they asked for something else. Lanny's fingers began to fly, and there came rippling out upon the air a stream of lovely notes, a beautifully woven pattern of sound, gentle murmurs in the bass and little bird-songs in the treble—the *Waldweben* from *Siegfried*. The Führer loved Wagner above all other composers, and the Nazis had taken him over, drums and trumpets, slide trombones, bass tubas, and all. Wotan the Thunderer was their god, Freya was their sex dream, and Loki, the tricky one, was the head of their propaganda department. Siegfried was Germany incarnate, and when the spear was driven into his back every German thought of 1918. The Nazis were in the process of rewriting the legend, bringing the young hero back to life and making sure that this time he would be properly armed and guarded.

Lanny said: "Herr Kannenberg brought his accordion and sang for the Führer." He gave them a sample: "*Tiroler sind lustig, so lustig und froh.*" They gathered round and joined in, and that was a pleasant way to pass an evening that otherwise would have been one of nervous strain for Lanny. "There Was a King in Thule," "When the Spring

Comes and Looks from the Mountains," "Ah, How Is It Possible for Me to Leave You?"—and so on and on—Lanny had sung these old songs when he had visited the Meissners as a boy, and if he didn't know the accompaniments he could make something up as he went along. When his repertoire was exhausted, they suggested others, and after he had heard the first verse he could play the rest. No matter how many verses there may be, no German is ever known to tire; nor will you find any one of them in the plight of most Americans, who know the first two or three lines of their national anthem, and then have to sing "La-lá-la-la-lá."

There came a pause, and Lanny said: "I will play you something that these old walls have heard before." He pounded out the tune that he had played on his first visit: "*Ah, ça ira, ça ira, ça ira—les æristo-crats à la lanterne!*" Only Rörich would know what it was, and Lanny looked at him and grinned. In his soul the husband was crying: "Trudi! Trudi! This is for you! I am coming!" Was she there, and could she hear it? He asked his subconscious mind but got no answer; instead, he played and the rest of the company joined in singing: "*Mein Heimatland, du schönes, du he-errliches Land.*"

The Germans have a poem to the effect that when you hear singing you may lie down in peace, for evil men have no songs. The Nazis were using this as one more camouflage, but for Lanny tonight it held good.

VI

The company broke up shortly after eleven and the refugee retired to his room. This was the worst period he had to spend, for he was alone, and could not sleep. He sat in a chair and tried to read; then he got up and paced the floor, back and forth, like a tiger in a cage. He had had weeks to think of every possible thing that might go wrong, but now he thought of more. The Graf had not come home; perhaps he was spending the night with his lady, but, on the other hand, he might come in late, or very early in the morning. Just what would Lanny say if his host should find him in the act of opening a pair of French windows in the library? "I am very restless, *Ihre Hochgeboren.* I couldn't sleep. The news is bad. I want to walk out-side." That would be all right; Lanny didn't care if they thought him a coward. But what would he say if the Graf caught him in the act of penning up the dogs? "They were barking, *Ihre Hochgeboren.* They kept me awake." Not so good!

So many, many things might go wrong! They had picked a moonless night, and that wasn't subject to change; but there was a wind blowing, and the opening of a door or window might create a draft and cause some other door to bang. It was apparently blowing up a rain, something to be expected in this part of France in November; if the ground was wet, he would leave tracks in the house and so would his fellow conspirators. In the general excitement, would they remember to clean their shoes? And then that unanswered question of a night-watchman! What would he be, an old servant or a young SS man?

Resolutely Lanny picked up the book of the Leipzig professor, and forced himself to read a paragraph. Then he realized that he didn't know what he had read, so he went back and read it again. This learned scholar, after decades of investigation, had convinced himself that the phenomena of psychic research were genuine. "All minds are One in some last resort,"—such was the conclusion he drew. But all this meant to Lanny at the moment was: "Why doesn't Trudi send me a psychic message?" Then he would wonder: "Did she get any of my psychic messages to her?"

His thoughts moved on to the musical signal, his Blondel song. If she had heard it tonight, she had probably heard it the previous time, and what had she made of it? A long wait between signals, and she must have become discouraged; perhaps she had decided that it was merely a coincidence. After all, there were plenty of people in France who knew the tune of the *Ça ira;* it was in the books, and some German might have been curious about it, or perhaps have thought of making up Nazi words for it!

Lanny was trying to retrace Trudi's thoughts, using psychology where telepathy had failed. He had promised her that he wouldn't endeavor to find her; but perhaps she would understand that this promise was beyond his power to keep. Would that worry her, or would they have broken her spirit to the extent that she would want to be rescued? Perhaps she wouldn't have mind enough left to want anything, to know anything; they might have driven her entirely insane.

Oh, devils, that were committing such horrors upon human beings! Lanny recalled the seven men with whom he had just dined. All were "gentlemen," in the sense that they had good manners, they ate their food properly, they listened to Beethoven and Wagner, they smiled and discussed world events. Then they went down into the cellars of this building and applied physical and mental tortures to a woman, to break her will and reduce her to a cringing wreck, an imbecile or a gibbering idiot! They did it, not because they were savages at heart, but because they had been taught it as a duty; they had been drilled in a creed of diabolism, the vilest perversion of faith and morals since the Spanish Inquisition.

Lanny had taken up a feud against it, and was leading a raid upon it. But he was not at one with himself, because he doubted the wisdom of his course. He had got himself into a position of danger, and was getting two other men into a position even worse. If they should get caught, he would have three persons to worry about instead of one, and he would have a long and costly campaign on his hands. Trudi might forgive him, but could he ever forgive himself if he destroyed his position of advantage in the struggle against the Nazi terror? Cold reason told him that at this moment he ought to be in Berlin, finding out what he could regarding Hitler's intentions as to Austria. He ought to be dancing with some diplomat's wife or mistress, picking up gossip, instead of being shut up in a room by himself, holding a book in two hands which trembled, looking at his watch every minute or two, then listening to make sure it hadn't stopped running. Verily, "Time travels in divers paces with divers persons," and right now Lanny Budd was the one for whom it "stands still withal."

VII

When the lagging hands at last arrived at one-thirty, all these doubts and debates came to an end. All Lanny's faculties were needed now for the job of outwitting his enemies. He put on his overcoat and hat, also his kid gloves; he must wear gloves through all these operations, to avoid leaving fingerprints. Into the coat's capacious pockets he put the two bottles of cognac, also a tiny flashlight not much bigger than a fountain pen; you pressed a button at one end and a thin beam came from the other. Also, he had a handkerchief with a piece of twine securely tied to one corner; also a tape measure, and a well-drilled brain—such were the accessories required for Plan 147B.

He put out the light in his room and went to the door. Holding the knob firmly, he turned it and opened the door. Outside, a dim light burned in the hall; there was a row of doors, all closed, and behind them slept some of the Nazis, Lanny hadn't made sure which. Softly he closed the door and stole down the carpeted hall. If anyone met him, he had his formula ready; he was jittery and couldn't sleep.

Down the stairs, one at a time, stopping to listen. A night light in the entrance hall, but no sound. There might be a watchman inside the building, but he was not to be seen. Lanny had learned the arrangement of the rooms thoroughly and he slipped silently into the almost dark library. Everything quiet here, except for the thumping of the intruder's heart. He couldn't be sure whether that was loud enough to be heard upstairs.

The third window from the northwest corner of the building. Lanny had studied it from the outside and made sure there could be no mistake. French windows are like two narrow doors, and one of them is enough for a man to pass through. The one on the right opens first, and that was the one on which Lanny worked. He hadn't dared try the bolts in advance, and had wondered if they might be rusted in place. He tried the one at the top, holding his thumb under it to keep it from snapping suddenly. It was free, and he drew it carefully down. Then the one at the bottom, and last the one in the center, which held the two parts together. He opened it, and a blast of air struck him in the face. He reached his hand outside; there was a handle whereby the door could be opened from the outside when the bolt on the inside was pushed back; having tested this and made sure he would not be locking himself out, he slipped outside and closed the door behind him.

High up overhead, on the wall of the building, was a shaded floodlight of moderate intensity, shining directly down on Lanny's head; illuminating the loggia, the terrace, and the shade trees in the background. Lanny had been prepared for this, having seen it more than once from the road at night. He started a stroll which he hoped would appear casual. He could be sure at least that the noise of the wind would keep anybody from hearing the pounding of his heart!

Around a corner of the building was a second light; no doubt he would find one on each side. Visibility was good, as the airmen say. The sky was black and mysterious, and so were the trees in the distance; but all around the house was a belt of light and anyone approaching would stand out as if in bright moonlight. Lanny strolled around another corner, watching carefully, prepared for anything. This side had a porte-cochere; under it was shadow, and from this shadow came a challenging voice: "*Wer geht da?*"

VIII

Lanny had been prepared for this, and he met it with his best society manner. "Herr Budd," he answered, and came toward the porte-cochere. He was careful to keep his hands hanging, the palms open and the fingers extended; a harmless position, but not ostentatiously so. "*Sie sind der Nachtwächter?*" he inquired.

"*Ja, mein Herr.*"

"*Heil Hitler!*"

"*Heil Hitler!*"

"I am a guest in the château. You know me?"

"*Ja, Herr Budd.*" The servants had talked, of course.

"I couldn't sleep. I had to come for a walk."

"*Eine böse Nacht, mein Herr.*"

"You have heard perhaps what has been happening in Paris—the arrest of our friends?"

"*Ja, Herr Budd; sehr unangenehm.*"

"I am very much upset about it. I may be in danger, too. I had papers they may have found."

"*Leider, Herr Budd.*"

"You walk at night?"

"*Die ganze Nacht.*"

"May I walk with you?"

"*Gewiss, Herr Budd.*" Never one sentence without the "Herr," so Lanny knew it was an old-fashioned German. A man in his fifties, too old to be a perfect Nazi; perhaps a family servant of the Graf. He would have heard that Americans were free and easy in their ways, and would not be surprised if this one chatted as they strolled. Without doubt he had heard the visitor thoroughly discussed in the servants' hall; his riches, his clothes, his manners, his love of dogs, his playing and singing, his having visited the Führer.

"It is a terrible thing to know that your friends are being arrested and perhaps mistreated. I couldn't sleep and I couldn't read. I didn't want to disturb anybody, and I thought maybe if I got myself tired, I could get to sleep."

"*Ja, ja, mein Herr.*"

"I tried taking a drink, but I'm afraid of taking too much. I need to have my wits about me in the morning." He laughed, and took out one of the bottles of cognac, opened it, and took a pull, a small one. He put it back into his pocket. "It is easy to take too much when you are nervous."

"*Ja, mein Herr, das weiss ich gut.*"

IX

They strolled, and Lanny chatted freely, as he had learned to do with all sorts and conditions of men. "I don't suppose you can read French newspapers"—the guest set out to make himself a substitute therefor.

He told about the Cagoulard conspiracy, and how important it would have been for Germany to get a new government in France, one that would break off the alliance with the wicked Reds, which of course was aimed at Germany and could have no other meaning. "They want to do what they did in the last war, compel Germany to fight on two fronts at once, and of course the Führer will never permit that."

So the genial American explained French politics and the world situation to a humble *Diener*, and the *Diener* was impressed by his kindness, and every now and then would say: "*Ja, ja, mein Herr,*" or perhaps "*Herrschaft,*" which is equivalent to the English quality, or gentry, and is the same whether you are many or one. "*Was wünschen der Herr?*"—what does the quality desire?

Lanny desired another pull at the flask, and when he had taken it, he held it out to the man, saying: "*Wollen Sie trinken?*" This, of course, was unthinkable in Germany, and the man was taken aback and tried to refuse; but the genial American insisted that it was no fun to drink alone; he stopped while the man took a nip, and then, laughing, said that wasn't enough and made him take a real one, *einen richtigen.* "I have had too much; you take the rest."

He made the watchman drink until he coughed and sputtered; and after that they were real friends, and, as they strolled, Lanny told how the wicked Reds were working in Paris, with traitorous Germans to help them undermine the Fatherland, and how Lanny had tried to help in getting a new French government that would put down these evil Reds; but now, *leider*, the effort seemed to have collapsed, and Lanny didn't know what would happen; he might have to flee into Germany and give up his labors in Paris, at least for a time. It was extremely sad and he became a bit melancholy, and stopped and took another nip, and saw to it that Max—the nightwatchman's name—took a good one to brace him against the chilly damp wind of a November night. "Finish the bottle," Lanny said, and added, with a slightly tipsy chuckle: "I have another." Max obeyed.

It is well known that men who are in trouble are tempted to drown their sorrows in drink; but a serious and well-trained *Nachtwächter*, charged with a heavy responsibility, cannot afford to do such things, and *der arme Max* pleaded his duty. Lanny let up on him, and they took another circle of the château. The American *Herr* giggled and said he had had too much, but Hans would watch out for him; surely that was one of the duties of a proper *Wächter*. Max admitted that he had had to perform it upon occasions. He made a truly valiant effort to keep sober according to his honor. He was broken down only by

Lanny's assurance that this wasn't real cognac, only an imitation; what tasted like alcohol was only a flavoring, and it wouldn't make any able-bodied man really drunk. Have one more, in the name of *Gemütlichkeit!*

After a while the guest said that he was tired, and they might try sitting for a while; so they sat under the shelter of the porte-cochère, and Lanny took out the other bottle, loosened the cork, took a very small swig, and with laughter and mischief persuaded his companion to take a large one. *Ja, gewiss*, it couldn't possibly do any harm! He kept this up until he was sure the man had got as much on board as even a German could carry; then he said: "I feel warm and sleepy; let's rest." He deposited the bottle between them, and rested his head against the wall and began to breathe heavily. Presently he heard Max taking the bottle and heard a gurgling sound, so he felt sure his game was won. In a very few minutes the man was snoring loudly; then Lanny took the bottle and slipped it into his pocket and stole away.

X

One more duty, a dangerous one. Somewhere in these extensive grounds the dogs were roaming, and the visitor had to find them. Until they were penned up there was no possibility of entrance for any stranger, even in a Nazi uniform. When Lanny was a sufficient distance from the château, it was safe to call, and he did so. "*Ho, Prinz! Komm, Lizzi!*" He heard barking, and moved in that direction, calling now and then. It was so dark, and the wind in the trees so noisy, that the animals were almost upon him before he knew it. A moment of real fear when he heard them; but he mustn't permit that, for he had read that fear has an odor which betrays it to dogs.

Really, the visitor had no cause for worry; he had made sure of these friends, and now he spoke their names and they came in a tumult of greeting. They were perfectly trained and did not leap up on him and put mud on his clothes; they whimpered their delight and no doubt tried to shake their tails off, though he could not see it in the dark. He greeted all four by name, and patted them, and they crowded against him and had a lovely time with all the smells they had learned to know and which told them that this was a friendly god, coming to keep them company in the dark.

Of course they would follow him, along the familiar path back to the familiar kennels. It wasn't their usual time for entering, but if the friendly god opened the gate and took them in, it was not for them to question why. Both pairs knew their pens and their snug little houses, with fresh straw and old home odors. When the friendly god so commanded, they would crawl in out of the cold wind and sleep. The god would take all the responsibility upon his divine shoulders. He did so, and went out, fastening the gate behind him.

There was a corner of the château grounds bordering the highway which Lanny and his fellow conspirators had chosen because it was far from the gatekeeper's lodge and sheltered by shrubbery. Lanny would come to this spot and then count seven posts, which brought him to the one on which he would tie the handkerchief for a signal. Getting there in pitch darkness wasn't easy, but now and then he ventured a moment's flash from his light. The fence was of steel, and he counted the posts by hand, pushing his way past the bushes. Number seven had been chosen because it was plainly visible to anyone passing on the highway, and Lanny took out his tape measure and measured up six feet from the ground, and precisely there he tied the handkerchief, leaving a slipknot so that it could be untied. Six feet from the ground meant: "Everything is clear." Five feet meant: "Come again half an hour later." Four feet meant: "An hour later." Three feet meant: "The plan is off until tomorrow." Two feet meant: "Off for good."

Lanny's part was done, and it was his job to get back to Max and make sure the man's slumbers were not disturbed. If by ill chance he should awaken, Lanny would be ready with more brilliant conversation and the rest of the second bottle. The library had been chosen as the place of entrance because it was on the opposite side of the building from the porte-cochère, and it had been agreed that if there was a watchman Lanny would lure him to the latter spot and keep him busy there. If in any extreme emergency it became necessary for Monck or Hofman to call Lanny, they would give a faint imitation of a hoot-owl.

XI

The watchman was slumped over and still snoring. Lanny felt pretty sure that he could be counted out for several hours. The conspirator himself had nothing to do but keep still, and try not to let his teeth chatter, whether from cold or the excitement of a desperate adventure. Nothing to do but sit and imagine his friends coming up in their car, their lights dimmed to avoid attracting attention; they were supposed to make a round of the place every fifteen minutes, beginning at a quarter to two o'clock. When they saw the handkerchief, they would park their car a safe distance away.

They had in the car a light rope ladder, with hooks at the top, and Hofman, the smaller man, would stand on Monck's back and set the hooks and climb to the top, then pull the ladder over to the other side. Monck would hand up the box of tools and Hofman would take it down to the ground. Then he would climb up again, and keeping his perch on top of the spikes as best he could, let the ladder down on the outside for Monck. Hofman would slide down on the inside, and Monck would come up, drop the ladder inside, and slide down. All this would be done in darkness and silence, and if a car came in sight at the wrong moment, they would both have to hide in the bushes. Everything had been carefully rehearsed, and Lanny didn't need any telepathy to see it happening. But things might go wrong, and he saw those, too, and telepathy didn't tell him which was "reality."

The amateur burglars would have no trouble in finding their way to the château, for its gray walls stood up well lighted in the darkness. They would have to come into that floodlight and cross the terrace and loggia to the windows of the library. They would walk with dignity and assurance, having a story carefully prepared; Hauptmann Branting —that was to be his name—had come from Berlin with a confidential communication for Seine Hochgeboren. Hofman was his secretary, and they had had a breakdown of their car, and not wishing to disturb anyone so late they were prepared to wait under the porte-cochere. If they were caught inside the building, they would say they had found a window open; if it was a servant who caught them, the Hauptmann would overwhelm him with his authority: *Gestapo, Geheimdienst, zu Befehl, Herr Hauptmann, undsoweiter!* Only an officer would be able to meet such a charge of *Autorität*.

But suppose one of the officers happened to be restless, and to come downstairs as Lanny had done? Suppose the Graf himself happened to arrive inopportunely? These were chances the conspirators had to take, and now they were fears that Lanny had to confront. He had read of people's hair turning gray under this sort of strain, and he wondered if it was happening to him. He would have liked to have another nip of the cognac, but was afraid he might need it for the *Nachtwächter*.

The snoring continued, so loudly that if it had been a still night it might have awakened some of the sleepers in the rooms above. But the wind continued to roar and the trees to sway and creak. Lanny kept saying to himself: "It's all right now. Stop worrying!" He said: "Trudi! Trudi! We are coming!"

He didn't permit himself to stir until he was sure that half an hour must have passed since he had hung up the signal. That was time enough for the two men to have climbed the fence and got inside the château, and Lanny stole away from the stupefied watchman and around the building to the library windows. Softly and carefully he opened number three, and stepped inside; he closed it quickly to stop the draft, and then flashed his tiny beam of light upon the carpet. There on the green velvet carpet lay the coin that he had been seeing in his imagination for weeks. A French franc, with the figure turned up, meaning that his friends were inside the building! Oh God, oh God!

Lanny slipped out again, shut the window, and stole back to keep watch over the watchman. He sat on the steps of the porte-cochere, resting his chin in his hands to stop both the chattering of his teeth and the shaking of his hands. For the first time in his life he began to pray. "Oh, God, help them! Oh, God, help Trudi! Let them find her! Help me to bear it till they find her! Oh, God, have mercy!"

And then, after the fashion of modern man, he added: "Oh, God—if there be a God!"

13

My Life on Any Chance

I

THE hardest of all things to do in a time of danger is to do nothing. If Lanny had been under the necessity of talking to the nightwatchman and keeping that functionary's mind busy, that would have kept Lanny's mind busy, too. But just to sit there and listen to the man snore and watch for indications that he might be waking up—that indeed was a strain upon the nerves. Who might be awake inside this château at half past two in the morning? Somebody tending a furnace? Somebody keeping watch over prisoners? And what would they make of a strange Hauptmann Branting and his commission to investigate the contents of the dungeons and interview the prisoners therein? Would they obey orders and help him, or would they turn and run and alarm the household? Such problems offered endless scope to the imagination, and Lanny's mind hardly waited to complete one alarming episode before it started another.

Every now and then he would take out his watch and flash the tiny light upon its face for a moment. Never since the invention of clocks had a pair of hands moved so slowly. He had set himself a half hour as the proper time to allow, but he couldn't stand it; at the end of twenty minutes he got up and stole around to the library windows and slipped inside to look at the coin on the floor. If it had been turned over, it meant that the burglars had completed their errand and gone; it would then be Lanny's duty to put the coin in his pocket, go out and release the dogs, then re-enter the building, fasten the windows securely, and get back to his room as quickly as possible. But, alas, there was Marianne, or liberty, or the republic, or whoever it might be—still sowing the seeds of revolt, or enlightenment, or prosperity, or whatever that might be. The burglars were still at their work, and Lanny had to go back to his vigil at the porte-cochere and resume the imagining of difficulties.

He had heard Horace Hofman talking for hours about locks ancient and modern, and the kind one might expect to encounter here. Old ones might have been taken out, of course, and new ones put on. Vaults might have been built, with steel walls and modern safe locks, time locks, anything. These would present difficulties and take time, perhaps more time than could be counted on. The Meister-Schlosser had told many stories of human lives depending upon the speed of fingers which were insured for a hundred thousand dollars; so far, he had never lost out, but this might be where the record was broken. They had set four o'clock as the hour beyond which it would be unsafe to stay. Darkness lingered long at this time of the year, but the estate was a small farm, and farm workers go by the clock and not by the sun—at least they would do so in a well-ordered German establishment.

So Lanny went back to his post, crouching out of the wind and drawing his English tweed overcoat tightly about him; his hands were trembling but the palms were moist, so it wasn't the cold. The snoring began to be broken and replaced by mutterings, and Lanny's heart began to pound with a new fear. The watchman turned over, he made an effort to lift himself on one elbow. "*Ach, wer ist's?*" he groaned.

Lanny took out the bottle and uncorked it. "*Hier! Wollen Sie trinken?*"

"*Nein, nein!*" The man tried to protest, but Lanny bent over him, held his head, put the bottle to his lips. "*Trinken Sie! Er ist gut!*" When the man opened his mouth to protest, Lanny pushed the bottle in and lifted it. There was a gurgling sound, and presumably the liquor was going down his throat and not his windpipe. "*Gut, gut!*" Lanny

kept saying, which is soothing to a German; at last the man sank back
with a heavy sigh. That would do him for a while.

II

There had been a play called *Alias Jimmy Valentine*, about a safe-
cracker who betrayed his identity by opening a safe in which a little
girl had been accidentally locked. This man was supposed to have sand-
papered the skin of his finger tips until they were raw; but Hofman said
that was nonsense, for pain would destroy those delicate sensitivities by
which you became aware of the dropping of a tiny tumbler. Ordinary
locks you could open, as a rule, without too great delay, because you
understood the principles on which they were constructed, and the
weak points; by delicate probing you could determine exactly the location of the locking bolt and of the tumblers. But it always took a certain amount of time, and you had to refuse to let yourself be hurried or
worried. Put your mind on it to the exclusion of everything else, just
as if it were a problem in chess. Monck, alias Branting, would mount
guard, and Hofman would forget there were such dangerous creatures
as Nazis in the world.

Such, at any rate, was the program. How many locked doors would
there be, and how could the invaders be sure which ones to open?
Would the Nazis lock the door or doors which led into the cellars?
Quite possibly; but again, it might be they would lock the doors of the
different rooms in which they stored food, wine, trunks, and other
property. If they had a number of dungeon cells, these would probably be in a separate part, and that part would be walled off and have
a steel door, or perhaps more than one, to keep the sounds from being
heard. Would they have a keeper inside this place at night, or would
they just lock their captives up and forget them till morning? The
French word *oubliette* means a place forgotten, or for persons forgotten, and the Nazis presumably would not let their slumber be disturbed
by worries over their captives. If one died, it would be no great loss;
but there might be one like Trudi Schultz who had vital secrets locked
in her mind, and they might take special care of her and keep her
guarded day and night.

Such had been the subjects of Lanny's thought for several months,
and of long discussions among the three conspirators. Now two of
them were finding out what they needed to know, while Lanny still
could only speculate. No news was good news to this extent, that no
alarm had so far been given. If that had happened there would have

been lights coming on in the rooms above, and surely someone would have called to the *Nachtwächter*, or come to look for him. If the two burglars had found a guard in the cellar, they would use their arts to persuade him that they were Gestapo agents and must be obeyed; only as a last resort would they overpower him and tie him up while they worked. Lanny's busy imagination pictured such a series of events—he pictured many different series, and some of them caused his teeth to chatter so that he held his jaw tightly cupped in his hands.

This was certain: if any violence was used, Lanny's position with the Nazis would be pretty certainly destroyed, for he could never persuade them that he had not admitted the intruders to the place. The same might be true if the occupants of the château discovered in the morning that their woman prisoner had disappeared without a trace. Lanny might protest ever so earnestly that he had been asleep in his room and knew nothing about it, but they would be sure to trail him for the rest of his days, or until they solved the mystery. He could certainly not live with Trudi again, whether in Paris or London or New York. He could hear Trudi saying: "Oh, Lanny, you shouldn't have done it!" and his only plea could be that he had loved her more than duty. What would be her attitude to this form of constancy?—or would she call it inconstancy?

Lanny would listen for a few moments to the snoring of the watchman, and then he would go off on another train of speculations, few of them happy, many of them melodramatic. If there were untoward events of any sort, the Nazis would be sure to question the watchman, and it was hardly conceivable that poor Max could withhold the fact that he had been drunk, or refuse to reveal that it was the American guest who had got him drunk. The guest saw himself being summoned before a board of inquiry consisting of Seine Hochgeboren and his staff. Just how had he spent the night, and how had it happened that he had got the watchman drunk while keeping himself sober—especially since he had given Rörich and Fiedler to understand that he got drunk with extraordinary ease? Was he accustomed to carry bottles of cognac around in his overcoat pockets? And just where had he been on the estate, and would he be so kind as to let them examine his shoes? Just when Lanny had got through assuring them that he had not been anywhere but on the loggia and the drive, he would find himself confronted with the fact that his footprints had been discovered at a corner of the estate close to the highway!

III

From scenes such as this Lanny's overstimulated imagination would return to the immediate present. He saw a vision of Hofman on his knees before a dungeon door, fiddling with the lock, putting in one skeleton key after another, shaking his head and muttering: "It is too much for me." Was that a case of telepathy, or just his fears taking form? Did he really see Monck standing with his lips to an opening in a cell door, whispering: "Is that you, Trudi?" Perhaps that was Lanny's own painfully acquired knowledge of how dungeons are constructed.

They have to have airholes, unless it is intended to suffocate the prisoner. There is always an opening at the level of the keeper's eyes, so that he can look in, and a larger one at the bottom, through which he can shove food and water. These are closed by sliding covers which cannot be opened from the inside, but only from the outside; they would have to be left open at night, and even if they were closed, they couldn't be locked. Monck would open them, and if Trudi was there, and was conscious, the would-be rescuers would tell her what they were doing. They wouldn't speak the name of Lanny Budd, but they might say: "*Ça ira*"; also the Latin phrase, "*Bella gerant alii*," which was the password Lanny had used in his effort to get Alfred Pomeroy-Neilson out of the Franco dungeon. He had told Trudi this story and explained the meaning of the phrase; also he had told Monck.

Another half hour had passed. Max was still in his stupor, and Lanny made another trip to the library windows. He held his breath as he turned his flashlight on the carpet inside, and something seemed to give way in the pit of his stomach when he saw that the coin had not been turned over. It was nearly half past three, and they were still down in those cellars—doing what? Lanny was free to go back to the porte-cochere, crouch out of the wind, and do all the guessing he pleased.

"Give me time, and don't worry"—so Hofman had said; but now Trudi's husband discovered that this was beyond the possibilities of his mind. He was so worried that it seemed to him he just couldn't stand it. Had the two men been overpowered? Or had somebody locked them in? A curious fate that would be for a locksmith! Or had they got lost! That was a new idea which hit the waiting conspirator with painful violence. The plans of the building which they had obtained did not show what was underground. Certainly the passages must be extensive, and there might even be difficulties deliberately constructed; there might be trapdoors, or trick doors which closed when you passed through them. What more likely than that the Nazis had protected themselves by some modern device of the photoelectric cell, to keep their prisoners secure and to trap any unauthorized person who ventured into forbidden premises?

A nasty idea, and the longer Lanny held it, the more havoc it made in his mind. He thought: "When they pass a certain spot or touch a certain door, it may ring an alarm bell in Hauptmann Bohlen's room!" Lanny hadn't heard any bell, but he wouldn't have heard it in the midst of this windstorm. Even at that moment the Nazis might have pistols at the heads of the two would-be burglars and be saying: "*Hände hoch!*"

IV

The time came when Lanny couldn't stand it any more. If the men were lost, he had to find them; if they were trapped he had to free them. He had to put an end to the suspense which had been tormenting him for the past three months, and know if Trudi was there, and if she was herself, able to speak and to know what was happening. He had become obsessed by the vision of her behind a steel door, whispering through the aperture, and Hofman on the other side, unable to solve the secret of the lock. If that was the case, Lanny would get her out if he died for it; he would get Jean to hire half a dozen of the leftists among the village men, arm them with Budd automatics, and have them raid the château the following night, sever the telephone wires, hold up the inmates, and cut out the lock of the dungeon door with an electric torch!

Max was still in his stupor; and once more Lanny walked through the floodlights, turned the handle of the French window, and saw the curtains billow out in the wind. Quickly he closed the door and flashed his little torch. The coin was still heads up; and Lanny moved silently across the library and into the dining hall. Beyond that a pair of swinging doors led to a passageway; he had seen the waiters coming through these doors at mealtimes, and according to the plans of the building there was a large butler's pantry and beyond it the kitchen. From one side of the pantry a door opened to the cellar stairs, and that was as far as the plans showed. From there on Lanny would be groping his way.

The stair door was not locked. Lanny opened it with care, making no click, and stood listening. The silence was that supposed to be appropriate to the tomb. He flashed his torch for one moment and saw that the stairs were made of heavy blocks of stone, well worn by nearly two hundred years of use. One glance was enough and he shut off the light, which might alarm either his enemies or his friends. He went down the steps, one at a time, stopping to listen for the faintest sound, and using his utmost efforts not to make any. At the bottom was another door, and he tried it softly and found it was unlocked. Had Hofman unlocked it? He had said that they would close every door they found closed, so as to avoid attracting the attention of anyone who might happen to be passing.

The intruder flashed his light again. A long corridor, about six feet wide, running in both directions; walls of stone, and a number of doors of heavy wood, all having locks. Storerooms, no doubt; the locks were large and old, something that was to be expected. The conspirators had agreed that there would hardly be prisoners behind wooden doors without openings; also, a door which shut off the dungeon part of the cellars from the storeroom portions would almost certainly be of steel, or at least of heavy iron.

Which way had Monck and Hofman gone? Lanny might have told them to drop a scrap of paper for an indication; but the idea that he might follow them had never been contemplated. He had to make a guess, as they had doubtless done; he chose the direction in which he knew the main part of the building lay. Before he started he took a franc from his purse and laid it in front of the door. If his friends saw it, they might guess what it meant; in any case, it would serve to tell Lanny himself how to find the stairs again. He would count his steps, and make careful note of every turn he made.

One—two—three—four—five—six—seven. Lanny taking tiptoe steps, in black darkness, guiding himself by the walls; stopping every few steps to listen, and thinking that the crazy pounding of his heart must be echoing up and down the corridor like any other sort of pumping plant. He knew he was in the midst of dangers, and didn't try to deny to himself that he was scared. He wanted very much to be out of there, and all that held him was the desire to take Trudi with him. Try as he would, he failed to think of any plausible reason he could give Seine Hochgeboren for tiptoeing about in the cellars of that nobleman's country home at half past three in the morning. He could say that he craved a drink of liquor; but what about the half bottle of cognac he had in his pocket? Could he say he had found that in the cellar? They would surely ask him: "Where?"

V

Presently he came to a cross corridor, and there he stopped and listened long. Not a sound in this tomb. He felt about him with his hands and made certain of the layout; he had three directions to choose among, and no time to be wasted; he flashed on his light, down one corridor and then the next. He saw a shadow darting swiftly down one of them, and his heart leaped so that it hurt. A sound of scurrying feet—a rat. He and his friends had discussed this as one of the phenomena to be expected. "Rats go wherever men go," Monck had said; "they have better brains and will outlast us." The three had debated this idea; an ex-sailor, who had lived among rats and observed them closely, pointed out that men chose to think about a great variety of matters, but rats thought about nothing but taking care of rats. Their method was outwitting men and stealing their food. Also, they didn't fight one another, at least not persistently, and in armies, as men did. "And doesn't that prove they have better brains?"

Here they were, taking this old château for their own, and having nothing to do but burrow themselves into safe hiding places and get access to stores of food. Doubtless they compelled Seine Hochgeboren, and before him M. le Duc, to pay tens of thousands of francs every year for food for them. They had gnawed holes at the bottom of most of these wooden doors. Perhaps—oh, God!—they had got into the cell where Trudi had been confined, and eaten the ends of her fingers and toes on occasions when she lay unconscious. Doubtless there were cats also in these cellars; they do not concern themselves about strangers, and would make no trouble for Lanny—but one little terrier dog might bring all their plans to ruin.

Lanny went down one of the side corridors and found himself confronting a row of coal bins, filled to overflowing. This building had not been modernized, and all its rooms were heated by grate fires; the coal was shoveled into scuttles—here was a row of them. A large dumbwaiter, the invention of the American Thomas Jefferson, went up through the floor above. This was the rear of the building, and Lanny had stupidly guessed that it might be where the dungeons were situated—overlooking such commonplace necessities as coal chutes, and the delivery and storage of huge quantities of food and wine.

He retraced his steps, counting them carefully, seventy-four tiptoe steps, which are not so long. He found the coin on the floor and left it there; he went in the other direction, and it wasn't long before he came to another cross corridor. Again he felt about him, and listened, holding his breath. What sounds would his friends be making? Hofman would probably be crouched down, working on a lock, and the sounds he made would be so faint that he himself could hardly hear them. He might or might not be using a flashlight. Monck might be standing guard, or perhaps prowling in different directions to listen. Both men were wearing rubber overshoes. Both would be as nervous as Lanny, though their pride might forbid them to admit it. Certainly neither would thank him for sneaking up on them and causing their hearts to stop beating.

The explorer turned his tiny light down one of the cross corridors. It vanished into nothingness, and he tiptoed in that direction and found a large space piled solid with split logs: a store of wood for the great fireplaces above. Doubtless there was a dumbwaiter leading to a service room above. There was a great scurrying of rats here, and Lanny guessed that hundreds of generations of them had come to being in the interstices of those logs. Perhaps they never went out into the daylight, and had lost the power to see except in the dark. The thought came: "At what hour in the morning do the servants start to get coal and wood up to the floors above?"

VI

Lanny hastened his steps, exploring the anatomy of the ancient establishment of the Belcour family, favorites of King Louis the Sixteenth of France. Surely they had had enemies and the need to keep these enemies where they could do no harm. Even if it hadn't been so, even if they had relied upon the King to protect them, the architects would have put in dungeons, because dungeons were a proper feature of châteaux.

Lanny's gloved hands came to a door which seemed different from the others and he flashed the torch. Iron, black-painted, with rust in spots. He tried the knob softly, and it turned; the door came open, with the faintest trace of creaking. The intruder listened again; not a sound, not even a rat. He flashed his torch, and saw stone steps going down. Here was the place! He and his friends had agreed that if they could find a way to a second level in the cellars, that was where the dungeons would be. A place where the cries of the unhappy could never reach the guests in the banquet hall and on the dancing floor! A place where nobody could signal the unfortunates by playing Blondel songs on a grand piano!

Lanny took one step down, and then silently, oh, so carefully, closed the door, cursing its faint creaks. He didn't want to alarm his friends, and he could count upon it that they were here. Almost certainly the reason this door was unlocked was that the Meister-Schlosser had solved its mysteries.

As soon as the door was tightly closed, Lanny gave the signal agreed upon, an owl's hoot: "Hoo, *hoo!*" with the accent on the second syllable, long drawn. They had planned it for outdoors, where it would be more appropriate. Or was it conceivable that there were openings into these cellars through which owls might find their way? Would they be nesting in crannies up above the piles of logs, and pouncing on the rats that scurried on the floor? Just as rats have nothing to think about but rats, so owls would have nothing to think about but owls; and they, too, might outlast men, having brains enough not to fight their fellow-owls.

No answer to the call. With his gloved hands on the walls at each side of the narrow passage, Lanny went down, step by step—sixteen of them, and sixteen times he put his weight on the stones with painful slowness, for he had no rubber shoes to dull the sound. At the bottom the corridor went straight ahead, and he didn't dare to flash the light, but stood again and called, a bit louder: "Hoo, *hoo!*" This time he heard an answer, faint but prompt. Some other owl was in this subterranean tunnel!

Lanny wasted no fraction of a second, but went toward the sound, as quickly as he could on tiptoe. There was a turn in the passage, and when he came there, the beam of a flashlight appeared suddenly full upon him. He stopped, and flashed his own tiny light, and there was the spectacle he had been imagining for the past two hours; Hofman on his knees before a door, with his metal box of tools beside him, and Monck on guard behind him with a torchlight in his hand. One glimpse was enough for all three, and they shut off their lights at the same moment. Lanny came to the locksmith and whispered, barely audibly: "What have you found?"

"There is somebody in here."

"Is it Trudi?"

"We can't be sure. We hear groans; nothing else."

"Man or woman?"

"We can't tell that."

"Can you get the door open?"

"I think so. I am working." Not a word more; he went to work. Monck drew Lanny a short way into the corridor, so that they would not disturb Hofman. The German whispered: "Why did you come?"

"I thought you must be in trouble."

"The dogs are penned up?"

"Yes."

"Is there a watchman?"

"I have him blind drunk. I don't think he will move."

"Everything else O.K.?"

"So far as I know. Have you opened any of these other doors?"

"We haven't had time. We had to open three doors on the way here. I've listened at all the cell doors and heard nothing. All the slots are closed but this one, and that seems to indicate the others are empty."

VII

Hofman whispered: "Hush!" and they fell silent. He was working in darkness, guided by his senses of touch and hearing. He had some kind of instrument in the keyhole and was moving it ever so gently. Only he could hear the sounds, and know what they meant; that was his business, at which he had worked and played most of his life. Lanny would have liked to listen at those other doors, but he was afraid to move a muscle; Monck had listened, and that had to be enough. Time, which had stood still for Lanny, was now racing for all three of them.

Suddenly there came a clicking sound, and a whisper: "I have it!" The lock turned, and the door creaked on its hinges. In the second which that took, Lanny and Monck had moved to the locksmith's side, and when he flashed his torch into the cell, all three pairs of eyes were as one.

The place was about ten feet long and eight wide. It had no window; only the two openings, one at the top and one at the bottom of the door. The air was fetid, and had the smell of dried blood which Lanny had learned to know in Nazi dungeons. In the far corner, to the right as you entered, was an iron cot, and on it lay a figure covered with a dirty gray blanket. Hofman stepped in and they followed, all three with their torches turned on. In that bright light they saw that the prisoner was a man, stoutish, gray-haired, and with a straggly gray beard which might have taken a week to grow.

In the light the prisoner stirred and groaned, but did not open his eyes; he was alive, but perhaps not much more than that. There were wounds on his head, unbandaged, and the blood had run over his face.

Apparently he had been left here to die, if he chose to do so. Beside the cot was a plate with dry bread, a tin cup, and a pitcher with water. Whether he was able to help himself to these was apparently no concern of the men who had left him here.

"He looks to be a German," whispered Monck; but of course one couldn't be sure, since there are so many types of Germans, and they have been so thoroughly mixed with bordering and invading peoples through the centuries.

Lanny suggested: "Your uniform may frighten him. Better wait outside for a bit."

Monck went out, and Lanny poured some water into the tin cup, and sprinkled it into the man's face. He stirred and moaned, but did not open his eyes. Lanny whispered: "Lift up his head," and Hofman set his torch on the stand and did as requested. "The whole back of his head is bloody," he declared.

Lanny put the water to the man's lips and tried to get him to drink. Lanny had to take one gloved hand and press his jaw down to get his mouth open; then he poured in a little water and the man swallowed it. He began to moan: "*Ach! Oh weh!*"—which confirmed the guess as to his nationality. He laid his head down, but still he did not speak, and Lanny said: "I'll try a little cognac."

He took the bottle from his pocket and uncorked it. Hofman raised the poor fellow again, and Lanny poured in a few drops of the liquor; this started the man to coughing, and Lanny waited, then tried a little more. At the same time he murmured: "*Wir sind Freunde*"—we are friends; and then: "You have nothing to fear."

The man opened his eyes, which were pale blue; one had been badly bruised and may have been useless. Lanny went on whispering reassurances, but perhaps his words were not understood. There was terror in the prisoner's face, and he cried faintly: "*Nicht peitschen!*" Do not whip me!

Lanny repeated, over and over: "We are friends. Do not be afraid." But the prisoner began to whimper in a faint voice. Evidently nobody had come into this cell for any purpose but to torture him, and whatever else they told him would be a trick.

Hofman whispered into Lanny's ear: "We cannot stay. Our time is up." But Lanny had no idea of leaving without some further effort.

"I have an idea," he said. He pulled off the blanket, revealing a sickening spectacle; the man had apparently been whipped on both his front and back; the former was a mass of bloody stripes. But Lanny was hardened to Nazi methods and didn't stop for comment; he hastily folded the blanket, and said to Hofman: "Lift him up." He placed the folded blanket so as to prop the man's head up, facing forward; then he sat beside the victim, leaning over him, and flashed the tiny torchlight into his eyes. Lanny began to murmur softly: *"Wir sind Freunde,"* and *"Keine Angst!"*—don't be afraid. Then in a sort of singsong, slowly: *"Sie wollen schlafen"*—you want to sleep. *"Sie wollen schlafen, Sie wollen schlafen!"*—over and over. Lanny had read somewhere that you cannot hypnotize a man without his own consent; but perhaps a man in a daze like this wouldn't know how to refuse. Anyhow, why not try? He went on and on trying, in spite of Hofman's whispered protests.

The prisoner was staring into the light, and perhaps he was getting the words; his whimpering ceased, and apparently he was being calmed. Lanny began passing his free hand before his face, just below the beam, not interrupting it entirely. He changed his formula: *"Sie schlafen—Sie schlafen. Schlafen—schlafen."* It is a good singing word, with a broad "a" as the Germans say it; and after seemingly endless repetitions of it, the eyes closed. The man might be in a trance, or he might be asleep, or he might be dead. It wouldn't take long to find out.

VIII

Lanny shut off the torch and bent close to the man's face, whispering: "We are friends. *Freunde, Freunde.* We won't harm you. Tell me who you are. *Was ist ihr Name?"* He kept repeating these words, until at last there came a reply, so faintly that Lanny couldn't be sure whether he heard, or whether his own imagination was supplying it. He wanted Hofman to hear it too, so he said: *"Lauter. Noch einmal. Ihr Name."*

This time Hofman could hear, and what a jolt it gave him! First Paul, and then Teicher, the first name pronounced "Powl," in German fashion. The name that both Lanny and Hofman had heard in the séance room from the lips of the old Polish woman, supposed to be speaking for Ludi Schultz! The old man who was kind, and who had tried to help Trudi, and who was being tortured by the Nazis! This was he!

"*Sagen Sie, Paul,* there was a woman prisoner here?"

"*Ja—eine junge Frau.*"

"What was her name?"

"*Nein, nein!* She wouldn't tell! She didn't tell me! *Ich weiss nichts!*" Evidently this question terrified the victim.

"Don't be afraid, Paul. We are friends. Your friends and her friends also. Was her name Trudi?"

"They said that was her name."

"The Nazis said that?"

"But she wouldn't say. She wouldn't tell me." Still the terror.

"What did they do with her?"

"They beat her, but she never talked."

"Is she here now?"

"No, they took her away."

"Where did they take her?"

"To Germany."

"Why did they do that?"

"Because she wouldn't tell them anything."

"They didn't kill her?"

"I don't think so."

"Why did they beat you?"

"I tried to help her."

"What did you do?"

"She wrote a letter and I tried to take it out. They were watching me and they got it."

"Who was the letter to?"

"A French name, I forget. Long—something."

"Longuet?"

"That is it."

Lanny needed to ask no more. Manifestly, Trudi couldn't have written to him, or to any of her comrades of the underground. She had thought of Jean Longuet, editor of the Socialist newspaper in Paris; she had heard Lanny talk about him, and knew that Lanny had been sending him secret news from Spain. He was well known, and to name him would be revealing no secret to the Nazis.

Monck came in from his vigil in the passage. "It is a quarter past four and we are taking a grave risk."

"One moment," Lanny answered. Turning to the prisoner, he said, in a firm voice: "Paul, you will not tell anyone that we have been here."

"*Nein, mein Herr.*"

"You will not remember that we have been here. You will forget. *Vergessen—vergessen. Verstehen Sie?*"

"*Ja, mein Herr.*"

"You will sleep and get well. *Schlafen und gesund werden.*"

"*Ja, mein Herr.*"

With Hofman's help Lanny laid the victim flat again and put the blanket over him. With quick strokes of his handkerchief Hofman wiped the pitcher and cup, so that not even the marks of gloved hands might be left on them. Bending over the prisoner's face, Lanny whispered: "You will wake up." He snapped his fingers. "You are awake."

They couldn't delay to make sure. Monck took the American by the arm, guessing rightly that it was hard for him to tear himself from this scene, and that he might be a little weak in the knees. "Come," he commanded, firmly, and led him to the door. All torches went off, and they came into the corridor, and waited while Hofman fiddled with the lock. They heard it faintly click. "O.K.," he whispered, and Monck picked up the heavy box of tools, he being the sturdier man. They went down the corridor, softly but swiftly.

IX

No reason for delay now; they had only one thing to do, to get out. They went up the stairs, and closed the door at the top. Apparently Hofman had made a passkey, for he needed but a moment to lock it. In single file they went down the long corridor in the upper cellar, feeling their way by the walls. Had they counted the number of steps? Lanny didn't ask; it was enough that he had counted, and now counted again. He knew the turns, but didn't have to prompt the others, for Hofman, in the lead, took them straight to the proper door. Lanny flashed his tiny light for the fraction of a second, just long enough to pick up the coin which he had laid on the floor. Hofman opened the door softly, and when the others had gone through, he closed it behind him, but did not stop to lock it; he was willing to let it be supposed that some careless person had forgotten to lock it.

They went up the flight of stairs on tiptoe, and waited while Hofman slowly and carefully opened the door which led into the butler's pantry; he held it open a fraction of an inch, listening. This was a moment of danger, for there was a good chance that some servant might be getting early to work. But there was no sound, and Hofman opened the door all the way. When the others had passed through, he closed it, and again did not stop to lock it. Lanny didn't ask if it had been found locked; he was sure that Hofman knew his business, and time was galloping for them.

Into the dining room, and past the long table of French walnut at which Lanny had eaten a meal and might eat more; past the historical paintings upon which Lanny had discoursed to Rörich. A dim light pervaded these rooms, and the three intruders looked in every direction, all their senses alert. Across a wide hall, and then into the library, and over the soft velvet carpet to the third window from the northwest corner. Hofman stooped and picked up the coin, and then opened the half-window, really a narrow door. A blast of wind, a long blast, while three men slipped through; then he closed the barrier behind them.

Had the watchman awakened? Had the dogs been turned loose? These were chances they had to take, and there was nothing to be said about them. "*Au revoir*," whispered the locksmith, and Lanny replied: "See you in Paris this morning." The two started across the floodlighted loggia, a paved and uncovered space in front of the château. They did not run, but moved with the dignity appropriate to an SS Hauptmann charged with secret duties by the Gestapo. Hofman was now carrying the tool kit—for of course it was unthinkable that an officer would perform such menial service. Lanny did not wait to watch them, but walked with his practiced casualness around the building to the porte-cochere.

The watchman was still breathing heavily, and that was to the good, though Lanny's peril was still far from over. He had to wait for a period of ten minutes, that being their estimate of the time required for the men to get to the steel fence and climb it. Once they were out of the light, they could carry the box of tools between them and make good time. The ladder was hidden in the bushes, and it wouldn't take them long to get it up and climb over. But there was the possibility that some car might be passing; a peasant cart might delay them quite a while. It wouldn't do for them to be seen climbing the fence with a heavy box, and still less would it do for the dogs to be turned loose until they were safely over.

X

So Lanny had to sit there and think about Trudi, and realize that he had proved all the worst that he had imagined. In that cell, or in one of the others adjoining, she had spent something like three months, being whipped and tortured by those half-dozen cultivated monsters with whom Lanny had eaten meals and might have to eat more. A feeling of nausea came over him, and he had to clench his hands and set his teeth tightly together. He wished that he had brought along his Budd automatic in his bag; he saw himself carrying it in his pocket when he went down to breakfast, and suddenly producing it and shooting down those men in a row. But no, it wouldn't do the least good; he was fighting not men but a government and a system of thought, a set of ideas. The day might come when guns would be used, but it wouldn't be one gun; it would be millions and perhaps tens of millions.

He had got here too late. The delay was something he would never be able to forgive himself. But what could he have done? Everything had depended upon his becoming a guest in the château, and how could he have managed that a day earlier? Should he have tipped off the Socialists in the French government as to the Cagoulard conspiracy and thus caused the raid earlier? Possibly he might have done so; but the idea had not occurred to him until the telephone call had come from Annette de Bruyne. He couldn't have given his name in an accusation which involved the de Bruyne family; and would the French cabinet have acted upon the basis of anonymous charges? No, that was just a crazy idea, one of many with which Lanny would torment himself, because he had to blame somebody for this tragic *dénouement*.

He had failed completely, and forever, so he told himself, with sickness of heart and soul. The Nazis now had Trudi inside the vast dungeon which was Germany. They had taken her there to kill her, because they couldn't break her will, and killing was what they did with the bravest and best. Lanny had no way to find her, and would never even know what had happened to her—unless some day she would appear at the foot of his bed in the night, or unless she would speak to him with the voice of Tecumseh. All Lanny's elaborate efforts had been for nothing; all the time and expense, bringing Hofman from New York and Monck from Spain; all Lanny's own time and labor, when he might have been really doing his job as presidential agent.

It was good to crouch there in the darkness and shiver with cold and grief and rage all combined; it helped to pass the time, which was again standing still. All Lanny could hope to save out of this misadventure was the ability to go on deceiving the Nazi-Fascists. He still might fail at that, for Paul might not obey the hypnotic suggestion, or Max might stay drunk and tell who had got him drunk. The dogs might make a disturbance, the two burglars might be delayed in getting over the fence, somebody might see Lanny coming in at the library windows—oh, yes, there were plenty of mishaps to be imagined, and to keep Lanny looking at his watch. It might even be that some of the Nazis would be using hypnotism or telepathy, clairvoyance or trance mediumship. Two could play at that game, and Hitler had men who knew all about it. You fought the devil with fire, and then discovered that he had discovered a new and hotter kind!

Oh, God, oh, God, poor Trudi! Lanny would have to give her up; yet, no sooner did the idea cross his mind than he knew that he couldn't do it. Already he began thinking about ways to find her in Germany. Who would have her in charge—Hitler himself, or Göring or Goebbels or Ribbentrop or Himmler? Could Lanny find that out if he stayed with the Graf and cultivated his friendship? Poor fool—so the son of Budd-Erling called himself—sitting here dreaming about such achievements, before he had even made sure that he could escape detection and the complete ruination of his career!

XI

The little imps or hobs or whatever they were that were sitting on the hands of Lanny's watch and keeping them immovable at last had to let go; the ten minutes' period was up, and Lanny arose and walked quietly to the rear of the building and back to the kennels. Nobody was there, at least not in sight. The dogs heard him coming and were on the alert; they weren't used to being turned out at this hour, but whatever the friendly god did was all right. He opened the gates and they followed him; he closed the gates behind them and told them to run, and away they went into the darkness. They might find the scent of the men and might lead their keepers to discover the tracks, but if the invaders had got away in their car there would be no solving of that mystery.

Lanny returned to the porte-cochere. He grabbed the watchman by the shoulders and shook him, saying: *"Aufstehen! Aufstehen!"* The man began to groan and protest; no doubt he had a headache that he wouldn't forget for a long while. He must be roused sufficiently to get on his feet, and be made to realize his own danger, that of losing his job, a terrible thing to an elderly citizen of Germany, where everybody is regimented and his life-time record is on file. Lanny kept on shaking him, more and more vigorously, and commanding sternly but not loudly: *"Wake up! Aufwachen, Sie Esel!"*

Lanny ventured a flash of his torch. By one of the pillars of the porte-cochere was a hydrant, used for sprinkling the flowers and washing the drive. Lanny turned it on slightly and got a little water in his handsome Homburg hat and went and threw it into the watchman's face. He did it a second time, and by dint of more shaking and pulling he got the poor fellow onto his feet. "Now, walk!" he commanded. "*Sie sind betrunken, Sie armer Narr!* If they find you this way, you will be sent back to Germany. *Verstehen Sie?*"

"*Ja, ja, mein Herr.*"

"All right then, keep walking. Don't let anybody know you have been drinking. Don't say anything about me, or they will get it out of you. You understand?"

Poor Max began to stagger along, with the American half holding him up. *Ja, ja,* he understood everything, and was terrified; *ach leider,* and *Herrgott,* and *bitte um Verzeihung, Herr!* And then *Oh weh, oh weh,* which is the equivalent of the English woe, and *bitte sehr,* which is please very much—everything a poor terrified elderly *Diener* could think of. "We have left undone those things which we ought to have done; and we have done those things which we ought not to have done; and there is no health in us,"—so runs the English formula, and this abject Pomeranian made it all up in his own language. Lanny would shove him along and catch him when he stumbled, and keep saying: "*Vorwärts, marsch, machen Sie sich auf die Socken!*— Keep moving and don't sit down or you will fall asleep again and they will find you drunk."

"*Ja, ja, mein Herr! Danke schön, mein Herr!*"—and so on. Lanny knew there were still a couple of hours before dawn in the middle of November, and if the man could be sufficiently frightened and would keep on his feet, he would get over his spree and get to his bed without attracting attention. Lanny walked him all the way around the château, and then dared not stay with him any longer. He gave a final set of injunctions and obtained a final set of promises, and then went up to the loggia, scraped his feet thoroughly, and went in by the library window. Inside, he closed the window carefully, and fastened all the bolts; he took one glimpse around to make sure that the coast was clear, and then went quietly to the stairway. Still there was nobody about, so far as he could see. He went softly up the stairs and walked down the corridor to his room. He hadn't failed to note which was his own door; he turned the knob and slipped silently in; he closed the door and locked it, and then went to the bed and dropped upon it and began to weep softly to himself—partly for Trudi, and partly in reaction from the frightful strain under which he had been laboring, not for three hours, not for three days, but for the three longest months of his life.

XII

Lanny did not sleep at all. He lay on the bed and rehearsed his night's or rather his morning's work, and tried to see if there was any flaw in the perfect crime. He searched his overcoat for smears of blood which might be difficult to explain; he found several on the sleeves, but they were small, and he rubbed them with a damp handkerchief. Fortunately tweeds do not show stains conspicuously. He washed his hands thoroughly, not forgetting his fingernails; he scraped and polished the soles of his shoes, and saw to it that the scrapings went down the drain. He hung his hat over his reading lamp, with the light turned on to dry it quickly. He shaved and put on a clean shirt, and when he went down to breakfast he looked reasonably fit and self-possessed.

Did any of the Nazis have anything on their minds? If so, they were as good actors as Lanny. The morning papers from Paris were there, and everybody looked into them eagerly, and then talked about what he saw. Arrests were continuing, and *l'affaire Cagoulard* was occupying the attention of all France. *L'Action française*, which espoused the cause of these bold brave heroes, charged in flaring headlines that the exposure was the result of base betrayal, a jealousy vendetta by the partisans of the Croix de Feu. It was a feud between Léon Daudet and Duc Pozzo di Borgo on the one side and Colonel de la Rocque on the other, and the Nazis at breakfast agreed that it was conclusive proof of the impossibility of dealing with the French, so feminine and unstable, so poisoned through with the virus of individualism and democracy.

Lanny agreed with everything; and after he had had coffee and toast, and felt better, he borrowed one of the papers and sat in the library to read it. Incidentally he had a good look at the third window from the northwest corner and made certain that the carpet was not too dirty and that the long velvet curtains hung properly. When his reading was finished he sought out Eduard vom Rath in the office, and said: "Herr vom Rath, I have been reading the news and thinking things over, and I have made up my mind that this is one of those tempests in a teapot, of which I have seen so many in this unstable nation. I no longer feel that I am in serious danger, so long as I go about my art business and keep away from those who are having trouble with the police."

"*Ich verstehe, Herr Budd.* It has been a real pleasure to have you with us."

"I know that Seine Hochgeboren is disturbed at having me here, and his reasons are obvious and proper. Will you be so kind as to present him my compliments and let him know of my decision?"

"*Selbstverständlich, Herr Budd.*"

"I know that courtesy requires me to thank him personally for his hospitality, but under the peculiar circumstances it would not be wise for me to call on him, or even to telephone or write him."

"*Ja, ja, das wird er einsehen.*"

"If he calls up, you can tell him that the guest has departed, without using my name; and when you see him, convey to him my deep and sincere gratitude for his courtesy."

"With pleasure, Herr Budd."

"Do not mention to anyone that I have been here, and be sure that I shall be no less careful."

"Your discretion is appreciated, Herr Budd, and we all enjoyed your company."

"Be so kind as to say my *Lebewohl* to the rest of your staff, since I do not wish to interrupt them at their work. *Heil Hitler!*"

"*Heil Hitler.*"

XIII

Speed the parting guest! Lanny went up to his room and put his few belongings into the bag. His car was brought under the porte-cochere, scene of never-to-be-forgotten experiences. He drove away, never to return, or so he hoped; at least, not until this château had again become French, and he might undertake the marketing of some reasonably good paintings.

The conspirator had made so real to himself the possibility of being involved with the Cagoulards that he took the precaution of phoning Hofman at his hotel, to ask if everything was all right. The locksmith met him on the street, and after making sure they were not being trailed, they took a taxi to Monck's hotel. There, what a bull session they had! Three veterans of a war—and all the world knows how old soldiers like to fight their battles over again. They wanted every detail of Lanny's story: how he had managed to force himself upon Graf Herzenberg, and the various persons he had met in the château, and how the dogs had behaved, and the nightwatchman. All these matters had been the subject of anxious speculation, and now to hear the true story was like being taken behind the scenes of history.

They had failed in their purpose, but they had done their best, and Lanny hastened to assure them that he realized this. The task he had undertaken had lain beyond his power; both Hofman and Monck had been convinced of that from the beginning, and had told him so. They saw no hope for the woman artist, and as sensible men they could not pretend otherwise. A locksmith could break into a French château, but not into the citadel of Nazism; as for Monck, alias Capitán Herzog, alias Hauptmann Branting, he said that he had a company of hard-fighting men waiting for him up in the red hills of Aragon, and that was the place where Trudi Schultz could be saved if anywhere.

The trio enjoyed a sleep, and then a bath and a meal. In the evening Lanny had a talk with each of them separately. Monck insisted that he had failed, and that the sum paid to him should be reduced accordingly; but Lanny said that the Capitán had done everything he had agreed to do, and the failure was not his but Lanny's. Monck had got into touch with his wife through the underground, and she and the children were expected in Paris in a couple of days; they settled on the arrangement that Lanny was to get a hundred thousand francs from his bank, about four thousand dollars, and during the next few days Monck would occupy himself in changing these for notes with different serial numbers. With one half he would purchase American Express Company checks for the use of his family, and the other half he would turn over to the underground for the continuing of Trudi's work.

Professor Adler, he reported, had somehow got wind of Trudi's kidnaping and had fled from Paris, but now he had returned. He had raised a gray beard, and was no longer a clarinetist, a conspicuous occupation; he was living in a different workingclass district and planned to support himself by doing translating. Only three persons were to know about him, Lanny, Monck, and that injured man about whom Monck had told Lanny in Spain. Lanny was to write Adler a code letter and they were to meet on the street, as in the old days. This was like having Trudi back again—the most important part, so Trudi would have told him, and so the Trudi-ghost would continue to assert. At least it would give him a reason for selling more pictures and making more money.

XIV

Hofman had not been told that Trudi Schultz was Lanny's wife, and so it was necessary for Lanny to conceal his grief when the locksmith was present. The locksmith had become convinced that Trudi was dead, and he said so flatly. As for Monck, he considered it the part of kindness to convince Lanny of the fact, in order that he might not go on wasting his efforts. When they were alone together, he said this, and Lanny thanked him, saying: "You may be right, and I fear you are; but surely I have to make certain before my mind can feel at peace!"

"How do you expect to make certain?"

"I have an idea that I am going to get Hitler to tell me." Then, seeing his friend's surprise, he added: "Don't think I'm crazy. So far it's just an idea, but it might work out. Hitler is a believer in occult phenomena, I've been told; and if I can get him interested in spirit communications, he might take the trouble to verify them."

"*Por dios!*" exclaimed the Capitán. "If you pull off that one, will you promise to let me know about it?"

"We'll have a dinner somewhere, and I'll tell you the story. But meantime, don't forget, all this is as close a secret as anything on this earth."

Later on Lanny had a private talk with Hofman, who still insisted that he didn't want any payment for his part of this job; he had had a delightful trip to Paris, had seen the sights and heard the news, living *en prince* in the meantime; what more could a man want?—especially when he had failed in the job.

Lanny replied: "You opened every lock."

"I got a free education," countered the Meister-Schlosser—"in two different subjects, psychic research and the insides of Nazism. Both are worth while to me, and I wouldn't take a lot of money for them."

"Do this," suggested the host. "Follow your hobby for a few days here in Paris. I have to wait for my father, and meanwhile you may find some old locks that you would like to add to your collection; if so, let me buy them for you and feel better in my conscience. I might need you again some day, you know."

XV

Lanny had to go and see his Red uncle and wind up matters there. The nephew was teaching himself discretion, and didn't tell Jesse the story of what had happened at the Château de Belcour; he just said: "That enterprise failed to come off, so you can pay Jean and tell him to forget it and move out of the mill." He didn't ask for an accounting and Jesse didn't offer one.

They talked about the Cagoulard exposé, as everybody in Paris was doing at the moment. Lanny was afraid the delay had spoiled his uncle's story, but Jesse declared: "If I had sprung the news in the Chambre everybody would have said it was a *canard;* but when the government springs it, some of those scoundrels get at least a few days of jail—damn their dirty souls!"

The *député de la république française* went on to reveal an amusing aspect of the affair. A very discreet representative of the Croix de Feu had come to him and explained how they were planning to expose their traducers; they had heard rumors that M. Block-léss had been collecting information along these lines and they wanted it to add to their own and turn it all over to the government. At first Jesse had been unwilling to trust the man, but the latter had managed to convince the deputy of his good faith; he wanted the data so badly that he offered to pay, and Jesse actually sold a copy of his notes for ten thousand francs, a most unexpected contribution to a Communist campaign fund. "Every little helps," he said; and Lanny replied with an even more pointed adage: "Extremes meet!"

Hofman knew where to look for locks, and he found a collection of ancient Egyptian contrivances which a dealer was holding in the certainty of some day interesting a rich American. Hofman told Lanny, and that rich American was interested. It appeared that the pyramid makers had designed such a good lock that no one had ever been able to think of a better idea. The only difference was that modern lockmakers had steel and precision instruments, whereas the Egyptians had had only wood. Hofman explained:

"They fastened their doors with a long hollow bolt and staple made of teak, the hardest wood they could find. Into the upper part of the staple, or housing, they fitted several loose pins that dropped into matching holes in the bolt and held it in place. The key was a flat stick of wood, generally thirteen or fourteen inches long for a street door, with pegs on the end to correspond to the pins in the bolt. To unlock the door, the Egyptians stuck the key through a round hole in the wall, lifted the pins until they cleared the bolt, then drew back the bolt by pulling the key which held it by pegs sticking in the pin holes. Egyptian locksmiths carried their finished keys about on their shoulders like a bunch of fagots."

"What does this dealer want for his collection?" asked Lanny.

"He wants sixty thousand francs, but that's much more than I would let you spend."

"I would pay it cheerfully," said the son of Budd-Erling, in whose pockets money always burned a hole. "But you can be sure your dealer doesn't expect to get his asking price—not even from an American. Offer him thirty thousand."

"I offered thirty-five and he laughed at me."

"Did you give him your name and address?"

"I did; and I told him I was leaving for New York in a couple of days."

"Bide your time. He hopes to get fifty thousand, and will take forty; but don't say more than thirty-five until you report to me. Remember, I've been buying and selling art works in this city for some fifteen years."

Hofman took the advice, and bought the collection for thirty-eight thousand francs of Lanny's money. He brought the locks home and spread them out on the bed and explained them to his friend. They had been used, no doubt, to secure the granaries or other treasure houses of some wealthy Egyptian, perhaps a pharaoh, nearly three thousand years ago. They had been carefully cleaned, and still worked, and the Meister-Schlosser was as delighted with them as a child with a big doll which shuts its eyes when you lay it down. When these two parted, it was indeed *"Au revoir"* and not "Good-by." Hofman said: "If ever you have anything as novel and entertaining as your last assignment, don't fail to let me know." He grinned, and added: "When I was a boy we used to say things like that, and finish with: 'I don't think!'"

BOOK FOUR

In the Midst of Wolves

14

The Jingling of the Guinea

I

ROBBIE BUDD arrived in Paris. He had got news of the arrest of the de Bruynes on board the steamer, and on the boat-train had got the newspapers and brought himself up to date. The French police had arrested a hundred or more conspirators, and at least a score of them were persons of wealth. Robbie's sympathy was with such persons, anywhere in the world and regardless of what they had done, provided that it was for the benefit and protection of their class. The government of France had Socialists in the cabinet, and that was enough to prove it incompetent and dangerous. Men who had tried to get rid of it might have been indiscreet, but you couldn't really blame them.

Robbie was in an especially embittered mood just now, because the near-Socialist government of his own country had broken his proud will. He had announced that he would go out of business before he would have anything to do with labor union organizers, but when it came to a showdown, he had felt himself obliged to consider the interests of his stockholders. There had been sitdown strikes all over the country, and the New Dealers were trying their best to prevent any more of them. Robbie had been plainly told that he wouldn't be allowed to have one; there was that most outrageous "Wagner Act," having to do with labor relations, and there were dark hints that delays in the placing of government orders might be experienced by employers who refused to meet union representatives and work out agreements.

Robbie was having a hard time, and he simply couldn't have gone on without government orders. It was humiliating, outrageous, an insult to his dignity as a man and his right as a citizen; but he had been forced to bow to the will of these new tsars, the bureaucrats, and their allies and political supporters, the walking delegates, the labor union racketeers. It was a political conspiracy; these fellows had put up half a million dollars to elect Roosevelt, and now they came to collect their price. It meant the death and burial of what Robbie had learned to call the "free enterprise system." It didn't occur to him to mention what amounts he and his associates had put up in the effort to defeat Roosevelt, or the use they had made of the government in the good old days when nobody had disputed their control.

Lanny had had many a wrangle with his father over such questions, and was resolved never to have another. He listened to the story of how Robbie, unwilling to meet the usurpers himself, had delegated the unsavory job to one of his vice-presidents and a couple of super-intendents; how then, greatly to Robbie's discomfiture, the usurpers had succeeded in persuading this trio that their men earnestly desired to increase and improve the Budd-Erling product, provided they could have some reasonable say about the conditions of their labor and a fair share in the profits thus earned. Poor Robbie had found himself backed up against the wall. "Big Steel" had surrendered to this hold-up, and so had General Motors. What could a poor "little fellow" do?

And so, Budd-Erling had become a union shop; the racketeers had the right to tell Robbie whom he could employ—or rather they had the right to say that the new employee couldn't go to work until he had got a union card, and had agreed to let the company deduct a percentage of his pay and turn it over to the union. The "check-off system," it was called, and the money would be used to extend the power of the union to other plants—or perhaps to enable the gangsters to have free trips to Florida, who could say? The hypocritical Lanny remarked that the world was changing, and nobody seemed to know how to stop it.

II

Denis de Bruyne and his sons had tried to make some changes in their French world, and apparently had got themselves into serious trouble. Robbie wanted to hear all that Lanny knew about it; he was deeply distressed, and perhaps it was his duty to go and visit the prisoners; would Lanny come along? The son replied that he had thought the matter over and decided against going. This was a fac-tional quarrel of the French, the most bitter that could be imagined, and they wouldn't want foreigners mixing in it; Lanny's business as an art expert would be knocked into a cocked hat if he were suspected of doing so.

What was really troubling Lanny was the possibility that the de Bruynes might say something to his father, indicating how deeply

Lanny had committed himself to them. Robbie wouldn't understand that, and Lanny couldn't very well explain it. "If I were you," he said, "I'd think twice before calling at the prison; it surely wouldn't do you any good with the government. You must realize that the Cagoulards had a hanging list, and many members of the government know that their names were on it. Their fury is easy to understand."

"What do you think they'll do to the prisoners?"

"Keep them in jail a few weeks to frighten them; but I doubt very much if they'll ever be brought to trial. There are too many important figures involved, people who will be moving heaven and earth to suppress the story."

"After all, I don't suppose there's anything I can do for Denis or the boys."

"Not a thing in the world. What is done will have to be done by Frenchmen."

So the cautious businessman remarked: "Perhaps it might be the part of wisdom for me to wait until I have seen Schneider, and found out what he wants."

"I should advise that strongly. The de Bruynes know the situation, and their feelings won't be hurt. They understand that we can't help them, and they don't need anybody to cry over them."

"Frankly, Lanny, I'm having a hard time. The recession is getting worse every day. I've taken a huge gamble in the belief that aviation is going to increase. It would be a great load off my mind if I could get a real order from the French right now."

"Well then, you had better keep away from the Cagoule. Many of the army officers sympathize with it, but dare not show their feelings at present, and Pierre Cot, the air minister, is a leftist, and one of those who are fighting in the Cabinet for the full exposure of the conspiracy. You are up against much the same sort of thing as at home: *le New Deal*, the French call it."

III

Robbie had telegraphed Baron Schneider from the steamer, notifying him of his impending arrival; and now at the hotel was an engraved card requesting the honor of the company of M. Robert Budd at the town house of the Baron that same evening. Lanny had received a similar invitation at his hotel. Beauty's heart would have been broken if she had been left out of such an affair, so Lanny telephoned the Baron's secretary, saying that his mother was in town and asking if it would be agreeable for him to bring her. The result was another card arriving by messenger within the hour.

Robbie got out his "tails" and had them pressed, and with one of his waggish grins asked his son: "Shall we wear hoods?" Lanny replied that the Baron would slip money to secret conspirators, but would not invite any of them to his home in this crisis. There one would meet the most fashionable crowd, plus the politicians of the center and right, and any sort of famous persons who might enjoy the favor of one of the most powerful men in France. The same sort of evening affair that Robbie had seen in the days when Lanny had been "Mr. Irma Barnes," and they had leased the palace of the Duc de Belleaumont, so that Irma might learn the duties of a *salonnière* under the guidance of Emily Chattersworth.

They engaged a uniformed chauffeur from Denis's taxicab company to drive Lanny's car and deliver them in proper state before the doors of the mansion. There between nine and ten o'clock was *tout Paris* arriving, with the traditional red carpet under its feet and striped canvas canopy overhead. Black-clad gentlemen with the correct white ties, and others in uniform with chests covered by decorations; the ladies in the much greater splendor permitted to them: gorgeous furs from every part of the earth and jewels from its depths; evening gowns of every hue, and snow-white or pink bosoms and arms and backs; coiffures so elaborate that the ladies exhausted themselves sitting up to have them prepared and then dared not lie down for a moment's rest. A splendid scene, as Lanny had foretold, comparing it to a dead fish such as he and his father could see on the beach at Juan on a dark night, shining with gold, silver, green, purple, shimmering and pulsating, fascinating to the eye—so long as you kept to windward of it.

The Baron received them cordially and said that he had been looking forward to the meeting with Robbie; would he and his son come to lunch on the morrow? "I don't suppose I have to introduce you to anybody," added the host, "since you know so many in my country. Consider yourselves at home,"—the utmost a Frenchman could say to foreigners.

Robbie Budd, who had been doing business as a munitions salesman in Europe since the beginning of the century, had met most of these military gentlemen and knew what their insignia and decorations meant. He had been a steel man, so he could talk shop with François de Wendel; he had been an oil man, so he could exchange greetings with Sir Henri Deterding, and chat with him about what had happened since their meeting at The Hague. He had attended several of the great international conferences in the interest of Budd Gunmakers, then of New England-Arabian Oil, and more recently of Budd-Erling; so he could chat with the diplomats and politicians, also with the great ladies, the duchesses and marchionesses and countesses who favored them. Beauty knew them, too, and had paid many a one to bring to luncheon or dinner some general or cabinet minister or great capitalist whom it was important for a salesman or promoter to meet privately.

IV

The great world of Paris was fluid, almost as much as that of New York. Persons of prominence lost their influence and new ones took their places. Writers and other intellectuals, musicians and other artists lost their vogue, and one met them in the cafés but no longer at fashionable soirées. Speculators lost their money and disappeared; others made sensational gains, and they and their chosen ladies made their appearance, having been properly coached and equipped by couturiers and modistes, and by ladies of fashion who had fallen into need and lived by giving help to the newly arrived. All this was especially true of politicians; they began, as a rule, by making violent speeches of a leftist character, and when they had got the votes, they accepted "campaign funds" from the big businessmen; each one acquired a rich *amie*, and after he had been taught how to handle a knife and fork, he made his entrée in the salons, where people were curious to meet him because his name had been in the newspapers.

Of late it had become the fashion for successful statesmen to go to the Comédie Française for their favorites. This state-owned institution had been since its founding two and a half centuries ago a lure which drew the most beautiful and charming ingénues from all over France. On the stage they enacted roles of luxurious passion, and off-stage they enacted the same roles with even greater ardor—this being even more essential to their careers. Their eyes were turned in the direction of the prominent politicians, and especially the Cabinet ministers, who had the appointing of director and assistants, and whose word could determine the assignment of roles, of publicity in the press, and all the other desirabilities of *la vie parisienne*. Intrigues went on incessantly, shifts took place, and a great part of French public life was occupied with speculation concerning who was who and with whom.

Lanny was behind the times with that sort of news; but when Beauty came to Paris she hurried off to lunch with one of her smart friends and to tea with another; she would come back loaded up with information

—and don't call it "idle gossip," for a deal in airplanes might depend upon the good disposition of one of these young creatures, and the first job of a businessman might be to go to the theater and see her in the embraces of some lover, and note the fine points of her technique. Nowhere in the world was acting more conscientiously rehearsed or traditions of the stage more religiously preserved, and if you understood these matters you were a person of culture, and knew how to flatter a popular actress and cause her to speak well of you to her patron. You might be ever so staid a family man from the land of the pilgrims' pride, but you had sowed your one wild oat when you were young, and here was your shrewd and well-trained ex-mistress, knowing the great world of Paris and London and Berlin, and ready to take your arm and be escorted about a drawing-room, whispering information into your ear, and introducing you to exactly the right ones. It wouldn't hurt you in the least to have this *grand monde* know that the mother of your son was still your friend; this *monde* would believe what in Newcastle, Connecticut, would be called "the worst," but here it would be considered a touching instance of fidelity, which ladies of maturing years, trying to hold onto their lovers, would observe with envious sorrow.

Beauty would say: "That is Yvonne Roux; she is seen everywhere with Herriot. The one next to her, in cerise crêpe-de-chine, is Hélène Manet —she is always invited with Tardieu." Later, on the ballroom floor: "You know Georges Mandel, I believe; that is Angelique Beaulieu he is dancing with—she also is a *pensionnaire* of the Comédie." After they had taken a turn or two: "There is Mlle. Poussin with Yvon Delbos, the new Foreign Minister." Robbie would observe a youngish man, tall and thin, pale and timid-looking. "He was a professor before he became a politician," the well-informed Beauty would add. "He is believed to be very conscientious, and intends to marry her. Right now she is playing in one of the Molière comedies."

There were wives present, also, and now and then Beauty could point out one in the same room with the *amie*. The contrast would be pathetic, not to say tragic, for the wives were what the politicians had been able to get when they were young and poor and had not the same range of choice. Now the wives had grown old along with their partners, and some of them were stout and some were gawky, and no art of dressmaker or cosmetician could conceal their defects. What heartaches they must suffer to see their life partners publicly disporting themselves with young hussies, and leaving the wives to such tenth-rate chances as they could find! There is an old song which tells about after the ball is over, after the dancers gone; many a heart is weary, many a heart is sad—and it might also have been recorded that many a husband is getting the very dickens from his wife.

V

In the library Lanny came upon a group of gentlemen and two or three ladies who preferred serious conversation. The center of the group was a shortish heavy-set man with dark overhanging eyebrows, dark straight hair beginning to thin, a long nose and a wide drooping mouth which gave him a somber, not to say melancholy appearance. Lanny knew him, because he had been a professor of philosophy in Nice, and one of the ornaments of Emily's Riviera salon. In that drawing-room a tactful hostess had guided the conversation, calling upon this person and that and making sure that each had a chance to display his intellectual wares. But here was no such circumstance; here two or three persons had asked the writer, Jules Romains, what he thought about the situation of the country, and others had joined the group and stayed so long as they were interested. There was nothing unusual about this; Lanny had seen the same thing at one of Emily's lawn parties at Les Forêts, where a troop of lovely ladies had listened spellbound while Anatole France poured out a flood of ironic wit; again in London, where Bernard Shaw had kept a roomful of people entertained for a full hour without one of them interrupting; again at the Genoa conference, where Frank Harris had produced a monologue about Shakespeare, like a stream of molten gold with rubies and emeralds and diamonds shining in it.

Here it was different, for this was a deadly serious man, delivering a message to a nation in serious trouble. M. Romains, now in his early fifties, was a voluminous writer, and among his output were volumes of plays and poems which were called "Rabelaisian," a French way of permitting what in English would be called "off color." But now he was at work upon a series of novels portraying the manners of his time; and in between these labors he was carrying on a crusade of a dignified and exclusive character to save his country, according to the best lights of one of her eminent philosophers and littérateurs. Here he was telling the story of his efforts to a dignified and exclusive audience; the sort of people who knew the inside workings of the machinery of statecraft, and set the switches and pulled the levers which determined the destiny of France.

M. Romains had taken many journeys in his country's interest and at his own expense. He had talked with the statesmen of fourteen European lands. Three years ago he had traveled to Berlin and delivered a lecture under government auspices. Brownshirted leaders had been summoned from all over the land to hear him, and one of the top-flight Nazis had said to him: "You know, no private individual has ever been received like this in Berlin." The philosopher-novelist had also been welcomed by the King of the Belgians, who had discussed frankly that country's attitude to the gravely threatened war. As M. Romains told about these matters, you couldn't doubt that he was patriotically in earnest, but also you couldn't help feeling that he was intensely impressed by his own importance.

His plan was the one known as *le couple France-Allemagne,* and it meant reconcilation with Germany, by the simple method of giving the Nazis whatever they demanded. For example, he had had the idea that the Allies should have got out of the Saar without the formality of a plebiscite. Lanny happened to know that Briand had been trying to work out some compromise on this question as far back as ten years ago; but apparently M. Romains didn't know that, and certainly it wasn't up to Lanny to correct him on his facts. The philosopher-novelist seemed to have the idea that the Saar settlement had been a matter between France and Germany, and that the plebiscite had taken place under French military control, whereas the fact was it had been a League matter, and French troops had been withdrawn nine years before the plebiscite was held.

Among the members of that attentive audience was Kurt Meissner, who had met the Frenchman many years ago in Emily's drawing-room. Evidently he had put his opportunity to good use, for it was just as if M. Romains had sat in a seminar conducted by the Wehrmacht's agent, had absorbed the entire doctrine, and was now giving an oral dissertation to demonstrate what he had learned and get his degree. His discourse embraced the complete Nazi program for the undermining of the French republic: warm protestations of friendship; unlimited promises of peace; the sowing of distrust of all politicians and of the entire democratic procedure; and, above all else, fear of the Red specter. The Reds kept faith with nobody, their country was a colossus with feet of clay, their army a broken reed upon which France persisted in trying to lean. The republic had to choose between Stalin and Hitler; between an illusory military alliance and a secure and enduring peace.

The words burned Lanny's tongue: "M. Romains, have you ever read *Mein Kampf?*" Of course, Lanny couldn't say them; but he wondered, how would this somewhat self-conscious idol of the bourgeois world have replied? Lanny recalled the Max Beerbohm cartoon in which a drawing-room fop is asked if he has read a certain book, and replies: "I do not read books; I write them."

VI

The next day Lanny drove his father to that same mansion, and they had a lunch in which a whole pheasant was put before each of them. Afterwards came a quiet chat in which two men of large affairs had a chance to develop their acquaintance. The munitions king of Europe spoke with frankness; he was gravely concerned about the state of his country, and the developments in military aviation which seemed about to put all other kinds of military equipment on the shelf. He didn't speak to Robbie as a big man to a little man, but rather as one who might become little to another who was certain to become big. This was immensely flattering to the visitor, but Robbie wasn't the one to swell up and burst; he knew what he had, and had worked many years to get it; also, he understood how business is conducted, and that when a big man invites you to his palace and offers you his finest old vintage wines, he wants something and wants it badly.

Robbie Budd was an associate of General Göring, and had been taken into the inside of the new German Air Force, and no injunction of secrecy had been laid upon him. Quite the contrary, it was Göring's policy to frighten his opponents and get what he wanted without having to fight; therefore, technically equipped visitors were encouraged to come and look and then go out and talk. This was Robbie's game, too, and had been ever since he had listened to his father's instructions as a boy; the way to sell munitions was to go from one country to the next, and tell each how far ahead the others were. So Robbie laid the paint on thick, and Charles Prosper Eugène Schneider looked at the picture and shivered deep within his soul. Yes, even though he knew the game as well as the son of Budd Gunmakers, having been taught it by *his* father and grandfather—and he was older than Robbie.

France's deadly rival had outdistanced her, and was leaving her hopelessly behind. Germany had become that which every gunmaker in the world had dreamed all his life, a country putting everything it had into armaments; reducing the wages and lengthening the hours of all its workers and bidding its munitions men to build all the plants they could, in the certainty that they would receive all the orders they could fill, and keep their machines going at full speed twenty-four hours every day, Sundays and holidays included. Most favored of all was the

Air Force commander who, while he looked like a comic stage character and dressed like one, was at the same time one of the most competent executives in the modern world, driving his subordinates with a
whiplash and getting the orders of his Führer carried out with utter
loyalty and no scruples.

That was a nightmare, a nightmare, exclaimed Baron Schneider; it kept
him awake night after night, seeing the calamity that hung over France.
His miserable, incompetent government, hopelessly corrupt—who knew
that better than the Baron, who had been buying it for half a century?
But of course he didn't say that to his visitors. What he said was denun-
ciation of the wretched system of prototypes to which the French air
ministry was committed; the economical illusion, the pinchpenny in-
sanity of having models of the very best planes, and the means of making them quickly, and imagining that that was national security!

"You can't fight battles with mating-jigs," said Robbie, dryly.

"Of course not! And now these politicians have taken over my
plants, having no idea how to pay for them and at the same time asking
me how to run them! We have all this confusion and miserable wran-
gling—and right in the midst of the gravest peril our country has faced
since Sedan."

VII

What was it this badly worried monarch of munitions desired? Well,
first of all he wanted Robbie to tell him the truth about the performance of the Budd-Erling P11, about which he had heard fabulous reports. When Robbie told him, he shook his head sorrowfully, saying
that the best of the French prototypes, the *Morane*, couldn't equal that.
Then he wanted to make sure if Göring had these secrets, and what use
he was making of them; Robbie could answer the first part of this
question, but said he could only guess about the second; *der dicke Hermann* was wide awake and not missing any tricks. Robbie said he had
given first chance to his own country, and then to the French and the
British; he named the men he had approached and who had turned him
down. "That left me no recourse but the Germans, if I wanted to keep
in business."

"Of course, of course," said the Baron. "It is too bad you did not
come to me. I had some power in my own country at that time. Now
I am not allowed to do anything, or to own anything except bonds. I
am supposed to be laid away upon a shelf. But being a man of action,
I am not happy there, especially when I learn what Thyssen and Krupp
von Bohlen and the rest of them are doing."

The munitions king of Europe went on to explain that he could not persuade the French air ministry to buy enough planes of French man-ufacture, and it was even less possible to persuade them to buy foreign planes, for then to the reluctance of a semi-pacifist government to spend money would be added the opposition of great French private inter-ests. It had been the idea of the Baron to buy personally a hundred or two of the very newest Budd-Erlings, and train men to fly them pri-vately; then in case of an emergency he could present them to the army. But now had come this wretched exposé of the Cagoule, which the Baron took as an infringement of his personal privacy, just about as Robbie took the C.I.O. invasion. There was no helping it, of course; a sensational press was playing up every item it could unearth, and would rush to proclaim that the master of Le Creusot was setting up a private air force and training it, for the purpose of threatening Paris and forcing the government to obey his will.

"I have to think of myself as an outcast from my own country," de-clared the great man, sadly. "I have to go abroad in order to save France from itself." He explained that he still owned Skoda, which was in the town of Pilsen, and the Czechs still granted him the right to make goods and to buy and sell as he pleased. Would Robbie be will-ing to manufacture a hundred fighter planes for immediate delivery in Czechoslovakia, and would he go in on some sort of arrangement to send his experts to that country and assist in establishing a factory for the manufacture of Budd-Erlings?

Robbie of course was delighted to get a large order, and said that be-cause of his sympathy with the Baron's cause he would give it priority over everything else. He would be proud to be associated with so dis-tinguished a concern as Skoda in the fabricating of planes, and would make the Budd-Erling patents available. But the Baron must understand that certain features of the Budd-Erling were protected by General Göring's patents, which were not under Robbie's control.

The Baron sighed and said it was too bad that the Germans had got ahead on everything; it looked as if the French would have to make friends with them, willynilly. "I have been talking on the subject with this well-informed son of yours. It is a question whether their Führer is a man whom we can trust. What do you think, M. Budd?"

"My son has had the advantage of knowing Herr Hitler personally," replied Robbie, cautiously. "I have not."

"Eh, bien, M. Lanny?"

Said Lanny: "Anyone would be assuming a grave responsibility who gave advice on that subject, M. le Baron. All that I can say is that you have to make up your mind to be either an ally or an enemy. It is not possible to be half-way between."

"It is extraordinary what discretion this young man possesses, M. Budd, and what an insight into our French situation."

Robbie was surprised, for he had never given his son credit for such valuable possessions. He remarked, deprecatingly: "Lanny has lived all over Europe, and has had unusual opportunities to hear opinions."

"One can hear all sorts of opinions in my drawing-room, M. Budd; the problem is to sort them out and select those which are sound. I should be glad if your son would come to see me now and then and tell me what he has learned; and this applies to you also, for I perceive that you are a man who has foreseen how the world is moving and has placed himself in a strategic position."

That was high-class flattery, and not to be rejected. Robbie perceived that Baron Schneider, ten years older than himself, was looking for someone to carry burdens for him. He had intimated in a delicate way that he would expect to pay generously. Robbie said he would think over the proposals and be ready with definite offers in a couple of days; the Baron replied that he had no doubt they would be fair, and he would have his technical men work over the details and his lawyers assist in drawing up the papers. He sent his visitors away happy; Robbie remarking to his son: "This may prove the biggest thing that has ever come my way."

VIII

Beauty Budd was still in Paris, and she wouldn't have been herself if she hadn't been thinking her own thoughts and scheming her schemes. The incomparable Lanny was involved with some woman, and was keeping her hidden, even from his adoring mother who had never failed to excuse everything he did. Manifestly, the reason could only be political; this woman, a German, was doing some of that dangerous underground work which had so frightened Irma and had caused the break-up of Lanny's marriage. At present Lanny was heavyhearted and preoccupied, and what could it mean except that the woman was in trouble, and perhaps Lanny also? Could it be that she had gone back into Germany? Most probably so, for Lanny stayed in his apartment a lot, read endless newspapers, and played the piano in a restless and distracted way. Beauty knew him so well that she could tell his moods by what he played and how he played it. She was right in the same hotel, watching him like a hawk; she knew that he had been away only one

night, and that certainly would not have been the case if the woman he
loved had been available. He was much more assiduous than that, and
accustomed to having what he wanted.

Perhaps right now was a chance for Beauty to have what she wanted.
Sophie Timmons, Baroness de la Tourette, had come up from the
Riviera for a lark, and now Beauty phoned to Emily Chattersworth,
who came to town, and those three old stagers put their heads together.
They had done so on previous occasions, trying to decide the destinies
of this eligible but provoking man. Here he was thirty-eight—the dark
secret was shared among the three who had known him from baby-
hood—and still drifting around at loose ends, a prey to any designing
female who came along, instead of having a wife and settling down to
raise a family in some place where these three conspirators could have
the fun of watching. It was they who had made the Irma Barnes
match—so promising, they still couldn't understand how it had failed.

The new wife had to be an American, they decided. There was a
large American colony in Paris, and many visitors, and after due canvassing they pitched upon a damsel named Mary Ann Everly, a nice
old-fashioned name for a debutante, just out of Bryn Mawr and doing
her grand tour with her mother. She had soft brown eyes and a gentle
manner, a quiet young thing; they all knew that Lanny disliked the
noisy ones who would chatter while he wanted to read the speeches in
the previous day's Chambre. No less important, the family had scads of
money; old Philadelphia people, the father a banker, Episcopalian and
everything proper. The girl was modern—they all learn the facts of
life nowadays, and talk about whatever comes into their heads.

The way it was arranged, Emily was to invite the mother and daughter to lunch, and Beauty and Sophie were to keep out of the way, since
it would look too pointed if the whole crew were there to gang up on
Lanny. Not that they could fool him anyhow, but they must do their
best. Emily would keep the mother busy, and Lanny and the girl would
go for a stroll in a great beech forest, haunted by the ghosts of thousands of German soldiers—but the girl wouldn't know that, and Lanny
wouldn't mind, knowing how all France was haunted by the ghosts of
soldiers of every nation and tribe. Or he could take her paddling in a
canoe on a little artificial lake. The match with Irma had been made at
Sept Chênes, Emily's place above Cannes; the locale now would be
different but the strategy the same.

IX

Lanny had mailed a set of notes to Gus Gennerich, calling attention to the fact that his previous account of the Cagoulard conspiracy had been sustained in every detail; also predicting that there would be no prosecutions, and that the share of the army and air force in the conspiracy would be hushed up. Later he sent a memorandum confirming his statement that the Nazi embassy had a château near Paris where they held and tortured anti-Nazi Germans, and suggesting that it might be well for the F.B.I. to look into the rumors that such Germans in New York had been kidnaped and spirited on board the *Bremen* and other steamers.

Now he prepared a summary of the state of the French air force as compared with the German; adding that he had got this direct from Mr. Tailor and it could be accepted as authoritative. Going over all this in his mind, Lanny decided that it constituted a good week's work for a presidential agent. If all hundred and three of them turned in as much copy, F.D. would have his hands full indeed.

As usual Robbie had invited his son to accompany him to Germany, and this time the son accepted. Since he hoped to make use of Kurt on this trip, he stopped in at a music store and purchased a new four-hand piano arrangement of an orchestral work by Hindemith; then he phoned Kurt, asking if he should drop in and practice it with him. Kurt couldn't resist this temptation—despite the fact that the composer was a modernist; this poison had so infected Europe that not even a fountainhead of Nazi propaganda could entirely escape its effects. They sat side by side and pounded away for an hour or two, Lanny making some mistakes and Kurt correcting them; that was their old relationship, so they finished in a glow of satisfaction.

Lanny told of his plans, and said: "You know Robbie has an important deal with Hermann Göring."

"I have heard so," replied Kurt, whose business it was to know everything. "It's been useful to us, and still more so to Robbie, I imagine." A typical Nazi assumption, which Lanny accepted with due humility.

"Are you going home for Christmas?" he inquired, and when Kurt answered in the affirmative, Lanny added: "I expect to stay a while, because I've been neglecting Hermann's picture business and he may want me. We'll get Heinrich Jung, and have a regular old home week. Perhaps we can call on the Führer."

"I'll see if it can be arranged," said Kurt. "He's likely to have his hands full very soon. Schuschnigg has been making a lot of trouble and may have to be taught a lesson."

It was an indiscretion, of course. Kurt was human, in spite of being an exemplar of the master race, and he couldn't resist the temptation to show an adoring friend and pupil how much he knew about his great leader's purposes. Lanny would get off another rush note to Gus, saying that there was reason to expect an invasion of Austria in the new year.

X

Coming back from this visit, Lanny found a message to call Emily Chattersworth. He did so, and was invited to lunch at Les Forêts the following day; some friends she especially wanted him to meet. Lanny, suspicious as a much-hunted stag, guessed right away that the does were after him again; however, he couldn't say No to an elderly doe who had been a second mother to him, and was now growing feeble and didn't get about very much. All right, he would come; after all, yearling does are pleasant to look at, and it couldn't do any harm to browse for a while in company with a carefully selected one. Lanny went up to see his mother, and found her looking as innocent as any tame doe in a paddock. She asked how Kurt was, and was politely surprised by the news that Lanny had had a call from the châtelaine of Les Forêts.

Mary Ann of the Philadelphia Everlys proved to be about the nicest Everly ever. She was twenty but looked even younger; rather small, with the sweetest little round face, a tip-tilted nose, and wide brown eyes taking in every feature of this fascinating new old world. Of course she couldn't really be as innocent as she looked; one glance at her competent mother, and Lanny could be sure that Mary Ann had been told what she was here for, but perhaps with a warning that this was a dubious man, who had been divorced by a monstrously rich wife because of "incompatibility of temperament." But that wouldn't keep him from being an object of curiosity. Emily, old darling, wouldn't have failed to mention that he was an art expert of high repute, having some of the wealthiest collectors at home as his patrons.

Lanny knew that he was there to entertain these visiting ladies, and he pulled out his best bag of tricks. He talked about this very splendid home and the many interesting sights he had seen here: Anatole France discoursing on the lawn, and Isadora Duncan dancing in the drawing-room, with Lanny playing, scared stiff for fear she would notice how many notes he was missing. And the famous people who had frequented Emily's salons—a roster of the great names, not merely of France and England, but of far-off places such as India and China. Part of the time Lanny had been too young to understand all they were saying, but he remembered their faces, and what people had said about them, which was enough to constitute culture in the smart world.

He described Hansi Robin playing the violin here, and Lanny's half-sister Bess falling head over heels in love with him. He made a funny story of his proud New England stepmother, shocked by the idea of her daughter marrying a Jewish fiddler, and the surprise she had got when Hansi visited her home town, and everybody treated him as if he were the grandson of the Jewish Jehovah. Hansi and Bess were now in London, and next week Hansi was scheduled to play with one of the Paris symphonies; he was going to give his rendition of the Bruch concerto, which Lanny said was something not to be missed. Courtesy suggested that he should invite his hostess and her guests to hear it, and when the older ladies accepted, Mary Ann was so happy as to seem almost but not quite indiscreet.

She had come abroad to see the places and things she had been reading about since childhood, and was prepared to renew all the thrills she had ever experienced. Her eagerness was genuine and quite touching. After lunch Lanny took her for a stroll in the beech forest, and told her how a whole division of the German army had been trapped here; he described the scene of wreckage after the battle, and showed the stumps of trees which had been shot into splinters. He told about the elderly librarian, M. Priedieu, who had been so shocked at the sight of the boches dumping the Louis Quatorze furniture out of the windows that he had dropped dead.

When they came back to the drawing-room, Emily asked Lanny to play for them, and he obliged. Doubtless Chopin is well known in the Quaker city of brotherly love, but its topmost social set might have difficulty in fitting him into its code of etiquette and ethics. He was an impulsive and unhappy lover, and the invasive and dominating George Sand carried him off and broke his heart and then made a novel and autobiography out of it. He died miserably of tuberculosis, and the only joy he had was putting his melancholy and anguish into music, along with the glory of his proud race. He made for himself a style which in course of the years became synonymous with piano technique; the sweeping phrases fitting the instrument as a well-worn glove fits the hand.

Lanny played the F-sharp minor polonaise, which Liszt admired so extravagantly, and about which he imagined strange things. It is tempestuous music, full of martial clashes, and not easy to play; but if Lanny made slips, the ladies wouldn't know it. When he got through, there were tears in Mary Ann's eyes; she tried furtively to wipe them away, because a public display of emotion was so contrary to her mother's code.

XI

Beauty of course wanted to know everything that had happened; she always did, and complained because Lanny left out the most interesting details. She wanted to pretend that she didn't know whom he had met; he said: "Old goose! She's a very nice girl, and I invited them to the concert tomorrow. But I'm not going to marry anybody, and I've told you often enough. Some day I'll tell you the reason, but at present I'm not free to, so you'll just have to trust me and forget it."

He had a row of seats for the concert; he was taking Beauty and her husband, and Sophie and hers, and Zoltan, as well as the other three. Robbie didn't care for highbrow music, and anyhow he was to have a final conference with Baron Schneider before leaving for Berlin the following day. Lanny went to Hansi's hotel to meet the couple and swap news with them. They were among the few who knew that he was helping the underground, though he had never told them how. He told about Kurt and what he was doing, and about the de Bruynes, and what he had found out about the Cagoulard plot. On this account he mustn't be seen in public with either Hansi or Bess, but it would do no harm for him to attend the concert, or to come to this hotel after making reasonably sure he wasn't being followed. He had brought the Hindemith score, and he and Bess played it; Hansi listened but didn't care much for it. The ultraradical in politics was a conservative in music.

It seemed to Lanny that his brother-in-law had never been better than in his rendering of the melodious and charming Bruch concerto that evening. He always made a good appearance on the platform, tall, dignified, and wholly concerned with his art. His pale ascetic features and large dark eyes gave an appearance of melancholy appropriate to a Jew in these tragic times. He had had two rehearsals with the orchestra and his performance was impassioned yet without flaw. Concert audiences in Paris are fastidious, but when they get what they want they do not stint their applause. They called Hansi out half a dozen times, and he played as an encore one of his favorites, a movement from a Bach solo sonata, very austere, and difficult to make effective after the sonorities of a large orchestra. The audience gave him another ovation, and his appearance was a triumph.

What would be the effect of all this glory of art upon a young lady of susceptible age and romantic disposition? She sat next to Lanny, but he had forgotten about her, being concerned with the technical side of what his brother-in-law and friend was doing. So might a relative of the daring young man on the flying trapeze have watched his gyrations and held his breath at the perilous moments. But when it was safely over, Lanny noticed that Mary Ann wasn't applauding, but sat rigid with her hands clasped together tightly in her lap and the knuckles white. He knew that she was having an emotional experience, and thought: "Maybe she's fallen in love with Hansi—and if so, that let's me out!"

But no, it wasn't that way; Hansi was wonderful, but he was a god that had come down out of the skies and would return there—along with his wife. Lanny was the host who had selected this entertainment and provided the tickets; and the three elderly Norns who had taken charge of Mary Ann's fate had no idea of letting him retire to his solitude again. When the concert was over, Mr. and Mrs. Parsifal Dingle and the Baroness and her husband just disappeared without a word. The majestic Emily, accustomed all her life to preside over social arrangements, remarked to Lanny: "I'll take care of Zoltan and Mrs. Everly; you drive Mary Ann." It might seem a wee bit pointed, but the *salonnière* knew that Lanny was leaving for a long stay, and it was now or never.

XII

Had Mary Ann been told what was going to be done? Probably not. But the mother must have been told; she had looked this prospective son-in-law over, and had doubtless made inquiry concerning Budd-Erling Aircraft. So there was Lanny, driving on the brilliantly lighted boulevards of Paris, with this small-sized package of quick-burning powder on the seat beside him. Chopin and Max Bruch and a magnificent orchestra and *la ville lumière* and a thousand years of French history were all mixed up in her soul, along with a handsome man who still looked young and who spoke with a soft voice and seemed to have all the languages of Europe and all the culture of the ages on the tip of his agile tongue.

He wasn't supposed to take her home right away, of course; he could propose a drive, perhaps in the Bois, and if they stopped a while in a sheltered spot, that would be according to the etiquette of this automobile age. But without any such preliminaries he said: "Mary Ann, may I talk to you frankly for a minute or two?"

"Certainly," she replied, and shivered inwardly.

"You are a lovely girl, and if I were free I should fall in love with you, I am sure. But, unfortunately, my heart is pledged."

"*Oh!*" she said, and all the life seemed to go suddenly out of her voice.

"My mother doesn't know it; or rather, she doesn't want to know it, and keeps fighting against it. It is a very sad story and I'm not free to tell it; but I owe it to you to be frank, so that you won't think I am indifferent to the lovely qualities that I see in you."

"Thank you," she said; "I appreciate it." She didn't say: "You are presuming a great deal as to my state of mind," or any artificial thing like that. She didn't mind his knowing that she liked him.

"I am taking a great liberty, I know; but I have lived most of my life on this old continent, and I really know what I am talking about—far more than I am able to tell. Take my advice, see all you can while you are here, and try to understand what you see, but then go home and don't come again. And above all, don't ever think of marrying any European man."

"You really think they are that bad?"

"There are noble exceptions, but your chances of finding one of these, or of recognizing him if you found him, would be slim. In general, European men do not feel about women as you would expect, nor about love or marriage. But that is not the main thing I have in mind; I mean what is coming to Europe and its people. Don't tie your fate to it, and don't give your heart to anyone whose fate is already tied to it, as mine is."

"You mean another war?"

"I mean a series of wars and revolutions that may not be over during your lifetime. You may live to see this great city laid in ashes, or bombed to dust and rubble. You may see the same thing happen to many other cities, and half their populations killed, if not by war, then by plague and famine."

"Oh, how horrible, Mr. Budd!"

"I'm not free to tell you what I know; you just have to take my word that I have special information that has caused me to say to my best friends: 'Get out of Europe and stay out.'"

"How soon do you think this will begin?"

"Within a couple of years at the outside. It may be next spring; it depends upon circumstances which are beyond anyone's control or guessing. When it comes it will be like a series of strokes of lightning, and I'm not sure that three thousand miles of ocean will be enough to protect anyone from them. But go back to Philadelphia, and marry some man of your own set that you have a chance really to know."

She might have made a saucy answer, but she was frightened, and shocked out of all pretending. She said: "Mr. Budd, you are being really kind and I am grateful." He knew that she would be bound to assume that he was in love with some married woman, and that suited him. But evidently it didn't suit her entirely, for she added: "If ever you find yourself near Philadelphia, let us be friends."

15

To Have a Giant's Strength

I

ROBBIE and his son went by plane, because Robbie was in a hurry and the season was not favorable for motoring; they could just as well rent a car in Berlin. They put up at the Adlon as usual, and since they had telegraphed for reservations, the reporters were soon on hand. The Nazis proclaimed themselves revolutionists, bringing in an entirely new order, but the fact was they slavishly followed the customs of the bourgeois world in all things that had to do with power and prestige. When an American airplane manufacturer came to consult Reichsminister General Göring, it was an acknowledgment of Germany's newly won importance. When his son, an art expert internationally known, came with him, that was an event of lesser importance but not to be overlooked. Each newspaper had in its *Archiv* the items already published about the Budd family, and dug them out and wove them into the new story. Always Lanny writhed, thinking of his old-time comrades, now underground, reading these items and despising him as one of the renegades, the band-wagon climbers, the worshipers of the bitch goddess Success.

Robbie had telegraphed the fat General, and soon after their arrival came Hauptmann Furtwaengler of his staff to invite them to lunch at the Air Ministry. It was an enormous granite building, the ugliest in the city, which was saying a lot; the newspapers said it had three thousand rooms, but you could never count entirely upon Nazi newspapers. *Der dicke Hermann* had a palatial suite here, and welcomed them in a military costume of cream and gold suggestive either of interior decoration or a musical comedy chorus. He made himself such agreeable company that Lanny, who liked nearly everybody, had to keep saying to himself: "This is the man who burned the Reichstag; who ordered the blood purge in Berlin; who is going to turn Europe into a slaughter pit." Hitler, of course, was the driving will, the prime mover, but his function was mostly making speeches and devising slogans, while this great lump of lard was the executive and the preparer of all future executions.

Lanny had been raised in the midst of killing instruments and his privileged life had been based upon their sale at a profit; but he personally had never killed anybody, and it had always required a psychological effort for him to understand a killer, to imagine what must be going on in his mind. This fat Hermann had been trained for killing since early youth, and probably through his childhood had been taught worship of the old German heroes who had made killing their sole business on earth and had then been carried off to Valhalla to have their reward in the form of unlimited barrels of beer and barrel-shaped maidens. He had been a brave and skillful killer in the great war, but had been licked at it. Now he was going to have another chance, and this time he was going to win. That coming revenge was the sauce that flavored all the food he ate and the beer he drank; the expectation of it was the motive of all the prodigious labors he performed.

One other impulse drove him—personal vanity. He was the master executive, the great one to whom the others came for orders. All Germany knew this, and the rest of the world, both friends and enemies, would acknowledge it in the future. In this vanity lay the root of the great man's hospitality; he had to have people to admire him, to serve as mirrors in which he might contemplate himself. He personally designed and ordered his bright-colored uniforms, literally scores of them; they externalized his glory, and first he surveyed himself, so as to see what his visitors would be seeing, and when they saw it he read the admiration in their eyes.

Secretly, of course, they might be amused, but that did not trouble

Der Dicke too much. After all, it was a game they were all playing, and it was the mob they had to fool and impress: the great German masses which lined the sidewalks twenty deep when their old-style robber baron drove by in his huge six-wheeled automobile, baby-blue in color. These masses went into the factories and toiled twelve hours a day to make the equipment for the coming war; they gave their sons to be drilled and got ready to spread the fame of the fat General, soon to be Marshal, all over Europe; to enable him to ride in triumph into one capital after another in the baby-blue limousine—equipped, of course, with bullet-proof glass.

II

That was what these Budds meant to Hermann the Great. They came overseas to him—not he to them. The father knew a lot about planes, and had given some first-rate ideas, in exchange for second-rate ideas and enough cash to keep him going. The son went about in drawing-rooms of the enemy, and from his chatter much useful information could be gleaned. Both of them admired Hermann, gazed with open-eyed wonder at his marvelous works, and bowed before the future which he was preparing.

Did they really mean all the admiration and friendship they expressed? Probably not; for most men are motivated by greed and fear, so Hermann believed, and he took them as they were; at present he fed their greed, and in due course would teach them fear. Meantime, they were good actors, and we all enjoy attending a show now and then; so, press the button, and lackeys will come, wheeling tables loaded with broiled venison, also *Rebhuhn*, with asparagus grown under glass, peaches frozen in California, and other delicacies from those seven seas which *Der Dicke* intends to master with his new air force. While planning and arranging these matters he does himself well, telling his exploits past and future and laughing uproariously, boasting to Robbie of the wonders his scientists have invented, making jokes with Lanny which cause that ivory-tower dweller to blush slightly, accustomed as he has been to the sophistications of the old world and the crudeness of the new.

This old-style German robber baron is devoted to his Führer. He recognizes that it is Adolf Hitler who has shaped the Nazi doctrines and built the Nazi Party; who has bewitched and captivated the German peasants and middle classes, something which Hermann could never have done. Hermann began as a humble *Leutnant* in the trenches, and has risen to be General and is promised a marshalship, the highest of all military ranks. That is enough; Hermann will build the Wehrmacht, and especially the Air Force which is designed to be its crown and apex, the breaker of stalemates, the crusher of Maginot Lines and whatever else the foe may have.

Incidentally, it means that the marshal-to-be will make himself the richest man in the world; he has set up the Hermann Göring Steelworks, the biggest of all time, and will add to them everything his army may take. Privately owned, of course, with no nonsense about nationalization—for has not the Führer said that Bolshevism is the Public Enemy Number One? Isn't it fear of Bolshevism that is enabling Germany to undermine and destroy the governments of every country in Europe? So, why shouldn't Hermann get rich—and boast of his riches to poor Americans, who make thousands of dollars while he is making millions of marks?

"You must come and see my new airports," says the world's future owner; and then: "You must come to Karinhall. Emmy said not to fail to bring you." Emmy Sonnemann, former stage queen, has settled down and got started on the way to presenting her husband with an heir. Her picture is in the illustrated papers almost every week; an example for every German woman below the age of forty-five; what they are all urged and even commanded to do. Block-wardens in all the humble districts go the rounds inquiring of the women whether they are pregnant, and if not why not, and they had better produce good reasons or the government will take action in the matter. Birth control advocates are shut up in concentration camps and abortionists are executed without ceremony, for the Führer must have soldiers for his future task of ruling the world. Hermann adores Emmy, and as a reward for setting a proper example to the German *Volk* she can have anything in the world she asks for; she is the first lady of the Fatherland—the Führer being a bachelor, and, in the eyes of the German *Volk*, a saint.

III

They had a very good time at the luncheon, and it was prolonged while they sipped *Rheinwein* and Hermann and Robbie smoked long black cigars and talked about their business affairs. When they were through with the preliminary stages, they discussed the state of Europe, and when they came to France with its tricky and futile politicians, Lanny told a story which *Der Dicke* pronounced *kolossal*. As Lanny told it, his old friends the de Bruynes had got themselves head over heels into the Cagoulard conspiracy, and at the moment when Denis *fils* had been arrested and the father was fearing arrest, he had entrusted certain especially compromising papers to Lanny's keeping, thinking they would surely be safe in the hands of an American. But Lanny had been tipped off that the French police were watching him, and he had tried in a great hurry to think of some place where he could hide and be safe. It happened that a few days previously he had met Graf Herzenberg at the home of Lili Moldau, the actress, and he had the impulse, perhaps foolish, to seek shelter at the Château de Belcour. Lanny repeated the long argument which had taken place between himself and Seine Hochgeboren; really amusing, for of course the Graf had been badly scared at the idea of the French police finding Cagoulard documents in his home. Lanny told how he had sought to assure the Graf that he was a friend of Hermann's, and the Graf had refused to believe him, and how alarmed he had been by Lanny's proposal to telephone to Hermann from the château.

Lanny narrated all this in a way to bring out its humorous aspects. He didn't know, but thought it a safe guess that Hermann didn't like Seine Hochgeboren, and wouldn't mind his having been embarrassed in this sort of opera-bouffe adventure. Lanny said he realized that he hadn't been able to do very much to help Hermann in his work, but he had done his best, and had certainly done a great deal to help Kurt Meissner in meeting the right people in Paris. *Der Dicke* was gracious enough to say that Lanny had helped him considerably and certainly had the right to be protected in Paris. That was good to hear, for Herzenberg would be bound to meet the General sooner or later and to ask about Lanny; indeed he might already have asked—which was Lanny's reason for telling the story. Hermann wanted to know what had become of those papers, and doubtless would have been willing to pay a fancy price for them; Lanny answered casually that he had turned them over to a trusted friend of the de Bruynes, and was glad indeed to have got himself clear of the mess.

He talked freely about the Frenchmen who were most active in the plot, and Hermann asked if Lanny would object to his making notes of the names. Lanny said: "Certainly not; but I believe they are all well known to your agents in Paris." To this the fat General replied: "That may be, but I like to know things myself, and have a check on my agents." He had until recently been head of the Gestapo, but a former schoolteacher named Himmler had taken over these all-important functions.

Somewhat to Lanny's surprise, Robbie referred to Baron Schneider as one of the backers of the Cagoule; that was a weighty secret, and one which the Baron would hardly have wanted revealed at present. But Robbie had come here hoping to place a good cash order with Hermann, and he knew that the way to make sure of it was to let it be known that he had already placed a good cash order with Eugène; no confidences counted for anything in comparison with that, and so the name of the Baron went down on the list, along with those of Michelin the tire man and Deloncle and General Duseigneur and Comte Hubert Pastré and the rest; not forgetting Pétain, marshal of the army, and Darlan, admiral of the navy.

Lanny could see the Reichswehr marching into Paris as a result of those pencil marks which the Kommandant of the German Air Force was scribbling on a pad of paper. Robbie could see it, too, though probably not so clearly. He had made up his mind that he didn't care, provided he could keep America out of it, and have Budd-Erling put to work on a big scale for America's protection. That was Robbie's philosophy in a nutshell; take care of your own house, and to hell with Europe!

IV

Hitherto when Lanny had come to Berlin with his father he had had affairs of his own; but now he seemed to have nothing to do but accompany Robbie everywhere, listen to Robbie's conversation, and ask questions about what he saw. This was a most gratifying development to the father, and brought back to life a dream which had died long ago—that his first-born might decide to follow in his footsteps and take over part of his burdens. Robbie's two sons by Esther were active in the plant, and he had no fault to find with them, but they didn't have Lanny's imagination or his knowledge of world affairs. Robbie had to be careful not to show these feelings at home, but Lanny knew what was in his heart, and was touched by the older man's willingness to explain everything, his pleasure in his eldest son's company and in the fact that the dangerous Pink tinge seemed to have faded out of the son's mind.

Robbie had been told, or had read somewhere, that this was something entirely normal. The young had their fine enthusiasms, and then in course of the years they learned what was possible and what wasn't. With Lanny this process had taken so long that Robbie had come to despair about it, but now it seemed to have come about all at once, a quite magical transformation. Lanny no longer met any Reds or Pinks and no longer had their papers on his table; more important yet, he no longer made the "smart cracks," the cynical remarks by which you could recognize the type. The father had been deeply hurt because his favorite son had repudiated all his ideas; and now to have him reverse his attitude was heartwarming indeed.

So Robbie had talked freely about Big Steel and Little Steel, about Alcoa, the great aluminum trust, and the various power combines allied with it; about Standard Oil of New Jersey and its arrangements with Germany concerning patents on the making of artificial rubber; about the du Ponts and their sale to Germany of the discoveries of their vast research laboratories. All these matters concerned Robbie, because they had to do with airplanes in one way or another. Planes had to fly faster and higher, they had to be stronger and at the same time lighter—the safety of the country, the mastery of the world, might depend upon ten-miles-an-hour difference in speed, or a .50-instead of a .30-caliber machine gun.

At the moment the Germans had the fastest fighter, but Robbie had a new one in the "mock-up" stage that was going to knock them all cold. Robbie's only problem was to get the money to complete this new model, without having to run into debt and risk losing his company to some Wall Street syndicate, as had happened in the sad case of Budd Gunmakers. A distressing thing to come here to Germany and see the research men with all the resources of a great government behind them, and to know that at home people were asleep, and leaving the burden to be carried by a few farsighted individuals, nearly all of them "little fellows" like Robbie Budd!

V

The General sent Furtwaengler to escort his guests and show them the wonders of the newly completed D.V.L., the institute for aeronautical research. To Robbie it was one of the great experiences of his life; he got from it thrills such as Lanny would have got if in the National Bibliothek he had stumbled upon the hitherto unknown manuscript of a tenth symphony by Beethoven. Great Jehoshaphat, these people had built a wind-tunnel in which they could test their models for speeds up to four hundred miles an hour. (Three hundred and twenty was the best that Robbie's new model was expected to produce.) They were training their men in air-reduction chambers, accustoming them to electrically heated suits and oxygen pumped into their lungs, so that fighter planes could get on top of bombing planes, even those equipped with sealed cabins and superchargers. Air war was going to take to the stratosphere, and the nations that didn't get there first would never get there; they would be licked in the first day, or night, of combat.

Most of these improvements were foreseen, but they were supposed to belong to the future; the Germans, however, were going to turn the future into the present. They could do it because their men at the top had the vision; because Göring had been a flyer, and had gathered his old buddies about him and put them in charge. These men knew what air war was, and what it might be; they had been licked once, and knew why, and how to get ready for the next time. All German science, all German discipline, all German wealth, were being directed to this end, so that when *Der Tag* came along, the German army should have an air cover to protect it, first to drive its enemy out of the skies and then to crush his defenses and enable the Wehrmacht to march where it would.

Meantime, in the other countries, what? Robbie Budd didn't wring his hands, for he wasn't of that type, but verbally he did just that. Muddle, muddle, muddle! The Royal Air Force was good, what there was of it, but its control was in the hands of men who still thought in terms of the last war; men who had never flown, and who looked upon airplanes as a convenient but uncertain device to enable army commanders to find out what the enemy ground forces were doing. Brass hats on the land, and on the sea admirals loaded with gold lace, pacing the bridges of great battlewagons with magnificent dignity and resenting airplanes as lawless, impertinent, and bad form.

In France it was even worse; their air force was a pitiful farce, and their program of nationalization in the face of the German threat was lunacy. As for America, that was a story which Robbie had told his son a hundred times. We had an air force of the right size for a Central American republic, and after a manufacturer had met a hundred different kinds of tests, most of them three times over, and had filled out forty-seven blanks in quintuplicate, and had been insulted half a dozen times by men who knew one-tenth as much about planes as he did—then he might get an order for ten units and the promise that Congress would be asked to budget twenty more, but a subcommittee would cut it out.

VI

Aviation was something new in the world, and at every stage of its development it had broken the rules and defied authority. When Lanny had been a tiny toddler on the beach at Juan, two bicycle manufacturers in Ohio had built themselves a frail contraption out of sprucewood and canvas, and on the sand dunes of the North Carolina coast had learned to keep it in the air for several minutes. Nobody had paid any attention to them, because everybody knew that it couldn't be done. Even when they went back to their home town and in its suburbs were flying circles around a field, the newspapers refused to pay attention to the doings, because they had been hoaxed so often and the public was tired of "flying-machine men."

Such was the attitude manifested at every stage of air development. A decade or so ago the army had court-martialed and discharged its most capable flying general, because he not merely told what bombing planes could do to battleships, but proved it. The men who conducted those proceedings were in command of the army today, so declared Robbie Budd, and they would have court-martialed *him* if they had had any way to get hold of him.

But Budd-Erling had a few supporters in the air corps, and one of them, a colonel in the reserve army, happened to be in Berlin at this time. Charles Lindbergh was his name, and when he was a youth he had performed an unorthodox and presumptuous action, stepping into a little flivver-plane on Long Island and heading out across the Atlantic. When he landed at Le Bourget airport near Paris some thirty-four hours later, he was the first man to make a solo flight across the ocean, and had become one of the most famous men in the world. He was a shy and retiring person, and didn't enjoy it; when he found he couldn't walk on a street anywhere in his native land without being surrounded and mobbed, he grew irritated, and took to being gruff to newspaper reporters, an offense unprecedented in the vast overgrown village called America.

Then came the tragedy of the kidnaping and murder of his little child. The uproar of the trial was a crucifixion for the young airman, and after it he moved to England to live. He had made a lot of money, and had married a banker's daughter and become conservative in his political views; perhaps he was that anyway, because his father had been a "radical" congressman and his family life had been unhappy as a result. Anyhow, Herr von Ribbentrop, the Nazi champagne salesman who had been made ambassador to England, saw an opportunity to make use of a naïve middle-western American for his propaganda. The Nazis were getting ready to fight, but of course didn't want to fight if they could frighten the world into giving them what they wanted. It suited them to have the world believe that Germany possessed overwhelming might in the air, and a tall, dignified, and honest young Swedish-American was picked out as the trumpet to blow this news to the world.

"Lindy" was invited to be General Göring's guest, and apparently he found it possible to enjoy living in the General's country. He came a number of times, and was received with every honor, and even given a decoration. All doors were open to him and all secrets revealed—or so he was made to believe. He flew his lovely young wife in their small plane over Germany, and saw that all along the Swiss and French borders the Germans had built an airport every twenty miles. He was escorted through giant factories, and estimated that Germany was building twenty thousand planes a year, and could double the number at will. He examined the planes and decided they were better on the whole than those of any other nation. He had not been forbidden to tell these things, and since they seemed important he told them freely, and persons in other countries who didn't want to face the facts were greatly annoyed.

VII

Colonel Lindbergh was a man after Robbie Budd's own heart, and one whom he would have chosen to have as a son. They agreed in practically all their ideas; they were interested in mechanical constructions and bored by what they called "sentimentality" of all sorts. They accepted the Nazis at their own valuation, as "conservatives" whose function was to put down Communism. In spite of the fact that one had flown the Atlantic and the other was talking about planes to fly it every day, both belonged to the group which was coming to be called "isolationists." They desired to see their country settle down within its own borders and arm itself to such an extent that no country or combination would ever dare to attack it.

So now these two sat in the Budd suite and discussed what they had seen and learned in the four great nations of the Western world, the only nations that really counted, in their way of looking at things. They knew each other's minds, and didn't have to waste time in preliminaries; they spoke a technical language, and neither had to explain his terms to the other. This applied not merely to the different makes of planes, their performances, and the hundreds of complex gadgets they contained; it applied to the techniques of flying them and the places to which they were flown, the companies which owned them, the stocks and bonds and other financial affairs of these concerns, and the personalities of those who financed and administered them. The only thing the air Colonel had to explain was the term "perfusion pump," a device which he was trying to perfect for the surgeon Alexis Carrel, a kind of "artificial heart" which would be used in certain emergencies.

Lanny listened to all this, and tried to remember as much as he could of the things which seemed to him most significant. He wondered if he, too, was becoming "conservative" in his middle years; anyhow, he found that he agreed with his father more than he had ever thought possible. Since the last war he had believed himself a pacifist, and had been embarrassed to bear the name of one of the "merchants of death"; but now he was convinced that France, England, and his own country ought to have military planes, as many as they could get in a hurry—yes, even if it allowed Robbie Budd to make a fortune, and to say to his son: "You see, I was right!" Later, when occasion permitted, Lanny would shut himself up in his bedroom and make careful notes of what he had heard, and pin them in his inside coat pocket right over his own "perfusion pump."

VIII

The great six-wheeled limousine called at the hotel for the Budds—establishing for them, so far as concerned the employees and many of the guests, a status equal to royalty. They were covered with a bearskin robe and driven to the ministerial residence, across the way from the Reichstag building, whose burned-out dome had been left unrepaired as a reminder to the German people never to forget to hate the Reds. Lanny thought of the tunnel which connected the two buildings underground, and through which Göring's men had come to set the fire. This was a story so melodramatic that nobody but Reds would believe it, and if you had told it to anybody else in Germany you would have been turned over to the Gestapo.

The deviser of this clever political stroke emerged from the palace he had won. He looked more immense than ever in a voluminous blue military cloak, with a black fur collar and hat; the coat reaching to the ankles of the shiny black leather boots. The great man occupied a full half of the wide rear seat, and his two guests the other half. A staff car followed for their protection, and *Der Dicke* started asking Lanny about the attitude of the British toward Germany's newly declared resolve to protect her minorities in the lands to the east of her. Lanny told of discussions he had heard.

The British, like the French, had to make the difficult choice between Nazis and Reds, and the fat General grinned as he listened to Lanny's account of their perplexity. Their Foreign Minister, Lord Halifax, former Viceroy of India, had visited Berlin in the previous month, ostensibly to attend a sportsman's exhibition which the General and his staff had got up. Göring was Master of the Hunt and Game Warden of Germany, while Halifax was Joint Master of the Middleton Hunt, so they had been two buddies. They had wandered around in a vast hall looking at the stuffed heads of slaughtered game from all parts of the earth, and his Lordship had received on behalf of his government the first prize for a display of overseas trophies.

Two men more incongruous it would have been hard for any cartoonist to imagine: the English nobleman, tall and drooping, with a pale, cadaverous face; stiff and solemn, deeply pious and praying both publicly and privately over everything he did; Göring, on the other hand, a throwback to the ancient Teutons, a tub of guts and a pair of bloody hands, a bellowing laugh and a restless will unchecked by the smallest scruple. He permitted himself the pleasure of telling his American guests about this visit. The noble Lord had done his best to pin Germany down to an agreement to be content with practically nothing. That was the "appeasement" idea of the new Prime Minister, Chamberlain, who kept offering it, and wondering why it was not welcomed. There had been a time in the world's history when the British had wanted things and had taken them; but now they had persuaded themselves that nobody was ever again going to take anything.

Said Robbie: "I believe they will let you have a few things, provided you can convince them that nothing British is involved."

"We have given them that assurance many times," replied the host. "There are Belgian and Dutch and Portuguese colonies of which we might reasonably claim a share. As for the people of German speech and blood who have been cut off from us by the Versailles treaty—we simply do not understand why the British are so determined to keep them in exile. If the British cannot endure to see Germany grow strong again, they will have to enforce their idea with some something more powerful than Anglican High Church prayers."

IX

The horn of the car moaned its long blasts while they sped over the low flat land of Brandenburg and came to the Schorfheide with its forests and the well-fenced game preserve. It belonged to the German government, but the old-style robber baron had calmly taken over the use of it—and who was there to say him Nay? A hunting lodge had been good enough for the Kaiser, but not for Göring, who had turned it into a palace and named it Karinhall. A long graveled driveway brought the baby-blue limousine in front of a wide-spreading two-story building of stucco or concrete, having a doorway like an ancient castle narrowing to a sort of stone tunnel as if for defense—one of those vestigial architectural features which Lanny had explained to Leutnant Rörich at the Château de Belcour. There were elk's antlers over this entrance, and many sorts of hunting trophies on the walls of the great hall inside; for of course a military man has to keep in practice, and when he can't have men he uses animals, which are cheaper, but not too cheap to be good form, in Germany as in England.

Lanny had visited this place with Irma, but that had been three or four years ago, and many trophies had been added and many gifts received since then. The Führer had had printed a special edition of *Mein Kampf*, as big as an atlas and with the most elegant binding imaginable. This had been set up on a table of corresponding magnificence, with a candle on each side always burning, just as in a church. Behind it, on the wall, was a Madonna and Child, and this seemed to Lanny the oddest combination an interior decorator had ever thought up. Had the General and his associates overlooked the fact that the subject of this work of art had been a Jewess?

Also there was a ceremonial Japanese sword which Robbie and his son were invited to inspect and wield—at a proper distance. There was an album containing photographs of the Air Force Commander's "first seventy airfields," and Robbie, of course, didn't have to pretend his interest in this. There was the shrine to Karin, the Swedish baroness who had been Hermann's first wife, and for whom the place was named; candles burned before it, and outside was a marble mausoleum holding her remains, brought from Sweden with ceremonies at which Hermann and Adolf had marched reverently side by side.

Also there was the lion cub—always a new one wandering about the house, despite the fact that one of its predecessors in favor had mistaken the General's white trouser leg for a birch tree. Upstairs the visitors inspected the most elaborate playroom they had ever seen, a floor made into a toy village with trees and all accessories, and running around it and through it a triple railroad track with toy trains. The great man sat at a desk and pressed buttons, and the trains shot here and there, through tunnels and over bridges. "My child will play with these some day," he said; the pregnancy of Emmy was soon to be made known to the German nation.

They dined in the long hall, at a table seating twenty-four guests. Only half the seats were occupied, mostly by officers of the General's staff, including Lanny's old friend Furtwaengler. After the meal the great man excused himself for a while, saying that he had reports to read. Robbie sat down to study the album of the first seventy airfields, and Lanny wandered about looking at art treasures and wondering from whom they had been expropriated. They included immensely valuable Flemish tapestries, portraying naked ladies of the Rubens style of architecture. As the great man's *Kunstsachverständiger*, Lanny knew that his patron's taste fluctuated between the two extremes of the most magnificent costumes and none at all. At the foot of the table in the dining hall, facing the General and his wife as they sat, was a marble Aphrodite Anadyomene, and elsewhere in painting and statuary you observed naked Greeks and helmeted and bemedaled Germans, about fifty-fifty.

X

In the library before a fireplace the lovely Emmy Sonnemann had seated herself upon a sofa, and not in the middle. She said: "Come and talk to me, Herr Budd." Did she intend that he should occupy the other half of the sofa? He thought it the part of wisdom to take a chair three or four feet away.

He could look at her better from that vantage point; and she was meant for looking at. Maternity in its preliminary stages seemed to become her. She was a large woman, but well proportioned; she had played Brunnhilde at the Berlin Staats-Theater, and could have played the Venus de Milo if anybody had written a drama on that theme. She had regular and lovely features, expressive of gentleness and kindness; bright blue eyes, and blond hair which had not required chemical treatment. Of all the Nazis, she was the one who came nearest to their professed Nordic ideal.

She was the first lady of the Fatherland, and one of the best known of its public figures, owing to her long premarital career. All Germans had seen her on stage or screen, and felt that they knew her. Mostly they knew only good; for though she had taken up the duties of a queen, she played it as a stage role, and everybody had the comfortable feeling that she was that kind of queen. In private life she was easy-going, comfortable, a bit naïve. Theatrical folk are supposed to be bohemian, but when they become successful, they are glad to turn bourgeois, and that was Emmy Sonnemann. Millions of people in Germany would have paid half their worldly goods for a ticket of admission to Karinhall and the privilege of sitting on the other half of that sofa; Emmy wouldn't have minded, but would have chatted amiably with each, and given the money to the *Winterhilfe.*

She said: "You don't come to see us very often, Mr. Lanny Budd."

"I have had to stay at home and help my father," he apologized. This wasn't true, but he couldn't say what he had really been doing.

"Lanny is a very nice name," she remarked. "May I call you that?"

"All my friends do," he replied. Doubtless she would have liked to add: "Call me Emmy"; but her husband, *Der Dicke,* might not have approved.

"You had a wife when you were here before. Then I heard you were divorced. Tell me about it."

Was that royalty speaking, or the stage world? In one case it would be a command, in the other just normal curiosity. Lanny took it for the latter and said: "It's a complicated story. Our tastes were too different. Irma had been raised in a huge palace on Long Island, and I in a little villa on the French Riviera. I just couldn't get used to being so very formal and magnificent."

"Oh, how well I understand!" exclaimed the first lady. "Sometimes I am so bored, I think I can't stand it. But then I remind myself how it used to be at rehearsals—doing the same thing over and over, and never getting it quite right."

"The public seems to have thought you got it pretty right," remarked Lanny, gallantly.

"*Na, na!*" exclaimed the one-time star. "Everybody flatters me, but you don't have to."

"I assure you quite sincerely that I saw you in several of your roles, and you were always lovely."

"*Ja, vielleicht;* I was good to look at, when they fixed me up and got the lighting exactly right. At the end I was beginning to show my age, in spite of anything they could do."

Lanny exclaimed with all sincerity: "This is an experience unique in my life: an actress admits her age when she doesn't have to!"

"But you know all about me, Lanny. I was a successful ingénue when you were a little boy."

"You must have been a very young ingénue; and anyhow, I didn't know about you then."

"To tell the honest truth, I was never a very good actress. I tried desperately hard, but I lacked the temperament. The directors wouldn't give me emotional roles, and my feelings were terribly hurt; but now I have thought it over and realized that they were being kind to me."

Lanny didn't know quite how to take such a confession. She was being frank—but would it be safe for him to be? He remarked: "May it not have been that you were too good for some of the roles, Frau Göring?"

"*Ach, nun,* you are being beautiful. That is the very explanation with which I comfort myself. I have never hated anybody very much that I can recall, and certainly I have never wanted to kill anybody. I like to see people happy, and I do what I can to help them. But nobody seems to want to see people like that on the stage."

"It is not the fashion of the time," admitted the art expert, consolingly. "But you have got what you want out of it, and so you can look back philosophically." He wasn't sure if that was true, but certainly it was up to him to assume it.

XI

The first lady of Naziland had commanded him to be seated, and had taken charge of the conversation. Presumably she had some purpose, and etiquette required Lanny to give her a chance to reveal it in her own way. There was a lull, and he waited; then suddenly she remarked: "I am still playing a role, Lanny. I have to be a great lady, and the stage and screen directors taught me everything about it. But one thing they never did teach me, and that is to be entirely happy."

"Ah!" exclaimed Lanny. "Whoever could teach that role would become the greatest director in the world."

"I don't like cruelty," the woman went on. "I don't like to see people suffer, and I can't help suffering with them. I am not supposed to say this to anybody in the world; but I have the impression that you have the same sort of feelings. *Nicht wahr?*"

"Yes, that is true," admitted Lanny. "I surely don't like cruelty." He couldn't say less about himself.

"Tell me this: How do you feel about the Jews?"

"Some of my best friends are Jews," he replied. After he had said it, he remembered that in New York the Jews had taken that up as a sort of shibboleth, by which you could recognize the anti-Semite who didn't wish to admit his prejudices. But after all, what else could anybody say? And what more?"

"You know how it is in the stage and screen worlds. The Jews seem to love art; at any rate they know how to run it, and how to make money out of it. So I made friends among them; some of them I became really fond of, and now they get into trouble, terrible trouble, and they write or send somebody to me, begging for help; and what can I do? I try to help one, and before I succeed there are several more. They think I am all-powerful, but I am not, I assure you."

"I can believe you, Frau Göring."

"Tell me honestly, what do you think of our policy toward the Jews?"

This indeed was a poser for the son of Budd-Erling, here on Budd-Erling business, or supposed to be! Was he going to forget that this lady's husband was the founder and still the nominal head of the Gestapo? He believed that she meant what she said, and was not just trying to probe his mind and get something out of him that might be of use to her husband. But he surely mustn't go too far on that belief!

"*Meine liebe Frau Göring*," he said, "I have suffered over this problem just as you have. I have conceived the most intense admiration for your Führer, and confidence in his program as the salvation of German culture and a means of preserving order all over Europe. But I don't regard the Jews as anything like the menace that many people do, and I think the Nazis have harmed their cause with the rest of the world by what they have done."

"Hermann feels the same way," replied Hermann's wife. "If he had the power, he would put extremists like Streicher out of office. He tells me that you have Jewish relatives, and made some effort to help them get abroad several years ago."

"That is true," Lanny admitted. "Hermann was very kind to me indeed." Long practice had taught this presidential agent to keep a straight face while listening to statements which tempted him to irony. *Hermann der Dicke*, like many another man in a high position or a low, was telling his wife the truth but not the whole truth; he surely wouldn't want her to know that this magnificent Karinhall was full of art treasures which he had wrung out of Johannes Robin by torture in the cells of the old red brick police prison on the Alexanderplatz.

Said the first lady of the Fatherland. "I go to my husband and ask him for exit permits for this Jewish artist and that, and he gets them for me. But he has so many problems and works so hard, and I hate to burden him with more cares. A man has a right to be happy when he comes to his wife, don't you think?"

Yes, Lanny thought so; also, he thought the former star was being extraordinarily indiscreet, and that he was on a spot and must be extraordinarily cautious. He replied: "I am hoping that now, when the Party is so securely in power, these unfortunate incidents will diminish."

"I fear it will be exactly the opposite, Lanny. The Party is in power, but our problems are by no means solved. The lower elements take pogroms as a sort of sport; and some of them make money out of it, too, I have been told."

XII

This conversation was interrupted by Robbie, who came strolling into the room. He was invited to take the place next to Emmy, and he started asking about motion-picture salaries in Berlin as compared with those in Hollywood, a subject of which no one in the profession ever wearies. Lanny sat quietly, supposed to be listening, but his thoughts were far away; he was having one of his internal discussions with Trudi.

Some part of his mind was always on her, and especially so in Berlin, the city of her birth and of his meetings with her over a period of years. He could never approach the Adlon without seeing his car parked on a certain spot in front of the hotel, on that night when the Gestapo had been hunting her, and he had parked her there while he went inside to fix matters up with Irma. He and Robbie now had a different suite, but all rooms in a great hotel look more or less alike, and the Trudi-ghost—as well as that of his love for Irma—haunted the bed in which he slept. It is not a good thing to have two wives in the same bed—so any Turk could have told this grandson of the Puritans.

Lanny was thinking: "Emmy is sorry for the Jews and helps them to get passports. Mightn't she become sorry for Trudi, a blond Aryan like herself? A woman artist of extraordinary talent, who has fallen under the suspicion of the police because of the activities of her late husband!"

Lanny went through an imaginary scene in which he told the first lady of Naziland this plausible and most touching story. He had every right to have been on friendly terms with art circles in Berlin prior to the coming of the Nazis; just as much as Emmy had to have known the stage and screen personalities. And to have met some Socialists, just as Emmy had met some Jews! And to have taken up a young woman artist of talent, and made her work known in Paris, and helped her to earn small sums! Later he had heard a rumor that Ludi, her husband, had been arrested and interned. Trudi, he was sure, had never been politically active, her one preoccupation being to sketch correctly the lineaments of every unusual-looking person she met. "Would you not be willing to make inquiries about her, Frau Göring, and perhaps go and see her, and help her to get away to America, where she could not possibly do any harm to the Nazi regime?"

Thus Lanny's imagination, lively as usual. No doubt he could persuade Emmy to cause the ordering of a report on the case of Trudi Schultz. A dossier would be laid on the desk of the Reichsminister General, who, among his manifold duties, had charge of the government of Berlin. That dossier would be labeled: "Trudi Schultz, alias Mueller, alias Kornmahler, alias Corning, alias Weill—and perhaps other names that she had never told to her second husband. Not exactly consistent with the ivory-tower attitude! The dossier would reveal that she had been one of the most active workers of the Social-Democratic Party's underground; that she had distributed literature from a secret press, whose operators had been caught; that she had procured the purloining of confidential documents from the General's own office and had smuggled them out of Germany by some method unknown; that after her flight to Paris she had been the source of large funds for the underground, and the best efforts of the police had failed to discover where she had obtained these funds.

That last was the fact which would stick out like a sore thumb from any report the General might get: really tremendous sums of money, tens, possibly hundreds of thousands of marks, from an unknown source; and would the stupidest General in the Nazi army fail to exclaim: "*Ach, so!* She is friend and probably mistress of this glib-tongued and plausible American playboy!"

That was where all Lanny's flights of imagination ended. He had given Trudi his pledge that he would go on giving money to the underground, and risk nothing that might direct the attention of the Nazis to himself. He had certainly broken that pledge in Paris; and how many more times would his pitcher go to the well before it got broken?

XIII

Upstairs in their adjoining bedrooms, Robbie Budd and his son might have talked over the events of the day, as guests all over the world are accustomed to do when they retire for the night. But Lanny had warned his father: "Remember, there is nothing more likely than that rooms in Karinhall are wired for dictaphones." It sounded like melodrama, but Robbie well knew that such things were done, and not only by Nazis. There were sound-detecting devices which could be hidden under a bed or behind a dressing table, and would magnify and record in another room the faintest whispers. Father and son had agreed that their conversation must be of a neutral character, and that if ever they said a word about anyone in Naziland it would be complimentary.

Now Robbie went to his suitcase and got a sheet of writing paper. Using the back of his suitcase and not the desk which was provided in the room, he wrote a few words, and then beckoned to Lanny, who came and read: "Don't talk so much to the woman."

"*Gosh!*" whispered the younger man. He wanted to say, or to write: "She pinned me down," or something like that; but obviously, this was no time for argument.

The father wrote: "Remember Donnerstein's story?"

Lanny nodded. He wasn't ever going to forget that very lively woman friend of Irma, who lived all over Germany, picked up delightful gossip, and retailed it with eagerness which would have landed her in a concentration camp if she had not belonged to the highest social circles.

Robbie wrote again: "The Heilbronn dentist," and showed the words.

"O.K.," said Lanny—this being something it was safe to say out loud.

He had passed on to his father one of the Fürstin Donnerstein's choice tidbits, having to do with a dentist who had known Emmy Sonnemann in the small town of Heilbronn where she had been born, and had written her a letter congratulating her upon her splendid marriage. In the course of the letter he had named a total of eighteen different persons in the town, telling the news about them. All these persons, plus the loquacious dentist, had been arrested by the Gestapo and brought to Berlin, where they had been held and cross-examined for weeks. Not one of them had any idea what it was all about; and when the ordeal was over, they each received a hundred marks and carfare to their homes, with the injunction to say nothing about what had happened to them.

"Jealousy is madness," wrote the father; and the son nodded several times more, saying: "O.K., O.K." No matter what advances the lovely Emmy might make, she wouldn't get another tête-à-tête with the son of Budd-Erling. Not only is jealousy madness, but Hermann might become a madman on slight provocation. He had been a dope fiend after the death of his first wife and had been confined in an asylum in Sweden. Under the strain of the gamble for world power which he was taking, he might well have fallen victim to the habit again. In any case it certainly wouldn't help Robbie Budd in getting airplane contracts to have this world gambler pick up the notion that Lanny was making himself too agreeable to the first lady of Naziland.

The son took the paper and wrote: "You are right. Sorry." Then Robbie carried the paper into the bathroom, set fire to it with a match, and held it carefully until it had burned down to the last square inch. He pulled the lever and sent the ashes down to a region where it might reasonably be assumed the Secret State Police would not follow; and along with the ashes went the last trace of Lanny's notion that he might get Emmy Sonnemann to help him get Trudi Schultz out of a Nazi prison!

16

Fuming Vanities

I

BACK in Berlin, Lanny found messages awaiting him. One was from Heinrich Jung, and Lanny had several reasons for wanting to see this ardent young Party official. He called him up, saying: "Come to lunch," and Heinrich replied, in English: "Delighted." He was proud of his English, proud of his rich American friend, and proud of an invitation which took him among international smart society.

Sixteen years had passed since Lanny had first met a humble student of forestry, son of the Oberförster of the Schloss Stubendorf estate. Heinrich was rounder now, and even rosier in the cheeks, but otherwise not greatly changed; blue eyes, close-cut blond hair, a brisk manner. He lived on hope and enthusiasm, and kept a bland smile as a permanent feature of his landscape. He had just been promoted to a post of greater responsibility in the Hitlerjugend, and had a new uniform with new insignia. He was happy in it, but at the same time modest, attributing his rise not to his own merits but to the discernment of the great organization of which he was a part. He had hitched his wagon to a star. and that star had turned into a nova, brightest of shining suns.

Heinrich didn't have any important secrets that Lanny could extract from him, but he was interesting as the perfect type of the Nazi zealot, the finished product of the Hitler educational machine. Lanny watched him with the attention he would have devoted to an ant under a magnifying glass: a bundle of energy and zeal, laboring with blind fury all day and most of the night, responding precisely and automatically to various stimuli, and never stopping for an instant to question the ends he was serving. Heinrich had that peculiar Jekyll-and-Hyde quality of the Germans, which made it possible for him to be a warm-hearted and amiable friend, and at the same time capable of most shocking cruelty. Heinrich himself had never committed any murders, but he justified them all as serving the great German purpose, and Lanny could never doubt that if the Führer should give the order, Heinrich would draw a gun in the Hotel Adlon dining room and shoot off the top of Lanny's head. He wouldn't enjoy doing such a deed, but he would know that it was necessary; otherwise the greatest man in the world wouldn't have commanded it to be done.

The *Herrenvolk* were fulfilling their destiny, and Lanny was one of the comparatively few Americans who understood and honored what they were doing. Heinrich Jung was completely naïve about this; the idea never crossed his mind that a member of the American privileged classes might believe that it was *his* race rather than the German which was destined to come out on top in the great world dog-fight. No, because the Americans had their own job to do, and a full-sized one; the greater part of their continent was still in the hands of others, and the Nazis granted them full rights to it. There were some who were even willing to concede South America, also; Heinrich avoided that question, because the Germans were strong there, and what the Germans had got they had to keep. The greater part of American culture, all that was best in it, had been contributed by the Germans, and that was one reason why Heinrich could feel so cordial to Lanny Budd; Lanny was part German, and the *Herrenvolk* could take him in, and his countrymen could become equal members of the future ruling group—that is, of course, after the Jews and the poisonous Jewish influences had been eliminated from their country.

Heinrich talked, as he always did, about the wonderful organization he was helping to build all over the world, and its achievements in making over the youth of Germany, and those of German race outside. There had never been anything like it in history; it was modern science applied to mass psychology, under the guidance of a supreme genius in that field. Heinrich had attended the *Parteitag* at Nuremberg in September, a five-day jamboree which was for every Nazi what the pilgrimage to Mecca is to the devout Moslem. Heinrich described all the ceremonies, and repeated the gist of the speeches. Everything in the world was going to be made over, and the Nazis had begun with history. Heinrich had learned at Nuremberg an entirely new history of Germany, and of the rest of the world in relation to Germany; he didn't know any other history, and he never read any book, magazine, or newspaper except Party publications. Lanny had to exercise the utmost care never to say anything that would clash with this friend's firmly rooted ideas.

II

There was a peculiar way in which Heinrich Jung was connected in Lanny's mind with Trudi Schultz. Once on the official's desk Lanny had observed a copy of one of the underground pamphlets which Trudi had written and caused to be printed in Paris and shipped into Germany. Some loyal member of the Hitlerjugend had turned this wicked thing over to his superior, and Heinrich had communicated with the Gestapo about it. Now Lanny said: "Do you ever see any more of that anti-Nazi stuff of which you showed me a sample?"

"No," replied the other; "not for some time. I think that sort of criminal activity has come entirely to an end."

"You have a marvelously efficient police force, I know."

"It's not only that, Lanny; it's the *Zeitgeist*, it's something that you will feel if you stay for a while. The very soul of the people is changed; they have been made over in the Führer's image, and it is impossible for any German to stand out against this influence. They all see that he has solved their problems for them; everybody has work, everybody has security, everybody has a sense of pride in belonging to the Führer's great organization and sharing his wonderful dream."

"I feel it, believe me, Heinrich. I make it my business to talk with the plain people wherever I go."

"You should come to Stubendorf this Christmas and meet the people there. It would give you an insight into what is coming soon in European affairs."

"You know I have never wavered for a moment, Heinrich, in my attitude to the question of the return of Stubendorf to Germany. I resigned my humble post on the staff of the Peace Commission because

I didn't approve the decisions on that and other border districts. And don't think it was easy to do; I made a lot of enemies, and put an end to what might have been a chance for a diplomatic career."

"I have never forgotten it, Lanny, and never shall. The issue is coming rapidly to a head now, and not because of our propaganda in the border states, as you will read in the lying foreign press. It is simply because our Germans in exile also see the Führer's success, and want to be a part of this new order he is building. Stubendorf is like a boiler under which you build the fire hotter and tie down the safety-valve. Our people simply will not endure to be governed any longer by incompetent and corrupt Polish officials. You will not find a single person who will say anything but this."

In the old days, Lanny would have got off some wisecracks; for example: "It might be different if I could understand Polish." But now he was playing a game, and he asked: "Is it the same all along the border?"

"*Absolut!* From Gdynia and the Corridor, all the way to the south of Austria, and even into parts of Hungary and Yugoslavia."

"I suppose the first move will come in Austria. At least, that is what people seem to expect in England and France."

"What is coming is in the Führer's mind alone," replied the loyal servant. "He does not tell me state secrets."

"Have you seen him recently?"

"I don't trouble him unless there is some important reason. Many people who had the good fortune to know him in the old days presume upon that circumstance, but I have always been careful not to."

"Not many can say that they came to see him in prison, Heinrich."

"That is true, and he doesn't forget. But I do my job, and he knows that I am doing it, and that is enough."

"Would you like to take me to see him again?"

The official's face lighted up, but then quickly became shadowed again. "Do you think it would be wise, Lanny? He is in the midst of heavy labors and has to make difficult decisions."

"Well, I don't want to intrude, but it happens that I have met a number of important persons in England and have listened to a lot of talk. Also, I have been on the inside of efforts in France to set up a government that would break off the Russian alliance. General Göring found my story interesting, and the Führer might do the same."

Lanny told of his dealings with the Cagoulards, and of his flight to the country home of Graf Herzenberg. It pleased Heinrich greatly, because it showed Lanny definitely on their side, something which

Heinrich had been trying to bring about for sixteen years. He said that, and added: "You see why we Germans can never trust a nation like France, whose governments are so unstable that we never know what to expect."

"I suppose you are right. It is a real tragedy that our coup d'état failed."

"You couldn't help it, Lanny. Nobody could do in France what we have done in Germany. Our revolution stems from the people; it is a general movement, with a Führer who is of the people and understands their soul. The French are incapable of producing such a leader, or of recognizing and following him if he appeared. All you could get there was a subsidized conspiracy, a pitiful sort of *Putsch;* it was fundamentally reactionary, and if it had succeeded, you would soon have made that discovery."

"I am afraid you are right," replied Lanny, meekly. He was interested to observe that what Heinrich said about the Cagoule was almost identical with what Leutnant Rörich had said in the château. Had Dr. Josef Goebbels discussed this pitiful French *Putsch* over the radio, and had they both been listening? Or had they been taught out of the same Nazi textbook?

Anyhow, Lanny got what he wanted out of this meeting. Heinrich said: "I'm sure the Führer would be interested in that story. I'll call up and see if an appointment can be made."

III

Another of the messages at Lanny's hotel was from the Fürstin Donnerstein; she was having an *Abend*, and would be happy if Lanny and his father would come. Lanny said: "You will meet important people." So Robbie put aside some calculations which he had promised to General Göring, and they were driven to the white marble palace on the swanky Königin Augustastrasse, belonging to a Prussian landowner and diplomat of the *Kaiserzeit*. The princess was some thirty years younger than her husband, a nervous, high-strung woman who smoked a great many cigarettes and was bored by her life without knowing why. She had met Irma on the Riviera years ago and they had become pals; now she hadn't heard from the heiress for a long time, and wanted Lanny to tell her why. Lanny knew that she was a tireless tattletale, and what she really wanted was to probe the mystery of a divorce which had intrigued smart society in half a dozen capitals. But now, with many guests to welcome and entertain, was not the time to approach this subject. The tall blond Hilde said: "Oh, Lanny, you must come to see me—and soon! Do promise." Then, in a whisper: "I have the most delightful lot of gossip—*wirklich prima!*" Lanny said promptly that he would call up without fail.

He and Irma had been about in Berlin society, and a lifetime in Europe had trained him to remember faces, names, and titles. Also Robbie had met many of the leading businessmen, and had the same sort of training; his German was shaky, but he rarely had to use it, for practically all these people knew English. Presently father and son were engaged in conversation with a dark somber-appearing man who knew the steel industry of Germany to the last ingot, and who was greatly concerned to know the meaning of the present business slump in America; what was the government going to do about it, and was there any chance of the steel men in America cutting their prices on the world market? This was Fritz Thyssen, pronounced Tissen, one of Germany's great industrial masters, and, by his appearance, one of the saddest and most badly worried men in Naziland.

Presently he remarked: "I don't sell much steel abroad these days, but they have to let me sell a little, in order that I may have the money to buy postage stamps and other things that require cash." What a world of meaning was in that sentence, for anybody who understood the code! Here was the man who, more than any other, was responsible for putting Adolf Hitler in power; who had brought Adi to the Rhineland and got the steel men together at a secret meeting, so that an ex-painter of picture postcards could explain to them that he didn't really mean his terrifying program of "abolition of interest slavery" and "nationalization of department stores." Thyssen personally had put more than five million marks into the Nazi treasury at times when the Party had been on the verge of financial collapse.

And now for a matter of five years he had been making the discovery that Adi was a man who kept no promises and had no conception of loyalty to anything but his own "intuition." Now this Catholic steelmaster was in the position of a man who has got a mad bull by the tail; he cannot let go, but has to hold on with all his might and be dragged in a bone-breaking career. He had dreamed of making tractors and promoting German agriculture, but instead he was commanded to make cannon and tanks, and for these products he had to take treasury notes, which were promises to pay on the part of the Nazi government, and were good inside Germany for the reason that all other German big businessmen were in the same plight as Fritz. That was the reason he looked as if he wanted to cry, and why he risked his freedom and indeed his life by making snide remarks to an American manufacturer who was still free to produce what he wanted to produce—even though he wasn't always sure that he could sell it after it was finished!

IV

The Donnersteins had engaged a *Sängerin* from the opera to entertain their guests, and Lanny listened with pleasure to the rendition of a song cycle by Hugo Wolf. It appeared that music was the only thing he still had in common with the Germans. So long as you left out the large section of music which bore the names of Jews, you were free to sing and to listen freely, and to express pleasure or lack of it without fear of the Gestapo. Therefore, ye soft pipes, play on; pipe to the spirit ditties of any tune provided its Aryan!

Robbie hadn't much time in Berlin, and preferred to put that little to business uses. When Lanny came out of the concert-room, he found his father seated in an alcove in conference with another Nazi notable: a large powerful man of about Robbie's age and looking oddly like a cartoonist's idea of a Prussian Junker; a square, knobby head close shaven and a square bulbous face very red; a small gray mustache and large spectacles, watery blue eyes and a sausage neck with a prominent Adam's apple, enclosed by a tall and tight old-fashioned stiff collar. Every now and then this gentleman would give a violent swallow, and then a nervous adjustment to his collar, as if he thought his Adam's apple might have knocked it out of position. His gestures were of violence, even when his voice was a whisper.

It was the great Herr Doktor Horace Greeley Hjalmar Schacht, a financier with a craving for publicity, who had been on both sides of pretty nearly every political movement which had appeared in the Fatherland since the days of the Kaiser—and what a number of them had cursed that unhappy realm! At present the Herr Doktor was Finance Minister to the Nazi regime, which meant that he was the issuer of those treasury notes which the fear-filled Fritz had to take whether he wanted to or not. The minister was apparently engaged in a confidential talk with Robbie, for when Lanny approached, he fell silent in a rather obvious way, as if to ask: "Who is this *Eindringling?*"

Robbie said: "This is my son, Lanny," and the Herr Doktor rose to his feet, clicked his heels and bowed from the waist. Robbie added: "Bring up a chair, Lanny," and then, to the other: "My son is to be trusted as I am."

So the Finance Minister resumed his monologue. It appeared that he was in the same mental state as the steel king; extremely unhappy, and overwhelmed by an impulse to pour out his soul to an influential American. Dr. Schacht's country was heading straight for bankruptcy, and the highest financial authority in the government was as helpless to prevent it as the humblest German laborer who received paper marks in his pay envelope and hastened to spend them at the nearest *Kolonialwarenladen*. The Nazis were undertaking a program of military preparation, and at the same time another of public works; making cannon and tanks, and at the same time building swimming pools and monuments! "What do they mean to do?" queried the Herr Doktor, and Lanny couldn't be sure whether it was tears or just rheum in his eyes. "We go on blindly issuing paper of a dozen different sorts, and even now our short-term paper is at a discount on the market. When the long-term obligations fall due, how can we meet them? How can anybody imagine it will be done? I have figures showing that seventy per cent of our total national income is going into government work of one sort or another at the present time, and what is that going to leave for sound business as you enjoy it in America?"

This lamentation went on for quite a while. The great financier placed his hand over his heart, covering the gold swastika which dangled there; he swore that the flood of printing-press money was the work of the radical element in the National Socialist German Workingmen's Party, and that he, a man who had been backing sound finance all his life, assumed no responsibility for the measures to which he was driven and for the orders his pen was signing. "*Leider!*" and "*Unglücklicherweise!*" and "*Zu meinem grössten Bedauern!*" began or finished nearly every sentence the Nazis' financial wizard spoke. Robbie Budd wondered: Could he be thinking of forsaking his native land and asking an influential American to help him get a job in one of the great Wall Street banks?

V

When the *Abend* was over, the Americans walked back to their hotel, along Unter den Linden, with its seeming-endless double row of great tall pillars, each with a double eagle on the top. They went on foot, because they wanted to get some fresh air into their lungs and also because they wanted to talk over the evening's events. Robbie said: "What an amazing thing, that two of this country's biggest men should blow off steam like that! I thought you told me there was no free speech here!"

Lanny explained as best he could. "These are two very exceptional men. The first"—he wouldn't use names, even in a low tone on a nearly deserted boulevard—"I believe was sincere; he is about at the end of his rope, and my guess is he's due for a fall. As for the second, he is one of the world's greatest rascals, and all I can say is, if he wasn't engaged in fooling you, then he certainly managed to fool me."

"What could his purpose be?"

"I'll wager he has made that same speech to several hundred foreign businessmen in the course of the present year. He wants you to believe that Germany is on the verge of bankruptcy, so that you'll go home and spread that good news. The Herr Doktor is concerned to have Americans carry on in the good old way, and not imitate the shrewd devices which he has thought up which enable Germany to put seventy per cent of her income into purposes that would scare you to death if you understood them."

"You're giving them credit for a devilish lot of subtlety, Lanny."

"For just as much as I would credit the devil himself. They have as good brains as there are in the world, and have put them to the task of blinding your eyes while they get ready to cut your throat."

"And yet you say the fat fellow"—Robbie wouldn't name General Göring—"tells me all about his war preparations in order that I'll go out and frighten Englishmen and Frenchmen!"

"The fat fellow is thinking about the immediate situation—the moves which are planned against the border states during the next year. He wants to bluff England and France just as Mr. Big in Italy bluffed them over Abyssinia, and as they are both doing over Spain right now. But our financial Doktor is a long-term man, and his idea is to persuade you that the whole thing is a house of cards and is bound to collapse of its own weight. That being so, the democracies can go on taking things easy, and won't have to arm, or fight for their lives—until it's too late."

"Well, it's certainly a new line of talk from a banker," commented Robbie. "He'd have a hard time getting money in Wall Street with it."

"He knows that's all past and over; he's got all he ever can. What these people want now is to be let alone for two or three years more, and then they'll be ready for anything that can happen."

"You still hate them like poison, don't you, Lanny!"

"I understand that my father is here to get contracts, and I'm help-

ing him. But it's no good letting you fool yourself, and when you ask
me questions, I tell you how I see it. That's strictly between you and
me, now and in future, of course."

"Oh, sure," replied the father; "and I'm grateful for what you are
doing. At the same time, of course, I hope you're mistaken."

"Nobody could hope it more than I," replied the son.

VI

All this time, while Lanny was playing about with smart Berlin
society, a voice was crying in his soul: "Trudi! Trudi!" He was in the
same position as to her that she had been in as to her former husband;
she had endured some four years of grief and frustration, with nothing to do but wait and fear the worst. In the end Lanny had been
able to persuade her that if Ludi had been alive he would surely have
found a way to get word to her. In this case Lanny could be sure that
Trudi would make no such attempt; she would never whisper his
name, to say nothing of putting it on paper. He must count her
among the dead; one of many thousands of casualties in the secret war
on Nazism, a part of that age-old war for freedom which has been
going on ever since the soul of man awakened and discovered itself in
slavery.

A hundred times Trudi had said to him: "It is bound to happen;
and when it does, forget me, and go on and do your work." So here
he was, trying to find out what Hitler was going to do about Stubendorf and the Corridor, about Austria and Czechoslovakia; which would
come first, and how soon, and would they resist, and what action
would England and France take? In the course of this work Lanny
had to go about and meet the leading Nazis, eat their rich foods, drink
their choice wines, and never fail to wear an agreeable smile; whenever
he found this possible, his conscience would begin to gnaw, and he
would say: "I am being corrupted!" When he found himself enjoying
the goodfellowship of *Der Dicke* or the rapier wit of Reichsminister
Doktor Goebbels, he would have a sick feeling inside, and would
punish himself by driving home past the prison on the Alexanderplatz
where he had gone to see Johannes Robin, or the Columbus Haus
where he himself had once been held under suspicion.

Would they be keeping Trudi in one of these places? Or would they
have brought her to Germany only to kill her? Monck had insisted
that the latter must be the case, and had warned Lanny not to waste
his energies. Of course, if Lanny seriously believed in spirits, he could

go on with those experiments; but no more burglaries! So now, when the husband came home from an *Abend*, he would prepare himself for sleep, put out the light, and lie for a while in darkness and silence. He would compose his mind and say: "Now, Trudi." He would wait and watch, concentrating his thoughts upon her, saying without words: "All I want is to know where you are." But no voice ever spoke and no figure appeared at the foot of his bed. Darkness and silence in his soul as well as in his room.

VII

Robbie Budd left for home; he would spend his Christmas on the steamer. Kurt arrived in Berlin on his way to Stubendorf, and called Lanny at the hotel, inviting him to come along. But Lanny said No. He had already met Graf Stubendorf in Berlin, and no longer had any sentimental feelings about the Schloss or the Meissner family either; they were all German, and getting ready for war, and full of Nazi rage and Nazi propaganda shams.

Heinrich had telephoned, saying: "Our great friend will see you shortly; but today is not a good day, because something bad has happened and he is annoyed." Lanny knew better than to ask questions about such matters over the phone; instead he kept his promise and telephoned Hilde, Fürstin von Donnerstein, who exclaimed: "*Grossartig!* I am simply bursting with news! Will you come and have tea?"

He drove to the white marble palace, and found that his hostess had invited no one else. She was the mother of three children, but still young; her colors were fading and she made up for them with more cosmetics than Lanny found attractive. She was tall and thin for a German woman, with a nervous, distracted manner; she would rattle on for a while, and then suddenly stop and start off on a new topic. Her speech was ninety per cent English and ten per cent German, or vice versa, whichever you preferred. Lanny knew that in spite of her high social position she wasn't happy; he suspected that her marriage to a man a whole generation older than herself had not proved a success. However, she was proud, and talked only about other people's troubles; that was satisfactory to Lanny, who had met numbers of unhappily married ladies and had learned many stratagems for keeping himself a sufficient distance away.

Like Rosemary, Hilde had to know about her friend Irma, and why she and Lanny had broken up. He had to give her something in return for what he wanted, so he explained the differences between his temperament and Irma's, giving the latter the benefit of all doubts. Nothing about politics, of course; it was just that he was bohemian in his tastes, while Irma enjoyed only the most proper people. Hilde would be certain that there must have been another man or another woman, and would be alert for the slightest hint as to which it was. But Lanny insisted that with Americans a divorce could happen without any sexual trespass. Irma had since found the perfect husband, but really and truly, she hadn't had her eyes on Lord Wickthorpe when she had divorced Lanny. Hilde heard this with lifted eyebrows, and exclaimed: "*Ach, mein lieber!* If I had ever in my life met a man as trusting as that, I should have fallen in love with him *sofort*."

This might be what in café society in New York was known as "making a pass at him." He was supposed to say: "Is it too late?" or something like that. But this proper grandson of the Puritans remarked: "Irma and I always trusted each other, but I knew she wasn't happy, and was sorry about it. We agreed to remain friends, and never let our little daughter know there had been any trouble between us."

"What cold-blooded people, you Americans!" exclaimed the Prussian princess. "It seems to us *ganz unglaublich* that a nation should have set to work deliberately—*kaltblütig*—to provide a place where you can go and hide for a few weeks and come back with a new partner! *Schrecklich!*"

"It isn't quite like that," smiled the grown-up playboy. "We seldom create anything deliberately; we discover what we call a 'good thing,' and then a lot of people rush in to make use of it. Nevada is a large state which consists mainly of deserts and mountains. It has a small population who haven't many ways to get rich, and one of its frontier towns discovered that quick divorces and wide-open gambling would bring tourists with checkbooks in their pockets. It's about the same thing as Salzburg discovering that a music festival could be made to pay, and that tourists like to dress up in short brown leather pants and hats with a *Gemsbart* on them."

"*Salontiroler*, we call them!" laughed the Fürstin, who had a summer home in those mountains, and had been expecting a visit from Irma and Lanny on the very day when their marriage had gone *kaput*.

VIII

A maidservant wheeled the tea service into the drawing-room, and then departed, closing the door. Hilde poured the tea, and then, as part of the ritual, took the "cozy," a sort of padded tent which was put over the teapot to keep the heat in, and set this object carefully over the telephone. There existed in Berlin the widespread belief that the Nazis had some sort of device whereby they could listen in on conversations, even when the phone was disconnected. Lanny doubted very much if it was so, but his knowledge of electrical matters was not sufficiently great for him to risk his own life or that of his friends upon it. He had seen this tea-cozy procedure in more than one home, and was never surprised if any host or hostess rose suddenly and stepped silently to a door and opened it to glance outside. Sometimes the person would apologize, and sometimes go on as if nothing had happened.

Hilde took a peek out of two doors, and then drew her chair a foot or so closer and turned on the gossip spigot. "*Also*, Lanny, have you heard the news about *unser kleine Doktor?*"

There might possibly have been many little doctors in Naziland, but for Hilde and her guest only one. He was short and frail-looking and dragged a club foot; to make up for these defects he had a pair of keen observant eyes, a lightning-swift mind, and a mouth so wide that when he opened it and shouted, the whole world heard him. He was one of the two most dreaded men in Naziland, the other being Himmler, head of the Gestapo. Now Hilde was radiant with delight, and though she spoke in a half whisper her voice carried a thrill. "Jupp" at last had got what was coming to him—from a screen comedian who had objected to nothing more serious than Jupp's having forced the actor's young wife to submit to his advances.

The popular Gustav Frölich had lain in wait for Jupp and given him a sound drubbing; whereupon Jupp had appealed to Himmler, who had had the actor thrown into jail; whereupon the actor's friends had rallied and given Jupp an even more complete working over, so that now he was laid up, giving out that he had been hurt in an auto accident. *Herrlich!* The Moscow radio had got the story and broadcast it last night—had Lanny happened to be listening? *Die ganze Welt* listened to Moscow these days—it was the only way you could get the truth about Berlin. Magda Goebbels, the little doctor's wife, had got the facts that way, and now she was giving Jupp a third licking, the worst of all. *Unschätzbar!*

IX

Lanny had had the honor of meeting the Goebbels couple early in his Nazi career. In his efforts to aid Johannes Robin he had appealed to Heinrich Jung, who had taken him to Magda. Lanny never knew just what had happened after that. Apparently it had been Dr. Robert Ley, head of the Nazi Labor Department, who at first had the bright idea of grabbing a Jewish millionaire and his yacht; then Dr. Goebbels, who called Dr. Ley a drunken rowdy, got the bright idea of taking him away from Dr. Ley; then Reichsminister Göring, who called Dr. Goebbels a deformed monkey, had the bright idea of grabbing him away from Dr. Goebbels. Of course Lanny wouldn't say a word about this to Hilde; he just said that he had been in the Goebbels home, and had found the little doctor a witty and delightful companion.

"He is a double personality," commented the woman; "when he takes his public role he is so bitter, so *grausam*, it makes you shudder."

"I suppose he takes a professional attitude toward his work. He began as a journalist, and newspapermen all have to do what in America is called 'taking policy.' When such a man goes into politics, he carries over the same attitude."

"*Ach, ja*, but does he have to be such a *Raubtier* toward young women?" Hilde got up and went to the door of her drawing-room, opened it, and then came back. "This wretched deformity has the whole stage and cinema world at his mercy; it is part of his propaganda department, and every young and attractive actress must come to his bachelor apartment in the Rankestrasse and submit to whatever indignities he cares to inflict. And poor Magda has to hear about it over the Moscow radio—not to mention all the anonymous letters."

"The last time I saw her was at the Berghof," said Lanny. "I thought I had never seen an unhappier-looking woman."

"She greatly admires *Die Nummer Eins*," replied Hilde, who even in the privacy of her own home was afraid to say the word Führer. "Some say she goes there to pay the little doctor off; *aber*—it would be better not to say, even if one knew." A pause, while a struggle between loquacity and security went on in the soul of the Princess. Apparently the latter won, for she dropped the sex-life of the Number One Nazi.

"Do you know Magda's story? She was an orphan, brought up by a wealthy Jewish family—and what a strange reward they have received! She married an elderly millionaire, Herr Quandt, who took her to New York, hoping to distract her restless mind. She rewarded him by demanding a divorce with a handsome alimony. Then she became a convert to our new racial religion, and her income was found useful at Party headquarters. She became *Die Nummer Eins*' dear friend, and there have been many times when he was in fear of poison and she alone was trusted to prepare the vegetable plates with one poached egg which he adores. She was, as you know, *eine Schönheit,* and many men fell in love with her. I suppose she thought our Juppchen offered the surest road to wealth and fame. At that time, you know, Göring was not married, so she expected to become our first lady. When the cabinet was formed, and Hermann was in it but Jupp was not, she entered upon a period of mourning; but finally Jupp became a Reichsminister, and Magda began to bloom. You should see the estate they have acquired on the Wannsee; and the entertainment they gave there last July—*fabelhaft*—it was like *A Midsummer Night's Dream,* only much more of everything. An island called the Pfaueninsel, and you go to it by a bridge of boats, held in place by men in livery; and on the other shore you find the SS men all in white uniforms, and lovely maidens in white—what do you say? *Maillots?*"

"Tights."

"You see a thousand huge artificial butterflies lighted from within; a dancing stage for a thousand guests, and forty men mixing drinks, and such foods as you would expect only at a royal banquet; after supper a ballet and then fireworks—such a racket that all the diplomats wonder, does the Propaganda Minister tell them that all art and hospitality and *deutsche Gemütlichkeit* are to end in war?" The Fürstin interrupted herself. "What do you think, Lanny? Is it so?"

"*Liebe Hilde!*—you will have to ask the Reichsminister."

"*Jawohl!* It is so anyhow with *die arme Magda*—her happiness has ended in domestic war. Her mail full of unsigned letters, and broadcasts from Moscow concerning her husband's black eye! *Preis und Ehre sei Gott!*"

X

Lanny had to be careful while drinking tea with this free-spoken member of the Prussian aristocracy. In the old days he had been freespoken himself, and Hilde was proceeding on that basis. She was talking *to* him, but he had to remember that before long she would be talking *about* him. He took occasion tactfully to remind her that he was General Göring's art expert, and that his father was the General's business associate. "I have had to learn to keep my thoughts to myself in many different parts of the world," he said. "Don't expect me to express opinions on Nazi personalities." That must have disturbed her, for she said no more about Nazi personalities for a while.

Irma had told her about Lanny's psychic experiments, and now he mentioned the cross-correspondence they had got in Berlin, and how he had just revisited one of these mediums and got additional messages from his grandfather. Hilde wanted to know how such things could happen, and he told her his theories or guesses. She said the Nazis were trying to repress astrology and fortune-telling, on the ground that it was nonproductive activity; but several of their prominent leaders dabbled in all sorts of mystical and occult ideas.

"I have heard that stated concerning *Die Nummer Eins*," remarked Lanny, leading the conversation to where he wanted it.

"*Ja, wirklich!*" exclaimed Hilde—and again the gossip-spigot was turned on. "Do you know the story of Hanussen?"

"I have heard that he was killed because he made some unacceptable prophecy concerning a high eminence."

"*Nein, nein, glauben Sie's nicht!* That is the sort of story that people make up because it pleases them. My husband met Hanussen, and attended one of the séances he used to give for the Berlin élite. He was a Jew, you know, but that was in the days before *die neue Ordnung* was installed. Hanussen was an astrologer, and some sort of *Genie*, people said; when he went into a trance he foamed at the mouth, and the things he told were often quite terrifying. It is true that he predicted the death of *Die Nummer Eins*—but after all, we have to die some time, *nicht wahr?*"

"Why was he killed?"

"It is one of our dreadful stories. He became wealthy, and loaned large sums to Graf Helldorf, who was one of the first of our Prussian nobility to take up with the Nazis, and became president of our Berlin police. He is a gentleman of more extravagant tastes than his estates warrant; also he is one of those whose *Liebesleben* is somewhat different—I was going to say from the usual, but perhaps I had better say from the non-Nazi. Anyhow, Hanussen made the mistake of letting Helldorf give him notes; and when the sums had grown very large and the first of the notes was due, Göring had the Jew-astrologer killed, and the notes have never since been presented at any bank."

"You know, Hilde," remarked the visitor, "your *Nummer Eins* has said that he is building a regime to last for a thousand years. I should say——"

"*Ja, Lanny?*" said the woman, expectantly. She had heard him say clever things, and was eager for his comment.

But it was one of the times when Lanny bit his tongue. He had been on the verge of saying that what Adi had done was to provide Hollywood with plots for a thousand years; but the Princess might consider that a *mot* and pass it on. He remarked, tamely: "I wonder if some fortune-teller made that thousand-year prophecy."

"I have never heard it said."

"Do you know if Adi consults such people at present?"

"I've heard no mention of the subject."

"I'd be much interested to know. I take these psychic matters seriously, and I am wondering to what extent his powers are derived from subconscious forces. He might use hypnotism without even realizing it; and it may be that his extraordinary self-confidence is due to his conviction that he has some kind of supernormal support."

"I haven't the least doubt he believes that, Lanny. He calls it his intuition."

"It is the same thing, whatever name you give it. Socrates talked about his *daimon*, and Jeanne d'Arc about her St. Michael. I'd be tremendously interested to know if this dynamism is supported by some medium, or by some psychic procedure, a ritual, or prayers, or act of worship. What does he do when he has a spell of discouragement?"

"They say he falls into a fit and chews the rug."

"Yes, but there is nothing medicinal in a rug. Sooner or later he gets up and goes to work to overcome his obstacles. I'm interested to know if there is somebody who goes into a trance, or who sits over a magic spring and breathes gases like the Delphic oracle, and tells him that he is a man of destiny and that all the world is going to belong to him before his end."

"I'll see if I can find out for you," replied the Princess. "One has to be careful asking questions about these matters, of course."

XI

Hauptmann Furtwaengler telephoned to say that Seine Exzellenz was having a shooting party at Rominten over the week-end, and would Herr Budd like to accompany him. Lanny said: "*Mit Vergnügen!*" He knew that Robbie had made an excellent deal with *Der Dicke*, and would wish the intimacy to be cultivated—but not with Emmy! This time would be safe, because Rominten lay away to the east from Karinhall, and in Germany ladies as a rule do not go on shooting parties; especially not ladies who are on the way to presenting their nation with an heir apparent.

The baby-blue limousine called again, and now Lanny and the General had the rear seat to themselves, except for a bearskin robe. It was a cold afternoon, and a light snow was falling; the mournful horn sounded incessantly while the great man went on pumping Lanny dry on the subject of French and British statesmen of all parties. Hermann's body might be lazy, but his mind was surely not; he was better educated than any other of the Nazi leaders whom Lanny had met, and whatever he heard he retained.

Rominten was what the British call a "shooting box," and had a thatched roof like a peasant's hut; but inside it was roomy and comfortable. Besides Furtwaengler and the other adjutants and aides-de-camp there was one of Göring's Swedish brothers-in-law, Count Rosen. Maidservants waited upon them and brought a supper consisting of half a dozen choices of game. Afterwards, Lanny played the piano and they sang, as at the Château de Belcour. Never again would he sing German songs without remembering the mental strain of that earlier occasion; he could play with one part of his mind, and with the other be thinking: "Trudi, where are you?"

Trudi had been taken away from Belcour, and this fat man with the bellowing voice was her keeper. When he retired to his bedroom to read "reports," was there one about Trudi Schultz among them? Or had he already ordered her killed, her body burned, and her soul forgotten? "Dead men tell no tales" has been the creed of tyrants and criminals since the beginning of human time, and the formula includes female as well as male saints and reformers. Lanny's face wore a smile and his fingers tripped lightly over the notes of a sentimental love song, while the mind which controlled them was thinking about pressing the trigger of a machine gun.

In the morning the company was called before dawn, and Lanny was put into a sleigh, along with the Hauptmann and an Oberstjäger-meister, also a keeper who had charge of the particular beat they were to visit. Outside was complete darkness, except for the stars shining like jewels; the two-horse sleigh sped silently along a wood-road through a deep fir forest, and meanwhile the keeper told them where they were going and what they were expected to do. Their goal an open glade, the haunt of a great "sixteen-pointer," a stag which was expected to come out with his hinds to feed upon what grass could be got by pawing in the snow. Herr Budd, as guest, would have the first shot, and the Hauptmann would be second; the "Colonelhunter-master," being attached to the estate, had to be content with shooting the partridges, hares and other small game which appeared upon the table three times a day.

XII

They came to the *Hochstand,* a platform some twenty-five feet high with a ladder at the side. They climbed up silently and mounted guard, not speaking even in a whisper, flexing their muscles to keep warm, and peering by the gray light of dawn to make out the forest and meadow. It was bitterly cold, and the first thing they saw clearly was the white streamers of their own breath. But soon the scene grew clearer, the fir forest, carefully kept, so that only the great trees and the proper number of smaller were left. Presently the animals put in their appearance, and they, too, were carefully kept, fed from hayracks when grass could no longer be found; the hinds were never killed, and the stags only when they had attained their full growth. It was a great honor to be invited to have a shot, and a great fall in prestige if you missed.

Lanny had to wait a considerable time for a clear shot; for of course it would not do for him to hit the wrong animal. The leader of this herd could have no idea of his danger, but it really appeared as if he were purposely keeping one of his ladies between himself and his foe. The men were tense with excitement, standing rigid as if they were parts of the *Hochstand.* Lanny was excited, too, but always there was that other part of him, saying: "What would Trudi think of this waste of time and money?" He recalled how she had urged him to cultivate the fat General; some other of her comrades had been doing the same, and had stolen precious documents from *Der Dicke's* files. While Lanny's eyes watched the stag, the underground part of his mind was saying: "I wonder would Monck know who that person was? And could he put me in touch with him?"

"*Achtung, die Herrschaften,*" whispered the keeper. The great antlered beast had taken a couple of steps forward, exposing his front half, and Lanny raised the rifle which had been put into his hands that morning, and which he had never fired. He knew all about guns, and had been taught to shoot in his boyhood; he had visited other shooting-boxes, and had studied a book which gave diagrams of the bodies of stags and showed the location of the heart from several angles. "X marks the spot," and Lanny raised his rifle and aimed at it with care. He pulled the trigger, there was a report, and the great creature dropped in his tracks. That was all there was to it, except that the two officers wrung his hands and patted him on the back. The rest of the herd had vanished into the forest, so the hunters descended from the stand and drove back to the "box" to learn what had happened to the other parties.

They went out again before sundown, and waited at another stand. This time there were two stags in sight, and Lanny offered the first shot to the Hauptmann, who had done him many favors. They argued in whispers, but the officer insisted that it would be displeasing to Seine Exzellenz; so Lanny shot first and got his, and then, as the herd did not run, Furtwaengler got his, and all were happy.

Sledges came and brought in the carcasses, and laid them on the lawn in front of the house. A bonfire of pine branches was built, and the Jäger wearing dark green uniforms and carrying horns in their hands, stood lined up behind the trophies, while the Hauptjäger read off the list of the kills and the names of the killers. The keepers of the herd had a name for each stag, and Lanny learned that he had killed first Heinie and then Stax. The General made a brief speech of thanks to his guests for the service rendered, and then the Jäger raised their horns and sounded the *Hallali*, or death of the stag. The notes were echoed back by the tall trees of the forest, and in the starlit night the scene was so beautiful that all parts of Lanny's mind forgot his wife for a few minutes.

But not so a little later, when Göring asked if his guest would like to have the head mounted and take it to his home. Lanny said: *"Danke schön, lieber Hermann."* He remembered the time when he had smuggled Trudi's stolen documents out of Germany in the back of one of Hermann's paintings for which Lanny had found a customer in America. A stuffed and mounted stag's head would offer an ideal hiding place for papers or jewels or whatever it might be. Lanny would ask the hotel to store the trophy for the present, against some emergency which might arise in the career of a "P.A."

Dangerous Majesty

I

"I T IS a great honor the Führer is doing you," said Heinrich, in that formal manner which he assumed when speaking of the greatest man in the world. "He hardly ever sees foreigners nowadays, except diplomats in his line of duty."

"*Gerade drum!* It'll be good for him to have a change of scenery now and then." Thus Lanny, with that free and easy American manner which half-frightened and half-fascinated a Party bureaucrat.

The appointment was for four, at the Chancellery. The weather had turned mild, the sun was shining, and they walked from Heinrich's office, past many cold white marble monuments to German glory. New buildings were going up, mostly of gray Swedish granite; they were part of the public works which the Herr Doktor Schacht had lamented. Lanny was committing no breach of confidence when he told of the Finance Minister's anxieties. Heinrich commented: "These mighty structures will be here long after the Herr Doktor's name is forgotten, and everyone will recognize them as one more proof of the Führer's manifold genius."

There was the "Old Chancellery," which had been built for the Hohenzollerns, but had not been good enough for a one-time painter of picture postcards. He had added to it the so-called "New Chancellery"; three-storied, massive, and rectangular, looking like a military barracks transplanted to the Wilhelmstrasse. In its upper stories were halls devoted to his greatest works, the models of the new city hall, the administration buildings, and of stadia and baths, layouts of whole cities, *Prachtbauten* which he was going to cause to arise. Heinrich had brought his friend early, at the great man's own suggestion, in order that these marvels might be shown to him.

The stern-looking SS guards gazed suspiciously at all visitors, even one in Heinrich's uniform. However, this pair had the proper cards of admission, and Lanny displayed the proper fervor as they wandered through the vast corridors with red marble floors and Gobelin-tapestried walls. Precisely on the stroke of four they presented themselves to the double guards in front of Der Adolf's private study. Over the double doors was a sort of coat-of-arms with "AH" inside the design. The visitors were passed in to the secretary, and by him ceremoniously into the inner sanctum.

In the Berghof and the Braune Haus the Führer had chosen modernism and simplicity; but here he had apparently been overcome by the spirit of Berlin, which is that of barbaric magnificence. He had set himself to outdo Mussolini in the colossal size of his office. It was paneled in dark wood, and had high broad doors leading out to the park of the Chancellery. There was a capacious fireplace, with a lifesize Bismarck over the mantel and a statue of Frederick the Great near by. The Führer's desk was at the left, an awesome distance away; it was flat-topped and large, and on it Lanny observed books of military strategy, a magnifying glass, a row of colored pencils, and, unexpectedly, a pair of spectacles, never worn in public for reasons of prestige.

Enormously high ceilings and glittering chandeliers, heavy draperies and thick rugs rather dwarfed the ex-painter, who was nothing much to look at. He was clad in a blue civilian suit with white shirt and black tie, and if you had passed him on the street and hadn't seen him in the newsreels you would have taken him for a reasonably successful grocer or a *Beamter* of the lower ranks, say a customs official like his father. He had grown stouter since Lanny had seen him last; his cheeks were rounder and also his nose; the little dark Charlie Chaplin mustache must have been growing also, but that could be reduced with less trouble than *embonpoint*.

He was in his amiable mood; indulging himself in the luxury of meeting one of his adoring followers, and a visitor from the land of wild Indians and cowboys. In his youth Adi's favorite reading had been a German romancer by the name of Karl May, whose endless volumes dealt with the noble redskin and his conquest by German emigrants on the plains. Since then the subcorporal of the World War had learned that America had heavy industry and could produce cannons and shells, but his thinking about the continent was still colored by his early imaginings. He would have been glad to have Karl May's America for his friend, and the son of Budd-Erling meant to him a glimmer of that hope. So this was not just a social call but a diplomatic *démarche*.

He shook hands with both his guests, and when he had them seated, he opened up on Lanny at once: "I thought you were going to send me a Detaze."

"I assumed you would have forgotten all about it, Herr Reichskanzler," said the art expert.

"Why should you wish me to do that?"

"I thought you were just being polite."

"I can be polite in less expensive ways. I wanted the painting because it will give me pleasure, and because I am doing what I can to promote friendship between the two countries, and to bring our two cultures together."

"I owe you an apology for my negligence. I will gladly make you a present of one of our best Detazes."

"You made that offer before and I told you I could not permit it. You said the pictures were for sale and I asked to buy one. I am not a rich man—you perhaps know that I do not take any salary for this office I hold—but the German people read my book, and I derive royalties from the sales, and can afford to indulge my taste in art to a modest extent. Tell me, what do Detaze landscapes bring on the market?"

"The prices have varied considerably, Herr Reichskanzler." Lanny did some quick mental arithmetic. "Some of the smaller works have sold for as low as eight thousand marks; on the other hand, at our show in New York, before the great panic, we sold several for as high as forty thousand marks."

"Let us compromise," said the Reichskanzler. "Would you consider thirty thousand marks a fair price to pick me out one of the best land and seascapes?"

"In view of the advertising it would bring, Herr Hitler, I should consider I was taking an unfair advantage of you."

"Not many people get an opportunity to do that, so you had better make use of it. Send me the painting with a bill in regular form and it will be paid."

II

The Führer talked about art for a while, and the efforts he was making to promote sound taste in the Fatherland. He didn't defend his tastes, he just stated them with quiet finality; in the course of five years nobody had ventured to dispute his authority on the subject, so it was perhaps only natural that he should consider the matter closed. Art existed for the purpose of inspiring the people with sound Nazi

ideals; it was a branch of Dr. Juppchen's Department of Education
and Propaganda, and the fact that Juppchen was just now laid up with
a black eye didn't invalidate his principles nor stop the work of their
inculcation. The Führer had that very morning received a visit from
his old and dear friend Magda and had laid down the law to her in
the plainest terms; there was to be no divorce and no more scandal
in the *Parteileitung;* as soon as Jockl—so the Führer called the little
doctor in the doctor's Rheinland language—was out of bed again he
would be summoned to the presence and have the law laid down to
him: he would live on terms of outward amity with his wife and he
would assign parts to young actresses on their merits and without any
other price: otherwise the Führer would apply to Jockl the Nazi laws
requiring sterilization of all persons who possessed hereditary physical
defects, which included clubfoot.

Of course Hitler didn't say any of that to his visitors. It was Hilde
who would tell it to Lanny at their next meeting; it might be that the
detail concerning sterilization had been added by Hilde herself, or by
the person who had passed the delicious tidbit on to her. It is not only
in Naziland that the great and famous are the subject of gossip, and
that it has a tendency to grow like the fish that gets away from the
angler.

Adolf Hitler forgot very little that was of importance to his cause,
and he remembered that at their last meeting he had charged the son
of Budd-Erling to inform the French people of his friendly intentions
toward them. Now he listened with pleasure while the visitor told how
he and his friend Emily Chattersworth had helped Kurt Meissner to
meet persons who were socially and financially prominent in Paris, and
how all three had helped to spread the message of peace on earth and
good will toward Germany. It was of course important for Hitler to
understand the Cagoulard movement, how strong it was and what reli-
ance he could place upon it; and here was a man who had, apparently,
lived in the very center of that movement.

Lanny talked freely, and Adi listened attentively. He trusted few
persons altogether, but he had to trust many part way, and to determine how far in each case was the first duty of a man of affairs, a
seeker of power. The last time this plausible American had come visiting, his rich wife had been enthusiastic for National Socialism, while
the husband had been reserved and noncommittal. Now he had
changed, and said it was because he had seen the wonderful work the
Führer was doing. And that was all right; many persons were being
convinced by that method, and not all of them were climbers and self-

seekers. Some were idealists, a type to which Adi considered himself as belonging. Because of his social position this middle-aged playboy from overseas could accomplish a great deal without any special effort. In these days of complex organization an engineer who understands a great machine can do more work by pushing a button than a thousand laborers can do by all their toil and sweat. The Führer of the Nazis was looking for such social engineers, and as he listened to Lanny Budd he was thinking, first: "Is this the real thing?" and second: "How can I harness him and put him to work?"

III

Lanny talked about the French statesmen, their incomes, their connections, their financial and journalistic backing, their lady loves and other weaknesses. He talked about the men at the top in the money world of Paris, the inner circles of the two hundred families. He told of Baron Schneider, and that uncertainty which tormented the soul of a munitions king, who knew that he had either to co-operate with Hitler or else get ready to fight him, and couldn't make up his mind which. This amused the Führer, and he rubbed his hands together and slapped his thighs, as was his way when pleasurably excited.

Then Lanny got launched on his story of the de Bruynes, and how he had got the news of their arrest, and had sought refuge in the home of Graf Herzenberg. That was a priceless tale, and Adi bubbled with delight, and abandoned some of that caution which he was trying to teach himself, never with entire success. Seine Hochgeboren was one of those haughty Junkers whom a humble army sub-corporal was now having to battle and subdue to his will; one couldn't expect a man who in his youth had been reduced to sleeping among the bums not to distrust, and in the depths of his soul to hate, one of those great estate owners who kept their land and their privileges through all wars and revolutions, and now were tolerating a mob-leader, a rabble-rouser who could be made to serve their purposes for the moment.

Adi had known this rich American for a matter of ten years, and he knew that Kurt and Heinrich had known him since boyhood. There could be no question that he really moved in the circles of which he told. Let him go on and talk, as he seemed to enjoy doing, and reveal his tastes and his ambitions. That was the way to win men, and to keep them in one's service. If right now, for example, this man could be tactfully caused to pay a visit to Vienna, he might meet on intimate terms the associates of a statesman whom Adi called "*dieser verdammte*

Schuschnigg," and ascertain what promises of support he has received from Mussolini, and how far the Italian windbag could be trusted—if at all!

IV

Just as the Führer was trying to make up his mind to approach this delicate subject, his visitor suddenly shifted the conversation. "*Eure Exzellenz*, I have been having some unusual experiences along the line of psychic research, and it occurred to me you might like to know about them. I have heard that some years ago you carried on experiments along this line."

"I am still a believer in many occult ideas, Herr Budd; but I have had to discourage these activities in Germany, because I have found such a mass of fraud connected with them, and credulous people are swindled unmercifully."

"No doubt that is generally true, though I myself have been fortunate in escaping it. Eight years ago my stepfather discovered a medium in New York, an old Polish woman, and we brought her back to the Riviera with us. She has lived in our home ever since, and we have had every opportunity to check on her activities. I have kept notes of my sittings with her, and my stepfather has done the same. Many days we drew blanks, but on others events took place which took my breath away."

"That interests me of course, Herr Budd. Tell me more about it."

"One of our friends who sat with this medium was Sir Basil Zaharoff. They met in a hotel room in Dieppe, where he had come as a stranger, and I am sure that Madame had no idea who he was. As soon as she went into her trance she began crying out about guns going off, and people shouting curses at the sitter. Then she introduced relatives of Zaharoff, and it was embarrassing, for they accused the old munitions king of actions which he denied. Finally the spirits made it so uncomfortable for him that he jumped up and left the room. Subsequently I verified one of the charges in the files of the London *Times* some fifty years back; it seems that he had pleaded guilty in the Old Bailey police court to the charge of having converted to his own use one hundred and sixty-nine sacks of gall belonging to a merchant in Greece. The medium had given the number of sacks, though I doubt if she had ever heard of gall as an article of commerce. I know I hadn't."

"That is certainly an extraordinary story, Herr Budd."

"Zaharoff was so impressed that after a long interval he came back, and for years he used this medium to communicate with his dead wife, the Duquesa de Marqueni. Early this year I happened to be having a séance with Madame at my hotel in Paris, and I was told that the spirit of Sir Basil had just arrived. Afterwards I went out and got a paper with the news of his death."

"I have never had any experience so convincing as those. Where is this medium now?"

"She was in Paris when I left. My mother was intending to take her back to our home."

"Would it be possible for me to see her sometime?"

"Surely, if you are really interested. Would you like me to bring her to Berchtesgaden?"

"I should be most grateful. If you would let me pay the cost of the trip——"

"Do not trouble about that. We have taken her to visit friends in London and other places, and have never failed to be rewarded by some interesting development. I must give you fair warning—the spirits are no respecters of persons, and Sir Basil is not the only one of our friends who have been embarrassed by what has come out in a séance."

"I am one who has nothing to hide, Herr Budd—unless it be matters of state, of course."

"In those the spirits manifest little interest. But I think you would like to hear of one incident which occurred to me some three and a half years ago. I was having a séance with Madame in my studio at home— the building which was used by Marcel Detaze. I take her there because it is quiet and the influences seem to be soothing. The paintings are Marcel's, and a fine library on the walls was willed to me by my great-uncle who was a Unitarian minister in Connecticut. This was on an afternoon, and the mistral was blowing outside, rather noisy in the pine trees and cypresses of the Cap d'Antibes. Madame gave a violent start, as she does when anything painful comes up. Her control, an Indian chieftain called Tecumseh, doesn't usually let himself be upset, but now his voice trembled as he said: 'A spirit has just come over; a little man in civilian clothes. He has just been shot. I see him lying on a couch covered with yellow silk; blood is pouring from a wound in his neck, and from other wounds. It is a great room with high ceilings; he is an important man. Others are running in excitement, some trying to help him, others crying out. I hear the word Doll—is that a name? He is not a doll, but a small man. He calls for a priest, but none comes. He fingers a rosary, and so I think the man is a Catholic.' Such was the scene, Herr Reichskanzler, and I made my notes of it; the date was July 25, 1934, and as soon as the séance was over I called up the newspaper office in

Cannes and got word that Dollfuss had been killed in Vienna about three hours previously."

"An amazing story, Herr Budd; truly, it deserves to rank with Swedenborg's clairvoyant vision of the great fire which destroyed so much of the city of Stockholm. You know that case, I suppose?"

"I have read it somewhere. I do not tell this particular experience very often, because it rests on my word alone, and people find it too hard to believe."

V

The fact was that Lanny had never told this story before, and didn't expect to tell it again. The reason was, no such séance had taken place; he had made the story up because he wanted Hitler to talk about Austria, and this was the bait. There was no risk involved in the telling, for Madame never knew what went on at her séances, and by Lanny's own account no one else had been present. Now he waited, in the mood of a fisherman who looks over the side of his boat and sees a large black bass approach the bait, and taste it or smell it, whatever a bass does. Finally, he takes it into his mouth. Glory hallelujah!

Said the Führer of all the Nazis: "You doubtless know, Herr Budd, there are people who say I had something to do with the killing of poor Dollfuss. I assure you, he had plenty of enemies of his own, and they needed no hint from me."

"I can readily believe that, Herr Reichskanzler; the situation in Austria is a miserable confusion."

"Basically it is quite simple. The Austrians are German people, and belong to the *neue Ordnung* which I am establishing. Some of them have been misled by false propaganda, originating in Moscow or other poison centers; but as soon as the Austrians understand what I am doing and planning, they will see where their true interest lies, and nothing will be able to keep them out of my Reich."

Lanny had laid a train of powder and set fire to it, and now all he had to do was to sit and watch it burn. He knew from previous experience that whenever the Führer got started, he became spellbound by his own eloquence, by his clear and logical train of thought and the vision of the wonderful things he was going to do with Europe when he had got it. His plans were so rational, so perfect, that no man could reject them when he understood them, and no man could fail to understand them when they had been explained as the Führer was explaining them now. That some men preferred what they called "liberty" to what the Führer called "*Ordnung*" was a sign that they were men of abnormal minds, and such minds could not be tolerated; if they refused to be convinced, there was nothing to be done but to exterminate them. That was a messy business, and the Führer was strongly disinclined to it; what he wanted was for people to submit peaceably, and he wanted this especially in Austria because German blood was sacred in his eyes. He wanted this clever American to confirm his own conviction that the mass of the Austrian people would be pleased to come in with their German brothers, and would repudiate the little group of self-seeking aristocrats, headed by Schuschnigg, the Jesuit-educated Chancellor who was in alliance with the Mediterranean and therefore racially inferior Mussolini.

VI

"Are you familiar with Vienna, Herr Budd?" inquired the Führer, suddenly.

"I have paid a few visits there in the course of my professional work. I have seen a number of fine paintings in those old palaces in the quiet secluded third and fourth Bezirk."

"That reminds me of something I have long had in mind. I should like to have several good Defreggers, and I have been told that there are some to be found in Vienna."

"I have seen several there. Vienna is surely the place to buy paintings now."

"His genre pictures of peasants give me great delight. You know I was born in that country, and look over a good part of it from my windows."

"Be assured I have not forgotten that magnificent view. As to Defregger, I have several of his works listed in my cardfile, but unfortunately I did not bring it with me to Berlin."

"If at any time you should happen upon a representative work, you might let me know. Don't mention my name, of course, for that would raise the price."

"I never name my clients under any circumstances, Herr Reichskanzler."

"Vienna is an interesting place just now," continued Adi, with seeming casualness. "Unless I am misinformed, important events are impending there."

"I doubt if you are misinformed," replied the American, with a quiet smile. "Other people await events, but you make them."

It was not easy to resist such tactful flattery. The Führer realized more and more clearly that he was dealing with a personality, and he

ventured a further advance. "It is true that I have sources of information; perhaps I have too many, and am too familiar with their weaknesses, their desire to impress me with their omniscience. When I put
their reports side by side, it is as if I employed a score of astrologers to
tell me what is going to happen, and their readings increase my uncertainty."

"We have a way of saying it in America, which I might translate:
Alle verschieden und keine zwei ähnlich."

"That is it exactly. If at any time you should find yourself in Vienna,
and be in position to meet some of the key people, I should be interested to know your reaction to them. In making the suggestion, I
assume that men in your position, and that of your father, have an immediate interest in the effort I am making to keep Bolshevism from
spreading into Western Europe."

"You do not have to explain that to either of us, Herr Reichskanzler."
Lanny said it hastily, for he knew that mention of this subject was like
pulling the trigger of an automatic gun—and one so heavily loaded that
it might go on shooting for the rest of the afternoon. "Give me an idea
what information you would like to have, and I'll do my best. I gather
that the situation in Vienna changes rapidly, and persons whose opinions and intentions are important one day may be of no consequence
the next."

"I see you know the city well," remarked the Führer.

Lanny smiled inside himself. He had learned a lot, and was learning
more every moment that he listened to this discourse. There was no
way Hitler could say what he wanted to know about Austrian affairs
without revealing what he didn't know, and what he feared. He
wouldn't say why he wanted his information, but that wasn't necessary,
for Lanny could be sure that his purpose in life was not the collecting
of Austrian painters. The fact that he was so direct and so urgent
meant that the crisis was coming to a head. The fact that he didn't
trust Mussolini, with whom he had made a deal only a few weeks ago,
meant that he was thinking of exploding the Italian windbag and wondered whether the explosion would kick back in his own face. The list
of those Austrians whom the Nazi Führer didn't trust proved to be a
complete roster of those now active in the country's public life, and
the things he wanted to know about them were like a row of big letters
on an illuminated signboard, spelling one single word: "ANSCHLUSS."
To give its full meaning in English would require a dozen words: "Invasion, and incorporation of the Austrian republic into the Nazi Third
Reich."

VII

When Lanny had got everything he wanted, he rose to leave, saying politely that he hoped he hadn't taken too much of a busy man's time. The busy man replied, even more politely: "Not at all, Herr Budd. I have talked for an hour without a break, and hope I haven't worn you out. It is my weakness, due to the intensity of my convictions."

"I have rarely been more interested in my life, Herr Reichskanzler," —and the secret agent wasn't lying in that.

"When may I hope to see you again?"

"I have to go to Switzerland on a picture deal, but that shouldn't take more than a few days. Then I will go on to Vienna, and see if I can find you a good Defregger, and anything else of interest. I'll come and report, and if you are still interested I'll have my mother put the Polish medium on a train and send her to Berchtesgaden or wherever you say."

"*Herrlich, Herr Kunstsachverständiger!*"

The great man turned to his adoring official, who had sat in a chair for two solid hours without once opening his mouth. "*Nun, Heinrich, wie geht's bei Dir zuhause?*" When Heinrich replied that nothing could be better with him, the Führer patted him on the back, exclaiming: "*Mit tausend Männern wie Du könnte ich die Welt erobern.* How do you say it in America—'lick'?"

"I could lick the world," supplied Lanny, and so the two visitors went out laughing.

"*Herrgott, Lanny!*" exclaimed the Oberförster's son. He was walking on air, so thrilled by the interview he had witnessed, and the secrets he would carry in his bosom from that hour on. He wanted his friend to come home with him and celebrate, and offered to open his best bottle of wine; but Lanny said No, he had several matters to attend to before leaving for Geneva, and the Führer's business was urgent, as Heinrich knew.

As a matter of fact Lanny had only one thing to do, which was to sit in his hotel room and go over in his mind all the information he had gathered. The reason he was going to Switzerland was to write it out and mail it in a free country; he would never put anything on paper in Naziland. He had tried to think of some way to send a letter out by his father, but he knew that the papers of travelers were examined, and anyhow he didn't want Robbie to become familiar with the name and address of Gus Gennerich. The thing to do was to step into a night express, and in the morning be in Switzerland or Holland where mail was safe and nobody searched your hotel room in your absence.

Also, Christmas was only two days off, and Lanny was lonely. He didn't know a human soul in Naziland to whom he could voice his feelings, and the Trudi-ghost was poor company at this season. The Germans still celebrated Christmas, but the Nazis did their best to turn it into a pagan festival; anyhow, after Lanny had been among them for a while the food they served him began to turn sour on his stomach. Hansi and Bess were giving a concert in Geneva, and after that in Zurich, and they were among the eight or ten persons who knew Lanny's true convictions, and to whom he could talk out his heart.

VIII

So, up into those high valleys, full of clear blue lakes which feed the Rhine and the Rhône and the Danube and the other mighty rivers of Mid-Europe. *Auf die Berge will ich steigen, wo die dunkeln Tannen ragen!* In the morning Lanny looked out upon a dazzling white landscape which quickly became painful to the eyes. Tier upon tier of towering snow-clad peaks, glittering like Christmas-tree tinsel; they had been here hundreds of thousands of years before he had been here to look at them, and they would remain for hundreds of thousands after he was gone. The thought made him feel lonelier than ever, a stranger in a world that was strange in many different senses. Nature, so beautiful in some of its aspects, was harsh and frightful in others, and Lanny was one of those softhearted men who desire that the human insects which have taken possession of the planet and call it their own should help one another to meet and overcome the menaces of nature, instead of creating others even worse, the new scientific ferocities called *Machtpolitik* and *Blitzkrieg*.

The train followed its course around the shore of the ice-clad Lac Léman, and came to the old city of watchmakers and moneylenders which Lanny Budd had visited so many times over a period of years. His first action was to ensconce himself in a hotel room, set up his little portable, and put upon paper a dangerous and exciting sequence of words. Everything he had learned in Germany, including details as to the strength of the Luftwaffe, and the fact that Adolf Hitler, by his own statements, was going to be in possession of Austria within the next couple of months; by some trick if he could devise it, or otherwise by invasion. He was quite sure that Mussolini was too heavily involved

in Spain to interfere, and that the British and French governments were
in the hands of men who wouldn't like it but would have to lump it.
Presidential Agent 103 agreed with these expectations, and cited evidence of a first-hand character to support them.

The "P.A." made only one copy, and he didn't leave it in the machine or his bureau drawer. He sealed it tightly in a double envelope,
addressed it to Gus Gennerich, marked it by way of a French steamer,
and mailed it at the post office. Then he went for a walk on the wind-
swept avenue which fronts the lake and struggled against a fit of profound depression. He had done a long and difficult job, far indeed
from what he would have preferred to do. He had done it under the
command of the Trudi-ghost, and also of his own conscience; but
could he persuade himself that he had accomplished very much? Granting that F.D.R. received these reports and read them, how long would
he remember what he had read, under the pressure of ten thousand
other duties? And what would he do about it? Lanny had been getting
the New York papers both in Paris and Berlin, and it seemed to him
that Roosevelt was following the program which some French wit had
attributed to Léon Blum: "One speech forward and two steps backward." Under pressure of bitter attacks from the isolationists, the President had taken back a good part of his "quarantine speech," and since
then he had kept quiet. That was all the dictators wanted, of course:
for their opponents to do nothing, and leave it for them to do everything.

IX

The old city of Geneva had been a center of world discussion and
sometimes of world action for the past seventeen years; and now the
League of Nations had just completed and was putting to use its fifteen-
million-dollar peace temple. It was spread wide, with magnificent terraces and flights of marble steps; a long white structure of four stories,
built on three sides of a rectangle and having heavy columns which
suggested the Greek, even though they were square. Lanny, who had
visited Greece, and studied its history as well as its art, knew that the
Greeks had had Amphyctionic councils which had sought to reconcile
the jealousies of a score of tiny states, but without success. Proud
Athens and stern Sparta had fought a deadly war, and then, after an
interval of preparation, a second and deadlier. It seemed to Lanny that
there were many parallels to the Peloponnesian Wars in the present
rivalry of Britain and Germany; he knew they were preparing to smash

each other's cities into rubble and dust, and here in this shining new temple of peace men were laboring with such brains and conscience as they possessed to avert that horror.

Lanny ate his Christmas dinner in the home of Sidney Armstrong, who had been a permanent official of the League since its start. Lanny had first met him on the staff at the Peace Conference; a young liberal, but one who had chosen not to protest when the time for protest came. So he had got a job, and was holding on to it, still not protesting when the time for protest had come—and gone, so it seemed to the son of Budd-Erling. At the same time, Lanny reminded himself that he enjoyed independent means, whereas Sidney had only his salary, and had acquired a wife, three children, and an expanded waistline.

Janet Sloane was the wife's name, and she had been the official's secretary; an efficient and at the same time very lovely young woman, with fluffy brown hair and lively brown eyes not easily to be forgotten by Lanny Budd. He wondered, had Janet ever told her husband about that little passage of love which had taken place between her and Lanny shortly before her marriage. He had taken her to dinner, and found her so interesting that he had driven her all the way around Lac Léman, a matter of some ninety miles. When they were parting she had asked him to kiss her just once. It was while his heart was pledged to Marie de Bruyne, otherwise he would very probably have married her; and what a difference that would have made in his life! No Irma Barnes, with all the contacts with the smart world that she had brought; no Trudi, with all the dangers she had brought! Indeed, it was hard for Lanny to think of anything in his present life that would have been the same; in all probability he would have settled down in Bienvenu, and extended his own waistline, and had three lovely children—though of course they wouldn't have been the same as these three.

The Armstrongs were a comfortably settled couple, and to all appearances happy. Janet considered her husband a well-informed and useful publicist, and she was helping him by entertaining and cultivating the stream of important personalities who came to the various Assemblies and Councils of the League, and often stayed to serve on this committee or that. She was bound to be thinking how different her life might have been if she had married this brilliant and fascinating grandson of Budd Gunmakers; but Lanny was most discreet, and did as little as he could to disturb her imagination. He ate his share of Christmas goose, and of plum pudding which had been sent by Janet's family in America; he played the piano for the children, and afterwards sat for hours listening to the conversation of a practicing exponent of international order and security, a bureaucrat who was fighting not merely for his job but for his faith.

The bureaucrat was, as Lanny found, not too greatly discouraged by a succession of failures. The League still stood, and its new palace, which provided its permanent officials with sumptuous offices, was a symbol and a permanent promise. True, many small states, mostly Central and South American, had withdrawn, but that was because they were poor and had fallen behind with their dues, politely called "quotas." Germany had withdrawn a few months after Hitler took power, and Japan after she had been censured for her raid on Manchuria. Italy had withdrawn just a couple of weeks ago, after using the League as a platform for the denouncing of all who opposed her invasions of Abyssinia and Spain. But Sidney, on the whole, was glad to have them go, for they had behaved as rowdies and bullies and not as reasonable men. The permanent official admitted that Europe's affairs were at a crisis, but it would be weathered, as others had been. A way would be found to teach the dictator states that they could not get along without their neighbors.

Lanny would have liked to ask: "What way is there but war?"—but of course that wouldn't have done. This serious-minded, middle-aged chair-warmer with the round, rosy face and horn-rimmed spectacles blamed most of the world's present woes upon America's failure to join the League and put its immense influence upon the side of law and order. He deplored the bloody conflict in Spain, but insisted that the Communists were in full control in Valencia, and thought that when Franco had won, as he was bound to, he would settle down and become a conservative statesman. He had hoped the same from Hitler and Mussolini, and was waiting to see the decent elements in those countries arouse themselves and take control.

To Lanny he was a mine of information about the various personalities prominent in international affairs. Occasionally he would say: "Don't you think so?" and Lanny would reply, discreetly: "I haven't your sources of knowledge, Sidney," or: "You are the one to tell *me*," —and found that this satisfied the permanent official. After an afternoon and evening, Lanny was in position to return to his hotel and prepare another report for Gus Gennerich—important and interesting, but without a single ray of sunshine in it.

X

Hansi and Bess arrived; they didn't put up at the same hotel with

Lanny, nor appear in public with him, but he would go to their rooms and stay, and listen while they rehearsed their recital. For Lanny it was like coming home; he kept little from this couple, only his dealings with Roosevelt and Trudi. He had told them that he was collecting information for an important purpose, and they took it for granted that this meant Rick—as in part it did. Bess still wondered why he didn't get a wife, and was prepared to co-operate with Beauty to this end; but she didn't bother Lanny about it, and both musicians listened gladly to what he told them about Europe's affairs.

When it came to Communism, Lanny would say: "Well, maybe so; I'm not taking any sides." They knew it was a polite evasion, and had learned to accept it and avoid arguments. They had their formulas, simple and satisfying. Nazi-Fascism represented the last stage of capitalism on its way to collapse; the Nazi-Fascists were gangsters whom the capitalists hired to protect them, just as Henry Ford and other great capitalists of America had done in the effort to keep labor unions out of their plants. If these gangsters now and then took to blackmailing their employers, that, too, was according to precedent. When finally the gangsters were overthrown, capitalism would fall with them, and there would be nobody but the Communists organized and able to take control.

Lanny would smile and say: "Well, I have a sister who will become a commissar, and a brother-in-law who has been made a Distinguished Artist of Soviet Europe; so I'll probably get by." Meantime, he would go on sending data to Eric Vivian Pomeroy-Nielson, who wrote under the pen-name of "Cato," and was quite sure that when the British people had been sufficiently informed, they would turn out the semi-Fascists and appeasers of Fascism and install a democratic regime; also to Franklin D. Roosevelt, President of the U.S.A., who pleaded that he couldn't go any faster than his people would let him, and asked his friends to trust him while he gave the dictators rope enough so that they could hang themselves.

Lanny sat quietly and inconspicuously in a large audience and listened while Hansi and Bess played a Mozart sonata, and then the very fine César Franck, which was one of Hansi's favorites, and which he had chosen to play on a notable occasion of his life. Two sensitive Jewish lads had come to Bienvenu to meet the wonderful Lanny Budd, about whom their father had been telling for years; two dark-eyed shepherd boys out of ancient Judea, transplanted magically to the French Riviera, playing fiddle and clarinet instead of harp and shawm. Hansi had been so nervous that he had hardly been able to hold his instrument; but as soon as he had got going and the lovely first theme came floating to Lanny's ears, Lanny realized that here was a musician who combined tenderness with dignity, and whom no demonstrations of technique would distract from the great purposes of art.

Now here he was, a recognized master; and again the lovely theme came to Lanny's ears, full of memories of which a French organist, its composer, had known nothing. Lanny saw little Freddi Robin, sitting near and watching his older brother, his hands locked tightly together, his whole body turned to stone with fear that one finger might be misplaced by the hundredth part of an inch; dear gentle, sensitive Freddi, who had grown up to be a steel-nerved hero and had been tortured by the Nazis to the edge of his dreadful death.

Strange are the whims of fate, and stranger still the alchemies of the spirit which turn suffering into beautiful art! "For deeper their heart grows and nobler their bearing, whose youth in the fires of anguish hath died." The soul of Freddi Robin had passed into his brother and sister-in-law, and when they played the music he had loved, something magical came forth from strings of gut and wire, and even casual strangers such as this audience in Geneva felt that they had been taken into some temple and were witnessing some valid rite. That is what art is, a process of creation, which makes itself a part of life, and builds new life in its own image, immortal and eternally operating within the soul of man. One accent of the Holy Ghost the heedless world hath never lost!

XI

The concert team moved on to Zurich, and Lanny traveled on the same train, for it was on his way to Vienna, and he needed the sustenance of great music to give him the courage to face another bout with the Nazis. He knew, of course, that when he entered that hell of intrigue and greed, when he put himself on exhibition as a court favorite, a privileged guest not merely of *Die Nazi Nummer Eins* but also of *Die Nummer Zwei*, he was bound to stir into life a million little demons of jealousy and suspicion. Who was this handsome and elegant stranger, and by what right did he intrude into the Holy of Holies, violating all the canons of national exclusiveness and racial domination? What did he want?—for manifestly nobody comes to visit a sovereign who does not want great prizes, either for himself or for others. His father was an airplane manufacturer—but couldn't the

Fatherland make its own planes? And what secrets could a Yankee sell that were half so precious as those he would wangle or steal? Watch him closely, for he is a menace—so a score of court favorites would decide, persons who would have given their eye teeth to be invited to Karinhall or Rominten, to say nothing of spending two hours with the Führer in his splendid study in the New Chancellery.

So Lanny did not visit two Red musicians on the train, but sat quietly reading a safe book on the psychic researches of the sound and racially respectable Baron Schrenck-Notzing. In Zurich he went to a separate hotel, and then phoned for Hansi's room number, and went to it without giving his name at the desk. They had their meals in the Hansibess's rooms, and Lanny went into the adjoining room while the waiters brought the trays. None of these precautions seemed excessive to the musicians, for they knew the Nazi spy system, and that only their international reputation kept them safe from harm. Anybody might be a spy or worse, and when this Red pair were driven to the concert hall, their agent accompanied them and had two able-bodied male friends along with him. Such was life in a city which lay only a dozen miles or so from the Nazi border.

Lanny was sitting in the lobby of his hotel, reading the news from Vienna in the local German-language newspaper. He chanced to look up as there passed him a slender, blond-haired woman; her blue eyes met his brown, and both gave a start of recognition; then she passed on swiftly, and went to the desk and got her key and disappeared into the elevator—called also the lift, *l'ascenseur*, *der Fahrstuhl*—for Zurich is a city where you are never sure what language you are speaking. If you go south, you will have Italian thrown in; if you go east you will hear a Tirolean dialect which will puzzle you unless you know German very well; in remote valleys you will hear varieties of Romansh, a language which has come down from ancient Latin.

Lanny sat thinking about Magda Goebbels. She it was, without question; and what was she doing in Switzerland? The last time he had seen her was at Hitler's retreat, Der Berghof; he had thought then that she was the unhappiest-looking woman he had ever seen, and he thought the same now. He could not say that she was pale, for the ladies do not leave themselves that way; but she was as thin as ever, and haggard and *harcelée*. She was out of Germany—and did it mean for good?

Lanny wasn't much surprised when a bellboy brought him a tightly sealed note, and he read, in English: "Dear Mr. Budd: Could I have the honor of a brief talk with you? Room 517."—and no signature. He said to the boy: "No answer," and sat for a while in further thought. She wasn't likely to be a spy; she had troubles enough of her own, and would be wanting advice, help, money—or possibly just to pour out her heart. To listen to high-placed, unhappy ladies was surely part of a presidential agent's job; and Lanny was free to do it, for this was international Switzerland, and not America, where high-class hotels catering to the family trade maintain a guardian angel on every floor to make sure that no gentleman enters a lady's room unless he is registered as the lady's husband or father or son. Here no one would pay any heed if Lanny entered the elevator and stepped off *au cinquième* or *Nummer Fünf*, and went to a certain door and tapped gently.

XII

"*Wie schön dass Sie kommen, Herr Budd!*" exclaimed Magda, with intense feeling; but there wasn't any gush about it, and she didn't stop for social formalities, to offer a drink or to ring for *Kaffee*. No, she was in grave trouble, and said: "*Bitte, nehmen Sie Platz*," and then: "*Ich muss mich entschuldigen.* You remember when you came to my home in Berlin, and asked me for help, I did what I could—it turned out not to be very much, but that was not my fault, it was out of my power."

"So I understood, Frau Goebbels."

"I have never forgotten how you told me the story of poor Johannes Robin and his terrible trouble. You may not know it, I was brought up by a Jewish family and have a host of Jewish friends; you cannot imagine what I have suffered to see their plight and to be helpless to do anything about it. Now my own turn has come—I am in the most awful distress, Herr Budd."

"I am sorry to hear that, Frau Goebbels."

"I have the keenest recollection of your kindness—that was four and a half years ago, if I remember—but I have not forgotten what I thought: here is a really kind and generous man, trying to get something for somebody else, not for himself. I have not met so many since then, Herr Budd."

"They are not so easy to find in our so-called *grosse Welt*."

"*Ja, leider!* If only I could have known it when I was younger! I have nobody to blame but myself for the wreck of my life. I have been a vain and silly woman. I had a kind husband, and a most elegant estate in Mecklenburg; my every whim was indulged, but I did not have sense enough to know that I was well off. I was taken in by formulas, by high-sounding phrases. I had dreams of glory, I thought I was going to make my mark on history—in short, I was ambitious."

"It is a common failing," said Lanny, consolingly.

"It should be left to men! Women should ask nothing but to be safe from the evils that men inflict! Nothing but a home, and a place to hide from horror and shame! I suppose you know what sort of man I am now married to. All the world has heard it over the radio."

"I didn't happen to listen; but I have heard talk."

"I cannot stand it any more. I am prepared to die rather than stand it. I have brought my dear children out of Germany, never to return. I have nobody to help me but my two maids, and I desperately need advice. Where are we to find safety?"

"That is a difficult problem, Frau Goebbels." Lanny had decided in advance that he would take time to think that problem over!

"*Um Gottes Willen,* you must help me! At least give me the benefit of your knowledge of the outside world. Not for my sake, but that of these pitiful children, who must not be made to pay for their mother's vanity and folly. If only you could know what I have suffered! What has been told over the radio is not the hundredth part of it, Herr Budd." The woman got up suddenly and stepped to the door of her room, opened it swiftly, and peered out. She closed and locked it, then took her costly fur coat, which had been flung upon the bed, and spread it over the table on which the telephone stood. All this was the familiar ritual in Naziland, the preliminary to confidential conversation.

XIII

Magda Goebbels drew her chair close to Lanny's, and lowered her voice. "*Mein Freund,* will you permit me to tell you just a little of the realities of National Socialism? And will you promise never to hint at me as the source?"

"Most surely, *gnädige Frau!* And will you, in return, never mention that you have talked to me?"

"That is only fair. I am throwing myself upon your mercy; what is it you say?—throwing discretion to the winds. I am desperate, and do not care what becomes of me—only for my poor little ones." She caught her breath and then rushed on: "I do not know what is in your heart concerning our *neue Ordnung,* and be sure I shall not ask you for the smallest hint, not even watching the expression on your face. All I will do is to tell you what I have experienced. My first husband was one of those who joined with Thyssen and other magnates in putting up money to aid a certain great man—I won't use names——"

"The Big Shot, we say in America." Lanny could still smile.

"*Richtig!* I listened to him shoot, and the thunder deafened my ears. I thought: This is the greatest man in the world. This is the man who is going to make over Germany and bring order to all Europe. I became completely converted, completely demented—what is it—the devotee of some cinema idol?"

"A fan."

"*Das ist's!* I make no excuses for myself; I was a vain and silly fool, but at the same time there was genuine admiration, a desire to help and serve. The human heart is not simple, you know."

"Indeed I know, Frau Goebbels, and I am prepared to make allowances. Nobody can question that the Big Shot is an orator, and a dynamo of energy."

"I came to Party headquarters to work, in order to be near him. I gave my money to the cause. I aspired to be known as the perfect *Parteigenossin.* I demanded a divorce from my husband, and broke with my old life entirely. I dreamed of the day when the Party would come to power and my hero would be able to accomplish in Germany all those wonderful promises. I gazed upon him with adoring eyes, and he saw it, of course, but he did not respond, and I thought it was because he was a man of saintly life, a consecrated man, thinking only of the German people and the National-Socialist cause; so I adored him all the more. I began to hear rumors that there had been women in his life, and still were, but they were such dreadful stories that I refused to believe them—I even denounced to the police one person who had repeated them. You have heard those stories?"

"I have heard many."

"They are all true, the very worst; but I didn't find it out until later, too late. Jockl fell in love with me—I was beautiful in those days, and he was an ardent wooer. He has a brilliant mind and can be most charming when he wishes. It was all for the cause; I would help him, I would become his first assistant, I would be put in charge of women's fashions in Germany—all sorts of things like that. I thought I could do great things, and wanted to be admired and to have titles and honors. *Die Nummer Eins*—the Big Shot—came to me and asked me to marry Jockl, and become some day the first lady of the Fatherland. This was before the Party took power, and long before Göring's marriage. So I became Frau Josef Goebbels and bore my darling Helga; and almost at once I made the cruel discovery that my husband cheats in love as he does in everything else in the world. He is one of those lewd men who want every young woman they see; he wants a new one every night—he must have the thrill of conquest, the excitement of unveiling, the novelty of solving a new problem, discovering a new set of reactions. I stood it because I had to; I was a woman among the Nazis, and there must not be any scandal in the *Parteileitung*. Am I boring you, Herr Budd?"

"Not in the least. You are not surprising me, either."

"You saw me at the Big Shot's home in the mountains, the evening you came there with your wife. Did that surprise you?"

"Not especially; but I thought you looked very unhappy."

"I was in such a state of terror that I could hardly keep my teeth from chattering. I came very near asking to be allowed to go away with you and your wife. It is the most horrible thing—I can hardly bear to speak about it." She got up and went to the door again, opened it and looked out, then returned, and lowered her voice almost to a whisper: "You know, perhaps, a little concerning sexual pathology?"

"Surely, Frau Goebbels."

"The great man is impotent; he, the most powerful in the world, cannot accomplish what his commonest soldier, his humblest *Diener*, can do. He is frightfully humiliated, he struggles against his frailty; he becomes excited, hysterical; he raves, he foams at the mouth; he blames the woman. He makes her do unspeakable things; and she obeys because he is the master, because his will is the only law in the land, because there is no one who would dare to help her, because, if she defied him, he would have her whipped until the skin had been stripped from her naked back. If she should escape to a foreign country, he would have her relatives seized and tortured—because you see, he demands loyalty, and does not permit scandals in the *Parteileitung*. Such is our *neue Ordnung*."

XIV

So at last Lanny had the truth about matters which had puzzled him greatly. A presidential agent had information which he wouldn't put on paper, even in Switzerland, but would deliver *viva voce* in that room in the White House. Said he: "It is a tragic story, Frau

Goebbels. You must know that it is a very old story, and is in the medical books."

"I am not going back to it. I have made up my mind—I will end my life first. What I want is to go to America, where women are safe. What I am asking from you, Herr Budd, is advice about getting to America."

"It is not especially difficult. You can go into France and take a steamer from a French port."

"But I must have passports, and that troubles me; the delay, and the danger in the meantime. I shall be in terror every moment; I dare not let my children out of my sight. Can you not help me to get passports quickly?"

"I am terribly sorry, *gnädige Frau;* I have no influence with the State Department, and would have no idea what to do except to follow the regular routine. Also, I must point out to you that I am an unmarried man, and if I became active on your behalf, the gossip-mongers would have a story ready to their hands, and one that could surely not help your case."

The second lady of Naziland sat with her hands locked tightly in her lap, staring ahead of her as if turned to marble. Her lips barely moved, as she whispered: "*Gott in Himmel*, what am I to do?"

He answered: "I will make a suggestion. My former wife, Irma Barnes, is now Lady Wickthorpe, and a person of influence. It would be a simple matter for you to travel through France and enter England as a tourist. Then ask Irma to see you and help you."

"Will she remember me?"

"She remembers you well, and has spoken of you often. I would advise you not to say anything to her about the Big Shot, because she is one of his ardent admirers. But she has doubtless heard about your husband's misconduct and will be prepared to sympathize with a wronged wife. She has the same reason for gratitude to you that I have, with the difference that she is a woman and therefore not a cause of scandal. She undoubtedly knows the American ambassador in London, and would actively interest herself on your behalf."

"Thank you, Herr Budd. I was sure that you were a kind man."

"It is difficult to be kind nowadays, and often dangerous. Let me suggest that you do not mention our meeting to Irma, or to anybody else—ever."

"I have promised that, and you may count upon it."

"It is not wise for me to stay longer; so—*Auf Wiedersehen.*"

He went out into the corridor, and observed, standing near the elevator, a gimlet-eyed man of a type which all Europe was learning to recognize—the Nazi in civilian clothes. Lanny didn't go to the elevator, but turned into the stairway and went down fast to his own floor. In his room he packed his belongings, rang for his bill, paid it by the bellboy, and left the hotel by a rear entrance. He stepped into a taxi and was driven to the depot. From a telephone booth he called Hansi at Hansi's hotel and said: "Something has happened which makes it better for me to be elsewhere. Write me to my home. By-by and good luck."

BOOK FIVE

Extravagant and Erring Spirit

18

Après Nous le Déluge

LANNY BUDD stepped from the train into the old, large, and poverty-smitten city of Vienna, which he had once described as a head without a body, the result of an anatomical experiment which had been tried under his youthful eyes by the surgeons of Versailles. First they had dissected the Austro-Hungarian body into two halves; then they had dissected away the greater part of the Austrian extremities, and the flesh from its bones, and tossed out what was left to sink or swim, live or die, survive or perish. Eighteen years had passed, and the almost bodiless Vienna had still managed to keep going.

More than a million and three-quarters of townspeople had only four or five million country people to support them; and it might be doubted whether ever in history so highly organized and cultured a group of humans had been suddenly plunged into such extreme and hopeless poverty. A good part of the middle class was condemned to extinction, by a process rapid or slow; rapid if you had no job, for then you had to sell your possessions one by one in order to get the price of a meal; slow if you had a job, for then you could buy enough food to keep you from starvation, and could keep your respectability so long as your clothing held together and you could get enough pieces to patch it with. When your white collar, symbol of social status, became dirty, you washed it yourself and pressed it against your mirror. When it became frayed, you trimmed it with scissors, and confronted with dismay the prospect that it would fall to shreds; for you could not be seen on the street without it, and if you stayed in your room, you would starve.

This socio-surgical experiment had succeeded in producing a fierce class struggle. The workers of Vienna were Socialist, and exercising their democratic franchises they had put their trade-union leaders into political office and proceeded to tax the rich for the benefit of the poor. Lanny had visited here with Irma six years ago, and had never forgotten the horror with which her fashionable friends had told of being taxed for having servants; a graduated tax, increasing with the number you had, and twice as much for men as for women! Owners of great estates and many palaces had known nothing so cheap as servants, and had taken it for granted from childhood that this was the natural condition of the masses; but now came a tax collector, requiring a list of names, and spying, asking questions of your gardeners and footmen, suspecting you of falsifying your reports! Irma had agreed with her friends that Pink Vienna was hardly to be distinguished from Red Moscow.

The situation was complicated by the fact that Socialist Vienna was surrounded by a Catholic and reactionary countryside. The same aristocrats who owned the white marble palaces on the Ringstrasse and in the third and fourth Bezirk also owned great tracts of timber and wheat lands, and they closed their palaces for economy's sake, and moved out to the countryside, out of reach of a confiscatory municipal government. There with the help of the priests they proceeded to organize their peasantry and marshal its votes into a strong conservative party; when this proved not enough, their hotheaded sons proceeded to form the younger peasantry into the Heimwehr, or home guard, which soon became the same thing as Fascism, only it was native Austrian, and supported by Holy Mother Church, as in Spain. As the saying was, they led the village taverns against the Vienna cafés.

Six years ago Lanny had inspected with enthusiasm great blocks of workers' apartments, built by the city of Vienna out of the proceeds of taxes on higher-rent houses and apartments. Two years later he had read with personal grief of the bombardment of these homes by the Heimwehr troops, financed with money put up by Mussolini, and commanded by reactionary officers under the direction of the Catholic Premier Dollfuss. This devout little statesman had suspended the parliament, in which he commanded a majority of one vote; and thus died one more republic and came one more dictatorship to the unhappy old Continent. From that time the history of Austria was a struggle among three kinds of Fascism, each bent upon exclusive rule: Mussolini's, Hitler's, and the native brand run by landowners and capitalists who wanted to keep the almost bodiless head for their private consumption.

II

On his previous visits to Vienna Lanny Budd had been an ardent young Pink. Now he came as an ivory-tower esthete, son of an American millionaire and perhaps one himself, associating only with persons of his own social rank. Such an evolution is generally accepted as normal. All he had to do was to avoid his former bohemian and workingclass acquaintances, and this was easy, because many of them were dead and others in exile or hiding underground; if by chance one sought him out and tried to borrow money, Lanny would give it, but strictly as charity, and with such a manner of reserve as did not encourage a second call. He sought no publicity, but announced his presence by a note to his old friend and client, Graf Oldenburg, who had been living for the past six years on the price which Lanny had got him for a small Jan van Eyck.

Lanny judged that the funds would have run out by now, and this guess was confirmed by the promptness with which the agreeable and self-indulgent old aristocrat replied. He invited the American to lunch, and the food was plain, but prepared with elegance and served by an elderly valet in faded livery and clean white cotton gloves. The wine also was old, and the conversation was about the glories of old Vienna, when Franz Joseph, longest-lived of emperors, had set the tone of society, and the archdukes had entertained the loveliest actresses in the Hotel Sacher. Swarms of two-horse Fiakers had raced through the Prater, a cause of much complaint; everybody danced to the music of Franz Lehár, and a Hungarian nobleman by the odd name of Nicholas de Szemere de genere Huba won more than a million crowns from Count Potocki in a single night of gambling at the Jockey Club.

This invitation to lunch was a small seed from which sprang up almost overnight a garden of the loveliest flowers. Word spread, literally by lightning—since Benjamin Franklin had found out what it was and another American had taught it to carry messages over copper wires. Leisure-class Vienna learned that there was a wealthy American in town, one who was socially presentable, and indeed had a sort of charm which made him almost Viennese. "You remember, he used to be the husband of that frightfully rich heiress—twenty-three million dollars, the papers said—no, not schillings—dollars, I tell you—and he must have kept some of them. His father makes the Budd-Erling airplane, and the son buys paintings—he says they are for clients in

America, but nobody can be sure about that." So everybody who owned a Defregger, or knew anybody who owned one, wanted to meet Lanny Budd. Invitations poured in, and without loss of a day he found himself in the fastest-moving section of the social whirl.

Since the Socialists had been put down, a degree of prosperity had returned to the almost bodiless head. The owners of wheat and timber lands, and of a mountain of iron ore, made money; and those who controlled the marketing of such products, and the speculators who were clever enough to guess the course of prices, all could reopen their palaces. In Vienna luxurious pleasure-seeking had become a sort of delirium, the most hysterical that Lanny had ever encountered. Everybody seemed to know that the present situation couldn't go on much longer; everybody wanted to spend his or her last schilling on one last fling of enjoyment. *Après nous le déluge!*

It appeared that five years of war, followed by eighteen years of economic dislocation, had undermined the sexual defenses of many of the ladies of Vienna. Nowhere had so many in what was called good society pressed their knees against Lanny's when seated beside him at the dinner table. It had always been his habit to wear a pleasant smile when dealing with the other sex, but here he decided that it wouldn't do, and took to looking stern. But that didn't do so well either; that made him appear masterful and military. He remembered the story he had heard about Brand Whitlock, who had been American ambassador to Belgium immediately after the World War. The ladies in the Palace Hotel of Brussels, owned by the King of Spain, had made a practice of knocking upon the doors of unattached gentlemen, and proved embarrassingly hard to get rid of, until the diplomat had the bright idea of purchasing a pair of lady's shoes and putting them outside his door every night along with his own boots to be polished!

III

The founder and chief of the Austrian Fascist army had been Ernst Camillo Maria Rüdiger, Prinz von Starhemberg, who traced his ancestry back to robber barons of the tenth century; the successful robbers had left him a total of thirty-six castles. He was a nephew of Graf Oldenburg, and Lanny met him at a dinner party. He was a man of Lanny's age, tall, vigorous, handsome in a greenish-gray military uniform with a blackcock's tail in his hat. He had served in a dragoon regiment in the war, and ever since had been active in political war against the people's movements of his part of the world. He was one of those whom Lanny had seen marching in the streets of Munich in Adolf Schicklgruber's abortive beer-hall Putsch. Later he had broken with the Nazis and become Mussolini's man in Austria. He was bold, haughty, and opinionated; a reckless gambler and popular with the ladies—in the latter activity it was easier for him to have his own way than in politics.

With him came his latest flame, the young and very lovely actress, Nora Gregor. She sat next to Lanny at the table, and did not try secretly to hold his hand. It was plain that she was completely fascinated by her rather boyish and primitive-minded aristocrat, who was in process of divorcing his wife in order to marry her; this was something unprecedented in the society of Catholic Austria, and meant that Ernst Camillo Maria Rüdiger was through in politics. This he admitted, saying that he was sick of its stupidities and shams, and Austria could go to hell, or Hitler could have it. This, Lanny knew, was sour grapes; Ernst's hated rival with the unprepossessing name of Schuschnigg had ousted him from command of the Heimwehr, and had disbanded this dangerous private army, in the face of Ernst's public statement that it would be done only over his dead body.

Nora Gregor had lovely soft white shoulders, revealed by a filmy pink tulle dress. She had a sweet gentle face, a caressing voice, an innocent manner—in short, the perfect ingénue, in private life as on the stage and screen. She was expecting to become a princess, but said that she was afraid of the world of great affairs, and would much prefer to live in some quiet place in the country. Perhaps it was so— it was the mood of Hollywood, and Nora had been there.

After the fashion of stage people, she talked frankly about her love; she made it seem very lovely—and Lanny wondered, was she saying what she had rehearsed so many times on the stage and before the camera? Manifestly, a woman cannot very well spend her professional hours learning to imitate the tones and gestures of passion, watching her performance before a mirror and trying it out before audiences, without carrying over into real life some of the consciousness of technique. Or was it the other way around—had she given her heart to this arrogant and domineering playboy-politician, and then enacted before her audience the tones and gestures she had practiced upon him? Lanny asked her, and she laughed and said that the web of life was complicated, and she lacked the skill to unravel its many threads.

This much a presidential agent learned for certain: Ernst Camillo Maria Rüdiger, Prinz von Starhemberg, was out of politics to stay, if his future princess had anything to say about it. That, she declared, was a statement never rehearsed before any camera, but straight out of her heart. She told how Ernst had traveled to Rome to interview Mussolini and try to get Il Duce's support against Schuschnigg's intrigues, only to discover that Ernst's own supporters had sold him out, in return for office and promotion. That was the kind of thing that made politics so odious, and caused a star of stage and screen to desire to flee from the *grand monde* and live in a cottage. At any rate, so she told the son of an American millionaire, at the dinner table of a Viennese nobleman, with several men-servants in livery coming and going on velvet carpets, placing reverently before her the choicest wines and most exquisitely prepared foods. Lanny Budd, a devotee of the theater, might well have wondered whether this, too, was a play, and if so, how soon was the curtain to be rung down.

IV

It was a "P.A.'s" business to meet Schuschnigg, the Jesuit-educated doctor of laws who had taken over the destinies of this unhappy country. Lanny wanted it to come about naturally, and without an appointment; he went to one splendid reception after another, and let the word spread that he had recently talked with Hitler. So it wasn't long before members of the government were seeking him out; and when he was introduced to the Chancellor at a musicale, that worried gentleman took him off into the library. Seine Exzellenz was a tall blond intellectual of about forty, with blue-gray eyes, a small light-brown mustache and tortoise-shell spectacles. When he smiled, he revealed even white teeth, and gave the impression of an amiable college professor, a younger Woodrow Wilson.

He started right away asking questions. What did that most dangerous and inexplicable Führer of the Germans really mean? Lanny answered that he really didn't know, and didn't think Adi knew quite yet; Adi was a man of impulses and intuitions. The Chancellor Doktor appeared to shrink at these words. He was extremely apprehensive, and made no attempt to veil or disguise his feelings. He was a man of no great personal force, Lanny gathered; he ruled "with an iron hand," as the saying was, but that seemed rather easy—the police and the military did the dirty work, and the head of the government could smile, or say his prayers if he preferred. It was a form of government familiar to Old Austria—despotism tempered by *Schlamperei*, that is, slackness, inefficiency.

This amiable-mannered Exzellenz talked as if he would like to put his too-heavy burdens off on his visitor. Austria, he insisted, had been created by a *Diktat* of the Allies, who had won the World War and now refused to accept the responsibilities which their victory entailed. "What will France and Britain do, Herr Budd?"—and Herr Budd had to admit the fear that they were in a mood not to do very much.

"Why, a few years ago France threatened war merely because the Germans talked about a customs union with us!"

"I know," said Lanny; "but a lot of water has flowed under the bridge since then. Hitler has built an army, and General Göring a lot of planes."

"*Ach, du lieber Gott!*" exclaimed the pious Catholic. "And what do you in America expect? You came here and broke us down—it was your armies which landed at Salonika and forced the capitulation of Bulgaria—and that was the beginning of the end."

"You may be sure it will be a long time before we do anything of the sort again," declared Lanny, reassuringly. "We thought we were setting the people of Europe free, and hoped they would govern themselves."

"With us," replied the Chancellor, "freedom is taken to mean Marxism, and presently it becomes Bolshevism, and no more freedom for anyone but the commissars. America will have to send us some wise man who can solve that problem for us."

Lanny was sorry, but could not pretend to be that man. Even so, Seine Exzellenz wanted to talk to him, more at length than was possible at a musicale. Would he come to the Ballplatz on the morrow?—and the visitor said he would be very happy. He went and listened to an earnest appeal for American, British, and French protection of Austria; apparently the Chancellor had been told that Lanny possessed wealthy and influential friends in each of these lands. He wanted it understood that while his country was now under a one-party dictatorship, it was a benevolent one, a Christian one, for the good of the country, and having the backing of all the sound elements of the public.

After saying this, the dictator began asking his American visitor how it was that Hitler and Mussolini had managed to get so large a part of the workers behind them. Lanny knew that Schuschnigg had in mind the forty per cent Marxist vote which had been cast in Austria, and which was now sullenly opposed to his regime. Lanny ventured: "If you don't mind my speaking frankly, may it not be because the Führer and the Duce have taken such pains to put forward a social program?"

"*Aber!* I too have a social program, Herr Budd, the best in the world. I am following the program of Pope Pius XI, in his encyclical *Quadragesimo Anno*, which favors neither the rich nor the poor, but seeks equal justice and fraternity between them."

"Unfortunately," replied the visitor, "this appears to be an irreligious age, and a program to be popular has to be rougher and more noisy."

Seine Exzellenz explained that it had long been the desire of the Austrian people to join with the German people in friendship and on equal terms; but to be dragged in by force, and to be governed by such rowdies and gutter rats as the Nazis were hiring here in Vienna—that they would fight *bis zum Tode*—to the death. They would never submit to it, *niemals, niemals*—the Chancellor spoke the word a dozen times in the course of his declaration, and Lanny wondered, whom was he trying to convince, his visitor or himself? Surely he couldn't expect to convince Hitler at this long range!

V

The Führer's ambassador in Vienna was Franz von Papen, known as "the gentleman jockey," a man who had set out to exemplify by his life the formula of Hamlet, that one can smile, and smile, and be a villain. In the first half of the World War this Prussian aristocrat had been an attaché of the German legation in Washington, and had busied himself hiring saboteurs to blow up munitions plants. Shrewd, but never quite enough so, he had kept the stubs of his checkbooks to prove that he had expended the money honestly. On his way back to Germany the British had captured him and his papers, and had turned the latter over to the American government. So now Fränzchen couldn't visit his many friends in Washington and New York—there being a grand jury indictment standing against him.

Lanny had met him first at a reception in the Berlin home of General Graf Stubendorf; afterwards at the Goebbels' and other places. Slender, pale, blond-gray with a blond-gray mustache, urbane and elegant, with a long "horse-face" deeply lined but always smiling, he would tell you whatever he thought you wanted to hear, and he must have the memory of an encyclopedia to remember what he had told each one in the course of years. Once in his life he had tried the experiment of telling the truth and had nearly paid for it with his life. A year or more after the Führer had taken power, the super-diplomat had decided that the regime was through, and had made a speech calling for freedom of the press; as a result, he had been attacked in his office during the Blood Purge and had several of his teeth knocked out.

Hitler would never trust him, but would use him, with a curb-bit and tightly held rein. A year and a half ago he had signed with Schuschnigg a solemn agreement of the two governments to be friends and to let each other's internal affairs alone. A Catholic Chancellor had to assume that the Germans meant to keep their word. But if so, why had the number of their agents in Austria been doubled, and why were they coming and going day and night at the palatial offices of von Papen in the Metternichgasse? Why was the German Travel Agency, with headquarters in the Hotel Bristol, importing salesmen, technicians, students, professors, and plain tourists in constantly increasing numbers? And what was that "Committee of Seven," with headquarters at No. 4, Teinfaltstrasse, composed of the most ardent Nazis, actively buying supporters and never in need of funds?

VI

"Fränzchen," as Papen was called, approached Lanny at one of the smart receptions, chatted amiably, and invited him to lunch. Lanny was pleased to accept, for he was beginning to think that he, too, was a smart fellow, and could get as much out of a gentleman jockey as a gentleman jockey could get out of him. Had Fränzchen by chance learned of Lanny's visit to Hitler? And did he wish to know about it for his own satisfaction, or had Hitler requested him to check on a too-plausible American? Or did Fränzchen suspect that Hitler had sent the American to check on a too-plausible Prussian? Oh, for a practicing telepathist, who could give a glimpse of the system of wheels whirling around in that narrow aristocratic head!

Lanny talked generalities, which must have been irritating to his host, who was paying for an elaborate luncheon in a private room of the Jockey Club. Lanny said that the prosperity which Adolf Hitler had brought to Germany was the wonder of the world. The ending of unemployment was a social contribution; Lanny told what he had heard important men of affairs say on the subject—including his own father. Let Fränzchen quote that to his Führer if he wished!

After a while the guest paused to let his host ask questions, and thus reveal his mind. It soon became evident that Papen was concerned to know what Lanny was doing in Vienna; evidently he didn't believe it was to get prices on Defreggers and photographs of those whose prices were right. Lanny explained that Vienna was a delightful city to live in; the music was of the best, the conversation sophisticated, the ladies beautiful—and the dollar commanded a great advantage over the schilling. To all this Fränzchen smiled assent, and probed more persistently. Whom had Herr Budd met that pleased him especially?

Lanny's fancy had been taken by Nora Gregor; lovely creature, off-stage as on. He mentioned her husband-to-be only incidentally. The Viennese reported him as *borniert*, that is, limited; the Viennese were subtle, and could be counted upon to find exactly the right word. Prinz Ernst was really a man of simple mind; he hated the city, and was much happier among his own sort of people, wearing yodeler's pants and a green cap with feathers in it. In the parliament, before it had been shut down, people had called him "the Loud Mouth," but in private his manner was one of easy familiarity, even gaiety, when he was not worrying about the upkeep of his many castles.

Whom else had Herr Budd met that appealed to him? *Jawohl*, he had had a delightful *Unterhaltung* with the Countess Vera Fugger von Babenhausen, who had just come down from her castle, bringing her four little Fuggers to spend the winter in town. Lanny wouldn't gossip, of course; he would wait until the well-informed ambassador mentioned the love affair which had developed between this wealthy lady and Seine Exzellenz Doktor von Schuschnigg. What an odd thing that both wings of Austrian Fascism should have been loaded down with a divorce scandal at this critical time! The Chancellor himself was a widower, but unfortunately the Countess's husband was still living, which made necessary a tiresome and complicated ecclesiastical procedure.

Lanny knew that Papen himself was a Catholic, so he ventured no comment upon the ingenious devices whereby Holy Mother Church denies divorce to her humble devotees, but can always find a pretext upon which to grant an annulment of a marriage to the heiress of a great fortune—to say nothing of a statesman who was in position to protect the funds which the Church had gained by the sale of such favors to rich ladies. Lanny asked politely how the matter stood now, and learned that the annulment had been approved by the ecclesiastical courts of the city and of the nation, and that a favorable decision was now hoped for from the Rota Court in Rome.

Lanny had carefully studied the technique of giving information which his hearer already possessed, or which could do no harm. He had practiced it upon General Göring, and had managed to establish himself as well-informed and at the same time discreet. Now he employed the method upon one of the world's most cunning intriguers, and must have annoyed that gentleman not a little. Papen wouldn't believe in any man's good faith, of course; but what would he believe? Would he think it over and realize how many clues he had given the American, by the questions he had asked as well as by those he hadn't? It may be true that language was created to conceal thought; but when there are so many thoughts to be concealed—when, indeed, there is nothing of importance which does not have to be concealed —then the most casual word may be loaded with dynamite, and there may be nothing for a super-diplomat to do but eat his lunch alone and in silence.

VII

Lanny rarely ate alone, because there were so many persons in this old city who had fine homes and wanted to hear news from abroad; or perhaps they had fine homes but no money to keep them up, and wanted an American art expert to find purchasers for their paintings. He listened to many people, some of whom spoke in whispers, and casting glances over their shoulders now and then. He collected masses of information and sorted it out in his mind, trying to decide what to believe. He had learned that where freedom of the press has been abolished, rumors thrive like weeds in a garden. One starts, and spreads from mouth to many ears, and next day comes back in a form such that its own creator would not recognize it. Never had the son of Budd-Erling heard so many wild tales as in Vienna under a benevolent Catholic dictatorship. No way to check them, for always the people who knew the truth were people you couldn't ask.

This circumstance caused Lanny to miss what might have been a remarkable "scoop." One morning while he was shaving he received a call from a certain Herr Grüssner, whom he had met six years ago as a dramatic critic for one of the newspapers. Lanny said for the gentleman to come up to the room, and was shocked by the change in his appearance. He had lost his position and was going downhill like so many thousands of others; what hair he had left was white, his face was lined and haggard, and he had a cough. Lanny assumed that this was to be a "touch," and being sorry for the poor devil, was ready to reach for his purse.

But it wasn't that. Herr Grüssner came quickly to the point, as if fearing that this wealthy and elegant American might begrudge him time for a tactful approach. He had certain journalistic connections, concerning which he was not free to give any hint; suffice it to say, he had come upon a piece of information of the utmost urgency—he began to grow agitated as he told about it, and traces of color appeared in his waxen cheeks. He had heard that Lanny had talked with Seine Exzellenz the Chancellor, and this item of news was of such gravity that Seine Exzellenz ought to know it at once.

"You don't know any Viennese who can tell it to him?" inquired the American, surprised.

"You do not understand the situation in our unhappy country, Herr Budd. Anybody who passes such a story on assumes a certain amount of responsibility, and I am a poor wretch who cannot afford to make powerful enemies. I come to you because you are an outsider, and in a position not to be harmed. *Bitte, um Gottes willen,* hear what I have to tell."

"Certainly," said the outsider; "I will hear, but I cannot promise to do anything about it."

Came the ritual of looking outside the door, and then the lowered voice, laden with fear. The story had to do with that Committee of Seven, the Nazi activists who made their headquarters at Nummer vier, Teinfaltstrasse, and were about ready to bring affairs in Austria to a head. Their plan was the old reliable one of provocation; they were going to organize a riot in front of the German embassy, and then blame it upon a prominent anti-Nazi, a member of the Austrian Legion. Ambassador von Papen would be shot, and this of course would excite indignation in Berlin, and divisions of the Reichswehr which were near the border would march in.

"I know, Herr Budd," persisted the one-time critic, "it sounds like melodrama, the sort I have seen many times upon the stage and have considered as deserving my critical contempt. But I assure you it is the truth—I know it as well as if I myself had been present in the office of Dr. Tavs, the secretary and leader of this Secret Seven."

An alarm bell was ringing in Lanny's mind. This might be anything. It might be Fränzchen, trying to find out Lanny's attitude to himself; again, it might be Schuschnigg doing the same; or it might be true—who on earth could guess? Plots within plots, like a set of Chinese puzzle boxes! No doubt the Nazis would be perfectly willing to sacrifice the life of a "gentleman jockey" whom they could never count upon, in exchange for a plausible pretext for seizing the timber and wheat and iron ore of Austria. But, on the other hand, it was just as likely that some enemy of Dr. Leopold Tavs and his committee was seeking to get them into trouble with the police of Vienna. One thing and one only was clear—it was no affair for an American *Kunstsachverständiger!*

Lanny said, very gently and tactfully, that he was here to find a good Defregger for a client, and if Herr Grüssner knew of any, he would be pleased to pay him a small fee; but as for Austrian political affairs—surely Herr Grüssner could see that it would be hopelessly bad taste for a visitor to mix in them.

Tears came into the eyes of this poor sick man. He pleaded that he was thinking about the safety of his country, and what could he do, even by risking his pitiful life? He could not get access to the Ball-platz, watched day and night by the Infantry of the Guard. If he talked to any subordinate, how would he know that the message would get to Seine Exzellenz? The government was honeycombed with spies and traitors; there were Nazi agents everywhere—"literally everywhere, Herr Budd; they may be searching your room, or spying on your callers. For a man like me to act in this matter would mean to be marked, and if they succeed in their plans and some day march into Vienna, I go to a concentration camp."

"I am very sorry, Herr Grüssner, but I cannot take any part in your country's political struggles." Thus Lanny, severely. He weakened to the extent of giving the ex-critic a few schillings, and saw him torn between pride and desperate need, thanking the rich American and begging his pardon for being an unfortunate wretch, *ein jämmerlicher Kerl.*

Lanny might have told this tale in an unsigned letter and sent it off by airmail to Rick. But he doubted its truth, and spent several days wondering what net of intrigue somebody might be trying to spread about his feet. Then all at once the cafés of Vienna were buzzing with the news—only partly told in the controlled press; the police had raided the headquarters of Dr. Tavs and seized a mass of documents proving a conspiracy of the Nazis to stage a raid upon their own embassy in Vienna. Several different revisions of the program had been found. The one to shoot Ambassador von Papen was signed "Heinrich Himmler," and included the idea of blaming it on the Communists. The one to have the Reichswehr divisions stationed near Munich march in was signed "R.H.," which people agreed meant Rudolf Hess.

VIII

The information which Lanny had collected was not so confidential that he was afraid to mail it, of course unsigned. A letter to Gennerich, saying that Austria would be annexed to Germany in the course of the next month or two; that Schuschnigg threatened to resist, but almost certainly wouldn't; that Mussolini knew what was coming, but would pretend not to, because for him to know was too humiliating; that it was the definite policy of the British government to permit this coup to happen, while publicly protesting against it; that Britain wouldn't let France do anything, even if she wanted to, which she didn't. Lanny sent a carbon copy of this report by air mail to Rick, and then took a train for Berlin.

Back at the Adlon, he might have communicated directly with the Führer, but as an act of courtesy he consulted Heinrich, who had been his means of access hitherto. Heinrich thanked him, but said it would be better for Lanny now to make his own approach; it wasn't a good thing for a subordinate to know too much about a great man's affairs, or to seem to thrust himself in where he wasn't needed. The cautious official didn't know anything about mediums and spirits, and maybe the Führer wouldn't want him to. This much advice Heinrich would give: Better to wait a day or two, for again there was trouble in the *Parteileitung* and important persons were in a bad temper.

Whenever this was the case, the person to call upon was Hilde von Donnerstein. "*Ach, grossartig!*" she exclaimed. "Berlin is the most interesting city in the world! Come and have coffee!" So Lanny went, and along with his *Kuchen* was offered a delicious *bonbonnière* of scandals. General Werner von Blomberg, Minister of Defense, the man responsible for the rearmament program, had married his secretary. For a high-up Junker this was unthinkable, but Die Nummer Eins and likewise Die Nummer Zwei had stood by him and publicly committed themselves by attending the wedding. Now the haughty warrior was enjoying his honeymoon in warm Capri sunshine, and here in ice-cold Berlin it had been discovered that the bride in her early days had been a lady of easy virtue, to say the least. Number One was furious, and was chewing the costly rugs on the Chancellery floor, according to his practice when his subordinates misbehaved.

Lanny asked about the subject of psychic research, and Hilde said she had talked to several persons who ought to know, but had not been able to learn of Die Nummer Eins having any astrologer or medium in his entourage at present; in fact, one man denied that the great person had ever been interested in this subject, it was all just idle gossip. However, Rudolf Hess, known as the Deputy Führer, lived surrounded by fortune-tellers all the time. Hilde had learned that he was now pinning his faith upon the prophecies of an old woman, a certain "Elsa" in Munich, and that at times he consulted a Berlin "professor" of the occult arts by the name of Bruno Pröfenik.

Hilde didn't know where he came from or what sort of name that was, but he was much talked about by smart ladies. "How could I find him?" inquired Lanny, and she replied: "He ought to be in the telephone book,"—which proved to be the case.

IX

More gossip. The Fürstin told about the latest developments in the Goebbels ménage. "Did you know that Magda fled to Switzerland?" she asked, and Lanny said: "I heard it." If he had been playing fair, he would have said: "I met her there,"—and then what a lovely time they would have had! Instead, he allowed Hilde to report that two husky Nazis in civilian clothes had approached Magda in a Zurich hotel and intimated that unless she returned at once something terrible might happen to her children; so she had come back to Berlin, and she and her "Jockl" were living once more in amity, at least publicly. "*Arme Frau!*" exclaimed Hilde.

A sad world, and the Princess Donnerstein was sorry for all women, herself included. She began telling Lanny about her own situation—concerning which he had learned in the past through Irma. He would have preferred not hearing any more, but to say so would have been rude. Hilde had been married very young, and really a girl didn't know what she was getting in for; titles and worldly glamour produced a great impression on the young, but they didn't make for everyday happiness, not if one had a heart. The Fürst was a stern disciplinarian, and expected his wife to obey him as a sort of higher servant. Hilde had spirit and a will of her own; they had quarreled bitterly and now they rarely spoke except in public—just like Magda and her little Doktor. "Of course Günther"—that was her husband—"goes where he pleases and does what he pleases."

Lanny had no trouble in guessing what all this was leading to. Hilde had considered an American's state of solitary bachelorhood and was sorry for him. She thought that Irma had treated him badly, and could not understand how any wife had been willing to break with such a husband. She wanted Lanny to know how she felt about him; she was paying him compliments, and he had to be appreciative. Just now Günther was away, attending to business matters of his estates which occupied most of his thoughts; no doubt he had some young woman there—the Prussian aristocrat never had any hesitation about asking for what he wanted, it being an ancient custom.

An eligible bachelor, who had been young for many years and still kept that appearance and feeling, had confronted a number of emergencies such as this, and carried with him an arsenal of pretexts, from which at a minute's notice he would choose the most plausible. In each case a friendship would be at stake, and Hilde's friendship was of value to Lanny. He could have told her that his mother had picked out a bride for him; but that might not have made much difference to a lady who was more than slightly neurotic, and whose motto in life was *Carpe diem*, or, as the German song phrases it: *"Pflücket die Rose, eh' sie verblüht."* To have talked about any sort of moral code would have been to claim that he was better than she was, which would have been insulting and might have ended this valuable friendship.

So now, with the most tender consideration and touching frankness, Lanny spoke of a mysterious weakness from which he had begun to suffer, and of certain treatments he was taking. He hoped that Hilde wouldn't say anything about this, and for once he could be reasonably sure that she would comply with his request—for how would she be able to explain that she had gained such an item of information? No, she would be sorry for him, and slightly afraid of him, and the friendship would continue on its agreeable platonic terms.

X

The visitor returned to his high-priced hotel, and on its high-priced stationery wrote a note to Professor Bruno Pröfenik, who resided in a fashionable district of the German capital. Lanny explained that he was an American art expert, an old friend of the Führer and also of General Göring. For many years he had been a student of mediumship and its phenomena, and had heard reports of the Professor's gifts along that line. He was here for a short stay and would like to consult the Professor as a client and, if possible, to have enough of his time to discuss the many ideas which they had in common. Leaving no chance for misunderstanding, he stated that he was expecting to pay for what he was requesting. He sent this letter by special messenger, and was not surprised when the same messenger brought a reply saying that the busy man would postpone other engagements and receive Herr Budd that evening.

Manifestly, this mystic-master was making a good thing out of his talents, whatever they were. He had a fine home and at least one servant in livery. The first thing you saw in his entrance hall was a Japanese dancing demon, a crouched figure three or four feet high, carved

of black ebony polished until it shone like glass; it had malevolent
yellow eyes made of topazes, and two rows of white teeth carved
from ivory. At the end of the hall was a large niche like a shrine, containing not one god but scores; the Professor had been collecting all
over the world idols and sacred images of the religions, ancient and
modern, and his display would have done credit to a museum.

The master himself was elderly, and had a long gray mustache and
two beards, one drooping from each cheek; this made him look like a
Chinese scholar, and perhaps he liked the effect, for he wore a black
jacket of Chinese silk with small golden swastikas upon it. His eyes
were small, dark, and shrewd, and his expression one of cultivated
benevolence. With many bows, and greetings in German with an
indeterminate accent, he led Lanny into a spacious study which was
like an astrologer's junkshop, with globes and zodiacal maps and
charts, a cabinet with black curtains, a crystal ball, a ouija board, a
Tibetan prayer-wheel, a Congo panther-man's garb and iron claws, a
nail-studded cunjur-doll from Haiti, and in one corner a miniature
Alaskan totem pole.

On an uncarpeted spot of the polished floor, Lanny observed, marked
in black paint, a large double pentagon with a circle outside it. This,
so it was explained in course of the evening, was for the enticing and
capturing of werewolves—a very ancient practice. Left unexplained
was a lovely dark-skinned girl of perhaps fourteen, a Javanese or possibly Balinese, who went about in the comfortably warm study as
naked as the day she was born. She brought coffee, and a Turkish
bubble-pipe for her master; she evidently understood such orders, but
made no sound during the entire evening, so that Lanny wondered if
she was a mute. There was an open fireplace with a soft-coal fire in
a grate, and a large tiger skin in front of it. When the girl was not
doing errands she squatted on this, as motionless as a Buddha, with the
reddish light shining on her smooth brown skin.

XI

Seating his guest in an armchair and himself in another, the man of
magic expressed his pleasure at receiving a friend of the Führer's, who
was a mutual friend and had had sittings with him. He had never heard
of Herr Budd, he said, but would not ask any questions because he desired to cast the visitor's horoscope before knowing any more about
him. The practice of astrology had been forbidden, but doubtless the
law would be relaxed in favor of a foreigner and a friend of the great.

After casting the horoscope, the Professor would go into a trance—a special kind which he reserved for adepts—and see what the spirits would tell him about Herr Budd's future, and about his friends, of whom he no doubt had many in the world where we all have a place reserved.

All this sounded well rehearsed, and Lanny decided quickly that here was a smooth and plausible charlatan. But that didn't mean that he mightn't have real psychic gifts, and be working both methods according to circumstances. Lanny gave the day and year of his birth, and spent half an hour watching and listening while the astrologer prepared a chart analyzing his character and foretelling his very pleasant future. After that the old man entered the cabinet, drew the curtains, and went into a "special" trance—meaning, of course, one which cost more. There came forth some groans and sighs, followed by an astonishingly large booming voice announcing itself to be King Ottokar I of Bohemia.

The communications this personage gave would indeed have been remarkable if they had been genuine. With only slight delay the spirit of Marcel Detaze announced himself, and gave quite plausible messages for his stepson and his widow and his daughter. Marcel was pleased with the use which Lanny was making of his paintings—though on earth he hadn't cared very much about either fame or money. He expressed himself as pleased with Beauty's new marriage. He himself was happy in the spirit world, painting many pictures, better than he had ever done on earth. He had sent Lanny messages whenever he could, and would continue to do so. Also he sent a message to Robbie Budd, to the effect that the military airplane industry had a far greater future than any other branch of armaments production. Robbie was going to be an extremely rich man, and while money wasn't valued in the spirit world, and especially not by spirit painters, Robbie was helping his own country and Marcel's as well as General Göring's. Peace among those three great peoples was to be put upon a basis that would endure for a thousand years.

Most extraordinary; the only thing wrong being that there wasn't a name or a detail which hadn't been published in the Berlin newspapers within the past few years, and all the Professor would have had to do was to call up a friend in a newspaper office and ask for the contents of their *Archiv* on the name of the American Lanny Budd; or, more cautiously, to send his secretary in a taxicab to jot down the data and bring them back. Lanny hadn't the slightest doubt that something of the sort had been done; but it didn't bother him, for he hadn't come here for psychic research, but for an entirely different purpose.

So when the Professor emerged from the cabinet, the sitter told him that his revelations had been amazing and the séance one of the most satisfactory he had ever attended. That made them friends, and they spent the rest of the evening exchanging mystical lore. The Professor soon discovered that this wealthy amateur had really taken the trouble to know what he was talking about; he had a stack of notebooks at home and his memory was stored with significant incidents. His stories were the more impressive because they moved in such exalted circles: Sir Basil Zaharoff at Monte Carlo and Lady Caillard in London, a private yacht cruising in the Mediterranean, palaces all over Europe, a baronet's son being wounded in war and Chancellor Dollfuss being murdered in Vienna. Yes, Lanny told again that tale which he had made up for the benefit of Adi Schicklgruber. He told true tales which revealed the circumstances of his own life and environment—being willing for a Nazi mystagogue to pick up all the data he wanted.

The Professor did his share of talking. He, too, had had remarkable experiences and achieved extraordinary feats. Strange as it might seem, he, too, had been in contact with the monastery of Dodanduwa in Ceylon, and would be able to establish telepathic contact with it at any time. Yes, there were Germans there, and they were spreading the gospel of the *Herrenvolk*. Also, the Professor had known Sir Basil Zaharoff in real life and sometimes had messages from him in the spirit world; if there was any message Lanny desired to send, its safe delivery could be assured. Yes, the Professor had tried hypnotism in many forms, and had the power to hypnotize any medium and cause that medium's astral body to travel to any part of the world, even to Ceylon, and bring back information desired. He could command earthbound spirits as well as those of the celestial regions; in short, Prospero and Cagliostro and Nostradamus were amateurs compared to this National-Socialist wizard, who had all the techniques of modern science at his command —or at any rate all its vocabularies.

XII

Quite casually in the course of this swapping of ideas Lanny introduced the particular item with which he was concerned; putting no special emphasis upon it, and being careful not to dwell upon it too long. "Tell me, Herr Professor, have you ever had the experience of having spirits appear at your séances who seem to be lost, and who come again and again for no discoverable reason?"

"Yes, indeed," said the wizard—he would never admit there was any experience he hadn't had. "In the end I manage to find out who they are and what they want, and I give it to them if possible."

"I have several cases in my notebooks that you might be interested to work over. Shall I give you an example—or am I boring you?"

"Not at all, Herr Budd. It is a pleasure to meet a man who really understands the significance of such phenomena."

"Well there is a spirit who calls himself Ludi; he was a commercial artist here in Berlin, so he says. He died, a painful death, apparently; I cannot get him to talk about it. And either he does not know his last name or else is embarrassed about it. Whenever I press him with questions he fades away and does not return for months."

"Possibly he is a fragment of a dissociated personality."

"That is what I have thought. I ask him why he comes to me, and he answers that he knew me in Berlin. I cannot recall any Ludi or Ludwig who is dead. Of course, I have been about a great deal in Berlin, and have been introduced to swarms of people, sometimes scores at a single *Empfang*. And, of course, as a stepson of Marcel Detaze I have met great numbers of artists of every sort; we had a one-man show in Berlin about four years ago, and all the artists came, the famous and the humble, and in the course of a couple of weeks I must have met hundreds."

"Undoubtedly you met this man, and his thoughts became attached to you. You would have been important to him, because you and your stepfather together represented the things he wanted but couldn't attain to."

"That might be the way. But I haven't told you all."

"Pray go on."

"A month or two ago there came a woman who says she is Ludi's wife. It sounds unlikely—that there should be a couple named Ludi and Trudi—one would take it for a vaudeville team. But that is what the woman says: Ludi and Trudi Schultz; but then again she gives the name Mueller, and doesn't seem to know why she changes. She is looking for Ludi, and he for her, but they never meet."

"Surely your control ought to be able to arrange that!"

"One would think so; but Tecumseh is a peculiar sort of control. Somehow he understands German, but objects to its being used. Anyhow, he says these two spirits fade out when he talks to them, and he has got tired of them. I must admit I have come to have the same feeling."

"Perhaps they had some tragedy in their lives; some crime, or suicide."

"I think that extremely likely. They seem to be harmless creatures, and I try not to hurt their feelings; but they interrupt my researches and make themselves something of a nuisance, especially now that there are two of them."

"We'll see what we can find out about them, Herr Budd. Perhaps if we bring them together they will go their way."

"Spirit hand in spirit hand," said the visitor, smiling; and then, after a moment: "By the way, Herr Professor, I have been told that you have held sittings with Rudolf Hess."

"Many times. He is one of my oldest friends—from the days when the Nazi fortunes were not so easy to foretell as now."

"I can believe that, indeed. I had the pleasure of meeting Herr Hess at the Berghof the last time I was there. I expect to go again before long, and if I see him I will tell him about this meeting."

"I will send my astral body to make note of what you and he are doing, and will tell you about it the next time we meet."

"That will be most interesting, Herr Professor. You may count upon my following up this fascinating subject. I realize that I am only a neophyte, while you are one of the masters."

"A most promising pupil, Herr Budd, and I shall be happy to reveal to you any secrets in my possession."

The time had come for the visitor to take his departure, and he asked this teacher what was the proper fee for the evening's instructions. The Professor said he would make no charge, for he had learned as much as he had taught. But Lanny knew better than to take that seriously. He drew an envelope from his pocket and laid it quietly on the center table, alongside the crystal ball. It contained a check for two hundred marks, about eighty dollars; a reasonably good fee, enough to keep any teacher interested. The check was drawn on a Berlin bank, which gave the elderly wizard a further item of information, and put him in position to get more if he thought it worth while. Again Lanny didn't mind, for he wanted what he wanted, and was prepared to pay.

19

Vaulting Ambition

I

LANNY BUDD had a perpetual problem to wrestle with in his dealings with Adolf Hitler. He hated so to give this most dangerous of living men any information that would be of use to him; but, on the other hand, some information had to be given, otherwise the connection would soon be broken off. Apart from the matter of Trudi, it was surely worth while for a presidential agent to have access to the Führer's home, and a time might come in the future when it would be of crucial importance.

Manifestly, there could be no such thing as restraining this half-genius, half-madman. If Lanny told him things that were calculated to restrain him, he would become irritated; if Lanny persisted, he would fly into a passion and make a speech two hours long. Afterwards, he would realize that he had wasted his time, and would say: "No more of that *Taugenichts!*" No, if you wanted to keep the friendship of a mad king, you had to do like the other courtiers—tell him what he wanted to hear. Watch for the signs of what he meant to do, and then advise him to do it, and he would know you for a wise man. The consequences might be terrifying, but there could be no other way. F.D.R. had hit the nail on the head when he said that it would be necessary to give these dictators rope and let them hang themselves.

So when Lanny received his summons to the New Chancellery, he told Adi Schicklgruber pretty much what he had already written to Gus Gennerich: that the Chancellor of Austria was a weak man who blustered. There hadn't been anything confidential in Lanny's two talks with him; quite the contrary, what Schuschnigg had said was what he wanted the world to know. Lanny told it to the master of the Nazi world, and the Nazi-master beamed, for it was what he wanted to hear. This agreeable American art expert had gone into the heart of Hitler's problem, had talked with the key people, penetrated their thoughts, judged their characters—and come out with exactly the

391

opinions that Hitler held. "Why can't I get my own people to do things like that?" thought Adi—but he wouldn't say it, lest the agreeable American should get a case of swelled head and start raising his price. Two expensive paintings, a Detaze and a Defregger, were enough!

"I doubt very much if he'll resist if it comes to a showdown," said Lanny; and Adi burst out: "What has he to resist with?"

"Not much, I agree; but he could make it awkward—you don't want to kill people of German blood, and you don't want to make too much of an uproar in the foreign press."

"*Die verdammte Judenpresse!*" exclaimed Adi, and began moving restlessly about the room, with those nervous jerks that he gave when something had upset him. He started scolding at foreign journalists, comparing them to a pack of jackals standing around a lion and his kill. Adi, of course, was the lion, and Schuschnigg, presumably, the kill, though Adi didn't say so. What he objected to was the noise the jackals made—for in the neighborhood there was a rival lion, the British, and also a rooster, or whatever symbol you assigned to the French and their army. Hitler dropped his simile, and exclaimed: "My generals are not to be convinced that Britain and France will stay quiet."

"I have heard, Herr Reichskanzler, that your generals took the same position when you wished to move your armies into the Rhineland, and again when you started rebuilding the Reichswehr."

"*Sehr richtig!* The same men, and they made the same speeches—in the Old Chancellery then, and now in this very room."

"Generals are good advisers when it comes to military matters, but for political affairs it takes a different sort of mind, I should imagine."

"That is what I tell them, and I'm going to give them a shaking up that will make their teeth rattle! For five years we have been getting ready, and what is it all for? Am I expected to sit on my tail and let the German Reich go bankrupt because its army leaders haven't the courage to use the forces I have created for them?"

That was almost word for word what Lanny Budd had said to Roosevelt concerning Hitler's problem and his attitude. The "P.A." ventured to repeat: "If a man builds a bicycle, presumably his intention is to ride, and not to go sailing."

"*Ein ausgezeichnete Vergleich, Herr Budd!* You have a happy faculty of finding the word. I am forced to waste my energies arguing with men who have been brought up to obey rules, and who have never had an original impulse in their lives. I tell them: Empires are not made in that way."

II

Lanny wondered: Was the Führer of the Nazis unaware that he was being indiscreet, or was it a calculated indiscretion? Was he thinking of sending this plausible American back to Vienna, to report the iron determination of the Führer and thus frighten a conscientious Catholic scholar? Lanny had another purpose in mind, and he said: "May I make a suggestion, Herr Reichskanzler?"

"I am always ready to hear them from you."

"Why don't you invite Doktor Schuschnigg to visit you at Berchtesgaden? It is a short trip, and if you and he could talk matters over he might discover that your intentions toward the Austrians are not so alarming as he has been led to fear."

"That is what I instructed Papen to arrange, but he has not succeeded. Schuschnigg is afraid, he reports. Does he imagine I would do harm to a guest?"

"I do not know, Herr Hitler. The subject was not brought up in our conversation."

"Do you suppose you could persuade him to come?"

"I am afraid that if I made such an attempt I should destroy any usefulness I might have to you. My advantage lies in the fact that I am an art lover and a citizen of the world. I met the Doktor socially, and we talked as friends; he asked my advice and I gave it. If now I should turn up in Vienna with a message from you, I should forfeit that status and be definitely set down as your agent. When I went to London or Paris, that reputation would follow me, and I should no longer be in a position to hear what my friends in the British Foreign Office are saying, and what they are planning to do with regard to Vienna."

"I suppose so," admitted the Führer, reluctantly—for he hated to give up anything he wanted. Following Lanny's red herring, he demanded: "What *will* the British do?"

"I should say that fundamentally it depends upon one factor, whether or not you succeed in convincing Whitehall that your ultimate goal is Moscow."

"What more can I do to convince them? Have I not promoted and signed an Anti-Comintern Pact with Italy and Japan?"

"That is not quite the same thing as saying that you intend to use your armies against Russia."

"Do they expect me to say that? Where? And how? In a public speech? Do I have to set the date when the advance begins?"

Lanny smiled. "You men of great affairs have your own ways of making things known to one another, Exzellenz. Sometimes a nod suffices."

"*Zum Teufel!* I have nodded my neck out of joint. I have said to every statesman I met that my abhorrence of Jewish Bolshevism is fundamental, and the duty to destroy it is the first of all duties I recognize."

"Do you authorize me to say that for you, Herr Reichskanzler?"

"Indeed I do, and I will be grateful to you for the service, as for so many others."

III

That seemed a good place to leave the subject, and Lanny said abruptly: "By the way, Herr Reichskanzler, shall I report on the matter of the Defregger?"

"By all means," was the reply, and Lanny opened up a portfolio he had brought. He had gone to some trouble to get photographs of half a dozen paintings of which he approved, and now he spent an enjoyable half hour, delivering his suave lecture and hearing his client's responses. Adi really loved art, and never tired of telling his guests that he would have preferred to be an artist, and that if the world would let him he would now retire to paint landscapes and design buildings for the rest of his days.

He liked all these paintings, and said that he would be glad to own them if he could afford it. Lanny, who wasn't thinking about commissions right now, remarked: "The prices of two or three seem to me excessive, and I would advise you, if you are thinking of going into Vienna, to wait until you are established there, and I might be able to do much better for you." He grinned, and the future world conqueror began to laugh and slap his two knees; he looked at Lanny and went on chuckling, rubbing his thighs.

So clever and so disinterested an agent deserved his reward, and the Führer demanded: "What about that Detaze?"

"I have been thinking it over, Exzellenz, and what I want to do is to pick out half a dozen of our best landscapes and either send them or bring them to you and let you make a choice. I will return to the Riviera and attend to that errand now, if you like; and if you are still in the mood to try experiments with my Polish medium, I might bring her back with me. She is an old woman and is not used to traveling alone, especially in a foreign country."

"I am interested in what you have told me about this woman, Herr Budd; but I have to remember that I am the head of a state, and that what I do is an example which millions follow. I must on no account have any publicity to the effect that I am dabbling with spirits."

"There will certainly be no publicity as far as I am concerned, Exzellenz, and I assume that you can control your own entourage."

"You grant me a power which is unattainable by any public man. Whatever goes on in my home is whispered all over Germany in a very few days."

"Permit me to make a suggestion. I recently had a séance with Pröfenik, who tells me that he knows you."

"I haven't seen him for years, but I used to see a good deal of him in the old days. He was a friend of Hanussen, and they sometimes gave stage performances together."

"He mentioned that Herr Hess sees him frequently."

"Yes, Rudi is never satisfied unless some astrologer has approved what he is doing. He can always manage to find one to approve, if he lets them know what he wants."

"It occurs to me that Herr Hess might be the one to invite Madame Zyszynski. Presumably he would do that if you asked it."

"Rudi is my other self; my Deputy."

"Well then, Madame could come to Berchtesgaden as his guest, and you could give it out that you have no interest in her. If she was in the house and you wished to see her, that could surely be arranged without attracting attention."

"*Jawohl*," said the Führer; "bring her along. You see how it is—I am represented as a self-willed man, doing whatever he pleases, but in reality I am a slave to my German people, and am not master even in my own house."

"You belong to history, Herr Reichskanzler," said the American admirer.

IV

Lanny took the train to Paris, where he had his car and his friends. Zoltan had just come back from New York, full of news about the art shows there; they talked shop quite shamelessly, and had no secrets from each other—except that Lanny was not free to name the important person in Berlin who had just purchased a couple of Defreggers on his advice. Zoltan would assume that it was Göring, and that could do no harm. Inside his shrewd head must have been the guess that this grandson of Budd Gunmakers had not changed his Pink opinions, but was disguising them for some purpose important to himself. The only sign Zoltan ever gave was a slight smile curving the sensitive lips, under a mustache which had once been light brown but was now turning gray.

In the mail awaiting Lanny was a letter from his father, saying that he had made an advantageous deal with Baron Schneider and it would help him over a really desperate time. So Lanny would be doing a filial duty in having lunch with the Baron.

He called at the Paris mansion. When he mentioned that he had had talks with both Hitler and Schuschnigg, the munitions king wanted to hear every word that they had spoken, and there was no reason why he shouldn't hear most. He was especially pleased with what Hitler had said concerning Russia; the pleasure lasted half-way through the meal, but by that time he had begun to wonder, could he believe it, and what did Lanny think on that point? Lanny said: "I would say you may believe it so long as you can make it to Hitler's interest to act upon it." This, of course, was according to the code of a man of great affairs.

In return for Lanny's frankness the Baron brought him up to date on French affairs, which were in a turmoil. The Chautemps cabinet had been forced out, and Blum had been trying to form a "National Ministry." Schneider said he had put his foot down; he wanted unity in France, but not under Socialist auspices, conferring prestige upon that dangerous party. So now there was another Chautemps cabinet, this time with the Socialists excluded; the Baron called that unity—disregarding the fact that the French workers were completely alienated, and ready to do whatever they could to sabotage another government of the *deux cent familles*. The franc had taken another tumble—thirty to the dollar now, and Schneider said it was the doings of the Britisher Montagu Norman. Premier Chautemps was asking for special financial powers and the Socialists were opposing him. Such was *la patrie*, torn in half by a civil war in the very presence of the foreign enemy.

Nothing had been done to punish the Cagoulard conspirators, except that they were still under confinement; the extreme rightist press was hailing them as martyrs, mass meetings were being held in their defense, and Lanny carried off as souvenir a leaflet headed: *"Libérez les de Bruynes!"* He wondered who had paid for the printing—Schneider, or Denis himself, or possibly Graf Herzenberg or Kurt Meissner? Lanny still didn't feel that it was the part of wisdom for him to visit the prisoners, but he drove out to the château to call on Annette.

This lovely young gentlewoman, living in the home which for Lanny had been consecrated by the presence of Marie, didn't know very much about politics, and had only one thought, to free her loved ones. To her the arrest was an outrage committed by the terrible Reds who controlled her beloved France; she went to see each of the martyrs twice a week—they were confined separately—and spent the rest of her time telephoning, writing, and calling upon ministers and persons of influence. She would always be polite to Lanny, but he was sure that in her heart she would never forgive him because he went about his own affairs, instead of dropping everything and trying to help these friends to whom he had stood in such close relationship. All he could say was: "I have assurances that they will never be brought to trial." Also: "I am a foreigner, Annette, and when a foreigner tries to do anything in French politics, it always works backwards."

V

One last duty: at command of the Trudi-ghost, Lanny got a hundred one-thousand-franc notes from his bank. Since they were all new, and the serial numbers consecutive, he spent the better part of two days getting them changed into smaller denominations—mostly by the method of purchasing inexpensive gifts for his family and friends in England and America. He wrote a typewritten and unsigned note to the ex-clarinetist, making an appointment for a dark street, and instructing the man to wear a red carnation and be prepared to give the name of two mutual friends. With the wad of bills wrapped up in a piece of newspaper, as if it were a pound or two of newly bought cheese, Lanny went strolling at the appointed hour, wondering as usual whether this would be the underground or the Gestapo.

The street was dimly lighted and had few persons out on a raw and windy night. There came an elderly gray-bearded German, wearing the proper sign, and Lanny turned and joined him, saying: "*Guten Abend.*" Promptly the man said: "Monck." Lanny said: "*Noch einmal,*" and the man answered: "Weill"—pronouncing it French fashion "Vay," as Trudi had done in Paris. That was enough, and Lanny slipped the package into his hands, turned sharply, and went off into the darkness, looking behind him frequently to make sure he was not being trailed.

VI

Two cords drew his heart to London: Rick, and his little daughter. One morning he climbed into a transport plane at Le Bourget field, and an hour later was set down comfortably at Croydon. What marvels man had achieved—and what use was he going to make of them? Nina and Rick met him in their small car, Nina driving, as always; the three of them squeezed into the space meant for two, and they had an hour in which nobody could intrude on their conversation. An old and tried friendship, this; a quarter of a century, or two-thirds of Lanny's life, since he and Rick had become friends. Lanny could tell them everything, save only the name of Roosevelt, and if they guessed that, no harm would be done.

For the first time he unburdened himself completely about Trudi; and if the tears came into his eyes he didn't have to feel embarrassed. "It's rugged, old chap!" said Rick, and that was enough from an Englishman. They listened to every detail of Lanny's adventure in the Château de Belcour, and at the end Rick's verdict was: "It's no go; you have to count her dead."

Lanny replied: "I suppose so; but I have to make sure. I can't go on wondering about her the rest of my life." He told of his plan to make Hitler tell him, and of the progress he had made to that goal.

"It's all right if you can get away with it," was his friend's judgment —"and especially if you can pick up news as you go along. That was a ripping story you sent me from Vienna; I had it in type two days later." Rick put the newspaper clipping into his friend's hand. He had got twenty pounds for the story, and wanted to go halves. Lanny refused it, for he knew that Rick needed the money, and might have got twenty pounds every day of his life if he had been willing to write for the press lords.

"You give me as much news as I give you," the American insisted. During the time he spent at The Reaches he got a pretty complete picture of the state of opinion in Britain among those classes which counted. The "appeasers" had won all along the line. As regards Spain, the "Non-Intervention" farce was continuing, and while France had been forced to close her border again, Mussolini and Hitler were sending the Franco crowd all the men and supplies they needed. Hitler would be allowed to expand his borders, provided only that he didn't take anything British. Reaction ruled the world, and the masses of the people weren't even allowed to know what was being done to them.

VII

Nina drove Lanny over to Wickthorpe Castle, and he spent several days verifying what the pessimistic Rick had said. The renovating of the castle had been completed, and Irma was safely launched upon that social career for which her life had been a training. Very interesting to watch her, so gracious and self-possessed, and to remember her first halting steps, and the guidance she had received from Emily and Margy and the other *grandes dames,* not to mention Beauty Budd and her son. Now she was intending to become the greatest of all the great ladies. Only one rival to dispute her future, another American, Nancy Astor; and Irma had the advantage, because her home was both comfortable and venerable, whereas Cliveden was merely comfortable.

It was in truth a public service to maintain a great establishment with all the comforts of a hotel, where persons of importance could come for stays long or short and discuss the problems of the Empire. Irma had the final say about who should be invited, but she was broad-minded about it, consulting not merely Ceddy and his intimates, but anyone of the right sort. If a guest should say: "You ought to know So-and-so," Irma would reply with easy informality: "Bring him along next week-end." She had forty bedrooms, each now provided with its bath. So-and-so might be a high official just returned from Sarawak, or an explorer from the Orinoco; he might be the exponent of a new scientific theory or the author of a best-selling novel; he might even be some notorious leftwinger like Rick, but an English gentleman even so. He might say what he pleased, and be ever so much in earnest, pro-vided he kept his temper and gave the others a chance to answer.

Certainly it was a privilege for Lanny Budd to have the freedom of this establishment. Lanny the man might not be entirely happy here, but Lanny the presidential agent was in his element. He listened to Montagu Norman, governor of the Bank of England, one of the most secretive men in the world, discussing with Gerald Albany the financial techniques by which recalcitrant foreign statesmen were compelled to serve the purposes of the Empire. Baron Schneider accused the British of having caused the collapse of the franc, and "the Governor" wasn't saying anything about it except to the right people. He took it for granted that the son of Budd-Erling, just back from a visit with Hitler, was among these.

Also, a chat with Philip Kerr, Marquess of Lothian, whom Lanny had come to know at the Peace Conference as the secretary of Lloyd George. Kerr, pronounced Carr, had paid a visit of state to Berlin a few months ago, and had come back a complete convert to General Göring's program of letting Germany alone in Central Europe in ex-change for a guarantee of security for the British Empire. His lordship was a Christian Scientist, and saw this deal with Germany as the way of reconcilement and readjustment. He was quite sure that when Hitler was satisfied, he would become conservative and gentlemanly like

Lothian himself. The Marquess talked on terms of intimacy with an American who had followed in his footsteps to Berlin and met all the right people. Almost without exception Irma's week-end guests agreed that the ex-painter of picture postcards—they called him a house-painter, sometimes a paperhanger, which they judged humiliating occupations—could not get very far in a career of conquest without tangling with the new Soviet Empire, and that was a spectacle which British Tories were prepared to contemplate with equanimity.

So smooth they were and so elegant; so well informed, and personally agreeable, many of them even charming! They had had an empire for four centuries, and had been trained for their jobs as masters. They were secure and easygoing; they had seen many upstarts upstarting in many parts of the world, but Britannia continued to rule the waves and a lot of the adjacent land. At the same time they were fair; they would listen, and would give way when they had to—no sooner than necessary, and not an inch farther than necessary, but enough to save them and their positions. No French or Russian or Spanish revolutions for them!

Lanny listened to a discussion between Lothian and an M.P. of the old-fashioned Liberal school; that saving minority of Englishmen who believed in morals in international affairs. This Liberal said about the Nazis all the things that Lanny would have liked to say; he said them with vehemence, and made some remarks which Lothian might have taken as personal. But the Marquess took no offense; he was courteous and persuasive, and made those soft answers which turn away wrath. He, too, believed in morals and in fair dealings among states; he wanted everything his opponent wanted, it was merely a question of tactics between them. Listening to this most plausible noble lord, you would have concluded that reactionary statesmen making deals with wholesale murderers were in reality tenderhearted humanitarians and crusaders for righteousness all over the world.

VIII

There was little Frances, several months older, visibly bigger, and still more eager to know about the wonderful world. She had one wing of a palace set apart for herself and her entourage. She was a stepchild, but had apparently not discovered the unhappiness of that status; the fact that her real father appeared only three or four times a year only made him seem the more delightful when he did come. There was a subtle and mysterious bond of blood between them; Ceddy could never take Lanny's place and was too busy to try. His lordship was like the proprietor and manager of a great hotel in which Frances lived, while Lanny was the Prince Charming who traveled all over the world and brought back delightful stories.

The child, too, saved up stories for him, but not much happened to her, she was so well taken care of; she didn't suffer from it, for her routine was normal and satisfying. There were horses and dogs, sheep and deer, rabbits and pheasants on this great estate. There was a French governess, and the child jabbered away to her father, reciting one of La Fontaine's fables. There was a piano teacher for an hour every day, and she played her little pieces for a tolerant judge. Most important of all, there was snow on the ground, and they had a grand time pummeling each other. She couldn't have a pony ride, because the damp snow would ball up under the pony's feet and he might stumble and throw her; but Lanny could pull her about on a sled, and if she fell off, that was a grand adventure to tell her mother about.

Grandmother Fanny, for whom the child was named, had broken her ties with Long Island, and she and her brother had a "lodge" of their own on the estate. The place at Shore Acres was for sale; but who would have the money to buy it? especially now when it appeared that New Deal spending was coming to the unhappy close which everybody had predicted for it, though nobody seemed to have anything to take its place. Just now had come a strange development: a would-be purchaser, the most unforeseeable and incredible of bidders, a large labor union proposing to use the property as a home for its superannuated members! They were actually offering one and a half million dollars, and half a million was cash which they had in their own bank! Word of this horror had got out among the fashionable neighbors, with the result that Irma and her mother had been deluged with cablegrams and letters of protest, and now the neighbors were subscribing to a syndicate to preserve one of the most select of New York's suburban districts. Really, it was a kind of blackmail, and everybody looked at his neighbor, wondering who would be the next to turn up a walking delegate with a yen for high-class real estate.

Frances had heard talk about this, and wanted Lanny to tell her what was so bad about these people. Then she wanted to know: "Papa, will I be an English girl?" He told her: "You will be whatever you want, and you will have plenty of time to decide." He had an idea that the world might change a lot in the next ten years. Stocks might continue to slump and income taxes to rise; the Barnes fortune might cease to be such an impediment to independent thinking. It might even be that

Wickthorpe Castle would come on the market, and some British labor union might have a hundred thousand pounds in its own bank!

IX

A plane returned the traveler to Paris, and his car took him over the well-worn *route nationale* to the Riviera. There Beauty was waiting eagerly to know every detail of the life of her darling. First, Lanny would tell all he could recall, and then she would start complaining because it wasn't enough; she must hear every word that had come from those precious little lips. She would plague Lanny with questions: What did they feed her? How did they dress her? What did she weigh now? Was she really happy? What did she talk about? Men are so uncommunicative; and it was such a shame that Fanny Barnes could have the grandchild all the year round, while Beauty couldn't have her except by disarranging all her affairs and going to camp out in England!

This wasn't exactly accurate, for she and Mr. Dingle could have a cottage on the Wickthorpe estate any time they chose, and a proper quota of servants to wait on them. As for traveling, it had been the major delight of Beauty Budd's life ever since her son could remember. The truth was, it was now the height of the season on the Côte d'Azur, and Emily Chattersworth wouldn't give up entertaining and couldn't keep it up without Beauty and Sophie Timmons to help her. Later, when the hot weather came, Beauty would transport herself and her New Thought husband to England, whither the height of the season would also have moved; there she would divide her time between Wickthorpe Castle and Bluegrass, the home of Margy, Dowager Lady Eversham-Watson, where Sophie also would have installed her husband. These old cronies, all four of them Americans, hung together, unconquered by time and unwilling to give up the delights of spending money and showing themselves to the world—even though they themselves shuddered when they looked at the spectacle in the mirror. Emily was well in her seventies, and Beauty was the only one of the gang who hadn't passed sixty.

Visiting at Bienvenu were Lanny's half sister, Marceline Detaze, and her husband. Marceline had returned because she was going to have a baby; a girl likes to have her mother around at such a time, and Marceline was for the moment less the self-assured and willful playgirl. But her chronic want of money continued, and it was agreeable news to her that Hitler was paying a high price for a Detaze; one-third of this price would be hers, and when would he pay? She started her old refrain: Why couldn't her brother take a little time off and sell a lot of those paintings, as it would be so easy for him to do?

Lanny knew that it was Vittorio who was putting her up to this; it meant that Vittorio was gambling again—if indeed he had ever stopped. He would make glib promises, but what did any promise mean to a Fascist? Evading them was a part of that creed which they called *sacro egoismo*. Il Capitano di San Girolamo was one of those weakminded persons who are always discovering a new "system" for breaking the bank at the casino of whatever city or town they happen to be in. Lanny, who in the course of life on the Riviera had known scores of such persons and seen them all go bankrupt and disappear, strove to convince his brother-in-law that there are laws of mathematical probability which never fail in the long run, and that the odds on a roulette wheel have been calculated on that certainty. But what did it mean to be a Fascist hero, if you had to admit the existence of laws superior to your own desires?

The Capitano had been granted a month's furlough to accompany his wife. He considered that he had earned it, spending a whole year in that God-forsaken hole of Seville where prices had tripled and quadrupled in wartime, and where pleasure was almost unobtainable. Vittorio had begun to open his eyes and discover that it wasn't all a picnic, pulling chestnuts out of the fire for the good-for-nothing Spanish aristocracy and the filthy-rich Juan March; he wondered what Italy was going to get out of it, and especially what a one-armed hero was going to get. He could never fly again, and had to take a desk job which bored him greatly, especially with a small salary and promotion unreasonably delayed. Vittorio was beginning to think of asking for a discharge and settling down on his wife and mother-in-law. If only he could get enough cash to try out the infallible new system which had been explained to him by a lounger in the casino bar!

But none of these personal dissatisfactions ever touched the fundamentals of the Capitano's creed. The ancient Impero Romano was being restored, the Mediterranean was to be "Our Sea," and statues of Il Duce would be set up on the shores all around it. Nice, Savoy, Corsica were the immediate Italian demands, and "Nice" meant this Côte d'Azur as far as Toulon, a necessary naval base. Vittorio's way of strutting, as well as his dogmatic tones, informed the people of Bienvenu, of the Cap, and of Juan and Cannes, that he was to be the future master of this soil. Some day soon the Party would recognize his special qualifications and make him a confidential agent at a high salary. Meantime he sponged on Beauty's rich friends and borrowed money from them, and had his moods of boasting, and other moods of wondering weakly why the French Fascists didn't take him up and admire him, overlooking the fact that the polo-playing and pigeon-shooting *jeunesse dorée* of the Midi had their own program of expansion, which included Italian Sardinia, Italian Tripoli, and even a slice off the Ligurian shore.

Since Lanny had come back from seeing Hitler and was going again, he was well established as a convert and recruit to the Axis, and the Capitano asked questions about the Nazis, their party organization and especially their air force. He revealed that he disliked all Germans intensely, considering them interlopers who had taken over the Duce's ideas and techniques. But there could be no doubt that they had great resources and industrial power, and had a right to expand; only let them do it toward the east, and leave the Balkans and the Mediterranean to the discoverers and creators of Fascism. All this Vittorio expounded at the dinner table of his mother-in-law's home, and Lanny listened courteously. Beauty, no longer sure what her son really believed, was satisfied to see him keeping the peace in the family, and leaving her free to give her thoughts to a soirée at Sept Chênes, where he was to play accompaniments for a singer from the opera company in Cannes.

X

A round of social duties completed, Lanny packed up half a dozen of the best Detaze landscapes and shipped them by express to the Führer at Berchtesgaden. He telephoned to make sure the great man was there, and that a visit would be convenient; then he told Madame to put her belongings into a couple of bags and come for a journey with him. He didn't say where they were going, just to the mountains of Southern Germany; that was enough to set her old heart a-flutter. He wouldn't risk motoring her through the Alps in February. To her it was like a romance, to be with the man whom she adored and who looked so much like the son she had lost. She hoped and prayed that Tecumseh would come on this journey, and not Claribel; so far he always had come, by yacht or train or motorcar. He didn't say how he did it—he was just there, at your service.

These oddly chosen traveling companions got along well, because Lanny liked to read, and Madame liked to play Patience for hours, and then to doze in her seat. They reached Munich safely, and as Lanny had telegraphed the hour of their arrival, there was an elegant limousine awaiting them, with a Nazi chauffeur in uniform and a Death's Head Leutnant riding beside him. "Herr Budd?" inquired the latter, and then: "*Bitte*, may I see your card?" Lanny showed him an engraved visiting card, smaller than it would have been had he been a German. The officer inspected it, and then: "*Bitte, einzusteigen.*" They drove all the way to the town of Berchtesgaden, a matter of a couple of hours on one of those modern superhighways completely cleared of snow. During the trip no word was exchanged; the Führer's guests shared his high status, and were not spoken to unless they spoke first.

From the town the road to the Berghof climbs steadily. Lanny had traveled it two and a half years ago, when he and Irma had taken Trudi out of Germany, and Irma had been so furious about it that she had taken a train to Bremen and a steamer to New York. Such had been the end of Lanny's first marriage—and, as you might say, the beginning of his second, though he had no idea of this at the time. Then it had been night, and the lights of his car had turned here and there with the winding of the road, sweeping over mountainsides covered with tall fir trees. Now it was daytime, and the slopes and trees were covered with deep snow, sparkling in bright sunlight; the air was clear and laden with forest scents.

The private road into the estate was guarded even more carefully than on the previous occasion; there were men of the Death's Head Brigade on patrol every couple of hundred yards or so and they gave their "Heil Hitlers," which the Leutnant returned. At the elaborate main gates they were halted and no chances were taken; not even a Death's Head Leutnant could bring two persons into the Berghof on his own word or guess. Lanny Budd had to present his visiting card again, and to submit to the humiliation of having the fur robe lifted from his knees, lest he might have someone concealed thereunder. The trunk of the car was likewise searched; and all this time the machine guns, one on each side of the steel gates, were kept turned upon the car. The grandson of Budd Gunmakers had had much to do with machine guns in the course of his life, but never before at the wrong end.

When the gates were opened they drove slowly, an SS man walking on each side of them. Lanny had heard that attempts had been made on the Führer's life, and the control had become far more rigid than on his previous visit. He took no chances of making a false move, and at the front door of the residence did not step out, American fashion, but waited for instructions.

There came waddling down the steps of the mansion a rolypoly of a man with a face as round and red as a newly risen harvest moon. Being a Nazi, he said: "*Heil Hitler!*" and then, being a Bavarian, he added: "*Grüss' Gott, Herr Budd!*" It was the one-time Kellner of the

Bratwurst Glöckle in Munich who was now the Führer's majordomo;
he knew Herr Lanny Budd, having played the accordion and sung for
him on his last visit. Were they afraid that some would-be assassin
might have slugged and kidnaped the real Lanny Budd, and with his
visiting card be now presenting himself at the Führer's retreat?

"*Grüss' Gott, Herr Kannenberg*," said Lanny, returning the con-
tinuous smile. "Allow me to present my friend Madame Zyszynski." So
it was all right; the SS men opened the doors of the car, the guests
stepped forth, and their luggage was lifted out for them. Lanny had
time for one look about, enough to see that the construction work
which had been going on in the autumn of 1935 had been completed,
and the simple châlet once called Haus Wachenfels now had a long
two-story wing added on each side, so that guests would never again
have to sleep in tents. He remarked to his escort the excellent taste of
the new work, and the majordomo replied with a tone and expression
as if he were singing a psalm in front of an altar: "*Unser Führer ist der
grösste Architekt der Welt!*"

XI

Lanny hadn't told Madame to what place she was coming; that was
his practice, and she understood that every visit was a test. She couldn't
fail to observe all this pomp and circumstance, and perhaps had seen
photographs of Der Berghof in the picture papers which she patronized; certainly she would know the most publicized of all faces, commonplace except for a fleshy nose and a Charlie Chaplin mustache. But
she wasn't going to see that face for a while; she was coming to visit
a different gentleman, whose name was Hess, but it had been arranged
that his name also was not to be spoken. The moment she entered the
house she was taken in charge by a maid who spoke English, and who
escorted her to a room and provided her with every comfort, including lunch and a chance to lie down and rest after her trip.

The rolypoly ex-Kellner took Lanny up in the elevator to another
room, and after he had had a bath he made his appearance in the reception rooms on the ground floor. The largest of these was the "great
hall," an architect's dream of comfort and elegance. The greater part
of its front was of glass, giving a view of the piled-up mountains of the
Austrian Alps. The ceiling was paneled, with a dozen heavy beams in
one direction and another dozen crossing them, forming squares. They
were of some beautifully carved dark brown wood, and from them
hung chandeliers, each a ring of thirty slim white candles with electric

bulbs in the tops. At the far end was a raised platform, like a terrace, three steps high and perhaps twenty feet deep, extending all the way across the room and along part of one side. Here was a great open fireplace with high-banked lounges in front of it. The walls of the room were wainscoted three or four feet high, and above were paintings, well spaced, and here and there tapestries for which an expert would have undertaken to get several million dollars—but he assumed that they were not for sale.

Awaiting the guest in this sumptuous apartment was a man in a Brownshirt uniform. He was known as the *Führerstellvertreter*, and Lanny had last seen him on a very solemn occasion—standing on the platform before one of the giant Nazi assemblies, calling the roll of the martyrs, those Party comrades who had been killed in the course of more than a decade of struggle for power. He had stood very straight, a tall athletic figure in the simple Brownshirt uniform, and now he wore the same in his Führer's not so simple home. He was a Reichsminister, chief of the Nazi Party, and Number Three man of the *Regierung*, but he did not go in for stage costumes like the Number Two. Following his master, he did not drink or smoke, but set an example to the Party rank and file, and despised and spurned those many who did not follow it.

Walter Richard Rudolf Hess had the face of a fanatic; a mouth which was a straight line, with hardly any lips at all, and another line made by bushy black eyebrows meeting over the top of his nose. His deep-set eyes were a greenish gray, and he was famous for being able to outstare any erring Party chieftain; they were all afraid of the contempt which they saw on his olive-skinned features. There was no trace of the Nordic about him; his hair was black and very thick, and at the top of his head was a long scar where no hair would grow—he had got it in one of those *Saalschlachten* in the early days of the Party, the beer-cellar meetings which had turned into battles with the Reds, and one of the enemy had hurled a beer mug at the head of Adi Schicklgruber's most faithful bodyguard.

He had been first an infantry officer and then an aviator in the World War, and afterwards, hearing the ex-corporal make a speech at one of the Munich meetings, had become his adorer and faithful secretary. For his part in the attempt at revolution he had been sentenced to the Landsberg fortress, along with Hitler; and being a man of better education than his master, he had patiently written down every word of the master's outgivings and shaped them into a book. Adi had proposed to entitle this work: "Four and One-Half Years' Struggle Against

Lies, Stupidity and Cowardice"; but Hess, with better judgment, had suggested "Mein Kampf." From then on the pair had been inseparable, and when Gregor Strasser had almost wrecked the Party by resigning and attacking the Führer, it was Hess who had been put in charge and authorized to speak in the Führer's name.

For four years now he had done so, becoming more dour and grim with each day of contact with the frailties of Nazi nature. He seldom appeared at social affairs, having no use for that sort of flummery; so the only time Lanny had met him was here at the Berghof with Irma. On that evening he had had almost nothing to say and had sat looking very glum, watching the two American visitors as if strongly disapproving the Führer's wasting his time on such people.

XII

Lanny had been told that this man could be friendly and even charming when he felt like it, and the visitor wanted very much to see him in that role. "Herr Reichsminister," he began, speaking English, which he knew the other understood and spoke fluently, "you may be interested to know about the first time I ever heard of you. It was at Christmas of 1924, and Heinrich Jung came back from Landsberg and told Kurt Meissner and me of two very wonderful men he had met in the fortress."

"*Wirklich?*" said the dark man; he could hardly say less.

"Kurt and I have been friends from boyhood and I was visiting him at Stubendorf. Heinrich is the son of the Oberförster there, as you perhaps know, and from that time on he never let up on me. I used to get some of your Party literature at least once a month. I stood out against it for years, but in the end I fell under the spell. So you see, Herr Hess, I am a sort of pupil of yours."

This from a guest only four years younger than himself was the extreme of graciousness. The hardest man has something in his soul about which he is sentimental, and that something with Hess was the period he had spent in prison with Adi and the other heroes of the NSDAP. The tight, almost lipless mouth relaxed into a smile, and the man of many suspicions remarked: "Those were great days."

"Greater, I believe, than any of us can realize as yet," replied the visitor. From that time on he was a member of the brotherhood, and no longer felt the eyes of the Deputy Führer following him about with suspicion.

Seated in one of the capacious leather armchairs of which there were a score in the hall, Lanny told about his eight years of dabbling in psychic research. He knew that his host was a believer in spiritualism; when he read that roll of the martyrs to the assembled Nazi throng, he was certain that the spirit of every one of those men was hovering over the scene and thrilling with the same pride as the reader. So now Lanny took that line; Tecumseh was a genuine spirit of a one-time Amerindian chieftain. Lanny had heard also that Hess was a "Moral Rearmament" man, a follower of Buchman, who had come back to America saying: "Thank God for a man like Hitler!" So Lanny spoke of having attended Buchmanite meetings in England, and having recently talked with Lord Lothian.

Lanny knew furthermore that Hess was a believer in faith healing, and had braved the ridicule of the other Party leaders to call a congress on that subject. Lanny knew the language of these many cults, because his stepfather had been teaching him for more than a decade. He told stories about the extraordinary cures which Parsifal Dingle had achieved. The visitor explained his belief that the "faith" which healed had no necessary connection with the Christian religion or the Jewish Bible; it wasn't faith in Jehovah or any other tribal deity, but faith in the creative principle which rules the universe and is in all our hearts. Lanny wasn't sure whether his host believed in Wotan and the old Teutonic panel of gods, but he was careful to leave them out of his condemnations. Also, being socially well trained, he was careful to give his host an opportunity to narrate his own experiences and to set forth the conclusions he had drawn from them; thus they spent a pleasant couple of hours, and at the end of the time were friends.

XIII

The American brought up the subject of Bruno Pröfenik, and told of his visit there. Hess said: "He is a man in whom I would not put too much trust"; and Lanny, not wishing to commit himself, replied: "I know there is fraud in every part of this field; also, I have reason to believe that there are mediums who at times produce genuine phenomena, and at other times, when the phenomena fail to appear, yield to the temptation to help the spirits out."

Hess agreed with this; he had kept his interest in Pröfenik because he was sure the old wizard had produced genuine trance phenomena, and in fact wouldn't dare to produce any other sort for the Deputy Führer. There was a menace in this for the wizard, and Lanny laughed and said: "Don't be too harsh with any of them! Remember that a man or woman in a genuine trance might cheat without being aware of it, or being able to help it."

The Nazi leader said he had never thought of that, and Lanny explained his idea that the subconscious mind has many levels and a variety of forces in it, some good and some evil. "We all have impulses to lie and cheat, and some of us yield to them on the conscious level." He skipped over this quickly, hoping that it wouldn't be taken as an allusion to a literary work of which his companion was joint author. "Why can it not happen that some sly and tricky subconscious personality should take control of a medium in trance, and seek to build up its own prestige and importance by making the medium do and say whatever it finds profitable?"

"That is providing them with a pretty broad alibi," remarked the Deputy Führer, shrewdly.

"Those who are conscious cheats will use everything they can think of. But I am not at all sure that Rudy Schneider ever became a deliberate cheat, or that Eusapia Palladino ever knew that she sometimes helped out her 'ectoplasm' with her foot."

These were cases in the books, and Hess didn't know the books, so Lanny told the stories. Then he said: "Pröfenik volunteered to send his astral body to the Berghof to find out what you and I are doing. It'll be interesting to see if he can make good on that. I wrote him that I would be here today, so no doubt he is trying his arts on us."

"Well, it oughtn't to be hard to guess that we are sitting in two chairs in this hall and talking about him and other mediums."

"I have thought of that," replied the American. "If you are interested in such experiments, let us do something a bit different, and beyond his guessing powers."

"What do you suggest?"

"I have thought of several things. They tell me you are an athlete, and keep yourself in condition. When I was a boy I was taught what was called 'French wrestling,' and what I have since been told all German schoolchildren practice. If the old wizard can say we were doing that, we can be sure he has some supernormal power."

"Either that, or else he has a spy in this household," remarked the dour Deputy.

They took off their coats and took their stand on a vacant part of that well-polished oaken floor; facing each other, but each somewhat to the other's right, with Lanny placing his right foot against the outside of Hess's right foot. They each took a firm stance, with the left foot back, and Lanny took his opponent's right hand in a firm grip with his right hand. So they were ready, and the trick was to keep your own balance while trying to push or pull your opponent off balance; you won a round when you succeeded in forcing him to lift his right foot off the ground. There are many tricks to take him by surprise, but Lanny never used one more than once, for Hess was quick in his reactions and had muscles of steel. Lanny, for his part, was a tennis player, which kept his grip firm; also he played the piano, which is harder work than most auditors realize.

That is what they were at when the master of this household entered the room. They stopped, but he wanted to know what they had been doing, and they went on while he watched them; he wished he had tried this form of diversion in the trenches, he said, when for months at a time there had been nothing to do but wait. However, he didn't offer to try it now; he looked to be flabby, and Lanny had heard that he took no exercise except walking. It wouldn't do for the Führer of all the Nazis to take any chance of being bested at anything. Lanny wasn't sure that his Deputy would have enjoyed such an experience either, and was glad that Hess was able to hold his own so well. When they quit, they were both of them breathing hard, and their Führer said, indulgently: "You are still nothing but boys, both of you." But they were *his* boys!

20

Mohammed's Mountain

I

IN THE course of a fortunate life Lanny Budd had been a guest in elegant homes in various parts of the world, and the thing which struck him about them was that the resemblances were so much greater than the differences. There had come to be a standard of leisure-class life, much the same in all great centers. Transportation and communication were responsible for this, and the greatest of these forces was the motion-picture screen, which transported everything and communicated it to everybody all over the world. If the rich man in America had some new luxury, the rich man in Tasmania or Iceland saw it and ordered it. The result was a general level of comfort and culture, with nothing very new or startling to any visitor; the furnishings in the Berghof might have been transported to a mansion on Nob Hill in San Francisco, or on the Avenida Rio Branco in Rio de Janeiro, and would have fitted there.

The same thing had happened to manners and morals. Everywhere were quiet and well-trained servants, and a household seeming to operate automatically; everything was spotlessly clean, and if there was mud outside, everybody wiped his feet before he came in. Everybody spoke in a well-modulated voice and tempers were rarely lost. There might be a great deal of drinking, but people had learned to carry their liquor; they drank until they were beginning to be stupefied, and then went up to their rooms and slept it off. Costumes likewise had been standardized; the gray trousers and blue sport coat which the Führer wore at his lunch-table would have served for an informal meal in the town called Newcastle in Connecticut, or England, or Australia; and the same was true for the white tie and tails of a ceremonious affair.

With few exceptions, the statement applied also in the realm of ideas. The average man of wealth and power took the same attitude toward politics the civilized world around. Details and techniques might differ, but what the rich and great wanted was to keep what they had. That was why Robbie Budd could travel to Paris and Berlin and get along so well with Baron Schneider and General Göring; that was why the movement which had started in Italy had spread so swiftly to Germany and Poland and Rumania and Austria and Spain, to Brazil and the Argentine and Japan; why the Führer's agents could report to him a continuing spread of his propaganda in France and Britain, and in the great democracy which called itself the sweet land of liberty. Those who had property and enjoyed privileges wanted to hold onto them, and when they found labor beginning to organize, call strikes, and use the ballot in its own interest, the masters began to look about for a strong private police. "Fascism is capitalism plus murder,"—so the leftwing Rick had declared after his first interview with Mussolini, eighteen years ago.

II

The household in which Lanny was now a guest appeared to be even more decorous than the average. Its master did not drink, and did not permit anyone to smoke in his social rooms; his guests had to retire to their bedrooms or go outside on the terraces to indulge that evil practice. At the table he served them the customary generous meals, but had put before himself a specially prepared vegetable plate with one poached egg on top, and a one per-cent beer brewed for him. He was so gracious to everybody at the long table, including three women secretaries, that Lanny had to keep saying to himself: "This is the murderer of Trudi, and of Ludi, and of Freddi Robin."

Not that he had killed them with his own hands; but he had established the system and given the orders which included them and thousands of other victims. He was planning at this time the murder of a nation of six or seven millions, and the various generals and officials who came here were giving information and getting instructions bearing on this project. Yes, it was like visiting in the home of Beelzebub, known as the Father of Lies. He, too, no doubt, had a modern and perfectly appointed residence, and his manners were above reproach; but at what moment would the floor crack open and flames and the smell of brimstone burst forth?

After dinner Rudolf Hess asked if it would be convenient for him to make a test with Madame, and Lanny went up to arrange it. He told her that the room was to be dark, and that a gentleman would enter and take a seat; this gentleman was friendly, and would be polite to Tecumseh or whoever might come. Lanny had already explained the procedure to the Deputy Führer, who didn't need much instruction, being familiar with séances. The American would have liked to be present, but was afraid to take the chance; he had got into a jam with Zaharoff through being a witness to his humiliation, and wasn't going to make that mistake with anybody here. What they had in their subconscious minds was their secret. Lanny said, lightly: "Remember, don't blame me if the spirits are impolite." The other smiled and promised readily.

So now Hess disappeared, and the other guests and members of the household were invited into the projection room to see a movie. The Führer was fond of them, and oddly enough preferred American pictures, of course with German titles; he did not understand English, except for "O.K., Chief," and other such standard phrases. This time it was a comedy called *It Happened One Night*; Hitler had had it run several times, and never tired of it. From it he could learn how people traveled on autobuses in America, and how they liked to have their own way—which was something he would surely not wish to introduce into the Fatherland. Lanny wondered, how seriously did he take

American comedies? Had he got the idea that the daughters of American millionaires were accustomed to run away from home and marry some poor but honest young fellow whom they picked up on the road? So far, it hadn't happened in Newcastle, or in the neighborhood of Shore Acres.

When the showing was over, Hess was pacing up and down in the great hall; he took the guest by the arm and led him away, saying: "The Führer also wishes to hear my report." They went quietly to Hitler's study, which was on the second floor, at the front. Seated there before the fireplace, the Deputy said: "Herr Budd, this is really remarkable. Are you certain that nobody has told that old woman my name?"

Lanny replied: "I cannot be certain of that. I can only tell you that I haven't told her, nor told anyone else but you and Herr Hitler. If she got your name, it could only have been from someone in this household."

"That could not have happened, I am sure."

"It is a doubt which troubles everyone to whom I take Madame. Poor Zaharoff tormented himself with it all his life. I can only tell you that I take these experiments seriously, and give you my word of honor that I gave her no hint. Members of my family knew that I was shipping paintings to Herr Hitler, but all I told them about Madame was that I had a friend in Germany who wished to try some experiments. They are used to that, as Madame is."

III

The Nazi *Nummer Drei* proceeded to describe the spirits with whom he had spent the past hour. The first had been a certain Franz Deek, or some such name—Tecumseh was never good at foreign names. Dieckhoff, it was, and Hess had forgotten him, but the spirit brought him to mind; he had been one of those SA men who had aided Hess at the time of the *Putsch*, some fifteen years ago. Hess had not marched in that ill-fated parade through the streets of Munich; it had been his job to kidnap two of the ministers of the Bavarian government, called by the uneuphonious names of Schweyer and Wutzelhofer. The pair had been forced into automobiles and carried off into a near-by forest; they had been blindfolded and stood up to be shot, but had been spared, and carried off to another forest, and stood up again—a form of torture which had been meant to frighten them so that they would obey Nazi orders in future.

"We were naïve in those days," remarked the dark Deputy; "we hoped that we wouldn't have to kill many people."

Lanny thought: "The floor is cracking, and here are the flames and the smell of brimstone!"

Hess told the story of that exciting day. At a crossroads he took the precaution to telephone to Munich and learned that the military attempt had failed. So he turned his captives loose and fled to the mountains, where he remained a fugitive for several weeks. But finally he gave himself up—and that was the most fortunate decision of his life, for they sent him to the fortress where he became a fellow-prisoner with Hitler. They were treated well—allowed liberty within the fortress, and all the books and papers they desired. Hess smiled and said: "No faction could be sure their turn might not come next day, so it was better to be polite to your opponents." Adi smiled at everything his faithful follower said. These two addressed each other with the familiar "du,"—Hess being the only man who took that liberty with his Führer.

Now had come this Franz, or his spirit, reminding the Deputy how frightened he had been when he realized that his opponents were still on top in Munich. At his trial Hess had declared that he never had any intention of killing the two ministers; but Franz knew otherwise, and in the séance joked with him about it. The whole thing had been amazingly convincing. The spirit had spoken with a good Bavarian accent, and Hess wanted to know, did Madame know any German? Lanny replied: "Only a few words that she has heard me use. The spirits use her vocal cords." Ordinarily he would have added: "At least, that is the theory,"—but now he was taking the spirits at their own valuation.

A remarkable sitting, indeed. There had come a World War comrade, one who called himself Hans, and had been with Hess in the trenches at Verdun, and been killed a few minutes after Hess had been shot through the lungs. Hess didn't remember him, but then, there had been so many—fed into that year-long inferno like meat into a sausage grinder. This man had produced evidence, for he had quoted a line of a poem which Hess had written in the trenches. "*He, Franzmann,*" it began, which in English is about the same as: "Hey, Frenchie!" It told this Frenchie in simple language the brute facts about *Lebensraum:* the Frenchies had the land, but the Germans needed it in order that they, instead of the Frenchies, might survive.

Lanny had never heard that Hess had written poetry, and said so. Hess answered modestly that it wasn't really poetry, just doggerel— but Lanny knew better than to assent. It is in this way that the great are betrayed by their greatness; try as they will, they cannot but absorb some of the flattery which is a part of the atmosphere they have to breathe. Before Lanny got through with this soldier turned party chieftain, the latter had become convinced that his doggerel was a genuine expression of the German *Geist*. Lanny would have said more, only he knew that Hitler would be bored—he, too, having written doggerel, but never having summoned the courage to let it be published.

IV

The Führer agreed that this was a significant psychic demonstration, and he wanted to go at once to Madame's room and make a test himself. But Lanny explained that this elderly woman was exhausted after a séance, and would hardly be able to produce results now; let her have a night's sleep, and any time tomorrow would be all right. Adi preferred the evening; he wanted to sneak into her room and not have any of the servants know it. The presumptuous American grinned and remarked: "For the sake of your reputation, it's a good thing she is so old!"

Hitler always slept badly, therefore he went to bed late, and liked to have company in the evening. These three sat for a long while discussing the nature of the universe and the possible destiny of the human insects which swarmed upon one of its insignificant planets. Hitler did most of the talking—for what else does it mean to be great? The other two listened respectfully, and gave their opinions when asked. Rudi, doglike in his devotion, invariably agreed with every word his divinely ordained Führer spoke. Lanny might venture to disagree, but always in the form of a question, calculated to start *Die Nummer Eins* on another discourse.

Adolf Hitler believed in God; not in the God of any of the established religions, and certainly not in the Hebrew God, or his Son the Christian God; but in the creative force, or spirit—yes, even personality, if you cared to say that—which worked behind the appearances of this mysterious universe. This spirit dwelt in us all, and could be used by us; to say that it answered prayers was merely another way of indicating this use. For a while Lanny might have thought that he was back in Bienvenu, listening to one of the New Thought discourses of Parsifal Dingle. Speak to him, thou, for he hears, and spirit with spirit can meet!

But quickly it became apparent that there was a difference between the transcendentalism of Tennyson and the National-Socialist *Mystik*.

Adi was a practical man, and had a world to conquer and to rule, and his God was approved and worshiped because He was willing to help with this job. No German tribal deity, the Führer hastened to explain, but a pragmatic One, to be judged by His works. That God had a purpose for the Aryan race to fulfill was proved by the fact that He had made them superior to all other races. The Führer said Aryan, for he included the Anglo-Saxons in his classification, and desired nothing so much as a union with the British and American peoples to carry out the great purposes which he envisioned. He didn't say so, but Lanny observed in all his conversation the secret envy which he held for the English with their long-tested traditions of rulership. Men like Lord Halifax and the Marquess of Lothian inspired him with a sort of embittered awe. The last of the Kaisers had had that same feeling, and had aspired to nothing so much as to be an English gentleman; he had got into a war with them, half by accident and half because they had patronized him.

God was a force, said the religious Adi, speaking here in the intimacy of friendship; God was the greatest of personal forces and likewise of social forces. Adi knew the former, because when he retired to his chamber he called upon this force to give him courage and vision, and it responded. Adi knew the latter, because he called upon this force in the hearts of the German people, and got his response in the form of national enthusiasm, will, and power. It was the duty of the seer, the mystic, to make that force real in his private life, and it was the duty of the statesman and the general to bring it into action in the masses. When you had those two personalities in one, then you had a really great leader, the man of destiny, the Führer of the *Volk* and the maker of history—"such as God has chosen me to be," said Adi Schicklgruber, not vaingloriously, but humbly. He never quoted the Hebrew Bible, and perhaps had never read it; but Lanny knew it, and remembered the experience narrated by the prophet Isaiah:

"Also I heard the voice of the Lord, saying, Whom shall I send, and who will go for us? Then said I, Here am I; send me."

V

This God-chosen man went on to discuss the other God-chosen men of history. There had been some who had failed, because they had had only spiritual force, and no way to make it effective; such had been Jesus, whose failure had been most abject—not merely had he been crucified, but his teachings had been perverted and the churches which operated in his name had no interest whatever in what he had believed and taught. The same was true of Buddha, whose doctrines had been even more perverted—his priests had had more time in which to forget him. On the other hand, there were great leaders like Alexander and Napoleon, who had built empires only to have them crumble, because they had relied upon the sword alone, and not upon the spirit, upon God. They had had nothing to teach mankind but materialism, the dog-eat-dog civilization of the moneychangers, the international Jews.

Lanny shivered when he heard these words, fearing that his host would get off on that special private madness of his. But no, Adi was in a constructive mood; he was not fighting his enemies, but building new states, empires, worlds. Said he: "The greatest man who has lived before me is Mohammed." Lanny was startled by this, for in thinking over the Führers of the past he had decided that Mohammed was the one whom this one-time sub-corporal and painter of picture postcards most closely resembled; and of course when Adi called the Arabian prophet the greatest man who had lived so far, it was the same thing as saying that he bore the greatest resemblance to Adolf Hitler. The Nazi Führer explained his prototype: a self-made man who had found God, and had not been content merely to preach Him, but had laid down His law and seen that it was obeyed; in other words, a holy book in one hand and a sword in the other. The result was that the religion Mohammed founded had endured and still endured; his book was still read and his law was obeyed, precisely as he had set it forth. "Do you agree with me, Herr Budd?"

"Indeed I do," replied the guest. "It may interest you to know that I have had this same thought about you, ever since I first read your great book."

"Thirteen centuries have passed since Mohammed died, and the world has changed greatly. It needs a new set of laws, a new revelation. And believe me, I am not relying merely upon the sword, I am not merely forcing people to obey me. I am training their minds and inspiring their souls; I am founding a new religion, one that will last for a thousand years, perhaps ten thousand—until such a time as God may see fit to send a new prophet to supersede me. I am not giving this revelation all at once, but little by little, as God gives it to me, in His good time. I tell you about it, Herr Budd, because you are a man who sees and understands these inner forces and will respect my vision."

"I understand exactly what you mean, Excellency," said the American, reverently.

"The masses of the people cannot live without guidance; they cannot solve the problems of life for themselves, but have to be told what to do. Also they must have a reason for obedience; they must have a faith; they cannot live without God. Rudi has been telling about this fellow-countryman of yours, Buchman—by his name and his ideas I take it that he is of German descent, and it is evident that he understands the religion I am founding, and is preparing America and Britain to accept our National-Socialist crusade. Do you know his Moral Rearmament movement?"

"I have attended some of its house-parties, and I had a talk with Lothian about it a week or two ago. I have had the good fortune to know Lothian—since my youth." Lanny had been about to say: "Since the Peace Conference in Paris," but he realized that this was another of Adi's phobias, and the mention might set him off on a tirade that would last the rest of the night!

VI

Lanny had a hard time getting to sleep that night; he lay contemplating a world pushed back to the seventh century. Adolf Hitler's world would have all modern improvements, such as telegraphs and telephones, radio and cinema and airplanes, but they would all be used for the more rapid subjection of mankind to the will of the new Prophet-Führer. Whereas the Mohammedan crusade on horseback had been stopped in Hungary in the east and in Spain in the west, the Nazi crusade by bombing planes and submarines might not be stopped by either the Atlantic or the Pacific ocean. Lanny composed in his mind a report to Gus Gennerich, to the effect that Adi Schicklgruber was the most dangerous man who had appeared in the modern world.

There was a list of rules posted on the door of Lanny's room, just as in a hotel. One of the rules was that guests were to appear for meals within two minutes of the ringing of the bell. Lanny hoped this didn't mean that he had to appear for the seven o'clock breakfast; he took the liberty of waiting for the second, which the Germans call the "fork breakfast," at nine, and for this he was not corrected. There the Führer took a glass of milk and a couple of rolls spread liberally with marmalade; also an apple. Then he retired to his study, and Lanny was told by others that he spent the morning going through state papers and giving orders to his adjutants. He had private telephone lines to Munich and Berlin, and mail came by plane night and morning.

There was a large staff at his mountain retreat, part of it permanent, and part coming by motorcar or plane whenever the Führer's weariness of office duties and state functions caused him to take flight from the cities. Lanny observed that without exception all these people were young, and he understood this as part of the psychology of a world rebuilder. The old and the middle-aged had been miseducated, they were cranky and set in the desire to have their own way. For almost two decades Adi had been training the young not to want their way, but to want *his* way, and these were the persons he liked to have about him. His military adjutants were a colonel, a commander, and two captains; the former pair under forty and the latter pair under thirty-five. There were three ordnance officers and two personal attendants, one a lieutenant and the other a sergeant; Lanny felt certain that all of these were under thirty and most of them under twenty-five. All were good-looking Aryans, and the same thing applied to the women secretaries and the maids, of whom the visitor must have seen eight or ten.

The Führer's personal physician, also young, took an interest in the guest from overseas. Possibly he had been told to do so; anyhow, he took Lanny in tow and showed him the art treasures of which the châlet was full, told him what he knew about them, and listened with interest to his comments. Later the young architect, who had carried out the new constructions under the Führer's orders, invited the guest to inspect the work which had been done on the estate in the period since his previous visit. Beside the two wings there was the widening of the main terrace and the building of a summer house above it, a garage built into the side of the mountain, barracks for the SS guards, a residence for the staff, and a sumptuous new guest house for important official persons. Everything was of harmonious design, having the background of fir-clad mountains and a view over the tumbled and snow-covered Austrian Alps, including a valley with the lovely little city of Salzburg.

All very splendid, a combination of nature and art; the fairy-story dream of a stepchild who had been neglected and thwarted, of a youth who had wanted to be an artist, but had never been able to get any training, except in the art of killing his fellowmen. He had known abject poverty, unemployment, and the life of a wastrel in a shelter for bums. In the trenches he had been forced to live in rain and mud, in freezing cold and summer's dust and heat, to be bitten by lice, to be blasted and shot at, to suffer wounds and be filled with terrors; all this for year after year—and at the end defeat and humiliation.

Such had been the training of Adi Schicklgruber, and it was hardly to be wondered at that he was a neurotic, and had to take drugs to put himself to sleep, and had moods of exaltation followed by others of suicidal depression; that he fled from his fellowmen in boredom and exasperation, and then fled back because he could not face the thoughts which haunted him alone. Ten thousand murders on his conscience; murders of his best friends, of men who had been his comrades on the battlefield and in the camps, of women who had given him love, or tried to. He believed in spirits, but hesitated to call them because the wrong ones might appear; he believed in God, but had to make Him into a God of war, because Adi himself had never been able to get what he wanted save by threats of war. He could not eat food without elaborate precautions against its being poisoned; he could not go for a drive in the streets of the cities he loved without the thought that at any moment a bomb might be dropped upon his head; he could not take a walk in his beloved forests without looking behind to make sure his sharpshooters were near, and that they were really his own sharpshooters and not his enemies!

VII

In the latter part of the afternoon the Führer had completed his day's labors and went for his daily dose of fresh air and exercise. A "constitutional," Lanny had heard it called by his great-uncle Eli Budd in Connecticut, and now he used this word and explained it, to his host's amusement. There came bounding three beautiful shepherd dogs, also getting their constitutionals; they paid no attention to Lanny, for they were one-man dogs—something the Führer required of all creatures near him. They raced here and there in a pack, and Lanny guessed that it would have gone ill with any stranger venturing into this preserve. A keeper followed to give the dogs orders, and a little farther behind came two of the Death's Head men. The customary automatics in their belts were not enough; each carried a rifle with a telescopic sight, and apparently the Führer had given information as to the route of his walk, for Lanny observed other armed men on the way.

"I am going to show you something that I don't show to many," remarked the master. They started up a mountain path which made him puff not a little, and after a while they came to what was evidently a newly made road, a two-lane highway carved out of the steep mountainside. The snow had been scraped from it, and Lanny could see that it was paved, and also that there had been traffic on it recently. They walked upon it, climbing steadily, admiring view after view. "This is the work of my wonderful Todt, who has constructed all my

Autobahnen. This time he was kind enough to build one for my private use."

Lanny recalled what he had heard from Hilde Donnerstein and others, that the Führer was building himself a secret retreat on a mountaintop called the Kehlstein, and that before this work could even be begun, it had been necessary to construct a road ascending more than half a mile higher than the Berghof itself. This labor had taken some two years; and now Lanny walked around one hairpin turn after another, and looked over the side of precipices a thousand feet deep. The road was beautifully balanced, tilted this way and that so that a fast-moving car would always be safe. Lanny remarked: "General Göring showed me his toy railroad, but you have the real thing." That did not fail to please the host.

He gave out, and stopped at one of the turns, saying: "It is too far to climb this afternoon; but some day next autumn, when it is done, I will take you to it. *Schauen Sie mal!*" He pointed to a spot high up on the mountainside, to what appeared to be a gray cliff. "*Sehen Sie etwas?*"

Lanny could see nothing, and his host explained that he wasn't supposed to; the entrance to the Kehlsteinhaus was expertly camouflaged and invisible from below. The road wound up there and entered into a tunnel cut into the mountain. When it was done, there would be bronze doors that opened automatically at the approach of a car and closed behind it. Inside was a shaft going straight up through the mountain, a distance of some two hundred meters. There was an elevator in the shaft, now used by the workers; when the task was completed, it would be replaced by a guest elevator accommodating eighteen persons. Everything would be run by electricity, of course. At the top would be a real retreat, where nobody could ever interfere with the meditations of a dreamer of new worlds. The house would be small, with just room for the Führer and a couple of attendants. The living room would be glass on three sides, and would overlook these Alps for a hundred miles. "Believe me," said Adi, "the scenery is not to be forgotten."

"It appears that you Germans have the love of mountains in your blood," remarked the visitor.

"That is true. My great teacher, Professor Haushofer, has shown me on a map that our people, emigrating to the east and southeast, have always avoided the lowlands and settled in the higher and more wooded country. And you know what a part mountains and forests have played in our legends and our art. When the gods ascend to Valhalla on a rainbow, it starts from a mountaintop."

"I will play you the music when we get back to the house," said the smiling Lanny. "Will you permit me to suggest a name for your retreat when it is finished? Perhaps others wouldn't understand, but you and I and Herr Hess can keep it as our secret. Call it 'Mohammed's Mountain.' "

The Führer of the Nazis looked at his guest for a moment, startled; then he began to laugh, and was so pleased over the *Witz* that he chuckled all the way around a half-turn in General Todt's masterpiece of road construction.

VIII

After dinner the Führer indicated his desire for some music. Brassin's piano transcription of *Siegfried* was produced, and Lanny played first the *Waldweben* and then the *Feuerzauber*. This music of forest and mountain was directed at Adi, a reminder of their recent conversation; it might have been in these Alpine forests that the little bird had sung to the young hero, and it might have been on the Kehlstein's top that the magic fire had protected the sleeping maiden. Beautiful beyond expression was the soul of the German hero, and tragic was his doom, to have a spear driven through his back by a treacherous foe. Truly the time had come for a new dispensation, a legend in which that doom should be averted; someone should warn the hero, and let him be the first to throw the spear!

The music over, the Führer disappeared, and Hess signed to Lanny, who went to Madame's room and told her to be prepared for another visitor. Afterwards Lanny went to Hess's apartment, close to the master's, and they sat and talked while awaiting developments. Lanny was interested to probe the mind of this silent man and learn about his life. He had been born in Alexandria, Egypt, and Tecumseh had talked about seeing a blue sea with many ships, and a dark people; this had sounded mysterious—but Lanny soon decided that, so far as Hess was concerned, the mystery was all on the outside, and that the intelligence behind it was commonplace.

Rudolf Hess was the perfect subordinate; he had only one thought in the world, which was to please Hitler and help him. Hitler had told him to run the Party and make it a fit instrument to run Germany; all right, the Deputy had taken up that burden—which meant filling his mind with the details of thousands of personalities and as many jobs, making sure that the round pegs got into the round holes and the square into the square. He would follow the pattern of Adi himself, and become furious and terrible, and so get his orders obeyed. He wasn't naturally a cruel person, Lanny judged; he did what his job required. The same thing was doubtless true of Hitler, who had a sentimental streak and was devoted to children, also kept a great many pet birds and was sad when one of them died. Perhaps it could have been said of Mohammed: he would never have killed people if only they had been willing to submit promptly to the will of Allah as revealed to Allah's prophet.

Concerning psychic and occult matters the Deputy Führer was not very well instructed, and Lanny thought it would be easy to take him in, if ever he wanted to—and he might. Hess had accepted the idea of spirits naïvely, and apparently didn't know that there were other theories by which the phenomena might be accounted for. He asked questions about these, and Lanny told what he had read, without committing himself either way. "I don't know" is easy to say, but is unsatisfactory to many minds; and Hess had by now made up his mind that he had talked to the spirits of Franz Dieckhoff and the soldier Hans. Why should a man's own subconscious mind want to play tricks upon himself? It was a silly idea. Lanny could have pointed out many things that seemed equally silly to him, but were in the book which the Führer and his Deputy had composed. They had told the German *Volk* how they were going to deceive the German *Volk*, and had told Germany's enemies how they were going to thwart and defeat those enemies.

"Tell me a little about Pröfenik," suggested the guest, "and why you don't trust him."

"I don't think he has ever played any tricks on me," replied the Deputy Führer. "But he produced physical phenomena for persons I know, and they thought the whole thing was faked."

"I found him interesting," declared the American. "He talked about matters which had puzzled me, and I think he threw light on them. How would it do if you and I were to pay a call on him, sometime when we are in Berlin?"

"By all means let us do it. I'd be interested to see what you make of that old fellow."

IX

Somewhere inside Lanny was a shivering all this time—because Adi was with Madame, and what might be happening? It might be the worst—and so indeed it proved. There came a tap upon the door—one of those good-looking young secretaries, betraying agitation. "The Führer wants you at once; in his study." Hess leaped up without a word and left the room with long strides.

Lanny hurried to Madame, and found her slumped in her chair, writhing as if in pain, and moaning. He knew what that meant; something had gone wrong with the séance, and he had a long job of comforting and consoling to do. She had come out of her trance, and he put his arm about her flabby old shoulders and took one of her trembling soft hands and started talking to her as to a sick or badly frightened child. "Never mind, Madame; it's all right, there's no harm done. I am here and you are safe."

She went on groaning; she suffered pain whenever a séance was broken off abruptly. Lanny half lifted her and half led her to the bed, and there she curled up, weeping; it was a nervous spasm, which she described as something clutching her stomach; he judged it was the solar plexus. He got a bottle of smelling-salts which she kept on her dresser. He went on murmuring words of sympathy and affection, for that was what a poor, lonely, and frightened old woman most needed in the world—somebody to be a son to her and care for her, even if these shocks, which enraged Tecumseh, should cause him to desert her and so ruin her psychic gift.

Presently she murmured: "Who is that man—that terrible man?" Lanny went and shut the door of the room, and then said: "Never mind, Madame; he is a sick man, and perhaps the spirits offended him."

"When I came out of my trance he was rushing up and down the room, cursing and screaming. What is the matter with him?"

"He is a very unhappy man, and something must have pained him deeply; some memory."

"I never heard of such behavior. I am afraid of him. I don't want to stay in the house with him."

"He won't do you any harm, Madame, I assure you. I won't let any harm come to you."

"He heard me groan and he shouted to me to shut up; then he rushed out of the room. I don't want him to come near me again."

"I doubt if he will want to. Don't worry; it will come out all right.

People have unhappy memories, things they cannot bear to be reminded of. Perhaps the spirits insulted him, as they did Sir Basil the first time."

"I am no longer so young as I was, and I cannot stand such things. Tecumseh will be furious, I know."

Lanny had to go on soothing this near-child, teasing her a little, also. He told her that her performance must have been extraordinarily good —really it was a compliment that was paid her, for a man didn't get excited about any revelation unless it was true. She was the most wonderful medium that Lanny had ever met, and he had tried dozens of them. Even if she never produced another spirit she had earned her place in the books—Lanny was going to have somebody write a book about her some day, and it would have her picture as a frontispiece. So on until he got her calmed, and she promised to go to sleep and not worry about the incident any more. But she would surely lock the door of her room on the inside!

X

Next morning the Führer appeared at breakfast, affable as usual, but apt to become preoccupied without notice. He said nothing to Lanny about what had happened; Hess, meeting the guest in course of the morning, remarked: "You must excuse that little mishap. Our Führer has many painful memories in his past."

"I understand, Herr Reichsminister. He has suffered everything the German people have suffered; if it were not so, he could not represent them and redeem them as he is doing." A carefully thought-out remark, which proved to be exactly right. The Deputy was gratified, and Lanny could be sure he would repeat the words.

"I hope the old woman was not too much upset, Herr Budd."

"I saw her this morning and she is all right. You can be sure she hasn't the least idea of what goes on at a séance—her trance is complete. So she couldn't talk about what happened even if she wanted to."

"Thank you, Herr Budd. I should like to try her again myself, if it would be agreeable."

"Certainly—and any of your friends, if you wish. That is what we came for."

Lanny went to reading the morning papers, which were flown from Berlin and motored from Munich, along with the mail. He thought the unfortunate episode was closed, but he failed to allow for the power of gossip in a small community. Humans are gregarious animals, which have lived in herds and hordes and households for millions of years; what each of them feels and does and says is of importance to the others—and especially whatever goes on in the mind of the Old Man of the Tribe, upon whose whims the life of all the others depends.

Lanny had received some mail forwarded from Bienvenu, and went to his room to write a letter; there he found one of those attractive young Aryan females, engaged in making the bed. She had already had a chance to look upon him, and had evidently found him good; her smiles told him that if he were to close the door and lock it, and then kiss her, she would not reject his advances. This was in accordance with the Nazi sex-code, but Lanny didn't want any of it. He got what he needed out of his suitcase and was about to leave the room, when the girl said, in a low voice: "*Herr Budd, darf ich etwas sagen?*"—may I say something?

Lanny stopped and said: "*Ja, freilich.*"

She came closer, and whispered: "What happened last night: it was Geli."

"*So?*" replied Lanny. "*Wirklich?*"

"You know that story?"

"It is better not to talk about it," said the proper guest, and went out quickly.

XI

Oh, yes, Lanny knew that story; one which was whispered everywhere by the refugees and other enemies of the *Regierung*. He had never before heard it referred to inside the Fatherland—perhaps because it was too terrible and too dangerous. Greta Raubal had been the child's name, and Hitler had called her Geli, pronounced "gaily." She was the daughter of his half-sister Angela, who had been his housekeeper, first here in the Berghof, after the release from prison, and then in Munich during the days of the Party's hard struggle for power. The child had flowered into womanhood in those desperately unhappy and abnormal times. Had she fallen in love with the dreamer of a new order, or had the dreamer made love to her, in his own strange and terrifying way? The story varied, according to who was telling it.

This much was certain: there had been an affair, permitted by the mother, beginning when Geli was very young and continuing to her death at the age of twenty or so. She was blue-eyed and fair, a tall Nordic blond according to Adi's ideal; she was gentle and submissive, and he, wildly jealous, ruled her with the whip which he liked to carry,

even in public. "When you go to woman, forget not the whip,"
Nietzsche had written, and Adi had read or at any rate heard of this
philosopher, another tormented dreamer on the road to madness.

There had been no happiness between uncle and niece, only fear on
the girl's part and in the end a desire to escape. But if any man came
near her, Hitler drove him away in fury. Otto Strasser told of such an
experience; but people distrusted Otto, knowing that he hated Hitler
as the murderer of Gregor, Otto's older brother. Another Party member, employed as a chauffeur, had learned the story and blackmailed
the Führer to the tune of twenty thousand marks and an important
Party position; this had been an especially unkind cut, since the Führer
had praised the man in *Mein Kampf* as one who had defended him in
the *Saalschlachten*. "My good Maurice!"

Nobody knew exactly what had happened at the end. Geli had tried
to get away and go to Vienna to study music, and the uncle had flown
into one of his hysterical tantrums; he had sent the mother away, and
the girl had been found on the floor of her room with a bullet through
her heart. This had been shortly before Hitler had become Chancellor,
and in Munich he was a powerful man. Göring had flown to the scene
and there had been no police investigation; it was called a suicide and
hushed up. The body had been buried in Vienna, in consecrated ground
—which could hardly have happened if the priest had not believed
that someone had killed her. Subsequently, Gregor Strasser had stated
that the priest on his deathbed had pointed out this fact to him.

So there it was, and you could take your choice: either Adi Schicklgruber had murdered his niece or he had driven her to suicide by
incestuous attentions. For days he had been near to suicide himself.
Too late he had made the discovery that she had been the great love
of his life, and no other woman could take her place, try as they would.
The tortured man had got a permit to visit Vienna incognito, and had
stood by her grave in the Zentralfriedhof late at night and dropped
flowers upon it. Now, half a dozen years later, he was master of all
Germany, and wanted to go to Vienna again. Lanny wondered if that
obscure grave was one of the forces which drew him.

What had happened in the disturbing séance? Had the free-spoken
Tecumseh, a ruler in his own right, dared to say what he thought
about incest and murder? Or had Geli herself appeared, and driven
her whip-wielding uncle into one of his frenzies of grief and fear? "He
that ruleth his spirit is greater than he that taketh a city." But then,
Adi rejected the old Hebrew prophets and did not read them. Suppose
the spirit of Freddi Robin had come and spoken such admonitions? Or

one of Adi's victims, such as Röhm, whom, after a stormy interview, he had had shot in cold blood? Or possibly Gregor Strasser, organizer of the Sturmabteilung. Lanny had once met Gregor in Adi's Berlin apartment, and had heard him get a sound dressing-down from his Führer. Later, after he had been killed in the Blood Purge, his spirit, or what claimed to be that, had been reported by Tecumseh; so evidently he was hovering about this bloodstained scene.

Lanny wondered how this story had got about in the Berghof. Had the beautiful blond secretary been listening at the keyhole? Or did the trusted "Rudi" have some confidant to whom he had whispered the single word Geli? Or had the young Aryan physician been called in to administer restoratives? Anyhow, the rumor was all over the place, and creating such excitement that a beautiful blond maker of beds had risked her job and perhaps her life by whispering to a guest about it. So much for Adi's fond dream that he could sneak into a room at night and consult a spiritualist medium without having the German *Volk* know anything about it!

The son of Budd-Erling realized that in his desire to ascertain the fate of his wife he might have gravely imperiled his privileges as a presidential agent. Hitler would hardly forget this episode; even though he could not blame Lanny for it, he would associate him with it in his mind, and this would surely not increase his desire to see the person. Might it even be that his tormented and suspicious mind would begin to wonder whether some enemy had deliberately prepared this shock for him? And what should Lanny do about the matter? Should he mention it and try to patch it up? Or should he drop some remarks indicating that he had no idea anything had gone wrong?

XII

The guest went down into the great hall and sat in one of the leather armchairs, looking out over Austria. A storm was coming up and dark clouds were scurrying over the tops of the mountains. Political storms, also, were gathering over Austria, and the master of these storms was in the room just over Lanny's head, planning and directing them. He might be standing at his window, said to be the largest in Germany, looking out upon this same scene, watching the swiftly moving clouds. He might be humming the *Walkürenritt*, one of his favorite tunes. Here in these mountains, with dark forests all about him, his mind was full of the myths and images of Richard Wagner, and in his predicament he must wish for Wotan to lend him a thunderbolt, or Loki, god of lies, to come whisper some wily stratagem into his ear.

A limousine came rolling up the drive and halted before the châlet. An officer in SS uniform got out and opened the car door for a woman passenger, tall, elegant, bundled in a heavy fur coat. Recognizing her, Lanny gave a start. Magda Goebbels!

Something new to wonder about! Was this a coincidence, a kindness that chance was doing an overwrought Führer? Or was it a royal command? Had Adi, unable to sleep in spite of his drugs, telephoned to Berlin and ordered consolation brought without delay? Magda would have left Berlin by plane early in the morning, and arrived in Munich an hour or so later.

Lanny rose as she entered the room, this being his duty. When she saw him her sad face revealed dismay for just a fraction of a second. Then, recovering herself quickly, as a woman of the great world learns to do, she greeted him: *"Grüss' Gott, Herr Budd."* He replied: *"Welche Überraschung, Frau Magda!"*

She shook hands with him, which she needn't have done. He saw that she was delaying, to let the SS officer and the man carrying her bags pass on. Then she leaned toward him and whispered, in a voice of tragedy: *"Ich konnt' mir nicht mehr helfen!"*—I couldn't help it— and then swiftly passed on out of the room.

21

Der Führer Hat Immer Recht

I

THE Detazes arrived, and a busy Führer found time for a one-man show. He ordered one wall of the main room cleared and the six French works hung in a row. There they were, land and seascapes, transporting the beholder from the white snowstorms of the Alps to the sun-drenched colors of the Riviera. Everybody was invited to inspect them, even the servants. It took Lanny back to the good old days of German *Gemütlichkeit* which had so impressed him as a boy, when the old Graf Stubendorf had assembled his *Diener* and *Knechte* and made them a speech on Christmas morning. Lanny wondered about this sudden geniality. Was the Führer saying to his household: "You see, this American visitor did not come just bringing an old witchwoman and a bagful of spirits; he is the stepson of a famous painter, and you can observe for yourselves and have something worth while to talk about"?

Lanny had taken the liberty of including one of the paintings which derived from the cruise of the *Bluebird* to the Isles of Greece: an old peasant standing in front of the hut which he had made out of brush, and holding under one arm a baby lamb. The Führer was much taken with this and wanted it. In fact, he wanted them all; a Detaze collection in his Bechsteinhaus, the châlet he had built on the estate for the use of official guests, would tend to show the world how sincere he was in his admiration of French culture, and how desirous of promoting the unity of Europe.

"I want you to understand, Exzellenz," said Lanny, "I didn't bring six paintings here with the idea of selling them all."

"Are they for sale, Herr Budd?"

"Yes, but——"

"Very well; I want to buy them. What is the price of the six?"

They had one of those bargainings in reverse; the Führer making an offer, and Lanny insisting that it was too much. They finally compromised on a price of a hundred thousand marks, a handsome enough figure. Lanny wondered more than ever. Had the great man some errand in mind, or was this just a retaining fee for a high-class agent? Lanny was familiar from childhood with aristocratic methods of hiring; he had listened to innumerable conversations between his mother and his father, and had watched Robbie's devices, such as playing a very poor game of poker, or making a wager on some preposterous thing, such as that the day was Thursday when he knew it was Friday. Adi's method was dignified and honorable in comparison, and perhaps Lanny was oversuspicious; but he could not believe that the Führer of all the Germans would ever do anything that did not contribute in one way or another to his world purpose.

The steward was instructed to obtain a draft on a Paris bank to the honor of Herr Budd, and Lanny was invited to go over to the Bechsteinhaus and see to the proper hanging of the masterpieces. Paintings considered to be inferior were taken up to the bedrooms—a custom prevailing among wealthy art collectors. In his bedroom in the Berghof Lanny had three very commonplace specimens of contemporary

German painting, and he wondered if Hitler had been personally responsible for their choice.

II

Franz von Papen showed up from Vienna and was closeted in his Führer's study. Other personages kept arriving, generals three or four at a time, and no effort was made to keep an American visitor from learning that the screws were being tightened on the Austrian government; Lanny even heard the designations of various Panzer units which were being moved to the border. He took the precaution to ask Hess if he was by any chance in the way, and the answer was, not in the least; the Führer esteemed it a great favor to have the two guests in his home.

The Deputy himself was having a sitting with the medium every evening, and was reporting results to his chief. He was telling Lanny some of the things, but not the most important, Lanny guessed. Hess's doubts had been completely dissipated; he was having secret conferences with the spirits of old-time *Parteigenossen*, those martyrs whose names he called at every *Parteitag*. Lanny wouldn't have been surprised if some day either the Führer or the Deputy had invited him to put a price on Madame Zyszynski; if he had done so, and agreed to say nothing about it, no doubt Madame would have stayed right there, regardless of whether she wanted to or not!

Lanny tried to imagine what was going on in the mind of the new Mohammed. For seventeen or eighteen years, ever since Adolf Hitler had taken control of a political party with seven members, he had been engaged in a guessing game with fate. He had tried violence once and failed abjectly. Since that time he had acquired a passion for "legality," and all the violence he had used had been in putting down those individuals and groups inside his party who rebelled against his determination to preserve the forms of *Gesetzmässigkeit*. Every crime he had committed had been in the name of law, and any aggression he would ever commit would be in the cause of peace.

Each decision was a step in the dark, a gamble for life or death. Can I trust this man, or must I have him killed? (No use to put men in jail, for when they come out, they are more dangerous than ever; but dead men tell no tales, nor do they undertake any coups d'état.) Every move on the chessboard of diplomacy meant a risking of Adi's future; for after all, his new Reich was a have-not nation, its resources were limited, and its Führer could not afford the luxury of a single blunder.

And if there was any way to lift the veil of the future, or to poke even the tiniest hole in it, how foolish not to make use of that method! If there were people who possessed that gift, why not hire them—especially when their price was absurdly small. Whatever it had been in the past, divination was now the poor man's way.

This ex-painter of picture postcards and possibly of houses believed in astrology, in fortune-telling, in spirits, in the whole kit and caboodle of occult tricks—for he had no means of sorting out the true from the false. His closest friend, his publicly announced Deputy, believed even more implicitly, and right now the pair of them were at a crisis, perhaps the gravest of their common career. Adi was in a struggle with practically his entire military entourage; all the trained intellectual power of the *Wehrmacht*, which he was making into the greatest army in the world. These were the heirs of Germany's greatest tradition; they had spent their lives preparing themselves to carry it on—and now came this upstart, this *Gefreite*, a sort of sub-corporal, or private first class, setting his authority against theirs, and bidding them commit an action which they considered dangerous to the point of madness.

But—it had happened before! They had advised against militarizing the Rhineland; they had advised against the Führer's bold announcement that he was going to double the size of the Reichswehr, and again that he was going to introduce conscription. But each time the inspired leader had had his way, and Britain and France had done nothing but enter protests.

And now, here it was again, over the question of the Anschluss. Adi was going ahead; his *daimon* told him to, and was not to be restrained. Just prior to this trip to Berchtesgaden he had shaken up his Cabinet and his army command, in order to get men who would obey him without hesitation. He had taken Ribbentrop, one-time champagne salesman, away from his job as Minister to Britain and made him Foreign Minister—because Ribbentrop was so sure that he had succeeded in bemuddling the British ruling class and that they would take no action to save Austria. He had deposed his oldest and most competent generals and given the command to others who were pure Nazis. He had made Göring a Field Marshal, giving him the right to carry a jeweled baton—all because Göring agreed with him and would back him in this contemplated gamble.

But up in that study alone, looking out of the large window over the land of his birth, what agonies of uncertainty must be tormenting the soul of this new Prophet-Führer, this man of destiny without peer in modern times! And in a room under the same roof was an old woman of a nationality whom the Führer despised—but some whim of nature had given her the power to call spirits from the vasty deep. Spirits of friends and of enemies alike—and who could say what they might know, what secret insights they might possess? Even the murdered ones, the former friends, would be Germans before they were enemies; even Röhm, or General Schleicher, or Gregor Strasser who had organized and trained the SA—even such spirits might be appealed to in the name of the holy Fatherland to say what Germany's fate would be, and what was the wise course for her Führer who dared not be wrong.

So what more natural than that Rudi Hess should be stealing off night after night to sit in a dark room and listen to what this stout old Polish woman was saying in her trances! Lanny wondered, could it be possible that Hitler himself was sneaking into that room, keeping the secret even from Madame's patron and paymaster? There was nothing to prevent it; all he would have to do was to make up his mind to endure in silence whatever insults and humiliations the spirits might inflict upon him, for the sake of the secrets they might consent to reveal.

And Hess sitting by, making notes in the dark, or by a dim light behind a screen; writing shorthand, as he had once written down the words of what had become the new German Bible! Would he now get a New Testament, a Book of Revelations of the NSDAP? "Blessed is he that readeth, and they that hear the words of this prophecy, and keep those things which are written therein: for the time is at hand." If anything of the sort should happen, they would surely have to discover that Madame Zyszynski was a changeling, and of pure Aryan blood; or at least that she was illegitimate—the device by which hundreds of Germans with Jewish names had managed to get themselves established as good Nazis!

III

Tension was increasing at the Berghof, increasing hour by hour; you felt it in the air, you saw it in the faces of everybody, high and low. Papen had departed in haste for Vienna, and word spread that he had orders to bring Schuschnigg to the Führer at all costs. Would he be able to do it? Everybody speculated, everybody had an opinion, no matter how presumptuous. It meant so much to them—for here they were, right on the very border; all they had to do was to slide downhill, as it were, and they would be in Austria. The people there were of the same race as themselves, speaking the same language, listening to the same music, eating the same sort of food and wearing the same sort of clothes; they came and went across the border—the German workers going every morning to the Austrian salt mines and coming back every evening. How preposterous that they couldn't be one country!

Lanny had found it pleasant to sit on the high-backed lounge in front of the fireplace and read the newspapers and magazines. Here he would be joined by someone of the household; young officers who had never visited the outside world were curious about it, and discovered that this American visitor knew the key people and possessed a fund of anecdotes. They didn't know why he was there, but they could be sure it was for some purpose important to the Führer, and they treated him as a member of the family. So it was no indiscretion when the young doctor remarked that *Der Paffenknecht*—meaning Schuschnigg —had only three days in which to make up his mind whether he wanted his baroque palace bombed about his ears.

Lanny could have guessed as much from the copy of the *Völkischer Beobachter*, the Führer's newspaper, which lay upon the table at this moment. The newspapers of Hitlerland were like so many searchlights, controlled from a common center and all focused upon the same spot at the same moment. Just now the spot was the Chancellor of Austria. They held this pious lawyer-statesman responsible for all the evils of Europe, and threatened him with dire and dreadful punishments if he did not step out of the pathway of the Nazi chariot of progress—or perhaps in these modern days one might better say the *Hermann Göring Panzer Abteilung*.

It was a technique of provocation which the Japanese had inaugurated in China in the previous autumn: commit an act of violence, blame it on the victims, and then set up a nationwide, a worldwide clamor for the punishment of the aggressors. In the case of Vienna, the criminals were the police who had uncovered the conspiracy of the "Committee of Seven." Dr. Tavs was in jail, with some of his fellow conspirators, and that made them heroes, and their cause was spread over the front pages of all the newspapers of Germany. The demand was that Schuschnigg should reform his Cabinet, putting in an Austrian Nazi as Minister of the Interior, in charge of the police. The conspirators would of course be released, and thereafter the Nazi rowdies would be free to beat up and kill their leading opponents.

IV

Such was the program; and Lanny had to watch it being carried out, without showing any trace of the dismay and disgust which boiled in his soul. He would stand in front of the mirror in his simple but elegant bedroom and whisper the Nazi formulas, watching his features in the meantime to see if he was betraying any trace of improper feeling. Really, he would be equipped for a leading role in any theater when he had got through with this assignment! He came down for the "fork breakfast" on the morning of Friday, the eleventh of February, and found the long table in a clamor with the news: "Schuschnigg is coming tomorrow!" He had no trouble in wearing a look of exultation, for he had guessed what the news would be, and had been rehearsing his comments not five minutes earlier. "The Führer is always right!"—so said the American guest to the magnificent Reichswehr officer who sat beside him at the table—General Wilhelm Keitel, newly appointed Adjutant to the Führer, with cabinet rank. "*Ja, Exzellenz, hier sehen wir wieder einmal: der Führer hat immer recht!*"

Unparalleled excitement throughout the household. Most of the furniture was taken from the great hall, including the fireplace settees on which Lanny had been so comfortable. A large table was moved to the center of the room and on this was spread a great relief map of Germany and all the border lands; "The Distribution of German Population and Culture in the States of Europe" it was labeled, and showed Germany and Austria in bright red, and the border states as pink with so many red spots that you would think they had the measles. The masterpieces of painting were taken down from the walls and in their places were hung greatly enlarged photographs of the damage done by the bombing of Guernica, Valencia, Madrid and Barcelona. The visiting lawyer-statesman was going to get a postgraduate course in the new science known as *Geopolitik*, as well as in the older science known as *Schrecklichkeit*.

Lanny thought it was the part of tact to take Hess aside and say: "I fear that an *Ausländer* will be out of place at this time." But the Deputy hastened to reply: "*Absolut nicht, Herr Budd*. The Führer trusts you, and would be sorry to have you take Madame away at present. May I tell you something in the strictest confidence?"

"Everything you tell me is confidential, Herr Reichsminister."

"I had a most extraordinary séance with Madame last night. The spirit of Hanussen came and foretold the outcome of these negotiations."

"That is indeed extraordinary!"—and Lanny didn't have to lie about it. Hitler, launched upon a campaign which had for one of its declared objectives the expulsion or extermination of the Jews of Vienna, was relying for guidance upon the spirit of a Jewish astrologer whom Göring had had murdered as a means of canceling the debts of his dear friend who commanded the Berlin police!

"I hope the prognosis was favorable," Lanny ventured.

"The Führer is greatly encouraged, and I am sure we shall see action before long."

V

Lanny went out for a walk in the forests which had once been the haunts of the witch or evil fairy named Berchta and were now witnessing the birth of a new religion of the sword. He was in the privileged position of those nobles of the *ancien régime* in France, who were admitted to the queen's bedroom to witness her *accouchement* and certify to the genuineness of the event. That would be something to tell to F.D.R., and perhaps to Lanny's grandchildren in the course of time; but just now he was sick of blood and terror, and permitted his mind to wander off to the subject of precognition, popularly known as fortune-telling. A new development in the mediumship of this Polish woman; the spirits she produced had hitherto been content with the present and the past, and never before had ventured upon what George Eliot described as "the most gratuitous form of error."

From the naïve point of view of Hess it was quite simple; the spirit of Hanussen was there, and had been able to foresee the future now as it had while in the flesh. But Lanny was trying to persuade himself that this self-styled "spirit" was in reality some form of subconscious activity, a fabrication or construct of the mind of Madame, combined with that of her sitter and perhaps of others. We speak of "levels" of consciousness because we are unable to think except in terms of space; but in reality the mind occupies no space, and there is no reason for thinking that one subconsciousness must of necessity be partitioned off from all others. It is purely a question of fact: Is it so or is it not? Lanny considered that he had been accumulating evidence disproving the partition hypothesis and proving some sort of commingling.

Why had Madame suddenly taken to foreseeing the future? Lanny guessed it was because a sitter had gone to her firmly convinced of the reality of this power, and consciously as well as unconsciously willing that the "spirits" should tell him what lay beyond the dark veil. Lanny had become convinced, not from any slip of the Deputy's, but from the general tenor of his conversation, that the Führer himself had been stealing into Madame's room, perhaps imitating Hess's voice, and anyhow behaving himself discreetly and taking whatever came. And Hitler was a man of driving will, both conscious and subconscious; perhaps a medium himself, perhaps a hypnotist, and certainly a man with a subconscious personality which drove him and guided him and taught him how to drive and guide others. Lanny had proved that it was possible to hypnotize Madame and direct what spirits or constructs should appear; and now Adi had gone in and commanded that the spirit of his old-time astrologer should be produced, and made to behave as he had when he had been so indiscreet as to announce that Adi had only a few years to live.

What would be the validity of the communications which this fabricated entity would deliver? Would the Hanussen-spirit tell his old-time patron what that patron wanted to hear? Would it have the power to do anything else? The answer depended in part upon whether you accepted the average man's idea of time as something absolute and real in itself, or whether you could manage to accept the teaching of philosophy and of modern physics that time is a form which our minds impose upon reality. Perhaps there is a level of our subconsciousness which is not limited to that form, and therefore a "spirit" might be no more ignorant of the future than of the past. Again it is a question of fact. Do we, or do we not, have dreams which correspond to future events? Lanny had read the books of J. W. Dunne, who had not merely proved by experiment that we do, but had proved by mathematics that we can.

This much any student of history must admit: the *daimon* of Socrates had guided not merely Socrates, but many of the youth of Athens, and later, by the power of the written word, had guided millions of men for a score of centuries. And this *daimon* had known he was doing just that; it had been a living force, foreseeing the future and helping to make it by its own intelligence and will. The same thing was true of the *daimon* of Adi Schicklgruber, when he sat with a medium and mingled his subconscious forces with hers and constructed a future which might be the true and real future because Adi was going to make it that. By will and imagination he renewed his spiritual and mental energy, and became the more able to carry out the purpose he was determined upon. Such has been the role of soothsayers through all time, and Lanny guessed that Adi was going to prove Madame right, and then marvel at her supernormal power.

VI

A stream of visitors kept arriving all that day: General von Reichenau, commander of the Reichswehr divisions stationed near Munich, together with two of his aides and a secretary; then Joachim von Ribbentrop—he had adopted the "von" of an aunt when he married the heiress of a great wine business; then a limousine full of professors, all of whom clicked their heels and bowed from the waist when an American *Kunstsachverständiger* was introduced; one was a geographer, one an agronomist, one a specialist in the history of Central Europe. Evidently they were here for the purpose of arguing with Schuschnigg—but Lanny would have been willing to wager his hundred-thousand-mark bank draft that Hitler would never give one of them a chance to get in a word; and Lanny would have won.

Consultations went on all day and most of the night; Lanny wasn't invited to attend, and thought it the part of good taste to keep entirely out of the way. There had been a thaw and then a freeze, and the snow was hard, so he took a long walk in those dark forests for possession of which Richard Wagner and the Witch Berchta contended in his heart. *Gemsböcke* leaped on the heights far above him, and *Rebhühner* rose with a whir of wings from almost under his feet; he came back tired but exhilarated. Then he looked over the library of the Berghof, and selected from an encyclopedia the volumes "M," "I," and "P," took them to his room, and read all they had to tell him about Mohammed and Mohammedanism, Islam and Pan-Islamism—wishing to know what it was that Hitler so admired, and thus to foresee the future of the world in which he had to live.

The Austrian Chancellor was scheduled to leave Vienna early next morning, and the drive would take five or six hours. He brought with him his Foreign Minister, Dr. Guido Schmidt, at heart a near-Nazi and a poor support; also a military aide and a secretary. Two cars full of private detectives followed, but Hitler ordered these stopped at the border and their place taken by a squad of SS men under the command of an officer who was a renegade Austrian. The party reached the Berghof about noon, by which time the Führer was pacing about biting his fingernails, and members of his staff were slipping outside onto the terrace to smoke a cigarette now and then.

Lanny was invited to take part in the reception. He wondered, did Adi wish to make sure that his guest had been telling the truth about his meetings with Schuschnigg? If so, Lanny would take pains to satisfy

him. He would not speak first to the pale and harassed-looking statesman, but would wait to be recognized. Schuschnigg must have been
surprised to see an American here, for his face lighted up and he exclaimed: "*Grüss' Gott, Herr Budd.*" The art expert replied: "A happy
accident, Exzellenz."

The Führer apparently meant to proceed on the principle that mo-
lasses catches more flies than vinegar. After the fashion of country gentlemen the world over, he took his guests to show them the beauties of
his estate. Lanny tagged along; and when they went into the Bechsteinhaus—named for the rich widow of the piano manufacturer who had
been Adi's main financial support in the early days of the Party—the
Führer called attention to the new paintings on the walls, and remarked: "This is my new Detaze collection. Perhaps you do not know
that Herr Budd is the stepson of this painter. He came here to bring
me these fine works." The Austrian staff would make note of this and
perhaps be fooled by it—who can say who believes what in the game of
Machtpolitik? Presumably they believed Adi when he said that he was
going to build *Wolkenkratzer* (cloudscrapers) in Hamburg, just to
show the Americans that he could do whatever they could. Also he
was going to build a great bridge there; a tunnel would have been much
cheaper, but he wanted to deprive the Americans of the honor of having the longest bridge in the world.

They returned to the Berghof, and the world's greatest *Machtpoliti-
ker* exhibited the relief map, a revelation of his life's dream. Perhaps it
might have been wiser to use some other color than red; however, all
would understand that it was the red of German blood and not of
Jüdisch-Bolshewismus. The thin red lines with arrows at their tips ran
from Berlin to various centers such as Alsace and Schleswig, Prague
and the Sudetens and the Corridor; one of them ran to Vienna, and Adi
didn't have to point it out. He was tactful about it, and didn't say:
"All this is going to be mine." His formula was: "*Unsere gemeinsame
deutsche Erbschaft,*" our common German heritage.

And the same with the greatly enlarged photographs on the walls,
showing the ruin wrought by General Göring's *Luftwaffe* wherever it
had had a chance to try itself out. Adi didn't say: "This is what I am
going to do to Vienna if you refuse to obey my will." No, he said:
"This is what modern war is coming to; a terrible thing to have to
destroy cities like this." He didn't say: "I have had these put up especially for your benefit." He left it to be assumed that this was the
spectacle upon which he fed his soul day and night!

VII

The Führer took the Chancellor and his minister up to his study; Ribbentrop accompanied them, but not the Austrian subordinates or the American art expert. These last sat in the great hall, chatting about the trip from Vienna, the obliging weather, and what other polite nothings men hit upon when they are under extreme nervous tension and are anxious not to show it. Every moment the tension increased and the conversation became harder to keep up; for over and under and in between their polite, well-modulated words came a distant rumble as of thunder, irresistibly commanding their attention and making it impossible for them to think, to say nothing of formulating thoughts into words. They would fall dumb, and then would realize what extremely bad taste they were showing in seeming to listen to what they were not supposed to hear.

Adolf Hitler was making a speech. He had shut the door of his study, and had set armed SS men on guard outside the door, but that made little difference to the laws of acoustics. His voice came down the stairway—or perhaps it came through the floor, or both. It seemed to have echoes, which produced a sort of blurred and booming effect—but then that had always been a characteristic of Adi's oratorical thunder. He had been practicing it for thirty years—yes, fully that, for he had learned to shout down opposition in the shelter for bums, the *Obdachlosenheim* in Vienna before the World War, and had been more than once thrown out because he wouldn't or couldn't keep quiet. After the war he had practiced addressing thousands in the noisy beerhalls which were Munich's meeting places—since no South German could think or even hear without a stein in front of him. In those days there had been no such things as microphones or loud speakers, and survival in politics had been dependent upon the power of the naked voice.

Here today Adi was using that voice upon two persons who were presumably daring to differ with him, to oppose his will. It could happen even without that, as Lanny knew well, having brought it on himself more than once by mere mention of the Jews or the Versailles *Diktat*. He had discovered that, once the Führer got started, an audience of one was the same as one thousand or one million. It wasn't the Führer speaking any more, it was his *daimon*, which perhaps couldn't count; or perhaps it took the mystical view that in the eyes of the Creator one soul is as important as one million. Anyhow, here was that

Supervoice, exactly as all Germany and indeed all civilized mankind had heard it booming and bellowing over the radio. More than ten years ago Adi had told Lanny Budd that he would make the whole world listen to him; recently, when Lanny had reminded him of that, he had replied: *"Mit Gottes Hilfe, ich hab's getan!"*

The Austrian military aide and the secretary had to give up all pretense of not listening; and so did Lanny. Impossible to hear every word, but whole phrases came clearly. The Führer of the Nazis told Dr. Kurt Schuschnigg and Dr. Guido Schmidt that they were a pair of traitors to their German *Blut und Rasse*. He informed them that they had made for years a practice of submitting people of their own blood and race to indignities and outrages, for no offense but that of defending their heritage. The Führer had at his tongue's tip a long list of such outrages, and he brought them up, and with each one his frenzy mounted and his voice became more raucous and more confused by echoes. Now and then would come a pause, in which it might be assumed that the Chancellor or the Foreign Minister was attempting some reply; but it never did any good to reply to Adi—it only made his anger greater and his next speech louder and longer.

VIII

This went on for a couple of hours, until a bell rang, and silence fell. Adi had ordered lunch prepared for his guests, and it was one of the laws of this household that when the bell rang, everybody dropped everything and came trooping downstairs as one company. Adi himself would turn off his rage as if it were water from a spigot; which seemed to suggest that it wasn't something which controlled him, but which he used as a matter of policy. He became once more the gracious host and escorted these blood-and-race traitors to the elevator and thence to the dining hall, where at the long table the Kanzler was seated at the right hand of the Reichskanzler, and the Auslandsminister on his left. Ribbentrop sat at Schuschnigg's right, and then came Hess, and then the Generals and then those of lesser military rank, with Lanny among them, *ars inter arma*. It was the Führer's intention to establish his *neue Ordnung* by whatever force it took, but never to forget that thereafter would come peace and the greatest flowering of culture in all history—so he had assured his art-loving guest.

The Führer had his vegetable soup and vegetable plate and near-beer; the rest of the company had *Hasenpfeffer* followed by *Apfelstrudel*, a very plain meal, almost insulting. Also—and this was the severest part of the ordeal—poor Schuschnigg was a chain-smoker of cigarettes, and here he had no chance for one over a period of nine hours. Immediately after the meal he and his minister were taken back to the Führer's study; the discussion began again—and in a few minutes Hitler was launched upon another tirade. Most of the staff members, the experts and others, retired to their rooms, ostensibly to have a smoke and perhaps a drink; they stayed for another reason—they wanted to hear what was going on without being observed to be listening. When Lanny went to his own room he noted that practically every door in the corridor was open—but just a crack, and heads that were close to the crack disappeared suddenly when his footsteps were heard. All the world knew of this visit to the Berghof, and was waiting to know the outcome; to expect those inside the building not to hear it if they could was to ask more than human nature could achieve.

What had happened in the study Lanny heard later on from Hess. The lawyer-chancellor had brought along a briefcase full of documents which proved to his legal mind that the Committee of Seven had been conspiring to overthrow his government. Hitler shouted at him: "What have I to do with that committee?"—and Schuschnigg, assuming that he really wanted to know, brought forth documents to show that the committee had been financed and directed from Berlin. Of course Adi flew into one of his worst rages—and after that Hess didn't need to tell Lanny any more, for he had been able to stand inside the partly open door of his room and hear the Führer of the Germans telling two Austrian statesmen what he really thought of them and their government and their population.

It was an opinion unprintably low. Adi Schicklgruber called the Viennese a cityful of café loungers and *Bummler*, drunken dawdlers in the *Heurigen* and women-chasers all over the town. As a result of their *verdammte Geilheit* they were a race of mongrels—Czechs, Hungarians, Slavs, Turks and gipsies, niggers, God alone could say what else—all mixed with Jews and dominated by Jew politicians, dancing to Jew music, eating Jew food, sleeping in Jew beds. When Adi got to describing the sexual conduct of the Viennese, he used the language which he had learned as a boy in a village of the Inn valley where they raise cattle, and his similes were such as only a countryman could understand. The louder he shouted, the more raucous his voice became— the effect of a gas injury during the war.

It appeared that Adi's spies had brought word to him that Schuschnigg had been making approaches to the labor leaders and Socialists of the city, with the idea of getting their support. Less than four years ago

Dollfuss had bombed and shot this *Gesindel* into submission and now Schuschnigg was proposing to bring them back into power; that was treason to the German *Volk*, that was *Jüdisch-Bolshewismus*, no less, and brought the loudest screams yet. Hitler said there would be no Red intrigues going on anywhere on his borders, and before he would permit it he would send three hundred planes and bomb Vienna until not one of its elegant buildings was left with a roof over it.

What Adi was demanding was to have Seyss-Inquart, Führer of the Austrian Nazis, become Minister of the Interior, in charge of the police. If the demand was refused, the German army would march. Schuschnigg backed and filled, and finally said he would have to phone to President Miklas in Vienna. This he was permitted to do, and came back reporting that nothing could be decided without a full Cabinet meeting. At this Adi's screams of rage rang through the house; this was *eine Ausrede*, this was *eine Schurkerei*, this was *eine Frechheit!* He shook his fist in the unhappy Chancellor's face and told him that he and his *verdammtes Kabinett* had forty-eight hours in which to make up their *blödsinnigen*—imbecile—minds.

All this Lanny heard, and shivered a little while Hitler told what he would do to the members of the Austrian government if they compelled him to use force. It bore a startling resemblance to what the son of Budd-Erling had just been reading in the encyclopedia under the title "Islamic Institutions." Unbelievers were invited to embrace Islam, and if they did so, their lives, their families, and their property were protected. If they refused, they had to fight, and if they were defeated, their lives were forfeit, their families liable to slavery, and all their goods to seizure. Such was the code, enforced this time, not by lightly mailed horsemen armed with javelins and swords, but by technicians driving mechanical monsters which shot steel and spat flame, and by others flying in the sky and dropping heavy packages of death and destruction. "Under which king, Bezonian? speak, or die!"

IX

It wasn't until night that Adi's near-prisoners were released and allowed to drive home. Then the tension in the Berghof was released, and men emerged from their rooms and admitted that they had heard what they couldn't have helped hearing—or so they could pretend. Dinner was late, a rare event; it was like a birthday celebration—for everybody considered that victory had been won; that miserable pettifogging lawyer would never dare force his country into a war with the

Führer. Or would he? Lanny could sense uneasiness underneath the blustering. How could this story appear to the newspapers of the outside world? Once over the border, the lawyer would be free to tell it as he chose; and what would Britain and France say? What would Mussolini do? Would Czechoslovakia mobilize? And Poland? The military men revealed a tendency to draw off by themselves and talk in low tones.

These were trying days for the Fatherland, and Lanny was not surprised when the Deputy Führer told him that he desired to try another séance with Madame that evening. Was it the Führer himself who was going? It was no part of Lanny's duty to spy, and he didn't; but he heard with interest the report next morning—that the spirit of Paul von Beneckendorff und von Hindenburg had talked with Hess, and had reported himself entirely satisfied with what the Führer was doing. That had surely not been the case during the old gentleman's last days on earth; he had been wont to refer to Adi Schicklgruber as "the Bohemian corporal," a term of contempt and not according to the facts, for Adi was Austrian and had never got as high as corporal. But now the great Feldmarschall was rested and rejuvenated, and with his intellectual powers restored he realized that the German *Volk* were in the best possible hands. All this the Deputy Führer said with a perfectly straight face, and the American visitor heard him in the same fashion—but inwardly wondering if they both hadn't passed through the looking-glass with Alice.

Hess reported that the Führer was obliged to leave for Berlin at once. Would Herr Budd care to come and bring Madame, both to be the Führer's guests? Lanny started making excuses—for he wanted to get off a report to Washington, and couldn't send it from Berlin. He said, quite truly, that Madame was not happy in a foreign environment; the severe climate in the Alps kept her indoors, and she was yearning for the sunshine and flowers of the Riviera. Lanny had some picture business to attend to at home, and would leave Madame there, and proceed to Paris and possibly London. "In a couple of weeks I'll join you in Berlin and we'll try those experiments with Pröfenik, if you're in the mood." Hess replied: "O.K."

That afternoon the two visitors, plus Tecumseh and the spirits, were bundled up and driven to Munich and put on board the night express for Milan. Snow was falling, but it didn't matter to great electric locomotives; snowplows went ahead, and they took their heavy loads of passengers and mail and freight up into the Alpine passes, and through the wonderful tunnels, and down the long winding gap known as *Der*

Brenner, or *Il Brennero,* according to which side you were coming from. The Germans asked if you knew the land where the lemons grew, and sighed to be taken there; the Italians, on the other hand, voiced their fear of invading barbarians who came out of the snow and ice of the north. These barbarians had now taken over the Fascist political creed, but even so, no Latin would ever like them.

X

At Bienvenu all was well. Marceline was in the *hospice de la maternité* in Cannes where Frances Barnes Budd had been born eight years ago; Marceline had a baby boy in her arms, and was proud and happy. As for Vittorio, he was at the bursting point; everything was coming his way—not merely was he a father, but he had won several thousand francs by a new gambling system he had discovered, and the newspapers were reporting a series of victories by his armies, which were pushing down from the north, threatening to reach the sea and cut off Valencia from Barcelona. That dreadful Spanish war had been going on for more than a year and a half, and everything Lanny had hoped for was being crushed and ground into the bloody red dust of the Aragon hills. He found the vauntings of his brother-in-law all but intolerable; but he had to put a grin on his face and keep it there—just as in the Berghof.

His recourse was to pour out his heart through a typewriter onto sheets of paper. Not too many sheets, for he must remember that the Man in the White House had at least one hundred and three confidential agents, and thousands of other people trying to get his ear every day—but surely not many who had been listening behind the door while the Führer of the Nazis browbeat and mauled the Chancellor of the Austrians. Lanny tried to hold himself to the facts; but one of these facts was that relief map, showing the German-inhabited lands which Adi meant to take into his Third Reich. Austria would be the first bite; the second would be the Sudetenland, and the third the Polish Corridor. Meantime Spain was becoming a Fascist state, and a future flying field and submarine harbor for the new Mohammed. "Get ready to meet that," wrote "P.A. 103."

He told his mother what amount of money he had got from Hitler, about forty thousand dollars, but advised her not to let Marceline know, except by slow stages. The child—Lanny still thought of her as that, although she was twenty—didn't really need thirteen thousand all in a lump, and Vittorio would get it away from her and lose every cent of it in one night. Better let them think they were poor, and dole it out to them at intervals. So long as Marceline could live at Bienvenu she wouldn't suffer. Lanny added, with a smile: "I'll keep your share and dole it out to you." Beauty's heart was in a state of deliquescence just now; she was so excited over that marvelous new baby that she couldn't refuse any request of the young madonna.

Lanny took the trouble to cultivate his Fascist brother-in-law for professional reasons. There was quite an Italian colony in Cannes and thereabouts, and Vittorio's friends included several officers recovering from wounds, and several agents promoting Il Duce's cause in the Midi. They talked freely in the presence of Vittorio's rich brother-in-law—why not? Thus Lanny was able to learn the number of Italian troops in Spain—about three times what Mussolini admitted; their armaments, their losses, and the reinforcements expected. They were shipped from the harbor of Gaeta, between Rome and Naples; a small town, rarely visited by foreigners and therefore fairly secret. The cost had been terrific, a couple of billion lire so far, but of course Mussolini would never accept defeat; he had put his hand to the plow and must go to the end of the furrow.

That was what Bernhardt Monck had said nearly half a year ago, sitting under a tree on a hilltop near the doomed town of Belchite. Germany and Italy had to win, and would send whatever men and supplies it took. The Loyalists had men, but no supplies—so now the Italians and Moors had broken through; thousands of those ill-clad and hungry men whom Lanny had seen were dead, and perhaps Monck among them. The presidential agent could have shed tears of grief and rage over these thoughts, but instead he set himself at his typewriter and sent off another report. He permitted himself one sentence of what might have been called propaganda: "Men are dying there in those cold red hills to give us time to wake up and get ready."

XI

On all this Coast of Pleasure, now at the height of a gay and costly season, Lanny Budd knew only one person to whom he could express his feelings. He went in to Cannes, and from there telephoned to Julie Palma, making an appointment to pick her up on the street. He drove her out into the country, and heard all she had to tell about her husband and what he was doing in Valencia. He couldn't write freely, on account of the censorship; anyhow, he was of an optimistic nature, and would go on believing the best in spite of any defeat.

Lanny said: "If the Rebels break through to the sea, the people in Valencia will be trapped. Raoul had better come out now while he can."

"He won't," replied the wife. "He is a Spaniard, and feels that his duty is there."

"Tell him I say he is needed to run the school. He can accomplish many times more that way."

"It would do no good," was the answer. "Right or wrong, he thinks he's needed where he is."

This competent little brunette woman, an Arlésienne, told the news of the school, a center of anti-Fascist agitation in the Midi and greatly hated by the reactionaries of all groups. It had been named to Lanny by Vittorio's friends, and he mentioned this to the woman, warning her again of the importance of keeping his name out of it. Gone were the good old days when Lanny could come to the school and talk to the gang; when the little Red and Pink urchins would greet him on the street. Now he was supposed to have gone the way of the rest of the rotten rich. "The Communists class-angle you," said Julie Palma, with a smile.

He put an envelope into her hands, containing enough bank notes to keep the enterprise going until his next visit. She had invented an imaginary rich relative in Paris who was supposed to be the source of these funds, and she told him about the comments of the school on this lucky find. It made Lanny sad, for he was by nature a sociable person, and now there were so few persons he could talk to. He hadn't told either Raoul or Raoul's wife about Trudi; and now, for what reason he couldn't guess, the Trudi-ghost came no more. One of the first things he had done on reaching Bienvenu was to make a try with Madame, but he got only Zaharoff and Grandfather Samuel and his other familiars. Parsifal got Claribel, and the inmates of the monastery of Dodanduwa. The Trudi-ghost had apparently got lost somewhere on the road between Paris and the Cap.

XII

Vittorio had been driving Lanny's car, which meant that it needed repairs; Lanny waited for these, and then set out for Paris. He had a round of social duties there, and pleasures, if he could take them as such. Selling paintings to the Führer of all the Germans was from the professional point of view no small feat, and Zoltan was delighted to hear about it. Being sent by the Führer as an emissary to Vienna was a feat from another point of view, and Lanny would not fail to tell Kurt and his secretary about that; also Graf Herzenberg and his actress *amie*. It immensely increased his rating with them to know that he had been allowed to stay as a guest in the Berghof while the negotiations with Schuschnigg were going on; from that time on they would talk freely to him and he could pick up many items.

The de Bruynes were out of jail. The agitation of the reactionary papers of Paris had been a source of embarrassment to the members of the Cabinet, some of whom agreed with the prisoners' ideas, and considered them guilty merely of an indiscretion. In other words, the storm had blown over, and so Lanny could visit his old friends without any publicity. All three looked well; they had been allowed every comfort consistent with being in prisons. But all were indignant because they had been compelled to dismantle their lone fortification and agree to purchase no more arms whether at home or abroad, an unprecedented interference with the right of rich men to spend their money as they pleased.

They, too, were interested in hearing about the visit to Berchtesgaden. Lanny was able to reduce their mental distress by pointing out that Adolf Schicklgruber had bought arms and had attempted a *Putsch* and had been imprisoned and compelled to agree to a course of "legality." But that hadn't kept him from getting power. Denis de Bruyne said that meant going into politics, and might be all right for Germany, but in France the politicians were so hopelessly corrupt, they sold out not merely their country but their employers and even one another. The de Bruynes were so depressed concerning the state of *la patrie* that Lanny wondered whether they were ready to invite Hitler in to clean it up. Certainly they were not in the least disturbed by the prospect of having him move into Austria. It was plain to all the world that he couldn't move far to the east or southeast without running into Russia, and that was the development upon which all hearts were set.

There was a long letter from Robbie, telling the news of the family and the business. This man of constantly expanding affairs stressed the importance of his deal with Schneider, so it became Lanny's not unpleasant duty to eat a well-prepared luncheon at the Baron's town house and tell about the various meals he had eaten at the Führer's country house. There was nothing he wasn't free to reveal about this visit, except a few things such as the screaming and bellowing at the Austrian Chancellor; the son of Budd-Erling, well-bred and tactful, would tone that down, so that the Baron might not have the idea that he would go out from the Baron's home and betray secrets.

XIII

So important did the master of Schneider-Creusot consider this account of Hitler's personality and ideas that he asked if Lanny would consent to tell it to a few of the Baron's friends. So, three days later, Lanny was guest of honor at a formal and most elegant stag dinner, served by half a dozen footmen in pink plush livery, and attended by a dozen of the leading industrialists and financiers of Paris. These were the men who really governed the country, putting up the electoral funds, naming the members of cabinets, and being consulted as to all measures of importance. François de Wendel, Sénateur de France and head of the great mining trust; Max David-Weill, representing the bank of Lazard Frères; René Duchemin of the French chemical trust; Ernest Mercier, the electrical magnate—men like these. Not merely the French empire in Africa and Asia, but their satellite states in Central Europe, where their government had loaned many billions of francs and their banks and industries had made even greater investments—all these treasures and dominions were at stake, and the crisis was such that it rocked the political world, and divided even these masters among themselves.

Was this Adolf Hitler a statesman like all the others, whom you could buy at a price low or high? Or was he a madman, one without any price? Here was an American, young compared with those present, the son of a man whom many of them knew, and he had actually lived in the madman's house for a week or more and heard his intimate conversation. They wanted him to tell everything about Adi and what to do about him—provided of course that Lanny would tell them to do what they wanted done. The guest explained that he was embarrassed, for he was no politician but an art expert; his errand to Austria had been to purchase a Defregger for the Führer and his errand to Berchtesgaden had been to take the Führer some examples of the work of Lanny's late stepfather, Marcel Detaze. (Not a bad advertisement for a high-class business, incidentally.)

The story of this dinner would, of course, go back to Berlin very soon; so Lanny had to be careful what he said. He had no objection to describing Adolf Hitler's well-appointed home, his agreeable manners, and what he ate and drank. It was all right to say that Hess believed in spiritualism and mental healing; but better not anything about Mohammed! The facts about the ultimatum to Schuschnigg had been in all the newspapers of the world, so they could be discussed freely. The relief map of German population and culture had been reproduced as a poster and was now being circulated by Dr. Goebbels, so there was no harm in that. The Führer had told Lanny to say that he loved France and hated Russia and that both these feelings were undying; so Lanny carried out these instructions. On his own authority he said that Hitler was determined to control and perhaps annex not merely Austria, but all the adjoining lands whose population was predominantly German; those who did business with him would have to do it on that basis.

After coffee and liqueurs had been consumed, the discussion went on for an hour or two, and even after the guests adjourned to the library they gathered around the guest of honor and wouldn't let him go. There was another Cabinet crisis impending in France, brought on by the Austrian situation. Chautemps was tottering, and Blum was plotting to come in again; these masters had to find somebody to keep him out—but first they had to make up their minds what they wanted done. They were all worried, and Lanny knew of old that men of this sort are the world's best worriers. In reality they were helpless, on account of the firm position of the British Cabinet, which had sold them out in favor of Hitler—at least that is how they saw it. Britain was playing Germany against France according to the ancient practice of *perfide Albion*. Why shouldn't France play Germany against Britain? But then, wouldn't that be playing the game of the Soviets?

They didn't come to any decision that night; but Lanny thought it a good enough story for Roosevelt that in this crisis the secret rulers of France hadn't yet been able to make up their minds whom they wanted for their friends and whom for their enemies.

22

Foul Deeds Will Rise

I

ADOLF HITLER summoned his tame Reichstag into session, a
device which he used when he wished to address the world. The
Reichstag had two things to do: first, to hear him make a long speech,
and second, to vote its endorsement of everything he had said. This
vote never failed to be unanimous—since any member who presumed
to voice disapproval would be sent off to a concentration camp before
that afternoon's sun had set.

This time Adi told the world pretty much the same things that
Lanny had told the guests of Baron Schneider. He set forth at length
his undoubtedly genuine loathing for the Soviet Union. "We see in
Bolshevism more now than before the incarnation of human destructive forces." It was not the poor Russian people who were to blame
for this world calamity, he said. "We know it is a small Jewish
intellectual group which has led a great nation into this position of
madness." And then those Germans on the outside, who had been
separated from the Fatherland by the wicked Versailles *Diktat*. "In the
long run it is unbearable for a World Power, conscious of itself, to
know there are racial comrades across its border who are constantly
being afflicted with the severest suffering for their sympathy or unity
with the whole nation, its destiny, and its philosophy."

This was a question of philosophy at the moment, for Adi wanted
the British Tories to keep quiet while he got Austria into his grip,
and then he would take up the next subject with them. But he gave
an idea what that was; for when Adi got going, it was hard for him
to stop, and when any one of his phobias was mentioned it became
impossible for him to control his feelings. He always delivered these
tirades extemporaneously and had never yet been known to read a
prepared speech. The British press was presuming to criticize his
ultimatum to Austria; this was called "freedom of the press" in Britain,
and it meant "allowing journalists to insult other countries, their institu-

452

tions, their public men, and their government." The Führer gave plain warning that he wasn't going to stand this. "The damage wrought by such a press campaign was so great that henceforth we shall no longer be able to tolerate it without stern objections. This crime becomes especially evil when it obviously pursues the goal of driving nations into war."

The British public might have foreseen the result of such misconduct; but the Führer saw fit to tell them in plain words. "Since this press campaign must be considered as an element of danger to the peace of the people, I have decided to carry through that strengthening of the German army which will give us the assurance that these threats of war against Germany will not some day be translated into bloody force." So there it was! Germany was being forced to arm by the British press, and nobody could ever again say that Germany had wanted to do it. Nor was there any use talking any more, so long as the press was free to build up a public opinion, and statesmen in democratic lands had to do what public opinion demanded. Said Adi: "Under these circumstances it cannot be seen what use there is in conferences and meetings as long as governments in general are not in a position to take decisive steps irrespective of public opinion."

II

Lanny listened to this address on his radio while motoring to Calais. It made him rather blue, and his feelings were not improved by a stormy Channel crossing; he was seasick one of the few times in his life, and went to the nearest hotel to spend the night and recuperate. There in the morning papers he read that Anthony Eden, chief object of the Führer's attack, had resigned from the British Cabinet. That would be taken in Germany as an act of submission; in Britain it was taken as a protest against the Prime Minister's course—a very decorous and reserved protest, in the British manner. The Prime Minister received it "with profound regret," and tried to make it appear as a protest against Italy's continued breaches of the Non-Intervention Agreement in Spain.

Lanny motored to Wickthorpe Castle and was welcomed as usual. He played with his little daughter, and in between times read in the newspapers of the hot debate going on in Parliament over the government's course. Secure in his Tory majority of more than two to one, Chamberlain stood firm in his policy of "appeasement"; and over the week-end the politicians and public men gathered at Irma's house-party to discuss what had been said and what was going to be done.

There was a general hush-hush atmosphere, for few Englishmen liked what they were doing. You took things for granted and didn't put them into words, except to a few of the innermost insiders. Germany was hell-bent upon taking back those eastern borderlands which she had lost after the last war; many Britons hadn't approved of taking them from her, and now, to keep them from her would mean a war that Britain wasn't ready for and didn't want. France, which had heavy investments there, would just have to write them off. There had been some sort of understanding with the Nazis—perhaps not in writing, just a gentlemen's agreement with men who rejected that classification. There were hints of it in Hitler's speech; he had said that Germany's colonial claims would be "voiced from year to year with increasing vigor"—which of course was "double talk" for the statement that they weren't being pressed at present. That was the thing which the British ruling class would never stand for—having Hitler become strong overseas, and establish airplane and submarine bases. On land they might have to let him have his way, provided he didn't go too far—but how far would he go? Who could say?

Right at this juncture came Lanny Budd, fresh from a sojourn in the home of this statesman of whims and frenzies, this genius-madman, this uncertain ogre. Incredible, but true; there could be no doubt that he had been there, for he described the pictures on the walls, the decoration of the bedrooms, the size and color and contents of the vegetable plates which the ogre ate. "Upon what meat doth this our Caesar feed, that he is grown so great?" These grave English gentlemen and political ladies thronged about an American art expert and plied him with questions, and some of the most exclusive asked if he would come to their homes and tell another select company what he had seen and heard.

Irma was quite taken aback by her ex-husband's social success. What had come over him? Could it be that he had really changed his mind and dropped his crazy radical notions? Or was this a super-subtlety that he had acquired? From the point of view of a week-end hostess it didn't make much difference, so long as he gave the facts and was so discreet, never intruding his own opinions, but leaving it for his hearers to draw their own conclusions.

Inside this venerable castle was every comfort, and complete protection against the winter's cold; but one heard the fierce gales blowing about the chimneys and rattling the windows. One knew also that political storms were rising, and no amount of English courtesy and reserve could keep out awareness of the people's discontent. There were mass meetings in Albert Hall, and huge crowds in Trafalgar Square in spite of unsuitable weather. Mobs shouted against the murder of the Spanish people's government, and British freedom of speech and press was used to print and circulate leaflets, pamphlets, and books denouncing the Fascists and warning of the wars they were preparing. The small ruling group which controlled public policy was being denounced under the name of the "Cliveden set," after the very elegant country home of the Astors. Of course these people vigorously denied that they exercised any such power, and even that there was any such set; Rick in one of his caustic articles had written: "They deny there is a Cliveden set, but will they deny there is a Cliveden sort?"

Irma mentioned this controversy more than once in her ex-husband's presence, and Lanny wondered: Was she a little peeved because Nancy was getting more than her share of public attention? He did not forget that Irma had had several years in café society, both before and after their marriage; and would she have been secretly pleased if the Red and Pink press had taken to denouncing the "Wickthorpe set"? Nancy had the advantage that her husband was a press lord, and she herself a member of Parliament, whereas Irma's husband was a career man in the Foreign Office, and had to preserve an atmosphere of aloofness and impartiality in his home. So that had become Irma's tone, and when she spoke of her rival it was in a gently patronizing vein.

III

Lanny motored to The Reaches, and then what a blowing off of steam there was! All the accumulated pressure of some of the most eventful weeks in the history of both the world and Lanny Budd. He could tell here how Adi had bellowed at Schuschnigg, and even give an imitation of the sounds—which sent Rick and Nina into gales of laughter, for it doesn't take much exaggeration to make German sound funny to English ears. He could tell about the new Mohammed, and what Islam had done to infidels and would still do if it had been able. He could even tell of the dreadful confession of Magda Goebbels, and the degenerate practices of which he had knowledge among the Nazis.

Also he could pour out his heart about Trudi. He hadn't succeeded in getting the information he sought, but he was close to getting it, he believed. "I'll be much surprised if Professor Pröfenik doesn't make use of every tip I gave him," he declared.

"I hope you *do* get it!" exclaimed Nina. "It is such a cruel thing to be kept in a state of uncertainty."

"It is what Trudi herself endured for four years or more. Thousands of others are still enduring it, and will for the rest of their lives."

"I know," said the woman; "but it makes a difference when you know the persons." Womanlike, she was interested in what was going on in the hearts of men, and added: "Tell me how you stand it, Lanny."

"Well, you learn to stand what you have to. It's not so bad in my case, because I'm doing Trudi's work, and I have the feeling that she's always with me. I know exactly what she'd say to everything that comes up, and when I give some money for the cause I feel her satisfaction."

It couldn't be the same, Nina knew; but she forebore to say so, for that would be like probing into a wound that he was managing to heal. Just as the body walls off a foreign substance which has got under the skin, so the mental body walls off suffering. So this gentle woman thought, and Lanny, an old friend, knew the meaning of her silence.

"Our case is hard to understand," he told her. "Few lovers were ever so impersonal. Trudi was so completely absorbed in her cause that really it seemed as if she had no life outside it. I would see her sitting silent, and would never have to offer a penny for her thoughts; I knew that her mind was on the comrades in the concentration camps, or those who were risking their lives circulating our literature. I would try to beguile her, and now and then succeed, but not often—for the pressure was always on her, there was always some new thing coming up that brought the whole tragedy back to life in her heart."

"It's inhuman to be like that, Lanny!"

"Of course it's inhuman; but so are the Nazis, and we who fight them have to be the same."

"What's that going to mean to the future?"

"I leave the problems of the future for the future to solve. The fact is now that we're at war, and have to feel the emotions of war and make the sacrifices of war. The Nazis are not going to be overcome except by men who are as stern as they, and as determined to prevail. There'll have to be a lot of anti-Nazi fanatics, and some of them will be women who think more about saving their comrades than they do about making their husbands happy. Isn't it so, Rick?"

"Right you are!"

"I haven't made up my mind whether I believe in immortality," said Lanny, "but I know that Trudi's spirit lives on in me. I think about her all the time; I suppose it's what the religious people call 'communing.' When I get in a stroke against the Nazis, I hear her saying: 'Good for you!'—and always: 'What next?' The Nazi terror goes on, and our resistance cannot slacken. I suppose I'm becoming one of the fanatics, too."

Nina wanted to exclaim: "Oh, *don't!*" but she was afraid it wouldn't be polite. Instead she asked: "Suppose you learn that they've killed her. Will you go on mourning for her, or will you find another love?"

"A fine chance I'd have to make a woman happy—or to discover one who would live my life!" Lanny smiled—he seldom talked long without finding some occasion to smile. "Did you ever read Sir Walter Scott's 'Outlaw's Song'?" He quoted:

> Maiden! a nameless life I lead,
> A nameless death I'll die!
> The fiend, whose lantern lights the mead,
> Were better mate than I!

IV

Lanny telegraphed Rudolf Hess, asking if a meeting with Pröfenik would now be agreeable, and the reply came promptly that an appointment had been made for two days from that date. So the agent motored to the Channel and had another stormy crossing at the beginning of March. He reached Calais—a town whose name had been written on his heart by the tragedy of the Robin family. An unseasonable snowstorm was making it dangerous to drive, so he put his car in storage and took the train so as not to miss his date.

He was invited to be the guest of the Deputy, but thought it the part of tact to put up at the Adlon and not be in the way. He knew from the newspapers that both Adi and his most loyal supporter were absorbed in what was for all practical purposes a war with Austria, being carried on inside that unhappy country through the agency of Seyss-Inquart and another Nazi who had been forced into the Cabinet. It might have been taken as a comedy war if it hadn't had such grim meaning for the future. The Austrian Minister of the Interior and Public Security granted to the Nazis of Styria the right to wear swastikas and to shout "*Heil Hitler!*"—and then the Cabinet of which he was a member canceled the order. He went to Graz and reviewed fifteen thousand Nazis, many of them in uniform and all giving the Nazi salute in what was an illegal parade. Nobody who knew the Hitler movement could doubt what this meant.

Lanny found the newspapers of Berlin full of clamor concerning the mistreatment of Germans in Austria. Those hateful Nazi newspapers, filled full of lies and abuse! Such a thing as factual reporting was entirely unknown in Hitlerland; it was all the poison propaganda of the crooked dwarf "Juppchen," whom Lanny had come to think of as the vilest human being he had ever shaken by the hand. One glance at any front page in Berlin and you knew what new move the Nazi machine was preparing and who were to be the next victims: Jews, Austrians, Czechs, Poles, Bolsheviks—and now and then a turn at domestic enemies, speculators, black-market operators, refusers of *Winterhilfe*, doubters of the Führer's wisdom—and then pacifists, Catholics, Protestants, Free Masons, and of course Jews and Reds everywhere and all over again.

V

Lanny reported his presence in town and confirmed the appointment; Hess would call for him that evening. Also he called Göring's office, and reported to Hauptmann Furtwaengler that he had orders for two paintings which the Feldmarschall had commissioned him to dispose of. That was always pleasant news; *Der Dicke* had become the richest man in Germany—"But nobody ever has enough money," observed Lanny, and the SS officer chuckled appreciatively. He, no doubt, had had opportunity to observe.

Deputy Führer Hess had not provided himself with a six-wheeled chariot enameled in baby-blue. He rode in a black limousine with a red standard in front and a gold swastika on the doors. A staff sergeant drove, with another SS man beside him for protection. Perhaps the windows were of bulletproof glass—Lanny had no objection to this being the case for the night. As they rode he discussed the Austrian imbroglio, of course blaming Schuschnigg—for what was the sense of appointing a Minister of Public Security and then doing everything to make him insecure? It simply meant that you didn't mean what you said, and the Führer was sick of dealing with people who kept no bargains. The Austrian Cabinet was going to get another shaking up, and this time the double-dealers would be shaken out on their heads.

They talked about Pröfenik, and Hess said the old fellow had had plenty of time to prepare and no doubt would put on a good show for them. It was so hard to find honest and competent mediums—and why did they have to be Poles and low-class people like that? Lanny said he didn't know, but it appeared to be a fact that many of them did come from those Central European lands. The most careful and dependable researchers appeared to be Germans; Lanny named Driesch and Schrenck-Notzing and Tischner. Hess made note of these names, and Lanny wondered if they would receive decorations and be put in charge of a *Forschungs Anstalt für Parapsychologie*.

Before they went into the building Lanny said: "I want you to know, I have not communicated with Pröfenik, or told him anything about you."

The Deputy Führer replied: "He knows plenty about me, and can find out more. But, by God, if he tries any monkey tricks on me, I'll have him skinned alive!"

VI

In that house of mystery nothing had been changed. The black-clad servant took their hats and coats, and the elderly Chinese-appearing gentleman received them with bland courtesy and escorted them into the dimly lighted room. He asked after their health and the Führer's, and said: "We are witnessing great events. I have cast the Führer's horoscope again, and this is the month for him." Hess answered, rather dryly: "He thinks so."

Lanny, watching the wizard closely, noted that his eyes moved warily from one to the other of his guests. "Gentlemen," he said, abruptly, "you have come for advice, and the auguries are favorable. Let us proceed to work, before anything is said that might influence the supermundane forces."

That suited the pair, so without another word the old man entered the cabinet and drew the curtains. They waited, and presently heard a moaning and sort of faint snoring; then all of a sudden the deep bass voice of the "control" who called himself King Ottokar I. Speaking German, he declared: "There is an elderly gentleman here. He has white sidewhiskers but his chin is shaven; he wears a uniform of cream-colored broadcloth with a large gold star on his bosom. He claims to be a great ruler, and gives the name of Franz Josef. Do you know any such person?"

"I have heard of him," replied Hess, not too cordially.

"He is unhappy; he says that terrible things are coming to his beautiful city. The Prussians are marching once more against Austria. He says: 'I don't mind if you kill some of the people—there were always too many of them; but spare my palaces, for they were built to last for a long time.'"

"Tell him that nobody wants to hurt his palaces."

There was a pause, presumably while the old Emperor talked; then the voice said: "He says that if it had been intended that men should fly they would have had wings on their shoulders."

"Tell him," said the Deputy, "that if it had been intended for men to live in palaces, they would have had them growing on their backs, like snails."

Again a pause, and then: "He declares that is no way to talk to *Majestät*, and you will have to be respectful if you desire the honor of his communications."

"I apologize," said the Nazi, for Lanny had impressed upon him that spirits have to be humored. "Ask Seine Majestät if he can tell us what is coming to his country."

"He says many sorrows before any joys; but in the end the name *felix Austria* will be justified."

"That is rather vague. Ask him, please: Will the Viennese resist?"

"He says: 'The Viennese resist everything.' He says, again: 'They have their own peculiar way, which others might not recognize.'"

"What we want to know is, will they resist with guns?"

"He says they will resist with arrows of ridicule; and that it is always better to persuade your opponents."

"Is that all he has to tell me?"

"He says that he really loved the city of his dreams,—'*die Stadt meiner Träume*.' He says: 'I did the best I could, but the world changes too fast for the mind of any man.'"

"Tell him that his place in history is secure," said the Deputy Führer of the NSDAP—and nothing could have been handsomer. "Ask him if he has any suggestions on his mind."

"He wishes you to know that his grandnephew Otto would make an excellent successor to the throne."

"We have heard of the young man, but he has been exiled from his Fatherland—and not by us. Anything else?"

"Seine Majestät thinks that the American gentleman might be interested to know there is a very fine portrait of his Imperial Majesty in the possession of the family of a painter named Husak, in Vienna."

"Ask him for the address," Lanny ventured.

"It is difficult to make out," declared the voice; but finally he gave it, spelling the name of the street. The American gentleman, making notes as best he could in the dim light, did not fail to get this information down. It was the first time the spirits had ever sought to do business with him and he wondered, had somebody offered the Professor a commission on a deal? If so, he was taking a bold chance for a small amount of money, for the communication was certainly not likely to fool the Deputy Führer.

VII

The aged Habsburger faded back into the realm or substance or whatever it was he had come from. They were not sorry to have him go, for his dynasty had never been celebrated for wit or charm. In his stead came a personage who rarely failed Lanny: the Knight Commander of the Bath and Grand Officer of the Legion of Honor. For the first time in his career in this world or the next he addressed Lanny as "Mr. Budd," and for the first time he reported himself as happily reunited with his duquesa. Apparently King Ottokar I was a dispenser of bliss—he had been extremely dictatorial on earth. Lanny was polite, but inwardly skeptical, until the spirit gave him a message for its earthly successor, Baron Schneider, and then a reference to Sir Basil's part in finding the gold of the *Hampshire*.

This was the devilish thing about the business of psychic research; just as you had decided that some medium was a fraud, you would get something that startled you, and then, likely as not, you would think it over and change your mind yet again. Had Robbie Budd's dealing with the owner of Le Creusot been mentioned in any of the Berlin newspapers? Certainly there were important persons in the city who knew about the matter; and that meant also their secretaries and underlings. The same was true regarding the cruiser *Hampshire*. Lanny had told Pröfenik about Sir Basil, though not about this gold; however, it had been only ten years since the treasure-seekers had set out, and the vessel had been equipped in Germany; it had returned to Hamburg, and Horace Hofman had been dined in Berlin, where he had met prominent persons, including Doktor Horace Greeley Hjalmar Schacht. So, if anybody set out to do a research job on Zaharoff in Germany, that was one of the things he might be expected to come upon.

VIII

All these thoughts were driven suddenly out of Lanny's mind, for here came the thing that he was waiting for; his heart began to pound uncomfortably, and he was glad the room was not well lighted. Said the thirteenth-century King of Bohemia: "There is a couple here, Germans and rather young; they speak in low voices and seem embarrassed to trouble Herr Budd. They say they troubled him once before, and now they want him to know that they have found each other."

"What are their names?" inquired Lanny; and really, he could hardly keep from trembling, for suppose this was a genuine medium, and suppose Trudi didn't know that Hess was present, and should blurt out: "I am your former wife." It wouldn't be like the Trudi of the real world, but who could guess what spirits might remember or forget, or how much they might know about the political situation? Truly it was taking a chance to have Hess sitting by—even though the communications might be only constructs of Lanny's subconscious mind!

He was proceeding upon the guess that Pröfenik was no medium, but a shrewd old scamp, making use of the material Lanny had given him. And apparently this was the case. The voice of Ottokar replied: "It is the man speaking and his voice is low. *Bitte, lauter, lieber Herr!* The name appears to be Schultz. Do you know any such person?"

"I cannot recall him."

"He gives the name Ludwig; then he says he is called Ludi. He tries to tell you about the place where he met you. It was in a large drawing-room, many persons present; they served coffee and other refreshments, and his wife was one of those who served as hostesses."

"Does he give the wife's name?"

"She was called Gertrud."

"I cannot recall any Gertrud Schultz."

"He says she was also known as Mueller. I ask, is that her maiden name, and he says no, she changed her name. I ask if they were divorced, and he does not say; apparently there is something very unhappy in their lives. He wants you to know that they are reunited now, and the pain is forgotten."

"Can they tell you anything more about the circumstances of their meeting with me?"

"He says they were artists, both of them, and they told you about their work; you showed an interest, very kindly, but they did not follow it up, because at that time they did not know that you were the stepson of Marcel Detaze, or that you were yourself such a distinguished expert."

"Thank them for me, and say that I wish them well; but I do not understand why they should come to me."

"They had come before and they feared that they had troubled your mind."

"Not at all; I have to confess that I had forgotten them. Have they any art works that I could see and might be interested in?"

"No, they are humble about their work. Ludi says that he was a commercial artist, and such work is only for the day."

"Does he wish to tell me anything about the cause of their unhappiness? Is it a story that I could have heard?"

There was a pause. Then: "The woman is weeping. She says she cannot bear to have it talked about."

"They aren't Jews, by any chance?"

"No, Aryans."

"Jews do not always look like Jews; and they take Aryan names —it is one of their favorite tricks."

"They say they are not Jews."

"Could they have been in any political trouble?"

"They don't want to talk about it; they are turning away; they have their arms about each other, as if they wanted you to know that they love each other deeply."

IX

The rest of the séance didn't amount to much. It was Hess's turn, and the spirit of Horst Wessel announced itself. The Nazi hero-martyr spoke of the song he had written, and was proud of this service to the cause. He told some of the circumstances of his earthly life, but did not mention that he had been a pimp. He made predictions as to the future triumphs of the Party and in general spoke in a way to warm the heart of a Party Führer. His last sentences were a triumphant prophecy that Austria would soon be joined to the Fatherland. He had studied for a year at the University of Vienna, and knew that frivolous people, he declared.

The wizard came out of his trance and emerged from the cabinet. He did not ask anything about what happened, but perhaps he could feel in the atmosphere that he had not scored a hit. He offered to cast the Deputy's horoscope, but Hess said that had been done many times, and he had more important business. Lanny asked if the Professor had tried to send his astral body to the Berghof, and the old man said that he had done so, and had seen Lanny and Hess gazing out over the mountains, and also at something which looked like playing cards—which they hadn't done. No mention of French wrestling!

As they went out, Lanny left an envelope on the table; he noticed that Hess failed to do the same, and wondered if Party chieftains enjoyed the privilege of free séance tickets. When they were in the car, the Deputy said: "That seemed to me pretty thin stuff."

"I agree," replied the other.

"All that about Horst Wessel—he could have got it out of a pamphlet which the Party sells for five pfennigs."

"Zaharoff always called me Lanny; never 'mister' in his life."

"That King Ottokar is a new one to me. Did you ever hear of him?"

"He was a king of Bohemia when it was one of the German states. Grillparzer wrote a play about him."

"No sense in any of it that I can see. We wasted an evening." There was a pause; Lanny waiting to let his companion bring up the crucial subject. He thought it would come, and it did.

"And all that about the Schultz couple. Did you make anything out of that?"

"Not very much. But one thing comes back to my memory—I believe those same people appeared in a séance I had nearly a year ago with a woman medium here in Berlin. There was a spirit who called himself Ludi Schultz, and he was wandering around trying to find his wife who was called Trudi."

"Did you tell Pröfenik about that?"

"That's what I'm trying to get clear in my mind. You see, I had a long talk with him, two or three hours. I mentioned the fact that a number of times I had had reports of spirits who seemed to be just drifting in and then out again. They insisted they had met me somewhere, though I couldn't recall them. It is possible that I may have given the names of the Schultzs; I can't feel sure."

"It makes all the difference," declared Hess. "If you told him, he could easily have made up the rest."

"You know how it is when something seems to be just hanging on the edge of your mind, and you think you've got hold of it but you can't quite. There's that business about women serving coffee and refreshments; there were several places where I was asked to give a talk on art, and of course I met no end of art people, and heard a lot of names."

"Pröfenik could guess that without trouble," insisted the Deputy.

"I know; but I keep reminding myself of this: If a man gets certain facts consciously, those facts are in his subconscious mind also, and they are just as apt to come out in a genuine trance as anything else.

Suppose Pröfenik had read a five-pfennig pamphlet about Horst
Wessel, his subconsciousness might weave those facts into a personality
without the least dishonesty."

"I never thought of that, Mr. Budd. Few people realize how complicated this subject is."

"You bet! It's a whole universe, whose laws we are only beginning
to guess at. Every now and then I have an impulse to follow up some
clue. Perhaps you can advise me: would there be any chance of finding a list of commercial artists in Berlin during the last few years? Do
they have an association or anything like that?"

"I don't happen to know, but I can find out. There are no associations in Germany that we don't know about."

"It seems to me that would be a good way to check upon Pröfenik.
He gave a number of details; and certainly not many Ludis have
married Trudis."

Again Lanny waited, and again the trap he had set was sprung.
"By the way," said Hess, "didn't the old rascal say the woman was
called Mueller also?"

"Yes, I recall that."

"Why should she have two names?"

"That is one of the things we may find out. Often artists take
brush names, of course."

"That might be. But a man in my business thinks of another possibility. A lot of artists and people of that sort have been opposing
our *Regierung*, and we've had to be rough with them. Maybe we
might find that she has some sort of police record."

"By heck! There's an idea! Could you have it looked up, do you
suppose?"

"Of course I could. We have a master cardfile."

"I don't want to put you to a lot of bother——"

"No bother at all. I'll tell my secretary to call up the police in the
morning, and if there are or were any such persons I'll have the data
within an hour."

"I never expected to have the help of the Gestapo in my psychic
researches!" chuckled the son of Budd-Erling.

X

Lanny walked into the Hotel Adlon with his feet hardly touching
the floor of the lobby. He didn't want to sleep; he wanted to lie on
his back in the dark and whisper silently: "Trudi! Trudi!" Once more

he felt that she was close to him, and that if he reached out a little farther he would make contact with her. He would say: "Are you there?"—and then argue: "Why should I have to wait on the Gestapo?" He thought of some of the phantasms he had read about, phantasms of the living as well as of the dead. Such stories went back as far as recorded history; also, you would hardly mention the subject in any company without finding some person who had had such an experience, often while refusing to believe it. Lanny had told Trudi a lot about it; she had never known whether to believe it or not, but surely now she would be thinking about it and trying it as he was.

He kept staring ahead of him into the darkness at the foot of his bed, but he saw nothing, he heard nothing, and at last he dropped off to sleep. Then he dreamed about Trudi. Did that mean that she was dreaming about him? Men had been wondering about dreams since the beginning of time, and weaving all sorts of fantasies on the subject. Now came the Freudians, with an explanation which they called scientific; but what would become of their theories if you admitted telepathy into the psyche? A bull in a china shop could do no more damage. Lanny had heard that of late Freud had become convinced of the reality of telepathy, but how could he explain dreams when they might have hopped in from the mind of any other person on earth? Lanny thought about this while he was shaving, and wished that while in Vienna he had called upon the learned Jewish doctor and asked for the answer to that question.

Lanny looked over the morning papers, full of denunciations of the treacherous Austrian government, with demands for immediate action by the insulted Reich. Lanny knew that no Nazi editor ever clamored for action until Dr. Goebbels had tipped him off that action was coming soon. He tried to read on, but could hardly think about Austria's troubles this morning; he thought only of the telephone. What time did Hess reach his office? The Gestapo, of course, would be open all night; its agents came and went, and its favorite time for pouncing upon its victims was at three or four in the morning.

The mail was brought to his room; also a cablegram, which proved to be mysterious and puzzling. It was from New York, and read: "Honored relative will call"; the signature was: "Bessie Budd Host." Lanny didn't have to figure long to realize that this was code for Johannes Robin, who wouldn't risk embarrassing Lanny by signing a name so notorious in Germany. Lanny had taken many agreeable trips on the yacht *Bessie Budd*, and had not forgotten who had invited him and paid the bills. If Johannes had signed the message "Bessie

Budd Owner" or "Bessie Budd Proprietor," that might have sounded phony; but "Host" was an inconspicuous word and might be a name—indeed, Lanny had once met a man who bore it, and if he had married Lanny's half-sister, her name would have been Bessie Budd Host!

Any relative of Johannes was, of course, a Jew; and all Jewish relatives were honored, that their days might be long in the land. Alas, their days promised to be short in Germany, and also in Austria! This would be some person in trouble, of course. Lanny felt a sinking of the heart, for he couldn't help any Jews now, he had another job—and how could he explain matters to his old friend? It might be that all the caller would want was money, and that would be easy enough. But usually what Jews wanted was to get out of Germany, and that might take a lot of money, more than Lanny had in Naziland. Also, they wanted passports to America; and Lanny was one of a hundred and three persons who could make no move along that line.

XI

The telephone rang; the secretary of Herr Reichminister Hess, desiring to know if Herr Budd could call this morning at the Herr Reichminister's office. It was then eleven, and Lanny said he had an engagement to lunch with General Göring, but would come at once and hoped that he could have the interview without delay. He stepped into a taxi, and gave his destination, the headquarters of the NSDAP; then he leaned back in the seat and closed his eyes to the traffic and the signals. Silently, and without movement of the lips, he read himself a lecture and taught himself a role. "*Now!* You're going to get bad news, and how are you going to take it? You might as well make up your mind that she's dead! There's not a chance of anything else; and what are you going to say? You've got to talk telepathy, or spirits, and not show any feelings—not have any feelings, because if you do Hess will know it. Watch every movement, every word, every thought; for this is dynamite."

Silently and without motion of the lips, Lanny practiced what he was going to feel and say if Hess told him that Trudi was dead; then—a still harder task, because less expected—what he would say if Hess told him that she was in a concentration camp. This went on all the way to the large building over which the Deputy and Party Führer presided; all the way up in the elevator; all the way through the closely guarded anterooms and into the great man's presence. Hess wore the simple brownshirt uniform, probably the same he had worn the night before. He looked stern and impressive at his large flat-topped desk with several telephones and many buttons, the symbols of authority in the modern world. Lanny was treading in one of the centers of the most cruel authority in centuries; this dark, tight-lipped man with the bushy eyebrows meeting over the bridge of his nose might cause serious trouble for a presidential agent unmasked. Or would he do any unmasking? If he had penetrated Lanny's secret, would he not be more apt to keep it to himself and his dread organization, and give Lanny rope with which to hang himself? Treason within treason, and treachery piled on treachery!

The Deputy got down to business, having been told that his visitor had no time to spare. Open before him was a portfolio with many papers and one hand was resting upon them as he spoke. "Mr. Budd, we have uncovered something interesting here. It looks as if the spirits knew more than we gave them credit for."

"Is that so, Herr Reichsminister?"

"I find we have a long record on these people, and of the blackest sort. They were Social-Democratic agitators, Marxists of the reddest dye, over a period of ten years or so."

"Oh, my God!" said the well-rehearsed visitor.

"The man was caught early, and committed suicide in Oranienburg. The woman got away, and caused us trouble for three years or more. She was center of a well-organized seditious group. She took the name of Mueller, and several other aliases—I won't tell them to you, because it might be interesting to see if you can get them through Madame or any other medium."

"By all means! What happened to the woman?"

"She fled to France; but recently she made the mistake of coming back into Germany. She died in Dachau two or three months ago."

So there it was; and Lanny never blinked an eyelash, never changed color by the slightest shade. He spoke the words that he had drilled into his mind: "*Herrgott!* This is really a case of supernormal power!"

"I think we have to admit it. That old bastard has got something after all."

"Well, that's the way it goes, Herr Reichsminister—you meet with disappointments and you are bored night after night; and then, just as you are ready to quit, you run into something like this. I am deeply grateful to you for digging this story out for me."

"Not at all—I am just as much interested as you. We'll go back and try again sometime and see if we can get more details."

"I'll try with Madame, also. Truly, it's a fascinating thing, and when you once get started, you are drawn in deeper and deeper. Imagine those two spirits going off hand in hand—and not wanting to tell their story in your presence! I wonder if they are still afraid of you."

"It's comforting to know they are where they can't do any harm to our cause." Lanny wondered, was this entirely true? Or was there something deep inside Hess that was afraid of what that couple might do to him from the spirit world? Or after he himself had entered that world!

XII

Lanny had time enough to walk to the Ministerial Residence, and he needed it to work off the grief and rage which possessed him. No forecast, no accumulated imagining, could equal the reality of knowing that Trudi was gone forever; that his efforts of the past six months had been futility, and his hope of seeing her again was vain. The scientific monster called Nazidom, the beast with the brains of an engineer, had got her in its clutches, and had treated her as it had treated so many thousands of other victims. Images of what they had done to her swept over him, but he struggled to put them aside—for that way lay madness. He must hate these Nazis, but it must be a cold and quiet hatred, rationalized and organized, scientific like their own.

He told himself that it was war; Trudi had been a prisoner of war, and they had treated her according to their code. They had waged war upon her in their dungeons, first in Paris and then in Dachau, trying to break her spirit, to force her to betray her party and her friends. In this they had failed, Lanny was sure; the fact that he was here, a free man in Berlin, and about to enter the home of the Nazi Number Two, was proof enough of that. With all their ingenuity, their knowledge of physiology and psychology applied to breaking the human will, they had not been able to break Trudi's. She had won that war—or so she would feel, and Lanny must train himself to feel the same.

It was a question about which men would always argue, according to their temperaments and their creeds. The Führer of the Nazis had declared that the greatest spirit could not function when the body in which that spirit was housed was beaten to death with rubber truncheons. Thus the new religion of the sword; and all the soldiers of that religion were taking their prophet's commandment and acting upon it. But Lanny had read Emerson in his youth, and had been assured that the heedless world had never lost one accent of the Holy Ghost. Which was the truth? Which was the word of God and which of Satan? Satan rebelling against God—that was not just a legend, a poet's imagining; that was something that went on every hour in the heart of every man alive. Here, in this Satan's world, with "truth forever on the scaffold, wrong forever on the throne," a man had to fight for his faith in God, and risk his happiness and even his life in the worship of the Holy Ghost.

This much was certain: the spirit of Trudi Schultz lived on in Lanny Budd, and the Nazis could never kill it there unless they killed him—or unless he let it die. It would live on in the hearts and minds of Trudi's comrades both inside and outside of Naziland. It would live in the hearts of other people, if ever the time came that Lanny was free to tell Trudi's story and spread her message. Such was the real and authentic magic of the spirit. Even the Nazis had discovered it, and had their roll of martyrs which they solemnly read, and their song about Horst Wessel, a rowdy whom they had made into a hero because he had been killed in street fighting with the Communists.

The Nazi religion was for one nation, one *Herrenvolk*, which aspired to rule all others. They called themselves a "race," but that was just a piece of nonsense which their fraudulent scientists had invented to make themselves more important; there was no such thing as "Aryan"; there was only German, and even that was open to question. The correct word was Prussian, or more precisely East-Elbian—a little group of proud and bigoted aristocrats whose power was based upon the ownership of huge estates, in a part of Europe where the armies of Napoleon had not penetrated to break up land monopoly. These proud Junkers, nearly all of them high-ranking military men, were using Adi Schickl-gruber the gutter-rat as their newest tool, their rabble-rouser and mob-deceiver, and when they were through with him they would send him to join his tens of thousands of victims.

National Socialism versus true Socialism, racism versus humanity— that was the struggle between Satan and God in the modern world. Trudi Schultz had been what her predecessor Heinrich Heine had called "a good soldier of humanity." She had lived and died for her cause, and had passed on her sword to her husband, who must keep it sharp and clean, and use it with that skill and determination without which battles are not won. Lanny would keep the Trudi-ghost alive in his heart, and somehow, someday—perhaps with the help of Franklin D. Roosevelt—he would see that spirit of justice and brotherhood spreading over the world and conquering the forces of bigotry and despotism.

XIII

Right now it was Lanny's job to clench his hands, set his teeth, compose his mind, and go into a granite palace and entertain a big fat lump of vanity, greed, and arrogance dressed up in a pale blue broadcloth uniform with white stripes down the pants. He might have telephoned and said that he had been taken suddenly ill, but that would have been the act of a weakling. Göring was an important man to a presidential agent; from him Lanny got not merely money for the cause, but information and prestige enabling him to get more whenever he wanted it. The Trudi-ghost inside him said "Go!"—so he put his best man-of-the-world smile upon his face, and went up the steps of the splendid building from which the Reichstag-fire criminals had operated. He was welcomed by his old friend Furtwaengler, who, he learned, had just been made into an Oberst—lower rank would not be proper in the exalted regions to which Hermann Wilhelm Göring had recently been raised.

Lanny was escorted to the *Nummer Zwei's* private office, and went to him with hand extended, crying: "*Heil, Herr Feldmarschall!*" and then: "*Darf ich seine Eminenz noch Hermann nennen?*" In reply the great man put his arm over the visitor's shoulder and led him to the flat-topped desk where the jeweled mace of office reposed. He gave an American a chance to see how it felt, and Lanny wielded it with spirit, pointing it in front of him and commanding: "*Vorwärts, Kameraden! In die Zukunft!*"—into the future. He knew where the Nazi future lay, and looking at *Der Dicke* he added, with a grin: "*Nach Wien!*"

They always enjoyed each other's company, because Hermann had a sense of humor, and Lanny the easy-going informality which is supposed to be American. While he ate his broiled salmon and then his breast of chicken with wine sauce, he told his adventures in Austria and at the Berghof. It was easy enough to make fun of Schuschnigg and Stahremberg; and when Lanny came to narrate how the Führer had dressed the former down, and how everybody in the house had stood all day with his ear in a crack of the door, *Der Dicke* roared with laughter so that he came near to choking. Lanny even ventured to imitate the Führer's *forte fortissimo* tones—something which no German would have dared, but which was good clean fun from the land of unlimited possibilities.

Later on they talked seriously, of course. The new Feldmarschall wanted to know all about how England felt and how France felt regarding the Austrian situation. "England," of course, meant the group at Wickthorpe Castle, and "France" meant that at Baron Schneider's stag dinner. Lanny told about both in detail, hereby adding greatly to his social stature. So much so that before they parted *Der Dicke* said, paternally: "*Hör mal, Lanny!* It is absurd for a man like you to be wasting his time selling paintings. Why don't you let me pay you some real money and do some real work for me?"

"*Na, na, Hermann!*" replied the younger man, in filial spirit. "We have had such a pleasant visit, and you want to spoil it! Don't you know that you would feel differently about me if you hired me? Then you would start demanding things, and would think I was lazy and a *flâneur*. But when I come in once in a while like this and enjoy your company, you have a friend and not just one more agent. You learn a lot more from me, because I have been visiting other people in the same spirit—and telling them all about you."

"Nothing bad, I hope," said the fat man, with mock concern.

"What do I know that is bad?" grinned Lanny. "You enjoy my jokes, you have a beautiful wife who is going to present Germany with an heir—and you own the Hermann Göring Stahlwerke!"

BOOK SIX

A Full Hot Horse

23

Les Beaux Yeux de Ma Casette

I

IF LANNY had been a newspaper correspondent or a sight-seeing tourist, he would have headed for Vienna again, for it was obvious that the "big story" was going to break soon. Schuschnigg, casting about in desperation, had hit upon the idea of a plebiscite; the people of his country would be invited to say whether or not they wanted *Anschluss* with Hitler Germany. Nothing could have been calculated to bring matters more quickly to a head, for Adi knew that the people of Austria would vote three to one against him, therefore he took the proposal as a defiance. Schuschnigg must have expected this, for he allowed only four days between his announcement and the proposed vote. The newspapers of Berlin burst forth with stories of Communists in possession of Vienna, mobs attacking Germans on the streets, and Czechoslovakia sending artillery to support the Red uprising.

Lanny knew that this meant immediate action, but it wasn't his job to witness it. Experienced newspapermen would be flying there, and the story of whatever happened would be laid upon F.D.R.'s breakfast tray each morning. It was Lanny's job to find out what was coming next, and he thought he knew. He was seized by a desire to report once more to Washington, and try to persuade his Number One to take some step to stop the new World War before it had spread any further. It was still not too late; if America would show the way, and get England and France together, the smaller states would join, to say nothing of the Soviet Union. The dictators might be halted—and who could guess how many millions of lives might be saved?

Lanny had a picture to get from Furtwaengler, and while he was waiting for this the telephone rang and a man's voice said: "Herr Budd, have you received a cablegram from Herr Host in New York?" When Lanny replied that he had, the voice inquired: "Would you be so kind as to meet me this evening? I will be in the Hotel Eden lobby at eight." Lanny, experienced in conspiracy, replied: "I will be there."

He had not recognized the voice, but assumed that the stranger would know him. He dined alone, looked over the evening papers, and then went for a walk, making certain that no one was trailing him. At five minutes before the hour he strolled into the spacious lobby of the Eden and took a seat. Promptly on the stroke of eight there came a man whom he knew well, though he had not seen him for years—Aaron Schönhaus, elder brother of Rahel Robin, Freddi's widow. Lanny waited until he had passed on, then got up and followed him outside and around the corner. They walked for a block or so, until Lanny was satisfied that no one was following; then he walked faster and caught up.

"Well, Aaron," he said, "glad to see you. How are the old folks?"

"Not too well," was the reply. "Excuse me for meeting you this way. There are reasons which I will explain. I have a car, and it will be safer if we drive."

He stopped in front of a parked car and unlocked it, slipped into the driver's seat, and Lanny took the seat beside him. Lanny was destined to have a lot to do with that car, but he didn't know it and paid no special attention, merely noting that it was a medium-priced sedan of German make and apparently little used. There was a robe and he drew it over his knees while his in-law-once-removed—if there is such a relationship—started the car and drove at a moderate pace on a wide boulevard.

II

Lanny had met the Schönhaus family soon after Freddi's marriage a decade ago, but he had seen little of them, for they had no special interest in their daughter's Socialist ideas and no aspiration to move in the exalted circles which Lanny frequented. The father of the family was a lawyer on a small scale, and being a Jew, had been forbidden to practice after the coming of the Nazis. He had lived on the bounty of his son, who had some sort of commission business about which Lanny was vague in his mind. Lanny knew that Aaron had a family, and recently had heard that his wife had died; that was all.

The man was several years younger than Lanny, but looked older, for the years had heaped burdens upon him. He was smallish, with a smooth-shaven face and sallow complexion, and wore a black overcoat of no fashionable cut and a hat which showed traces of wear; but that was no proof of his financial condition, for most Jews kept themselves obscure in these dangerous times. He knew English, but not too well, and spoke German to Lanny. He told the status of the family. Mama had developed a cancer, and would not have many years to live; she was not able to be moved to America, and Papa would not leave her, but devoted all his time and thought to taking care of her. They had both been frantically begging Aaron to take his children and emigrate to America; he had money put away, and at any time the Nazis might seize him and torture him to make him give it up. At last he had yielded, and Johannes had managed to get the passport visas. Aaron had paid the necessary bribes here in Berlin and had his exit permits.

He asked Lanny about his sister, who was married again, to a man employed in Johannes's office in New York. She had another baby besides Freddi's son, little Johannes. Lanny reported that they lived with the old folks and got along well; he always saw them when he visited Connecticut. Little Johannes, just eight years old, was the image of his father, and a most lovable child. The Schönhaus family knew what Lanny had done in his efforts to save Freddi from the Nazis—no doubt that was Aaron's reason for coming to him now.

It wasn't a great favor the man wanted; simply to get a little of his money out of Naziland. Said he: "I have always been an independent man; and maybe I think too much about money, but it goes against my nature to land in New York a pauper. I can borrow from Johannes, of course; but he's a dictatorial man—without realizing it, I think—and I prefer to be on my own. You understand, I have made my own way in the world, and earned what I have by hard work. I don't see why I should turn it over to my racial persecutors if I can help it."

"Certainly not," declared Lanny, venturing that far out of his ivory tower.

"Under the Nazi law I'm allowed to take out only fifty marks, and that wouldn't get me and three children very far toward New York. But here is this car, which represents a good chunk of money. I'm guessing that you didn't drive into Germany this time."

"How did you guess it?"

"I read of your arrival in the *Mittag*, so I judged you had arrived in the morning, and I hardly thought you'd have been driving overnight in a storm."

"A good guess. I'm not driving, and I have a couple of paintings to take out."

"That fits right in. This car costs about five thousand marks when it's new, and it ought to bring at least half that in Belgium or Holland. That would be enough to take me and my children to New York and keep us there until I get to work. Nominally the car doesn't belong to me; I have a gentile friend who is so kind as to keep it in his name. He would sell it to you—that is, you wouldn't have to pay any money, but take his receipt for twenty-five hundred marks and the car would be yours. You would drive it to any place you say outside Germany, and I'd meet you there and pick it up."

So there was Lanny being tempted again! Out of the kindness of his heart he would undertake to help some oppressed person—and forget for the nonce that he carried the destinies of his native land and perhaps of the world in his keeping! —Or would he? Doubts assailed him, and he said: "I don't know the law, Aaron. Is a foreigner permitted to buy a car in Germany and take it out?"

"Why not? It's simply export, and the Germans are working like the devil to promote foreign trade. They'd figure they'd be getting good American *Valuta*, with which to buy copper and oil and rubber and cotton and other materials of war."

"But isn't there some sort of permit needed? And mightn't there be a tax?"

"If there's a tax I'll give you the money to pay it with. It wouldn't do for me to be making inquiries, but I'll have my friend, the nominal owner of the car, do it. Or since you have influential friends, you might ask and assure yourself."

III

That was the way they left the matter. In the morning, as chance would have it, Lanny received a cablegram about another of those paintings which Göring had confiscated from Johannes Robin's palace and which didn't happen to conform to the great man's artistic taste. Lanny called up Furtwaengler to make the deal, and at the end of the conversation remarked: "By the way, Herr Oberst, I came in by train this time, and I have several paintings to take home. I have a chance to buy a German-made car at a reasonable price, and I wonder what the regulations are on that subject."

"I don't happen to know," replied the SS officer. "But you don't have to bother about regulations in any case. We'll be glad to fix it up for you."

"I wouldn't want to bother Seine Exzellenz about so small a matter."

"Of course not. I know his wishes without asking, and I'll have the office fix you up with a permit that will enable you to go through without delay."

"That's very kind of you indeed," replied the visitor, and thought, how very convenient is dictatorship—for the dictators and their friends! He felt himself being seduced by the perquisites of office.

He had got the license number and other data on the car, and gave these to the Hauptmann over the phone. The permit, properly signed and stamped, was delivered from the office of the Reichsminister-Feldmarschall that same afternoon, and in the evening Lanny met his Jewish near-relative by appointment and told him O.K. Lanny had been intending to leave at once, but might be delayed a couple of days awaiting a cabled remittance on the new picture deal. Aaron said that was so much the better; he would arrange for the car to have a thorough checking to make sure that it was in order for the journey. They made their arrangements for the sale and the meeting in Amsterdam, where Lanny had word of paintings that he wanted to inspect. Lanny would set out early in the morning, and Aaron would take the night express with his children; they would meet at the Hotel Amstel. Lanny would have offered to crowd them into the car, as he had once done with the Robin family, but they agreed that this would be too conspicuous. A carload of Jews and a permit from Marshal Göring wouldn't fit together very well.

IV

It seemed delightfully simple. Promptly at eight in the morning Lanny paid his bill and had his bags and his carefully wrapped art treasures carried down to the door. There was Aaron, looking like a humble deliveryman, with the car and the bill of sale duly signed. He tipped his hat respectfully and walked off, while Lanny saw his belongings properly loaded. What more natural than that this important American should have bought a car in which to transport himself on a not too raw and windy day in March? He tipped the bellboys and the magnifico of the door, and they all bowed and smiled, and away he went.

"For God's sake, drive carefully," Aaron had said, "for this will be all I have left in the world." Lanny had attached no special importance to this remark, answering lightly that he had motored all over Europe since his boyhood—how many hundreds of thousands of miles he wouldn't attempt to figure.

The *Autobahnen* of the Third Reich had been constructed by General Todt, and their purpose was to take the mechanized armies of Germany to whichever of her borders might be threatened by a foe. Robbie said these roads were a mistake, because in a long war Germany would find herself short of both gasoline and rubber, and be forced to fall back upon her railroads, neglected for a long time. But Adolf Hitler didn't intend to fight any long wars; he intended to overwhelm his foes one by one, and his mind was attracted by everything modern and repelled by everything old. So here were splendid four-lane highways, passing under or over all intersecting roads, straight most of the time, so that you could roll along at whatever speed you chose.

The new car was in perfect order, no rattles or squeaks and no missing of cylinders. The Germans were proud of their cars, and this one sped straight to the west at something like a hundred kilometers an hour. Lanny, used to driving, thought about other matters. Being a sociable person, he thought about the friends he was going to see on this trip; what he was going to tell Rick and Nina about Trudi, what he was going to tell his father about Hitler and Göring; then, the items of news about Austria in the papers which he had glanced at before leaving, and had brought with him for more careful reading. If F.D.R. had read his agent's reports, he would be thinking: "That fellow Lanny had it exactly right!" The fellow Lanny was entitled to what satisfaction he could get out of this reflection.

V

Without incident of any sort he arrived at the Dutch border. It was the second time he had driven up to that black-and-white-painted barrier with a permit from Göring's office in his hand. The first time had been by night and this time was by day, but otherwise there was no difference; the border officials fell into the same state of abjectness, and it was: "*Gewiss, mein Herr,*" and "*Selbstverständlich, mein Herr,*" and "*Bitte sehr, mein Herr.*" He didn't have to leave the car; he didn't even have to wait while the hood was lifted and the engine number checked. Anything that Göring's office ordered was right. "*Glückliche Reise, mein Herr!*" The barrier was lifted, the car moved on, and there were the Dutch border guards to inspect his passport with its visa.

It was afternoon, and Lanny was hungry; he saw what he judged was a clean and proper eating place on the outskirts of a town, and he stopped, parking his car by the curb and locking it. He took the Berlin papers with him and read them while disposing of an omelette and a salad. Schuschnigg had invited the people of Austria to vote on the question of their independence and had proposed to present them only a ballot marked Yes. If they wanted to vote No they would have to bring their own ballots. But this had caused such a clamor at the last

minute that it had been decided to make the ballot secret and to provide
spaces for both Yes and No. Lanny thought, how the job-printing concerns of Vienna must be working right now!

VI

His meal eaten and the check paid, he went out to the car. It was
still there, but alas, not the same! Some careless driver, or perhaps one
swerving to avoid a pedestrian, had struck Aaron Schönhaus's car at
the front, on the driver's side, farthest from the curb. At first glance
Lanny thought it must have been a terrific crash, for the bumper had
been badly bent and the fender crumpled like paper. Whoever had
done it had not waited for explanations or apologies; even in well-
ordered and law-abiding Holland they had hit-and-run drivers! A few
spectators, mostly children, stood looking at the damage.

Lanny's first thought was, had the wheel or the axle been bent? In so
serious a crash it was to be expected. But then he saw something that
he had never before observed on any automobile in his driving experience: where the fender had been crumpled and the enamel knocked
off, there was a bright yellow gleam, such as belonged to no metal
used in the manufacture of vehicles. And the bumpers, which are usually of steel with a handsome finish of nickel—where they had been hit
the outside finish had been knocked off, and there was the same gleam,
which could be only one thing in this world: *Gold!* Gold fenders and
gold running boards painted over with black, and gold bumpers painted
with some sort of silver—that was the car which Aaron Schönhaus had
prepared for his near-relative to drive out of Naziland under permit
from the Field Marshal in command of the German Air Force! "By
heck!" said Lanny Budd to himself—again and then again.

The wheel was apparently uninjured, and Lanny realized that it
hadn't been so serious a crash as he had thought. Gold is soft, and the
driver of the other car must have been astonished by the results of a
moderate bump. And now, here were people staring—and did they
know gold when they saw it, and what were they making of the
spectacle? Lanny unlocked the car and slid into the driver's seat; he
started the engine, released the brake, and gently tried the car. It
moved, and without ceremony he started and left the sightseers behind.

Rolling westward, thinking busy thoughts. So long as he drove,
no one would pay attention to a battered car; but as soon as he stopped
again, someone would note one of the most exciting of all spectacles.

And of course the same thing would happen in any garage where he might take the car for storage or repairs. Lanny was repeating on a small scale the experience of that humble laborer in the high sierras of California who had been working at repairs to a saw mill, and had noticed the same exciting gleam coming from the bed of a small stream.

Manifestly, the first problem was to cover up that secret. Coming to a town of larger size, Lanny hunted up a paint shop and bought a small can of black enamel and one of silver paint, also two small brushes. Already another crowd had gathered about the car; he left them behind, and outside the town stopped at an unfrequented spot and carefully covered all the exposed surfaces of the gold. He knew that the wind would help to dry the paint, and meantime it would gather dust and look less new and shiny; he would no longer have a treasure car, but just one which had been run into—a sight to be gazed at, but not with revolutionary thoughts, such as of wrenching off a piece and sticking it into your pocket!

VII

The traveler drove, chastened and slow, for he had plenty of time to reach Amsterdam, and must do nothing to risk another crash or to attract attention. Meantime, he did some mental arithmetic. The United States government paid thirty-five dollars an ounce for gold, which fixed the world price; nobody would sell it anywhere for much less. Thirty-five times sixteen is five hundred and sixty dollars a pound. Lanny guessed that the outside appendages of this car, when made of the ordinary material, would weigh at least a hundred pounds. He knew that gold weighs two or three times as much, so it was safe to guess that the clever Aaron had managed to smuggle out of Naziland well over a hundred and fifty thousand dollars!

How had he achieved the making of these parts? It couldn't have been an easy matter, for they are not hammered out by hand but stamped by great machines. It would have to be done where there was an electric furnace, and perhaps in the plant where the car had been made. A group of workmen might do it at night; it would be risky, and involve the payment of a lot of money—to say nothing of the problems of purchasing and turning over to workmen such an amount of gold. Somehow the job had been put through; and Lanny promised himself an interesting story on the morrow. He might have considered that Aaron had played a rather shabby trick upon his near-relative, but he decided to overlook that. He had "got away with it," and no doubt Aaron meant to offer him a fee—which he wouldn't take.

There was nothing to do now but put up at the Hotel Amstel. Lanny took the car to the garage himself. The garagemen were sympathetic about his accident, and asked if he wanted repairs made, but Lanny said No, he had to leave the next day, and would have the work done at home. The damaged parts looked all right, and anyone who noticed the fresh paint would assume that the American traveler had tried to make his car look a bit more respectable. Lanny shivered at the thought of leaving a fortune like that lying unguarded overnight, but it was what the owner had told him to do, and he had no choice. He diverted his thoughts with the afternoon papers and an American movie, and then went to bed and slept the sleep of an honest anti-Nazi.

VIII

Next morning there was *De Telegraaf*, delivered with Lanny's breakfast tray; also *Het Volk*, the Socialist paper, not usually called for by the guests of palace hotels. Both gave news from Vienna; the plebiscite had been called off, and Hitler was demanding Schuschnigg's resignation. Lanny didn't need to read any correspondent's explanations of the whys and wherefores. He could imagine Adi's ravings— perhaps directly to Schuschnigg over the telephone. He could imagine Papen besieging the Chancellery, and the swastika mobs parading, singing about how the world was going to belong to them, and shouting denunciations of that vile form of political sham known as democracy. They would be smashing windows and plundering Jewish shops as proof of their own political and racial superiority.

Lanny bathed and shaved and dressed, and was ready for his guests. The train from Berlin was due, and he could be sure that Aaron wouldn't delay very long to make certain that his treasure was safe. He would probably phone from the station. But no call came, and Lanny decided that the train might be late, or that Aaron was taking a taxi and coming to the hotel. He read a magazine; then he called the office, and learned that the train had arrived on time and other passengers had reached the hotel. Lanny felt a sinking inside him; he didn't need to ask anything more, for he had been through it all nearly five years ago, in Calais where he had waited for the yacht *Bessie Budd* to arrive with the Robin family and it hadn't arrived.

Neither did Aaron Schönhaus arrive, and Lanny never heard from him, directly or indirectly. The art expert spent a miserable day waiting in his room for a telephone call, watching train schedules and imagining calamities. Certainly if anything had delayed Aaron's starting, he would send a telegram, or call Lanny on the phone, or have his trusted gentile friend do that service. Silence like this, a complete blackout, could mean only one thing—that the Nazis had grabbed the unfortunate Jew as they had grabbed his father-in-law at the outset of their *Regierung*. There just wasn't any possibility that with all that treasure at stake, its owner would have failed somehow to get word to its trustee.

What could have happened? Had the Gestapo got word about the gold car? If so, why hadn't they stopped the car at the border? Had Lanny just got through by a few seconds or minutes? And if so, what would be the effect upon Lanny's future? They would surely take it for granted that he had been a fellow-conspirator and was sharing in the loot. And would *Der Dicke* be furious? Or would he roar with laughter, discovering that the son of Budd-Erling wasn't the noble idealist he pretended to be, but was as greedy for gold as *Der Dicke* himself?

Or could there be some other reason for Aaron's arrest, having nothing to do with the car? Had he been so foolish as to try to bring out some money on his person? Or had the Nazis grabbed him on general principles, because he was a Jew, and must have money hidden somewhere. Did they play a cat-and-mouse game with such poor devils, letting them bribe officials and then not get what they had paid for? No, for that would stop the sources of good income. There must have been some other reason, some slip that a too-clever schemer had made at the last moment.

In the case of Johannes and his family Lanny had gone into Germany and worked hard to help them; but he couldn't do that again. His situation had changed and he was no longer a free man. Moreover, he had been heavily in debt to Johannes, and Freddi had been his comrade, whereas Aaron was a comparative stranger—one of thousands of unfortunates whom Lanny was trying to help wholesale but couldn't help individually. He must arrange for the packing and shipping of his paintings, and then go on to his job.

He sent a cablegram to Johannes Robin: "Property here but owner not arrived circumstances compel proceeding England taking property for safety address care Rick." He signed this "Bessie Guest," and did not send it from the hotel but from a telegraph office. If by any chance a Gestapo agent was trying to find the car, there was no reason to make the task easier.

Lanny drove to Calais, where the Channel crossing was short, so that he wouldn't have to leave the car on a ferry-boat all night. He drove to The Reaches, where he told his story to Nina and Rick and discussed what should be done. Obviously, no one in his right mind would desire to drive a gold car, especially when it was damaged; there could be no safe place to store it, and the thing to do was have the gold parts taken off and melted. Rick agreed to attend to this, and if Lanny hadn't heard from Aaron or Johannes in the meantime, Lanny would take a bank draft to Connecticut and turn it over to Rahel Robin, her brother's heir if he was dead. Lanny was never going to put anything into writing about this matter, and would make sure that neither Rahel nor Johannes talked about his part in it.

IX

The English newspapers were full of the details of sensational events in Austria. Schuschnigg had resigned, and the Nazi Seyss-Inquart had assumed authority. "Tourists" who had been visiting Vienna had suddenly turned into *SS Standart Neun und Neunzig,* and occupied the public buildings of the city. All night Nazi mobs had been parading through the streets, screaming *"Sieg heil!"* and the battle-cry of *Anschluss,* which was *"Ein Volk, ein Reich, ein Führer!"* The new government invited German troops into Austria to preserve order—and that, of course, was the "legality" which was Adi's special fetish. At dawn the long motorized columns crossed the border at various places and sped toward the capital. Later that Saturday the Führer himself entered by way of the town of Braunau, where he had been born; the people strewed flowers in his path and hailed him as their deliverer. He visited the graves of his father and mother and told the assembled crowds that he was carrying out "a divine commission." To Rick and Nina Lanny said: "Mohammed!"

It was the end of Austria. The very name was abolished; it was to be the Ostmark, and Seyss-Inquart was to be *Statthalter.* On Monday, March 14, Hitler was driven into Vienna. A plot to shoot him had been discovered, so he showed himself only for a few minutes from the balcony of the Hotel Imperial, and did not make the expected speech. Next day he flew back to Berlin, where he had work to do.

Now was his chance to show the world what a "plebiscite" could be. He would hold one for the whole of Greater Germany, including the Ostmark, asking the people if they approved the *Anschluss;* he would carry on a whole month's campaign of parades, mass meetings, and speeches, in which he would tell the people that this was "a holy vote." And meanwhile the plundering and killing of Jews would go on all over the newly conquered land; women of refinement would be compelled to take off their underwear and get down on their knees and scrub the pavements and gutters with the garments. Thousands were fleeing to the borders, but only a few got across, and many committed suicide.

And not only Jews, but all of Adi's political opponents—for he had no forgiveness in his nature and the idea of chivalry never crossed his mind. Schuschnigg was a prisoner, undergoing torture and destined to be driven insane. A former Vice-Chancellor and Commander of the Heimwehr was murdered, along with his wife and son and even his dog. Other opponents were murdered and called suicides. The men who had killed Dollfuss became national heroes, and the Nazis of the Ostmark were put in command of concentration camps and charged with the duty of tormenting their former jailers. Things like that had been happening in this part of Europe as far back as history goes, but never had there been anything so scientifically organized. It wasn't long before Feldmarschall Göring issued an order to stop the private robbery of Jews, explaining that this was a prerogative of the government and must be carried out "systematically."

X

Interesting indeed to visit Wickthorpe Castle and hear what the ruling class of England had to say about all this! To hear the tall, lean, and long-faced Lord Halifax exclaim: "Horrible, horrible! I never thought they would do it!" Lanny would have liked to say: "Why did you go to Berlin four months ago and give them the green light?" Lanny learned that Ribbentrop had come to London in one of Germany's fast bomber planes, only three days before the march into Austria, and had been wined and dined while carrying on "exploratory negotiations" for a permanent understanding between Germany and Britain. He had talked with Ceddy Wickthorpe and Gerald Albany, and told them about his session with Halifax on the previous day, also with the Archbishop of Canterbury, whose endorsement of the Nazis as the future destroyers of Bolshevism was no secret from anybody at either Wickthorpe or Cliveden.

On Friday, with Hitler's troops poised on the border and ready to roll at dawn, the Nazi champagne salesman had seen the King, and had lunched at Number 10 Downing Street with Prime Minister

Chamberlain. Among the guests had been Lord Londonderry, who was Göring's chum and perhaps the most ardent pro-Nazi in England; Sir Samuel Hoare, the friend of Franco; Sir Alexander Cadogan, pronounced Cadúggan, Undersecretary of State; also Lord Halifax and Sir John Simon and the wives of all these. Several of these noble ladies and gentlemen had revealed to Lanny Budd their belief that the one-time *Gefreite* or sub-corporal named Adi Schicklgruber offered the best hope of safety for the British Empire, provided he could be persuaded to give up his demand for colonies overseas and turn his attention to the east. These ladies and gentlemen were shocked by the rape of Austria, because they had supposed they were at the stage of "exploratory negotiations," and hadn't realized that it was the time for action. For them it was unlikely ever to be the time for action. Why should it be, when they had an Empire on which the sun never set, and all the estates and securities they personally needed; when they all spoke with the right accent, and enjoyed freedom to play the delightful game of political power inside their snug little preserve?

These bitter observations were not Lanny's; they were those of a baronet's son who had the qualifications and might now have been a member of the Cabinet, had he been willing to be tamed and trained like other budding statesmen who had had socialistic inclinations in their youth. Lanny came back to The Reaches and reported what he had seen and heard in his ex-wife's castle; and after he had listened to his friend for a while he said: "When you want to criticize the English, get an Englishman!"

Rick answered, with a smile: "Don't try it otherwise!"

XI

Sir Alfred Pomeroy-Nielson had his man of all work, whose father and grandfather before him had been in the service of the family, take off those unusual car fixtures and cart them away to an electric furnace. Rick had made arrangements and went to see the job honestly done, and then to escort two or three hundred pounds of gold "pigs" to market. While this was going on, Lanny read and played the piano, took long walks and looked at the beautiful country of Hertfordshire which hadn't changed a particle since his first view of it, a quarter of a century ago. Also he thought a bit about his future, and in this had the advice of a wise gentlewoman who had known him since the days when the "Zepps" had been dropping bombs on London. Nina's hair had been light brown in those days, and now was several shades darker; her complexion, too, had faded, but there was so much kindness in her face that she would always seem a lovely woman. She had managed to keep her interest in ideas, while carrying the burden of a household full of individualists. Sir Alfred had to be amiably checked in his impulse to let his collection of the contemporary British drama crowd out everything else in a rambling old house; in his private study there were so many manuscripts and documents which he intended to read and classify that often he could find no place to sit down. Rick also had a den, where nobody but himself could find anything; and there had been four children, now all at school, and eight servants to manage, and a score of fires to be kept going in the month of March. Yes, Nina had to be a firm and yet tactful character; she knew the facts of life, and looked into your eyes with a frank and steady gaze when she spoke of them.

She came into the library while he was reading. She had her sewing with her, and when that happens, a man knows that he isn't going to read any more. "Rick agrees that I ought to talk to you, Lanny," she said.

"There's no law against it, old dear," he replied. He had told them both the story of how he had got from Hess the definite news of Trudi's death. So now he knew what Nina wanted to talk about. He said: "There's no cure for grief but time."

"Friendship helps," she answered, and he said: "You bet! And when I get too lonesome I head my car in this direction."

"I think you ought to let me advise you, Lanny. You know you won't go on all the rest of your life without love; and neither Rick nor I want to see you make another bad guess like the Irma one."

"I'm not apt to, Nina. I'm older, and also, my circumstances have changed. I have a duty, and I'm doing it. But it makes me a hard matrimonial problem. No woman could get along with a husband who hops from England to New York, and then to Paris, Juan, Berlin, Munich, Vienna, and so on all over again."

"A woman would want to know what her husband was doing on those journeys, of course; but if she was sure it wasn't some other woman, she could stand it. Here on this island of sailors we have thousands of women who don't see their men except at long intervals."

"I know, Nina; but my problem is a special one. I'm playing a role, and getting deeper and deeper into it. I have to be a Nazi; and how is any decent woman going to tolerate that? I can't marry a woman who doesn't know or care anything about politics, because she would bore me to death. I can't marry a woman of the leisure class, because

I'd be lying to her, as I was to Irma, and sooner or later she would find it out and be furious. I can't marry a leftwinger; I can't even meet one without risking the work I've pledged myself to do."

"It isn't a simple problem, I admit, but you exaggerate the difficulty. You are known as an art expert, and that's a respectable role. You don't have to talk politics to a woman the first time you meet her."

"I have to before long. If she shows any serious interest in me, and I don't tell her, I'm giving her a rotten deal."

"Not if she's a leftist. You can keep your pose as a reactionary, tactfully and carefully, and let her try to convert you if she wants to."

"What she'd want to do is to tear my hair out," said Lanny.

"If she does that, you'd know that she was in love with you."

Lanny couldn't keep from laughing. "I suppose it's better to have our rows before we're married than after," he admitted. "You're outlining a unique sort of courtship."

"I'm just showing you that you could meet some woman with brains and character, and find out about her without committing yourself or betraying your secret. If the time ever comes that you're seriously interested, you can give her a hint that she is beginning to persuade you. If she's a woman you want to marry, you would certainly have to trust her with your secret—at least as much of it as you have trusted to Rick and me. If you say to her: 'I have given my word of honor that I will never tell my secret to anyone,' that would be all right. Every Socialist knows there's an underground against the Nazis, and every true Socialist would be eager and proud to help it."

"You would," said Lanny, gallantly; "but I haven't met many like you, Nina." Then he added: "If you or Rick, either or both, know any woman you think I ought to know, I'll be glad to meet her, and be as friendly and polite as I know how. But I can't promise that either of us will fall in love."

"Of course not, Lanny. But it's so much more sensible to talk about love and know what you're doing, instead of just leaving it to chance, and a pretty face or the shape of an ankle."

"One sees a lot of ankles nowadays," said Lanny, with a grin, "but mostly what they support is a poor line of conversation."

XII

Lanny Budd set sail on a Cunard liner, carrying in his pocket a bank draft for forty-two thousand, six hundred and seventeen pounds, seven shillings and fourpence, payable to Rahel Robin. He had deducted the costs of the operation, including a hundred pounds for his friend who had dutifully made sure that none of the gold disappeared at any stage. Lanny had a passage stormy but otherwise uneventful, and was met at the steamer by Johannes Robin and his daughter-in-law. While Rahel wept softly, he told them the sad story. The Jewish man of affairs, already acquainted with sorrow, had guessed the worst and had forewarned the woman. A sum of money for which she had no need would do nothing to compensate for the loss of her brother, and perhaps of her mother and father—for it was a part of the Nazi creed that the sins of any Jew should be visited upon all his relatives.

And the three little ones—what did the master race do with children when they sent the parents to concentration camps? Were they turned out to feed out of garbage cans? Or were they painlessly asphyxiated, or perhaps sterilized and turned into slaves in some proper Aryan household? Lanny couldn't answer those questions, and it was perhaps the worst of Nazi tortures that so many people could never know the fate of their loved ones.

Lanny had invented a very exacting client in Washington, D. C., and said that as soon as he had satisfied this client he would visit his several families in Connecticut. He telephoned Gus Gennerich, and after some delay got an appointment for the following evening. He took the night train, and in the morning made himself comfortable in a hotel and typed out a summary of his recent political experiences—partly to put on the record, and partly to clarify his own memory. Later he took a walk in Rock Creek Park, going over in his mind everything he was planning to put into the mind of the most important man in the world. Mostly it had to be facts, but a certain amount of comment would be proper, and Lanny meant that every sentence should be a high-explosive shell, loaded with accuracy and care.

XIII

In newsreels and newspaper photographs Lanny could see President Roosevelt dressed as the rest of the world saw him; but when he met him face to face, it was always going to be in a pongee pajama coat, blue and white striped, with a knitted blue sweater or a blue cape over it. Apparently he liked to retire early and read in bed—or to hear reports from secret agents. He greeted his caller with a hearty hand-clasp and a wide smile; his face was rosy and his manner gay—amazing the way the man enjoyed his job and throve under it! Right now, with the stock market at the bottom of another slump, and the men whom he had helped now pouring blame and abuse upon him for the only kind of help that would have done them the least good—right now he was grinning with delight to see a visitor who had been in an ogre's den and counted the piles of human bones in the corners. "Hello, Jack of the Beanstalk!" he exclaimed.

Soon he became serious, and declared: "I want you to know, Lanny, I've read what you sent me. My actions may not show it now, but they will in the end."

"That's what I have to hear, Governor," said the secret agent. "With that, I can keep going for a while longer."

"Tell me what's coming next, Lanny."

"Undoubtedly the Sudetenland."

"Was that taken from Germany?"

"No, it belonged to Austro-Hungary; but Hitler tells the world that it was Germany's, and that he is determined to have it back."

"What has it got?"

"Minerals and forests, and positions vital for military defense. His excuse is a lot of Germans there."

"A majority?"

"It varies from district to district, from village to village; it s all mixed up as if it had been shaken out of a pepper-pot. It's exactly the same as in Stubendorf, where I used to visit my friend Kurt Meissner when I was a boy. That's farther to the east, and was given to Poland. The Poles in the district are mostly peasants and laborers; the Germans are the property owners, the educated people, and so the ones who can make the propaganda."

"You are sure the Czechs will come first?"

"Hitler didn't say it in so many words. You have to listen while he raves and note whom he raves at longest. First came Schuschnigg, and then Beneš. That tells you."

"And will the Czechs fight?"

"I can't tell you that. You know Jan Masaryk—ask him."

"Of course he says they'll fight, but that may be because he wants them to."

"If you're asking for my guess——"

"I'm asking."

"I think the British will make them give way."

"God Almighty, what is Europe coming to?"

"It's coming to Hitler. You can't imagine the present British Cabinet until you listen to them talk. They aren't ready for war, they don't want it and they won't believe it even when it comes. They have made up their minds that Hitler has to be like themselves, because that would be so convenient for them. They are going to 'appease' him, by letting him undo the blunders they made at Versailles—or that the French forced upon them. They are disgusted with the French politicians, because they are greedy and corrupt. They are afraid of the Russians, mainly because of the effect on British labor of letting the Communist experiment succeed. They are sure that sooner or later Hitler is going to come into conflict with the Reds, and then they are going to lie back in armchairs and sip whiskies and soda and enjoy the show."

"How do they think Hitler is going to get by Poland?"

"They don't talk about that very much, because it wouldn't sound good. They expect to appease Poland with part of the Ukraine, which she claims. There's enough land there to satisfy everybody, and it would be saving the world from Bolshevism."

The smile had gone out of the great man's face, and he said in a grave voice: "Lanny, you can surely see why the American people are so determined to keep out of that mess."

"I can see why they want to," replied the secret agent, "but whether they can do what they want is a different question. What will they do when Hitler takes Brazil?"

"Is that on his schedule?"

"Everything is on his schedule until he is stopped. If we let him take Spain, why not Northwest Africa? And when he has the bulge of Africa he's within flying range of the bulge of Brazil."

"We should have to stop him before then."

"Yes, but could we? Remember, it would be air forces, not navies. I can't find anybody in this country except my father who has realized the effect of aviation upon our military situation. From Africa, Hitler would be two or three times as near to Brazil as we are; and he has his agents and his German populations being organized all over South America. Those countries would fall into his lap like so many ripe plums; and we should have the job of landing armies there in the face of land-based aviation. It looks to me, Governor, as if you are going to share the fate of Woodrow Wilson and have to turn your attention from social reform to military strategy."

The frown on the "Governor's" face showed that he didn't relish this prospect; and the visitor went on to add: "It puts me on the spot personally, because my father is making fighter planes and it happens that I own a few shares of stock in the company; so I am one of those 'merchants of death' that I used to be so cross with a few years ago. I would sell the shares, only it would hurt my father's feelings. I'm letting him have the idea that I agree with him these days."

"That's all right, Lanny," said the President, smiling again. "I'll promise never to suspect you."

XIV

A greatly overworked executive was concerned to know how much time he had before these new burdens fell upon his shoulders. Time was urgent, for he could get only limited amounts of military appropriations from Congress. "How long will Hitler wait before his next move?"

"I'll give him six months to digest Austria. He has to put his men into the key positions, and they have to learn their jobs. He has to take over the big industries and fit them into his economy. There's a mountain of iron ore, and Göring will have that; there are steel works, and he'll put them to making cannon. There are huge forests, and Göring was telling my father just recently of the miracles their chemists are doing with wood; all kinds of substitutes, plastics, fibers, and even food, not merely starches but proteins. And food is a weapon, of course; you can say that everything is a weapon, one hundred per cent of the German economy, and it's all working while we sleep."

This line of conversation was calculated to interfere with the sleep of the most powerful man in the world. Lanny was doing it with premeditation—it was why he had crossed a stormy ocean. He went ahead to explain that the "digestion" of Austria would not preclude the softening up of Czechoslovakia. "My guess is that as soon as Hitler has finished with his plebiscite the German press will start up about atrocities in the Sudeten. You understand how it is worked—they send their bullies into the country to provoke disturbances, and when the police put them down, that's an atrocity. By next autumn Hitler will be ready to move; and of course he'll do it legally if he can—but his Panzer divisions will be on the border, and he will be threatening to lay Prague in ashes in an hour. They have rehearsed it on a dozen cities and towns in Spain and they know exactly what they can do."

"Horrible, horrible!" exclaimed F.D.

"Exactly what Lord Halifax said the other day," replied Lanny. "The whole civilized world will say it, but that won't worry Adolf Hitler. He would love to destroy Prague, because it is full of monuments of Czech culture, which he despises. But he won't bomb Pilsen."

"On account of the beer?"

Lanny smiled. "On account of Skoda, which is probably the biggest munitions plant in Europe. Hitler is going to have that, and poor Baron Schneider has guessed it by now, and is sitting in Le Creusot worried sick."

Lanny told about his talks with the munitions king, and the stag dinner in his Paris mansion. He presented his Chief with a new list of code names. "I don't like to use important names in my reports, for one can't trust even the mails entirely, and if a single letter fell into the enemy's hands it would ruin me. But you can count upon the fact that when I tell you I know something, I have got it from some top man."

Lanny had prepared a report on his recent visit to England, and what Lothian and Halifax and Londonderry had said about the raid on Austria. He took his hearer to Vienna, but not for long, for Schuschnigg was now a "dead duck" in the American slang—meaning dead not physically but politically. Better to move on to Berchtesgaden and Berlin, where the live duck was quacking. F.D. had listened to Adi Schicklgruber's recent ravings over the radio, so he could appreciate Lanny's account of scenes in the Berghof while the Führer had been putting the Chancellor of Austria through the softening-up process. The President with a sense of fun guffawed over Lanny's imitation of Adi's bellowings. *Bummler—Geilheit—Gesindel—Schurkerei—Frechheit* —all those were funny words to an American, even though he didn't know what they meant.

Lanny added: "Please be careful and don't tell any of all this to your friends. Remember, the German embassy is very active, and they have a fortune to spend; they know all about you and your jokes, and they have a good idea of what you know about them. If the slightest whisper goes out that you know more than you ought to, they'll start trailing every American who has ever been near the Berghof or Karinhall—and believe me, there aren't very many."

"You are depriving me of some happy hours," replied the President, "but I get your point, and mum's the word."

XV

The President of the United States was never without a sea story or a "whodunit" by his bedside, and perhaps he stole looks into them when he should have been reading grave state papers. Now he listened to a mystery story from real life—the effort to find Trudi Schultz in a Nazi hideout in Seine-et-Oise. That part of a great man which had refused to grow up hung on every word of it, even though he was stealing time from his sleep. When the story came to its bitter climax, tears started down Lanny's cheeks and he did not try to hide them. The grown-up part of his auditor realized that this was a distillation of thousands of tragedies which were going on wherever the Nazi power had penetrated. The unhappy old continent was getting itself ready for another blood-bath, and nowhere within its confines was there sufficient moral or intellectual force to avert the calamity.

"Believe me, Lanny," said the President, "I sympathize with your feelings; but my position as I explained it to you remains unchanged. I have to think about the needs and the demands of a hundred and thirty millions of our own people, and I have only a limited amount of time and thought left for those outside."

"All right, Governor; I have to accept that. But I came to tell you— it means another World War, and we can't possibly keep out of it. What do you want me to do next?"

"I want you to go right on as you have. I cannot go to these different countries, and your travels are an extension of my eyesight. I renew my offer to put you on my secret payroll."

"No, I manage to make picture deals wherever I go."

"Living off the enemy's country," said F.D., again with a smile.

Lanny rose. "I ought not to keep you up any longer, Governor. I expect to be at my father's home for the next couple of weeks, and you could send me an anonymous note, if you wished."

"I doubt if there will be need of that. Just remember that I'm watching you, to see how your prophecies come true!"

"It doesn't need any prophet, Governor; it needs only an understanding of German economy, such as I have obtained from Göring and Thyssen and Schacht and others I meet through my father. I repeated to Hitler what I had said to you, that when a man builds a bicycle he has to ride and he can't sail a boat. Hitler accepted those words as exactly right. He has made the German economy into a war economy, and now he'll be doing the same for the Austrian economy. It's nonsense to say that he will stop when he has got the border territories where the Germans live; for what is he going to do with them? He can't feed the people on machine-gun cartridges and airplane bombs—not even I. G. Farben is equal to that miracle of *Ersatz*. Even if Hitler should die tonight, Göring or Hess would be driven by the force he has created; they have to go after the potato fields of Poland and the wheat fields of the Ukraine, the minerals of the Balkans, and the oil of the Caucasus."

"That's quite a program," said the President, no longer smiling. "Watch him, keep me informed, and trust me to make the best use of the information that I can."

24

God's Footstool

I

LANNY thought that he had earned a holiday, and it occurred to him that he would like to renew his limited acquaintance with his own country. He went up to Newcastle, where they would always find a spare room for him, put a car at his disposal, and let him make noises on the piano at reasonable hours.

The town had grown uncomfortably fast; the staid oldest inhabitants looked upon the changes with displeasure, and found the increase in bank deposits and retail sales a poor compensation for the crowds on the streets and the impossibility of finding parking space. They shut themselves up in their old frame or brick mansions and refused to have anything to do with the new world growing up around them: noise and confusion, bad taste, corrupt politics, unmanageable young people. It was the age of the "jitterbug"; a round-faced Jewish musician stood on a platform and wailed on the clarinet, and the young people swayed their shoulders and swung their hips, or sat in their seats with their eyes closed and their lower jaws dehiscent. They listened by radio all over the land, literally by the millions; Lanny listened also, trying to call it music and to find out what it meant to them. The most popular song of the moment was called "A Tisket, a Tasket." He knew what the first and third word meant, but failed to find the others in the dictionary.

Robbie Budd was partly to blame for conditions in Newcastle, having started a new industry in a town with old and narrow and winding streets; the older Budds—of whom there were many—considered that he should have asked their advice, and they still looked upon him as a headstrong and unsafe man, and were glad they hadn't put any of their money into crazy contraptions to fly in the air. Right now there was a slump, and these seventy- and eighty-year-olds—and two nineties —all said: "We told you so." The men among them still referred to Lanny as "Robbie's bastard," and looked upon him as a young rapscallion; but they were interested to hear him tell about the wickedness of Paris, London, and Berlin.

Robbie played poker with some cronies every Saturday night, and went out with his wife "once in a coon's age," as he phrased it, but otherwise he had no life outside his business. Modern competition called for that, and Robbie glorified it, and was proud of his ability to stand the pace. He had got capable young fellows, including his two younger sons, and drove them hard, and set them an example by knowing every detail of what they were doing. The Budd plant was country and God to them, and the fact that the B-E P12A was now the fastest and most maneuverable fighter on the market was the theme of a song which a girl stenographer had composed and which was sung at banquets, picnics, and other company occasions.

Never would Robbie give up the dream that Lanny would some day be caught by this enthusiasm. Whenever he came, the father would expose him to the contagion and watch for signs that it was taking. He had never been so hopeful as now, for the Pink tinge had faded entirely from his first-born's conversation, and he showed real appreciation of the place of military planes in a competitive world. Of course Robbie wanted to know all about his conversations with Göring and Schneider and other business people; as for Adi Schicklgruber, the idea of visiting that ogre's lair and selling him paintings and buying some for him in Vienna—that was really a tale, and Robbie told it over town, with the result that everybody wanted to hear it, and Lanny became a social lion for the second time—the first having been when he turned up with a twenty-three-million-dollar bride.

People wanted to give him dinner parties in their homes, or at the country club; they didn't ask him to stand up and make a speech, but they would get him talking and then the rest of the table would fall silent, except for questions. The ladies found him fascinating, and were ready to fall in love with him, and not only the single ones. This was a serious matter in these modern days, for it was no longer a question of coy glances and sighs; these were emancipated ladies, who went right after what they wanted. They would press him too closely while dancing, and try to be led off to one of those nooks which architects had thoughtfully provided; if he showed the slightest interest they would think up some pretext to take him somewhere in a car—each of them had her own—and then anything might happen, and with disconcerting suddenness.

II

Esther Budd, daughter of the Puritans, now several times a grandmother, knew all about her home town and had been obliged to adjust her thinking to the changes going on. In Lanny's youth she had distrusted him as a product of the Coast of Pleasure, but now she had decided that he had turned out much better than her fears, and she accepted him as "family" in good standing. She knew how strong a hold he had upon her husband's heart, and she desired to play her difficult role of stepmother with generosity and grace. Lanny had been a grass-widower now for two years and more, a sufficient time for all the proprieties and even some of the dangers. Esther decided that it would be a stroke of statecraft if she could be the means of persuading him to marry in Newcastle and settle down. Already he came two or three times every year, and seemed free to prolong his stays at pleasure.

Esther Remsen Budd was a pillar of society in this city which remained a small town in its mind. Her father had been president of the First National Bank and her brother had recently succeeded to the post. She was tireless in church work and in every form of what was called "good works." She had been brought up to believe that woman's place was the home, but since women had been dragged into politics and forced to vote they had better vote well than ill; so Esther had joined a woman's club and inspired it to take a stand for clean government—which, rather alarmingly, had threatened to bring her into conflict with her husband's business interests.

They had worked out a compromise, and it had had the rather odd outcome that this tall and gray-haired, dignified and reserved Puritan lady became as it were the political boss of her town. When the time for nominations came around and the local party heads brought Robbie the proposed slate, he would take it to his wife, who would conscientiously investigate the records of every candidate, and if any of them were "too raw," would cross them off. Of course a secret like that cannot be kept, and power like that cannot be held without a lot of hard work and bother. Deputations would come for this or that, and candidates to make known their qualifications. And then the barbecues and political picnics! "You asked for it!" Robbie would say, with a malicious grin. But the streets were kept clean, and no man who had ever stolen public funds or neglected his wife and children could rise to political favor in Newcastle, Connecticut.

III

Esther's way wouldn't be to have a heart-to-heart talk with Lanny, after the manner of Nina Pomeroy-Nielson. In her world these matters had to be arranged with carefully preserved casualness. Esther would try to imagine what sort of young woman would appeal to her difficult stepson, and would invite a specimen to lunch and watch for signs of a spark. If none flew, she would wait two or three days and try another, perhaps at dinner, to make it less obvious. She would make offhand remarks, letting Lanny know who was coming and pointing out her connections and qualifications. There is a saying that in Boston they ask you what you know, in Philadelphia who your ancestors were, and in New York how much money you have. Newcastle lay between Boston and New York, but Esther had the Boston idea and would never speak of money. However, you could be sure that she would never put on the carpet a candidate who didn't have a decent amount.

So Lanny had every opportunity to become acquainted with what beauty, spirit, and talent the land of his forefathers had to offer. Lovely girls and bright girls, some of them sharing his musical and artistic tastes, some of them astonishingly mature and well informed. One of the loveliest, oddly enough, was the daughter of that Adelaide Hitch-cock whom Lanny in his callow youth had been the means of turning out of a role in the country-club performance of *A Midsummer Night's Dream*. He had called her a "stick," and had put in Phyllis Gracyn, who had become soon afterwards a stage queen of Broadway and was now acting maternal roles in Hollywood. That social blunder had been forgiven him; and now—my, how time does fly!—here was Adelaide's daughter in early bloom, with her mother's large brown eyes and some of the life her mother had sadly lacked. She was related to Esther and would have scads of money, and when Lanny talked about smart life on the Riviera, she listened entranced. She had been trained for the glory of spending money, principally upon clothes, and wearing them in ballrooms and at dinner tables, and her young heart was a-flutter at the thought of getting started.

What could Lanny have done with such a bride? Leave her here while he went scouting over Europe? Or take her to his mother's home and leave her there? Keep his opinions from her, or else worry and frighten her as he had done with Irma? Certainly he couldn't tell her his new occupation; and when the time came that he got into trouble— as sooner or later he was so likely to do—what sort of time would she have then?

The devil of it was, he couldn't tell either the girl or his kind step-mother, nor could he give them the excuses he had devised for use among the age-old corruptions of Europe. He must be gracious but reserved—which only made him seem the more mysterious and attractive. The eldest son of Budd-Erling became the subject of anxious conferences in many a boudoir in Newcastle and near-by towns. Was he wholly lacking in human feelings? Or did he have some duchess waiting for him in Paris? Or was he perchance looking for another twenty-three million?

IV

Then came to Lanny one of those experiences which befall eligible bachelors, even in the land of the Pilgrim's pride. He had dined with one of the elder Budds, his father's uncle; a duty call, to oblige Esther. It was an early meal, to accommodate an old gentleman and his younger but by no means young wife; frugal fare, a "New England boiled dinner," served on ancient silver plate, in a dining room with a full-rigged clipper ship under a large glass bell, and trophies brought from all the ports of the China seas. Lanny listened to old family stories, necessary to his education; and then, coming home early, looking forward to a quiet read, he passed the central square of what might be called Old Newcastle. In one corner stood the public library, a square brownstone building, long ago the town's pride and now its embarrassment. Esther was one of the trustees and he knew of her efforts to get an appropriation for a new and more commodious building.

Lights were burning within, and Lanny remembered that he wanted some item of information which the meager resources of his father's library did not supply. He parked his car and walked to the building; people were coming out, and just as he entered the central room a bell rang and he saw people getting up—it was obviously the closing bell. The clock on the wall showed nine, and he hesitated, and was about to turn and leave when one of the ladies in charge came toward him. She was of that indefinite age which characterizes librarians and school-teachers; she was slender, and when he thought it over afterwards he guessed that her salary did not permit her to be otherwise. She was obviously very much a gentlewoman. "Can I help you?" she asked, and her voice was in character.

"I am afraid I am late," he replied.

"A few minutes won't matter, Mr. Budd." His picture had been in the local paper, with an account of his delightful occupation and his travels. She would know the vitally important fact that he was a stepson of the great lady upon whom the fate of the new building depended. "I am Miss Hoyle, the librarian," she said. "By all means let me help you."

"I am wondering if you have anything on Italian Renaissance painters —the earlier part of that period."

"We have Vasari," she replied, "and other works with chapters. I will show you."

She led him into an alcove, between closely crowded stacks. She showed him a row of books, and stood by while he glanced over the titles. Meantime, somebody was turning off lights in the building but obligingly left this alcove alone. Lanny was interested in the books and glanced hurriedly into one or two; of course he couldn't fail to be aware of a woman standing close to him, a quiet, self-possessed woman who did not keep up a chatter while he was trying to read, but left him free to make up his mind. When he said: "I think this might serve my purpose," she took out another and said: "You might find something in this, also." Only when he was through with his search did she start to talk, and in a few sentences disclosed the fact that she knew a lot about the Italian Renaissance and its painters. He took the occasion to look at her, and saw that she had delicate features, rather pale, with no make-up; dark hair, and large, dark, admiring eyes.

He knew that when she said: "You wouldn't remember me, but I had the pleasure of being invited to your father's home to see the Goya which you brought from Spain. That was one of the great events of my life. What became of it?"

"It was bought by friends in Pittsburgh."

"Also, I listened to Hansi Robin play at the country club. You have done more for us provincial people than you can have any idea of."

"It is kind of you to tell me," said Lanny. So there were persons in this home town who lived obscure lives and were poor according to his standards, but who eagerly reached out for cultural opportunities! Lanny would be a romantic figure to them. The women would know that manners and morals in France were different, and they might find him a disturbing figure.

Everybody had left, and they were alone, or so it appeared. Miss Priscilla Hoyle made out a card for him, and while she did so he watched her delicate slender hand moving swiftly, and also the fine little dark hairs at the back of her neck. When she gave him the books he said, on an impulse: "Could I have the pleasure of driving you home?"

She was startled, and revealed that there was blood in the marble cheeks. "Oh! But—it is out of your way."

"How do you know my way?" he asked, with a smile. "I have kept you overtime."

"It is kind of you," she said; and then, more precisely: "With pleasure."

V

She turned off the lights and they went together down the steps of the old building. Was Lanny right in his impression that she looked about nervously, to see if anyone was observing this unprecedented behavior? He offered her his arm and she took it; was he right in his impression that her hand trembled? He didn't know her voice well, but he knew it was full of feeling as she explained that Newcastle was culturally a backward town; its body was growing much too fast for its brain, to say nothing of its soul, and those who cared for the higher things of life had a hard struggle here. Lanny understood what this meant; the town librarian was close to the seats of power for a brief period, and if she could cause the stepson of Esther Remsen Budd to take an interest in her library's cause, the scales might be tipped in favor of the appropriation.

Lanny could imagine without being told how she had served for years at this post, coming every weekday for long hours and patiently telling all sorts of persons, old and young, rich and poor, whatever they wanted to know about books. The library was her life, and now she was fighting for it. But was that all? What were her thoughts about this handsome man who must be middle-aged but looked young because he had taken good care of himself; who wore a little brown mustache and was dressed so elegantly, spoke several languages, and had met all the great ones of the earth? She sat alone with him, almost touching him; a prim daughter of the Puritans, strictly brought up, a church member and almost certainly a virgin, or she could never have obtained this post in the town of Esther Remsen Budd.

She had given her address and he was driving, not at break-neck speed. He said: "I know about the library's need, and I'll say a good word for it."

"Oh, thank you!" she answered—and was that more soulful than needed? Was there a voice crying somewhere in this worthy soul: "Youth is passing, and your last chances"?

She had a sweet personality, and he thought it could do no harm if he laid one hand gently on hers, by way of expressing his appreciation.

Immediately then he got his answer to all the questions; she gave the faintest of sighs, and inclined toward him and rested her head on his shoulder. Amazing!

So he asked: "Shall we drive a little?" and she whispered: "Yes." He turned off the road and toward the river. He knew this drive well; there were wooded points, and lanes in which lovers stopped. He knew that there was a moon rising on the other side of the river, toward the east, as is the immemorial custom of moons. It had been a warm day in April, and spring was softening this stern and rockbound coast.

It was a silent petting party. Perhaps both of them knew that the less they said the better. He held her frail hand and it responded to his pressure. When he came to a quiet spot he drew up a little way from the road and turned off the ignition and lights of his car. He put his arms about her and she put hers about him; he kissed her, and she didn't murmur any conventional protest, or feign any reluctance; evidently she had made up her mind that it was now or never; she kissed him in return—delicately, even modestly, but unmistakably.

This was most agreeable; but the question always arises, how far is it to go? Was he meaning to seduce the librarian of his father's, and more especially of his stepmother's town? Seduction it would certainly be called, no matter how willing the lady might be. Once before Lanny had come to almost this same spot and gone through the same procedure, with a girl called Gracyn Phillipson, later Phyllis Gracyn. Then he had been only eighteen, and it had been possible to forgive him; but now he was more than twice that, and it would no longer be possible.

In the course of a fashionable career Lanny had met numbers of men who took their pleasure where they found it, and talked freely about their adventures. Among them more than one had made known that they put only one restraint upon themselves: they would never consent to be the first man. He recalled their phrases: "The first time means so much to a woman; they expect such a lot,"—and so on. These phrases rang a warning bell in the soul of Lanny Budd. If he "went the limit" with Priscilla Hoyle, she would expect him to call at her home, meet her relatives and friends, and escort her on Sunday morning to the First Congregational Church, thus regularizing their courtship. Esther would be astonished, but would accept the strange mishap in the all-powerful name of "democracy."

But again the problem, what would he do with his bride? Set up an establishment in Newcastle, and visit her several times a year? Invent some pretext for never taking her along on his many journeys—not even one honeymoon tour? She might make him a good wife—but how could he know? How could he guess what might be her reaction to his abnormal ideas? He hardly knew her mind; he hadn't even had a chance to ask her what she thought of Newcastle's pet phobia—That Man in the White House!

Thus conscience did make a coward of Lanny Budd, and thus his native hue of resolution was sicklied o'er with the pale cast of thought; thus his enterprise of great pith and moment had its currents turned awry and lost the name of action. The frequency of his kisses diminished, and he began gently stroking the forehead of this estimable lady. Presently he whispered: "This has been very sweet of you."

What had been going on in her own mind? Doubtless the same operations of the conscience; for she said: "Mother will be worried about me." An old-established device for the protecting and preserving of virginity—to mention "Mother"!

Lanny drove her home, asking if he might have the pleasure of calling upon her when he came to town again—he was under the necessity of returning to Europe in a short time, he revealed. Fair warning to Priscilla of the Puritans; the fiend whose lantern lights the mead were better mate than I! He left her with one more kiss, stolen in the darkness in front of the modest cottage in which she and her mother resided. She would cherish this in memory for the rest of her spinsterhood, and would associate the son of Budd-Erling with every line of love poetry she had read in the course of a life with books. Lanny, for his part, went away half glad and half sorry for his renunciation. Exactly the way he had felt about Janet Sloane, now Mrs. Sidney Armstrong, with whom he had had the same sort of perilous passage-at-arms so long, long ago!

VI

Hansi and Bess lived within comfortable motoring distance, and Lanny spent much time with them. He listened while they practiced for a new concert; then, while Hansi gave lessons to favored pupils, Lanny and his half-sister played four-hand piano arrangements. Bess was going to have another baby, and that was to be all, she declared. Americans had taken an old formula, "Two's company, three's a crowd," and applied it in a new field.

Lanny swore this couple to secrecy and told them the story of Trudi and his efforts to save her; it was a form of release to talk about her and have the sympathy of these dear friends. Lanny had got from his father's safe the sealed envelope containing his will and Trudi's photograph; he had destroyed the will and now carried the photograph with him. He showed it to Hansi and Bess; dwelling on the lovely delicate features, and telling about her ideas, her manners and way of life, until the young couple had tears in their eyes. Lanny was having the photo enlarged and would leave the copies here; he would not dare to take one with him on his travels.

Of course all this had the effect of setting one more woman to figuring over the problem of finding a proper mate for the incomparable Lanny Budd. Bess saw this dream-woman as a follower of the Party line, who would keep her erratic half-brother in the strait and narrow path. He, of course, treated this line with irreverence, insisting that it had been erratic, while he had held steadily toward the goal of democratic Socialism. But Bess wouldn't give up hoping; there were many ladies of wealth and culture who were classed as "fellow-travelers," and whenever Bess met a new one she wondered how Lanny might hit it off with her. Just how he could go on pretending to fellow-travel with the Nazis while his wife fellow-traveled with the Reds was something Bess hadn't figured out precisely.

Also Lanny visited the home of the Robin family, and kissed his Jewish near-mother, and told once more the sad story of Aaron Schönhaus. Not a word had come from the missing man, and carefully veiled inquiries of friends in Naziland had brought no results. Lanny had to think up an excuse for his own inactivity, and he said: "I am afraid I broke the law, and it would do Robbie great harm if I involved myself any further." Poor Jews, who had to take what crumbs of kindness anybody gave them!

Lanny played with the sweetly serious little eight-year-old boy who looked so much like Freddi Robin, his father. Little Johannes still remembered Bienvenu, and his playmate, Baby Frances, and Lanny told about her way of life in a grand old English castle. It sounded like a fairy tale, and Lanny left it that way; the tale was not apt to come true, for Irma would hardly consent to have her twenty-three-million-dollar baby renew the intimacy with German-Jewish refugees tinged with the hated Pink color.

VII

New York was near, and its call was loud. There was art business to be done, and more to be planned—which meant the acceptance of a certain number of dinner invitations and the pouring out of great gobs of social charm. In the story of Hitler and Schuschnigg Lanny had a passport to the wealthiest circles, and, just as in Newcastle, a full draw-ing-room would hang on his words and ply him with questions. The seizure of Austria had startled the world into attention and forced it to recognize the arrival of a new social force. Men and women who hated the New Deal with such vehemence that they became incoherent when they talked about it, found themselves wondering whether they might not have to follow the National-Socialist lead. If so, they wanted to know how to set about it.

Lanny gave them the benefit of his observations. Adi Schicklgruber had got power because he had spread in the sky of middle- and lower-class Germans a glittering rainbow of hopes. To be sure, he hadn't carried out his promises, save only the plundering of Jews; everything else had been just springes to catch woodcocks. He had caught these birds in the twin snares of nationalism and militarism, and now he had them fast. Lanny didn't say: "Do you propose to do the same to the American people?" He just fell silent and let them talk about when and how it could be done, and where on the political horizon was a leader who had what it took.

Amusing if it hadn't been so terrifying. Their problem was made almost impossible of solution, because they loved their money and their power so that they couldn't contemplate letting any demagogue say anything against it—not even for purposes of camouflage! What they really wanted was another conservative regime, another President Harding, the whole cycle of Harding, Coolidge, Hoover. Lanny was tempted to add: "And another Wall Street smash?" But no, they had forgotten that, and their gratitude to That Man who had enabled the banks to reopen. They just wanted twelve more years of peace and plenty, in which time they could get such a grip upon the nation's affairs as to make it impossible for another demagogue to get started.

They would take the conversation out of Lanny's hands and begin talking about some promising Republican governor in some reactionary state; the visitor would listen, and think that he was back in the days of the Sun King, who had proclaimed: "*L'état, c'est moi.*" But occa-sionally there would be one or two of more intelligence, who realized that this Europeanized American really had something for them; they would draw him aside and ask, where could they get the Nazi Party program to study it? They would fall to canvassing the rabble-rousers of America, in search of one who really had the stuff, and who might be depended upon to stay bought.

A chance for the son of Budd-Erling to learn something about his own country! Huey Long, unfortunately, had been shot; a shrewd devil, he had said: "It will be easy to bring Fascism in America. Just call it Anti-Fascism." That was something to be made note of! There was Father Coughlin—but unfortunately a Catholic couldn't be elected. There were Gold Shirts and Silver Shirts, Gray Shirts and Crusader White Shirts, Ku Klux nighties and many other odd costumes. There was an oratorical fellow named Gerald Smith—somebody ought to make a thorough study of all these friends of the "pee-pul" and choose one who knew where the butter on his bread would come from.

VIII

Departing from one of these Park Avenue parties, Lanny walked to his hotel. A pleasant evening in spring, and he liked to walk, and watch the speeding traffic on this wide avenue, divided into two lanes by a parkway with a four-track electric railroad underneath. He thought about the men he had been talking to; the masters of America—and what were they going to make of their country? They had business dealings with the German cartels, and knew that the German big businessmen as a rule were getting along with the Nazis, working day and night on war goods, earning big profits, and plowing the money back into plant. The gentlemen of Wall Street and Park Avenue were doing the same, and meant to go on doing it; they had the money, and knew that money talks, money makes the mare go, money pays the piper and calls the tunes. Right now they were Nazi tunes, raucous to Lanny Budd's ear.

Crossing a side street, he heard the shout of a crowd, and looking toward Lexington Avenue saw the gleam of torchlights; he stood listening to volleys of sound, and then turned and strolled in that direction. Curiosity, not altogether idle, for it was worth while to know what was going on in this city whose population exceeded that of whole lands such as Sweden and Austria, now the Ostmark. New York was the center of the publishing industry, and impulses which originated here were spread quickly over the three million square miles of America. April was not the time for elections, and this must be some sort of propaganda meeting—Red or Pink, Black or Brown, White, Gray, Silver, Gold, Green, or Purple—there was hardly a shade of shirts or pants which did not have social significance in these frenzied times.

It must be a religious meeting, Lanny thought, because he observed a large white cross standing above the speaker's head in the light of the torches. The orator was standing on a truck, a large man with handsome features and heavy black hair which he tossed now and then. He was evidently at the climax of a great effort, shouting in tones which drowned out the traffic of a busy avenue; the side street, close to the corner, was packed solid with auditors, and every sentence was punctuated by volleys of applause. Lanny was surprised to find an evangelist arousing such fervor in this cynical metropolis; but then he saw a banner: "Christian Front," and realized that this was American Nazism, and the orator a candidate for the attention of the Wall Street and Park Avenue gentlemen.

This one clearly had the qualifications; personality, voice, energy, cunning—and, above all, hate! Hate for everybody and everything that the poor man, downtrodden and ignorant, believed to be his oppressors and his enemies: hatred for the money power, the idle rich, the educated and cultured; hatred for the government, the New Dealers, the bureaucrats, the politicians; hatred for the Reds, the Communists, the Socialists; hatred for the foreigners, the niggers, and above all, the Jews. Roosevelt was a Jew, and his government was a Jew government. The New Deal was the Jew Deal: Morgenthau and J. P. Morgan, Felix Frankfurter and Frances Perkins, Baruch and Ickes—the tirade scrambled Jews and non-Jews, and nobody in the crowd knew or cared; they yelled for the blood of each one in turn.

"Is this America?" demanded the orator, and the answer came like the hissing of snakes: "Yes! Yes!" Then: "Are we going to give it to the Jews?"—and the answer like a thunder clap: "No!" "Are we going to restore it to Americans?" "We are! We are!"

It happened that Lanny had been reading *The Island of Dr. Moreau*, a story by H. G. Wells about a scientist on a tropical island who performs surgery upon animals, gives them brains and power of speech, and then teaches them formulas to discipline them and make them behave. So now these half-human creatures stood in the semi-darkness and shouted automatic answers to oft-repeated questions:

"Do we love our little kike mayor?"
"No! No!"
"Do we like to have his cops crack our heads?"
"No! No!"
"Are we going to surrender our rights as American citizens?"
"No! No!"—and sometimes *"Nein! Nein!"*

IX

Lanny, on the outskirts of the throng, observed those about him, screaming, shaking their clenched fists. Next to him a man stopped to catch his breath, and Lanny nudged him and asked: "Who is that?" The reply was: "Joe McWilliams, the greatest man in America." Then, without stopping for a glance at the questioner: "Bully-boy Joe! Give it to 'em, Bully-boy! Down with the sheenies! Kill the kikes!"

It made the son of Budd-Erling feel sick deep inside him. He knew every tone, every gesture, every emotion, every idea. He had heard it first in a huge Munich beerhall more than fifteen years ago; since then he had heard it at a score of meetings in various parts of Germany, and over the radio, and in the Braune Haus and the Berghof. The thought that the land of his fathers had to go through this dreadful cycle filled him with an impulse to flee to some desert isle. But no, there was no longer any refuge in these days of airplanes; this horror had to be faced and dealt with where it was.

So, when a thin-faced fanatical fellow with front teeth missing offered Lanny a copy of the *Christian Mobilizer*, he paid a nickel and put it into his pocket for future study. Then came a red-faced German with a copy of the *Deutscher Weckruf und Beobachter;* then a frail, half-starved girl, selling Father Coughlin's *Social Justice.* Lanny bought everything; even to a button with a white cross on it, which he pinned onto his coat as a preliminary to asking questions.

The speech ended with an appeal to the audience to enroll in the "Christian Front" and give their support to the salvation of America. Many gathered around the truck for this purpose, and it occurred to Lanny Budd that it might some day be useful to a "P.A." to possess a membership card in this organization. He gave his name, together with his hotel address, which wasn't permanent. The card was made out by an elderly woman wearing a black alpaca coat, frayed at the cuffs; she did not fail to note the elegant appearance of this new applicant, and said: "God bless you, brother! Come and see us and give your support to our holy cause."

The paper sellers were busily hawking their wares. There was a table loaded with pamphlets and books, prominent among them the *Protocols of the Learned Elders of Zion.* A strange social phenomenon that! An impecunious lawyer in Tsarist Moscow had adapted this document from a French work of fiction; the original version had had nothing to do with Jews, but the revised version was taken as gospel and had become a hate-weapon of Nazis all over the world. Henry Ford had distributed hundreds of thousands of copies, and wherever his cars traveled people learned on the authority of the world's richest man that the Jews had a secret international organization plotting to destroy Christian society. Later on the Flivver King had taken it back, but few people knew that, or cared. From other literature for sale at these tables you could learn that the Jews had a rite which required the blood of freshly killed gentile babies.

X

Along with other members of the dispersing audience Lanny strolled toward the west, and found himself alongside the hatchet-faced fellow who had sold him the *Christian Mobilizer*. "Hot talk, that!" remarked the visitor, and the reply was: "You said it, brother!"

This sadly depressed specimen of megalopolitan life gazed suspiciously at a spring overcoat of the latest cut and Homburg hat to match; however, he noted the little button with the white cross, and asked: "You one of us?"

"I carry a card," replied Lanny, and showed it in his hand; he didn't mention that he had carried it for only five minutes. "You find a good sale for the paper?"

"We've just started, but it's going big."

"Not with the Jews, I imagine."

Lanny said it playfully, but there was no play in this child of the gutters. "Sometimes we sell to the kikes. They take a good look at us an' guess they'd better."

Among the people walking on this cross street were several other vendors of literature, and others of a sort with whom Lanny would not have cared to be alone on any street. "Where do you go from here?" he inquired.

"We allus go to Times Square after meetings. We get the the-ay-ter crowd, and sometimes we teach the sheenies a lesson. Come along, if you want to see the fun."

Lanny wanted to see everything, and wanted to learn all he could about a "Christian Fronter." An Irish-Catholic boy, raised in the slum known as "Hell's Kitchen" and educated in a parochial school, Mike Raftery had been told by his priest that the bloodthirsty "Rooshians" were trying to destroy Holy Mother Church, and that they were all Jews, or at any rate Jewish-inspired. He had not the least difficulty in believing that Jewish Bolsheviks and bankers were in a common conspiracy to dominate the world; he had but the vaguest idea of what bankers did or what Bolsheviks believed; he had learned from Father Coughlin's papers that the bankers gave money to the Bolsheviks for the undermining of the Catholic religion and the American Constitution. Now he had shifted to the paper of "Bully-boy Joe," which was new and even more violent. "Speeches ain't enough," said Mike. "We gotta have action; we gotta make them kikes pipe down."

What constituted "action" Lanny saw quickly enough. Reaching Times Square, the sellers spread out on the various corners made by Broadway and Forty-third Street. They began screaming: "Buy the *Christian Mobilizer!* Save America! Down with the Jews!" Meantime the group of toughs, the "goon squad," moved from one seller to another; not conspicuously, but one here and one there; Lanny knew them, because he had walked a mile or so with them. When a Jew came along—preferably a poor one—a seller would approach him. "Buy a *Christian Mobilizer*—read all about the dirty sheenies!" If he didn't stop, the seller would try to step on his toes; if he did stop, the seller would poke the paper under his nose. "Save America from the kikes!"

The Jew thus assailed would do well to get out of the way quickly, and to keep his mouth closed. If he said anything angry, or tried to shove his tormenter out of the way, the man or woman would yell and the goon squad would leap in. They carried what appeared to be newspapers, but really were pieces of lead pipe with newspapers wrapped around them. They would bring these down on the victim's head, splitting it open, or cracking his arm if he tried to defend his head; they would leave him bleeding and perhaps unconscious on the pavement, and disappear into the crowd in a flash.

This went on night after night, Lanny was told; and it surprised him, for he had read little or nothing about it in the papers. The New York "cops" were in good part Catholic, and there was no law against their reading Father Coughlin's paper; they came from the same slums as the paper sellers, and in their boyhood had spit upon many a "Christ-killer." The mayor of New York was part Jewish, and was in an awkward position because he was a liberal and had been preaching freedom of speech all his life. The newspapers of New York lived upon department-store advertising, and reports of violence and especially of racial and religious violence were bad for trade; a large part of the buyers who came to the city were Jewish, and what if their wives became frightened and persuaded them to go elsewhere? As for Lanny Budd, playing the good Samaritan in the theater district would surely have been bad for *his* business.

XI

The presidential agent looked up the name of Forrest Quadratt in the phone book and called him. "I have just had the pleasure of spending ten days at the Berghof," he said. "I was there during Schuschnigg's visit."

"Oh, splendid!" exclaimed the poet turned propagandist; he didn't get a call like that very often. "Won't you come up to dinner? I have a friend, a high-ranking personality from overseas who happens to be in town, and I'll invite him. I know you'd like to meet him."

Meeting high-ranking personalities was Lanny's business, so the date was made. He took a taxi to the upper West Side, where the partisan of Nazism had an apartment on Riverside Drive, filled with the trophies of culture. The host had written a shelf of books, including a defense of the Kaiser, whose left-handed relative he was supposed to be. He was a smallish, near-sighted man, suave and gracious, caressing in manner. He had a sweet little wife about whom Lanny wondered, what did she make of the Nazi doctrines concerning her sex? Lanny had the suspicion that both husband and wife had Jewish blood, but this of course would never be put into words.

The other guest was a tall Prussian aristocrat with a round blond head, wearing a monocle and introduced as Kapitän von Schnelling. He had commanded a U-boat during the World War and been one of those who sank their vessels at Scapa Flow. He had most formal manners, and knew Stubendorf, Herzenberg, the Donnersteins, all Lanny's high-up friends in the Fatherland. What he was doing in America was made apparent during the course of the evening, and Lanny realized that he was dealing with a really important man and a shrewd one.

They wanted to hear about his adventures in the Berghof and he told them in detail. He didn't say anything about a spiritualist medium, or about having sold some paintings, which might have turned it into a business affair; he left it to be assumed that his long stay had been owing to the Führer's delight in his company. He talked about walks in the forest and the retreat under construction on the Kehlstein; about a great man's household, his eating habits, his visitors—there could be no doubt that the teller had actually witnessed these things.

Also he told about Vienna, the interview with Schuschnigg, and the misadventure of the lawyer-doctor in Berchtesgaden. Manifestly, no one would have been permitted to stay in the Führer's home at such a critical time unless he had possessed his host's confidence; nor was this confidence misplaced. The son of Budd-Erling was no *Emporkömmling*, a social climber, but understood the Führer's ideas and his high destiny. He spoke with respect and even awe of a crusader who had set out to chain the wild beast of Bolshevism and put an end to the age-long quarrelings among Europe's petty states.

So the Kapitän could see no reason for secrecy, and talked frankly about his responsibilities in America. He was a sort of inspector-general, making a survey of Nazi educational work all over the country, and at the same time lending his prestige and cultivated intelligence to the task of influencing highly placed Americans. He had completed a tour of nearly two months, in the course of which he had visited a score of cities, all the way from Seattle to Palm Beach, as he put it. He was greatly pleased by what he had found; in most cases the propaganda was in excellent hands and the results most encouraging; America was ripe for a fundamental social change, and with hard work and wise guidance there was every reason to expect that the strong German elements throughout the country would play their full part. The main trouble, as this polished Junker saw it, was the reluctance of the Nazi partisans to Americanize themselves; they wanted to follow the Nazi ways, and to force these ways down American throats, which couldn't be done. The Bund had been ordered to change its make-up, and to print the swastika in red, white, and blue. All this was hard, especially in the hinterlands.

Lanny agreed, but said that he had noted a great many native groups springing up, having the Nazi program, but not acknowledging it as Nazi, and in many cases not even knowing it. They called themselves "Christian" or "Protestant," "Yankee Freemen" or "American Patriots" —it didn't really make any difference, so long as they saw the Red peril and the Jew menace, and fought the New Deal. The Kapitän agreed, and Quadratt put in: "Citizens' Protective Associations and National Workers' Leagues are a dime a dozen in New York right now."

XII

This highly trained aristocrat spoke English without a trace of accent, and had no difficulty in "Americanizing" himself. He was here for America's benefit, he declared, to give the country a chance to profit by the lessons which had been learned in Germany. He had found Americans an extremely receptive people, especially those who were highly placed, and had more to lose from reckless experimentation. He talked interestingly about his meetings with such men. He had spent the better part of a day with Henry Ford, an unusual privilege, and found him in a generous mood. He had spent an evening with Colonel McCormick and found him, as he said, "most congenial." The same for Lammot du Pont in Wilmington; "a really powerful man, with whom we have done a great deal of business, as you know." The same for Mr. Rand, of Remington-Rand, in Connecticut, who had recently had a painful experience with a great strike, and was bitter as a result.

"My father knows him well," said Lanny; and the Kapitän was quick to take that lead. "I have heard a great deal about your father, and would esteem it a privilege to meet him." Lanny couldn't do anything but offer an introduction. Poor Robbie would have to take his chances with this suave and subtle Junker!

The greatest progress had been made in Washington, if you could believe the agent's story. He mentioned hostesses such as Mrs. McLean and Mrs. Patterson who had entertained him, and the senators and congressmen who had heard him gladly and assured him of their sympathy. He was amusing on the subject of Senator Reynolds of North Carolina, who had begun life as a barker in a sideshow, and had got elected by accusing his rival of the crime of eating caviar. "Do you know what caviar is? Fish eggs! Do you want the Tarheel State to be represented in Washington by a man who eats fish eggs?" Now the Senator was congenial to the Nazis, though of course not carrying the label. He was planning a paper to be called the *American Vindicator*, and had shown the Kapitän his idea of the layout. "Pretty poor stuff, I thought it; but I judge the standard of education in the Senator's part of the country is not very high."

Lanny wished that these misguided statesmen might have heard what a Nazi agent really thought of them in private. "Senator Wheeler appears to hate the Administration even more than he loves the Anaconda Copper Company." And then: "Senator Nye, I gather, has been a pacifist for a long time. Now the Führer has got him bewitched, and he is a pacifist for everybody but us." Then a congressman with the odd name of Ham Fish. "I am told that he comes from an old and wealthy family, and was a great football player when he was young. He should have stuck to that."

Forrest Quadratt took up the conversation. He knew Fish very well, and reported him as amiable, but bumptious, and stupid beyond belief. There was a convenient American arrangement known as the "franking privilege," by which congressmen could send out mail free of charge; there was no limit upon it, and some had even shipped their furniture and liquors by that method. Ham Fish had turned over the matter to his secretary, and the secretary had given Quadratt the use of it, a device whereby unlimited Nazi speeches, pamphlets, and books could be distributed to the American people at their own expense. The ex-poet urged his Junker friend to realize the importance of this, and told about a publishing house which he had set up in a small town of New Jersey. It was carefully camouflaged to look American, and Quadratt showed his guests several books which he had written under pseudonyms and published through this concern.

On another shelf of the same bookcase was a row of the decadent poets of France, Germany, Austria, Italy, England, and America. Lanny's eyes ran over them: Baudelaire, Verlaine, Dowson, Symons, D'Annunzio—and Quadratt's own youthful volume, *Eros Unbound*. The ex-poet saw Lanny's glance, and remarked, nostalgically: "There used to be a day when I could recite whole pages from those books; now, alas, I have had to become a reformer, and my mind is a card catalogue of names and personalities all over my native land." He meant America, and repeated the wheeze which was his stock-in-trade, that he was trying to interpret the land of his birth to the land of his forefathers, and vice versa.

XIII

The "inspector-general" of the Nazis had been invited to meet some of what he called the "key personalities of the American movement." This was to be on the following evening, and Quadratt offered to get an invitation for Lanny, who accepted with pleasure. The Kapitän never made public speeches, he said, but was glad to talk confidentially with the leaders, and especially those who were in position to put up the funds, so essential to the building of any new movement. The gathering was to be in the home of a Miss van Zandt, on lower Fifth Avenue, now mostly pre-empted by the dress-making and book-publishing industries. Quadratt explained that this elderly lady was "slightly cracked, but harmless, and lousy with money." He added that in America it was the women who had the money, and you had to put up with a certain amount of boredom and inconvenience in order to get it. Lanny remarked that it was not so different in Germany; he mentioned the Bechsteinhaus at the Berghof, named in honor of the widow of the piano manufacturer, who had financed the Führer all through his early struggles. It was a worthy precedent.

At eight on the following evening Lanny descended from a taxicab in front of an ancient brownstone mansion, and the door was opened before him by an aged servitor in black. There he met and listened to the oddest assortment of upper-class intellectuals it had ever been his fate to encounter. His hostess, tall, thin, white-haired, and wearing pince-nez, greeted him in the entrance to her drawing-room, clad in a full-length and long-sleeved black silk dress in which her great-grand-mother might have attended funerals in Grace Church. This lady's ancestry went back to New York's early Dutch beginnings, and she had inherited a small family farm, now covered with skyscrapers paying enormous incomes. When she went for a walk she carried a black silk umbrella faded green, and when she invited guests she gave them rather cheap refreshments, but would not hesitate to write a check for five thousand dollars when a plausible ex-poet persuaded her that he had a new book which would help to oust the Reds from their entrenchments in near-by Union Square.

To this soirée the "slightly cracked" lady had invited persons of wealth whom it might be worth while for a Nazi Junker to meet: among them a White Russian count—White in the political, not the geographical sense—with the difficult name of Anastase Andreivitch Vonsiatskoy-Vonsiatsky. (Lanny never did find out the wherefore of the repetition with variation.) He was a giant of a man with huge hands and thick lips from which came a deep rumbling voice. He had married a wealthy widow more than two decades older than himself, and now he had Nazi Stormtroopers drilling on her immense estate in Connecticut. There also he edited and published a Russian-language magazine called *The Fascist*, and sent arms to the Mexican Gold Shirts —all this quite openly, boasting of it in loud bellows.

And then a round-faced, soft-voiced American with graying hair and the aspect of a scholar, who had inherited a fortune from the paper-manufacturing business and purchased a literary magazine and turned it into an organ of American Fascism. Seward Collins politely explained to Lanny Budd that he had been converted by Hilaire Belloc to "distributionism"; he wanted to go back to the Middle Ages and have everybody cultivate small plots of land. He hated capitalism, and tolerated the Nazis because he thought they were destroying that evil system. He considered anti-Semitism an error, but even so had set up a bookshop for the sale of all sorts of Fascist literature.

Leading brain-truster among this company was a Georgian—the American, not the Russian variety—dark and curly-haired, a Harvard graduate and employee of the State Department in the happy days before the New Deal. Lawrence Dennis had written three books advocating and predicting Fascism for his country, and he now published from a downtown office a bulletin called the *Weekly Foreign Letter*. He was prepared to defend anywhere the thesis that "democracy" was an evil dream, for the masses never had been capable of self-government and never would be. He was ardent in defense of Franco, and in this was supported by two other guests, an elegant old gentleman, Mr. Castle, who had been Undersecretary of State under Hoover, and a shrewd and forceful Mr. Hart, who, Lanny was told, was paid ten thousand dollars a year by certain big corporations to oppose whatever forms of social legislation might come up.

The Army was represented in this gathering by Major-General Moseley, who was treated by everybody with great deference, being looked upon as the future "Nationalist" party's candidate for President; he contributed to the discussion the idea that refugees coming from Europe should be sterilized. The Navy was represented by Lieutenant-Commander Spafford, who, in accordance with Navy traditions, had little to say. The Press was represented by the city's smallest newspaper with the largest circulation.

One of the women guests at this high-class social event delivered Lanny to his hotel, and on the way remarked that if the wealth represented there were totaled up it would amount to a couple of billion dollars. Lanny went to sleep in a state of deep depression, and next morning, to cheer himself up and to pacify the Trudi-ghost he put a thousand-dollar bill in an envelope, together with a typed unsigned note: "To be used for the combatting of anti-Semitism in New York." He mailed this to a liberal clergyman of the city, the same to whom, more than a year ago, he had turned over the profits from the sale of the Goya painting. Before sailing for Europe, the secret agent wrote a report to his Chief, concluding with these words: "America has everything that Germany had during the period that Hitlerism was in the egg."

25

Slings and Arrows

I

LANNY took a steamer to Le Havre, and a very slow train to Calais, where he had stored his car. He drove to Paris, where he met Zoltan, just returned from London with news about the sales at Christie's and other art matters. They went to the spring Salon together, looking for new talent and finding mostly commonplace, for they were two exceedingly fastidious gentlemen. When they got too discouraged about their world they would go to the Louvre or the Petit Palais and commune with the old masters, who had really known how to paint, or so the experts thought. They would have lunch together in an outdoor café at the Rond Point; the spring sunshine was delightful, the crowds gay, and now and then the pollen of chestnut blossoms would be wafted down onto their table, supplying their food with extra quantities of vitamin A. They talked about deals they had made and others in prospect, and life seemed good—so long as you thought only about your personal affairs.

The political situation was truly depressing to any Pink. Franco's armies had cut their way to the Mediterranean, thus dividing the Loyalist forces in two. Everybody agreed that the government's position was hopeless; that is, everybody except the Spanish people, who refused to realize that they had to become slaves. In spite of continual bombing of cities and killing of thousands of civilians, the Valencianos and Madrileños went on fighting desperately in their sector, and the Barcelonese in theirs—something considered irrational and exasperating by all members of the governing classes of Europe. The British and the Italians, having come to an amicable agreement on this and other subjects, put pressure on the French and forced the closing of the border once more. Red Catalonia would be starved until it came to its senses—or rather to British and Italian senses.

A part of the agreement had been over Abyssinia: Mussolini's triumph was to be legalized, and the 101st League of Nations Council proceeded to pass what was in effect an act of suicide, the renunciation of its last hope to prevent war. In harmony with the hypocrisy of the time, it would do this in the name of peace, and the ultra-pious Lord Halifax was chosen as the man for this job. "Great as is the League of Nations," he announced, "the ends it exists to serve are greater than itself and the greatest of those ends is peace." His white Lordship was answered by a frail little black man who looked oddly like a Jew, Haile Selassie, Negus of Abyssinia: "The Ethiopian people, to whom all assistance was refused, are climbing alone their path to Calvary."

Affairs in France stood on the same plane of fraudulence. The Chautemps government had been forced out, because the Socialists had refused to vote it the "special powers" it demanded. On the day that Hitler had invaded Austria, *la grande nation* had been without a government. Then Blum had formed one which had lasted less than a month. Now France had what was called an "anti-Red" Cabinet under Daladier, and for Foreign Minister had a politician named Bonnet, lean and sallow, with a bald head and one of those long beaked noses used for smelling money. Lanny wondered, was any of it Nazi money? The Minister's wife was one of Kurt Meissner's intimates, and Lili Moldau was her constant companion.

The party of these men called itself "Radical Socialist," but had long ago become a party of bribe collectors and distributors. "Envelopes" was the polite word; they were handed to journalists, to publishers, to political manipulators, to ladies who had any sort of influence. They would contain a proper number of bills—never a check that could serve as evidence. Bonnet had a great banking firm behind him, and when public funds were not sufficient for his purposes, the bank would make up the quota.

That was how France was governed now, and when you heard the inside story you despaired of the republic. There were patriotic and honest people left, but they were out of power, and their protests had become stereotyped; the great public, which craved novelties, was bored by them. Blum was a Jew, which damned him, and his party quarreled with the Communists, who repeated Russian formulas and urged Russian techniques—in face of the evident fact that its class enemies had the arms, the planes and bombs and poison gas, and in any attempt at uprising it would be the Fascists and not the Communists who won. The mass of the people read the great press, having no idea that the contents of these papers were for sale to the highest bidders, in many cases the agents of the Fascist and Nazi governments.

II

Lanny had obtained orders from clients in New York and thereabouts, and was planning to set out on another trip into Germany; but something occurred which changed his program in a few minutes. He was strolling, as was his custom, from one fashionable picture dealer's to the next, looking at what they had to offer; this was important, for prices varied from time to time and from place to place, and Lanny's success depended in part upon this knowledge. It wasn't enough to say: "This is a genuine Monet, a worthy example of his art." It would be necessary to add: "I saw one of his works offered in Paris last month for four hundred thousand francs." Right now the franc was down to thirty-four to the dollar, and that made Paris an excellent place to go shopping for art.

The dealers all knew the son of Budd-Erling, and hastened to point out their best. One of them remarked: "I have something that might interest you, M. Budd: a very good seascape by Detaze."

"Indeed?" said Lanny, surprised—for these paintings did not often come upon the market. "I should like to see it."

He was still more surprised when he looked at the painting. He knew all of them by heart, as it were; every brush stroke, of which he had watched so many thousands being put on. He was quite sure that he had had this particular seascape in his hands during his last visit to Bienvenu.

"M. Bruget," he said, "I am embarrassed to have to ask you to set this painting aside and not sell it until I have investigated the matter. I am practically certain that it was in my mother's storeroom less than two months ago; and she never sells a painting without consulting me."

"*Mon dieu, M. Budd!* You mean that it has been stolen?"

"I don't want to say until I have made inquiry. Would you mind telling me where you got the painting?"

"Certainly not. I bought it from the dealer Agricoli in Nice. I thought that was a natural place for a Detaze to be found."

"Did he have more than one?"

"He said he had had three, but had only this one left."

"Would you be willing for me to see the back of it?"

The man hastened to unscrew the back of the frame; and on the canvas, in addition to Marcel's signature, which was always put on both back and front, was a lightly painted number, 94. "That is my catalogue number," Lanny explained. "I have a cardfile at Juan, with the data on every Detaze that I have ever known of. I am sure that I had this one in my hands on my last visit to the storeroom, for I considered it as one of a lot which I was taking to Germany for sale."

"I am greatly disturbed, M. Budd," declared the man. "I hope you understand that I had no means of knowing and no reason to suspect anything wrong."

"Certainly; that idea could not occur to me. I wonder if you would permit me to call my mother's home and pay the charge. I may be able to get some information at once."

Lanny put in a call; and since long-distance service was never very prompt in France, he strolled about and looked at other paintings until he was summoned, and heard his mother's voice. He asked: "Have you sold any of Marcel's works since I was last at home?" When she answered "No," he inquired if she knew of anyone else having sold any. Then he said: "Please do not say anything to anybody about this call until you see me. I will be home late tonight."

"Is something wrong?" Beauty's tone was full of concern.

"I can't be sure until I have talked to you, and to others. Please promise me, nothing until I arrive."

She promised, and the dealer agreed to lock the painting up until he heard again. Lanny took a taxi to his hotel, packed his belongings, and set out on the Boulevard Champs Elysées to the familiar *route nationale*.

III

Lanny drove straight through, and Beauty was waiting up for him when he arrived. While waiting, she had been trying to guess, and he discovered that they had guessed the same thing. He told her what he had learned in Paris, and received once more her assurance that she hadn't given anybody access to the storeroom. He consulted the cardfile which was kept in his room while he was away. Number 94 was marked with an "S," which meant that it was supposed to be in the storeroom. The keys were kept in the top drawer of his chiffonier, and he looked and found them in the proper place.

Getting a torch, he hurried over to his studio. Doors and windows appeared to be intact, and he let himself in, first at the front door, then at the one which led from the main room to the storeroom in the rear. Everything appeared to be as he had left it; rows of deep shelves ran around the walls, and the paintings were ranged on these according to number. It took but a moment to make sure that 94 was gone; what others were gone would require a checking against the cardfile.

Lanny locked up again and went back to his mother. "Somebody has taken one painting, probably three, and possibly more. Either the thief is an expert at picking locks, or he had access to our home and knows where I keep the keys. Either he worked in collaboration with Agricoli, in Nice, or he made that dealer believe he had come by them honestly. I note that he went to an Italian, and that seems to me significant."

"Oh, Lanny, it *can't* be true!"

"I don't want to say that it's true. I'll have a talk with Agricoli in the morning, and see what I can learn. This much I know, and you know it, too—that a man who gambles is always exposed to temptation, and I can't see Vittorio as a very heroic resister. Where is he now?"

"Asleep in their room."

"Well, let them sleep; there's nothing more to be done now."

"Oh, it will be so dreadful if it's true! What shall we do, Lanny?"

"It's always a waste of time trying to cross bridges before you come to them. All I want to know is my own position in the matter. Legally I have no rights in the paintings; they are your property by Marcel's will, and I am merely your agent."

"That is not so, Lanny. I made a definite agreement with you to handle the pictures and divide the proceeds three ways, you, me and Marceline. I should have put it into writing, and I'll do it now."

"Have you paid Marceline all the money that is due her on the Hitler sale?"

"No. I have been giving her a little at a time, as you suggested. She wants more, of course. Oh, Lanny, do you suppose it is possible she could have known about it?"

"My guess is it was Vittorio's own bright idea. But it's futile to speculate. The only sensible thing is to go to sleep, and not worry about troubles that you may never have to face."

"If Marceline doesn't know about it, she will be so horrified!"

"It is important that we don't give either of them any sign that we have noticed anything wrong. The thing for you now is to go to bed. Count your blessings and say your prayers!" The mother had become quite religious under the influence of her husband's example, and when any good thing happened to members of her family, she piously attributed it to her spiritual exercises. Lanny wondered if she had prayed for Vittorio to succeed with his "systems" at the casinos? If so, her faith had been sorely tried!

IV

Lanny didn't sleep much himself. He got up early, dressed, and got a bite to eat, served by the black-clad lame Spaniard who had taken over the management of the home, and who looked upon the young master as one who came down out of the skies in a chariot. After the fashion of servants, José had figured out the relationships existing among the members of this family; unlike most servants, he kept his thoughts to himself, out of loyalty to Lanny. Did he know or suspect anything about the paintings? Lanny didn't hint at the subject; he took a glance at the morning papers, with news of bombings in Barcelona and Valencia, and remarked: "A good time to be in France, José." Then he went out to his car and drove off. He wasn't in the mood for play-acting with the young couple.

In Nice he found the art shop not yet open, and sat in his car reading items of depressing news from all over the world. At about ten there arrived a stoutish, round-faced Italian, with a pointed black beard and the proper morning coat and pin-striped trousers. It was a warm morning, and he had been walking, and wiped the perspiration from his forehead. He did it several times more when the highly respected stepson of Marcel Detaze followed him in and opened up with the tidings that he had been receiving stolen goods. "*Dio mio, Mister Budd!*" exclaimed the dealer, several times without variation.

"Let me relieve your anxiety, Signor Agricoli," said the suave expert. "I don't want to have any publicity, or to make any unnecessary trouble. If you will deal with me frankly, I will consider you an ally and a friend—and I am sure you will find it better that way."

"*Si, si, Mister Budd, sicuramente—naturellement*—with my heart." The frightened man seemed not sure whether he was speaking Italian, French, or English, so he said it in all three.

"I want two things: first, to get the paintings back, and second, to find out who took them, so that I can stop the leak. So far as the money losses are concerned, I am prepared to deal generously with you."

"*Merci, M. Budd—grazie*—I thank you—I will do everything—*tout possible!*"

Hearing the story, Lanny realized that the man had reason to be worried. He had bought three Detazes at an absurdly low price, and had sold them for half what he might have got at the sales rooms of the Hotel Drouot in Paris. Such a procedure seemed to indicate a fear that the paintings had not been honestly come by. According to his story, a young Italian of good appearance had come to him, giving the name of Gigliotto and saying that he had three French paintings which had belonged to his recently deceased father in Genoa. He professed not to know the name of the painter, but had been told that the works were valuable, so he had brought them to France. The pair had bargained back and forth, and the stranger had twice gathered up the canvases and gone out of the shop; finally the dealer had agreed to pay eighty thousand francs. He had the bill of sale, and Lanny inspected it but did not know the handwriting, or recognize the seller from the description. He was interested, however, when the dealer said that he had seen the man two evenings later, coming out of the casino with another young Italian, who wore an officer's uniform with the left sleeve empty.

The dealer named the customers to whom he had sold the paintings. He had carbon copies of his bills of sale, and showed his books, in which purchases and sales were entered. That was all he could do, and all Lanny wanted. Said he: "The paintings are my mother's property, and under the law you will be bound to reimburse the persons to whom you sold them. You will probably not get much back from the thief— since it appears that he frequents the casino. But all this would involve publicity, which my family does not want. I prefer to settle the matter quietly, and I make you the offer that if you will see your customers and buy the paintings back from them, I will reimburse you for the eighty thousand francs you paid to the thief. Does that seem to you reasonable?"

"*Si, si, M. Budd*, most generous—*vraiment. Però*—are we not breaking some law?"

"I don't think the law will trouble itself, if no one complains. I am pretty sure I can find out who the thief is, and persuade him to get out of the country and stay out. The French law would be satisfied with that."

"*Mille grazie, Mister Budd*. I will do my best—*sans delai*."

"It will mean a trip to Paris for you—for I think it would be the part of wisdom not to put anything into writing. M. Bruget, I am sure, will be amenable; and if either of your other customers questions your good faith, you may tell him to call my mother's home on the telephone, and either she or I will confirm your statements."

V

So the matter was settled. Lanny drove back to Juan, where he found his brother-in-law on the porch, absorbed in the reading of a yellow-backed novel which he hurriedly shoved into his pocket on Lanny's approach. Il Capitano Vittorio di San Girolamo had a taste for pornographic fiction which he knew his relative did not share. The latter said: "Be so good as to come down to the studio. I have a matter of importance to talk over with you."

Lanny had had time to think over his procedure, and wasted no breath on preliminaries. He motioned Vittorio to a chair and took one himself, then opened up: "Your friend who calls himself Gigliotto has just told me his part of the story, so you might as well tell me yours."

The Capitano had barely touched the chair; now he bounced out of it. "That is a lie!" he cried.

"Don't waste words, Vittorio. I assure you I am in no mood for nonsense. You have one chance to keep out of jail, and that is to tell me the whole story frankly."

"I haven't the remotest idea what you are talking about."

"All I want to know is, did you take any paintings except the ones that fellow sold to Agricoli?"

"It's a God-damned lie. I never——"

"All right, Vittorio. If that's your line, I'll give the police a chance to handle the matter. They are better equipped for such cases than I am." He got up and went to the telephone on his desk, and had got so far as to take down the receiver when the Capitano descended from the aristocratic perch on which he habitually sat. "Oh, all right, I'll talk." So Lanny hung up, and the other resumed his seat and said: "I took three paintings, no more. I was sick of seeing you holding back Marceline's money."

"I'm not going to discuss Marceline. But I point out to you that if you took more, I'll find it out. It's just a matter of checking against my records, which I haven't yet had the time to do."

"You can save yourself the trouble. I only took three. That was all I could carry at once. Marceline was broke and so was I."

"Did she know what you were doing?"

"Of course not. And I hope you're not going to tell her; it'll only make her unhappy for nothing."

"How much of the money have you left?"

"Not a sou."

"What did you do with it?"

"I tried a new system, but I didn't have enough. Just when I got to the point where one more turn would have put me on the road to success, the money was gone."

"It has happened that way ever since the roulette wheel was invented," remarked Lanny. "Now let me inform you, I have arranged to pay Agricoli eighty thousand francs and he will get the paintings back for me. You, for your part, will give me your demand note for the amount."

"What good will that do you?"

"I will put it away in a safe place, on the chance that you may ever have a claim against any member of my family."

"Very clever of you!"

"I hope it is. The other request I have to make is that you will invent a telegram ordering you back to your duties in Spain. In that way you can avoid giving Marceline the information which, as you say, would only make her unhappy for nothing."

"You are going to try to break up our marriage?"

"Just the opposite. If I tell Marceline the truth, it might well break things up; but on the basis I am proposing, she will be free to follow you to Spain if and when she wishes; that will be for you and her to settle. The one thing I have to make certain is that you do not ever come back into France."

"Oh, so you pass a sentence of exile on me!"

"Italy is your native land, and Spain is going to be your colony. There ought to be glory and money enough for you there. I propose that you leave France for my mother and myself."

"Very subtle indeed—but it seems pretty close to blackmail to me."

"I don't know the exact name for the method by which you have been getting your gambling money from my mother and her daughter, and I don't want to bandy words with you. I simply tell you that unless you agree to take the night train to Marseille and a steamer for Cadiz, you will spend tonight in the Cannes jail."

VI

Vittorio de San Girolamo was a young gentleman who thought extremely well of himself; it came naturally to him, and a fond mother had encouraged it. He had pale, well-cut features, and a little sharp-pointed black mustache of which he took great care. He had several medals and decorations which he wore on all occasions, and he had manners which made an impression upon the ladies. Of late he had been feeling himself master of Bienvenu, and had perhaps not been taking the trouble to manifest his best qualities. It occurred to him that now was a time for the quickest possible turning on of his charm.

"Lanny," he began, humbly. "You are taking a very harsh attitude to me, and I beg you to stop and try to understand my position. I may have made a blunder; yes, I know I have, I admit it freely, and truly regret it—but you must realize that it wasn't quite the same thing as a crime. Marceline has a claim on those paintings, much better than your own. She is Marcel's daughter, his own blood; and when she tells me that she is being badly treated, am I not supposed to pay any attention to what she says?"

This was a subject which had been discussed in detail, and Lanny was tired of it. Said he: "Are you ready to give me your answer, or do you want time to think it over?"

"I see that you are hopelessly prejudiced against me, Lanny. How am I to get the money to travel?"

"If you let me know early enough, I will have my friend Jerry Pendleton meet you at the Cannes station and put into your hands a railroad ticket to Marseille, a steamer ticket to Cadiz, and a thousand francs so that you can eat on the way, and travel to Seville. The army, I am sure, will welcome you."

The deflated ex-aviator sat staring in front of him, occasionally biting his lip. He looked like a surly and greatly vexed Fascist, and Lanny thought: "May there be more of them in that state!" Always he saw this brother-in-law in the role of which the brother-in-law was proudest—of dropping bombs upon undefended Abyssinian villages, and mustard gas upon roads where barefooted natives walked.

"You are giving me a rotten deal, Lanny. You must know that Marceline loves me, and wouldn't want this to happen."

"You are at liberty to tell Marceline about it, if you think it will help you; but that won't change my attitude. I am offering you a chance to keep your name clear, and to start life over again, if you have it in you."

"But what in God's name is Marceline to do—and the baby?"

"Marceline is a free agent, and the choice will be hers. If she wants to go with you tonight, I will give her the money. If she wants to stay here and come later, I will give it to her then."

"But sooner or later Marceline will want to come back to visit her mother; and what excuse can I give for not coming with her?"

"I suppose you can plead your military duties. Marceline will be welcome to her mother's home, but you will never come here so long as I live. There is no statute of limitation on felonies, and there will be none on my determination. These paintings have been safe in their storeroom for more than twenty years, and I want to know they will be here the next time I come back."

"You won't accept my word that I am truly sorry, and will never again touch them?"

"Excuse me, Vittorio—you have taught me that your word is worth exactly nothing. My mother has given you money on your pledge to quit gambling, and you have broken it again and again. A home is a place where people believe in and trust each other; and you have excluded yourself from ours."

"Do you want to know what I think about your behavior, Lanny? You're still a Red in your heart. I've believed it ever since you came into Spain to help that God-damned snake Alfy."

"You can believe whatever you please, Vittorio, but don't make the mistake of talking about it. Remember that you took money to do your part in freeing that snake."

"I took the money, but I never did anything. I went to watch you, and make certain that you didn't do any hurt to our cause."

"That's your story; but don't fail to realize what a weak one it is. Your camp is full of spies and traitors, and if you once get that tar on your fingers you'll have a hard time rubbing it off. I'll tell you about myself—I have seen so much of the crookedness of politicians in all the camps that I have decided to attend to my own affairs and let them alone. So far as you and I are concerned, I think it's a fair bargain for me to say nothing of what I know about you, and you to say nothing of what you guess about me. Do you want to give me your decision?"

"Oh, I'll go, of course—what else can I do? I don't want to bring disgrace on my wife, or to handicap my son's future. But I'm telling you, I'll come back to France some day—and on my own terms."

"Perhaps you'll come at the head of an army. If so, I'll hope to get out before the bombs fall."

Lanny seated himself at his desk and wrote: "On demand I promise to pay to Lanny Budd the sum of eighty thousand francs for value received." He dated this, and the Capitano signed it and stalked out.

VII

In the village he took the tram to Cannes, and from there telephoned his wife, saying that he had received at the Italian consulate a telegram ordering him to return to Seville at once; he had made a mistake and overstayed his leave.

Marceline, of course, was greatly upset. What was she to do? Surely she couldn't take a young baby on that long trip, and stay in war-torn Spain, with the midsummer heat coming so soon. "I'll have to wait a while, Vittorio; and perhaps wean the baby and leave him here."

"Oh, Lanny, what have you done!" exclaimed the softhearted mother, in the privacy of her boudoir. "Don't you know how she loves him?"

"It's her hard luck that she made a bad guess," replied the tougher-minded son. "She made her own bed—and she doesn't have to lie in it one night longer than she chooses."

"In Southern Spain, that ghastly climate—and all the mosquitoes! You shouldn't have done it, Lanny! It was too drastic!"

"Hold your horses, old dear," he replied—a phrase he had learned in the rude land of the Yankees. He didn't tell her just how "drastic" he had been, leaving her to guess that the young husband was departing because of his painful embarrassment.

Vittorio explained to Marceline that he had a lot of business to attend to in Cannes, and asked her to pack up his belongings and drive in and meet him. Also, would Lanny be kind enough to have the travel bureau attend to the matter of his accommodations?

Lanny was happy to oblige; he called up his old friend Jerry and promised to mail a check on receipt of bill. He gave Marceline a thousand francs in an envelope, and that was the end of the matter for him. He was glad he didn't have to be a witness of the parting, and persuaded his mother to send her farewells by proxy. Let the young couple have their last hours together and work out their problems in their own way. Lanny himself had no tears to shed; he had always loved his mother's home, but had lost interest in it since a Fascist ex-aviator had been free to spread his ego there. Now Lanny would stay awhile, and go fishing with Jerry, and play tennis, and swim, and let a little of the joy of life seep back into his heart.

VIII

But he couldn't keep out of politics. He had to get in touch with Julie Palma, and take her for a drive, and read the letters that had come from her husband. The government had been moved to Barcelona, and Raoul was there, being bombed almost every day; a strange thing, you got used to it—apparently human beings could get used to anything. You heard the whistle of the bomb, and you closed your eyes for a moment or two—that was automatic; then came the explosion, and the house across the street might be turned to rubble in a fraction of a second. Hundreds of people were being killed in a single day, or worse yet, maimed and pinned under wreckage which might take fire. There wasn't a pane of glass intact for blocks around Raoul. Yet people stayed on and did their jobs, women refusing to leave their men.

Raoul might easily have come out, but he, too, refused. His little wife closed her eyes and the lids quivered as she said: "I won't ask him to come. It's his duty, and I won't be the one to break him down. It's the people's war; it's freedom, it's everything we believe in. We asked for it and we have to stick by it."

Lanny gave her some money and then went back to his home, deeply moved, and troubled in his conscience because he was taking a holiday in a terrible time like this. It was the Trudi-ghost, still working in his soul and giving him no peace. It wanted Lanny to become a fanatic like itself. It filled him with rage at the hypocrisy in high places, at the spectacle of class interest masquerading as patriotism, as piety, as love of peace. He knew how quickly these peace-lovers would start a fight, the moment their own privileges were threatened. You could see that in Spain and hear it talked in smart society on the Côte d'Azur, where the wealthy Spaniards were waiting for their homeland to be made safe again, and where the rest of smart Europe expressed its hearty sympathy.

The farce of "Non-Intervention" went on all that summer, and so, also, did the seeking and finding of pleasure. The French Riviera was now fully established as a summer resort; villas were leased for the year around and hotels and rooming houses were filled to the last garret. The drums thumped and the stopped trumpets blared all night across the Golfe Juan; all day the women lolled in the sunshine with two narrow strips of cloth around them, and the men strolled by and looked them over and took their pick. Day or night it was hard to get near the gaming tables for the crowds, and the dancing floors were so packed that, as the disgusted Sophie put it, you had to learn to dance on a sou.

She was one of those who had bought a luxurious villa on the Cap d'Antibes, planning to spend a life of mild enjoyment, and now resented the invasion of vulgar hordes. The only thing to do was to stay away from public places: entertain your own little group of friends; eat in one another's dining rooms and dance in one another's drawing-rooms, or outside on the loggias. Along the shore were quiet spots with white or pink villas perched upon the rocks, and other villas dotting the slopes of the hills, many of them with extensive and beautiful grounds. The residents divided up into sets according to their wealth and the mysterious thing called "social position," and kept others out in spite of no end of heart-burning. Many who had been considered "fast" when they were young had become pillars of conservatism in their later years, and were now shocked by the doings of the younger set.

Sophie, Baroness de la Tourette, had been a wild one, with henna hair and a loud voice; now she had let the hair turn gray, her laughter was subdued, and her principal diversion was playing bridge for money which she didn't need. Beauty Budd was one of her cronies, and it was a misfortune that Beauty's husband wouldn't learn to play cards. They would try their best to rope Lanny in, and failing in this, would take Marceline. All Lanny wanted was to sit in a corner with a book, or to wander down to his studio and pound on the piano; but this was contrary to the ladies' idea of a social life, and every time they got him here, even for a few days, they would start scheming to interest him in some member of their sex. They wouldn't say "wife," because that had a terrifying sound; but some girl to sit out with on lovely summer nights, and to take sailing on dark blue water whose millions of wavelets sparkled like silver in the moonlight and like gold in the sun.

Just now it was a visiting grand-niece of Sophie's, a lissome young thing just out of finishing school in Mobile. She was a dream made out of the different varieties of roses—cream and pink and red, with the almost black kind for her hair; she had the loveliest soft drawl, if you had time to listen to it, and ran the consonant of one word into the vowel of the next just as if she were French—only the French did it in half the time. Sophie was determined that this was going to be a match, and the bunch of roses was apparently willing to be plucked. Lanny would be invited over to dinner, and then left to stroll in the garden, and he did—but after they had talked about the people they knew and the things they were doing and the places they had been to, what on earth was left?

IX

A funny thing happened. Sophie and her husband, the dignified Mr. Armitage, were in the card room finishing their second rubber with Beauty and Marceline, having won several dollars from their guests. Lanny was sitting outside on the terrace, listening to Lucy Cotton's account of her home on Mobile bay, where the magnolias were now in bloom and the mocking birds singing the whole night long. There came a sound of motorcars and a flashing of lights; two cars stopped under the porte-cochere—it was the fashion to drop in, most any time before dawn, for the nights were delightful, while the afternoons were hot, so you took a long siesta. In the evening, after you had danced, or gambled, or been to a show, you would drop in on friends, and sit for a while sipping iced drinks, and gossiping about the people you knew: She has scads of money— They say her grandfather was a miner— She said this and I said that— And have you heard about Dickie, he's drunk again and Pudzi is threatening to leave him— I have a date with my *couturier* tomorrow, and what are *you* going to do?

One of this company appeared to be different from the rest. For one thing she had no make-up, and for another she wore glasses, which no smart lady will do if she can see to walk down the street without them. This one was of the indeterminate age between twenty-five and thirty-five, a small, birdlike creature, quick in her glances and speech. Lanny had never seen her before, and her name, Miss Creston, told him nothing. He saw that she was watching one after another of the company, and when her eyes met his, she did not avert her glance in the usual ladylike way, but met his frankly, as much as to say: "Well, who are you, and what do you want?" There is a term applied to such a manner; it was "forward."

When she had finished looking at Sophie Timmons, the hardware lady from Cincinnati who had married a French baron and wished she hadn't, and at Sophie's second husband, the retired engineer, and at the one-time professional beauty whose friends had given her that unusual name, and at this too-well-known lady's son and daughter, Miss Creston started inspecting Sophie Timmons' drawing-room, the paneling, the draperies, and the pictures on the walls—which wasn't exactly polite behavior. Then she got up and looked at the books in the bookcase—which was really just like saying that the conversation bored her. Lanny knew how Sophie's books had been chosen; she would get one that people were talking about, and start to read it, but rarely finish, because by that time people were talking about some other.

It happened that somebody mentioned Hitler, and a speech he had just made denouncing the mistreatment of Germans in the Sudetenland. What did the man want, and where was he going to stop? One of the company remarked: "Ask Lanny; he knows him." Another, a stranger, interjected: "You mean, personally?" The reply was: "He was a guest at Berchtesgaden just recently."

That brought Lanny into the spotlight, and the lady with the glasses stepped in and joined him there. Turning from the books, she exclaimed: "My God, do you mean one can actually visit that man?"

Said Lanny, mildly: "One can, if one is properly introduced."

"And how does one get introduced?"

"Well, it happens that the Führer is an admirer of my stepfather's paintings, and I took some there and he bought them for his guest house."

"Oh! It was a business matter!"

"Partly that, but social, also. You would find him a quite charming companion, I assure you."

"I suppose he's fond of little children, and all that!"

"It happens that he is especially fond of children."

"And how does he have them prepared?"

For once Lanny wasn't quick on the uptake. All he could say was: "How do you mean?"

"I mean: How are they cooked? What sauce are they served with?"

The company had stopped all other conversation to listen to this colloquy. Polite persons all, they must have been taken aback, even as Lanny was. However, he managed to smile, and replied: "It happens that he is a vegetarian. The only babies he eats are chicks before they have begun to be; in other words, a poached egg on his boiled vegetables. But he will serve you baby lamb or calf if you desire it."

The woman stood there, as conspicuous as if she were making a speech; and nobody offered to interrupt this duel. "Tell me, Mr. Budd," she said; "do you approve of this charming vegetarian's political procedures?"

"I am an art expert, Miss Creston. I help to find beautiful paintings, mostly for American collections. I have found that it is necessary for me to deal with people who have all sorts of political opinions, and I try not to force mine upon them."

"But you must have a few opinions of your own, don't you?"

Rather awkward for Lanny Budd, who couldn't afford to have the members of this group go out and say that he had evaded such a challenge. This duel was something to be talked about, and would be talked about all over the Cap before the day was over—it was after midnight. He had to make a flat answer, and it had to be one which would satisfy the Fascists and Nazis who swarmed on the Coast of Pleasure.

Said the son of Budd-Erling: "I used to have political opinions when I was young; but when I arrived at years of discretion I found that they disturbed my digestion and my judgment of art works. So now I confine myself to my chosen profession and let more qualified persons run the world's business affairs."

"And if you found that one of these persons was getting world power by means of wholesale murder and lies, that wouldn't disturb you in the least?"

"I am afraid, Miss Creston, I should have to remain in my ivory tower, and leave it for you to deal with that dangerous person."

"Ivory tower, Mr. Budd?" snapped the woman. "It seems to me you might better call it a cave, and yourself a troglodyte."

You could feel the shock run through that well-bred company—for that word had a terrible sound, even though not many knew its meaning.

Lanny still took it amiably. Said he: "My understanding is that the troglodyte was a hairy man, and I could hardly qualify for that."

This gave the company a chance to laugh, and broke the tension. The ladies started to talk very fast about something else; and Miss Creston, realizing that she had said a mouthful, returned to her seat.

X

Lanny's job had brought him close to that state known to psychiatrists as schizophrenia; two minds living in the same body. He was a perfect reactionary, and felt all those emotions—he had to, in order to make them real to an audience. Then he would go apart by himself, and be the perfect rebel. Now he sat quietly, stealing an occasional glance at this stranger, and thinking: "Gosh, what a nerve! Here's a woman who hates every hair on the Nazi beast, and she doesn't mind saying so among people who would like to poison her!"

He remembered the picture which Nina had drawn, of himself being converted by some ardent anti-Nazi girl, and then marrying her! He could be quite sure that Miss Creston would undertake the first part of the job, at least. But how could this operation be carried on, here in one of the world's leading gossip centers? As the story stood at this moment, it was exactly right for a presidential agent: a Red vixen had challenged him, and had called him a troglodyte! "What is that?" the horrified dowagers would ask, and when they were told, "A caveman," they would say, "Oh!" and forever after be sure that Lanny was a good fascist. But if the story were to have a sequel: "Oh, my dear, what do you think? He went to call on her and took her motoring, and they say they are fast friends now,"—no, manifestly that would brand Lanny for the rest of his days.

Or could he call this lady up and ask her to meet him secretly? Not very well. Could he say: "I am completely in sympathy with your ideas, but for reasons of state I have to pretend otherwise?" He would need to know a person very intimately indeed before he could speak such words.

XI

Driving home with his mother and half-sister, he heard what they thought about this episode. "That perfectly odious creature!" exclaimed Marceline; and: "Did you ever hear such insolence in your life?" demanded Beauty.

"Who is she?" Lanny inquired.

"Sophie says she is from New York, and writes stories for the magazines."

"How does she come to be here?"

"She's related to those people who brought her. I'll wager they don't bring her to Sophie's again."

"They won't need to," said Lanny with a chuckle. "She studied the house and everybody in it. We'll all find ourselves in a short story some day."

"I never wanted to scratch a woman's eyes out so much!"—this was Beauty.

"I rather admired her nerve," remarked the wayward son.

"Oh, you would!" countered the mother. "It would be like you to look her up and fall in love. You always did pick out the people who insulted you and patronized you."

"Don't worry, old darling; I don't like that aggressive type. If ever I fall in love again, it will be with some gentle, submissive damsel."

"I'll believe that when I see it," retorted Beauty, so far from gentle or submissive herself. "There's that lovely Lucy Cotton, ready to adore you if you would give her the least encouragement."

It was necessary to deal respectfully with a relative of good old Sophie. Lanny said: "It's not easy for a man to be sure about these amiable young things. They turn out so different after you know them a while. Take Marceline. When she was young, I thought she was the sweetest and gentlest ever; but now you see, she knows exactly what she wants and never gives up until she gets it."

They had been discussing the subject of money on the way over to the party; and in the interim Marceline had lost several dollars because of her mother's card blunders. Now she took up the challenge, in a manner not so different from the Red vixen. "Sell my third of the paintings now and give me the money, so that I can go and live decently in Seville, and you won't ever again be bothered with the problem of my temperament."

"There now, you see!" said Lanny to his mother.

26

Pleasure Never Is at Home

I

BEAUTY had made all her plans to spend the summer at Wickthorpe Castle, and with Margy at Bluegrass, renewing her acquaintance with little Frances and enjoying the delights of visiting London. But here, unexpectedly, was the problem of Marceline and her infant, doubly dear because it had been named Marcel. The young mother couldn't very well be taken on this tour; she couldn't be left here alone, for she had never been alone, and had no resources within herself. Moreover, she dared not stay too long away from her husband; she said that men were weak and undependable, and Seville was full of idle and predatory women. Marceline agreed with General Sherman on the subject of war.

What she wanted was for her mother to give up the trip and stay in Bienvenu and take care of the baby while Marceline joined Vittorio. It was a lot to ask, but Marceline had never let that stand in her way. She had been brought up to be beautiful, and to live by that beauty; to take care of it, dress it, have it admired and waited upon. She had been taught that only rich people were of consequence, and now she had many rich friends and couldn't keep up with them;

she wouldn't have any other sort, because she looked down upon the others and found them depressing. An unhappy situation for a young woman to be in, and Marceline blamed everybody but herself for it. She complained persistently, and set out with dogged determination to get what she wanted.

Lanny had learned how to meet that attitude to life; he said No and meant it, and let Marceline know that he meant it. But poor Beauty couldn't do that; she said No and meant it, but then gave way, which was the same as not meaning it. She pleaded that it was her duty to see Frances, and not to let that dear child forget her entirely; but Marceline said that was rubbish—what Beauty was thinking about was Ascot and Ranelagh and the balls and parties at Margy's town-house. It would cost a lot, and Marceline wanted that money to live half-way decently in Seville, where you paid five prices for every-thing, and maybe ten by now. She argued and nagged: it was just this one season; those hateful Reds couldn't go on with their mad fighting much longer, and then Vittorio could come back with honor, and find something to do that would pay him more than a beggar's wage.

Knowing that she was going to get her way, the young mother pro-ceeded to wean her baby; and Beauty was just on the point of writing letters to call off her trip, when there came an emotional cyclone which turned both mother and daughter on their heads. There had been delivered at Bienvenu a letter addressed to Vittorio; a letter in an unfashionable envelope, addressed in a woman's handwriting of an inelegant sort. Lanny had dutifully readdressed it to Seville and thought no more about it. Then had come a second, and he had re-peated the procedure. Now came a third, and this time it was ad-dressed to Marceline, and she received it without Lanny's seeing it. The first notice he got was in the form of a scream, and then a storm of rage and weeping from his mother's room. He went in and found his half-sister lying on her stomach on the bed, kicking her feet in the air, alternately shrieking and biting her handkerchief which she stuffed into her mouth. Beauty was there, pale and bedraggled with-out her morning make-up; she didn't say a word, but handed Lanny the letter, which Marceline had crumpled up in her rage and then thrown into her mother's lap.

Lanny spread it out. It was in French, and the substance was that the writer had learned Vittorio's real name and had written to him twice that she was pregnant and about to lose her position. She needed help, but Vittorio had left her letters unanswered, and unless the family would make him come to her aid she would be forced to resort to the law. Celestine Lafitte was the name, and the address was a small café in Cannes.

At one moment Marceline proposed to rush off and tear the bitch's eyes out; at the next she wanted to travel to Seville and perform the same operation upon the faithless husband. She used astonishing language, the sort that wasn't printed until the last few years; Lanny was surprised to discover that his half-sister knew such words, not merely in English and French but in Italian. It was like an explosion in a sewer.

"Marceline, dear!" exclaimed the shocked mother. "The servants will hear you!"

"To hell with the servants!" cried the hysterical girl. "To hell with the whole rotten world! That's what I get for marrying a broken-down wreck of a man and sticking to him in spite of every misery and discomfort! The dirty stinking two-timer!"

"You don't even know that he's guilty, my child."

"Of course I know he's guilty; he's a skunk, a wolf! He can't keep his eyes off any good-looking woman—I've watched him, I've given him plenty hell for it. I've heard the talk of those Italian officers when they didn't know I was near."

Lanny would have liked to say: "I told you what the Fascists were,"—but that wouldn't do any good, and he had to leave politics out of it.

"He couldn't wait while I had a baby—that's the sort of dog he is. Jesus, how I hate him! Let him have his Celestine—let her be the one to go to Seville and be his camp-follower! Not me!"

II

It was a long drawn-out scene. A woman who had been petted and spoiled through her almost twenty-one years had had snatched away from her the thing she most wanted, and her way of taking the blow was without dignity or even pathos. She wanted to punish the two persons who had robbed and humiliated her, and the only idea she could think of was that Lanny should go and see this woman, and give her money to travel to Seville, so that she could make Vittorio miserable for the rest of his life. "Give her a gun and tell her to shoot him if he refuses to support her!"

Lanny said: "In the first place, Marceline, I doubt if the woman could get a visa into Franco Spain. All French passports are now stamped: 'Not valid for Spain.' And in the next place, Vittorio couldn't support her in Seville on his pay, even if he wanted to. She and her child would starve to death."

"All right, let them!"

"You overlook the fact that the woman might find some way to get her story into the newspapers. The Red press would find it very much to their taste."

"I don't care what they say—I'm through with Vittorio, his bitch and his bastard."

Lanny, a bastard himself, said no more. He knew that he would have to see this woman, and if she had any evidence that the child was Vittorio's, he would give her enough to tide her over the period while she was incapacitated. He would count that a small price for getting completely rid of a Fascist brother-in-law. When Marceline had got over her hysterics, he thought it the part of wisdom to tell her the reason why her husband had so suddenly departed for the wars. When Marceline heard that, she decided that she had been made a fool of by all the members of her family, and that from this time on she would look out for herself.

She was the child of Marcel Detaze, and somewhere within her was steel. She dried her tears and put war paint on her face, and announced that she was ashamed of her lack of self-control, and from this moment on nobody would see her shed a tear. What she wanted was a divorce from Vittorio as quickly as it could be arranged under the French law. Mlle. Lafitte would presumably serve as a witness, and in that way might earn the money to have a baby. "After all, I'm sorry for the poor brat," remarked the bitter young wife, and then winced, realizing that her own precious infant had the same father.

Lanny thought it over and decided that this was a matter for the family lawyer in Cannes. He consulted this gentleman, who invited the restaurant cashier to his office and found her amenable; she agreed to receive the sum of two thousand francs a month for a period of a year in return for her testimony that she had been seduced by the Capitano. She had some notes in his handwriting, and the lawyer pointed out to her that she would not be compromising her claim against the officer; after the war was over he would presumably return to his homeland, and she might follow him there and bring suit for the support of the child. So everything was "jake," as Robbie Budd would have said if he had been present. The suit was filed, and notice sent to the ex-aviator; then the daughter of Marcel Detaze said to her mother: "Let's give a party right away, a good one, and invite all our friends, so that I can show them I'm not down and out!"

III

The dénouement of this tangle of events was something which nobody could have foreseen. Sophie, Baroness de la Tourette, undertook to give the party, because she had a much larger dancing floor, and admired the "child's" nerve, so she said; she had known Marceline since the hour after her birth, and had helped to keep her a "child" all these years. Sophie made a suggestion that was practically a command: the way for a "child" to display her *insouciance* to the smart world was to do some of that lovely dancing that she and Lanny had displayed off and on for the past ten years.

For Lanny, also, this was a command. Grieving over the already-consummated murder of Austria and the all-but-consummated murder of Spain, he would find it like dancing on a grave; but there was nobody he could say that to, and he really wanted to help his half-sister in this time of trial. He hadn't done any dancing for quite a while, but had kept himself in condition by tennis and swimming, and Marceline had danced even while she was pregnant. Now she fell to practicing in a sort of frenzy. It was a way of defying the world, of answering all the patronizing, the sneers and jibes which she knew were being made behind her back; it was a way of punishing Vittorio, of telling him to go to hell. The daughter of Marcel Detaze was coming back into the *grand monde* again, she was going to have another début and score another triumph.

She and Lanny rehearsed those gay and graceful forms of bodily expression which Lanny had begun while playing with the fisher children on the beach at Juan; which he had disciplined at the Dalcroze school in Hellerau, and had set free again while watching Isadora Duncan through the years. He had begun teaching Marceline when she was just able to toddle, and they had played together on a hundred dancing floors, until they had become as one person, knowing each other's every impulse even before it was born. This ease and grace gave delight to any sort of audience; and Marceline, an extrovert, living to be admired, would catch the crowd excitement, be swept away by it and dance like one possessed.

Of course the gossips had been busy with her story; everybody in this fashionable company knew that her man had "done her dirt," and everybody knew that this was her defiance, her announcement that she wasn't going to whimper or weaken. They admired her for it, and called her out again and again, and warmed the hearts of both the dancing pair. Lanny saw once more what his half-sister was meant to be; and Marceline had known it for a long time.

The consequences were immediate. At lunchtime next day—or rather, that same day, since they had danced until long after midnight —the telephone rang, and a man announced himself as M. Cassin, proprietor of the Coque d'Or, one of the smartest of the Cannes night clubs. He wanted to know if he might come over to talk with M. Budd and Madame Marceline—so he called her—about the possibility of their appearing in his floor show. Lanny said that he might come, and Marceline pretty nearly blew up with delight. She forgot her ice-cold melon and began capering all about the room. The shocked Beauty exclaimed: "My child! Would you be willing to dance in a place like that? And for money?"

"Hell!" said the child. "What do you suppose I would dance for?" Then, seeing the pained look on her mother's face: "Didn't you pose for painters for money?" She didn't have to add "in the altogether," for Beauty knew that several years ago, rummaging in the storeroom, Marceline had come upon that painting of her mother which Lanny had found in an art-dealer's shop and had purchased, but which the respectable widow of Marcel Detaze didn't wish him to hang upon any wall in Bienvenu.

Brother and sister talked it out. Lanny said that he hadn't the time and didn't care for the life. But Marceline begged and clamored; he must do her this one favor, just this one, and she would be off his hands forever; just help her to get a start and she would never trouble him again. This was what she wanted, to be a dancer; she had everything that it took, youth, beauty, grace, verve—she said it herself, knowing that it was true and that Lanny knew it. She wanted money, and this was the way to get it; she wanted independence, a career, a chance to make the headlines and to shine. Never mind if he approved it or not; just grant her the right to be herself, and give her one good push.

Beauty suggested, feebly: "If you would do it for charity——" and the daughter replied: "Charity, the devil!" But Lanny pointed out, it was important to keep her social prestige, to be a Budd as well as a Detaze; she would get more money that way. So then she said: "I'll let it be announced that the engagement is for charity and that will set the tone; then after the first week there can be an engagement for *me*. Oh, Lanny, you *must* do it! Just one week! Then if I make a hit I can get somebody else. You can pick any charity you please, and make all the arrangements. I'll do whatever you say. Oh, please, please!"

So finally Lanny said: "All right; but let me do the talking to that fellow."

IV

M. Robert Cassin introduced himself as an "impresario," and said that he had been told about the triumph which the dancing pair had achieved last night. Previously he had seen them dancing at the casino and other places, and knew about the family and its exalted social position. There was much curiosity concerning the pair in those circles which would like to get into smart society but couldn't. M. Cassin knew that he couldn't tempt them with money, he said, tactfully, but they would give refined pleasure to a great many people, and might help to raise the standard of dancing on the Côte d'Azur, which was far from high at present.

Lanny replied: "This is something quite out of our line; but my sister enjoys dancing, and people enjoy seeing her. If we do it, the money will go to the fund for the widows and orphans of fishermen here on the coast, some of whom were my playmates in boyhood. You might advertise that fact."

"*Magnifique, M. Budd!* That will be *très snob.*" The French had managed to find a worthy significance in this word.

"And how much would you offer us?"

The "impresario" hemmed and hawed. For charity—for widows and orphans of the men who were injured or drowned in these sometimes stormy waters—one would have to be proud to contribute. Would ten thousand francs a week——?

Lanny answered promptly that it wouldn't. That was only about three hundred dollars, less than fifty dollars a night. "My idea is a round fifty thousand francs for the week."

M. Cassin was shocked, or so pretended. They had an argument on the subject of how many smart people would come to the Coque d'Or and how much they would spend for food and drink. At the end they compromised on three thousand francs a night, to be paid each night in cash to the secretary of the fund. The proprietor said he would make a ceremony out of it, he would pay the money after the last of three appearances by the couple, and tell the audience what he was doing. A master of ceremonies likes to have things to talk about, and this would confer great *éclat*.

Lanny added: "If the engagement is a success, my sister might wish to continue. I would not be interested myself, because I have other work which keeps me busy; therefore I suggest that you feature her in the billing. She will use the name Marceline, and you may point out that she is the daughter of one of France's most eminent painters."

"You might add that some of his paintings have been sold for as high as two hundred thousand francs apiece," put in Marceline. Even if she wasn't allowed to sell those paintings, she was surely allowed to advertise them!

V

The hour when this child of fortune first stepped forth as a professional performer was the greatest hour of her life so far. She was shivering with nervousness, but nobody was allowed to see it; she knew what she was doing, and was perfectly right in her statement that she had what it takes. In a night club you perform only for the rich, and Marceline had been one of them all her life, and they knew it. Many in her first audience were the same friends for whom she had danced at Sophie's, and before that at Emily's and in her mother's home. Lanny accompanied her modestly, doing everything he could to put her forward and display her charms. The affair went off like magic; word went out that here was a new sensation—and when the bored victims of *snobisme* discover a new sensation, they pay for it gladly. The night-club gentleman was delighted with his bargain, and told Marceline that he would be happy to have her continue with any partner of her choice.

So, after a few hours' sleep, the new sensation had herself driven to the casino at Nice, where she entered quietly and sat for an hour watching the gigolos, the dancing men who were hired by ladies who because of age or lack of charms had nobody to companion them. Marceline went from one place to another, looking for a boy who was young and agile, and had a reasonable amount of talent; she was going to hire him permanently and train him. She knew what she wanted, and found him without too much delay, brought him to Juan and put him up at a hotel, took him every night to the Coque d'Or to watch her performances, and then, in the afternoons, had Lanny drill him and teach him the steps.

He was an eager if somewhat corrupt youth, and did reasonably well. Within two weeks after the close of the engagement with Lanny, Marceline was ready to show her new partner to the "impresario," and they bargained again; this time Marceline took charge, for she said she might as well learn. She got a two-weeks' engagement at twenty-five thousand francs a week, and there wasn't any nonsense about charity this time; the night club was to have the option to renew for as many weeks as it pleased at the same rate, and that was all right with the dancer, because she could live at home free of charge, and she liked to dance for people she knew and to chat with them between the turns. As for her new partner, she was paying him two thousand francs a week, which was more than he had ever seen in his life before; he had agreed to work for a year on that basis. One other proviso in the agreement: No love-making! "That nonsense is out for me," Marceline told him; and in the privacy of her family she added: "If any man ever makes love to me again, he's going to pay for it, I'll tell the world!"

So that was that, and Lanny could consider that the problem of his half-sister had been solved; no longer would she be complaining, and blaming him for her frustrations. All he could do for her now was to help her think up new ideas—for of course she wouldn't want to go on doing the same old things. She wanted to know about Isadora, and how she had made such a sensation. There would be no "Red" nonsense in the career of Marceline, of course, nor would she waste herself getting drunk, or trying to start a school and teach children; enough if she could teach herself and one indispensable man. When the winter season came, she would want to go to Paris; and what would be the best place for her début, and would Lanny try to pull some strings for her? Emily would give her an engagement at Les Forêts; and what about Baron Schneider, and the Duc de Belleaumont, and Graf Herzenberg, and Olivie Hellstein? Marceline would accumulate a cardfile, like her brother; and Beauty would begin pulling strings—just as she had done for Robbie's munitions, and then for Marcel's paintings, and then for Lanny's old-masterings!

VI

While sharing these events, Lanny was not entirely idle politically. He met influential Fascists on the Riviera, and listened while they discussed their plans for the undermining of the North American states and the taking over of those in South America. As soon as Franco's rule was secure—and it couldn't be long now—his state would become the motherland of a new Spanish-American empire, built upon the Fascist formula. Spain had always been the cultural center for these lands, and Spanish Fascism, standing upon a firm Catholic foundation, would not antagonize the somewhat primitive peoples of South America as Nazism had done. This was explained to the Norte Americano by a Spanish bishop in exile to whom Lanny listened attentively, giving the Most Reverend Father cause to hope that his listener was on the way to becoming a convert. Afterwards Lanny went home and wrote a report—but not for El Papa.

If you stayed on the Riviera long enough, you met "everybody"—meaning, of course, everybody who was rich and important. At Sophie's Lanny ran into Charles Bedaux, Franco-American millionaire who had been one of the guests at Baron Schneider's dinner in Paris. An extraordinary person, he had emigrated to the United States as a penniless laborer and worked as a bottle-washer in a New York waterfront saloon, then as a "sandhog," boring tunnels under rivers. With his eager and alert mind, nothing could keep him down; he had devised a method of timing the motions of every sort of labor; the "Bedaux system" had been installed all over the world, and he had made so much money he had a shooting box in Scotland and palaces all over Europe where he entertained the great and famous.

He knew Lanny's father and mother and Lanny's former wife and everybody in their great world. He had just come back from Salamanca, where he had talked with Franco and Juan March, Franco's money backer. Bedaux admitted that he, too, had invested heavily in Spanish "Nationalist" bonds. He had a châlet on the Obersalzberg where he had spent the previous summer and had visited the Berghof frequently; the home of the Donnersteins was near by, and Hilde was one of his intimates. A big man with a fat face, an eager manner, and a loose tongue, he was a goldmine of information about the big-money world and its denizens. He was all tied up in the Nazi-Fascist schemes, and with money-making on an international scale—always a bit dubious —but he had no reserves with the son of Budd-Erling, merchant of death. All Hitler's intimates, Göring and Goebbels, Ribbentrop and Abetz and Wiedemann, even Max Amman, the Führer's publisher, were investing huge sums outside Germany, and Bedaux was their adviser and silent partner. After talks with him, Lanny had a long report to write.

Also, with his stepfather he continued experiments in psychic research. He tried out the idea of hypnotizing a medium and endeavoring thus to shape the developments of a séance. Perhaps he overworked Madame, or produced confusion in her various subconscious minds; anyhow, the results were one of those dreary stretches which try the patience of psychic investigators. Lanny had been fortunate over a long period of time, but now he got only scraps and irrelevancies, with just enough that was real to tantalize him and keep him trying. Tecumseh resumed laughing at him; and could it be that this malicious old personality was deliberately destroying Madame as a medium, the source of his own being? Was she really the source, or could he wreck her and then go off and enjoy himself elsewhere? Lanny reread Morton Prince's *Dissociation of a Personality*, the case record of a young lady of Boston whose subconscious mind had developed five different personalities. One of them, called "Sally," was a demon, a mischief maker identical with those one read about in ancient fable. Dr. Prince was able to kill her in the mind of Miss Beauchamp, but Lanny's efforts to kill Tecumseh only caused that grim old Amerindian to express scorn.

VII

Also Lanny read the newspapers of London and Paris, which reached him one day late, and watched the slow preparation of that tragedy which he had foretold to F.D.R. Poor compensation to be able to say: "I told you so!" Rick sent him a beautifully written article about the people who had maintained for many centuries the ancient kingdom of Bohemia, and now had built the modern republic of Czechoslovakia, and were trying to protect it in the midst of many angry dictatorships. Lanny had never visited Prague, but he had seen pictures of that romantic old city and had imagined it while listening to Smetana's tone poem of the River Moldau. In Paris he had met Professor Masaryk, son of a coachman and a cook, who had begun as apprentice to a locksmith and a blacksmith, and had ended at the age of eighty-five as founder and president of the most liberal democracy on the Continent. His foreign minister and successor, Beneš, pronounced Béhn-esh, was a peasant's son, one of the few diplomats of Europe who said that he spoke the truth and spoke the truth when he said it.

Now the great boa-constrictor called Nazism was getting ready to swallow this small mountain-girded state. Hitler had had his agitators among the Sudeten Germans from the beginning; their Führer was a bank-clerk named Henlein who had become head of the *Turnvereine*, the gymnastic societies which were camouflage for Stormtroop armies all over the world. Their technique was identical with that used in Austria: agitate, organize, make trouble, and then, when you are suppressed, clamor against "persecution." The Germans in Czechoslovakia were citizens with equal rights and liberties, and that suited most of them; but not the Nazi agitators and terrorists, who had money, arms, and propaganda literature in an unending stream. The Hitler borders had been increased in length by the taking of Austria, and the position of the Czechs was exactly that of a soft woolly lamb in a boa-constrictor's mouth.

Lanny had thought it was all over in the month of May, for Henlein came to London and was received by the leading Tories, and spent a week-end at Wickthorpe Castle. Rick wasn't invited there any more, but living not far away he heard the gossip, and wrote that Chamberlain had definitely decided to deliver the Sudetens as the price of peace in Europe. Hitler declared that this was the last demand he had to make on the Continent, and the British Tories wanted desperately to believe him.

But they had reckoned without the Czechs, who thought something of their liberties and didn't intend to be given away. When the Nazi armies moved toward their borders, the Czechs mobilized and announced their will to fight. The French were pledged to come to their aid, and the Russians were pledged to join the French. Europe hung on the verge of war, and Hitler wasn't ready for it; he backed down, his first big defeat—and Lanny imagined the rug-chewing that must be going on in Berchtesgaden, and wished he had stayed to see the show. But that joy in his heart didn't last very long; he knew that Adi would never give up his purpose, and Rick wrote that the Tories would give up anything that wasn't British. Lanny burned letters like these, taking no chance that they might somehow fall into the hands of his enemies.

VIII

Beauty could be spared now, since Marceline had her career for company, and had got a competent nurse to take care of the baby. Lanny agreed to drive his mother and stepfather to London, with some necessary stop-overs. One was at Le Creusot, gigantic forge of Vulcan; the couple stayed in a smokestained hotel while Lanny spent the night at La Verrerie. He had been asked by his father to cultivate Schneider, and had assented gladly, for the Baron was a pipeline into the center of French financial and political affairs. What this elderly hawk-nosed moneymaster believed and desired affected the destinies of every Frenchman alive, and of millions of other persons who had never even heard his name. It seemed to Lanny Budd a defect in education for democracy, that the people knew so much about the politicians and so little about the men who made the politicians and paid their fares on the bandwagon.

The munitions king had just determined the destinies of Europe, at least for a time. He told Lanny a spy story, a regular movie thriller. He

had a "man" in Berlin, evidently a very good one indeed; on Friday, the
21st of May, this man had called the Baron out of bed at two o'clock in
the morning, to tell him that Charlotte was ill with appendicitis. Those
were not the exact words, the financier remarked with a smile, but it
was something like that, and it meant that Germany was mobilizing.
Furthermore the man said that Doktor Henry and Doktor Schmidt
were in disagreement about the case—again those weren't the right
names, but it meant that the British ambassador had had a row with
Ribbentrop and accused him of deception, and was now ordering special trains to take British residents out of Berlin—meaning, of course,
that he expected war.

"*Mon dieu*, could I let Hitler have Skoda?" exclaimed the Baron. The
answer was, "*Jamais*," so he had routed Foreign Minister Bonnet out of
bed and told him that France must definitely announce its support of
Prague. Said the munitions king: "*Ce malin chauve*"—that bald-headed
malicious one—"thinks about nothing but keeping his job and saving
the franc; but what will be the value of all the francs if we lose our
eastern alliances?"

Now in Lanny's presence the moneymaster was assailed by doubt
and depression. He couldn't make up his mind who was his more dangerous enemy, the Brown devil or the Red. "Hitler will never give up,
will he?"—and Lanny felt free to say: "Hitler and Pan-Germanism are
one and the same."

He suggested that his friend should read Adi's book and see what the
Führer had to say about himself. Strange to say, that idea had never
occurred to the Baron, and he found it most original. Lanny told about
the personality of Rudolf Hess, the real author of the volume; at least,
he had seen to it that the greater number of Adi's sentences had a verb
in them, and an ending. It did no harm to tell about Hess's interest in
astrology and spiritualism, since all the Fatherland knew it; but nothing
about the Führer's secret visits to Madame Zyszynski.

All this was of importance to Robbie Budd, since his deal with the
Baron involved Pilsen and its great Skoda arms plant. The first thing
Lanny did on reaching Paris was to type out an account of the munitions king's distracted state of mind, and mail one copy to his father
and the other to Gus Gennerich. He had already warned Robbie that
war could not be postponed more than a year or two, and that Robbie's
financial arrangements should be based upon that certainty. It was a
sign of the changing times that Robbie now took such advice seriously.

IX

There were going to be great doings in Paris; the newly crowned King and Queen of Britain were coming for a visit of state; they would be banqueted and presented with French orders and decorations, and would confer British equivalents upon French statesmen. But Lanny didn't care for public spectacles, and Beauty was aching to see her darling Frances, so they drove to the Calais ferry, and direct to Wickthorpe without stopping for any of the delights of London. Beauty and her husband were installed in a two-hundred-year-old cottage on the estate—it had been remodeled, of course, and had all modern conveniences, but still had a thatched roof and low ceilings, and doorways that you had to stoop slightly to pass through. Now, in July, it was delightfully rustic, like camping out; there was a vine-covered summerhouse where Parsifal could say his prayers all day and night if he wanted to. Frances was having a holiday from her tutors, and could come over and spend all her time prattling away to her grandmother, who was so happy that she became a child herself, and neither would bore the other.

Meantime Lanny put up at the castle, a mass of round towers of many sizes, and having crenelations on top; the modern parts were at one side, so as not to spoil the effect. After a brief visit to his daughter, Lanny became absorbed in his own unusual kind of work. He had happened along at a moment of importance, for the Earl of Wickthorpe came back from town, bringing a guest to whom Lanny needed no introduction, having met him at the Berghof at the time of the Schuschnigg visit. He was one of the Führer's aides-de-camp, and enjoyed a specially favored position because he had commanded the company in which Adi had been a sub-corporal during the World War. Captain Fritz Wiedemann was a large, powerfully built fellow with heavy dark eyebrows and lantern jaws; a fanatical Nazi, but also a suave man of the world. From him Lanny had made certain that he knew exactly what was going to happen to Austria—in fact, he had been one of the military men called in to tell the Austrian Chancellor what was going to happen to *him*.

Gerald Albany had just returned from a highly confidential visit to Hitler, Ribbentrop, and Göring; undoubtedly he had taken some important proposals of the British government, and now in all probability Wiedemann had come with the answers. Lanny had read of the Hauptmann's arrival in the London morning papers, together with the offi-

cial denial that he had any diplomatic errand, or had talked with anyone of Cabinet rank. That, of course, meant the opposite of what it
said, for British diplomatists proceeded upon the formula that a lie was
an untruth told to a person who had a right to know the truth, and the
British public was not included in that sacred roster. Before that evening was over Lanny heard from Wiedemann's own lips that he had
had an interview with Lord Halifax, the British Foreign Minister, on
the previous day. Halifax was accompanying the royal visit to Paris, so
Lanny could guess that he was carrying the German proposals to the
French.

X

Here was a presidential agent, in the very heart of the intrigue which
was to determine the fate of Europe for a long time to come. Never
had he had to step more warily, not even on that hair-raising night
when he had been helping to burglarize the Château de Belcour. He
judged that neither Ceddy nor the discreet Gerald would discuss
these ultra-secret affairs in the presence of other guests or of servants; Lanny's problem was to get some one of the group alone, and
contrive to have the subject brought up by this person and not by
Lanny. Often a man would drop hints without realizing the full significance of his words.

The first thing was to establish Lanny's sociopolitical position, as it
might be called. Exercising his privilege to bring up a new subject of
conversation, he said: "By the way, Wiedemann, you remember that
you expressed skepticism on the subject of psychic phenomena. Have
you had any chance to talk with Hess since he tried his experiments
with me at the Berghof?"

"No," said the German. "How did they turn out?"

"One thing that might be of interest to a military man: Rudolf got
what purported to be a communication from a soldier who had been in
the trenches with him at Verdun, and had been killed a few minutes
after Rudolf himself was wounded. Several details were given which
Rudi confirmed, and he told the Führer about them in my presence. It
made a great impression on both." Then, turning to Irma: "That was
Madame, our old Polish medium. I took her to Berchtesgaden for Hess
to try his luck."

They talked for a while on a subject which was fascinating and at
the same time entirely safe—since the spirits had never been political, at
least not so far as Irma or Lanny knew. She told of communications
which were supposed to have come from her father; Ceddy told about

a ghost which was reputed to appear now and then in the oldest tower of this castle, but which had possibly been disturbed by Irma's recent alterations, since it hadn't shown up of late. This conversation served two purposes of a subtle intriguer. It would enable the Hauptmann to go back to the Berghof and report that the son of Budd-Erling was an intimate of the earl and the countess as he had claimed; and, no less important, it settled in the minds of Ceddy and Gerald any doubts as to the truth of Lanny's claims that he had been in the Berghof at the time of the Schuschnigg visit.

XI

After the coffee and cigars the Foreign Office men excused themselves and took their guest into his lordship's study. That left Lanny alone with Irma, something which might have been awkward for some "ex's," but not for this socially trained pair.

"You have changed your opinions very greatly of late, Lanny," the woman remarked. "It's hard for me to realize it."

"Well, I had to grow up sooner or later," he said.

"If you had made it a little sooner, we might not have had our breakup."

That was kind of her, and Lanny wanted to be no less so. "Then you wouldn't have had this grand old castle," he countered, with a smile.

Irma was *enceinte*, as the polite word had it, and had reached the stage where she moved slowly. "Shall we pay a call on Beauty?" she suggested, and of course Lanny offered to accompany her. They strolled across the grounds through lovely English twilight, which comes late in the month of July. Frances had been taken to bed, for she lived on a strict schedule. It was quite like old times, with Beauty and her husband, and Irma and her "ex." They talked about the child for a while, and then Beauty, most tactful of guests, suggested that Frances' other grandmother might like to share the conversation. Mrs. Fanny Barnes occupied a villa on the estate, where she lived with her brother, the elderly retired stockbroker whom Lanny had learned to call "Uncle Horace." To Lanny he was the world's worst bore, but fortunately he had a touch of the gout and couldn't come.

The large and important widow of the American utilities king summoned her chauffeur and was driven a quarter of a mile or so to "Glavis," as the cottage was called—for some reason that was buried under the debris of time. She proposed a rubber of bridge, and politeness required Lanny to oblige. In former days the two elderly ladies had played against Irma and Lanny, but now Fanny's sense of propriety brought it about that mother and daughter played against mother and son, and won handily. Truth to be told, it was hard for Lanny to keep his mind on his mother's signals, when it wanted to speculate on what the three conspirators over at the castle might be deciding as to the fate of Czechoslovakia. And anyhow, it was always tactful to let Fanny Barnes win.

XII

Luck was kind to Lanny, for when he got back to the castle he found that Gerald Albany was taking Wiedemann back to London that night, and Ceddy was staying on. That meant that after the important guest had departed, the lord of the castle sat in the library with his wife's former husband, and rang for whisky and sodas and a bite before retiring. Did he fear that he might have seemed discourteous in excluding an old friend from a conference? Or was there something that he wanted to get out of Lanny without Lanny's knowing it?

The art expert had thought out his plan of attack while dealing bridge hands, and now he went right to it. "Ceddy," he began, "may I talk to you frankly for a minute or two?"

"Certainly, Lanny—always."

"Why doesn't the British government make up its mind and do something to settle this miserable wrangle that is making every sort of progress impossible in Europe?"

"It doesn't rest entirely with us, Lanny."

"That's where you are making your mistake. You don't realize the position of Britain at the present time, or how much depends upon your decisions. The French simply don't know their own minds; they are staggering around like a lot of drunken men, knocking one another over. I had a talk with Schneider only three or four days ago. Honestly, it is tragic; the man can't keep his mind made up through an hour's conversation."

"Tell me what he says, Lanny."

Was that what the British Foreign Office wanted to know on this critical evening? If so, Lanny would be happy to favor them, in consideration of a fair return. He told what he had heard at La Verrerie, and what he knew about French opinion from other sources. "The French ought to be told what to do and made to do it, and they'll be relieved to get it off their minds."

"It is the most complicated situation we have ever faced, Lanny— perhaps in the whole of England's history."

"I agree with you; but no decision can be so bad as indecision. That means leaving everything at loose ends, and helps nobody but the forces of disorder. I don't feel myself a stranger to Europe, and I suffer from the confusion like all the others, rich and poor. Everybody I know keeps asking: why doesn't England make up her mind? Either say to Hitler: 'Stay where you are or it means war'; or else say: 'We blundered at Versailles, and you can have your border territories back, and let's start over again and be friends.' "

"If it were only that simple, Lanny! But here are all these nations and tribes, like so many wild beasts in a cage, ready to fly at one another's throats. We confronted the possibility of a general war two months ago. And our people don't want war; we aren't ready for it and we don't want to have to get ready."

"All right then, make up your minds to a settlement. Decide what territories you are willing to let Hitler have. Put your cards on the table and say: 'You can have this, and this, and no more.' Put it before the French, not for squabbling over, but as an ultimatum: 'This is the settlement, and you can come in or we make a deal with Hitler instead.' Say to Czechoslovakia and Poland: 'This is our decision, and you have to take it or wage a war by yourselves.' "

"I wish I were free to talk to you about these confidential matters, Lanny——"

"That's all right, old man—it doesn't make any difference, because I'm going back to Paris in a few days, and whatever Halifax is saying to Bonnet, Schneider will tell it all to me in ten minutes. The old gentleman's nerve seems to be broken; he is possessed by the horrid idea that if Hitler gets Pilsen, he will refuse to recognize those pieces of paper which guarantee title to the Skoda plant. So he wants some of my father's fighter planes to protect his property; also he wants somebody to let him cry on his shoulder. Instead of trying to keep secrets from me, Ceddy, it would be more sensible to tell me what you people want and let me help you get it. All I want is to see peace in Europe, so that people can have time to think about paintings again."

"You really do know a lot of the key people, don't you, Lanny."

"It's my blind luck that Budd-Erling is tops right now in the race for speed and maneuverability. Robbie has proudly demonstrated it at several military airfields; so, when I go to Berlin, *Der Dicke* invites me to Karinhall and tells me the most shocking things—I mean, diplomatically speaking. And as for Hitler, when he gets started he tells everybody what he's going to do for the next thousand years. I think it's a calculated indiscretion with him—he's working a gigantic game of bluff." Lanny paused for a moment and added, with a grin: "Would you like me to take a plane to Berlin and send you back a complete report of what Gerald offered to the champagne salesman?"

The Earl of Wickthorpe couldn't keep from smiling in return; it was very disarming. "I don't mind telling you, Lanny, that we've come to be of very much the same mind as yourself. It appears that we have no choice but to let Hitler have a readjustment of his entire eastern boundary."

"And Wiedemann is here to tell you what they demand; and Halifax is taking it to Paris. He is a man of the most upright character, but can he pound the table hard enough to impress those French buccaneers?"

"Many of them require no persuading, Lanny; and Halifax can be stiff-necked when he wants to."

"I hope so. Would you like me to call on Schneider and try to convince him that it's to his best interest to accede to your proposals?"

"I haven't any authority to suggest such a thing, Lanny——"

"Of course not! You don't have to talk protocol to me, Ceddy—that's our Washington slang, as you may know. I'm talking off the record, as one friend of peace to another. I'm not asking for state secrets—there'll be plenty of leaks in the next few days and I don't want to be a possible source. But if I'm to talk to Schneider to any purpose I have to be able to say this and have it straight: Is Britain going to help him preserve his title to Skoda, or is she not?"

The handsome and dignified nobleman looked at his guest with a steady gaze and delayed replying. So presently Lanny added: "I think I ought to make you acquainted with one set of facts, Ceddy. My father has a deal with Schneider, by which Schneider has the right to build Budd-Erling planes in a new plant in or near Skoda. It was a cash deal and my father has no interest in the concern. It would be all the same to him if the Nazis were to grab the plant, for he also has a deal with Göring; thus Göring wouldn't gain anything he hasn't already got, and Robbie wouldn't lose anything he hasn't already sold. I think you ought to know that, so that when we talk about these delicate matters, you won't have the thought that I may be concerned about some family interest."

"I'm glad to have that knowledge, Lanny,—though I had no such thought. You understand, my lips are sealed as to what is going on at the moment, and I would prefer that you didn't mention to anybody that you have talked to me. But, as one friend to another, it can do no harm for me to tell you that Baron Eugène will have to take his chances along with the rest of us. The British government is certainly not prepared to go to war to protect his titles to Skoda, and if France holds out from the settlement we are working out with Hitler, France will have to do her own fighting, and find whatever way she can to help the Czechs. We, unfortunately, lack the means to get there."

"That is plain enough, and I'll tell him," replied the secret agent. "It will have a pacifying effect, I am sure."

Said his lordship: "We can only hope and pray that Hitler means what he tells us, that this will satisfy him, and that he will settle down and reorganize his economy on a peace instead of a war basis."

So Lanny drove up to town next morning and got a room in a hotel, set up his little portable, and hammered out a report to President Roosevelt, setting forth the fact that the republic of Masaryk and Beneš was the next chunk of appeasement that was going to be fed to the Nazi wolves.

BOOK SEVEN

The Things That Are Caesar's

27

Fever of the World

I

LANNY BUDD was living in a world which did not please him; which indeed seemed to be far on the way toward madness. The job he had chosen—or which perhaps had chosen him—obliged him to meet people whose company he could hardly tolerate, and forbade him to meet anybody he really wanted to know. As a result, he stayed alone except when he was collecting information, and found his pleasure in music, or in books, which he was free to read without permission of the Nazis. He was forced more and more in upon himself, and had to fight against moods of depression, and a tendency to brood over his failures and the tragic scenes he had witnessed.

For example, that poor devil he had left behind in the dungeon of the Château de Belcour. It wasn't that Lanny blamed himself for having left him. There wasn't a thing those three intruders could have done; to have carried the man out would have given the whole thing away and ruined the career of a presidential agent. It might have been the part of kindness to smother him to death; but Lanny had never killed anybody, and hadn't even thought of it. Now he kept wondering: was the poor devil still alive, and still being tortured for having tried to give help to Trudi?

The broken figure became a sort of symbol of the cause which Lanny loved and believed in. Not merely the German people—the good Germans, the good Europeans among the Germans—bound, gagged, imprisoned, and condemned to years of torment; but all the other unfortunate peoples whose fate Lanny had been watching: Italians, Chinese, Abyssinians, Spaniards, Austrians—and now the Czechs, the next on the list, standing helpless, watching the assassins gathering about their house. The unhappy Paul Teicher became multiplied in Lanny's imagination by thousands, by millions, by hundreds of millions. It was the destiny of the peoples of Europe and Asia to have their lands invaded, their young men slaughtered and their women raped, their fields ravaged and their homes burned about their heads, their cities bombed to rubble, their leaders and intellectuals shot or hanged or beheaded or shut up in stockades. Such had been the events in incubation during the whole span of Lanny's life—this wonderful new twentieth century which had called itself "modern" and had hoped so much from itself and for itself.

The state of affairs had been getting worse year after year; the crimes had been increasing in arithmetical progression. And now it seemed that what had happened so far was merely a shadow of the holocausts and desolations ahead. The hopes of Spain were going to be completely extinguished. That cold methodical murderer, General Franco, would continue to receive killing materials from Italy and Germany and to blast and rend the bodies of his fellow countrymen, until there was no longer left in Spain a single person of intelligence, of even common decency. Every man and woman in the land who believed what Lanny believed would be slaughtered, or shut up in a dungeon to perish slowly of the diseases of malnutrition. Every child in Spain would be taken and turned into a pious robot, saving his soul by letting some black-robed priest mumble ancient magic over his poor little lice-infested head.

And now it was happening to Austria. *Wien, Wien, du Stadt meiner Träume!*—Lanny heard gorgeous waltz music every time he thought of it; and now it had become a Nazi headquarters, and was being *gleich-geschaltet*—co-ordinated—which meant that in a thousand dark holes were being repeated those hideous iniquities which he had witnessed in Munich and Berlin. And now the beautiful old city of Prague, and the Czechs, one of the most intelligent and democratic-minded peoples of Europe—whose only offense was that their ancestors, nearly a thousand years ago, had permitted many Germans to enter their country and to purchase lands and other property.

These accumulated horrors caused Lanny Budd to ask questions of the universe into which through no intention of his own he had been so suddenly and strangely projected. What ruled this complex of phenomena—a Providence of any sort, or just blind chance? Lanny hadn't seen any works of art or of artisanship brought into existence by blind chance, so he had to believe that there must be some intelligence at work; some mind must have contrived the production of two billions of human creatures on a small planet revolving obscurely in vast and complicated stellar and galactic systems. What that intelligence could be, and how it worked, and above all what it wanted, became harder for Lanny to imagine the older he grew and the more familiar with massed human misery.

Presumably, that Providence or God wanted each human to do his best; and for Lanny that could only mean a great deal of puzzling and worrying. Perhaps this puzzling and worrying was part of the process; perhaps God meant for each of the two billion creatures to go on striving until it learned to think more clearly, and to organize and co-operate with its fellows. Yes, that must be so—but it seemed such a wasteful, a ghastly process. Why couldn't they have learned to co-operate from the beginning? Why couldn't they have been born with enough sense in their heads—instead of with a desire to dominate and oppress, to rob and to kill?

When you asked questions like that, there was only one answer: "God knows." Since God wouldn't tell, that didn't get you very far. The two billion humans were here on this planet, with no wisdom or guidance save what they themselves could devise and provide. If they were ever going to stop dominating and oppressing, robbing and kill-ing, it would be because some among their number had sufficient intel-ligence to persuade the others to settle down and produce wealth for themselves instead of trying to take it away from their neighbors.

To Lanny's mind this seemed to call for an international government and a world police force. But then he found himself thinking: "Good God, suppose there should be a world police force set up by the new Mohammed!" That was to him just the most horrid thought in the world; and every day seemed to be bringing the possibility nearer to mankind.

II

Politics in England had become so hot right now that Lanny was afraid to go from Wickthorpe Castle to the near-by Reaches. He drove into London and called Rick from there, asking him to come to town; Lanny met him at the station and drove him for a while, as the safest way to discuss the meaning of the Wiedemann visit and the errand of Lord Halifax to Paris. Lanny really didn't have much to tell that was new; the leftwing press had a pretty clear outline of the Nazi-Tory plot to give Hitler what he wanted, in the hope of steering him toward the east. But the leftists couldn't prove it; what they published was shame-lessly denied, and the "appeasers" went right ahead with their plotting. Lanny could confirm Rick's ideas, but he couldn't let him publish the evidence, or even hint at it, because Ceddy knew that Lanny and Rick were friends. The playwright would have to do what he had done on previous occasions—pass the information on to others, a little here and a little there, so that in the end readers of the opposition papers would get a fairly clear outline of the picture.

Lanny told about his discontent, and pleaded for the privilege of being with friends for a few days. Why couldn't Nina and Rick take time off and come with him for a motoring trip? Why not drive north and see that Lake District where Wordsworth had managed to live a peaceful life through all the horrors of the Napoleonic wars? "The world is too much with us," Lanny quoted. They would keep off the beaten paths and avoid the fashionable folk who would know them. Rick said "Topping!" and they met by appointment without telling anybody, and felt as gay as three schoolchildren playing hooky.

The Lake District is in the northwest part of the tight little isle, a couple of hundred miles from London. That would have been a week's comfortable journey in the poet's day, and he had taken it rarely during his eighty years. In Lanny Budd's reckoning it was a forenoon's drive if he was in a hurry; but this holiday party took it slowly, stopping to look at ancient landmarks of which every schoolchild hears. The English countryside wore its midsummer dress of dark green, and the natives called the weather hot, but it didn't seem so if you had been reared in the Midi. All England was having a holiday, apparently; a startling thing to come to the land of a contemplative poet's quiet dreams, and discover his roads paved, his lake shore lined with villas and hotels, and the lakes sprinkled with rowboats and canoes. They had to drive some distance away in order to find accommodations.

The poetry of Wordsworth had been given to Lanny at the age of seventeen by his great-uncle Eli Budd in Connecticut, and he had read and marked it dutifully. Rick, whose education had been more of what he called "mod'n," didn't know it so well; however, Lanny had brought along a copy, and they allowed themselves time to read long passages and look for the features described. It was too late in the year for the golden daffodils, and they would hardly have recognized the peaceful vale; but they heard the twofold shout of the cuckoo, and saw the buzzard mounting from the rock, deliberate and slow. They sat upon one of the multitude of little rocky hills and looked down upon the tiny lake of Grasmere, a mile or so long, with its one green island and its rocky shores. They saw the silver wreaths of curling mist, and the earth and common face of nature spake to them, exactly as to the youthful worshiper a century and a half ago.

Ye presences of nature in the sky
And on the earth! Ye visions on the hills!
And souls of lonely places!

III

But there was a limit to the time that men of this age could spend in the contemplation of natural phenomena. More even than in the poet's day they were besieged by the fretful stir unprofitable, and the fever of the world. Just as the mind of the poet had been haunted by the menace of Napoleon, so the mind of Lanny Budd was haunted by Nazi-Fascism, and he wanted to exclaim to Rick: "O friend, I know not which way I must look for comfort!" Surely now, if ever in recorded time, England was a fen of stagnant waters, and all the poet's other phrases of grief and despair applied as well to this new age.

The Englishman answered: "Yes, but we survived the Napoleonic wars, and I fancy we shall pull through again."

Said Lanny: "Every time I go to Germany, and see the preparations the Nazis are making, I grow more doubtful. I don't think you have ever been in such danger as you are today—certainly not since the time of the Spanish Armada."

Rick agreed, but added that there were some wide-awake men in the government, and some real preparing was under way. "Alfy knows some of the Air Force chaps, and they are working hard, I can assure you."

Lanny revealed his personal discontent; he couldn't keep himself persuaded that he was accomplishing anything, that anybody was paying real heed to the information he brought. His friend told him earnestly: "I don't know what you may be accomplishing in the States, but I can assure you you're being helpful here. It bucks me up to get your confirmation, and to know exactly who our enemies are and what they are planning. I pass on the facts to one key person after another, and if we all have a clear view of the situation today, we owe some of it to your efforts. Certainly you are accomplishing more than if you were to kick over the traces and come out on our side; you could never again go into Germany, or enter the drawing-room at Cliveden, or meet people like that in France or the States."

"That's true," Lanny had to admit. "But just now the whole task seems so immense—so hopeless."

"I'm tempted the same way," admitted the playwright; "but I shan't give up to it, and neither must you. The house is on fire, and we don't know whether we can get the people out, but we have to give the alarm, as loud as we can, and as often."

Said the son of Budd-Erling: "In New England they have a heavy iron ring the size of a wagon wheel; they hang it on a chain from a sort of scaffold, and when there's a fire they hit it with a blacksmith's hammer."

"Righto!" replied the other. "You're the chap who comes running with the hammer, and I'm the one who makes the racket. The townspeople are fat and lazy, and hate to have their dreams disturbed, but we keep on banging and little by little we rout some of them out."

IV

Margy, Dowager Countess Eversham-Watson, had been begging Beauty to come and spend a while with her, and Beauty wanted to take Frances, at least for a week-end. Irma and her mother had never got over their memories of the Lindbergh kidnaping, and the precious darling rarely went off the estate; but Lanny agreed to take her and bring her back, and since he possessed the legal right to do so, Irma had to be content with having the child's governess and the child's maid go along. The theory was that everything Frances could need was provided at Wickthorpe, but Lanny observed that nothing could take the place of the outside world; whenever the little one was taking any sort of trip, she was always wild with delight.

When Margy Petries of Kentucky had become the second wife of Lord Eversham-Watson, she had rebuilt and enlarged the mansion and renamed the place Bluegrass. When her husband known as "Bumbles" had died, Margy's stepson, the new heir to the title, had occupied the mansion, and Margy had built herself a villa on another part of the grounds. Beauty was to stay there along with Frances, while Lanny was to be a guest of the stepson, whom he had played with as a boy.

David Douglas Patrick Fitzgerald, seventh Lord Eversham-Watson, was a big, handsome fellow as his father had been; jovial, easy-going, and untroubled by intellect. An ardent sporting man, he had taken over the management of his father's racing stable, whose pure-blooded Kentucky horses had been one of Margy's contributions to the family prestige as well as to its exchequer. The books showed that they had won close to half a million pounds since the World War. Davy, as he was called, was pure-blooded English, but had always had Americans in his home, and delighted himself with American slang.

He was impressed by Lanny's attainments and liked to hear his stories, especially since the 'report had got around that this art expert had become a pal of the Nazis One, Two, Three. Everybody wanted to hear about them right now while they were making such bally nuisances of themselves, and Davy had filled up the house with people who wanted to ask questions.

So Lanny spent a week-end in the society of England's "sporting set." Most important among them was a short little gentleman, old, almost doddering, with a fringe of white hair around a bald head and a little white mustache decorating a benevolent smiling mouth. "Old Portland" or "dear Portland" was the way everybody referred to him, for he took them back to what they believed was a kindlier age, when there had been no income and death duties. He had been a duke for more than sixty years and had been Queen Victoria's Master of the Hunt. William John Arthur Charles James Cavendish-Bentinck was his name, and he was K.C., P.C., G.C.V.O., Baron Balsover and Cirencester (pronounced Cizeter), Viscount Woodstock, Earl of Portland and Marquess of Titchfield. He had shot one thousand stags, been in at the kill of as many foxes, and had served ten thousand banquets. All in himself he was an era.

In boyhood Lanny had been taken by Margy and some of her friends to see the enormous Welbeck Abbey, home of this duke; it was in the Midlands, where he owned close to two hundred thousand acres, including coal lands and the sites of several villages. To a boy the most interesting fact was that the Duke's father had been possessed by a passion for building things underground; an underground ballroom a hundred and sixty feet long, an underground carriage road which took him secretly into his village of Worksop, a mile and a half away. He had a garden with ovens built into the walls so as to heat it and ripen fruit quickly; a skating rink for the maidservants of the Abbey; a riding school with four thousand gas-jets to light it. A boy does not forget oddities like these.

You ran into them frequently in the ruling-class world of Britain. They were individualistic people, especially when they had a great deal of money; they did what they damned well pleased, and there was seldom any law against it. Some of them had come to New England, and their names had been Budd, and Lanny had learned about them and so was used to the idea of eccentricity. He knew there were dukes who set the fashion in clothes, and others who wore any old thing that pleased them. He had heard the great Duke of Norfolk tell a story on himself—how he had been strolling on the grounds of his estate, which he maintained as a park for the public, and had been rebuked by a member of that public for walking on the grass. "Can't you read? Don't you see that sign that says: 'Keep off the grass'? It's people like you that will cause this place to be closed to the rest of us!"

V

There was one of these ill-dressed noblemen among the company at Bluegrass. He appeared in a blue serge suit, worn shiny at the elbows and the seat of the pants, and a hat made of plaid cloth, of a shape known as "ratcatcher." When he dressed for dinner, his black tie was crooked. He had a thin nose, a wide mouth, and a mass of dark hair thrown to one side and having a tendency to fall over his left eye. He looked for all the world like a poet or painter from a Bloomsbury lodging house—of which he would soon own hundreds, perhaps even thousands.

His name was Hastings William Sackville Russell, and when his aged father died he would be twelfth Duke of Bedford, Marquess of Tavistock, Earl of Russell, Baron Russell of Thornhaugh and Baron Howland of Streatham. The father lived quite alone in a Bedford-shire mansion, and Lanny had heard that it was full of old masters, including eighteen Canalettos in a single room. He decided to culti-vate the son for this reason, but the son told him it was no use; the old gentleman had sixty rooms ready for guests, and sixty more for him-self, but he occupied only three or four, and preferred the company of giraffes and zebras, of which he had a herd. It had been his practice to drive the zebras in harness, and his park was given up to a great number of llamas from the Andes, with a fence around them and guards in green uniforms and cockaded hats to watch over them. Also he had lions and tigers and panthers and what not, and had had an armored train built so that he could drive among them in safety. He could afford to indulge such whims, because he owned large chunks of land on which the city of London had been built, and this land was "entailed"—that is, it couldn't be sold, but only leased, and was handed down to the eldest son.

Thus the Honorable Hastings William Sackville Russell had come honestly by eccentricity. He himself was a lover of birds, and had specialized in the breeding of beautiful parrots. He had been an army officer, but at the outbreak of the World War had decided that he was a pacifist, and had become dishwasher in a Y.M.C.A. canteen. He was still a pacifist, but of that peculiar kind like Senator Nye of

North Dakota, who seemed to except Hitler from his code. The Honorable was greatly interested in the Führer, and Lanny wondered if his haircut was intentionally identical with Adi's. A dozen other noble ladies and gentlemen sat and listened to the questions he asked, and the American was left in no doubt as to the contents of their minds. The familiar problems: Which was the less dangerous, the Brown ogre or the Red, and what were the prospects for getting the pair of them to kill each other off? Lanny thought of that German fairy tale about the little tailor who threw clods at the two sleeping giants and thus provoked them to terrible combat with each other.

VI

The visiting father drove his little daughter back to Wickthorpe, with the governess and maid in the rear seat. All the way the little one chattered about the good time she had had; the beautiful horses, the long-haired shepherd dogs, the kind and friendly people. She asked a string of questions, and again Lanny watched the miracle of a young mind unfolding, a character and a point of view in process of making. He would have liked nothing so much as to take her away and teach her what he believed to be the truth about the world she was to live in. But, alas, he wasn't free to speak a word of that truth, even to hint at it. When she asked about poor people, and why they were that way, what could he answer? If he said anything about the atrocious English land system, the two attendants would hear it and spread the news all over the castle. If he waited until he had the child alone, she would surely blurt it out to her mother: Papa says this, and Papa doesn't think that. He would be breaking faith with Irma, and she would feel it her duty to warn her husband: "Be careful what you say in Lanny's presence; he is still a Red at heart."

No, Frances Barnes Budd must have her mind so shaped that she could live under the English land system without any qualms of conscience. She must believe that by right of birth she was a superior being, entitled to draw off immense sums from the product of other people's labor, and that whenever she returned any of those sums to the people it was an act of benevolence for which they were duty-bound to admire and even love her. There were kindhearted countesses and duchesses in England, and some who used their fortunes to carry on Be-Kind-to-Animals crusades. If an elderly white-haired lady leaped from her limousine to stop a carter from beating an old horse with a stick, it might be "Dear Portland's" wife, whom Frances

had met at Bluegrass, and who had told her about the pit ponies of the
miners which she allowed to fatten themselves on the meadows of her
estate at Welbeck. Little Frances might be made into a Lady Bounti-
ful like that; she was being trained by tutors and family to become
the proper bride of some one of the great nobles of England, and the
best that Lanny could hope was that she wouldn't happen upon one
of the eccentrics.

It was a system which had endured since the battle of Hastings, a
period of eight hundred and seventy-two years. The dukes and earls
and barons were descendants of the Norman conquerors, while the
miners and tenants were descendants of the Saxon losers. The two
languages had become merged, but in the everyday speech you could
recognize the differences between the two groups from a single sentence, sometimes from a word. If the English system had survived and
spread all over the world, so that now the sun never set on it, the
reason was that the governing classes had possessed the wisdom to
yield when they had to, and to treat all conquered peoples with a
share of generosity.

Lanny, reading history and watching the events of his time, decided
that this was the difference between the British Empire and those
which Hitler and Mussolini and Franco and the Son of Heaven were
setting out to build. The British always took with them, wherever
they went, a saving minority of dissidents, whereas the modern dictators shot theirs, or shut them up in concentration camps and suppressed their ideas. The British practice meant to Lanny that his little
daughter had a chance to hear some humanitarian ideas—even without
her father's intervention.

VII

The visitor made himself agreeable to the family and guests of this
well-run household. English fashion, he was let alone and let everybody else alone. He took long walks, read books from an extensive
library, and when the guests wanted music he played for them—nothing too long or too noisy, but properly selected *Salonmusik*. And
whenever the occasion presented itself he listened to discussions of the
Empire's affairs. He could hardly have chosen a better seat from
which to view the procession of events, and to hear them interpreted
by those who were directing them, or trying to.

Among other guests at the next week-end came an elderly gentleman who until recently had been plain Mr. Walter Runciman, but

now had succeeded to the title of Baron. He was a tremendously rich shipowner and had been a member of the Asquith Cabinet. He had just been yachting at Cowes, where he had acquired a healthful coating of tan; but now the Prime Minister had summoned him and put upon him a duty, which Runciman himself whimsically described as being put adrift in a small boat in mid-Atlantic. He was one of those Englishmen with a wry sense of humor, the sort who read *Alice in Wonderland* and frequently quote it. His forehead was high and wrinkled, his round head visible with little interference from hair. His thin lips smiled frequently, but his eyes betrayed anxiety, for he was going to Prague, supposedly unofficially, but really to persuade the Czech government to assent to the settlement which the British Cabinet had worked out through Gerald Albany and other emissaries.

He had come to Wickthorpe to consult with Gerald and other persons familiar with the fine points of the negotiations. They didn't invite the son of Budd-Erling to their conferences, but they couldn't keep from dropping hints, and then Lord Runciman abandoned pretenses by drawing Lanny off into the library on Sunday afternoon and plying him with questions about the different Nazi leaders whom he might expect to encounter on his mission. Did Lanny by any chance know Henlein? Lanny replied that he didn't, but had heard much about this former bankclerk turned agitator; he told what he knew of such fanatics.

And Ribbentrop? Yes, Lanny had met him several times, but only casually. Doubtless Lord Runciman knew the story of how he had behaved when he had been appointed Ambassador to London; presented to the King, he had given the Nazi salute and exclaimed: *"Heil Hitler!"* The King had gazed at him in amazement, and twice more he had repeated the performance, apparently trying to force His Majesty to return or at least acknowledge the salute. He had been treated to the iciest of English frosts, and ever since then hatred of the country has been his principal diplomatic motive.

"Undoubtedly," said Lanny, "he is the Führer's most evil counselor. Göring is cautious, and pulls back on the reins whenever he can; but Ribbentrop is brash, and tireless in insisting that England will not fight, and cannot if she wishes. Unfortunately the champagne salesman is on top at present, so I am told."

"How can such a man be handled?" asked his lordship; and Lanny had to say: "I am afraid that the program of appeasement which you wish to promote is only likely to encourage his arrogance."

Impossible for anyone to ask questions like these and not betray the secret thoughts of his heart. What was apt to be Hitler's reaction to this proposal and to that? Manifestly, these were the proposals which Baron Runciman of Doxford had been commissioned to make; and before their talk was over he had pretty well abandoned the pretense that the details of the settlement were secret. The British Cabinet didn't want Hitler to get Skoda, for example; but they wanted to give him the mountains in which the Czechs had built fortifications from which alone the Bohemian plain could be defended. "Why," asked Lanny, "should a burglar take the trouble to break into a safe unless he means to carry off the treasure?"

VIII

Rosemary, Countess of Sandhaven, wrote a little note: "Why don't you come to see me, Lanny?" She had a right to ask, being one of his oldest friends, and he having been in the neighborhood for a month. He couldn't think of an excuse, so he went and had tea. How lovely she looked in a light summer dress, with those bold flowered patterns the women were wearing! They sat on a shaded terrace, with two big dogs sleeping at her feet, and drank their tea and chatted about families and friends, and what they had both been doing. Rosemary was interested in people, and events had a tendency to become personal when she talked about them, because she knew the persons who were making the events, and explained everything according to the persons' temperaments and desires.

She was a year older than Lanny, and had three nearly grown children, but showed none of the effects of age; her skin was as fair as when he had first known her, and her two ropes of straw-colored hair had never been cut, but were wound like a coronet about her head. She had taken good care of herself all these years, and had never engaged in any conflict with her fate. She was kind, gentle, serene, and to Lanny a boyhood dream. Her husband had other women, and she had let him go his way, according to the modern custom; she had always been easy-going in sexual matters. Why did Lanny stay away from her?

The political views he now professed were those which Rosemary took for granted, so they could have got along quite harmoniously. If he needed any particular item of information, she would have helped him to get it. They would have had to be what the world called "discreet," meeting in London and traveling together only on the Continent; their friends would have known about it, and no one would have been shocked save a few old-fashioned persons who did not count in their world. The arrangement would have been comfortable, and, from the world's point of view, sensible.

The wrong lay in the fact that Lanny had come to hate that rich and smart world; a parasitic group which didn't even know itself to be that, which hadn't enough brains to realize what it was costing the human race. Some day Lanny was going to break with that group, openly and completely; he couldn't foresee how or when, but meantime he didn't want to compromise with it in his soul, he didn't want to take any chance of weakening his inner resistance. To hold in his arms a woman whose ideas he despised was fair neither to the woman nor himself.

So, talk about the Budd-Erling business, in which Rosemary had a few shares of stock; about paintings which Bertie owned, and for which he wanted too much money; about the Runciman mission—Rosemary knew "Old Walter," as she called him, and said that he was a shrewd trader, for all his whimsical manner, and would probably come away with Ribbentrop's shirt. Rosemary knew the champagne salesman, too, and reported with a smile that he had tried to make a date with her the last time they had met. That had been at Cliveden, and Rosemary talked freely about the visitors there, and what they had said as to the importance of getting France away from the Russian alliance and into some kind of settlement with Germany.

All this was important to Lanny, and he wished the damned business of sex hadn't stood in the way. He had to think up an excuse that wouldn't hurt an old sweetheart's feelings, and on the spur of the moment he told her that he had found a happy love, but was under solemn pledge not to breathe a word about it. Of course that set her on edge with curiosity, but he stuck to his story: Not a word! He could soothe his qualms of conscience by telling himself that it was Trudi he meant. It was really the Trudi-ghost who stood between him and the Countess of Sandhaven.

IX

Lanny studied the newspapers, not only those of London, but those he got from Paris and Berlin. The Runciman mission arrived in Prague and was received at the railway station by the entire Czech Cabinet in top hats. The German papers did their best to make it appear an official effort at "mediation," despite Runciman's own insistence that he was "a purely private person." Also the Berlin papers were full of atrocities in the Sudeten—which meant that the Nazis were determined to have what they wanted, and were beating up the threat of war.

Hitler invited Admiral Horthy, the Hungarian dictator, made a secret pact with him, and showed him a review of the new German battle-fleet, a hundred and ten modern vessels, with the dreadnaught *Gneisenau* at their head. Then he put on a military parade which included huge field guns built so that they could be taken apart and the four parts carried on separate vehicles and reassembled in two hours. Hundreds of thousands of laborers rushed work on the Rhineland fortifications against France. There was a "trial mobilization" of trucks and motorcars, and a million Germans were reported under arms. *Deutschland über Alles!*

Zoltan Kertezsi arrived in London at this juncture. "Everybody" was out of town in late August, but he had some paintings to look at in a country house in East Riding, and Lanny drove him there. Zoltan himself didn't drive, and looked upon motorcars as dangerous toys; but he trusted Lanny, and they liked to be together. They had no end of shop to talk, and the Hungarian revealed that he had a nibble at a couple of Göring's paintings which Lanny had listed with him; he would have to see them, and how about Lanny's motoring him to Berlin?

The political pot seemed likely to boil over any day in Germany and it might be a good thing to be there. No doubt existed in Lanny's mind that Hitler was going to be presented with the western portions of Czechoslovakia, but the question remained, how long was he going to be content with them, and what would he take next, Prague or the Polish Corridor. This would be an important item of information for F.D.R., and Lanny would enjoy being the first to transmit it. It is that way with secret agents; they develop a competitive spirit, and number 103 wants to get ahead of his hundred and two rivals. Lanny said: "It's a date," and got a stenographer and sent off a batch of letters and cablegrams, informing his father and mother and various clients, including Feldmarschall Göring, that his address until further notice would be the Hotel Adlon.

There had been few months in Lanny Budd's life in the course of which he hadn't put his belongings into bags and stowed his bags into a car and driven to some other part of the earth. The procedure had become automatic, so that he could perform it while chatting, or meditating upon the problems of his own life and of the world. Indeed, he had developed two sections of his subconscious mind, one for Britain and the other for the continent of his birth and also for the land of his forefathers; he never forgot which place he was in and gave the wrong signal or got onto the wrong side of the road. It took a few moments' attention to enter a ferry on the left side and come off on the right, but once that was done it was as if a key had been turned, and the British section of Lanny's driving mind was locked away for the duration.

He never tired of rolling along the beautifully paved highways of France, Belgium, Holland, and so into Germany. The world became a panorama unwinding before his eyes; sometimes he noticed it in swift glances, sometimes it was absorbed into his subconscious mind through the skin, as it were. From years of experience he had learned where good food was to be had, and waited till he came to those places; the proprietors remembered and greeted him, and it was pleasant to let his eyes roll over a menu and his appetite indicate a choice. Yes, the world was a pleasant place in the year 1938—if you had looked out for yourself and put money in your purse, and refused to get into a dither over the troubles of the rest of mankind!

X

Arriving at his hotel, Lanny found an invitation from *Der Dicke* to visit him at Karinhall. He called up Furtwaengler and accepted, and at the same time arranged for Zoltan to view the paintings. If he had tried, he could have got an invitation for his colleague to Karinhall; but he didn't, because it was for him a business visit and its secrets could not be shared. The Hungarian was well content; he had affairs of his own, and would learn about *die grosse Welt* of the Nazis from his friend's lively accounts.

Lanny drove himself to the Schorfheide, and there was the fat *Nummer Zwei* and his fair lady, a trinity now, with a tiny baby girl who had been publicized all over Germany as an unprecedented achievement. Lanny, well-trained courtier, knew the proper ritual under such circumstances. He must ask and not wait to be invited to see this royal mite; he must cry out with pleasure the moment the sight burst upon his eyes; he must study every feature and debate whether it was derived from the father or the mother; he must overlook no charm which any of the three possessed, and must end by declaring that in all his experience with bundles fresh from heaven he had seen no one so promising of all the virtues. When he had completed this rite, with every evidence of intense sincerity, Karinhall would be his, and anything in it he chose to ask for.

What he wanted was no earthly treasure, but information, and he began by giving it in generous measure. What could be a better opening than to say that he had spent a week-end with a certain "purely private person," only a day or two before that person had set out on his purely public mission? Göring at once began to ply his visitor with questions. What sort of emissary was this, whose last act before leaving home had been a public prayer in Holy Trinity Church for the success of his mission? Did he really believe in that, or was it just politics in a land of *Dummköpfe*—blockheads? Was he really as rich as reported? He had brought his wife along, presumably to keep other women away from him. Did he drink or gamble, and was he fond of good food, or of money? And how did it happen that he had been prominent in the Liberal Party, but now was working with the Tories? A puzzling thing, this British political system!

XI

Once more it was proved that a man cannot ask questions without revealing what is on his mind. The fat Marshal betrayed to his visitor that behind the Nazi façade of bluff and defiance was a group of greatly confused men, sharply divided among themselves. Before Lanny departed from *Der Dicke's* country place, he managed to bring him to the point of frankness on the subject of Joachim von Ribbentrop; at least to the extent of stating that his country's Foreign Minister was a vain fool, a snob and a charlatan, an upstart, an intriguer, and a sycophant. He had become suddenly wealthy by marriage, and that eminence had gone to his head; he had managed to persuade the Führer by his glib tongue, and had been sent to England, where the aristocracy had twisted him around its finger—making him think that he, not they, controlled the foreign policy of the Empire, and that they were as clay in the potter's hands—a champagne potter!

"You know England, Lanny," said Göring. "Cliveden and Wickthorpe and the other country houses control up to a certain point, but nobody can ever be sure when the mob may rise up and force a reversal of their policy. It's like sailing a small boat on one of those Swiss lakes; everything is so peaceful and still, you think it's a washbasin; but suddenly comes the *bise* and upsets everything."

"I have seen it," replied Lanny.

He had been troubled in his conscience, for fear that he might have been agreeing too freely with the Nazis and thus giving them encouragement. It would be intolerable to think that by so much as a feather's weight he had helped to turn the scales in any of these recurrent crises. Now he saw a chance to tip the scales his own way, and he hastened to agree with Göring's opinion of the English "mob"— its instability, its liability to sudden frenzies, and the cowardice of the most powerful political leaders in the face of such a storm. An irresponsible press and an unsubdued labor movement had almost broken the Tory policy over Abyssinia, and again over Spain; now they might easily do it over Czechoslovakia, and Germany would find itself at war with Britain, France, and Russia all at once.

"Give us two years more to get ready," lamented the head of the Air Force, "and we shall be beyond danger. But no, we cannot wait! Ribbentrop is there, like Mephistopheles, whispering into the Führer's ear, insinuating doubts as to the judgment and even the good faith of those of us who try to restrain him, who plead for a little more time. It is a terrible thing!"

Suddenly the great man had a bright idea. "Why don't you talk to him, Lanny?"

"*Me*, Hermann?"

"You know England better than any of us, and he knows that you do. Tell him what you have just told me."

Lanny hadn't really told very much; he had listened to what Göring told, and put in a few words of assent now and then. But it wouldn't do for him to cast doubts upon his own authority. He replied: "You know, it's not easy to talk to the Führer when his mind is made up. *He* does the talking!"

"I know; but his mind isn't made up yet; the thing is hanging in the balance. You might find him in a mood to ask questions. You are one of the few persons he can believe to be disinterested; you have never asked him for anything, and I have told him he can trust you, for I believe you are a good influence upon him."

"Thanks, Hermann. I'm always honored to meet him, because I know he's a great man. You would be interested to see how people everywhere crowd about to ask me questions about him—and about you also. You are looming large upon the world's horizon right now."

"Far too large," replied *Der Dicke*, who had not permitted his high station to destroy entirely his sense of humor. "I am going to have to take a reducing cure. But seriously; let me call the Führer and tell him you are here, and tell him you have talked with Runciman and Wickthorpe and others. He will wish to see you without any suggestion from me. He will probably tell me to have you flown to Berchtesgaden."

"I have my car here," the visitor reminded him.

"*Das macht nichts aus*. We will fly you back here, or send your car to Berlin, or to Berchtesgaden, wherever you prefer. This is a serious matter—the fate of Germany, and indeed of all Europe, may be hanging in the balance."

XII

So it came about that Lanny saw Germany from the extreme north to the extreme south, quite literally a bird's-eye view; a gigantic map unrolling, slowly, silently, except for the roar of a great motor. He sat in the co-pilot's seat, beside a very young Air Force Leutnant, one of the world's best, so *Der Dicke* had declared, patting them both on their backs after he had introduced them. "Take good care of him; he is the Führer's friend,"—so he had told the officer.

So now, through the interphone, the pilot in charge of Lanny's destiny for an hour or so entertained him with the names of cities, towns, and villages, rivers, lakes, canals, forests, mountains, airfields, great factories—every feature of the map below, whether natural or made by man. The greater part of Germany, as seen by a bird, looks like a checkerboard, but with no two squares alike. Different crops have different shades of green or brown or yellow at different seasons of the year; roads are tiny gray ribbons; buildings have only roofs, and these vary according to their materials, and whether they are wet or dry. Such details constitute an airman's life while he is in the sky, and while he is studying photographs, or maps on a briefing-room wall. When he learns that his passenger's father makes the fastest pursuit plane in the world, he gets a thrill and asks many questions, and mentions that the factories of his own land are just on the point of exceeding that record by ten or twenty kilometers per hour.

Lanny was set down expertly on the Führer's private airport, Ainring. A car was awaiting him, and again he was driven into those beautiful mountains. The earth had performed more than half its annual swing about the sun, and early March had become late August. The snow was gone, and the evil witch Berchta had retired to her cave; the landscape was arrayed in dark green, shiny with gleams of the sun; all the good fairies, gnomes, and little men who haunt the German forests were hiding under the fern-fronds, and a million bees were collecting honey for the Führer's table. They had to work overtime, since he, non-smoker and non-drinker, was extremely fond of sweets, especially when they were made into cream tarts or puffs or other delicacies, usually considered more suitable for ladies' palates.

That was one part of the meal he served Lanny at lunch; a much better meal than he had prepared for Schuschnigg on his visit—and surely better than that luckless wight was now getting in the castle where Hitler had him confined. No more proclamations about plebiscites from him; no more insolence over the radio, imitating in a mocking voice the Führer's peculiar modes of speech acquired in the Innviertel! The outside world hadn't heard much about the ex-Chancellor's fate, but Lanny knew that he had been united to his Countess Vera—by proxy, in a ceremony in which his brother took his place, and bride and bridegroom were not permitted to set eyes upon each other!

The master of the Berghof welcomed his guest cordially; but Lanny knew him well enough to perceive at once that he was under great tension. The whole place was on pins and needles, as the saying is; people coming and going, talking in whispers, and watching to be sure that nobody else was listening. Hess was there, and the first thing he said to Lanny was: "You should have brought Madame. She might have been very useful to us now." Lanny answered: "I was planning to consult Pröfenik, but I got whisked away in too great a hurry."

XIII

Right after lunch the Führer invited the guest to his study and seated him in one of those extremely modernistic chairs made out of light stainless metal. "Göring tells me that you have just come from England. Tell me what you found there; it is important for me."

Lanny complied tactfully, beginning with every favorable circumstance he could think of. The British ruling classes were tremendously impressed by the diplomatic skill which a man of the people was so unexpectedly displaying; the military people were awed by the quality of Germany's new armaments; the great industrialists envied him the *Ordnung und Zucht* which he had managed to impose upon German labor. Lanny told of the parade of Mosley followers he had seen in the streets of London; of the admiration for the Führer which had been expressed by highly placed noblemen and their heirs; of the eager questioning by Lord Runciman of Doxford. The Führer beamed, rubbed his thighs, slapped his knees, and gave every evidence that his vegetable plate and temperance beer were setting well upon his stomach.

But then—a *but!* "Of course that isn't all the story, Herr Reichskanzler"—and the great man's face began to fall. "Hermann thinks I should tell you both sides, because you have a grave decision to make, and it is not the part of friendship to withhold any facts."

"By all means, Herr Budd, tell me the worst. What are the difficulties you see?"

Lanny referred to the British press, which boasted itself "free," and understood by freedom the policy of publishing whatever was likely to arouse reader interest and increase sales. A highly competitive press, dominated by commercial motives; under the influence of the late Lord Northcliffe it had thrown dignity to the winds, and gone in for headlines and sensations. There were, of course, still responsible papers. The *Times*, called "the Thunderer," was now owned by Lord Astor, who was the Führer's friend; the same was true of Lord Beaverbrook, who owned the *Daily Express* and the *Evening Standard*, and of Lord Rothermere, Northcliffe's brother, who owned the *Daily Mail* and the *Evening News*, and had gone so far as to give his support to Mosley's Union of British Fascists. All these could be counted upon in any crisis; but there were other papers, able to make a great noise, which catered to labor, to what they called liberalism, democracy——

That was enough to set Adi off, as Lanny knew it would. For a solid half-hour without one pause he poured out his loathing of that licentious capitalistic press and that bastard "liberty" which permitted it to batten on the degradation of the public. It was Jewish-owned and Moscow-subsidized—both these facts the Führer could prove, and it was part of the hideous conspiracy to bolshevize Europe and the entire world. To the thwarting of that conspiracy the Führer had dedicated his life; for that purpose Divine Providence had sent him in this crisis. A complete speech, with all rhetorical stresses and gestures; it might have been delivered with éclat to seven hundred thousand Germans on the *Tempelhofer Feld*, or to seventy millions over the radio, but it was delivered to one American and four dead walls—unless there was a household listening, as in the case of the Schuschnigg tirade.

The orator stopped as suddenly as he had begun—this being his custom, as Lanny had learned. "I am doing all the talking," he said, "and you have information that I need. Please pardon me, and go on."

"The facts I tell you are deplorable, Exzellenz," replied the visitor, deprecatingly; "but you must know that I did not create them. There is no greater service that can be done to a master of men like yourself than to bring him the truth."

"Certainly, Herr Budd; I am not a child and have no wish to be treated as one. Tell me frankly, and be sure that I will consider it an act of friendship."

"What I have to say, Herr Reichskanzler, is that a large section of the British public appears to be in a nervous and excitable state at the present moment; ready to be played upon by any demagogue who tells them that you are not going to be satisfied to get back the territories which are preponderantly German, but that you are aiming at conquests. I don't meet persons of that way of thinking, so I can't say this at first hand, but I know that the governing classes are worried, fearing one of those storms of public emotion that arise, as suddenly as the *bise* on an Alpine lake. It is their prayer that you will make matters as easy for them as possible. Will you give them time, so that the changes can be made with order and by mutual agreement? That is the question I have been asked a score of times in England; and, of course, if you care to give me an answer, I will be happy to pass it on to the key people."

The Führer of all the Nazis couldn't take a thing like that sitting still. First he began to snap his fingers and then to jerk his arms; then he hopped up, and began to pace about. He would stop and start to interrupt, then choke back his words and force himself to listen, as he had promised to do. When he could endure no more, he burst out again, listing the humiliations and insults he had endured from the people and government of England over a period of years, indeed ever since he, the son of Alois Schicklgruber, had become aware of what was happening in the world.

The son of Budd-Erling knew that he wasn't doing himself any good by becoming the target of such a tirade, and at the first break in the deluge of words he exclaimed: "Remember, Exzellenz, I am an American, and you are not to hold it against me when I tell you about people in England."

The great man took this as the occasion to end the interview. "You are correct, Herr Budd. I have to give the historic process time to work itself out. You have done me a service, and be sure that I appreciate it, and hope that you will never hesitate to tell me the truth as you see it. Stay with me a while now, if you can spare the time, and let me ask you for more information."

XIV

That was handsome, and Lanny went to his room with hope that he might actually be helping to bring peace to Europe. This mood lasted for an hour or more; until there came a tap on his door, and there was Rudolf Hess, also seeking information. "The Führer is in one of his black moods. What on earth did you say to him, Herr Budd?"

So Lanny told his story all over again. He wasn't sure what was the personal attitude of Nazi Number Three toward Nazi Number Two, but he thought it proper to state that Marshal Göring had considered his information from England of such importance that the Führer ought to hear it. Hess, who had been raised among Englishmen and knew their ways, assented to this at once; the situation was critical, and it was important that someone should take the onus of pointing it out to the Führer, who didn't know the English people, their language or their literature, and so was in danger of misjudging their attitude. Lanny, groping his way in the mazes of court intrigue, was pleased to discover that Number Three agreed with Number Two, and shared his hatred of the champagne salesman, who had never had a number officially assigned him, but had apparently established himself as Number Four and doubtless had hopes of pushing upward.

The faithful Rudi took it as his duty to explain the greatest man in the world, whose servant and admirer he had been for most of his adult life. Der Führer was a man of action; when the time for action came, he moved with the swiftness of a charging lion, and those were the times when he was really himself. At other times he was restless and uncertain and a prey to many sorts of moods, some of them even suicidal—it was no secret that Hess had had a hard time keeping him from destroying himself after the failure of the *Putsch*, almost fifteen years ago. He was impatient of every sort of detail, and left it to Hess or others upon whom he had conferred authority; he rebuked them when they brought him problems, and told them that all he required of them was that they should succeed—otherwise they were of no use to him and would be replaced.

The prime necessity of his being was solitude. That was the meaning of the long walks in the forest; that was why he had chosen the Berghof, and why, since it had become a great establishment, he had built the eagle's nest on the Kehlstein, where no one could possibly get at him. He had to hearken to his inner voices; he had to give his *Genie* a chance to incubate in secret and give him guidance. For weeks at a time he would be brooding, inaccessible, irritated when anyone forced himself upon him.

"I am sorry if I have made things harder for you," said Lanny, considerately.

The Deputy answered: "Not at all, we are used to it; we have learned to adjust ourselves to the moods of an inspired leader." And then, after a pause: "As a matter of fact, the one who is going to catch it has not yet arrived. I'll not tell him of your part in the matter."

"Who is it?" inquired the visitor. "Ribbentrop?"

"No, Dr. Franck."

Lanny knew the name of Karl Hermann Franck as Henlein's Deputy Führer in the Sudeten. "What has he done?"

"He has taken upon himself to issue a proclamation, canceling the previous instructions to our people there that they should forego the right of self-defense for the present. Franck has told them that they should resist attacks by Marxist terrorists. Of course they should do that, but apparently it is premature, and interferes with something the Führer is planning. He is in a rage, and ordered me to telephone for Franck to be brought here by plane at once. I would not care to be in his boots."

XV

Thus duly forewarned, Lanny stayed in his room. But he took the liberty of leaving his door slightly ajar, according to the custom of the Berghof as he had learned it. When, later on, he heard shouting downstairs, he took his post just behind the door, the best place from which to get an earful—and surely he got it. Apparently the Führer was in such a fury that he didn't wait to have the unhappy Deputy brought up to his study; he rushed downstairs and met him in the entrance hall—which meant that everybody in the place could hear every word.

At the beginning there were a few breaks in the tirade; one could imagine the frightened official trying to interpose explanations or apologies. But after that there were no breaks; the Führer was yelling at him —and never in all his life had Lanny Budd heard such sounds coming from a human throat. The dressing-down of Gregor Strasser, even that of Schuschnigg, had been a summer's zephyr in comparison with this tornado. The unfortunate Herr Doktor was called *Sie Trottel, Sie verdammter Esel, Sie Schweinhund*—and when such ordinary German abuse wasn't adequate, he was called foul names known to the Innviertel yokels. He had exceeded his authority, he had threatened with utter ruin and collapse the Führer's careful policies of legality. Germany might be plunged into war overnight by his insane presumption, and he alone, *der lumpige, abgesetzte, unsägliche* Doktor Karl Hermann Franck would bear the responsibility for it all. A traitor to his Fatherland and his Führer, he deserved to be taken out onto the drive in front of the Berghof and shot forthwith. Lanny heard the words *erschossen worden* at least a dozen times during that lambasting, and each time he could imagine a terrified wretch cringing and perhaps falling down upon his knees.

That should have been enough from any master to any servant, so thought the Anglo-Saxon; but it wasn't enough for a member of the *Herrenrasse*. The screams went on increasing in intensity; they became those of a panther rather than of a human being. Lanny had long ago decided upon "half-genius, half-madman" as a description of Adi Schicklgruber, but now he shifted the proportions in his mind; he began to wonder whether the Führer might not be physically attacking his victim, beating him with the horsewhip which for years he had carried in Munich—though he had abandoned the custom some time before taking public office. Lanny had heard from Hilde von Donnerstein and others how Hitler was said to foam at the mouth during such rages; his lips would turn blue and sweat would stream down his face. Now it was easy to imagine these things happening. Lanny was amazed by the ability of a human organism to endure such protracted effort and strain.

There fell a sudden silence; really quite portentous, and Lanny wondered, had Adi strangled his victim, or had he himself fallen unconscious? Apparently it was the latter, for he heard people running, and then he thought it proper to open his door and come out. He could see the stairway, and watched while half a dozen secretaries and staff members carried a heavy bundle upstairs and into the Führer's apartment. That was all the visitor heard for quite a while; he returned to his room and shut the door, cherishing the hope that it might be an apoplectic stroke, freeing Germany and Europe once for all of this mad Mohammed.

But apparently it wasn't anything out of the usual. When the dinnergong sounded, Lanny came down, according to the rules, and here came the Führer, freshly bathed, shaved, and dressed, smiling like any well-bred host. The unfortunate Dr. Franck did not appear and was not mentioned; Lanny was left to wonder whether he had been carried off to Stadelheim prison, near Munich, where Lanny himself had been shut up by an unfortunate mistake. But no, he was soon in the news dispatches again, performing his Deputy's functions in the Sudetenland, but presumably with care not to exceed his authority.

Lanny played, at request, *Elizabeth's Prayer* and the *Pilgrims' Chorus* from *Tannhäuser*, and then listened to Herr Kannenberg play the accordion and sing Bavarian peasant songs. Later he went to bed, telling himself that he had helped to prolong the life of the Czechoslovak Republic—possibly for as long as twenty-four hours!

28

The Stars in Their Courses

I

LANNY telephoned to Berlin, ordering his mail forwarded, and among the letters which came was one from Hilde von Donnerstein. She had a summer châlet on the Obersalzberg and invited him to visit there, adding that her mother was with her, so it would be quite *comme il faut*. The place was a good walk from the Berghof, if you liked hard climbing amid mountain scenery. Lanny paid her a call, and she took him to a summer house on a point of rock, from which you could see all around you, and make sure that nobody was eavesdropping on a shivery conversation. The Fürstin, who lived on gossip, wanted to hear the news about her many friends in England, including Irma, and in return she was ready to pay in kind.

The Führer of the Nazis lived in a glass house, it appeared. His servants told their sweethearts what was going on there, and even some of his secretaries and military aides were not above whispering secrets into one pair of ears. One pair was enough to keep the whole neighborhood informed; and furthermore, if you could believe Hilde, there were high-powered field glasses frequently trained upon that conspicuous house on the mountainside. Anyhow, Hilde knew all about the Dr. Franck episode, and was disappointed to learn that Lanny had been shut up in his room at the time. She knew, or professed to know, all about Geli Raubal, and half a dozen other young women whose happiness had been wrecked by the Führer's peculiar practices. She even knew what Juppchen Goebbels had said to Magda the last time she had come back from the Berghof.

More important to Lanny, some friend had told her what was going on in the Wilhelmstrasse. She knew about the acts of provocation in the Sudetenland, how they had been planned and how they were being handled in the press. She had heard who was going to be put in charge of Skoda when it was taken over—something that would surely be of interest to Baron Schneider! With a nervous glance around the landscape, and after swearing a guest of the Berghof to everlasting secrecy, she told about the recent visit of Count Ciano, Mussolini's son-in-law and Foreign Minister, who had listened to the Führer raving at the Czechs, and coming out, had thrown up his hands and exclaimed: "My God, that man believes his own atrocity stories!"

A curious phenomenon the visitor noted: this sophisticated lady, despising the crude men who had seized power in her country and willing to risk her family's safety for the pleasure of repeating smart gibes about them, was yet in her secret heart proud of what they had achieved. A cynical worldling, she was nevertheless a German. The Fatherland had to expand, she remarked, casually; they were a vigorous people, and had the misfortune to be penned up in a small territory, and shut off from the rest of the world by the British fleet. That fleet, the press reported, was about to flaunt its power in Germany's face by parading forty battleships in the North Sea; something which couldn't, by the widest stretch of words, be called courteous behavior.

Lanny was free to tell about his visits to Professor Pröfenik, omitting the Trudi part. The Fürstin said: "By the way, a friend of mine has just had an extraordinary experience with a young astrologer in Munich. Of course he doesn't call himself that, since it's against the law, but he will practice it for people he trusts. He told my friend the most amazing things about her past and her future—and some of the latter have already come true."

"I don't think much of astrology," answered the visitor. "I have never been able to find a rational basis for it."

"I know; but when things like this happen,"—and Hilde began a string of episodes, the sort of marvels that people tell, doubtless not always getting them quite straight.

The other said: "Hess believes devoutly in astrology. I wonder if he knows this man." He made note of the name, Reminescu—he was a Rumanian—and added: "Perhaps I'll give him a try. I know so many people who would like to have a look into the future right now!"

II

In the course of his dabbling in psychic matters Lanny had naturally met a number of believers in astrology. They studied elaborate charts of the twelve signs of the zodiac, and were firmly convinced that under whichever sign you had been born, your character and destiny were thereby determined. They would cast your horoscope and look enormously wise and speak a recondite and mystifying lingo. You could see on newsstands in London or New York a row of magazines, proving that there were great numbers of persons who believed in this ancient science or art and were willing to pay good money for it. The first time Lanny had heard about the subject had been as a boy, and he had asked the opinion of an old friend at Bienvenu, a retired Swiss diplomat, M. Rochambeau. This student of books and life had answered in words about as follows:

"You see a group of stars in the sky which suggests to you a certain shape, a scorpion or a lion, and you call that a constellation and give it a name. That pattern has not changed very much since the stars were first observed, and it was possible to imagine all sorts of mystical things about it—until modern high-powered telescopes revealed that the stars which make up Scorpio or Leo are millions of millions of miles apart and have no connection with one another, save that they exist in the same universe. It is as if you stood looking out of a window, and saw three flies on the pane of glass, and three leaves on a tree outside, and three birds in the sky and perhaps an airplane, and all these happened at some moment to make a figure, which looked to you like a coffin and suggested death, or like a shoe, perhaps, and suggested that you were going for a walk."

That had sufficed Lanny until long afterwards, when he had become convinced of the reality of telepathy and clairvoyance, and had been led to revise his thinking about all the practices called "occult." We know so little about how psychic phenomena are brought about, and what states of the conscious or the subconscious mind induce them. It might be that studying astrological charts, or the patterns of tea-leaves, or the lines in a person's hand, are forms of autosuggestion, of attaining concentration, of inducing mystical moods or feelings, which might cause some spark to fly, some energy to be released or diverted. Give it whatever name you please, the point is that these modern seers, or the ancients who had observed the flights of birds and the entrails of sacrificial beasts, may have found that they achieved some special mental state by such methods. The mere fact of believing ardently in bread pills has been known to cause some persons to recover from diseases.

So now, returning to the Berghof, Lanny talked with Rudolf Hess, and listened to his ideas about the stars in their courses which had fought against Sisera but now were fighting for Adolf Hitler and his

National Socialist German Workingmen's Party. Lanny remarked: "I have just been told about a remarkable fortune-teller in Munich, a young Rumanian by the name of Reminescu. Have you ever heard of him?" When the Nazi answered in the negative, Lanny said: "There are paintings I want to see in the city, and I might stop in and give him a try—if you don't mind my breaking the law."

"By all means go," replied the other, unsmiling. "We need all the guidance we can get in these critical days."

III

The outlawed interpreter of the stars had rented himself a rear parlor in a residential street which was gradually being converted to the uses of art and assignation. A small sign on the door described him as a "phrenologist," and his room was decorated with the customary charts of the head, and with framed letters from satisfied clients. A young woman answered the doorbell, then disappeared, and at once the astrologer came in. He was in his late twenties, Lanny guessed, a rather frail dark chap with sensitive features and a deprecating manner. He wore an ordinary dark business suit, and apparently went in for no hocus-pocus. When Lanny said that he wished to have his horoscope cast, and would promise to consider it strictly confidential, the other looked him over, and said: "You are a foreigner?" When Lanny replied: "Yes," he said: "My charge is ten marks." Lanny produced a bill and paid in advance.

Then began the usual rigmarole. The visitor gave the year, month, day of the month, and hour of his birth, according to what his mother had told him. The man produced his charts from a drawer and began conning them, making notes and calculations. Meantime Lanny watched him in silence, thinking: "He has Jewish blood,"—but one did not ask about that in Naziland. Lanny thought: "He looks worried and unhappy." He had been told that the Gestapo had all the mediums and psychics of the Fatherland on its list and was making life difficult for them.

Suddenly the man got up and moved a chair close to his visitor. "Would you mind if I held your hand for a while?"

Lanny consented and his hand was taken in one that was soft and warm, with delicate slender fingers. He did not look at Lanny's, but closed his eyes and was still. Lanny thought: "He does not trust his stars entirely." He wondered, as many times before, could there be vibrations of some obscure sort which passed from human hands, or from the brain? And if so, what was the sense that received them and interpreted them? Something happened, he was sure.

Suddenly the man remarked: "You are an American?" When Lanny replied, he added: "But I have a feeling that you were born very near here."

That was a bull's-eye, for Lanny had been born in Switzerland, a little more than a hundred miles from Munich. "Yes," he admitted, and the astrologer tried another shot. "The stars tell me that you were born rich, and have become richer."

That might perhaps have been inferred from Lanny's appearance and manner. He replied, discreetly: "Standards of wealth are decidedly relative." To this the other made no comment. Instead he remarked: "It appears that you have been married twice."

Now there were only four persons in the world who were supposed to know that secret: Nina and Rick, Monck, and the President of the United States. Even supposing that Reminescu had recognized Lanny, which was unlikely, how could he know about a secret marriage in England under assumed names?

Lanny took a chance and said: "Only once." The other shrugged his shoulders and replied: "I can only tell you what the stars report."

The client was curious enough to ask: "Will I marry again?" The answer was: "You may wish to, but I doubt if you will." Lanny thought: "Am I going to fall in love with the wrong woman again?" It had been his unfortunate habit.

The next statement came with the suddenness of a shot. "You will die in Hongkong."

As it happened, this remote city was little more than a name to Lanny Budd. He said: "I have no reason for ever going to that place that I can think of."

"You will find a reason," was the reply; "and you will die there. It is in the stars."

"I hope this will not be too soon."

The astrologer went back and studied his charts. Then he announced: "It will be when Saturn is in the constellation Taurus; somewhere between three and four years from now."

"I am not trying to be clever," replied Lanny. "I am sincerely interested in the possibility of precognition, and anxious to understand your methods. Suppose I were to accept your warning and were to refrain from going to Hongkong, would I not thereby cheat this destiny?"

"One does not cheat one's destiny. If you were destined to refrain

from going, it would not be in the stars that you would go. There will
be some reason for going that will seem to you important, and you
will go."

Lanny smiled. "You should not labor too hard to convince me,
otherwise you yourself might be thwarting the stars."

"If it were in my power to convince you, it would not be in the
stars. You will not accept my warning, but will go away saying to
yourself that it is nonsense."

"I'll surely remember it if I ever find myself on the way to Hongkong!" was Lanny's wisecrack.

IV

That was supposed to be the end of the session; but the visitor wasn't
satisfied. He had been intrigued by the statement that he had been
married twice—though he couldn't discuss or even mention it. He took
another ten-mark note from his pocket and laid it on the table. "I
am very curious about this subject, Herr Reminescu. Could I make it
worth your while to talk with me a bit longer?"

"Certainly, *mein Herr*. What can I tell you?"

"I am wondering just what part the stars play in your communications, and what part may be telepathy or clairvoyance or some other
means. Do you generally hold your client's hand for a while?"

The younger man admitted that when the stars did not give him
satisfactory guidance he got it by mysterious "hunches." He told a
little about himself and his training, and Lanny in turn gave his name
and identified himself as an art expert buying paintings in Munich.
They took a liking to each other and chatted for a while—even though
another client had arrived and was waiting. Lanny was about to leave,
when the astrologer suddenly exclaimed: "Herr Budd, I wonder if I
may trespass upon your kindness. I am in trouble, I fear, and greatly
need advice."

"With pleasure," Lanny said, and resumed his seat; whereupon the
other poured forth a story of difficulties with the German police. It
wasn't his illegal profession; that called for only the payment of a
little graft. It had been his practice to travel back and forth between
Munich and Bucharest, having clients in both cities; and now the police
were accusing him of having smuggled jewels out of Germany. Once,
he admitted, he had carried a small package for a wealthy client, but
he had had no idea what the package contained or that he was violating any regulation. He had been summoned three different times for

questioning, and now they wouldn't give him an exit permit, but kept him in a state of anxiety for week after week.

This was a common enough story, and not the sort of thing that Lanny could afford to mix in. There was nothing in the possession of astrological science or of genuine psychic gifts that would keep a man from doing a little smuggling on the side, and of course if he had done it, he would earnestly insist that he hadn't known what he was doing. No doubt the very efficient Gestapo was watching him at this moment, and Lanny didn't want to get on their list as a suspected associate of a smuggling ring. He said:

"I am truly sorry to hear about your trouble, Herr Reminescu. I have no sort of influence with the German authorities, but there is one suggestion I can make. I happen to know a prominent person who is interested in astrology, and if you were to give him a convincing horoscope, or a séance, as you prefer, you might gain his friendship and then tell him your story as you have told it to me."

"Oh, Herr Budd," exclaimed the other, "I have no words to tell you my gratitude! When will this gentleman come, and what is his name?"

"He may prefer not to give his name, but to come anonymously, as I did. I will tell him the circumstances and it will be up to him to approach you in whatever way he sees fit."

"*Vielen, vielen Dank!* I beg you not to delay too long—for you know how the Nazi police are—they move swiftly and one can never know what to expect."

Lanny had an impulse to ask why the interpreter of the stars did not cast his own horoscope and find out whether he was going to die in Stadelheim prison or the Dachau concentration camp. But that wouldn't have been kind, and the son of Budd-Erling would always be kind wherever he had a free choice.

V

Lanny went back to his friend the Deputy Führer and reported: "That is a really extraordinary astrologer. He told me a number of remarkable things—and I'm sure he had no means of knowing my name or anything about me. He told me I'm going to die in Hongkong, and that really gave me quite a start, because I have an old schoolfriend who lives there, and has been begging me to take a trip around the world and pay him a visit. I had been thinking quite seriously of doing so— but now I guess I'll lay off!" Lanny had invented this Hongkong friend as a substitute for his second marriage, which he took as a genuine case of some sort of mind reading, but which he couldn't tell about.

"What you say interests me tremendously," replied the dark Deputy. "I have many questions I would like to ask of my destiny at this moment."

"You'd better not delay," ventured Lanny. "I had a chat with this fellow after he got through with my horoscope, and it seems he's in trouble with the police, and asked me for help."

"Because of his practicing his profession?"

"No; they suspect him of having smuggled some jewels out of the country. He tells a plausible story, but of course I have no means of guessing how true it is. I told him I couldn't have anything to do with a matter such as that, being a foreigner. But I said I had a friend who was prominent in Germany and deeply interested in astrology, and I would tell this friend about the case. Naturally I didn't give him your name or any hint of your identity, so you are free to do what you wish about the matter."

"Thank you, Herr Budd. Give me the man's name and address, and I will make inquiries, and perhaps pay him a visit—or maybe send him the necessary data and let him work over the problem. I am frightfully busy at the present moment."

"The time when you are busiest may be the time when you need help from the stars," remarked the philosopher-friend.

VI

As when two mighty wrestlers struggle upon a mat, locked in an unbreakable grip, heaving and straining, exerting the last ounce of their forces; gasping and panting, they sway this way and that, and their muscles stand out in great lumps, and the cords are as if breaking through the skin, and the veins swell and the eyeballs seem about to spring from their heads; still they increase their efforts, and it appears that one is slowly yielding, but he summons new forces and holds his own; the spectators of this contest catch their breaths, and sway this way and that with the contestants, sharing through the power of the imagination the agony of the effort and manifesting even the physical symptoms of strain: so now it was in the diplomatic arena of Europe, where the once beaten champion Antaeus-like had touched the earth and renewed his forces, and now was coming back for another bout in spite of all the betting odds against him, he being determined, singlehearted and singleminded, while his opponent, grown soft through ease, was confused in his thoughts and hesitant to use the powers which he possessed.

Lanny Budd was watching this international contest from a ringside seat. Telegraph keys clicked, telephone wires hummed, dispatch riders came on motorcycles, important visitors were brought in cars—and the sum total of these communications spread in semi-secret whispers all over the Berghof. Nobody had ever been more skillful at making friends than the son of Budd-Erling, and being an American, he was regarded as a neutral, even a sort of arbiter, a court of appeals, a person not bound by precedents and conventions. "You see what they do to us?" the court physician would say, when some Sudeten German got hurt in a tavern argument and Dr. Goebbels spread it over the front pages of all the newspapers of the Fatherland. "*Sehen Sie, Herr Budd!*" exclaimed the Führer himself. "I take your advice and try to be moderate, and they drive my people to desperation." The man who believed his own atrocity stories!

The Führer took a plane and flew to the town of Kehl, in the Rhineland, to inspect the new fortifications which he was rushing to completion, fronting the Maginot Line. Kehl—the name rang like a bell in Lanny's soul, for it was on that bridge over the Rhine that the Nazis had delivered to him what was left of Freddi Robin after they had got through tormenting him. Only four years ago, and how much water had flowed under that bridge—and how many of the hopes of Europe had flowed away forever! The Führer came back in a towering rage because the French were answering his visit by sending more troops to the border. What else he could have expected was a question that nobody was supposed to ask him.

Diplomats and "purely private persons" were flying back and forth between Prague and Berlin and Berchtesgaden and London and Paris. Henlein and Ribbentrop came to report to their Führer, and Lanny got a glimpse of them. Hess told him they had brought word of new proposals which the Czech government was making. These represented a painstaking effort to satisfy the Germans by giving them every sort of equality, political and educational, and full local self-government in all the cantons—the utmost that was consistent with the preservation of the Czechoslovak Republic's integrity. But that was precisely what the Nazis didn't want, because they didn't trust the Czechs, but regarded them as a lower race of beings.

What interested Lanny especially was the part which Lord Runciman of Doxford was playing in this diplomatic wrestling match. This "private person" with all the prestige of his powerful government behind him was engaged in extracting from Prague a series of concessions which would mean for all practical purposes the end of the republic and its democratic institutions. For one thing, they were to abolish free speech in the country—since it displeased Nazis to have Communists and Socialists and Jews telling the truth about what Nazis were doing. Also, the alliances with Russia and France were to be ended, and there were to be commercial treaties with Germany which would force Prague into economic dependence upon Berlin. These were the things the Nazis were determined upon having, and the noble English gentleman had given up his yachting at Cowes to come and make plain to a long-time ally of Britain that it had to surrender and become a slave of Germany.

VII

As soon as Lanny had made sure of this information, he told his friend Hess that he had some more art business in Munich, and would take the occasion to pay another visit to the Rumanian astrologer. He would stay overnight to attend a concert, he added, and put a bag and his little portable into his car and drove away. But he didn't go into Munich; making sure that he wasn't followed, he turned south, into the high mountains of Austria and thence up the Inn valley to the Swiss border. Across the upper Rhine he stopped at a little inn and got a room and went to work on his big story—two copies, one for Rick and one for Gus. Being afraid that his typing might have attracted attention, he drove to another Swiss town where he dropped the letters at the post office and quickly disappeared. Needless to say, his name was not on them, either inside or out.

Next morning he drove back to Munich, and late in the afternoon called at the office of the stargazer. The young woman answered the door, and the moment she saw him exclaimed: *"Ach, Herr Budd! Die Polizei!"* Her manner was distraught and her face full of fear—which might have been for herself as well as for her employer.

Lanny said nothing until he had come into the room and closed the door. Then: "Tell me what has happened."

"Two Gestapo men came the day before yesterday and took him away, and that is all I know."

"They didn't say what the charge was?"

"They went upstairs to let him pack a bag. I didn't hear what they said up there. They said nothing to me and of course I was afraid to speak."

"You haven't made any inquiry?"

"*Du lieber Gott!* What could I hope for, except to get myself arrested too?"

Lanny told her: "I will make inquiries and see if I can find out anything." With that he excused himself and took his departure.

VIII

But he got only as far as his car. Just as he was in the act of stepping in, a taxicab hove into sight and drew up at the curb. Out of it stepped the astrologer, with a suitcase in his hand. "*Grüss' Gott, Herr Budd!*" he exclaimed. He paid the driver, and then turned to Lanny. "*Um Gottes willen, kommen Sie herein!*"

They went into the house, Reminescu using his key. He greeted the woman casually—his thoughts entirely on Lanny. Shut up in the room he sank onto a couch, exclaiming: "*Jesus Christus!*"—and took out a handkerchief and wiped his forehead. "*Was für ein Erlebnis!*"

"I hope they didn't treat you too badly," said Lanny, by way of being co-operative.

"They treated me as if I were Paracelsus, Pythagoras, and Trismegistus rolled into one," replied the astrologer. "But God preserve me from such hospitality in future!"

"Tell me about it," suggested the visitor, not embarrassed to reveal curiosity.

The still agitated young man lighted a cigarette and took a couple of quick puffs, then began a curious tale. "Two Gestapo men came, the day before yesterday, and ordered me to come with them, no questions asked. 'Bring all your charts and books,' they said, so I packed them up. They took me, of all places on earth, to the Vier Jahreszeiten Hotel, which I am told is now run by the Gestapo. I had a most elegant suite, with Cupids on the ceiling, and a Death's Head SS Major or something saluting me respectfully. 'My apologies, Herr Reminescu; I am carrying out orders from above. It is desired that you should prepare horoscopes for certain important persons. While you are doing this, you will be my guest, and will be supplied with anything within reason that you care to order. No harm will be done you, but unfortunately it will be necessary for you to remain in this suite until the work has been completed. I will put before you the birth data of twelve persons and when your work is done, I will have it delivered, and if it is found satisfactory you will be paid two hundred and fifty marks, and will receive the exit permit which I understand you have applied for.' Did you ever hear anything to equal that, Herr Budd?"

Lanny had to admit that it was a novelty in his experience.

"So, there is a typewritten list, and I spread out my charts and go to work. Such meals as I have never eaten, and such a soft bed with embroidered linen coverlets as I have never seen outside of a museum; and cigarettes, champagne, brandy—truly, I lived like the Shah of Persia, or maybe the Maharajah of Indore. But there I sit, and shivers run all over me, and the sweat stands out on my forehead, and I hardly dare to breathe; for I have run my eyes over the birth dates, and I dare not tell you what I see."

"I can guess, if you will permit me," smiled Lanny.

The other gazed about anxiously; then in a whisper: *"Bitte, sprechen Sie leise!"*

Lanny, replying in a whisper: "April 20, 1889." The other nodded, and fear melted the bones of both, for that was the day when a last and least satisfactory son had been born to the Braunau customs officer Alois Schicklgruber who had changed his name to Hitler.

"It would not be fair to ask me what the stars told me, or what I wrote down," murmured the astrologer, and the visitor replied: "I have not asked you."

After a few moments, Lanny went on: "Do you remember the other dates?"

"They took the list from me, but of course they could not take it from my mind. However, I would not dare give them to you, and it might be very dangerous for you to possess them."

"Quite possibly, Herr Reminescu. And you may be sure I will keep your secret, at least until you are safe in your homeland. I take it, your presence indicates that you managed to please the higher powers."

"I did my best, and the twelve horoscopes were taken away early this morning. A short while ago the officer came and informed me that the work was all right, but that some further questions were to be asked. He had these in writing and I wrote the answers on the same sheet; then he paid me the money and told me that I was free, and that my exit visa would be sent to me. So here I am, and I wait. Do you suppose they will really send it?"

"I do not know, my friend; but if I were in your place I would not mention this experience to anyone else. It happens that I am good at keeping secrets. I have an idea that what has happened was a result of my effort to assist you, and I think I had better not try any further.

I will just say that you were indisposed and unable to do any work for me today. Let me give you my home address in France, so that you can write me and we shall not lose touch with each other. Don't write it down, it is easy to remember."

The stargazer said that his memory was good, and Lanny told him: "Juan-les-Pins, Alpes Maritimes, France." Then they shook hands warmly and parted forever.

IX

Everybody in the Berghof who was entitled to have an opinion of the diplomatic situation wanted to discuss it with Lanny Budd. They had discovered that he knew practically everybody they could mention in England and France; so he found himself once more in the position which he had occupied at the Paris Peace Conference, an interpreter not merely of languages, but of personalities and national characteristics—of manners, climates, councils, governments, himself not least but honored of them all. Word had got about somehow that he considered the British populace to be in a pathological condition, and officers of the household, young Nazis who had been reared upon the idea of the Führer's infallibility, would stop suddenly in the midst of their vaunting and look at Lanny uneasily and ask: "Can it really be so in Britain? How can there be a great nation without any authority, without somebody who knows what it is going to do?"

It seemed to them a most dangerous thing, every bit as bad as Jew-Bolshevism, and indeed the same thing in subtle disguise. The Nazis were going to end it some day, and the only question was when and how? If the possibility occurred to them that they might be moving too fast and running into danger, they would dismiss it from their minds; for of course the Führer would know, the Führer was always right. How could it be possible that the British would be so foolish as to risk defying the German Air Force? And for such a political monstrosity as Czechoslovakia? *Unsinn!*

Adi himself was confronting one of the great decisions of his life; one which might lead him to triumph, or wreck everything he had accomplished thus far. He was in a continuing nervous crisis, and members of his staff kept out of his way when they could. His agency of communication with Lanny was Hess, who would ask this and that about Runciman and Chamberlain and Sir Nevile Henderson, the British Ambassador in Berlin. Once he inquired whether it might be possible for Madame to come to the Berghof again. Unfortunately Madame was laid up with the flu at Bienvenu, and could not travel, even to help determine the fate of Europe.

There came a royal command: Herr Budd was to take a motor ride with the Führer, late in the afternoon, the time when the great man usually went walking with his dogs and his *daimon*. This time he and his guest rode in the back seat, and a staff member in the front beside the chauffeur. They took a road which wound up a mountainside by a series of hairpin turns, and Lanny realized quickly what road this was. "I see you don't forget your promises, Herr Reichskanzler," he ventured, and the reply was: *"Niemals."*

They were climbing the Kehlstein; but within about five hundred feet of the top the road swung suddenly straight into the mountainside. There was a great bronze door, apparently operated by an electric eye, for it began to swing back, disclosing a grotto, carved out of the solid rock, a chamber paved and walled with concrete, large enough for several cars to enter and turn in. Indirect lighting flooded the place with a warm glow, and when Lanny descended from the car he saw at the far end another bronze door, which also opened automatically. He entered an elevator, large enough to accommodate eighteen persons; but this time only two rode. The Führer pressed a button, and they stood in silence while traveling upward through the heart of a mountain.

When the doors opened, they stepped into a large living room, part of a villa with bedroom, small kitchen, and rooms for two attendants, perched on the very top of a mountain, entirely invisible except from the air. Around it was a terrace from which you looked over what seemed to be all the mountains of Europe: a relief map of deep depressions and swelling protuberances; a study in deep greens, flecked with the bright blue of little lakes and the varied color of villages in the valleys and residences along the slopes. Lanny gazed, and cried several times: *"Herrlich! Herrlich!"*

Adi Schicklgruber, one-time *Gefreite*, had created this and owned it, and the idea that he should not be proud of it was one that had never occurred to him. His heart swelled, and the deepest chords of his soul began to vibrate—his love of the mountains and forests, of music, of the *Herrenvolk* and of his own rulership. He heard those grand open chords by which the Nordic gods ascend over a rainbow to Valhalla; he heard the music of the forging of Siegfried's sword: *"Nothung, Nothung, neidliches Schwert!"* How could a people who had such music calling them to glory ever fail of their destiny?

X

They sat in two striped canvas chairs and watched the sun go down in an explosion of gold and pink, changing to deep red and then to pale violet. Said the Führer of the Nazis: "That is the capitalistic era dying before your eyes. People think that I mean only the National half of my party's name, but believe me, I am not through giving the world surprises. Before I finish, I mean to keep every promise I have ever made."

"I believe it, Exzellenz. I lack the power to read that future in the stars, but I watch day by day to see it happen."

This was a trap Lanny was setting, and his host's foot slipped into it immediately. "Tell me, Herr Budd, do you believe in the influence of the stars upon human destiny?"

"It has always been a problem with me, Herr Reichskanzler. I cannot find any basis in scientific theory, yet it has happened to me to have astonishing predictions made, and to see them come true. The same thing has happened to friends of mine, and I am forced to conclude that there are powers which I do not understand. Just the other day, for example, I went quite casually to a young astrologer in Munich and had him cast my horoscope for me. I am sure he did not know me from Adam, and the things he told me could not possibly be guesswork."

"Tell me about them."

"Well, at the outset he told me that I was an American, but had been born near Munich. It does not happen that many Americans are born in Switzerland, and I am sure I do not carry on my person any signs that I did not enter the world at my mother's home on the Riviera or my father's in Connecticut."

Lanny went on to tell the wonder story which he had partly made up about Hongkong; and it was to be expected that the Führer should display curiosity concerning so capable an astrologer: his name, his age, his personal appearance, his character, so far as Lanny had formed an opinion. "Some of my friends are interested in this subject, and might wish to consult him," explained the great man; and Lanny accepted this tactfully. He wondered: Was Reminescu being considered for a court position? And if that fate fell on him, would he be invited or commanded?

But no, it wasn't that! The Führer of all the Germans had had a horoscope cast, and was trying to make up his mind to what extent he could trust it. In this most dangerous crisis, before which his innermost soul quailed, he needed the help of supernormal powers; but it was so hard to know when you were getting such help, and when you were being victimized by some shrewd self-seeker!

"My own attitude toward these so-called occult matters is very much like your own, Herr Budd. I have seen things which I cannot explain; but I dare not trust the practitioners, because there is so much deliberate trickery, and because even the honest ones might avoid telling me the truth, for fear of displeasing me."

"So!" thought Lanny. "Reminescu has given you a favorable horoscope and you want to believe it!"

Adi was going on: "In matters such as these I have had to learn to trust my own inner voices—intuitions, I suppose is the word to call them. I wait, I listen to all advice, I consider all the factors involved—and then suddenly it is as if an inner light were switched on, and everything becomes clear before my eyes. That is the moment to act, and I never permit myself to hesitate."

"That, Exzellenz, is what the world has agreed to call genius."

It was like touching the button which caused the elevator to rise through the heart of the Kehlstein. Adolf Hitler began to talk about genius. He discussed Richard Wagner, the greatest musician who had ever lived. He discussed Karl Haushofer, the greatest scientist, fortunately still living. He named Napoleon as a military and Bismarck as a political genius. Before long he was explaining the difficulty of combining these various kinds into one. That was something that happened only once in a thousand years or so, and when it did it meant a new epoch in human history. Such an epoch was now in process of being made by himself, the creator of the NSDAP.

The son of Alois Schicklgruber didn't apologize for saying this; he stated it in a matter-of-fact way, because it was the truth, and he always spoke the truth—excepting of course in political matters, where it was necessary to rear elaborate structures of pretense. But here, in the presence of a trusted friend, the former inmate of the home for the shelterless of Vienna told what had been revealed to him by that energizing spirit which dwelt in the deeps of his personality. Outwardly a soft-fleshed, rather flabby man with a bulbous nose and futile small mustache, he saw himself in his soul's mirror as a heroic figure in shining armor, and was carried away by this sublime vision. Standing bareheaded beneath the first pale stars of a twilight sky, he pointed to them and exclaimed: "You, heavenly bodies, once controlled the destinies of men! But now a man has come who will determine his own course, and —who can say?—perhaps, before he has finished, he may determine your courses as well!"

XI

Hess had invited Lanny to be his guest at the Parteitag, the tremendous week-long orgy of racialism and reaction which the Nazi chieftains prepared for their subordinates early in September of each year. It was held in the ancient city of Nuremberg, a hundred or more miles north of Munich. It offered no joys to a secret agent, but many opportunities to meet the Party leaders and hear their purposes revealed; so he accepted gladly.

Since many persons were going from the Berghof, he volunteered to take some members of the household in his car. Thus he enjoyed for several hours the society of three young SS patriots who had never known any other creed or code save that which the Party had taught them. They held rather fantastic ideas about the world outside, and became confidential and revealed to their host the opinion of the Berghof concerning himself—that he must be the person whom the Führer had picked out to become the *Gauleiter* of the North American continent. Manifestly, he had all the qualifications, and what else could be the reason for the favors showered upon an *Ausländer?*

The nine-century-old city has narrow and crooked streets and seems like a Grimm's fairy-story town of houses with high-pitched roofs, peaked gables, and chimney pots; churches with tall spires and every sort of Gothic exuberance; a five-cornered tower with the "iron maiden" and other instruments of torture on exhibition. Now its population of four hundred thousand was multiplied several fold by the swarms of Party leaders of every rank who arrived by train and bus and automobile. Whole tent cities had been erected on the outskirts of the town and army cooking outfits served millions of hot meals each day. Everything had been attended to with German thoroughness; the flags in the streets were like the leaves of a forest, and everywhere were bands of music and uniformed marching men with standards and banners.

Outside the city, on the immense Zeppelin field, had been prepared a breathtaking spectacle. Adolf Hitler, one of the world's greatest showmen, had been working on this for a decade and a half, rehearsing it each year and making improvements. Decorations and scenery like a Wagnerian opera, solemnity and holiness like a Catholic high mass; an appeal to every primitive sentiment, every memory dear to the hearts of the Germans in those dark forests where they had lived through the centuries while preparing for the conquest of the ancient Roman empire. It was Hitler who had devised the ceremony of calling the roll of martyrs, which Rudolf Hess performed early at each Party assembly. It was Hitler who had devised the mystical rite of the dedication of the flags, and he himself performed it, walking down the rows of flags and solemnly touching each with the sacred *Blutfahne*, the flag which had been carried in the Beerhall Putsch of fifteen years ago and was stained with the blood shed in that fight.

Blood was a sacred thing in the German mythology. It was the noblest and best blood in the world, and Germans shed it in battle, not merely for the protection of the Fatherland, but for the extension of its borders, so that there might be more Germans with more of the sacred blood in hearts, arteries, and veins. *Blut und Boden*—blood and soil—was the slogan. The ancient German warrier who died in battle was carried off to Valhalla, and that was a glorious death, whereas to die in bed was ignoble and disgraceful. The Führer was reviving all these ancient barbaric emotions, and his marching legions chanted incessantly about blood and iron and war. "Rise up in arms to battle, for to battle we are born!" The old German God was a God of war, who could never get enough of blood. And now was the time of times, as His favorite new song, *Deutschland, Erwache*, proclaimed. "Storm, storm, storm, storm! From the tower peal bells of alarm!"

XII

Lanny walked about the streets of this romantic old city, home of the Meistersinger, of Dürer and other great artists, now swarming with hordes of red-faced and sweating male creatures with fanaticism in their faces and rage in their hearts, the *furor Teutonicus* which the ancient Romans had dreaded. It made the American rather sick at heart, for he hated war and cruelty, he hated hatred—and these men had been brought up on it, they had been taught it systematically, with all the skill which modern science had put at the service of the teachers. All the arts of the psychologist and the advertising expert had been applied to the inculcation of fanaticism—one of Hitler's favorite words, rarely missing from any speech however brief.

Physically Lanny was made as comfortable as a man could expect to be on such an abnormal occasion. He was put up at the Deutscher Hof, the rendezvous of the Party great ones. At the meetings he had a reserved seat among the distinguished guests, which included the diplomats from all countries of the earth. For eight days he was deluged with Nazi oratory, conveyed to his ears by means of bellowing loudspeakers. The keynote was set in the opening proclamation, read for the Führer: "Party comrades! More threatening than ever, Bolshevist danger of the destruction of nations rises above the world. A thousand-fold, we see the activities of the Jewish virus in this world pest!"

Monday, Tuesday, Wednesday, Thursday, Friday—five days of incessant hate oratory, with the crashing of bands, the mass singing of songs, the parading of flags and banners. On Friday night, amid the glare of klieg lights in one of the enormous halls which had been constructed for these meetings, Lanny heard the Führer address a hundred and eighty thousand of his Party leaders of all ranks, and tell them: "At a time when there are clouds on the horizon, I see about me those millions of unflinching, nay fanatical, National Socialists, whose leadership you constitute and for whose leadership you are responsible. Just as I could rely blindly upon you in the days of our struggle, so today Germany and I can depend upon you."

And next day Feldmarschall Göring addressed the leaders of the Arbeitsfront, the Nazi labor battalions. To Lanny Budd, at the hotel where they stayed, he had expressed the same desire for caution and legality as in Karinhall, but under the influence of the crowd and the bright lights he lost his head and raved and bellowed for an hour and a half. He told them how he had saved up food for war and had conscripted labor to complete the *Westwall;* they might have to work ten hours a day for the glory of the Reich. "Our arms industries are going at high pressure in every branch." Referring to his Czechish neighbors he said: "This miserable pigmy race without culture—no one knows where it came from—is oppressing a cultured people and behind it is Moscow and the eternal mask of the Jew Devil." Lanny did not have a chance to ask *Der Dicke* about this sudden change of mood, for when he inquired at the hotel afterwards he learned that the old-style robber baron had been overcome by the violence of his efforts, and had been carried off to the country to recuperate from bronchitis and inflamed legs.

XIII

But the secret agent had plenty of chances to confer with other leaders and listen to their conversation among themselves; he made sure that one and all they were expecting to take over not merely the Sudeten districts but the whole of the Czechoslovak Republic. He heard Foreign Minister von Ribbentrop make statements on this subject which seemed to him so important that he was tempted to bolt to the French border and send off a report to Washington and The Reaches without delay. But such a move might excite suspicion—it would be inconceivable to Hess, to say nothing of the Führer himself, that anybody could leave Nuremberg just before the Führer's closing speech for which all Europe was waiting as for a blast from Gabriel's trumpet.

So Lanny stayed and heard that speech, delivered before what was said to be the largest number of human beings ever assembled in one place—well over a million, and claimed to be more. From the outskirts of the crowd on the Zeppelin field the Führer of the Germans must have seemed a tiny pin-point figure, but by the magic of modern electro-acoustics he had a voice like thunder in the mountains. Over the ether waves it was carried to the whole earth, and few indeed must have been the places where civilized men did not hearken. At the end of every two or three sentences the auditors would hear the wild-beast roar of that mighty assemblage: "*Sieg heil! Sieg heil! Sieg heil!*"

As usual when Adi had a great occasion, he talked at great length. As always, he recited the grievances of the German people; as always, he denounced the Bolsheviks and the Jews; as always, he stormed and threatened at all his foes. It was his purpose to terrify Europe, and especially the statesmen of Czechoslovakia and its allies, Britain and France. Of the Sudeten people he said: "These Germans, too, are creatures of God. The Almighty did not create them that they should be surrendered by a State construction made at Versailles to a foreign power that is hateful to them. . . . They are being oppressed in an inhuman and intolerable manner . . . brutally struck . . . terrorized or maltreated . . . pursued like wild beasts for every expression of their national life." Count Ciano, if he was listening, must have thrown up his hands again.

Adi went on to tell the world what he was doing to protect these Germans; building along the Rhine "the most gigantic fortifications that ever existed." He continued: "On the construction of the defenses there are now 278,000 workmen in Dr. Todt's army. In addition, there are, further, 84,000 workmen and 100,000 men of the labor service as well as numerous engineer and infantry battalions. . . . These most gigantic efforts of all times have been made at my request in the interest of peace. . . . The Germans of Czechoslovakia are neither deserted nor defenseless. . . . We all have a duty never again to bow to a foreign will. May this be our pledge, so help us God!"

XIV

Lanny would have liked to leave right after that meeting and drive all night to the border; but even that might have been dangerous. He had to sit up for hours and discuss the speech with a crowd of excited henchmen; drink beer with them, apologize for his lack of capacity, and endeavor in other ways to justify their idea of him as the future Gauleiter of the North American continent. In the morning he had to thank his host and request him to convey to a busy Führer the guest's compliments upon a magnificent and clear oration. Lanny explained briefly that he was off on a picture deal, and would return to Munich in short order to consult the astrologer and see what further light the stars might throw upon the future of the National-Socialist movement.

At last Lanny was free—as a bird on the wing, or as a motorcar on one of the *Autobahnen* constructed by Dr. Todt's army. Straight to the border at Kehl, where recently the Führer had viewed the most gigantic fortifications that ever existed. The son of Budd-Erling was not invited to view them, but no tourist passing through could fail to see the labors in process on the near-by heights, to hear the rumble of machinery and note the heavy traffic through the town. A hundred and sixty-eight years earlier it had been a tiny village, and in early spring a great cavalcade had arrived there, having traveled all the way from Vienna to bring the fifteen-year-old princess, Marie Antoinette, to marry the future king of France. There had been no bridge then, and several hundred heavy vehicles had had to be ferried across the river Rhine to the old cathedral city of Strasbourg.

Once again the secret agent presented himself at the barrier of the bridge. His papers were in order and he drove onto French soil. He did not go to the Ville de Paris hotel, because he was afraid somebody might remember his stay with Freddi Robin. He put up at the Maison Rouge, locked himself in a room, set up his little typewriter, and went to work to do what one man could to help Britain and America to realize their peril. Adolf Hitler, guided by his own mad *daimon* and egged on by the wounded vanity of Joachim von Ribbentrop, did not mean to rest until he had abolished democratic institutions from the soil of Europe. Said Lanny Budd, in his closing words: "He has the definite purpose not to leave, anywhere in the world, one single person free to criticize his party or his program."

29

The Hurt That Honor Feels

I

LANNY was sick of the Nazis; of the sight of them marching in uniform, the sound of them yelling and singing, the smell of them in closely packed mobs. He wanted nothing so much as to get into his car and drive to Bienvenu, to a studio in a quiet garden facing the sunsets. There was a piano, there were paintings on the walls and a couple of thousand well-selected books on shelves. The water would still be warm for swimming; he could go fishing with Jerry Pendleton, play tennis, and perhaps persuade Nina and Rick to come for a visit, take them sailing, and talk over old times.

But the Trudi-ghost said No. He had promised to help in keeping the underground alive, and in keeping the people of France and Britain from falling under the spell of the bad witch Berchta and her flock of sheep in human form. Regardless of his own happiness, he had to go on earning money and distributing it where it would count, and supplying Rick with information instead of tempting him to holidays. Also, that job he had undertaken at Hyde Park, a little more than a year ago. What excuse could he give F.D.R. for not watching the events that were shaking the world?

He got the London and Paris and Berlin newspapers. Two hundred thousand troops of the Wehrmacht had been moved to the Austrian frontier, facing Czechoslovakia; that country was shaped like a badly stuffed sausage, and the heavily motorized army, facing the middle of it, could cut it in half in a single day. They had done it to Austria, and all Adi had to do was to say the word and they would do it again.

All over the Sudetenland Nazis were attacking Czech public buildings and stoning Czech policemen; and this could only be under orders, its purpose being to work up feeling in Germany and justify the Führer in his next move. The French were mobilizing—could that be the rumble of camions and tanks which Lanny heard in the night under the windows of the Hotel Maison Rouge? If the war started,

Strasbourg would be one of the first points at which the Germans would strike, repeating the air smash they had rehearsed so thoroughly at Guernica and Barcelona and Valencia and Madrid. They might do it without any warning, a new technique called *Blitzkrieg* which Göring and his staff talked about freely. Make up your mind, Lanny! East or west doesn't matter—any place but No Man's Land between the two marshaling hosts!

II

He had left Zoltan in Berlin, promising to get in touch with him as soon as the visit to Berchtesgaden was ended. They had talked about paintings in Munich for which they might find purchasers; they would help each other and divide the commissions. Now Lanny telephoned, saying: "I can be in Munich this evening." The other replied: "I will take the night train."

The secret agent packed his belongings, paid his bill, and set out. Not wishing to attract attention to himself, he drove down the Rhine on the French side and crossed into Germany by the first ferry. To Munich was a couple of hundred miles, a pleasant day's drive, with time off for a leisurely lunch, and stops to look at the Black Forest and admire the snow-clad Alps from their foothills. In between these pleasures the traveler meditated upon the state of the world, and now and then turned on the radio to hear "spot news" of Europe's impending crisis.

The ex-bankclerk Henlein had decided to settle the problem by direct action. His followers had been plundering Jewish shops, and the Czech government had declared martial law. That Wednesday morning Henlein issued an ultimatum, demanding the withdrawal of Czech troops and police from the Sudetenland; when the government paid no attention to this challenge, his Stormtroopers attempted to seize barracks and public buildings, using hand grenades, machine guns, and even tanks which they had brought in from the Fatherland. Fighting went on all that day, and one or two hundred men were killed on each side; but the Czech government stood firm. By suppertime, when Lanny reached Munich, even the Nazi radios had to admit that the *Putsch* had failed. The Henleinists were everywhere in flight into Germany, where the Nazis hailed them as heroes and martyrs, and denounced the Czechs as terrorists and murderers.

Lanny didn't have any uncertainty as to the meaning of such a series of events. He could be sure that Henlein, and his Deputy, the well-chastened Dr. Franck, had not attempted a private revolution, nor was Juppchen Goebbels celebrating martyrs for any purpose of his own. Adi was getting ready to move; or at any rate he was telling the world that he was doing so—and it came to the same thing, since he couldn't afford to let his bluff be called a second time as he had done in May. He had discussed that episode in his Nuremberg speech, saying in substance that he had let it happen because he hadn't been ready; but now he had got ready, and the world was on notice. How long would he wait? Lanny guessed that he wouldn't wait more than a day or two, perhaps not more than an hour or two.

The traveler put up at the Regina Palast and got a light supper, with an evening paper to keep him company. When he went to his room he turned on a new gadget which had come on the market, a portable radio set which didn't have to be plugged in to a light socket or the generator of a car. With this he listened to an official statement from the British Foreign Office, given by the Munich radio both in English and German. Prime Minister Chamberlain had sent through his Ambassador in Berlin a message stating that he proposed to fly at once to Germany to consult with the Führer in an effort to find a peaceful solution to the existing crisis. He had asked the Führer to name a place for a meeting, and the Führer had replied accepting the proposal. "The Prime Minister is, accordingly, leaving for Germany by air tomorrow."

III

It was to be doubted if there was any person in the city of Munich to whom that news meant more, or who was in better position to interpret it. The presidential agent could transport himself in mind to Wickthorpe Castle and listen to Ceddy and Gerald planning the move—in all probability one of them had suggested it. They were in a state of bewilderment, almost of despair. It was hard for them to conceive of a man like Adolf Hitler holding power in a European country; they didn't know how to deal with him, and had even been reduced to the hope that an American art expert might be able to smooth him down and temper his rages. Sir Nevile Henderson, their ambassador, had been powerless to do it; Lord Runciman of Doxford was failing abjectly; the Marquess of Londonderry, the Marquess of Lothian, the Earl of Perth, Sir Alexander Cadogan, Viscount Halifax— a string of the noblest and most plausible of English gentlemen had been running to Berlin and Berchtesgaden over a period of years, with no results worth mentioning. And now plain Mr. Neville Chamberlain, a commoner who manufactured small arms in Birmingham, was going to make one last try.

Lanny had met this statesman only casually, but had watched him closely at public and social affairs. He was tall and lean, with thin sallow face, prominent nose, and long neck with conspicuous Adam's apple. He dressed in black, wore an old-fashioned wing collar, and might have been taken for an undertaker. Since he lived in a land where rain comes frequently, he never went out without a proper black umbrella, tightly rolled; the cartoonists, on the lookout for oddities, took this up eagerly, and before long the world had accepted a black umbrella as the symbol of a political point of view.

This attitude Neville himself called "practical," but more properly it might have been called "commercial"—of course on a large scale. He was a businessman, which meant that he bought things and sold them for more than they had cost; he believed in this procedure—of course on a large scale—and thought that if it was continued long enough and over the whole world, everything would work itself out and all problems would solve themselves. He came from an old family of trade aristocrats; he had been Lord Mayor of Birmingham, and so had his father and five uncles and a cousin. Personally, Neville was a dry and unimaginative old man, interested in birds and fishes more than in human beings. He was a pacifist who made instruments of killing; he thought he could go on making them on a large scale without having them used, and it had apparently never occurred to him that if his customers did not intend to use them, they would stop buying them.

IV

Lanny learned from the newspapers that the Führer was at the Berghof, and it was a safe guess that the conference would take place there. He might have called up Hess and got himself invited; but what good would it have done? He surely wouldn't be asked to act as interpreter at this supremely important affair, and he could be sure there wouldn't be any yelling in the house. Adi had great respect for the British ruling classes and desired most earnestly to have them consent to what he was determined to do. He had always been polite in dealing with them, and on this occasion would try his best to behave like a Birmingham undertaker.

Lanny could foresee what was going to happen almost as well as if he had been on the scene. This meeting, over which the whole world was agog, was in fact a sort of stageplay, of which Lanny had attended the rehearsals. The details of the settlement had been worked out by Gerald Albany in Berlin and by Wiedemann at Wickthorpe and Cliveden. Adi had made his demands and they had been granted. The present dramatic journey of the head of the British government had to do, not with the what, but rather with the how and the when. Could not Seine-Exzellenz be persuaded to display better table manners and not grab suddenly with both hands and thus risk upsetting the soup tureen? Could he not persuade the Sudeten Germans to endure a few days longer, while Mr. Chamberlain and his friends made clear to the French that they must repudiate their engagements with Czechoslovakia, and to the Czechs that they had not a friend in Europe and had no choice but to surrender?

That was what this dramatic flight would be for, and when the Führer conceded a few more days it would be a triumph for British diplomacy, heralded to the world with radio trumpets. The facts about it, hammered out on Lanny's typewriter in a London hotel, had been on President Roosevelt's desk for several weeks, and all that Lanny could get now was the melancholy satisfaction of saying: "I told you so." This being true, he would refuse to get excited over anybody's oratory, but would have his sleep, and in the morning would not suggest taking Zoltan to the airport to join the throngs who would cheer the Prime Minister's arrival. Rather the pair would go to view paintings, and would talk about prices and customers, just as if Europe were not supposed to be hanging on the verge of a second World War.

Zoltan's own mind was in a confused state. He was a man of peace, a man of international mind, a good European who had no quarrel with anybody on the ground of race, creed, or political ideology. He met people on the pleasant sunlit fields of art. His occupation, which was at once a business and a delight, took him all over the Western world, and he had learned to listen politely to what other people said, and, if they tried to draw him into controversy, to tell them that an art lover had to live above all battles. Now it seemed to him that the world was going mad, that civilization was committing suicide. He accepted at its face value the stageplay which came to be known as "Munich." Chamberlain was really trying to save the peace of Europe, and Zoltan awaited the outcome in painful suspense. Such was the mood of the average uninformed man all over the world, and Lanny had to join with millions of others in saying: "God help him!"

V

The man with the black umbrella landed at the Munich airport and was taken at once to the Führer's armored train, which carried him on to Berchtesgaden. Cheered everywhere by crowds, he was motored to the Berghof, and the Nazi radios told how the Führer had come out bareheaded in the rain to welcome him. For three hours the two states-men sat in Hitler's study, with only an interpreter present, and after-wards the official communiqué announced that they had had "a com-prehensive and frank exchange of opinions." Later on, telling the House of Commons about it, the Prime Minister said that he had there got the impression that "the Chancellor was contemplating an imme-diate invasion of Czechoslovakia."

Chamberlain went on to record: "In courteous but perfectly definite terms, Herr Hitler made it plain that he had made up his mind the Sudeten Germans must have the right of self-determination and of returning, if they wished, to the Reich." In these last words the Prime Minister was repeating one of Herr Hitler's favorite lies, and it was hard to believe that he was doing it naïvely; for certainly Gerald or Ceddy or some other of his permanent Foreign Office men must have informed him that the Sudeten Germans had never belonged to the Reich, not since they had left Germany nine hundred years previously. And as for "self-determination," those Germans had never been con-sulted; the Nazi agents and agitators had done the "determining," and among their determinations was that a fair plebiscite should never be held in that region.

Here was the author of *Mein Kampf*, demonstrating his thesis that the bigger the lie the easier to get it believed, and that all you have to do is to keep on saying a thing often enough and you can make it the truth. Adi had made it the truth that he was master of Germany, and he was going to make it the truth that he was master of all the lands where any number of Germans lived. Such was the *Blut und Boden* doctrine. Adi had moved two-thirds of his army to the borders of Czechoslovakia; and would he have dared to take that risk unless Brit-ish statesmen had "made it plain" that they were not going to defend the threatened country? Chamberlain expected the Commons to be-lieve that he would, and presumably they did so, for they let him con-tinue in his role of the statesman who was saving Europe from a devastating war.

The Prime Minister had obtained a promise that the German armies would not move until he had time to return to London and consult with his Cabinet, and also with the French. These consultations began, and continued day and night. Premier Daladier and his Foreign Minister, Bonnet, came to London, and there was endless speculation over the radio about what they were deciding. In Germany there were heavy penalties for listening to foreign broadcasts, but Lanny could lock the door of his hotel room and turn on a whisper and listen in safety; the gravity of the offense began when you told other persons what you had heard, and this he had no wish to do.

As a matter of fact there wasn't much to choose between Nazi and British radios in this crisis, so far as moral character was concerned; it was all "propaganda," serving the purposes of governments which didn't want their publics to realize what they were up to. Lanny knew the pale, flabby, and tricky politician who had become Premier of France, and likewise his Foreign Minister who was in his heart a Fascist and whose wife chose German agents for her intimates. Chamberlain wouldn't be having to spend a day and a night persuading such men to indorse a treacherous bargain. No, they would be talking as "practical" men. Just what promises could they get from Hitler that would make their surrender appear less abject? Just how should they present it to make the dose less bitter to the world? Such would be the subjects debated at No. 10 Downing Street, and it wouldn't be worth Lanny's while to fly to London for the details of such a conference.

VI

Tired of listening to lies, the "P.A." put on his rainproof coat and went for a walk. He had promised to look up the Rumanian astrologer, and this was an hour for consulting the stars, if ever. He found the rooms empty and the *Pförtnerin* not especially communicative; Herr Reminescu had moved out, and the young lady also, and had left no address; no, the police had not come, the tenants had just moved and said nothing. So that was that, and Lanny thought: "I will get a letter some day at Juan." But he never did get a letter, and never heard a word from or about the young mystagogue. That was one of the unpleasant aspects of dictatorship as Lanny had observed it in operation for a decade and a half. People disappeared, and that was the end of them so far as relatives, friends, clients, customers, and everybody else was concerned; it might be dangerous to ask about them, and unless it was someone especially dear to you, you decided that discretion was the better part of curiosity.

So, look at old masters and get prices on them, call in a stenographer and write letters and cablegrams to your clients and await their replies. There is no law against taking art works out of Germany, for the Nazis need foreign money to buy oil and tin and rubber and the other raw materials of war which the Fatherland lacks because other nations got there first and grabbed the desirable colonies. All that is going to be changed soon, and meanwhile we let the art-loving *Ausländer* come in, and we serve them politely and pretend that we like them; but *Der Tag* will come—it is not so far off now—and then we will take back what we have lost, with interest at rates which we shall fix ourselves.

There was good music to be heard in Munich, there were dramas to be seen, and paintings to be looked at; also charming people to be met —people who did not greet you with the Hitler salute and did not talk nonsense about blood and soil, blood and race, blood and iron, blood and guts. There was Baron von Zinszollern, from whom Lanny had bought a painting years ago while trying to get Freddi out of Dachau. The Baron's fine home was mortgaged, so he was glad to see an art expert again, and still gladder to see two. Since they were socially acceptable persons, he not merely showed them his collection and talked prices, but invited them to stay to lunch and spent most of the afternoon in conversation.

He was a typical Bavarian, with round head, dark hair and eyes, and plump features; genial but skeptical and worldly. He got pleasure out of life as he went along, and after he had made certain that he was dealing with two good Europeans, he told amusing stories about the kaleidoscope of history in which he and his fellow *Münchner* had been living for the past half century. A monarchy with mad rulers, a World War, a Socialist republic and a Communist revolution, a democratic republic and a Nationalist revolution—the Baron smilingly declared that he couldn't keep track of them all, and didn't remember the name of the particular kind which they had at this moment.

He was out of politics, but never out of humor, apparently. When he learned that Lanny was an investigator of occult matters he asked if he had met Fräulein Elvira Lust, a little old lady who lived on Nymphenburgerstrasse here in Munich; you would find her in the telephone book as a "graphologist," since astrology was forbidden. She was all tied up in knots with arthritis, but the Führer sent a car for her every now and again and had her brought to the Berghof. It was said that she was used by high-up Nazis to give him advice which he would take from the stars but not from mere humans.

Lanny didn't say that he had been a guest at the Berghof, for that might have stopped the flow of urbane gossip. He inquired concerning a young Rumanian astrologer whom Hess was reported to have patronized, but the Baron had never heard of that one. He declared that the best known of the *Regierung's* occult advisers went by the one name of "Elsa," and lived just across the street from the Führer's Munich apartment; she was toothless, and used a pack of black rubber cards without markings so far as anyone could observe. A friend of the Baron's had consulted her a few days ago, and had paid her ten marks to shuffle the cards and tell him that he had come to consult her about the chances of war—a safe guess about anybody at the moment. Her answer had contained only five words: "*Kein Krieg in diesem Jahr.*" The skeptical nobleman was not impressed, for he said that Hess and other members of the Führer's staff consulted Elsa frequently, and she quite certainly had information about his purposes.

So talked Baron von Zinszollern, and others of the well-to-do folk whom Lanny met during his stay in this capital of good beer and *Gemütlichkeit.* The Nazis had been able to abolish many of the liberties of the *Münchner,* but not their liberty to be amused. And yet, strange as it might seem, this pleasure-loving gentleman referred quite casually to Germany's need of colonies and her right to expand. Indeed it had been years since Lanny had met in Germany a single man or woman who didn't think that Germany had to expand. He had decided that the last of such persons must have got caught and been either beheaded or shut up in a concentration camp.

VII

On the morning of Monday, the 19th of September, the radios of Europe blared forth in a babel of languages the result of the deliberations of the British and French heads of government in London. It was an ultimatum which had been presented in Prague. With hypocrisy not often matched even in the diplomatic world, the two great governments informed a small and helpless government that it was to be torn into fragments in the cause of "the maintenance of peace and the safety of Czechoslovakia's vital interests." The small nation was required to turn over to the Reich "the districts mainly inhabited by the Sudeten Deutsch." A reply was called for "at the earliest possible moment," on the ground that "the Prime Minister must resume conversations with Herr Hitler not later than Wednesday, and earlier if possible." The ultimatum didn't say what would be done to the Prague government in the event of refusal to comply; presumably Herr Hitler would attend to that part of the procedure.

For Lanny Budd it was like finding out that Trudi was dead; he had been sure the news was coming, and still he was sick at heart over it. He shut off the radio and walked up and down his room for a while, swearing vigorously; then he reminded himself that he was a presidential agent, and called up Hess at the Berghof. He had already written a "bread and butter" letter to thank the Deputy for his hospitality. Now he said: "The Führer has achieved a great feat of diplomacy." The reply was: "He is far from certain about it. Come and tell him."

So Lanny drove, on a warm sunshiny afternoon, with a soft haze over the mountains and no breath of air stirring the millions of fir-tree needles. By the time he arrived, he had thought out his program carefully, and was once more the suave courtier and admiring friend.

The Führer was taking a bath, one of his aides explained; this was his practice whenever he was under nervous strain. Lanny agreed that warm water was relaxing, and didn't ask whether it was true, as reported in Munich, that the Führer took three baths every day. A certain "nature-cure" Dr. Bummke of that city had prescribed the regimen, and the Führer followed it although he had quarreled with the elderly adviser. It was as hard to know what to believe in Munich as it had been in Vienna—two cities where a sense of humor seemed to prevail over strict concern for facts.

In the great hall Lanny encountered a young woman wearing an English walking costume; a tall, straight blond with lovely regular features, the perfect embodiment of a Führer's Aryan dream. Lanny had met her once at a race meet in England, but she didn't recall him and he had to remind her of the occasion. She was one of the two daughters of Lord Redesdale, an ardent supporter of Nazism; her name was Unity Valkyrie Freeman-Mitford, and her sister was twice married to Sir Oswald Mosley, leader of the British Union of Fascists, the second time in Germany, with the Führer serving as best man. Unity made Nazi speeches in Hyde Park, and had got herself celebrated in the newspapers as one of Adi's infatuated admirers; she followed him everywhere he went, and gossip had it that she planned to marry him and thus bring about the union of the two countries. How far Adi went along with this program was uncertain, but it was well known that he liked to look at beautiful girls, and Unity was adapted to that purpose. She had golden curls hanging to her shoulders—at the age of twenty-four.

Lanny politely assumed that she had come for the same purpose as himself, to congratulate a great man upon his diplomatic triumph. He tried to make himself agreeable, talking about the wonders they had witnessed at the Parteitag; but he noticed that the lady seemed restless, and kept looking in the direction of the stairs. Abruptly she excused herself and went up, and at the same time Lanny observed Rudolf Hess entering the room. Without especially lowering his voice, the Deputy remarked: "I wish somebody would kick that bitch all the way down."

So once more Lanny observed that these little Nazi children did not always obey the injunction to love one another.

VIII

The hydropathic regimen had apparently not been entirely effective in this crisis, for when Lanny was escorted to the Führer's study he found him almost wild with nerves, pacing the floor, snapping his fingers, and manifesting a peculiar jerking movement of one leg. His face made Lanny think of those he had watched in the gambling casinos of the Riviera; faces of men and women who were staking everything they owned upon the turn of a card or the spinning of a wheel. Hitler was doing much the same, and a moralist might have observed that one does not achieve world power without paying for it.

"*Diese verdammten englischen Staatsmänner!*" he burst out. "Can anybody believe a word they say?"

"I think you can believe what they say in this case, Exzellenz," replied the visitor, mildly. "They have committed themselves before the world."

"Yes, but have you read the text of that statement?"

"I have heard it over the radio, in both English and German." This involved an admission, but Lanny didn't mind making it, for he was accepted as a member of the *Herrenrasse*, and the Führer would hardly object to his listening to news from whatever source.

"Do you see the tricks they have put into it? They mention a plebiscite, and the fact that the Czechs have objected to one; but they leave it as a possibility that the Czechs may change their minds."

"I thought the English were unusually shrewd, Herr Reichskanzler; they tell Prague that they are taking it at its word, and state clearly that they anticipate the method of direct transfer."

"But then they go on to talk about negotiations, provisions for adjustment of frontiers, and so on. I have never read so many weasel words in my life. They are making the greatest mistake if they think they can tie me up in red tape, and make me listen to the quibbling of what they call 'some international body, including a Czech representative.' I don't want any Czech representative anywhere near me—ever again while I live!"

"If you want my opinion, Exzellenz——"

"Of course; I am asking it."

"Well, you followed a course of legality for many years inside Germany, and I heard some of your followers complain that you had a 'legality complex.' But you know that it paid you well in the long run, and I think it will pay you to deal on a basis of legality with the British also."

"Is that what they tell you to tell me?"

Lanny didn't have to pretend to be shocked. "Nobody in England is in a position to tell me anything, Herr Reichskanzler. I am an American, and my only interest is in having peace prevail in Europe. You cannot expect to have friends unless you can bring yourself to trust them."

"*Ja, ja, Herr Budd, Sie haben recht.* You must understand. I am under heavy strain. They have kept me dawdling about this matter for months; and I am by nature a man of action."

"Of course; but could any man wish to provoke war when by steady pressure and patience he can gain the same ends without war?"

"You are right; I have to admit it. Tell me about this incredible Chamberlain. Can it be possible for any human being to deceive himself to such an extent as he appears to?"

So Lanny delivered a discourse which might have come out of Emerson's *English Traits;* he explained that peculiar combination of religiosity and sanctioned avarice which enabled a man to become Lord Mayor of Birmingham in the stage of capitalism's approaching collapse. Elderly English Tories dreaded the future, dreaded every sort of change, and in this crisis couldn't make up their minds whether to trust to their dreadnaughts or their prayers. Runciman had prayed publicly before setting out for Prague, Halifax prayed several times every day, and Chamberlain's wife had been praying for him in Westminster Abbey while he was in flight to Munich. At the same time the forty British battleships had been parading in the North Sea.

In answer to a direct question, Lanny said he had no doubt whatever that Chamberlain intended to see that the Czechs turned over to Germany those parts of the Sudetenland whose population was more than fifty per cent German. Any danger to the Führer's plans came, not from the insincerity of British statesmen, but from the volatility of British public opinion; it was possible, but not probable, that such a storm might arise that the government would be overthrown and the deal canceled. "If that happens, it means war!" exclaimed Adi; and his visitor replied: "They know it, and that is why it is unlikely to happen."

IX

It had been agreed that the next meeting of the two heads of government should be at a place nearer to England; Hitler had made the suggestion, so Chamberlain stated it, "to spare an old man another such long journey." The spot selected was a summer resort on the Rhine near Cologne, where the river is inside Germany. The place was Godesberg, which is old German for Hill of the Gods; the old gods, of course, those deities of *Blut und Eisen* whom the Führer and his chief mystagogue, Rosenberg, were bringing back to life. Godesberg was a favorite resort of the health-seeking Adi, and the newspapers reported that he had visited the Hotel Dreesen no less than sixty-seven times. It was in this place, a little more than four years ago, that he had received urgent and terrifying phone calls from Göring, as a result of which he had taken Goebbels and flown to Munich to order the murder of one of his best friends, Ernst Röhm, and a thousand or more others; those dreadful days and nights of the Blood Purge which had come so close to ending the career of a presidential agent before it got started.

Lanny might have hinted tactfully at the idea of being on hand for this new conference. He had thought of it but decided that it would not do. There would be a swarm of newspapermen on hand, and their presence was reason for him to be elsewhere. Many of the old-timers knew him from the days when he had been a "Pink," and he didn't want the job of explaining to them when and how he had changed his color. When any reporter sought to interview him he replied that his visits to the Berghof had to do with the sale of art works, on which the Führer was considered to be an authority.

The Godesberg conference began on the 22nd. Hitler stayed at the Dreesen, and the Prime Minister at the Peterhof on the opposite side of the river. Chamberlain crossed by the ferry, and they held council all afternoon, after which Chamberlain issued an appeal for patience and order in the Sudetenland. That was enough to start reports that all was not going well. Next day the pair met again, and later the Prime Minister went back to his side of the river, and they took to sending notes back and forth, a procedure which justified still more alarming reports. Chamberlain came back, and they argued all evening, and at half past one next morning, when they parted, Chamberlain stated: "I cannot say it is hopeless,"—which was about as ominous as could be.

Terror spread over all Europe. The French and British governments notified the Czechs that they could not "continue to take responsibility of advising them not to mobilize"—which was the same as telling them to prepare for war. The horrified Czechs proceeded in haste to obey, and the Goebbels newspapers went wild, reporting more outrages in every new edition. The Hungarians and the Poles put in demands for parts of Czech territory, and now the Russians warned the Poles that if they moved against Czechoslovakia the Russians would denounce their non-aggression pact with Poland. That was the way it was in unhappy old Europe; the nations were like a row of tin soldiers standing close together—you pushed the first one and down went the whole row. The French called up half a million troops, and in London gas-mask stations were opened and swarms of people gathered to be fitted. Armies of men began piling sandbags around public buildings, and digging trenches in the parks so that people might hide from flying bomb fragments. The government organization known as Air Raid Precautions began issuing elaborate instructions over the radio and with loudspeakers in the streets.

In short, it was war; and what did it all mean? Lanny could make a guess that Adi had voiced his strenuous objections to being "tied up in red tape" and forced to listen to "the quibbling of an international body, including a Czech representative." He was demanding the right of military occupation of the Sudetenland at once, and a praying English gentleman was trying to restrain him, claiming that the Führer was increasing his demands over what had been agreed upon in Berchtesgaden. Chamberlain was a man of his word, while Hitler was a man of what he wanted, and that was the difference which had caused them to take to sending notes back and forth across a river.

Of course they were trying to bluff each other; they both had shrewd bargainers with them, and were playing close to their chests, with the future of Europe as stakes. Both were afraid, Lanny could be sure, but he guessed that Adi had the advantage, because he was half mad and his rage would overcome his fear. Thinking the matter over, day and night, Lanny wondered whether this diplomatic duel was altogether sincere. Might not both parties have decided, perhaps without voicing it, that it was necessary to give the public another scare, to increase the demand for peace and reduce the protest of those elements in Britain and France which were denouncing the program of "appeasement"? Knowing what the diplomats had been discussing among themselves for the past several months, Lanny found it hard indeed to believe that anybody was seriously thinking of war over the issue of Czechoslovakia.

X

Munich had its share of the terror. The Czechs had an air force, less than a half-hour's flight away. Suppose those treacherous sub-human creatures should decide to strike first, instead of waiting for the *Herrenvolk* to do it! Marshal Göring's flyers at the Oberwiesenfeld warmed up their motors, and the young men of the city were put into uniforms, loaded into freight cars, and hauled away toward the frontier. The performances of the Führer's favorite comic opera, *The Merry Widow*, which were given every night at the Theater am Gärtnerplatz, with a very young and lovely dancer, entirely nude, rising on a platform through the center of the stage—these performances lost nearly all of their dancing men, and the promotion of what the Nazis called "a healthy eroticism" received a sudden check.

There was an annual event in Munich, the October Fair, beginning in the middle of September and running for a month. In the Theresienwiese, an enormous meadow below the Exhibition Park, was held a combination of all the various forms of public entertainment known to the Western world: Coney Island and Luna Park, Crystal Palace and Vauxhall Gardens, Mardi Gras, Barnum and Bailey, and the state fairs of the forty-eight United States of America. Anybody who wanted to be considered a good *Münchner* had to go and ride on roller coasters and merry-go-rounds, listen to the bands, throw coconuts at the heads of clowns, and learn to eat Bavarian horseradish along with pretzels and beer.

Lanny and Zoltan went on Monday evening, two days after the Godesberg conference broke up. A quarter of a million South Germans had come to enjoy themselves in the open air, and two foreign visitors wanted to watch them at play. The visitors forgot that this was the night which the Führer of all Germany had chosen to make his report to his people, and what that would mean to the festival. All day, and until the middle of the evening, joy was unconfined; huge crowds milled here and there amid bright lights and lavish decorations; they burst into singing on the slightest occasion and danced with their *Mädels* wherever there was a smooth floor or turf underfoot. Music echoed everywhere, the barkers of sideshows orated, bells rang, roller coasters roared, and people yelled with laughter or with simulated fright.

Then suddenly came the bellowing of loudspeakers; the Führer was about to address the world from the Sportpalast in Berlin. All other sounds died away as if by enchantment. Dancing stopped, talk stopped, and a quarter of a million men and women halted in their tracks. And it was the same with all other activity, everywhere in Germany; all work in factories, all showing of motion pictures, sales in shops, serving in restaurants, walking on the streets—everything halted, and seventy million people, excluding only the babies, listened to one monstrous Voice. To fail to listen or to walk away was a crime, and had landed many a person in a concentration camp. Said Adolf Hitler:

"If I am now the spokesman of this German people, then I know: At this second the whole people in its millions agrees word for word with my words, confirms them, and makes them its own oath! Let other statesmen ask themselves whether that is also true in their case!"

XI

This Voice, roaring over the hundred acres of the Theresienwiese and over the air waves of the whole earth, told not merely what the German people were doing at this second, but what they had been doing for the past twenty years and what their great Führer had been doing for them. In the course of an address of some six thousand words, the Voice used the words I, me, my, and mine a total of one hundred and thirty-four times. Said this Voice: "I have offered disarmament as long as it was possible. But when that was rejected, I then formed, I admit, no halfhearted decision. I am a National Socialist and an old front-line German soldier. I have in fact armed in these five years. I have spent milliards on these armaments: that the German people must now know!"

It was the policy of this supremely cunning statesman to deal with one enemy at a time. Therefore in this speech, an ultimatum to the Czech Republic, he set to work to eliminate methodically all other opposition. With Poland, he said, "permanent pacification" had been achieved. As to the English people, he hoped that "the peace-loving parts would gain the upper hand." As to France, there were now "absolutely no differences outstanding between us. . . . We want nothing from France—positively nothing!" With Italy, under the "rare genius" of its Duce, there had been established "a true union of hearts."

All these matters having been disposed of, the Voice came to what it described as "the last territorial claim which I have to make in Europe." This problem, it said, existed because of "a single lie, and the father of this lie was named Beneš." The lie was "that there was a Czechoslovak nation." This lie had been told to the Versailles statesmen and they had believed it. The rest of the long speech was a recital of the duel of wills between this liar and his lie on the one hand and the Führer of the Germans and his truth on the other. This struggle had now come to its climax. Said the Führer: "I have demanded that now after twenty years Mr. Beneš should at last be compelled to come to terms with the truth."

On October 1, five days later, the hated Czech was required to turn over the Sudetenland to Adolf Hitler. It was an ultimatum, and none of the rascal's wrigglings and evasions would do him any good. "Mr. Beneš now places his hopes on the world! And he and his diplomats make no secret of the fact. They state: it is our hope that Chamberlain will be overthrown, that Daladier will be removed, that on every hand revolutions are on the way. They place their hope on Soviet Russia. He still thinks then that he will be able to evade the fulfillment of his obligations.

"And then I can say only one thing: now two men stand arrayed one against the other: there is Mr. Beneš, and here stand I. We are two men of a different make-up. In the great struggle of the people, while Mr. Beneš was sneaking about through the world, I as a decent German soldier did my duty. And now today I stand over against this man as the soldier of my people."

The Voice went on to thank Mr. Chamberlain, and to repeat the final assurances which had been given him before, "that the German people desires nothing else than peace. . . . I have further assured him, and I repeat it here, that when this problem is solved there is for Germany no further territorial problem in Europe. . . . We want no Czechs!"

Then, at the end, this all-powerful Voice addressed his faithful flock throughout the Reich:

"And so I ask you, my German people, take your stand behind me, man by man, and woman by woman. In this hour we all wish to form a common will and that will must be stronger than every hardship and every danger. And if this will is stronger than hardship and danger, then one day it will break down hardship and danger. We are determined! Now let Mr. Beneš make his choice!"

As a piece of oratory it was vigorous beyond dispute, and as an example of diplomatic strategy—which precedes war or continues war

—it was a masterpiece. How did it seem to the German people? To Lanny it was as if he were witnessing a plebiscite being taken on the Theresienwiese. A quarter of a million Germans were asked if they wished to "be stronger than every hardship and every danger," and they cast their vote, not in words but in actions which speak louder than words. There was not one handclap, not one cheer, not even one smile. The quarter of a million Germans, assembled to enjoy the simple pleasures of the poor, had been invited to become heroic. The men, ordered to take their stand behind their Führer, man by man, behaved like dogs which had been kicked with a heavy boot; the women, ordered to take their stand, woman by woman, bore the aspect of hens which had been doused in a tub of soapy water.

Every particle of life went out of the October Fair. The merry-go-rounds started to whirl, but nobody wanted to ride; the barkers started shouting, but nobody listened; the sausages started sizzling, but nobody wanted to eat. The people strolled away and went home, or gathered in little groups, talking in low tones. There would be no chance for a pair of strangers to hear what they said, but their woebegone expressions were eloquent enough. Man by man and woman by woman, they took this speech to mean war; and full as it was of subtle falsehoods, it had contained one incontrovertible truth—that the German people desired nothing else than peace.

30

Hell's Foundations Tremble

I

THE next two days were a nightmare to the people of Munich. Everybody believed that war was certain; everybody who knew Lanny Budd wanted to ask what he thought, and he could only say that he didn't know any more than they. In his secret heart he was sure there wouldn't be war—not yet. Britain and France would give way, as they had done in case after case. But this was an opinion not to be voiced, even to Lanny's friend and colleague in art experting. His conclusions had long since been placed in the hands of Rick and F.D.R., so now he had nothing to do but listen to the radio, read the newspapers, and await the event.

The papers published a cablegram which President Roosevelt had sent to Hitler and to Beneš, pleading with them not to break off negotiations. Officially, the President could hardly avoid taking that position, and Hitler's reply was likewise according to formula—another long tirade, rehearsing his grievances against Czechoslovakia. Lanny pictured his Chief lying in bed in the White House, reading that sheaf of telegraph sheets—and what would he be making of them? Would he believe what he read, or would he have in mind the facts his "P.A." had provided?

The night after the Hitler speech the British fleet mobilized; that cost a lot of money, and certainly looked serious. Then Poland broke off with Czechoslovakia—which meant that Poland's dictator had swallowed the bait, sugared with flattery, which Adi had held out to him; Poland was going to take a chunk of the plundered country, and block off Russia from giving its promised aid to the victim. No doubt the British Tories were back of that action—since of all things in the world they wanted least to have the Soviet Union take part in a successful war on Germany and make it into a Communist state. Lanny recalled a conversation between Gerald and Ceddy during the crisis over Abyssinia; they had agreed that they couldn't afford to let Mussolini be unhorsed, because of the certainty that some sort of leftist government would take his place in Italy.

Lanny would have liked to be in London now, to hear what these friends were saying; but he knew it could do no good, for the crisis would be over long before he could get any word to Roosevelt. No, an agent's business was here, in the Führer's playground; the Führer would come back from this crisis with his heart high, and would boast about what he meant to do next. If there was anything one could be certain about in this mess, it was that Adi's statement concerning his "last territorial claim in Europe" was a piece of nonsense, a bait for suckers.

II

Two days after the Sportpalast speech, the British Prime Minister arose in the House of Commons to make his report. Solemnly, as if presiding at a funeral, he told the long story of his negotiations. His hands were full of papers, and trembled as he read them; the notes which had been exchanged, the proposals which had been made, the memoranda of his two visits and what had been said at them. He declared that he had cast aside all thoughts of self, and of the dignity of his office; he had sought to preserve the peace of Europe. He revealed that he had just sent one last letter to Hitler, offering to make a third visit to Germany, and pledging the power of the British and French governments to see that agreements arrived at would be "carried out fairly and fully and forthwith." Also he had written to Mussolini, begging him to join the conference, and to use his influence with Hitler "to agree to my proposal which will keep all our peoples out of war."

A dramatic incident. Just as Chamberlain had reached this part of his speech a messenger from the Foreign Office rushed upstairs to Lord Halifax in the balcony and delivered an envelope. Halifax read the contents and passed it on to Gerald Albany, who hurried downstairs and passed it to the Prime Minister. The latter read it, and a smile of relief dawned upon his haggard features. "That is not all," he announced. "I have something to say to the House yet. I have now been informed by Herr Hitler that he invites me to meet him at Munich tomorrow morning."

That was as far as the speaker got; the House forgot all its rules, and burst into a frenzy of cheering, clapping of hands and stamping of feet. The dry and frigid Prime Minister wept, and others of his sort made no attempt to restrain their feelings. There wasn't going to be a war after all! The head of the British government was going to forget his dignity once more, and give Adi Schicklgruber a chance to wring still further concessions from him. "It's all right this time!" cried Neville to the crowds who cheered him in the streets. The Queen Mother went out weeping; the whole nation wept—and nobody stopped to think how the Führer of the *Herrenvolk* might use this revelation of the great dread of war which possessed the "degenerate democracies."

III

For Lanny this arrangement was most convenient; he had decided against going to London, and now London was coming to him! Just as he finished reading in the morning papers the news of the dramatic scene in the House of Commons, two planes from the Heston airport near London arrived at the Oberwiesenfeld airport, and from them stepped the Prime Minister and his staff—including Lord Wickthorpe and Gerald Albany. They were to be put up at the Regina Palast, where Lanny and Zoltan had a suite; many persons had to be suddenly thrown out, but needless to say a friend of the Führer would not share such a fate. The two visitors received special cards which enabled them to pass the SS guards who surrounded the hotel, and outside in the streets they could know when the distinguished guests arrived, because of the thunderous cheers from crowds surrounding the building. Munich had come to life again, and the man with the black umbrella had taken a place even higher than the Führer in the hearts of all Bavarians.

Hitler had gone in his private train to the frontier to meet Mussolini, so that they could have a conference in advance. On their ride back the Duce labored to persuade his Axis partner to be reasonable, and at the railroad station there were more cheers for Il Duce than he was getting now at home. The Prinz Karl Palace had been hurriedly dusted off for the Italian staff, while the French were taken to the Vier Jahreszeiten, under the charge of the Gestapo. It happened to be a beautiful day, and flags flew everywhere, and the radio told the people where to go and whom they were to welcome. The heads of three great states had come at the Führer's bidding, and everybody knew what a triumph that was; everybody trusted the magic of their divinely inspired leader, who had brought them safely thus far and would guide them to a happy ending.

Lanny sent in his card to Ceddy, and was called to his lordship's room for an exchange of hurried greetings. The perfect blond Aryan was engaged in "washing up," and the visitor came close and handed him a tiny slip of paper with a typewritten message: "Don't forget that your room is pretty certainly wired." Ceddy read it, and lifted his eyebrows. "Really?" he said, in the English fashion which makes it sound like "rarely" without the second "r." Lanny answered: "Take my word for it," and then handed a second slip, reading: "Tell the Old Man to stand firm. The other side will back down if they have to." To that Wickthorpe replied by putting his ear close to his friend's and whispering: "I won't have a chance to. It's all settled." Lanny held out his hand for the two notes and tore them into small pieces; he dropped them into the toilet bowl and pulled the lever—a technique he had learned from his father long ago.

They had time for a few words about family matters. Lanny had read in a London paper the news that Irma had presented her husband with a son and heir to his great title and estates. Ceddy was extremely proud, and of course Lanny congratulated him cordially. Lanny said that he would be returning to England as soon as he had got through with some picture deals. While they were chatting, there came a summons for Ceddy; the visiting delegations were going to have luncheon at the Führerhaus, and after that the discussions would begin. "The people seem glad to see us," remarked his lordship out loud—that being a statement to which the Gestapo would take no exception.

IV

The rest of the day, and until after midnight, all the world waited upon that conference. It had been known in advance that the Führer was insisting upon military occupation of the Sudetenland on Saturday, four days later, but beyond that all was uncertainty. Lanny stayed in his room, to keep out of the way of the newspapermen who swarmed in the hotel, and who, in the absence of real news, would have been glad to get hold of a man who had been a recent guest at the Berghof. The radio would give the results as soon as there were any; and meanwhile, take the most interesting book you could get hold of and do your best to lose yourself and forget the agony of the world! Lanny had an American book, dealing with ranch life in the wide open spaces of the great southwest; some tourist had left it behind, and it had caught Lanny's eye on the open stall of a secondhand-book store. It was a part of the world which he had never visited, but it was his homeland nonetheless. In spite of mountain lions and rattlesnakes and tarantulas and bandits, he would have chosen it as a place of residence over any city of old Europe on the verge of war.

At one o'clock in the morning, such Germans as had stayed awake learned over the radio that their Führer had put his signature to a Four-Power Pact, providing the methods by which the Sudeten territory was to be turned over to Germany. The evacuation by the Czechs was to begin on the next day and to be completed within ten days. The German troops were to enter zone by zone to each of four zones marked on an accompanying map. Both sides were to release political prisoners, and the inhabitants of the ceded territory were to have six months in which to decide which citizenship they wished to enjoy. All these matters were to be in charge of an international commission, and the four heads of government agreed to guarantee the new boundaries of the Czechoslovak State against unprovoked aggression.

So there it was; peace in Europe had been saved. The three visiting delegations went home in rain, and when the British arrived there was a rainbow in the sky over Buckingham Palace, and crowds singing and shouting a tumultuous welcome. They told Chamberlain that he was a jolly good fellow, which must certainly have surprised his friends. In return he told the crowd that it was "peace with honor" and "peace in our time." Premier Daladier said afterwards that he had expected to be mobbed when he reached home; but he too was cheered and sung to, all along a twelve-mile drive into Paris. Arriving, he was carried on the shoulders of a multitude to the Tomb of the Unknown Soldier. Only a few grumblers and Czechs had any fault to find with the settlement, and Lanny Budd knew few of either. When, later in the day, he read that the Assistant Secretary of State of his own country had praised the achievement, he felt himself the forgotten man.

A tragic time indeed for clearsighted men and lovers of justice; the greedy ones were rubbing their hands and the butchers were sharpening their knives all over the world. Every gain that had been made in the World War had been thrown away, and every principle for which Woodrow Wilson had fought had been mocked. Each day became a series of fresh humiliations, and it took all the fortitude that a presidential agent possessed to keep him from throwing up his job and going back to lie on the beach at Juan and let the world go to hell in its own way.

The Führer went to Berlin, and of course had a triumphal progress. Promptly at the hour set, his troops crossed the border from Upper Austria, and soon afterwards he followed, the first day into Eger and the second into Karlsbad. At the same time Poland served an ultimatum, demanding Teschen—a district which, during the days of the Peace Treaty, Lloyd George had admitted never having heard of. The Poles had remembered it, and now they took it; also the Hungarians proceeded to take their bites out of the stricken carcass. The Nazis took everything they wanted, and the "international commission" in Berlin decided all disputes their way. The hated President Beneš resigned, since it was obvious that he could no longer do his country any good, and what was left of the carcass became a dependency of the Nazis. Pilsen was taken over in the very first days, and the great Skoda plant started making war materials for Hitler's next campaign. Lanny Budd got one feeble smile, wondering how Baron Schneider was enjoying that.

V

Life came back to Munich as to a drought-stricken garden after a thunder shower. The bands played and the merry-go-rounds whirled and the shoot-the-chutes roared on the Theresienwiese, and all good *Münchner* laughed and sang as of yore. Those who had permitted doubts of their Führer to creep into their hearts were shamed and tried to forget it; he was the world's greatest wonder-worker, and from now on they would follow him without question, certain that he could do whatever he wanted with the rest of Europe.

Zoltan had to return to Paris, but Lanny stayed on, because he wanted to catch the Führer in an unbuttoned mood, and the Berghof was the place. Sooner or later he always returned, generally on impulse and without notice. Meanwhile Lanny attended to his picture business, making money among the rich and friends among all classes.

Among those he had met at the Berghof was Adolf Wagner, Gauleiter of Bavaria, and one of Adi's oldest pals, having marched with him in the Beerhall Putsch and helped him in the Blood Purge. He was a big man and had an even bigger voice than Adi; he had taken pains to imitate every tone of his master, so he was officially known as "the Führer Voice," and read speeches for Adi on many occasions—among them always the opening of the Parteitag. He had a wooden leg from the war, but managed to get his great bulk around on it. "Big Adolf" was a political boss of the sort that cities in America are used to, but he had no law to interfere with him. When it rained in Munich, as it did frequently, and his stump ached, he would send some Catholic priest to Dachau; when, on the other hand, the sun shone and he had loaded up with *Münchner* at the great Artists' House which Big and Little had designed and built, his friends could get anything they wanted from him.

The artistic tastes of the Bavarian Gauleiter were not the same as Lanny Budd's, but Lanny had kept that fact to himself. The blusterous gang leader was proud of his love of culture and had appointed himself State Minister of Education, Culture, and the Interior; he patronized all the arts and all artists, especially those who were young and pretty. Anyone whom the Führer entertained must be all right, so Lanny had the keys to the city. He didn't care for Bierabends, and pleaded lack of capacity; but right now, when all Germany was celebrating, he had to accept some invitation, so he went for a raft ride on the Isar River, a unique sort of excursion.

The waters come down, clear and cold and green from the glaciers of the high Alps, and on them float logs from the carefully supervised state forests. When the stream is big enough they are tied together with chains, and presently there is a raft. When a political boss wishes to entertain his friends he has planks nailed on top of such a raft, and has a special car hitched onto a train and takes the party overnight to Bad Tölz, where he has a brass band to welcome them at the station and Aryan peasant girls to dance with them. After a breakfast of sausages washed down with the native beer they march to the raft, which has comfortable steamer chairs on it, also baskets of *leberwurst* and *schweitzerkäse* sandwiches and of course a keg of beer.

The raft is poled out into the stream and away it goes, under bridges lined with cheering crowds—no trouble getting people to cheer in Germany in October of 1938! You see a lot of fine scenery, and you have exciting times sliding down sluices past the various dams in the river. You stop at a monastery for a fry of river fish, and finally you arrive at Munich's favorite bathing place. There you go ashore, while the raft continues on its way to the beautiful blue Danube, perhaps to become part of a house in Vienna or Budapest.

VI

Feldmarschall Göring had built himself a châlet on the Obersalzberg, having had the bad taste to build it high and looking down upon his Führer's. To this place he had retired with his bronchitis and swollen legs, and now he had recovered and was sticking pigs in his forest. He invited Lanny for a visit, and Lanny was pleased to go, but preferred to watch the pig-sticking from a distance. He didn't lose caste by that, for the operation was admitted to be dangerous, and *Der Dicke* was satisfied to display his prowess and be admired by weaker men. The job was done on horseback, and two keepers with rifles rode close behind, to be ready in case of accident; but none happened, and three great shaggy boars were pierced through the heart by the fat man's well-aimed lance.

After supper they sat before a blazing fire, with a backlog so huge that it had to be brought on a little rubber-tired "dolly." They talked about the state of the world, and the marshal was as proud of his Führer's stroke of statecraft as he was of his own stabs at the pigs. "Was there ever such a man since the world began?" he inquired, and Lanny didn't try to think of another. He lent *éclat* to the occasion by telling what he knew of its risks; it had been touch and go, for the British statesmen had been almost broken by the pressure of public opposition.

It was all right for Lanny to say: "I had a few minutes with Ceddy Wickthorpe in the Regina Palast, just before he went in to the conference. He was a badly worried Englishman, *glauben Sie mir.*" That was slang in American, but oddly enough wasn't in German.

"I don't mind telling you that I had very little sleep for several nights," admitted *Der Dicke*. "The Führer is hard to deal with at such times; he has a way of calling you on the telephone when he can't sleep."

"What is he going to do next?" inquired the visitor.

"*Weiss Gott!* I doubt if he knows himself."

After such a question and such a reply, a skillful spy would pass on quickly, so as to seem casual. Said he: "The newspapermen pestered me so that I shut myself up in my hotel room all the time of the conference. I read a book about hunting in the American southwest, and one story seemed to have some bearing on what was happening at the moment. It was in the Rio Nueces country of Texas; a man had located a place where wild turkeys roosted at night, and he went just at sundown to get them. He tied his horse to a tree some distance away and crept to the spot and waited, and when the moon came up he shot six turkeys with his shotgun. He tied the turkeys together and hoisted them onto his back and started to carry them through the brush; but before he got very far he discovered that he was being followed by a mountain lion."

"They have lions in Texas?" inquired Göring.

"It is the panther, or cougar; it has a number of names—in South America the puma."

"I see."

"This mountain lion has a most terrifying scream, and the man realized that he was in grave danger; his shotgun would be of no use against a sudden charge in the dark. The creature had smelled the blood of those turkeys, and didn't mean to let them get away from him. So the man stopped and cut off one turkey and left it lying in the trail. That sufficed for a while; but then the man discovered that the lion was stalking him again, so he dropped another turkey. That went on, and every time the man dropped a turkey, he was safe for the time, but then to save his life he had to drop one more. Finally he used up his last turkey; then, by good fortune, he reached his horse, and leaped on, and, as they say in that country, 'tore a hole through the brush.' The story goes on that when he got home he told his wife of the adventure and she saw that he suddenly began to tremble; she asked: 'Why do you tremble now that you are safe?' He replied: 'It just occurred to me, suppose I had shot only five turkeys, what would have happened?'"

Der Dicke had got the point of this story before it was half told; at the end he burst into laughter, the loudest the visitor had ever heard from that capacious throat. "*Wunderbar!*" he exclaimed. "*Herrlich!*" Then he added: "The woman should have made an answer."

Of course it was up to Lanny to ask: "What would the answer be?"

"She should have told him: 'If you had not shot any turkeys at all,

the lion would never have troubled you.' " So then it was Lanny's turn
to chuckle, and the pair of them had a gay time over the plight of a
British Prime Minister whose shotgun was a black umbrella and whose
turkeys were called Abyssinia and Spain and Austria and Czechoslovakia
and Poland and—who could say about Number Six?

"Perhaps it will be called Turkey," suggested the son of Budd-Erling.

VII

Lanny thought that he knew the Nazis by now, and didn't expect any
more surprises; but Göring provided one. Lifting his considerable bulk
from an overstuffed chair, he went to a near-by cabinet and took out
a phonograph record. "Here is something that will answer questions
in your mind," he said, and put it on the machine and pressed the lever.
Then he resumed his seat, and Lanny listened to a voice discussing the
attitude of the British government toward the Reds and "their so-called
Socialist Soviet Republic." It was an English voice, cultivated, deliberate, with a touch of Oxford. It would say two or three sentences and
then stop, and another voice would translate the sentences into German. The English voice would resume, declaring that the British government would raise no objections to moves which the German government might make toward the east, provided that they would make a
satisfactory arrangement with the Poles; that the British government
were firmly convinced that Communism was a great menace, and
would be disposed to look upon the spread of its power as highly
deleterious to European civilization.

There was nothing new in this point of view; Lanny had heard it
expressed many scores of times by Ceddy and Gerald and their guests,
and by other highly placed ladies and gentlemen at Bluegrass and at
Cliveden. The voice to which he was now listening was speaking with
slow precision, evidently on some formal occasion; it was a vaguely
familiar voice, suggestive of Parliament, and Lanny thought: "It
couldn't be Londonderry. It couldn't be Runciman. Could it be Nevile
Henderson?" Not until a third voice broke in, asking a question in
German, did it suddenly dawn upon a "P.A.'s" mind what he was listening to. The English voice was that of the Prime Minister, and the
occasion was the first of his conferences with Hitler, in which he had
settled, or thought he had settled, the destinies of Europe for the next
generation.

The twelve-inch record was completed, and Lanny, younger and
more movable, got up and stopped the machine. He stood by it, star-

ing at the fat Marshal. "By God, you've got him over a barrel!" he exclaimed.

Der Dicke chuckled until he shook all over. "Can you imagine such a fool?"

"Does he know you have this recording?"

"*Herrgott, nein!* We have a new and marvelous invention, that catches the faintest whisper."

Lanny shivered inwardly, recalling the scene in Karinhall when his father had written little notes to caution him about being too cordial to Hermann's wife; also the occasions when he had gossiped with Hilde, and when he had been tempted to gossip with Ceddy in the Munich hotel. Had there been any place where he had yielded to the temptation?

"This is just a few extracts which we have put together on one record," added the Marshal, still grinning. "I would play you the whole thing, only it would take several hours, and would be very boring."

Lanny said: "I tried to keep myself busy looking at paintings while that conference was going on, but I found it difficult to keep my mind on them." Then, after a pause: "Tell me, Hermann, am I at liberty to tell my father about this?"

"I haven't asked you to keep it confidential, have I?"

"No, but there are some things that are understood among gentlemen."

"Put your mind on this situation. The British have been doing everything in their power to block our moves in eastern Europe. Everywhere we turn we hit our shins against obstacles they have set in our path. Some day in an emergency I may invite some of our Russian friends who understand English to listen to this recording; and it is barely possible that if Mr. Neville Chamberlain knew that we had it, he might be tempted to reduce the ardor of his diplomatic agents. You know, we don't want any unpleasantness that we can avoid."

"You have provided me with a delightful item of conversation at my next visit to Wickthorpe Castle," replied the son of Budd-Erling.

"You don't have to say where you heard the recording; just say what you heard, and the man with the umbrella will remember what he said."

Lanny went to his room convinced that he had indeed got a delightful item, but by the time he was ready for bed he had begun to wonder whether he had got anything at all. That was the way with the Nazi code of lying—they made it impossible to believe anything they said. What would be easier than for Göring to have had such a record faked? Some blackguard Englishman with a cultivated accent could be hired for a few pounds and be set to studying real records of Chamberlain's mannerisms. As for Hitler—well, if he didn't want to take the trouble to "frame" a record, Adolf Wagner could do it for him, and no Russian could tell the difference. Lanny decided that he would do some investigating before he helped to spread that delightful item.

VIII

Back in Munich, Lanny paid a visit to that crippled lady in the Nymphenburgerstrasse who enjoyed such a high reputation among the Nazi élite. Evidently the profession of "graphologist" was well rewarded, for the lady had a fashionable apartment and a maid in cap and uniform; Lanny was seated in a luxurious drawing-room, dimly lighted so that the waiting customers might avoid being stared at. When his turn came, the maid asked for his ten marks in advance, he being a stranger.

He was escorted to a table in a little cubicle, with some light on him and none on the lady; he could see that she was stooped, and wore a dark blue robe, hiding a crippled figure. "Be so good as to write a few words on the pad," she murmured, and he took a fountain pen which lay before him and wrote the German equivalent of: "Now is the time for all good men to come to the aid of the party." That had its meaning in Germany as in America.

The little old woman took the pad in her gnarled fingers and for a long time sat studying the script. Part of the time Lanny guessed that she was studying him. Finally she exclaimed, in a cracked voice: "What a strange man! What is the matter with you?"

The visitor guessed that was a rhetorical question, and did not answer. "You are an unhappy man," she went on; and then: "I do not like you!"

"I am sorry," he replied, humbly.

"You are two men, and they are at war. Presently you will not know which you really are. Make up your mind, or it will go badly with you. I see a tragic fate in store for you."

There was a pause; then Lanny asked: "Can you tell me where that fate is to be?"

He wondered if she was going to say "Hongkong." Even if she had, he wouldn't have been satisfied, of course; he would have called it "telepathy"—"that old telepathy!" in Tecumseh's phrase.

The woman said: "I am disturbed by your presence. I cannot do any more for you. I am sorry."

The rejected client did not ask for his ten marks back. He went out thinking hard about this strange world of the subconscious, so greatly neglected by orthodox science. Somehow he had taken it for granted that any power of mind-reading which a medium possessed would deal with aspects of his life such as a munitions-making grandfather or a Transcendentalist great-uncle. But suppose—just supposing!—that some old witch-woman should call up Gestapo headquarters in the Wittels-bacher Palace and report: "I have just been reading the mind of an American *Kunstsachverständiger*, and he is here for the purpose of spying on Number One, Number Two, and Number Three."

Lanny decided that for the present he would discontinue psychical researching inside the Third Reich!

IX

Rudolf Hess was back in Munich. He had his home here, with a family which he did not publicize as did others of the Nazi leaders. He was personally the most decent of those whom Lanny had met, the most agreeable because of his international upbringing and outlook. He was fanatically loyal to his leader, but where Party matters were not concerned he had a sense of humor, and with persons whom he trusted he put off his grim exterior.

Lanny paid him a call at the Braune Haus, the Party building which the Führer had purchased and made over according to his taste. It was on the Briennerstrasse, a fashionable neighborhood, with the papal nuncio right across the street. It was a four-story building, set well back and protected by high fences. Outside were SS guards, and inside was a riot of swastikas of all sizes, on grillwork, lamp brackets, windows, doorknobs, ceilings. Hess's office was simple and unostentatious; its windows looked out upon the Führerhaus, one of the magnificent structures which Adi had built since taking power, and in which the recent world-shaking conference had been held.

Naturally they talked about that event and its consequences. The Deputy Führer explained that for him it meant a great increase in duties and responsibilities; he had a new Party province to govern, and since the Party administration was everywhere more important than the political government, Hess had his hands full right now. He explained that the type of men suited to agitation and guerrilla warfare was not the same as that needed for administration after a victory, so he had a lot of demoting and promoting to do, and many heads to knock together. Lanny listened sympathetically, and was glad in his heart that he didn't have either to administrate or be administrated.

This was the period during which Hitler was increasing his demands on the Czech carcass day by day. The "international commission" which was supposed to decide disputes consisted of one Nazi official, one Czech, and the British, French, and Italian ambassadors to Berlin. These last were busy gentlemen, and didn't want to be bothered by complaints or talk about fair play. When the Nazis set up a claim that a certain section of the Bohemian plain had more than fifty per cent of German population, the ambassadors didn't go to make a count, nor did they pay heed to the fact that the territory contained some mineral resource or industrial enterprise which the Führer needed for his war preparations. They just voted the Czech delegate down and the German troops in.

Of course it meant friction, and lamentations from the Czechs, some of which got into the foreign press and annoyed the Nazis. Herr Goebbels had dropped his press campaign against this fragment of a state, but now he was taking it up again. Lanny said: "You can't get along with those people; they are too different from Germans."

"I am afraid you may be right, Herr Budd," conceded the Deputy.

"The Führer said: 'We want no Czechs'; but my guess is, he'll be able to find work for them if he has to take them over." The secret agent said this with a grin, and the dour Deputy grinned in return. No more words were needed between friends.

Lanny added: "I am wondering why the Führer had to go so far as to give a guarantee to Czechoslovakia. The British wanted it, of course; but did he have to give way?"

"He always knows what he is doing," replied Hess. *(Hitler hat immer Recht!)* "What he gave is a guarantee against unprovoked aggression, and you may be sure that if there is any, the Czechs will do the provoking." The smile had gone from the Deputy's face, and he meant this statement without any trace of irony. Anyone who heard him would have been glad not to be a Czech.

X

Adolf Hitler did not like the cold and formal city of Berlin, and stayed there only when ceremonies and diplomatic etiquette required it. Munich was his playground and the birthplace of his party; his own kind of people were here, and he would dump responsibilities into the laps of his subordinates and fly to his mountain castle. From there Munich was only a couple of hours away, and he would step into his black bullet-proof Mercédès, followed by three cars full of SS men, and speed away to his peculiar pleasures.

He liked to visit the Schwabing district, which was Munich's Quartier Latin, and dine in the Osteria Bavaria restaurant, where his vegetable plate was prepared by a chef who knew his tastes. He liked to put on black chamois shorts and a green *Loden Frey* hunting jacket and visit the October Festival, mingling with the people and being photographed with children around him—his plain-clothes guards keeping carefully out of the camera's eye. He liked to dress in black trousers and immaculate white jacket and visit the Theater am Gärtnerplatz —now giving Strauss's *Fledermaus*—and see his personally selected "Beauty Dancer" giving her performance in the second act. Adi would arrive during the intermission, and his Führer Standard would be hung from the railing of his box; before the performance was resumed, the plain-clothes men scattered through the audience would give the Hitler salute, and the entire audience would rise and make their thrilling response. Then, in the interest of a healthy eroticism, the Führer would sit with a pair of high-powered glasses fixed upon the young, supple, and entirely nude Dorothy van Bruck displaying her many charms.

Or perhaps he would visit the Künstlerhaus on the Lenbachplatz, which he had just rebuilt. This had been in the old days a clubhouse for world-famous artists, and Adi, who was pleased to be hailed by his adorers as the "Greatest Artist in the World," had made it over on a scale of magnificence suited to his New Order. A suite had been set apart for him, and when he discovered that a large Jewish synagogue interfered with his view, he ordered the building torn down and the site used for the parking of Nazi cars. All self-respecting artists stayed away from the place and it had become in effect a night club for the Party bosses. Beautiful girls with theatrical ambitions were always on call, and companies gave private performances at command. Such shows as the American Acrobats and the Can Can Ballet, with French dancers giving the Hitler salute with one leg instead of one arm—these helped to divert the mind of a world conqueror from his cares. The Number One would go home at three or four in the morning, and then the real fun would begin for his champagne-soaked subordinates.

XI

Such was the "Artists' House"; and still more grandiose was another structure just completed in the Englischer Garten, called "The House of German Art." It was, in a way, a monument to one of the most significant events in the life of Adi Schicklgruber, his rejection as an art student by a committee of judges in Vienna. All his youthful hopes had been centered upon such a career, and when he submitted his work and was coldly told that he had no talent, it had meant for him a sentence to sleep in the shelter for bums and to earn his bread by painting and selling postcards. When by his political genius he had made himself master of Germany, one of his burning desires had been to prove himself the Fatherland's greatest critic and patron of the arts. So had come that colossal marble structure, built on swampy ground at tremendous cost—but nothing mattered in the cause of proving how great had been the error of the Vienna committee!

After four years the work was done, and the wits of Munich had dubbed it the "Greek Railroad Station." It was an unusual art museum, in that it was also a restaurant, a beerhall, and a night club. Had not the Nazi Party been born in a beerhall, and had not all the Führer's early speeches been delivered in such places? The new order was pledged to the extermination of Christian-Jewish asceticism; eating, drinking, and making merry were the order of the new day, and all young Germans were told to build strong bodies and to bring new strong-bodied Aryans into the world as early and often as possible. Most Nazi temples provided an abundance of private rooms in which a beginning might be made at any hour of the day or night.

Lanny Budd visited this temple of art, and found it not easy to keep his shudders from becoming visible. Not that there were no good paintings to be seen, for Munich had been a home of art for centuries, and not all the good painters were in concentration camps. When they painted landscapes the places were recognizable, and when they painted Bavarian peasants they frequently revealed sympathy. But when they painted a naked Aryan Leda in the embrace of the swan, it made one think of the "feelthy postcards" which were peddled all over the Mediterranean lands. When they painted Stormtroopers in uniform and Nazi implements of war, it seemed that the work belonged in the Department of Propaganda and Public Enlightenment, presided over by a crippled little dwarf.

The visitor stood before a large and extremely bad painting called

The Spirit of the Stormtroopers, depicting a column of Nazi youths marching in the brave old days when they were engaged in making the streets free to the brown battalions. Concerning this work the gossipmonger of the old regime, Baron von Zinszollern, had told a most awful story, having to do with the festival called the "Day of German Art" in the previous July, when this and thousands of other new works had been revealed to the world. One of the curses of the Nazi regime had been homosexuality, and at the time of the Blood Purge Hitler had used this as his pretext for ordering the murder of Ernst Röhm and others of his oldest associates. It had been necessary to outlaw the practice, and the crime had been described in Paragraph 175 of the Criminal Code. Since it has always been the practice of civilized man to find some subtle way of alluding to things that are not nice, it had come about in Germany that *"hundertfünfundsiebzig"* had become the German way of whispering a reference to this form of abnormality.

And now, here came this magnificent art show, trumpeted to the world as evidence of Nazi love of the higher things of life. Several hundred thousand catalogues had been printed, intended to be sold for one mark, twenty-five pfennigs each; and was it the operation of blind chance or of some malicious trickster on the hanging committee that the number assigned to a painting entitled *The Spirit of the Stormtroopers* should be that much-whispered number? The discovery was made by an American correspondent, who reported it to the Gestapo, with the result that all the catalogues were destroyed, and if rumor could be believed, somebody high up in Munich art affairs lost his life. When the "Greek Railroad Station" opened, the marching Nazi heroes were found with a harmless number, while *hundertfünfundsiebzig* was assigned to a *Vase of Flowers.*

XII

Lanny Budd went to call on the Führer in his elegant Munich apartment in the Prinzregentenstrasse. He found the great man as happy as the cat that has swallowed the canary and has not been spanked for it. He did not refer to the fact that a wise and understanding American had advised him how to proceed, and Lanny was, of course, too tactful to hint at it; he judged that the occasion called for a good stiff dose of flattery, and he told the greatest statesman of modern times that the world marveled at the diplomatic finesse he had displayed; above all the sense of timing, which had been the essence of this most difficult job. Such a humiliation for a British Prime Minister—and such pitiful efforts in Parliament to dignify himself! There had been nothing like it since King Henry had come to Canossa.

The Führer behaved as cats do when they lie in front of a warm fire and have their fur stroked the right way. He appreciated the discernment of this sympathetic visitor, and presently when the visitor hinted that there might be a weakness in the Führer's position, he asked at once what it was; when told that it was the guarantee against unprovoked aggression given to Czechoslovakia, he smiled slyly and said that this was a guarantee against the aggression of other states. See how he had reduced the demands of Poland and Hungary for Czech territory! But that was far from meaning that the Czech politicians were free to carry on their intrigues against Germany abroad, and if they kept it up they would soon find they had no guarantee against German discipline.

"We Nazis have learned that diplomacy and war are two sides of the same shield," declared the Führer. "Very surely we shall not allow anyone to make war on us unpunished." He spoke of the fact that the Foreign Minister of Poland had just been to Rumania in an effort to make an agreement for mutual defense. Of course such an agreement could be aimed at no one but himself, declared Hitler, and proceeded to denounce the Poles as another subhuman tribe, victims of priestcraft and clerical intrigue. "The cross and the swastika cannot exist side by side," declared Adi. "The Versailles *Diktat* has put the Poles in position to blockade Germany from East Prussia, and who but our enemies could imagine that I will permit such a thorn to go on festering in the body of the Reich?"

"Aha!" thought the "P.A."—another territorial claim in Europe! Said he: "That remark interests me for a personal reason, Exzellenz. May I talk about my own plans for a moment?"

"I am always interested in my friends' plans, Herr Budd."

"A few months ago I was passing through the Corridor, and chanced to see a little place that I thought I would love to own. You know how it is—you proved it here at the Berghof, if you start with a place already built you save a lot of time; you have the roads, and the beautiful trees that would take a lifetime to get, and a place to live while you plan improvements. I inquired about this little property and found that it is within my means. Only one thing deterred me—I could not bear to live under a reactionary Polish dictatorship. I thought: 'I will wait and see what happens.'"

"You won't have to wait indefinitely, Herr Budd; that much I can tell you."

"I don't want to commit an impropriety and put myself in the position of a real estate speculator. If I should make the purchase, it would be to have a home for the rest of my days; and one of my reasons would be that it is in convenient driving distance of Kurt Meissner, and of yourself, if I may make so bold as to count upon your friendship. I should probably wish to become a citizen of your Third Reich."

"You will be most welcome, I assure you. And certainly you can count upon the fact that all the impositions of Versailles are going to be wiped off the books of history. If the place you speak of is in a district in which the Germans are a majority, or in which they were a majority before they were driven out by Polish misgovernment, you can be sure that it will come under my protection very soon."

"*Herzlichen Dank, Herr Reichskanzler!* There is no reason why I should pay more than necessary, so I think I'll wait until your intentions have become manifest, and the Poles will be more disposed to sell."

Lanny said this with a smile, and the Führer broke into a grin. He had a sort of ghoulish humor when it was a question of his ability to outwit his opponents. "Wait about six months, Herr Budd, and I will promise to soften the price of your future home!"

XIII

The Führer had just ordered the new puppet government at Prague to break off its Russian alliance, and the order had been obeyed. He said now that he hoped soon to see the French people come to their senses and realize that dalliance with the monster of Bolshevism could do them nothing but harm. This dalliance represented the nadir of depravity to which venal politicians could descend; French newspapers and Cabinet members had been bought outright by Russian gold, and so long as such men held power there could be no friendship between France and Germany. That was what the Führer meant by the statement that diplomacy and war were two sides of the same shield; the Russian alliance was a perpetual act of aggression against his *Regierung*.

Lanny remarked: "You are aware, of course, that many statesmen in both France and Britain are hoping that you will put down Bolshevism for them."

"While they sit and watch me bleed to death! Believe me, Herr Budd, I am nobody's monkey and pull nobody's chestnuts out of the fire. When the war on Bolshevism begins, they will help, and I'll be certain they are all the way in before I put in one foot."

"Tell me," said the visitor; "have you thought of the possibility that you might make a non-aggression pact with the Soviets? That would give Britain and France quite a jolt."

"Indeed it would; and be sure that I don't overlook any cards in my hand. I am well aware that Britain and France have been doing their best to set the Bolsheviks against me, and it is no part of my program to let my enemies move first."

"When I go to London," remarked the art expert, "Lord Wickthorpe is going to ask me as to your views. Shall I tell him that?"

"Tell him anything that I have said to you. That is the advantage of my position; I tell them the whole truth, and it is as if I had said nothing, for they do not believe me."

"You are something unique in the history of Europe, Exzellenz, and they do not know what to make of you. I have never before called you '*Mein Führer*,' but I think from now on I shall have to do so."

And after that, of course, a presidential agent was free to share in all the secrets of Nazi diplomacy!

31

Courage Mounteth with Occasion

I

L ANNY had got the information he wanted, and was through in Munich. He had found a purchaser for another of Göring's superfluous art works, and would drive to Berlin, pay for the painting, and take it out with him; he made it a rule never to ship anything from inside Naziland, dishonesty having become so rampant in the country that he was unwilling to trust even the German employees of the American Express Company. He would pay duty calls on several persons in Berlin such as Herr Thyssen and Dr. Schacht, who were free talkers; he would listen to General Emil Meissner tell about the newest technical achievements of the Reichswehr; also, he wouldn't fail to collect a few tidbits of gossip from the Fürstin von Donnerstein.

The day before he left the Bavarian capital a dreadful piece of news came over the radio. A Jewish youth in Paris, a refugee crazed by his personal sufferings and those of his people, had shot Eduard vom Rath, official of the Germany embassy whom Lanny had met in the Château de Belcour. The Nazi radio burst into a frenzy, blaming the crime upon the incitements of the British press, which had persisted in publishing stories about the persecution of the Jews in Germany. It happened that the day of the Paris shooting was the anniversary of the Beerhall Putsch, so all the Nazi leaders were in Munich. That night Adolf Wagner gave the order, and a wild pillaging of Jewish shops began; Lanny in his hotel room heard the crashing of glass and the yells of the Stormtroopers, and went out to watch the disciplined marauders smashing plate-glass windows and showcases with sticks and stones, filling their pockets with watches and jewelry, tying up bundles of furs, lingerie, silk stockings—whatever they thought might please their lady friends.

That wholesale looting went on the whole night, and many of the Nazis in their greed got badly cut with flying splinters of glass or with the sharp edges in showcases. Lanny witnessed one of the strangest of sights, a battle royal between the Stormtroopers and the SS guards of Marshal Göring in front of the Bernheimer establishment which dealt in oriental rugs, antiques, and objets d'art. He supposed it was a brawl over the possession of these treasures, but later on he learned that Herr Bernheimer was an "honorary Aryan," the only one in Munich; he had supplied the fat commander with all the furnishings of Karinhall, and thus was entitled to protection.

Next morning when Lanny set out upon his drive, the street-cleaning department of the city was engaged in sweeping up the broken glass and loading it into trucks, and the looting was no longer an enterprise for the rank-and-file Nazis, but was being systematized in proper German fashion. Members of the city's Kulturkammer had been commissioned to ransack Jewish homes and carry off to the museums all works of art of whatever character which might interest the Aryan public. All the male Jews of Munich were being rounded up by the Gestapo and carted off to Dachau; some who had learned what went on in that place of horror were shooting themselves or jumping out of windows.

It was the same all over Germany; more than sixty thousand Jews were put into concentration camps in this dreadful "November Pogrom," and the number who were murdered could never be guessed. Lanny, who had started late, stopped for lunch in Regensburg, home of one of Göring's great airplane factories. He there observed an elderly bearded Jew sneaking along the street like a frightened animal, doubtless trying to get to his home or some other place of hiding. A gang of half a dozen of the Hitlerjugend, boys of no more than four-teen or fifteen, set upon him with clubs and with their "Daggers of Honor." The poor man screamed for mercy, putting his head down and hunching his shoulders to protect himself from the blows. They beat him to the ground and then pounded and kicked him and slashed his clothing and his flesh with the daggers. They quit only when he was such a mess of blood that they could not touch him without ruin-ing their brown uniforms. They went off singing the *Horst Wessel* song, leaving the motionless form lying in the gutter.

There was nothing Lanny could do about it. He was safe because he was an Aryan and looked it, but he would have ruined his career for-ever if he had made any move to interfere with the German effort to protect their "racial purity." Grief took away his appetite, and he got back into his car, depriving the busy city of Regensburg of the two or three marks he would have spent in one of its cafés.

II

The same scenes were taking place in all the towns along the Munich-Berlin *Autobahn;* looted shops gaped with broken windows and empty shelves, and trucks were loaded with wretched Jews, many of them having faces and clothing red with blood. Nowhere was the situation worse than in Berlin; organized brutality prevailed for a week, and turned the cold and proud capital into a charnelhouse for Lanny Budd. Impossible to have any sort of pleasure there; impossible to read a newspaper, to take part in social life, to enjoy rational con-versation. Painting, poetry, drama, music, all had been poisoned by this systematized lunacy. You might say that you would go to a concert hall and hear great music out of the past; but Bach, Beethoven, and Brahms were mocked by modern Germany—their scherzos were like dancing on a grave, their adagios became the unbearable agony of a great and noble culture being dragged down and defiled.

Two cultures, in fact, the German and the Jewish, equally worthy, and reciprocally dependent. Lanny had met many Jews in the Father-land; all sorts, both good and bad, as was the case with Germans. He had observed that there were characteristic Jewish faults, as there were characteristic German faults, and he saw little to choose between them; he liked the domineering German just as little as he liked the devious Jew. On the other hand he liked the ardent idealistic Jew as much as he liked the genial and warmhearted German, and he knew that these types supplemented each other; he knew that they got along well together, for he had seen it happening.

The tragic events of the time were really a family quarrel, for the Jews had been in Germany for many centuries, and thought of themselves as Germans before they were Jews. They had prospered, and had their share in the country's history and the building of its culture. They had been proud of themselves, and looked down upon the Jews of Poland and Russia as an inferior breed. Now the Nazis were beating them down to a level below the dogs of Germany—for that same Hitlerjugend who had murdered the old Jew in Regensburg would love and cherish their dogs.

In Lanny Budd the souls of Heine and Toller, of Mendelssohn and Mahler, Marx and Lassalle, Ehrlich and Einstein and a hundred other great German Jews cried out against this horror. It was really not the German people who were perpetrating it, but a band of fanatics who had seized a nation and were perverting its youth and turning them into murderers and psychopaths. Germans would awaken some day as from a nightmare, and contemplate with loathing and dismay the crimes that had been committed in their name. They would do penance for centuries, having to read the pages of history on which these deeds were recorded; they would bow their heads and shed tears upon the pages, knowing that to the rest of mankind the name of German had become a byword and a hissing.

Lanny thought of cultivated and gracious Jews he had known in this nightmare land. Those in Munich who were not dead or in Dachau would be seeking refuge in the woods which bordered the river Isar, or in the Alpine foothills, depending upon the charity of the peasants for food. Those in Berlin, if they had not cut their own throats or jumped into the city's canals, would be hiding in cellars, coming out at night and trying to escape in a freight car or canal boat. Suppose one of them were to telephone to Lanny at the Hotel Adlon, saying: "I am in peril of my life. Help me!"—what would he answer? In the old days he had done what he could for the Robin family, but what could he do now for the Hellsteins or the humble Schönhaus family? He couldn't say: "I am a secret agent, and my duty is elsewhere." He could only mumble some excuse which would mean to the hearer: "I am a coward and a man without human feelings."

III

Lanny attended to his affairs in Berlin, and then on a day of heavy and cold rain he drove to the Belgian border, and straight on, without stopping except for a meal, to Paris. There, in his hotel, he wrote his latest report on Germany, and put it into the mail.

For a few days *la ville lumière* seemed like home; Zoltan was here, and Emily, old friends whose hearts were warm and whose minds were not perverted. His mother had gone back to Bienvenu, and he called her on the telephone and got the family news: Marceline was soon to get her divorce; she was dancing her head off; the baby was well; Madame had got over the flu. Lanny reported that he was going to London and then to New York, where he had a lot of business, some of it urgent.

There was the autumn Salon, worth a day of any art expert's time. There was a lot of nude flesh, but no marching Nazis, and the number 175 was represented by a harmless landscape with sheep. Also there was a visit to the de Bruyne family, eager to hear the latest news from *la patrie's* new ally; they deplored but excused the pogrom, and looked upon the Four-Power Pact as the most fortunate event in French history for many a year. The hated Franco-Russian alliance was for all practical purposes dead, and now Daladier had got emergency powers and was able to govern "by decree"; a plague of labor revolts would be put down without the customary weak compromises.

In short, French politics looked more hopeful to a family of French aristocrats than it had for a generation. They were proud of their personal martyrdom, and considered what had happened at Munich as their vindication. They talked freely, as usual, and Lanny listened to the latest details of wire-pulling by the "two hundred families," who collectively had decided upon a compromise with Hitler as the cheapest form of insurance. "It means the surrender of our power in Central Europe," admitted Denis père, sadly; "but we still have North Africa and the colonies, and we are safe behind our Maginot Line. Above all, we don't have to make any more concessions to revolution at home."

It wasn't Lanny's business to educate this self-made capitalist, but only to make remarks that would draw him out. The same was the case with Schneider, who was at his town house and invited the son of Budd-Erling to lunch. The elderly munitions king was carrying his burdens not too easily; he seemed worried and far from well. His interests were spread all over Europe, so he was not so optimistic as

Denis. He reported on the arrangements he had made about Skoda; he would remain the owner and get generous profits, but would not be able to take them out of Germany; he would have to turn them into extension of plant, or building of new plant, as a government bureau in Berlin would direct. "In plain words, I am giving my time and skill to making armaments for Germany; and if I don't like it I can sell out for what they offer me, which is practically nothing." The Baron shrugged his shoulders in the French fashion. "What can a man do, in these strange times?"

Lanny couldn't tell him what to do. He could only report what Nazis Number One, Number Two, and Number Three had said about what was coming to the rest of Czechoslovakia, and to Poland, and then to Hungary and Rumania and the other turkeys. The most staggering thing of all was the suggestion that if France and Britain didn't hurry up and make their peace with the Führer, he might turn to Russia for a friend; that truly was like seeing the world turned upside down and shaken. "Has the man no principles whatever?" demanded the master of Le Creusot. By his own principles he had managed to preserve his munitions plants from bombing during the World War, but he couldn't see how he was going to achieve that feat a second time. "Your father is the wise one," he remarked. "He got cash, and took it out of Europe!"

IV

One more report to Washington, this time on the situation in France. Then Lanny stored his car in Paris and took flight to London. At Wickthorpe he was welcomed, and inspected the lovely new baby and paid all the proper compliments. This tiny mite of life with the pink cheeks, golden down on the head and lips forever sucking, was the Honorable James Ponsonby Cavendish Cedric Barnes Masterson—named for various relatives, including his American grandfather. Already he had put Frances completely into the shade, and would keep her there the rest of her days.

Lanny could now talk safely in an Englishman's home, his castle in which there were no dictaphones. Interesting indeed to hear what had gone on inside the conference room of the Führerhaus in Munich; the little details of personality and manners of the four men who had settled the destiny of Europe. His lordship had been called in at one stage of the drafting, because he had made a special study of the courses of rivers and the boundaries of towns involved in the transfer. The discussion had been carried on in the German language, and every word had to be translated to the Prime Minister. Il Duce thought that he knew German, but his efforts were terrible, and did him no good with Hitler, who made faces. The Führer's own German was far from perfect, but that didn't trouble him.

Lanny had much to tell, and told it freely, on the principle that fair exchange was no robbery. To hear a permanent official of the Foreign Office react to Hitler's latest outbursts was to know pretty surely what the Tory government of Britain were going to do in the course of the next few months. (The government of Britain were plural—that was one way you could tell an Englishman from the rest of the English-speaking world.) The government were going to do everything possible to avoid offending a touchy Reichskanzler, even to the extent of censoring British opinion on the subject of "Munich." American news-reels which ventured criticism were barred, and a strict rule against censure of Chamberlain was being enforced by the British radio.

But the ghost would not stay laid; for there was no way to keep individuals from voicing their sense of outrage in print and at public meetings. Just now a hot controversy was going on over the part played in the settlement by Colonel Lindbergh and Lady Astor. "Lindy" had been in Germany in August, being shown all the secrets of the Air Force, and then he had gone to the Soviet Union and been treated as an honored guest. He had come back to England, right at the critical moment while the crisis was at its height, and, so the story ran, had told Nancy's guests at Cliveden that Soviet aviation was "utterly demoralized," and that Göring's Air Force could defeat the combined forces of Britain, France, Czechoslovakia, and the Soviet Union. That, insisted the critics, had turned the tide and brought about the decision to surrender; so now the "Cliveden set" carried on its already burdened shoulders the blame for the greatest diplomatic defeat in Britain's history.

A story ready-made for the Reds and their fellow-travelers! In all the pubs of Britain, and likewise in the drawing-rooms, the issue was debated with heat. Lady Nancy, *née* Langhorne of Virginia, Conservative gadfly of the House of Commons, declared that the whole story was "Communist propaganda." First she said that Lindbergh had not been at any Cliveden dinner recently and had not discussed the Soviet Union there. Then her memory was refreshed and she said that he had been at a luncheon, and had "talked about Russia in general," but she couldn't recall what he had said or who had been present. The makers of Communist propaganda found this unlikely, and it only added fuel to the flames.

Lanny knew that Roosevelt had met the mistress of Cliveden, and that he was interested in personalities; so a conscientious agent collected the names of those who had been present at the famous luncheon. Members of the "Cliveden set" found it amusing to be called that, and said that of course they had tried to learn all they could about German versus Soviet aviation, being concerned to protect their country from getting into a fight which it might not be able to win. War would be no bally joke these days, because it wouldn't be confined to the troops in the field but would involve everybody at home, and what was to keep a bomb from being dropped on Buckingham Palace or the House of Commons? What statesman would want to run such risks to oblige the Reds or their fellow-travelers—or to save for a mongrel nation like Czechoslovakia a strip of land which ought never to have been taken away from Austria, and which should go to Germany now because she had already got Austria?

V

In short, the British government were committed to the policy of satisfying the Führer, and must continue in that course, even though it meant stubbing their official toes many times. It meant being told that the Führer was highly incensed at a speech by Mr. Lloyd George, and then at British criticisms of a nationwide pogrom. It meant taking up a discussion of the limiting of air forces, and having the Germans express willingness, on the basis that they were to have three times the strength of the British. The government rejected this, but did decide to modify their building program to meet Hitler's wishes; they would have fewer bombers, meant for attack, and more fighters, meant for defense. When Gerald Albany told Lanny about that, Lanny's reply was that it would bring his father over to England in a hurry!

As part of the appeasement policy there must be a settlement with the Duce—all according to that world conqueror's wishes. They would recognize his title to Abyssinia and his right to intervene in the Spanish war. The Loyalists there were still holding out, in spite of Franco's frequent announcements that they were beaten. Now the British would recognize Franco's belligerency, and would force the French to do the same. Il Duce's reply to this courtesy was most elegant; when the French ambassador came before the Italian deputies to present the gift, the deputies shouted: "Tunisia!"—which meant that they wanted to take this French colony, presumably by the method of Hitler in Austria and Czechoslovakia. Outside in the streets the Fascisti were shouting: "Nice! Savoy! Corsica!" Those cries had special interest for Lanny Budd, who had not forgotten the idea of his ex-brother-in-law coming back to France with his army. In Nice, the city where Vittorio had disposed of the stolen paintings, he would be only ten miles from Bienvenu; and just where would his Duce draw the boundary line?

<h1 style="text-align:center">VI</h1>

For Prime Minister Chamberlain and his Cabinet, life had become "just one damn thing after another." The Führer had solemnly promised that if he got the Sudetenland with British help, he would forget the subject of colonies for a few years; but now he was talking colonies —and in that rude and harsh manner which he had brought into the diplomatic drawing-room. "We wish to negotiate, but if others decline to grant us our rights we shall secure them in a different way." And what were the British government going to do about that? It was the business of a presidential agent to meet the key people and tell them what he had heard the Führer say on the subject, thus luring them into stating their reactions. Needless to say, no British government ever gave up anything that belonged to Britain; but there were Togoland and the Cameroons, belonging to France, and perhaps the Führer might be contented with that brace of turkeys.

The inquisitive agent heard various suggestions, all having to do with sacrifices to be made by other nations. It was the British fleet which protected the little fellows in their colonial possessions; if Britannia ever ceased to rule the waves, what chance would there be for the French Empire, the Belgian, the Portuguese, or the Dutch? Was it not reasonable to expect these dependent nations to contribute at least one turkey to Adi Schicklgruber's Christmas feast? Lanny heard in British tea parties references to sections of the earth which hitherto had been mere names to him, and obliged him to consult the large globe in the library of Wickthorpe Castle. French Equatorial Africa, a huge territory, from which slices of dark meat could surely be cut. The Belgian Congo was likewise enormous, and very fat. Portuguese Angola was small, but then, so was Portugal; she had had a treaty with Britain for some six centuries, the oldest still valid treaty in the world, so Gerald declared. It had been several centuries since Portugal had been in position to protect herself, and surely now she might be asked to pay a long-standing debt. Security cost money in these times, said a pious high churchman.

Lanny went to London and met Rick, according to their new arrangement. They had lunch in a hotel room for greater privacy, and exchanged secrets which would surely have caused each individual Aryan blond hair of Ceddy or Gerald to stand on end. According to his custom, Lanny put a couple of hundred pounds into his friend's hands, to be used in promoting the anti-Nazi cause in England. Having friends among the Reds, Rick could reveal that Hitler had just recently made approaches to Moscow on the subject of a *rapprochement*. "Will they consider it?" Lanny asked, and the answer was: "Good God, no!"

Lanny wanted very much to believe that; but he was living in a mixed-up world where one could not count too much upon anything. He made this remark to his friend, who replied: "That is one thing I would stake my life upon. It is a question of ideological differences, utterly irreconcilable."

VII

For the first time in his life Lanny Budd found himself coming to think of America as home. America hadn't as yet got as far in corruption as old Europe; people were kinder there; less sophisticated, less highly cultured, perhaps, but also less dangerous. The social conflicts which were rending the old world were developing in the new, but they hadn't progressed so far; there would be at least a few years of respite. Lanny decided that he was tired of wandering, and might find a wife, or let his wise and kind stepmother find one for him; he would settle down, read some books, refresh his piano technique, and enjoy the luxury of saying what he thought.

He boarded one of the big ocean liners at Southampton and had a stormy passage near the end of November. The flight of time was accelerated by a charming widow from California, a state which Lanny had never visited; she looked and acted as if she had money, and made it plain that she liked the son of Budd-Erling and might be willing to console his mysterious melancholy. He danced with her, and avoided any chance of displeasing her by the expression of unorthodox opinions. But when she invited him to visit the Golden State, he told her that he had to be about his father's business—and did not intimate that it was the Great White Father in the Great White House.

Ashore in New York, he was driven to the airport, and called Gus Gennerich in Washington. He was shocked to learn that the man had died while accompanying the President on his trip to South America in the previous August. There had been no way to let a secret agent know about this. He was wondering what to do, when the voice, a woman's, inquired: "Are you calling on official business?" When he answered that he was, she said: "Call Mr. Baker," and gave a number. So Lanny put in another call, and when a man's voice said "Baker," he replied: "Zaharoff, 103, phoning from New York." The voice instructed him to come to a certain street number in Washington.

He had time before the plane left to call Robbie and report his arrival. He was off on a picture deal, he said, without saying where. He didn't want his father to get Washington fixed in his mind, and start guessing about Lanny's errands. Instead, he told what "Baron Tailor" had said about Robbie being so lucky; also the news that Britain had changed the proportion of fighters over bombers—which drove all other thoughts out of the father's head.

There being still time, Lanny called Johannes at his office, and promised him a load of news before long. All the family were well, its head reported; Hansi was playing in Carnegie Hall next week, and no news had come from Aaron Schönhaus. "Oh, Lanny, that awful pogrom!" exclaimed the exiled financier, with a catch in his voice. Lanny said: "I saw a little of it, and will tell you."

VIII

Up the movable steps into the luxuriously fitted plane, and then that miracle of flight to which Lanny could never grow indifferent. Younger men might take it for granted, but not one who had seen it born into the world. Lanny had been a grown boy when his father had taken him and Rick to see with their own eyes the dream of Icarus and Leonardo made reality. That had been on the Salisbury Plain in England, just before the outbreak of the World War; and now the mature man sat at ease and looked down upon the land of his fathers from a viewpoint which they had never been able to attain: cities and villages that were all roofs, roads with tiny dots moving on them, rivers with boats that seemed fixed in glass, farmhouses with painted roofs and fields dark with wetness. Then, in one hour, the white marble structures of the capital, ever multiplying as the interest of America shifted from business to politics, from Wall Street to Washington. More softly than a duck sliding down into the water the plane settled onto the runway, and Lanny stepped forth with his two light suitcases. He checked them in the station and stepped into a taxi.

At a small brick dwelling he rang the bell, and the door was opened by a vigorous youngish man with a businesslike manner. "Baker," he said, and Lanny replied: "Zaharoff." Invited in, the visitor said: "I only just learned of Gus's death."

"What is it you wish?"

"To see the Chief."

"You understand that you have to identify yourself to me."

"I am under orders not to give my name."

"I know that. You can tell me about Gus, and the procedure you followed with him."

Lanny recited all the details that came to his mind. "Gus Gennerich was a big blond fellow, quiet and decided in manner; he used to be a New York policeman, so the Governor told me. Gus never talked about himself, in fact he didn't talk to me at all. I met him on the street at night, by appointment; he picked me up in his car and took me into the White House by the 'social door.' We went up by the stairway to the second floor; always at night, and the Chief was in bed, propped up reading. He wears pongee pajamas, blue-striped or plain blue, and a blue coat sweater, but the last time he had a blue cape. He always has a stack of papers, and a mystery or a sea story. There is a typewriter in the corner at the right, beyond the foot of the bed. A colored valet sits outside the door. Is that enough?"

"You must understand, I wouldn't take any stranger into that room without searching him. After the Chief has O.K.'d you, it will be different."

"Certainly," answered Lanny. "Do you mean now?"

"I mean before we go in. I have made an appointment for you at ten tonight."

"That's all right. Shall I come here?"

"I'll pick you up as Gus did." The man named a corner, and Lanny jotted it down for safety. His mind was greatly relieved, for he had feared that he might not be able to get to the President without betraying his identity.

IX

The traveler got his bags and put up at the Mayflower. Then he went for a walk, to see the new sights of his country's capital, which had been nearly a century and a half a-building, and had grown more in half a dozen years than in its first century. White marble appeared to be *de rigueur*, and Adi's House of German Art in Munich was being put in the shade by a National Gallery of Art which was to cost fifteen million dollars and to house many great collections, beginning with the banker Mellon's. In the bad old Coolidge days this two-hundred-times millionaire had been called "the greatest Secretary of the Treasury since Hamilton," and it had been his sad fate to lead his country's finances into collapse, and then be forced to admit that he had no idea how to put Humpty-Dumpty together again.

Lanny dined alone, read the evening paper, and took another walk, to get clear in his mind what he wanted to report to his boss. He had made up his mind to ask for a release from further duties; he wasn't going to criticize what the boss was doing or failing to do, but merely to say that he didn't feel that he, the secret agent, was accomplishing very much. He wanted to throw off his camouflage, tell the world what he really thought about Nazi-Fascism, and do what one American could to arouse the democratic peoples to the peril into which they were drifting. If it wrecked the art-experting business, all right; the son of Budd-Erling had enough to live on. He might even go into the business of making fighter planes—upon which the future of the world appeared to depend.

Promptly on the minute he stepped into Baker's car. There was another man driving, and while the car rolled on, the new arrival was subjected to a going-over by swift and well-trained hands; not merely all his pockets, but under his armpits and in his trouser legs, where a small weapon might be concealed. Even the inside of his hat was not overlooked. "O.K.," said the searcher, at last, and apologized: "We don't take any chances these days."

"I hope not," replied Lanny, with feeling.

X

Once more he retraced the familiar journey and found himself in the presence of that big man with the powerful shoulders and the exuberant smile. His greeting left no doubt in the guard's mind that this was the real and right "Zaharoff." The man took his departure, closing the door behind him, and the visitor seated himself by the bedside and underwent the scrutiny of F.D.R.'s bright and lively blue eyes. "Well, Lanny!" said the warm voice with deep overtones. "You have waited a long time between calls."

"A lot of things were happening, and I kept on the trail of them. Have you received my reports?"

"Every single one, in order as numbered. I have them in a special file. Incidentally, I have them in my head. Tell me what is coming next."

"Hitler is going to take Prague and what is left of Czechoslovakia. You can place your bets on that."

"And how soon?"

"By the end of the winter, I should guess. That will be six months after his Sudeten move. It appears to take him about that long to consolidate an acquisition, and to carry on his softening process for the next one. According to that he should be ready for Danzig and the Polish Corridor by next autumn."

Lanny went on to give his reasons for these beliefs: what Hitler had said, what Göring had said, what Hess had said. In the middle of it the President broke in: "Hell's bells! Will you be telling me they have put you in charge of their military operations?"

Lanny laughed. "It is due in great part to my father's prestige; he has what they need and understand. That got me next to Göring, and when Hitler saw me solid with Göring, he thought I must be all right—and so it has gone. I lay myself out to entertain them, and I tell them things about France and England which they need to know. Also, I put in a touch of sauciness, of a sort they consider American; they have a peculiar attitude toward us—they envy us and imitate us, even though they wouldn't acknowledge it, even to themselves. Hitler, Göring, Hess, any one of them would smack down a German who dared say to them what I say. My turkey story, for example."

Lanny told the story, and his auditor threw back his head and laughed, almost as heartily as Göring had done. "That tells a lot," he commented. "Göring doesn't resent seeing his Führer as a beast of prey!"

"Göring always has a lion cub as a pet, and Hitler until recently carried a riding whip everywhere he went. They have a Death's Head brigade of the SS, and many such symbols of cruelty and terror. They have committed themselves to that course, and cannot turn back if they would."

Lanny went on with his recital. He told how he had watched the Munich crisis develop, and what the British and the French had said and done in the face of it. He described Chamberlain, Runciman, Halifax, Londonderry, Wickthorpe—appeasers all, and the part they played in the ignominy. As Lanny had foreseen, F.D. wanted to know all about Lindbergh and Lady Nancy, and just what had really happened; he was pleased by Rick's epigram that there might not be a "Cliveden set" but surely was a "Cliveden sort." He wanted to hear about Adi Schicklgruber's secret interest in the occult arts; the idea of locking an outlawed astrologer up in a Gestapo hotel and compelling him to cast a dozen horoscopes he called a story out of the Arabian Nights—but Lanny assured him it had really happened, and it really had.

This busy great man, with the cares of a hundred and thirty million people on his shoulders, took hours off from sleep to ply Lanny Budd with questions concerning events and personalities of Western Europe: what Schacht had said about German finances; what Thyssen had said about how industry was controlled; what Schneider had revealed concerning his Skoda arrangements; what the de Bruynes had told about Laval and Bonnet and their intrigues with Kurt Meissner and Otto Abetz; about Daladier's noble *amie,* the Marquise de Crussol, and her intrigues; about Ceddy and Gerald and their hope that the Nazis would keep agreements as to arms limitation; about "Old Portland" and "Young Bedford," and Mosley and his Blackshirts, and even about Unity Mitford and what she was doing at the Berghof. In the course of this unrelenting quiz Lanny could make sure once for all that not merely had his reports been read and digested, but that his ideas had become a part of the mental make-up of his country's Chief Executive.

XI

So the secret agent never got a chance to offer his resignation; or, at any rate, he never took the chance. The idea just quietly melted away in the warmth of this great man's sympathy and gratitude. The nearest Lanny came to a complaint was to say that he found it damned discouraging, wandering about Nazi-Fascist Europe and never meeting a person to whom he could speak an honest word. The President's answer was: "Consider yourself a soldier under orders. The scout who goes into the enemy's camp at night feels the same way, but he goes."

"If you put it that way," Lanny replied, "of course I have to stick it out. But sometimes I wonder if I am really doing any good."

Said the President, looking suddenly grave: "Do you imagine I never wonder about my job, Lanny?"

"At least you can do something now and then."

"Not as often as I want to, believe me! If you think otherwise, it is because you haven't given much study to the American Constitution, and to our political system. I am not only well checked and balanced,

I am under orders, as much so as any private in the army. The American people are my boss, and I have the job of finding out what they want, and doing it. I might bull something through, but what good would it do if the people repudiated it at the next election?"

"I suppose that is true," admitted the visitor.

"I know just how you feel in Europe, Lanny. You see the horrors piling up, and you send in your reports—and nothing happens! But you must understand, I am no Hitler or Mussolini whose will is law. I have my private opinions, of course, but I have to remember that I speak as the voice of the nation. Incidentally, I am the leader of a party. I have only two years more as President, and I cannot take an action without thinking what will be its effect upon the party's future; otherwise I might throw away my six years' work, and have the humiliation of seeing a successor undo the entire New Deal. If you saw the election returns early this month, you know that the Republicans made gains; so I have to stop and ask myself, what have I done to cause it, and what can I do to check the trend and keep it from becoming a landslide?"

"I must admit all that makes a difference," said the agent, greatly chastened.

"It is my duty to lead the people, but I can only lead them as fast as they will follow. As I think I explained to you before, if I go faster, I lose contact, and somebody else becomes the leader. Never forget that it takes time to change the thinking of a hundred million people, or even of the educated part of them. You go to Europe and see the events with your own eyes; but the people do not go, and the tragedy seems far-off and unreal to them. If I had denounced the rape of Czechoslovakia, and given any hint of aid to England and France, do you imagine for one moment that the American people would have got behind me?"

"Only a few, it may be."

"I should simply have been handing the government over to the appeasers and the reactionaries. When there comes some ghastly thing like this pogrom, I can voice my abhorrence; I have recalled our ambassador from Berlin, and shall probably not send him back—a gesture which your high-up Nazi friends will not fail to understand. Also, I can tell the Congress that these are perilous times, and that it is necessary for us to increase our means of national defense. That we are doing, I assure you. But for the rest, I have to await events, and the education which they will give to the people. Facts are the only teachers who will be heeded."

"What keeps me unhappy, Governor, is the fear that the lesson will be learned too slowly."

"Don't think that you are the only one who has that fear. It has kept me awake many a night, and tempted me to what are considered indiscretions. You saw what happened when I let you persuade me to make that 'quarantine speech.' I haven't been forgiven for it yet."

"I hope you have forgiven me," said the visitor, troubled in conscience.

XII

Lanny had been over this interview many times in his mind, and had stowed there a number of items that he wanted to "get across." Most important of all was this question of the time limit within which his Chief had to work; a schedule not of Roosevelt's making, but of Hitler's. Now, speaking earnestly, Lanny said: "Governor, I want to put a question which you may not care to answer. You don't have to, but you ought to have it in your mind."

"All right—shoot!" said this informal great man.

"The question is this: What, exactly, would you do if you should be waked up in the middle of the night and told that London has just been bombed to dust and rubble?"

There was a silence; then: "I don't think I could answer that question, Lanny—not without a lot of reflection."

"It would be wise to think it over. And this, also: Suppose the British Prime Minister should call you on the telephone and tell you that you have twenty-four hours in which to decide whether to send Britain aid, or else the fleet will have to be surrendered."

"Good God, Lanny! You mean that seriously?"

"I am quite sure it is one of the possibilities."

"And how soon?"

"I don't think war can be more than a year or two away. I can tell you for certain that that is what the Nazi leaders believe. Göring is the most conservative, and two years is what he is asking for. Of course I can't tell whether his Air Force can do what he thinks it can; but undoubtedly he means to try. The British leaders all know it, and that is why their bones have turned to putty. If he were able to wipe London out, I don't see how the British government could continue, except by taking the fleet to Canada. But what good would that do, unless we promised them support?"

There was a pause, while a Chief Executive who had learned caution weighed his off-the-record words. "I don't think the American people would ever let the Germans come to Canada," he remarked, at last. "Also, I admit the fact that our country has lived in safety for more than a century behind the shelter of the British fleet. We haven't realized it, but in such a crisis it might be possible to make the American people realize it. You understand, all this is for you alone."

"Rest assured, Governor, I have never quoted a word that you have said to me, or even mentioned that I have met you—not even to my mother or father."

The face which was usually so genial and smiling had become somber, and the man who was stealing time from his sleep sat staring before him, frowning. "Do you know the Bible?" he asked, suddenly. "There are some words—I think St. Paul's: 'God is not mocked.' "

" 'Be not deceived; God is not mocked: for whatsoever a man soweth, that shall he also reap.' "

"I think that applies to nations as to individuals, Lanny. I don't attempt to guess how it is coming, but I refuse to believe that men can commit such crimes as the Nazis have committed, and not raise up some agency of justice against them. If it should appear that the American people have to shoulder that burden, I trust they will not shrink from it."

Again a pause. Then the President, watching his agent's face, inquired: "Do you know much about Lincoln?"

"I am ashamed not to know my own country as well as I do Europe."

"Take my advice then, and read a good life of Lincoln. He was a man of peace who was compelled to fight a long war. Observe his wise patience, his shrewdness in reading the public mind, his skill in leading the people, one step at a time. If ever you are tempted to wonder about what I am doing in a crisis, you can guide yourself by the certainty that I am asking what Lincoln would have done. He saved the Union, he saved what he called 'government of the people, by the people, for the people'; and be sure he didn't do it solely for one people, but as an example to which all mankind would turn. Recall that to your mind when you are tempted to be lonely and discouraged, over there among the Nazi lions and the Fascist jackals."

XIII

So Lanny went out from the presence. Because he had a lesson to ponder, he did not go to his hotel at once, but took a long walk at random, lost in thought. When he came to, he observed in the distance a great marble structure which he knew to be the Lincoln Memorial; it stood, shining in a bright electric glow the whole night through. Lanny decided to begin his study of Abraham Lincoln without delay, and went to the building, entered, and stood looking at the nine-foot marble statue of the Great Emancipator sitting in the seat of judgment. At that late hour, there was no one in the building but the sentries, so his thoughts were undisturbed. He turned to the walls, where the Gettysburg Address is inscribed, and read the immortal closing words:

"It is rather for us here to be dedicated to the great task remaining before us; that from these honored dead we take increased devotion to that cause for which they gave the last full measure of devotion; that we here highly resolve that these dead shall not have died in vain; that this nation, under God, shall have a new birth of freedom, and that government of the people, by the people, for the people, shall not perish from the earth."

The son of Robbie Budd turned again to the great statue. There was exaltation in his heart; he was glad now that he was an American; he renewed his faith in democracy and resolved never again to waver. Once more his native land faced a crisis, and once more the people, with their deep understanding, had found a leader worthy of their trust.

Lanny's mind leaped back across the sea to that other man of great power whom he had come to know so well. Three times in the past year and a half he had traveled back and forth between Franklin Roosevelt and Adolf Hitler, and he knew that he had not made the last of these journeys. Suddenly the events of the time took shape in his imagination as a duel of wills between these two: one the champion of democracy, of government by popular consent, of the rights of the individual to think his own thoughts, to speak his own mind, to live his own life so long as he did not interfere with the equal rights of his fellows; the other the champion of those ancient dark forces of tyranny and oppression which had ruled the world before the concept of freedom had been born. It took no prophet to foresee that this struggle was not over; it was going on until it would involve the whole world and the whole future of mankind.

Roosevelt versus Hitler! These two had not created the forces, but led them and embodied them; they had made themselves, one the protagonist and the other the antagonist in a world drama, the like of which had never before been played in history. Lanny Budd resolved that as long as fate spared him he would play a part in that drama, the faithful friend and messenger of democracy's champion.

BOOKS BY UPTON SINCLAIR

WIDE IS THE GATE
DRAGON'S TEETH
BETWEEN TWO WORLDS
WORLD'S END
EXPECT NO PEACE
YOUR MILLION DOLLARS
LITTLE STEEL
OUR LADY
THE FLIVVER KING
NO PASARAN!
THE GNOMOBILE
CO-OP: A NOVEL OF LIVING TOGETHER
WHAT GOD MEANS TO ME: AN ATTEMPT AT
  A WORKING RELIGION
I, CANDIDATE FOR GOVERNOR AND HOW I
  GOT LICKED
THE EPIC PLAN FOR CALIFORNIA
I, GOVERNOR OF CALIFORNIA
THE WAY OUT: WHAT LIES AHEAD FOR
  AMERICA
UPTON SINCLAIR PRESENTS WILLIAM FOX
AMERICAN OUTPOST: AUTOBIOGRAPHY
THE WET PARADE
ROMAN HOLIDAY
MENTAL RADIO
MOUNTAIN CITY
BOSTON
MONEY WRITES!
OIL!

THE SPOKESMAN'S SECRETARY
LETTERS TO JUDD
MAMMONART
THE GOSLINGS—A STUDY OF THE AMERICAN
  SCHOOLS
THE GOOSE-STEP—A STUDY OF AMERICAN
  EDUCATION
THE BOOK OF LIFE
THEY CALL ME CARPENTER
100%—THE STORY OF A PATRIOT
THE BRASS CHECK
JIMMIE HIGGINS
KING COAL, A NOVEL OF THE COLORADO
  STRIKE
THE PROFITS OF RELIGION
THE CRY FOR JUSTICE
DAMAGED GOODS
SYLVIA'S MARRIAGE
SYLVIA
LOVE'S PILGRIMAGE
THE FASTING CURE
SAMUEL, THE SEEKER
THE MONEYCHANGERS
THE METROPOLIS
THE MILLENNIUM
THE OVERMAN
THE JUNGLE
MANASSAS, A NOVEL OF THE CIVIL WAR
THE JOURNAL OF ARTHUR STIRLING

Plays

PRINCE HAGEN
THE NATUREWOMAN
THE SECOND STORY MAN
THE MACHINE
THE POT-BOILER
HELL

SINGING JAILBIRDS
BILL PORTER
OIL! (DRAMATIZATION)
DEPRESSION ISLAND
MARIE ANTOINETTE